Mother
of the
Believers

Mother

of the

Believers

A Novel of the Birth of Islam

KAMRAN PASHA

WASHINGTON SQUARE PRESS

New York   London   Toronto   Sydney

Washington Square Press
A Division of Simon & Schuster, Inc.
1230 Avenue of the Americas
New York, NY 10020

First Washington Square Press Paperback edition April 2009

Washington Square Press and colophon are trademarks of Simon & Schuster, Inc.

For information about special discounts for bulk purchases, please contact Simon & Schuster Special Sales at 1-800-456-6789 or business@simonandschuster.com.

The Simon & Schuster Speakers Bureau can bring authors to your live event. For more information or to book an event contact the Simon & Schuster Speakers Bureau at 866-248-3049 or visit our website at www.simonspeakers.com.

Designed by Nancy Singer

Manufactured in the United States of America

10 9 8 7 6 5 4 3 2 1

Library of Congress Cataloging-in-Publication Data

ISBN-13: 978-1-4165-7991-5
ISBN-10:   1-4165-7991-5

"Paradise is at the feet of the mothers."

—Prophet Muhammad

Dedicated to my mother,
who is the living proof of these words.

Contents

Mother
of the
Believers

Author's Note

This book is a work of fiction. Though based on historical events, it is not a history of those events. Readers who are interested in learning more about the history of Islam and the lives of Prophet Muhammad and his wife Aisha are encouraged to read some of the wonderful reference works that I have relied on to write this tale. These books include the brilliantly crafted biography by Martin Lings entitled *Muhammad: His Life Based on the Earliest Sources*, as well as the excellent works by Barnaby Rogerson, including *The Prophet Muhammad: A Biography* and *Heirs of Muhammad*.

Those interested in seeking a Western scholarly perspective on Muhammad's life and legacy are referred to Montgomery Watt's seminal work *Muhammad: Prophet and Statesman*, as well as Karen Armstrong's influential book *Muhammad: A Biography of the Prophet*.

Readers seeking more knowledge about Aisha will find a wealth of information on her and other prominent Muslim women in Jennifer Heath's *The Scimitar and the Veil: Extraordinary Women of Islam*. For those fascinated by the military history surrounding the rise of Islam, a wonderfully readable analysis can be found in Richard A. Gabriel's *Muhammad, Islam's First General*. Hugh Kennedy's *The Great Arab Conquests* is also a fine resource for those seeking insight into how a small band of desert warriors improbably created a vast empire and a civilization that remains vibrant and influential in the world today.

Readers interested in a general introduction to the faith and practices of Islam are referred to *The Complete Idiot's Guide to Islam* by Yahiya Emerick and *No god but God* by Reza Aslan. Those who wish to gain deeper insight into the spiritual values of Islam and what the religion offers the world today are referred to *Islam and the Destiny of Man* by Charles Le Gai Eaton and *The Heart of Islam: Enduring Values for Humanity* by Seyyed Hossein Nasr. A deeper look at the spiritual heart of Islam can be found in *The Vision of Islam* by Sachicko Murata and William Chittick and in the classic text *Understanding Islam* by Frithjof Schuon.

There are many translations of the holy Qur'an on the market today, but I have found three to be particularly helpful to Western readers. Abdullah Yusuf Ali's *The Qur'an: Text, Translation and Commentary* is one of the most beloved of English translations and is helpful to those who are new to studying the Muslim faith. Muhammad Asad's monumental translation *The Message of the Holy Qur'an* is both scholarly and written from the point of a view of a European convert who understands how to explain the scripture to the Western mind. For those seeking a simple translation that is not bogged down with commentary, I recommend *The Qur'an*, translated by M.A.S. Abdel Haleem and published by Oxford University Press. An older but still popular translation is *The Glorious Qur'an* by Muhammad Marmaduke Pickthall, a British convert.

Writing a novel about the birth of Islam and the remarkable personalities of the Prophet Muhammad, Aisha, and the rest of the early Muslim community has been an extremely challenging and rewarding process. Compared to the limited historical data available on Jesus, the origins of Islam and the life of the Prophet have been documented with a degree of historical detail that is mind-boggling to many Westerners. It has been said that we know more about Muhammad than we do about any other man in history, as his followers meticulously recorded everything they could about their beloved teacher, from how he looked, to his daily mannerisms and eating habits, to surprisingly intimate details about his personal life with his wives. Much of this can be credited to the remarkable memory of Aisha, who was responsible for transmitting over two thousand individual hadiths, or oral accounts of her life with the Prophet and his teachings.

The corpus of historical data about the Prophet Muhammad is staggering in its depth and detail, but his life remains a matter of controversy. Believers and nonbelievers will obviously interpret the tales about Muhammad in accordance with their own perspective about the truth of his spiritual mission. And within the Muslim community it-self, interpretation of historical events is often hotly debated among the different sects of Sunni and Shia Islam.

For the record, I am a believing and practicing Muslim. Theologi-cally I consider myself a Sunni, and spiritually I am drawn to Sufism, the mystical heart of Islam. By lineage, I am a sayyid, a direct descen-dant of the Prophet through his daughter Fatima and his grandson Husayn. For me, this novel has been both a rewarding journey into the heart of my religious tradition and an eye-opening study of the pas-sionate and complex people who were my ancestors. They were simple men and women, living in a remote desert, who should have been for-gotten by history. And yet through the sheer power of faith, they man-aged to turn the world upside down.

I would like to take a moment to comment on one of the most controversial aspects of my story, at least for many modern readers. In recent years there has been a great deal of discussion regarding Aisha's age when she married Prophet Muhammad. Estimates of her age have ranged from early teens to early twenties. The most controversial ac-count is that she was nine years old at the time of her wedding, which some modern critics have attempted to use to smear the Prophet with the inflammatory charge of pedophilia. In response to these charges, many Muslims are now performing all kinds of historical analysis to attempt to clear his name and reputation. What is evident is that Aisha was a young woman at the time of the wedding, but that her marriage was not in any way controversial and was never used by the enemies of the Prophet as a critique in his lifetime, unlike his marriage to Zaynab bint Jahsh. So clearly whatever Aisha's age was, it was irrelevant to her contemporaries and considered mainstream in the social context of seventh-century Arabia.

In my novel, I have chosen to directly face the controversy over Aisha's age by using the most contentious account, that she was nine at the time she consummated her wedding. The reason I have done this is to show that it is foolish to project modern values on another time and world. In a desert environment where life expectancy was extremely low, early marriage was not a social issue—it was a matter of survival. Modern Christian historians have no problem suggesting that Mary was around twelve years old when she became pregnant with Jesus, as that was the normal age for marriage and childbearing in first-century

Palestine. Yet no one claims Mary's youthful pregnancy was somehow perverse because it is easy to understand that life expectancy was so low in that world that reproduction took place immediately upon menstruation.

An interesting anthropological analysis of the onset of puberty in ancient and modern times can be found in *Mismatch* by Peter Gluckman and Mark Hanson. Their study shows that modern social norms have evolved in ways that conflict with evolutionary pressures for girls to menstruate and bear children at a young age. These conflicts were less apparent in ancient times, when survival trumped other concerns. Girls in many ancient cultures were considered adult women immediately upon the onset of their cycles. To project modern social norms backward into that environment is disingenuous and reflects a failure to understand history and human nature.

It is for that reason that I have chosen to use the most controversial account as a framework for my story.

In closing, I should note that not all Muslims would agree with my interpretation of Islam in these pages or with my portrayal of the Prophet's life and of Aisha's role in Muslim history. And that is fine. I encourage those who disagree with my presentation to write books that reflect the truth as their hearts see it. In fact, I hope a day comes when novels about Prophet Muhammad, Aisha, and Ali become as commonplace in Western literature as the diverse and beloved books on historical figures such as Alexander the Great, Julius Caesar, Cleopatra, and Queen Elizabeth I.

My intention in writing this novel has been to give Westerners a glimpse of the richness that exists within the Muslim historical tradition and to invite all my readers to learn more about Islam and draw their own conclusions. To the extent that I have succeeded, the credit belongs to God alone. The failures, however, are all mine.

The
Beginning
of the
End

In the Name of God,
the Merciful,
the Compassionate

What is faith?
    It is a question I have asked myself over the years, dear nephew, and I am no closer to the answer now than I was when my hair was still crimson like the rising dawn, not the pale silver of moonlight as it is today.

I write this for you, because I know I am dying. I do not complain, for there are times I wished I had died many years ago or, better yet, had never been born. My heart looks at the trees, whose life consists of no more than dreams of the sun and memories of the rain, and I envy them. There are times when I wish I were one of the rocks that line the hills beyond Medina, ignored and forgotten by those who tread upon them.

You will protest, I am sure. How could I, Aisha the daughter of Abu Bakr, the most famed woman of her time, wish to trade in my glorious memories for the sleep of the deaf and the dumb of the earth? That is the tricky thing with memories, dear Abdallah, son of my sister. They are like the wind. They come when they wish and carry with them both the hope of life and the danger of death. We cannot master them. Nay, they are our masters and rejoice in their capriciousness, carrying our hearts with them wherever they wish.

And now they have taken me, against my will, to this moment, where I sit in my tiny bedroom made of mud brick, only a few feet away from the grave of my beloved, writing this tale. There is much I do not want to recall, but my memories cry out to be recorded, so that they can live in the memories of others when I am gone.

So I shall start at the beginning. At a time when one world was dying and another was about to be born. There is much glory in my tale, much wonder, and a great deal of sorrow. It is a story that I hope you will preserve and take with you to the farthest reaches of the empire, so that the daughters and granddaughters of those who are still being suckled today will remember. Much of what I shall relate, I witnessed with my own eyes. The rest I recount as it was recounted to me by those who were present.

It is a tale of great portent, and the bearer of my words must shoulder a weighty burden before God and man. And of all those who dwell on earth, there is none whom I can trust more than you, Abdallah, to carry my tale. In my days of honor and of disgrace, you have stood by my side, more loyal than any son of my flesh could have been. I look upon your smiling face and see all that I have gained and lost as the price of my destiny. A fate that was written in the ink of dreams when I was still a child.

I was six years old when I married the Messenger of God, although our union was not consummated until I began my cycles at the age of nine. Over the years, I became aware that my youthful marriage was considered shocking, even barbaric, by the haughty noblewomen of Persia and Byzantium, although none would have dared to say so to my face. Of course I am used to the cruel whispers of the gossipmongers. More so than most women of my time, I have been subjected to the hidden daggers of jealousy and rumor. Perhaps that is to be expected. A price I must pay as the favorite wife of the most revered and hated man the world has ever known.

Tell them, Abdallah, that I loved Muhammad, may God's blessings and peace be upon him, and that he loved me, for all that I proved unworthy of it. Of the many twists and turns that have guided the caravan of my life, there are none that I treasure more than my ten years with him as his wife. Indeed, there are many days that I wished I had died with him, that Gabriel would have taken my spirit with his and I could have left this valley of tears for others to conquer. I torment myself with the knowledge that many thousands would have lived had I simply died that day. An army of believers who followed me to their doom. Good men, who believed that I acted out of idealism rather than pride and a hidden lust for revenge. Good men like your father. Had my soul departed along with the Messenger, he and so many others would have lived.

But that was not my destiny.

My fate was to be the mother of a nation, even though my womb has never borne a child of its own. A nation that was chosen by God to change the world, to destroy iniquity, even as it is forever tempted to succumb to it. A nation that defeated every adversary, despite all the forces of Earth marshaled against it, and then became doomed to fight itself until the Day of Resurrection. A nation whose soul, like mine, is filled with God and yet consumed with earthly passion. A nation that stands for victory and justice, yet can never hide its own failures and cruelties against the terrible judgment of the One.

This is my *Ummah,* my nation, and I am its face, even though no man outside my family has looked upon my face since I was a little girl.

I am the harbinger of joy and anger. The queen of love and jealousy. The bearer of knowledge and the ultimate fool.

I am the Mother of the Believers, and this is my tale.

Book One

Birth
of a
Faith

I was born in blood, and its terrible taint would follow me all my life.

My mother, Umm Ruman, cried out in agony as the contractions increased in severity. The midwife, a stout woman from the tribe of Bani Nawfal named Amal, leaned closer to examine the pregnant woman's abdomen. And then she saw it. The line of blood that was running down her patient's thigh.

Amal looked over to the young girl standing nervously to the side of the wooden birthing chair where her stepmother was struggling to bring forth life.

"Asma," she said in a soft voice, trying to mask the fear that was growing in her chest. "Get your father."

Your mother, Abdallah, was no more than ten years old at the time, and she paled at Amal's words. Asma knew what they meant. So did Umm Ruman.

"I am dying," Umm Ruman gasped, her teeth grinding against the pain. She had known something was wrong the moment her water broke. It had been dark and mottled with blood, and the subsequent horror of the contractions was far beyond anything she had experienced at the birth of her son, Abdal Kaaba, so many years before.

At the age of thirty-eight, she had known that she was too old to bear another child safely and had greeted the news of her pregnancy with trepidation. In the Days of Ignorance before the Revelation, perhaps she would have turned to Amal or the other midwives of Mecca for their secret draft that was said to poison the womb. But the Messenger of God had made it clear to his small band of followers that the life of a child was sacred, despite the many pagan Arab customs to the contrary. She had sworn an oath of allegiance to his hand, and she would not go against his teachings, even if they meant her demise.

Unlike most of her neighbors and friends still clinging to the old ways, Umm Ruman no longer feared death. But she grieved to think that her child, the first to be born into the new faith of Islam, might not survive to see the sunrise.

Amal took her hand and squeezed it gently.

"Do not despair. We will get through this together." Her voice was kind, but Umm Ruman could see in the stern lines around her mouth that Amal had reached her professional conclusion. The end was nigh for mother and child.

Umm Ruman managed to turn her head to her stepdaughter, Asma, who stood frozen at her side, tears welling in her dark eyes.

"Go. Bring Abu Bakr to me," she said, her voice growing faint. She stroked the girl's still plump cheeks. "If I die before you return, tell him my last request was that the Prophet pray at my funeral."

Asma shook her head, refusing to face that possibility. "You can't die! I won't let you!"

The girl was not of Umm Ruman's flesh, but the bond between them was as strong as that of any mother and daughter. Perhaps stronger, for Asma had chosen her over her actual mother, Qutaila, who had refused to accept the new faith. Abu Bakr had divorced his first wife, for it was forbidden for a believer to share a bed with an idol worshiper. The proud Qutaila had left their home in a furious rage, vowing to return to her tribe, but Asma had refused to go with her. The girl had chosen the Straight Path, the way of the Messenger and her father, Abu Bakr. That had been three years ago, and Asma had not seen her mother since. Umm Ruman had felt sorry for the abandoned child, still too young to understand the enormity of her choice, and had raised the girl as her own.

She wondered what would happen to Asma once she was gone. Abu Bakr would likely look for a new wife, but there were only a handful of believers, and the Message was spreading slowly because of the need for secrecy. If the pagan leaders of Mecca learned the truth of what the Prophet was teaching, their wrath would be kindled, and the tiny community the believers had founded in the shadows would be exposed and destroyed. In all likelihood, Asma would be alone, without any foster mother to guide her through the journey of womanhood. The girl was past due for her cycles, which usually began at the age of ten or eleven for those born under the harsh Arabian sun. The menstrual flow would erupt any day now, but Umm Ruman would not be there to comfort her through the shock of first blood.

She ran her hand through Asma's brown curls, hoping to bequeath a soft memory with her touch that would comfort the child in the days to come. And then a shock of pain tore through Umm Ruman's womb and she screamed.

Asma broke free of her stepmother's grasp. She fell back, stumbling over one of the bricks that the midwife had placed at Umm Ruman's swollen feet. As Amal searched desperately through her midwife's stores for a salve to ease her patient's agony, the girl turned and ran in search of her father.

Umm Ruman closed her eyes and said silent prayer even as her body burned from within.

As her uterus contracted with increasing urgency, she could feel the baby shifting, preparing to emerge into the world. A process that in all likelihood would lead to her death, and possibly the baby's as well.

It was the beginning of the end, she thought sadly.

Umm Ruman was right. But in ways she could not have expected.

→　→　→

My father, Abu Bakr, walked through the quiet streets of Mecca, his head bowed low, his back hunched slightly, as if the weight of the world was on his shoulders. Which, of course, it was.

Tonight everything had changed. And he needed to tell someone. Normally he would have gone straight home after emerging from the Prophet's house, as their dwellings were next door to each other. But after what he had seen and heard tonight, he needed to take a walk.

And besides, his wife had entered labor earlier that day, and his home was now the exclusive domain of the midwife. Abu Bakr had learned through the birth of two sons and a daughter to give the tribe of women its privacy at such moments. A man could only serve as a bumbling annoyance or a dangerous distraction to the sacred rituals of birth. And the safe delivery of this child, the first to be born into the Revelation, was important not just to him, but to the entire Muslim community.

All twenty of them.

His child. Abu Bakr wondered for a moment what kind of world the baby would grow into. For years he had hoped that the Truth would spread discreetly and in secret until the masters of Mecca were surprised to see that their tribal religion had died in its sleep, to be replaced quietly with the worship of the One God. But tonight had shown him that whatever path Islam would take among these people, it would not be a quiet one.

He paused to look up at the heavens. There was no moon tonight and the sky was aflame with a legion of stars, the sparkling strands of a cosmic web that testified to the glory of the Lord. The foolish among his people believed that the future could be discerned in the shimmering patterns that played across the heavens. But Abu Bakr knew that such superstitions were a delusion. Only God knew the future. The greatest of storytellers, every day He surprised man with a new tale. Those who thought they could encompass His grand plan with their puny calculations were always humbled.

Turning a corner in the walled district of Mecca where many of the chieftains of the city lived, he found himself looking out past the hills that surrounded the desert valley to Mount Hira—the place where God had spoken to a man, even as He did to Moses at Mount Sinai to the north. The mountain, which soared two thousand feet above the desert floor, tapered into a rocky plateau, at the pinnacle of which was hidden a tiny cave. A small, cramped space where no light could enter. And from which Light itself had sprung forth.

When his childhood friend Muhammad, the orphan son of Abdallah of the clan of Bani Hashim, had emerged from that cave three years ago, he was transformed. He had seen a vision of an angel named Gabriel who had proclaimed him to be God's Messenger to mankind, the final Prophet sent to bring the world out of darkness into light. It was an audacious claim, one that would understandably invite ridicule had it been made by any other man. But Muhammad was different.

Abu Bakr had known him since they were excited boys traveling with a caravan to the markets of Palestine and Syria. And from the first day he had set eyes on the young Muhammad, Abu Bakr had known that his friend had a destiny. Raised in poverty and humiliation, the boy nonetheless exuded a dignity, a power, that seemed to emanate from another realm. While other youths quickly embraced the sharp business tactics of the Meccan traders as a means of getting ahead in the harsh world of the desert, Muhammad had gained a reputation as *Al-Amin*—the Honest One. His reputation for fair dealing brought him respect but little profit, and Abu Bakr had been heartbroken to see his friend live in destitution while less scrupulous young men advanced rapidly.

And he had been overjoyed as Muhammad's luck finally turned, when he won the heart of Khadija, a lovely—and wealthy—widow who had employed the youth to manage her caravans. Khadija had proposed to the penniless Muhammad, and Abu Bakr took great pleasure in seeing his boyhood comrade finally living in affluence among the nobles of Mecca. But Muhammad had never seemed comfortable around wealth, and his sudden prosperity and entry into elite society had only increased his concern for the many who remained poor in the desert valley.

Abu Bakr had spent many nights talking with his friend through the years as he expressed agitation over the worsening plight of the lower classes of the city. Women and children starved in the valley of Mecca, even as flourishing trade with the Byzantine and Persian empires to the north enriched its tribal chiefs. Muhammad had become increasingly distraught at the daily injustices he witnessed, as the strong preyed on the weak and men used and discarded women, leaving their bastard children to fend for themselves—in the worst cases, killing infant girls, whose birth was seen as socially undesirable.

Abu Bakr had not been surprised to see his tormented friend embark on a spiritual path, meditating every night and spending his days conversing with people of other nations and faiths he met on the caravan routes. Muhammad had never been interested in the religion of their people. The crude idols that the Arabs worshiped had repelled him, and he was drawn instinctively to the People of the Book, Jews and Christians, and their remarkable stories of the One God who stood for justice and compassion. And the People of the Book would remind him that this God had once also been worshiped by the ancestors of the Arabs, who had been descended from the prophet Abraham through his firstborn son, Ishmael. This God, whom the Jews called *Elohim*, was still known to the Arabs as *Allah*, the Creator God. But the Arabs now worshiped hundreds of other deities that were seen as intermediaries of Allah, who was too powerful and remote to care about the daily lives of men. Every tribe in the desert had its own god, and each held its god out to be better than the others, leading to division and warfare among the clans. These competing deities, like the untamed elements of nature they symbolized, were capricious and lacked any sense of morality or justice. Seeing the chaos engendered by these warring and cruel gods, Muhammad longed for his people to return to the old ways of Abraham and his simple, pure vision of Allah.

When Abu Bakr would come to visit him, Muhammad would often stay up late into the night sharing tales he had heard from these foreigners, stories about Moses and the haughty Pharaoh, Joseph and his conniving brothers among the Children of Israel, and Jesus the son of Mary, God's most recent Messenger to mankind, who had healed the blind and raised the dead. Abu Bakr was swept away by his friend's passion for this God and His prophets, which awakened within him a similar longing for the Divine. Like Muhammad, Abu Bakr found the gods of the Arabs to be petty and small. But Allah, this God of Abraham, had never spoken to the Arabs, and Abu Bakr longed to hear from this mysterious, invisible being who had forgotten the children of Ishmael.

And then it had happened. Muhammad's vision on Mount Hira had left his friend shaken and confused. Seeing the winged angel first inside the cave and then standing on the horizon, its wondrous form expanding in a cloud of light until it stretched to the heavens, Muhammad became convinced that he was mad or possessed by a djinn. He had wanted to kill himself in despair, but his wife, Khadija, had comforted him. She told him that a man of his character would not be misled or abandoned by Allah, and that his experience must be true. Over the next several months, the visions intensified, and the angel told Muhammad that he had been chosen to follow in his ancestor Abraham's path—to abolish idolatry and establish the worship of the One God among the Arabs, who would then spread the faith of their forefather to all mankind.

Muhammad was overwhelmed. He was being asked to undertake an impossible task. To turn a land of warring tribes who venerated hundreds of tribal deities into a unified nation under one God. How could he begin? Unable to find an answer beyond the loving circle of his wife and family, he had taken a risk. Muhammad had turned to his friend Abu Bakr and shared what was happening to him.

So it was that one peaceful evening three years ago, Abu Bakr had sat on the floor in the quiet of Muhammad's sparsely furnished private study as his old friend revealed the angelic visions and the Voice that had called to him from the heavens. As Abu Bakr heard him speak, he felt something stirring inside his heart. It was as if he had been waiting his whole life for this moment. It was as natural and inevitable as falling in love. Even before Muhammad finished speaking, Abu Bakr knew that his inner longing had been answered. Allah, the God who had spoken to Moses and Jesus, had not forgotten the Arabs, the children of Abraham. Abu Bakr had known Muhammad for over thirty years and had never had reason to doubt one word spoken by *Al-Amin*. If God would choose anyone to prophesy to the Arab nation, it would be this man. It had to be this man.

Without hesitation, Abu Bakr had accepted his claim to be the Messenger of God and promised that he would be Muhammad's right-hand man on his mission. And for the next three years, he had quietly spread the word to a few trusted friends and kinsmen that there was a Prophet in their midst, one who would bring their people to salvation. Abu Bakr acted in absolute secrecy, as the leaders of Mecca, whose trade was done in the name of the ancient gods, would have moved quickly to destroy this new religious movement.

While he succeeded in persuading a small handful of associates to accept Muhammad's teachings and join his faith, he was devastated that he failed to win over some in his own family. His first wife, Qutaila, had refused to break the idols of her gods and he had divorced her. And to add to his grief, his beloved son Abdal Kaaba also proved unwilling to turn his back on the ways of their people. Their arguments grew so bitter that Abdal Kaaba had left his home and gone to live among kinsmen, refusing to speak with him until Abu Bakr renounced his foolish new ideas. His alienation from his son weighed heavily on his heart, and the Prophet gently reminded Abu Bakr that Noah, too, had been estranged from his son, whose resistance to God's message had ultimately led to his death in the Flood. Abu Bakr understood that a father could not be responsible for the choices of his son, but his failure haunted him nonetheless.

Despite the personal losses he had endured in his family, Abu Bakr had not faced any major social consequences for his involvement in Muhammad's new group. The chieftains of Mecca had heard rumors that *Al-Amin* was quietly playing the role of spiritual teacher to a handful of locals, but they paid little attention. As long as his small band of followers kept to themselves and did not create trouble in Mecca, they could worship whatever god they wished, believe whatever they wanted. As long as Muhammad's teachings remained quiet and did not disrupt the profits of the tribal chiefs, everything would be fine.

But that had all changed tonight.

Abu Bakr turned away from the towering vision of Mount Hira and looked back to the Prophet's home in a distant corner of the city. The two-story edifice sparkled under the starlight, its white stone walls shimmering with a faint, unearthly glow. For the past few years, that house had been a secure gathering place for Abu Bakr and the nineteen other believers. There they prayed together and listened to the Prophet as he shared God's words that had been revealed through Gabriel. That home was their sanctuary.

It would now have to be their fortress. For the leaders of Mecca had learned tonight what Muhammad's true message was.

And they had declared war.

- ◆ - ◆ -

ASMA RACED OUT OF her father's home. She had seen Umm Ruman's ghostly pale face, the blood on her thighs, and had known that the birthing had gone terribly wrong. Asma had already lost one mother— she could not bear to lose another.

The girl ran down the steps and stepped out into the narrow alley between her father's home and the house of the Prophet. She splashed her feet in a pool of dark mud, residue of the rare and welcome rainfall of the night before. Her friends had all gone this morning to pray at the sacred temple—the Holy Kaaba—and thank their gods for the life-giving water that so rarely fell from the sky in the desert valley. But Asma had not joined them. Her father had taught her that the idols in the Kaaba were abominations, false gods whose worship angered Allah. The believers had gathered instead inside the Prophet's home to thank the One God in secret. They had bowed in unison, their foreheads touching the dark earth as the Prophet recited the most recent verses of the Qur'an, the Book that God was revealing to him bit by bit, in small poetic stanzas, every day.

Asma always enjoyed their services, partly because of the secrecy, the thrill of doing something that was forbidden. And partly because it was a special time that she could share with her father. Abu Bakr was a prosperous merchant who was forever busy inspecting caravans from

Yemen, buying and selling frankincense, carpets, and pottery in the marketplace, and serving as an arbiter of commercial disputes among the various trading parties of Mecca. She rarely saw him during the day and relished the few hours every night when he would set aside the ledger of a businessman and take on the robes of a believer.

Asma had always been amazed by how he would change in the presence of the Prophet at these meetings. Abu Bakr was a dignified man, masculine and strong, a man accustomed to quiet leadership. But in the presence of the Messenger, he became as a slave before its master—enthusiastic, nervous, anxious to please. The stern cynicism of the trader was replaced with wonder, the complete and absolute trust of a child. His long face, tired and worn from a day of haggling with Abyssinian, Greek, and Persian traders, would suddenly come alive with enthusiasm and joy. When her father had first approached Asma and told her of his new faith, she was too young to understand the intricacies of theology. But she saw how the Revelation had changed him, how it breathed life into a man who once seemed like a stone, perennially weary of the world, and she knew she that she, too, would embrace this path.

Her love for her father had given her the strength to turn her back on her mother, Qutaila, and her half brother, Abdal Kaaba, who had refused to join the new movement. When they left, a pall had fallen over the house of Abu Bakr. They were outcasts in their own home, adherents to a strange new religion that had the temerity to put the bonds of the soul before the ties of blood. Asma had felt her father's silent despair grow as his efforts to spread the Prophet's teachings among his kinsmen were met sometimes with incomprehension, more usually with laughter, and a few times with anger. As fewer and fewer of Abu Bakr's clansmen and family members came to visit their home, she had felt her own growing isolation. The girls she played with would sometimes whisper about the rumors spreading through Mecca, that Abu Bakr and his family had been possessed by djinn or had been placed under a spell by a sorcerer. She wanted to tell them, tell everyone in the city, the truth. That God had spoken to them, was speaking to them every day, through the lyrical voice of a man who had never before recited any words of power or poetry. That they were being told truths far greater than any relayed by the *kahins,* the mystical soothsayers who wandered through the villages of Arabia, sharing their visions for a price.

But her father had forbidden her to speak of their community and its beliefs. So she had kept silent, and the shared secret created a lasting bond with the few other believers. They were her new family.

A family that would now be torn asunder if her stepmother died. Umm Ruman had become a mother to the whole community, second only in importance to Khadija, the Prophet's wife and the first to embrace the new faith. The handful of believers turned to Umm Ruman for hope and inspiration. They relied on her patient ears to unload their tales of loneliness and sorrow, the price that came with their newfound faith. Her kind smile had lifted the hearts of many who had been consumed by grief and rejection, and her soft hands had wiped many cheeks of tears in the past few years. Her death would be a devastating blow to the faithful. But they would ultimately be consoled by turning to the Prophet and his family, the *Ahl al-Bayt,* the People of the House, who served as the heart of the new religion. The believers would move on, Asma thought ruefully, but she would be bereft of a mother. Again.

She ran down the narrow path toward the Messenger's home, stopping in front of the wrought-iron gate. As always when she approached the beautiful stone house, with its sturdy pillars and delicately tapered arches, she detected the distinct smell of roses in the air, although she could see no blooms in the courtyard. Asma caught her breath and glanced up. The silver latticed windows on the second floor, the family area, were dark. Although she knew there had been a large gathering inside earlier in the night, no sound emerged from within. The eerie chirping of crickets echoed around her mournfully. Perhaps the Prophet was asleep or immersed deep in prayer.

Even though she knew that her mission was one of life and death, she still hesitated to knock and disturb the holy family. Although her father always reminded her that Allah was merciful and compassionate, she had heard the frightening tales of those who earned His wrath—the tribe of 'Ad, which had mocked their prophet Hud and been struck down by wind and storm, or Thamud, which had hamstrung the she-camel of its prophet Salih and been consumed by an earthquake.

Asma realized that she was shaking. Whether it was from fear of losing her stepmother or fear of inciting God's anger by troubling his Prophet, she could not say. She took a breath and took hold of the silver knocker that hung just above her head. Asma rapped the gate three times and was surprised by how deeply the sound echoed inside.

For a long moment, she heard nothing. She tentatively reached for the knocker a second time, when the sound of approaching footsteps halted her. The gate swung inward and a shadow fell upon her. Asma looked up to see a handsome boy of thirteen with emerald-green eyes and hair the color of a starless night. She immediately knew who he was and for a second had difficulty speaking. His intense eyes seemed to peer straight through her in the dark, as if they were lit by their own fire. She blushed and looked down at her feet, and was suddenly mortified to see her slippers, feet, and ankles caked in mud.

"Peace be upon you, daughter of Abu Bakr." The boy spoke cheerfully, apparently oblivious to her embarrassment. He smiled at her softly, but what he was thinking as he looked at the panting and bedraggled girl on his doorstep, she had no idea. Ali, the son of the Meccan tribal chief Abu Talib, was a cipher, a mystery to even those closest to the Prophet and his family. He was the young cousin of the Messenger and had been adopted into the *Ahl al-Bayt* when the Prophet's elderly uncle Abu Talib could no longer afford to feed him. Muhammad was very close to the lad, perhaps viewing him as the brother he had never had, or the son who could have been.

But Ali was not like other youths, and he remained aloof from the boys of Mecca. He showed little interest in their sports, races, or kites, preferring to spend his time watching people in the marketplace as if trying to understand a strange and different species. As a result, the other young men of the city were always a little nervous and uncertain in Ali's presence. Even the believers around the Prophet were not sure what to make of him. He never quite appeared to be with them in spirit, even if he was there in body. Even now, Ali was like an apparition from a dream. She suddenly had a strange thought. What if Ali is the dreamer and Asma the dream? What happens to me when he awakes?

"I am looking for my father," she said, pushing the troubling thought aside. "Umm Ruman is ill. Her womb is bleeding."

Ali blinked at her as if he did not understand her words. Asma got the unnerving feeling again that he was not quite with her but was gazing at her from across some vast distance.

And then he nodded, as if suddenly snapped back to the present moment.

"I am sorry to hear that," he said softly. "I will inform the Prophet. He will pray for Umm Ruman and, if God wills, she will be healed."

Ali stepped back and moved to close the gate, when Asma shifted on to the threshold and took hold of its iron latch.

"And my father?" Asma insisted.

"Your father is not here," Ali said gently. "Abu Bakr went to see Talha and tell him the news."

"What news?"

The light in Ali's eyes seemed to brighten.

"It has begun," he said simply. And with that, Ali nodded a farewell to the perplexed girl and closed the gate.

Asma stood frozen for a moment. There was perfect silence all about her, and the air felt heavier, as if a mysterious blanket had covered the street. It felt as if time had somehow stopped during her brief talk with Ali and that the world itself had been holding its breath.

And then the crickets chirped again in a steady, flowing cadence. Asma shook off the uncomfortable sensation of having just returned from a strange and distant land and focused her mind on what she had to do. She turned and ran away from the Prophet's house toward the main streets of Mecca and her cousin Talha's home.

─   ─   ─

ABU BAKR WARMED HIS hands by the fire as Talha poured him some goat's milk in an old wooden bowl. The young man, recently turned eighteen, was one of the most recent converts to the new faith. The Prophet's teachings of charity and justice for the poor had ignited Talha's youthful idealism and had given him a cause more worthy of dedicating his life to than simply driving camels for his wealthy cousin. He was eager to share the Revelation with his young friends, to recruit them to the cause, but he had sworn a vow of secrecy. Talha had passionately counseled the Messenger to let him spread the word among the stable boys and shepherds of God's Word. He argued that the new way would be resisted by Abu Bakr's generation, long trapped in the rites of their fathers, but that it was among the *shabab* of Mecca, those too young to be subdued by the overpowering weight of tradition, that they would find their strongest supporters. The Prophet had smiled and gently admonished him to be patient. Allah had a plan and none could rush the Divine into action. They day would come, Talha had been assured, when they would emerge from the shadows and proclaim the One God openly in Mecca, and eventually the world.

And now, at last, that day had come.

"So he told the tribal chiefs tonight?" Talha's eyes glittered with excitement as he handed his elder cousin the bowl of milk.

"Yes." Abu Bakr held the bowl to his lips, softly whispering the invocation *Bismillah-ir-Rahman-ir-Raheem*—"In the name of God, the Merciful, the Compassionate." It was the sacred formula that the Prophet had been taught by Gabriel, the words by which believers began the recitation of their prayers. It was the blessing that they uttered every time they started something anew, whether it be as simple as eating or drinking or tying their shoes, or as meaningful and profound as making love. The *bismillah* sanctified even the smallest moments of life, elevating the mundane to the holy with every breath.

Abu Bakr sipped the milk, let its soft curds flow down his throat and cool the fire he had felt growing inside his belly through the night.

"What happened?" Talha leaned forward, his hands gripping the edge of the old cypress table that Abu Bakr had given him as a gift the day he embraced Islam.

Abu Bakr sighed and put down the bowl.

"The Prophet received a revelation from Gabriel that he must now openly proclaim the Message, beginning first with his own family members," Abu Bakr said, looking into the flames as he recounted the tale. "And so he asked Ali to gather the heads of Quraysh for dinner tonight."

The Quraysh were the Prophet's tribe, who had long administered the city of Mecca and organized the annual pilgrimage that brought Arabs from all over the desert to worship their gods at the Kaaba, the holy temple at the center of the city. They were the de facto rulers of the most important religious site in all of Arabia, and their support would have given Muhammad's new movement the prestige to win over the hearts of their countrymen.

"It was a sparse meal," Abu Bakr said softly, remembering the strange events of the evening with a hint of wonder in his voice. "Just a leg of mutton, the meat of which barely filled the bowl the Prophet gave to Ali. And one cup of milk that I saw him fill from an earthen jug. I asked the Messenger if I should go and bring more food from my house, for there was barely enough to feed one man, much less the gathered dignitaries of the Quraysh. He simply smiled and reached into the bowl, taking a small strip of meat. He chewed a morsel and then threw it back into the bowl. And then I saw him turn to Ali and tell the boy to take it in the name of Allah."

Talha clasped his hands eagerly as Abu Bakr recited the inexplicable events that had followed.

"Ali passed the bowl from man to man, thirty in all, and each reached in and took his fill. Yet the meat did not diminish and the bowl remained always full. Ali poured them milk from the goblet, filling each man's glass, and yet I never saw him refill his own."

Talha gasped at the remarkable tale.

"And you saw this? With your own eyes?"

Abu Bakr nodded. "It was like the tale the Messenger once told me when we were boys, a story passed along to him by a Christian monk he met on the caravan to Syria. A tale of the prophet Jesus, peace be upon him, who multiplied many fish and loaves as a sign from God."

Talha felt a chill go down his spine, and his heart began to thud in his chest. The Prophet had never claimed to perform any miracles, saying that the fact that God was speaking through an illiterate Arab was enough of a miracle in itself. Talha had accepted the truth of the Prophet's words because they touched his heart. He had never needed any such signs or proofs of his divine mission. But now, listening to Abu Bakr's tale, he fervently wished that he had been there tonight. But Talha was not a tribal chief. Far from it. He had little wealth or influence of his own and often regretted that he could offer little to the Prophet in terms of material support. But if what Abu Bakr was saying was true, perhaps their little community no longer needed material help. If food could rain down from heaven as it had in the days of Jesus, then the age of miracles had been reborn. Their new faith would triumph, shining a light on what was true and pushing away the darkness.

"Surely the Quraysh must have seen what was happening," Talha said excitedly. "Surely their hearts must have been moved by the miracle."

Abu Bakr looked down sadly. "Their hearts were indeed moved, but in the wrong direction. They hardened, like the heart of Pharaoh when confronted by Moses and his miraculous rod."

Talha was stunned. "They denied the sign?"

"When murmurs of surprise spread through the hall at the miracle, Abu Lahab, the Prophet's uncle, rose and proclaimed that their host had bewitched them." Abu Bakr shook his head at the memory of the old man's fury. "The tribal chiefs rose to leave, but the Prophet begged them to stay, to hear his message. He told them at long last the truth. That he was the Messenger of Allah, and that he had been sent to destroy the idols and false gods that had corrupted the religion of the Arabs. They were shocked and outraged, and for a moment I thought their fury would lead to a riot there in the very home of the Prophet."

Talha sat back, his heart sinking. "What did the Prophet do?"

"He called out to his clansmen and asked who among them would help him in his mission and thus become his brother, his executor and successor among them." Abu Bakr looked into Talha's eyes. "None spoke in his favor. And then Ali stood up before all the lords of Mecca and proclaimed that he would be the Prophet's helper."

Talha was perplexed. "Ali? He is just a boy."

Abu Bakr nodded. "A boy, perhaps, but with the heart of a lion. He showed more courage in that moment, standing firm before the jeering chieftains, than most men show in a lifetime. The Prophet touched Ali's neck and commanded the tribal chiefs to hearken to Ali and obey him."

Talha was speechless for a moment. Abu Bakr saw his consternation and smiled.

"The chieftains had the same reaction," he said. "There was a silence in the room, like the quiet that falls upon the earth before the wrath of heaven is unleashed. And then they began to laugh and mock the Prophet, who had ordered them to obey a boy whose voice had only recently hardened, whose cheeks were still without a beard. I looked across the room to see Ali's father, the Prophet's uncle Abu Talib, bow his gray head in shame, as the lords heaped abuse on his son and nephew. And then they all turned and stormed out of the hall, leaving us alone and in silence."

Talha shook his head in dismay. He ran his hand through his dark curls as if trying to pull off the cobweb of despair that had suddenly fallen on him.

"So now they know. And they will try to destroy us."

Abu Bakr nodded.

Talha looked across the small room that served as his only shelter in the barren valley of Mecca. He had only the table his cousin had given him and a small leather cot across from the open fireplace. That was the extent of his worldly goods. And he was considered richer than many of the believers. How were they going to stand up to the might of Mecca, whose lords lived like kings, whose coffers were filled with gold, whose clansmen were armed with the finest swords and spears?

"So what do we do now?"

Abu Bakr gazed out the small window of the stone cottage. Outside, the stars sparkled and danced across the firmament. A heavenly flame flew past his vision, followed by another.

"A new day is upon us," Abu Bakr said thoughtfully. "The secret has been revealed, and the world will now conspire against the believers," he said softly.

And then he reached over and touched Talha on the shoulder. "Like you, my heart was heavy tonight. But as I moved to leave the empty hall, the Messenger took me aside and comforted me. He said these words that had been revealed by Gabriel:

"In the Name of God, the Merciful, the Compassionate
By the flight of Time
Man is indeed in loss
Except for those who believe
And do good
And persevere with truth
And persevere with patience."

Talha felt the words flow through his heart, like a stream bringing life to the dead earth. These words, which rhymed with majestic poetry and perfect meter in Arabic, had been spoken by God Himself tonight. Tears suddenly welled in his eyes. The God of Abraham, who had chosen to speak to man one last time. And in His inexplicable plan, He had chosen to speak through them, a barbaric, uneducated, and primitive people. A nation forgotten by history and mocked by the grand civilizations that surrounded them. They were the worst of the sons of Adam. And yet He had chosen them.

Talha followed his elder kinsman's gaze at the stars outside. They had circled the earth for countless millennia. Had seen empires rise and fall, had seen mighty kings and warriors crumble into dust, their names forgotten, the songs of their deeds lost in the mists of time. And yet the stars remained firm, sparkling in the heavens, as a sign of that which would never die, that which would never be lost to time.

Talha understood. Though the entire world might work against them, God's plan would triumph. It was not for them to know the how or the when. Their task was to begin writing the tale, even though its final chapter was hidden from them.

Abu Bakr leaned closer to him and spoke softly, conspiratorially. "Do not sleep tonight, but stay awake and bow in worship."

Talha looked at him. "I will do as you say."

Abu Bakr nodded. He looked directly into Talha's eyes. "The Messenger said that there will be Signs tonight. The angels are writing the future of our faith even as we speak. The destinies of men and women will be inscribed in the Tablet of Heaven, and the writing will be made clear to those whose hearts are ready. For it is tonight that our faith will be born anew and shall light a fire that will consume the old world and bring in the new."

Talha nodded, his soul stirring with awe at Abu Bakr's words.

And then he saw the first Sign.

An angel clad in white, its gown glittering in the starlight, was flying down the path toward his home. Talha's mouth fell open. He stared at the apparition in wonder, like a parched traveler gazing at a mirage, hoping beyond hope that what he saw was real and not a ghost of his imagination

And then he saw that the angel was a child, whose face was white with fear.

"Father!" It was Asma, Abu Bakr's daughter, who cried to them from across the dirt road as she caught a glimpse of their silhouettes standing near the window of the tiny mud brick cottage.

Abu Bakr turned to stare out the window in surprise. And when he saw the look on his daughter's face, the blood emptied from his own. Talha watched in shock as his cousin's serene composure shattered and was replaced by a look of pure terror. Abu Bakr staggered toward the door, his heart in his throat. He stumbled and Talha reached to help him, but the older man swatted him away.

Abu Bakr threw open the small arched door to Talha's cottage just as Asma fell inside the threshold. He held his daughter close as she tried to catch her breath. But even before the child spoke, Talha knew what she would say. Her red-rimmed eyes burned their message to any who looked into them.

Abu Bakr stroked his daughter's brown curls softly, let her lean into his chest to gain strength from the power of his beating heart. A heart that was now thundering so loudly that Talha fancied he heard it pounding in his ears. Or was it his own?

"Umm Ruman . . ." Asma gasped, trying to choke out the words. "Umm Ruman . . . the baby . . . is dying . . ."

━ ━ ━

AMAL THE MIDWIFE WIPED the sweat-drenched brow of her unlucky ward. She barely noticed that her own face, indeed her arms and breasts, were bathed in sweat from her efforts to save the life of the mother and child. By all accounts, both should be dead by now. The blood from Umm Ruman's womb had flowed like honey from a beehive, slow, dark, and persistent. She had lost more blood in the past hour than Amal imagined could have possibly flowed through the veins of the tiny woman. But the delicate lady, with bones as dainty and small as a bird, had proven a warrior in spirit. Umm Ruman had screamed and screamed in agony, but she remained stubbornly alive, refusing to give in to the inevitable.

Amal had finally been able to stem the hemorrhage, which had drained the dark-skinned Umm Ruman and left her soft skin a sickly yellow, like a full moon low on the eastern horizon in midsummer. The midwife had breathed a sigh of relief and muttered a prayer thanking the goddess Uzza, when her patient sharply forbade her to mention the name of the divinity. "If you pray, do so to Allah," Umm Ruman had croaked out between labored breaths. Amal was surprised at the strange request. Allah, the High God, was too far away to hear the prayers of mortals. That is why their people worshiped His daughters Allat, Uzza, and Manat, and a host of other gods who had the time and patience to deal with the petty affairs of mankind.

Umm Ruman was clearly light-headed and confused from her ordeal, but Amal knew enough to remain silent. Now that the bleeding had stopped, she needed to help bring forth the remains of the baby. The child would in all likelihood be stillborn, but she needed to clear the dead fetus from Umm Ruman's womb and cleanse her of the poisonous afterbirth if there were to be any hope of saving her patient.

Amal had pressed her hand along Umm Ruman's stretched belly and was surprised to feel the unmistakable tremor of movement beneath her flesh. The child lived! Amal's heart soared with hope for a second and then was dashed as she pressed farther along Umm Ruman's stomach. She felt a soft pressure near the birth canal that she immediately recognized as the baby's feet. Her spirit sank. The baby was improperly positioned. If Umm Ruman pushed the child out feetfirst, it would suffocate before it had a chance to enter the world.

Amal knew what had to be done. She looked up at Umm Ruman, whose bloodshot eyes shone with grim determination. "The child . . ."

"I know," was all Umm Ruman said, and Amal knew that she understood. The tiny woman with the heart of a soldier grinded her teeth in preparation. "Do it."

Amal nodded. She hesitated and then made a loud prayer to Allah for the safe delivery of the child. She did not really believe that the Lord of the Worlds would take a moment from turning the stars in the heavens to care for the plight of one small, forgotten mother, but Amal wanted to give Umm Ruman hope. The odds were she would die from what happened next, but at least she would die with her heart satisfied.

The midwife took a deep breath and put her hands on Umm Ruman's belly. Remembering the ancient techniques taught to her by her own mother, Amal placed pressure on her patient's womb in order to turn the child headfirst.

Umm Ruman screamed, an agonized cry that echoed across the valley of Mecca and traveled high into the starry heavens.

—•— —•— —•—

ABU BAKR STOOD OUTSIDE his wife's birth chamber, shaking with fear. He could hear Umm Ruman's horrific wails, which seemed only to increase in intensity. Every fiber in his body cried for him to rush inside and comfort his dying wife through her final moments. But Talha held him back. "Let the midwife do her job," the boy had said, and Abu Bakr knew he was right.

He looked down at Asma, his loyal daughter, who had chosen him and his faith even over her own mother, and squeezed her tiny hand. She was strong, stronger than he would have been in her position. He had torn their family apart with his decision to follow Muhammad, and she had never complained. Abu Bakr had always been close to his own parents, and he had found it beyond comprehension how his young friend Muhammad had endured the horrific loss of his beloved mother, Amina, when he was only six years old. Abu Bakr's heart was heavy with the knowledge that he had orphaned Asma once already by renouncing Qutaila. And now, with Umm Ruman's impending death, the child would be doubly motherless.

He looked around the antechamber where they waited for the screams to abruptly end and the midwife to emerge with her dreaded tidings. It was well furnished, as befitted a prosperous merchant of Quraysh. Thick rugs imported from Persia covered the marble floors. The stone walls were whitewashed and held many trophies and trinkets from his travels on the caravan routes. Silver plates from Syria, their tiles swirling in intricate geometric designs, lined one wall, while another was covered in an assortment of swords and daggers from Byzantium, their hilts embedded with precious emeralds and rubies. The arched windows were covered in thick curtains made from Abyssinian cotton. Couches covered in rich silk brocade had entertained many nobles from Mecca and beyond in the years past, although now that Abu Bakr's true beliefs were known, he was likely to have few such visitors in the future.

Abu Bakr was by every account a wealthy man, but he would readily trade all the gold in his coffers for a miracle tonight.

Perhaps sensing his thoughts, Talha touched his shoulder.

"Let us pray the *Fatiha*. Perhaps it will be of help," the boy said softly.

Abu Bakr looked at the sensitive young man and then at his brave little daughter, and nodded.

The three believers stood in a circle, their hands upraised to heaven in humble supplication, and recited in unison the Seven Oft-Repeated Verses that the believers read daily in their prayers:

In the name of God, the Merciful, the Compassionate.
Praise be to God, Lord of the Worlds
The Merciful, the Compassionate
King of the Day of Judgment
You alone do we worship, and Your aid alone do we seek.
Show us the Straight Path
The path of those who incur Your favor
Not the path of those who earn Your wrath
Nor of those who go astray.

Abu Bakr, Talha, and Asma recited the prayer out loud, their voices melding in lyrical unison. They repeated it again, and a third time. Perhaps it was Abu Bakr's imagination, but each time he recited the sacred verses, the cries from the adjoining room seemed to lessen in intensity.

Again and again they repeated the holy words. And then, at the seventh recitation, a silence fell over the house, a quiet so sudden and so complete that Abu Bakr's heart chilled. Umm Ruman was dead.

Tears welled in his eyes, and his heart started pounding. She was his strength, his soul. How could he live without her? He realized that Asma was now crying openly, but he found he could not move to comfort her.

Talha moved to take the weeping child out of the room, to leave Abu Bakr to the privacy of his grief.

And then they heard it. A strange, impossible, glorious sound.

The cry of a baby.

Abu Bakr raised his head and stared at the door to the birthing chamber. There was silence again. Had he imagined it? And then the child wailed louder and he felt a burst of light illuminate his heart, like the sun emerging from behind the empty blackness of an eclipse.

Talha looked up at him in wonder. And Asma laughed, clapping her hands with the unfettered delight that only a child can know.

Abu Bakr felt his legs go weak, and he grabbed hold of an intricately carved chair made from Iraqi cypress. And then he stumbled forward and threw tradition to the wind. He flung open the door to the forbidden chamber and rushed inside.

Umm Ruman was still seated on the sharply angled birthing chair, her tunic covered in blood and the fluids of childbirth. Her face was sickly pale, but her eyes were open and alert. And she breathed deeply, like a woman trapped at the bottom of a well longing for air. She was alive!

Abu Bakr looked at her in wonder and she smiled weakly. He would remember that smile in years to come, when the storm clouds that had been gathering would be unleashed and the armies of men and the devil would seek to destroy the believers. It would give him strength and hope and power to battle on in the cause of God and His Messenger. For in a cruel world where the only certainty was death, their way was the way of life.

The child's cries turned his head and Abu Bakr looked at the midwife, who had just finished washing the baby and had wrapped it in a green swaddling cloth. Amal's face was haggard and she looked as if she herself had endured the pangs of childbirth. She looked up at him and nodded a greeting, the lines of her mouth too tired to form into a smile.

"I give you glad tidings of a girl," she said weakly. Abu Bakr saw the strain in her face and worried that she barely had the strength to hold the precious baby. He moved to take the child into his arms, and the midwife did not protest.

Abu Bakr took hold of the tiny child as Talha and Asma tentatively entered the birthing chamber. He looked down at the wrinkled face and ran a finger across the girl's cheeks, pink like a rose blossom. His daughter had a healthy brush of hair, a fiery red that glittered like copper in the pale torchlight. As Abu Bakr held his child, he realized that she was a true miracle—the first child to be born into the new religion. He wanted his first words to her to impart the truth he had come to believe with all his heart. He bent down carefully and whispered into the infant's ears the formula of faith: *There is no god but God, and Muhammad is the Messenger of God.*

The child opened her eyes for the first time at the sound of his words. Abu Bakr caught his breath. She had eyes unlike any he had ever seen before. Golden, like those of a lion, they seemed to glow with their own fire.

He felt rather than saw Asma step up behind him, and he turned to her.

"Come, see your sister," he said to his daughter, who looked down nervously at the little girl. Asma hesitated and then bent down to kiss the baby on its forehead. Abu Bakr turned to Umm Ruman, who weakly reached out to him. He moved to show their daughter to his wife, when the midwife made a cry of alarm.

"Manat protect us! The tidings are ill!" Amal squawked unexpectedly.

Abu Bakr looked over to see the midwife staring out of a small window facing east. Her eyes were wide, and she was slapping her head furiously in the ancient gesture of grief and terror.

"What's the matter?" Abu Bakr asked sharply.

"The baby . . . she is born under a dark star," Amal said. She pointed out the window to a constellation that was rising on the eastern horizon. It was a swirling cluster of lights, with the ominous red star Antares pulsating in its center.

Al-Akrab. The Scorpion. To the pagan Arabs, the stars of the zodiac were gods in their own right, beings that ruled men's affairs from the heavens and set their destinies at birth. And al-Akrab was the lord of death.

Before Abu Bakr could react, Amal rushed to his side, her eyes wide with fear.

"The child . . . cast it into the desert . . . bury it under stones before it can wreak its havoc!" she said, her voice frantic, her leathery face contorted with a kind of madness.

Abu Bakr felt his fury rise. He pushed Amal away from him forcefully.

"Get away from my daughter!" he said with terrifying ferocity. A mild and restrained man by nature, his anger was a rare and terrible thing to behold. Even Asma shrank back at the sudden rage in his voice.

Talha quickly moved forward and put a steady hand on the agitated midwife. "Do not utter your blasphemies in this house, which God has blessed."

But Amal ignored the boy.

"She is a curse . . . wherever she will go, chaos and death will follow her," Amal said, her eyes brimming with the intensity of her superstitious belief. "Slay her now, before the wrath of the gods is kindled!"

Abu Bakr held the baby closer to his heart, which was pounding with anger.

"I will slay your gods instead, and the wrath of the One will be kindled against your lies for all time!" Abu Bakr's voice boomed with such power and authority that Amal was struck speechless.

He turned to Talha, his eyes burning with righteous indignation.

"Pay this midwife what she is due, and then let her not darken my doorstep again," he said.

Talha pulled the trembling woman away and led her out of the birthing chamber. She bowed her head and did not struggle with him, nor did she make any move to take the gold dirham that he offered her. He finally pushed it into her hand and closed her fingers around it.

As Talha pushed Amal out the door, she looked up at him with her dark eyes, which now shone with the frenzy that he had seen among the *kahina*s, the medicine women of the desert whom the foolish people consulted for their oracles.

"The child will lead you to your death someday," Amal said softly.

Alas, poor Talha, how I wish he had but listened to her portent!

But he only looked at her with contempt.

"If that is the will of Allah, I will happily embrace it."

His confident response surprised the woman, who suddenly looked confused and lost. Who were these strange people who ignored the ancient traditions of the gods and put their trust in a God that no one could see or hear or touch? She turned and gazed out across the stone settlements of Mecca as if seeing the city for the first time. Amal looked up at the stars for an answer but found none.

"The child is the beginning of the end," she whispered. "It is all ending. Everything. And I cannot see what will take its place."

Talha looked at the strange woman and shook his head.

"The Truth," he said simply, before closing the door on the midwife.

Talha returned to find Abu Bakr leaning close to Umm Ruman, who now held the swaddled baby in her arms. The drama of the midwife appeared to be forgotten amid the family's joy at her safe delivery.

He went up to his kinsman and smiled.

"The madwoman is gone," he said.

Abu Bakr looked up at him and shook his head.

"She was not mad," he said softly. "This little girl *will* bring death."

Talha was stunned by these words.

"I don't understand" was all he could say.

Abu Bakr stroked his newborn daughter's soft cheek gently.

"She will bring death to ignorance, which will allow the light of knowledge to be born," he said simply.

Abu Bakr took the girl from Umm Ruman and held her close.

"In a world of idolatry, she is the first to be born a believer," he said softly. "She has already conquered death and has brought life." He gazed into the child's golden eyes, which were alert and seemed to exhibit an ancient intelligence.

"I will name her Aisha," Abu Bakr said.

A name that Talha knew in the old language meant "She Lives."

2 Mecca—AD 617

y first real memory is the day I witnessed death.

Ever since that day, I have been blessed—and cursed—with perfect memory. I can recall words said forty years ago as if they had been uttered this morning. The scent of a moment is forever impressed on my heart, as if I live outside time, and every moment of my life is now. The Messenger, may God's blessings and peace be upon him, used to say that I was chosen for that reason. That his words and deeds would be remembered for all time through me, the one he loved the most.

But there is a darkness behind every gift, like the veil of night that remains hidden behind the sun, waiting patiently for its moment to cast the world in gloom. My gift of memory is like that. For even as I can remember every moment of joy, every instant of laughter in my life, I can also remember the pain with absolute clarity. There are those who say time heals all wounds, but that is not so for me. Every wound I have suffered, I relive with terrifying precision, as if the knife, once embedded in my heart, leaves behind a shard of crystal sharpness ready to cut me again should I turn my thoughts in its direction.

It is that perfect memory that has made me the most prized recounter of *hadith*, the tales of the Prophet's life and teaching to be recorded for future generations of believers.

And it is that perfect memory that brought war upon my people and splintered our nation forever.

But every memory, even one as pristine as my own, must begin in earnest one day. Mine begins the day of the great Pilgrimage. My father had decided that I was old enough to attend the annual ritual, where tribes from all over Arabia descended on the arid valley of Mecca to worship at the House of God.

I ran shoeless out of the house when Abu Bakr called, and my father sternly sent me back, telling me that I could not accompany him unless I wore the tiny blue sandals he had bought from Yemeni traders earlier that summer. I pouted and stamped my feet, but Abu Bakr simply raised his eyebrows and refused to open the gate until I hung my head and sullenly went back inside in search of them.

I hunted through the house, trying to remember where I had thrown them in one of my tantrums earlier that morning. I searched in my small bedroom, beneath the tiny cot with its knotted rope fibers supporting the soft Egyptian cotton mattress. I looked through the mountain of dolls and toys that were piled in a corner, throwing the little wooden and rag figures everywhere and making a mess that my mother would assuredly chide me for later that day. But that inevitable reckoning did not concern me, a young girl who only cared for the moment. The future, as every child knows, is little more than make-believe. All that ever exists, all that ever matters, is now.

Frowning, I ran out of her bedchamber and looked in the main sitting room, underneath the emerald brocaded couches from Persia that were among the few luxuries that still remained inside our home. My mother told me that our house used to be filled with beautiful and expensive furnishings in the Days of Ignorance but that Abu Bakr had sold most of his worldly goods since I was born, dedicating his wealth to the spread of the Truth. I always wondered why spreading the Truth should be expensive, since it was obvious and free to all, but when I asked Umm Ruman once, my mother gave me the stern glance that was her practiced response to my litany of impertinent queries.

Looking around in frustration, I suddenly saw a hint of blue in a corner. I ran over, my crimson hair flying behind me. There they were! My Yemeni sandals were tucked behind an intricate vase that my mother said was made in a faraway city called Damascus. I paused to admire the swirling floral designs in carnelian, citrine, and olive that circled the ivory vase in crisscrossing patterns.

Umm Ruman had taught me the names of the different blooms depicted on the vase—hyacinths, jasmine and lotus—flowers that grew in faraway cities with mysterious names like Aksum, Babylon, and Persepolis. I loved flowers, but so few grew in the hot desert sun. I had yelped with delight a month before when I had found a small *abal* bush growing in a gulley just outside the perimeter of the holy precinct, at the base of the sacred hill of Safa. I had plucked its red, lantern-shaped blooms, which I had seen the older girls use to rouge their cheeks, but its thorns had torn into my tiny palm and I had run home crying.

My mother had gently removed the needles from my hand and salved the little wounds with dried sap from the thornbushes that grew in our courtyard. After drying my tears, Umm Ruman had gently chided me for wandering so far away from home. From now on, I was to play only within sight of their house. Mecca was a dangerous city for little girls . . . especially girls whose families supported the heretic Prophet in its midst.

I remembered her words as I grabbed the sandals and slipped them on. They were pretty enough, with little white stars woven though the tiny blue throngs, but I didn't like them. Although other girls were obsessed with shoes, spending hours in silly talk about the merits of various designs, the newest fashions arriving on caravans from north and south, I found shoes to be an irritant. Instead, I loved the tingly feeling of the warm sand on my bare feet, even the tiny pricks caused by the pebbles that littered the streets of the ancient city. Shoes made me feel restricted and caged, like one of the goats my father had kept in a pen behind the old stone house in preparation for the sacrifice at the apex of the Pilgrimage.

I ran back to my father, who was still waiting by the gate. Seeing the look of mild irritation on his face at the delay, I quickly kicked up my feet and showed off the little shoes, and then danced an excited jig around him, until his stern face broke into an exasperated smile. I always knew how to melt Abu Bakr's serious mood. I was too full of life to allow others the luxury of gloom.

My father took my hand and together we walked through the dusty streets of Mecca. Smoke rose from the chimneys of hundreds of small stone cottages and mud-brick huts, clustered together in expanding concentric circles around the central plaza known as *Al-Haram*—the Sanctuary. As we walked toward the heart of the city I saw children racing through the streets, chasing one another or a variety of animals—goats, lambs, and a few wayward chickens—that had escaped their pens.

I also saw dozens of beggars, mainly women and bastard children who had been abandoned by their fathers. They held out their hands, their pathetic cries for compassion largely ignored. My father handed an old woman a gold dirham. Her eyes went wide in shock at his generosity, for she had come to expect little more than a copper piece accompanied by a grudging look. We were suddenly surrounded by what appeared to be every beggar in town, their hands reaching out for this source of bounty. I was frightened by this excited crowd of young and old, dressed in rags and smelling worse than the rabid dogs that prowled the streets at night. But Abu Bakr was patient with them, handing to each a single gold coin from his leather purse until he had nothing left.

They followed him through the streets, pleading for more, but my father simply smiled and shook his head.

"I will be back tomorrow with more, *insha-Allah*," he said, using the phrase "if God wills" that was a signature of the Muslims. The Messenger had taught us that we should say *insha-Allah* whenever we spoke of the future, even if referring to events only an hour away. It kept man humble and forced him to acknowledge that he was not solely the master of his destiny.

My father managed to slip away from the more persistent and aggressive of the beggars, pulling me into a side alley and taking a circuitous route to the Sanctuary. We were now in the oldest section of the city, whose buildings were said to have stood for hundreds of years, since the earliest tribes had settled the valley. The ancient houses looked like grand towers to me, but in truth most were ramshackle constructions of wood and stone, few rising higher than a second story. I could see people standing on rooftop terraces, their eyes on the horizon as the steady stream of Bedouin pilgrims emerged from the dead hills in search of Mecca's gods—and its life-giving wells. My eyes went wide as I watched the strangers ride by, their camels covered in colorful mats of wool and leather, their faces cracked and blackened by years of harsh work under the unforgiving sun.

My father sensed I was dawdling and he pulled forward with a gentle tug until we had cleared the narrow stone alleys and stepped onto the red sand that marked the boundaries of the Sanctuary. The plaza was spread open in a wide circle and my eyes immediately fell on the Kaaba, the grand temple that was the heart of Mecca and all of Arabia. Shaped like a majestic cube, it towered forty feet above the ground and was the tallest building in the settlement. The granite walls were covered in a variety of rich curtains of wool, cotton, even silk—

crimson, emerald, and sky blue—that were brought by tribes from every corner of Arabia to mark their Pilgrimage to the sacred house.

As we approached the Kaaba, I saw my father frown. The plaza was covered with a bewildering collection of idols, stone and wood icons that represented the various gods of the desert tribes. There were 360 in all, one for each day of the year. Some were elegantly fashioned, chiseled in marble to an almost lifelike representation of a man or an animal—lions, wolves, and jackals seemed particularly popular. But others were little more than misshapen clumps of rock that required much imagination before any semblance of recognizable form could be imputed to them.

My eyes fell on two large rocks that looked vaguely like a man and woman entwined in the act of love. My friends had giggled and told me that they were once two romantics named Isaf and Naila who had consummated their lust in the Kaaba and had been turned to stone for defiling the Sanctuary. I was not sure why these two sinners who had been punished for their indiscretion should now be worshiped as gods, but they were apparently quite popular, and many young men and women bowed before them and tied tiny strings in the nooks and crannies, praying for the deities to win them the heart of their beloved, or at least bring ill fortune to their rivals in the game of love.

"Barbarism," my father uttered under his breath. He grimaced at the sight of middle-aged women kneeling before a red-flecked rock shaped like a pregnant woman with bulbous breasts and hips. This was Uzza, one of three "daughters of Allah" who were worshiped by the pagans. She was said to be the goddess of fertility, and her favor was much sought after by those who wished to conceive. The women, their eyes brimming with hope and despair, tore open their tunics and rubbed their naked breasts against the cold stone, pleading in loud wails for Uzza to reverse the course of time, to begin their cycles again so that they could bear the children that had been denied them.

I was fascinated by these strange rituals, but my father pulled me away and led me toward the Kaaba. A crowd of hundreds of pilgrims was steadily circumambulating the House of God, moving like the stars around the earth, circling seven times while praising Allah, the Creator of the Universe. The pilgrims were dressed in a variety of robes reflecting their wealth and social power, with the tribal chiefs wrapped in silk and endowed with glittering jewels commanding the right to walk closest to the temple, while others encircled at the outskirts in filthy rags—and a few even danced around the Kaaba naked.

"Don't look at them," my father warned sternly as my eyes fell on these hairy nude men, their organs hanging like the sagging genitals of a dog in the open. I giggled, but a stern look from Abu Bakr forced me to hide my amusement. We walked around the holy house at a steady pace, while my father prayed aloud for the mercy of God on his wayward and ignorant people.

When we finished the sacred rite, my father, who was now drenched in sweat from the noon sun, led me away from the Kaaba and guided me to a blue pavilion at the outskirts of the Sanctuary. Under the merciful shade of the tent was the well of Zamzam, which had provided the city with a steady supply of water since the days of the first settlers. Its miraculous existence in the middle of an otherwise dead wilderness had made Mecca a necessary stop for all trading caravans that traveled between the fertile lands of Yemen to the south and Syria to the north.

This strategic location and life-giving water supply had brought much prosperity to the city's traders—but not for most others. For the merchants of Mecca believed in only one rule—the survival of the strong. Those who were smart enough to take advantage of the opportunities provided by trade deserved to lord their wealth over others. Those too weak to do so best hurry up and die, freeing up the resources they left behind for those who were more worthy. It was this heartless mind-set that the Messenger of God had challenged, and his calls for economic justice and redistribution of Mecca's wealth were a direct threat to the philosophy of the city's ruling class.

As we joined the line of thirsty pilgrims eager for a drink of the sacred water, I saw a newly arrived caravan of Bedouin pilgrims approach the Sanctuary. Their leader, his face scarred and his beard dyed red, disembarked from a gray camel and helped the others of his clan climb off their horses and mules. Their faces had the dark complexions and high cheekbones of the men of Yemen, and I realized even at my tender age that they must have traveled at least twenty days in the harsh desert to attend the Pilgrimage. Their faces were covered in coarse sand that was turning into mud under rivers of perspiration.

As I watched them, I saw a tall man dressed in rich silk robes approach them, a blue turban on his head. Abu Sufyan was not the king of Mecca, but he certainly acted like it. He walked with a royal flourish, his hands held wide in welcome of the new arrivals. Beside him I saw a short boy of about fifteen years of age with a hooked nose and unblinking black eyes that made him look like a hawk. Muawiya, Abu Sufyan's son, was more reserved than his expressive father and looked over the newcomers with shrewd appraisal. I sensed that he was calculating their wealth and value to Meccan trade even as his father embraced the Bedouin leader as if he were a long-lost relative.

"Welcome my brothers, my friends!" Abu Sufyan's voice boomed with the practiced good cheer of a salesman. "Welcome to the House of Allah! May the gods bless you and grant you all that you seek!"

The Bedouin leader wiped his brow as the river of sweat threatened to blind him.

"We seek water, for the journey has been trying and the sun god merciless."

Abu Sufyan's eyes fell on the heavy emerald rings that covered he chief's fingers and he smiled greedily.

"Of course, my friend."

And then Abu Sufyan's saw that the traders were carrying arms. Swords and daggers in sheaths on their rough leather belts, and spears and arrows tied to the sides of their horses. Necessary protection for their journey through the wild—but a potential threat to order inside Mecca itself.

"But first, I must ask that you lay aside your weapons, for they are forbidden inside the precincts of the holy city," Abu Sufyan said with an apologetic smile.

The Bedouin looked at him for a moment and then nodded to his fellow pilgrims. They removed their various weapons and dropped them at their feet.

Muawiya stepped forward to pick up the blades, but the Bedouin leader moved to block him, his eyes filled with suspicion at the boy.

Aware of the sudden tension, Abu Sufyan immediately put on a gracious smile and stepped between the scarred Bedouin and the youth.

"My son Muawiya will take personal responsibility for all your weapons," the Meccan chief said smoothly. "He will hold them in trust at the House of Assembly, and will return them to you at the conclusion of your Pilgrimage."

The Bedouin spat on the ground at Muawiya's feet.

"We are warriors of Bani Abdal Lat," he said, his face hard. "We do not leave our weapons in the care of children."

Abu Sufyan's ingratiating smile vanished. The pride and power of his lineage suddenly shone through.

"My son is a lord of Quraysh, and there are no children among us. Only men of honor," he said, his cold voice suggesting that the Bedouin had overstepped the bonds of hospitality.

Muawiya quickly interceded. "I will serve as surety over your goods," he said, demonstrating the natural diplomacy that would serve him well in years to come. "If you do not receive them all back when you leave, you may take me as your slave in return."

The gruff Bedouin looked over the small boy, who gazed at him steadily, never breaking eye contact. The pilgrim finally nodded, satisfied.

"The boy is strong. He has the eyes of an eagle," the man said in clipped tones. "Your surety is accepted."

He nodded to his people, who stepped aside as Muawiya quietly gathered the blades, spears, and arrows. Abu Sufyan's gracious smile returned and he led the dust-covered pilgrims toward the tent of Zamzam. But when he saw my father and me standing near the well, a dangerous look came into his eyes. It was if he were communicating a wordless warning to my father. Abu Bakr met his gaze without flinching and then turned to me and held me up by my arms so that I could reach for the bucket of water he had pulled out of the well. I grasped a small bronze cup that hung from a ring at the side of the wooden bucket and drank to my little heart's content.

Abu Sufyan turned back to his visitors.

"Behold the sacred well of Mecca, which never runs dry, nor do its waters suffer from disease or pollution. A sign of God's favor on this blessed city."

The Bedouin gathered around the well and dipped their leather pouches into its waters, scooping up the precious liquid and consuming it in quick gulps.

My father looked at Abu Sufyan and then laughed loudly.

"You are a strange man, Abu Sufyan," my father said. "You acknowledge God's favor on Mecca, and yet you still refuse to obey Him."

The chief of Mecca turned red with suppressed anger.

The Bedouin leader saw his reaction and gazed at my father with sudden interest.

"Who is this man?"

Abu Sufyan turned his back on us.

"Just a madman spouting nonsense," he said, waving his hand in dismissal. "Unfortunately the time of Pilgrimage draws many such fools, like the flood brings out the rats."

Hearing him speak of my father like that ignited a fire in my child's heart. I broke free of my father's grasp and ran over to Abu Sufyan. "Don't talk about my father that way! You're the fool! You're the rat!"

The Pilgrims laughed at my childish outburst, and my father quickly pulled me back with a scolding look.

"Aisha! We are Muslims. We do not speak to our elders with disrespect. Even if they are unbelievers."

Now the Bedouin were intrigued. Their chief stepped forward

"What is a Muslim?"

Which was, of course, the question my father had been waiting to answer.

"One who has surrendered to God alone," he said solemnly, like a teacher imparting wisdom to a young pupil.

But Abu Sufyan was not about to let this happen. He stepped right in front of my father and looked down at him with fury.

"Do not pester these pilgrims any further, Abu Bakr," he said through gritted teeth. "They are tired and thirsty. Let them drink the sacred water of Zamzam in peace."

Abu Bakr looked at the Bedouin, quenching their thirst from the well.

"I will do as you say. If you can tell me why this well is so sacred."

Abu Sufyan stiffened.

"It is sacred because our forefathers have said so. That is enough for me."

My father turned to the Bedouin.

"Tell me, my brother, is that enough for you?" he asked softly. "Do you know why the water you drink is blessed?"

The Bedouin looked perplexed. He ran a hand over the scar that disfigured his left cheek.

"I have never asked. But now I am curious."

The Bedouin glanced at Abu Sufyan, but the tribal chief had no response.

And then my father turned to me.

"Tell them, little one," he said with a gentle smile.

I looked up at the dark and dusty men from the desert and recited the story I had been raised with.

"The well of Zamzam is a miracle from God, written in the Book of the Jews and Christians," I told them. "When our father Ishmael was sent into the desert by Abraham, his mother, Hagar, looked for water so that her child would not die of thirst. Seven times she ran between those hills."

I pointed to the peaks of Safa and Marwa that overlooked the city. Even then, dozens of pilgrims were racing between the hills as part of the Pilgrimage ritual, though they had long forgotten its meaning or origins.

"But when she could find no water, she came back here," I continued. "And the angel Gabriel appeared and told Ishmael to strike his foot. And the well of Zamzam sprang from beneath his feet, bringing water to the desert. And life to Mecca."

As I spoke, I could tell that I had caught the attention of the Bedouin. They listened raptly to the story I wove, which suddenly brought a new meaning to the ancient rites they had crossed the desert to perform.

Abu Sufyan snorted.

"A child's fable. Come, let me take you to the House of God."

The Bedouin looked at me and my father, intrigued.

"Perhaps it is a child's tale, but it is a good one," he said, his eyes wide with wonder.

Abu Sufyan could no longer hide his irritation. He pushed his Bedouin guests toward the Kaaba as if they were wayward mares. My father and I followed. Even though we had completed our rites for the morning, Abu Bakr had sensed that the Bedouin were ready to hear more about our faith. We would wait until the men had finished their circumambulation and Abu Sufyan attended to other newcomers. And then my father would likely take them back to the House of the Messenger, where they could hear the Truth and be saved.

But as we approached the Kaaba, where the perpetual whirlwind of pilgrims was in motion, I heard shouts from across the Sanctuary. The enraged, booming voice of a man echoed through the plaza and drowned out even the loudest of prayers.

"What is it?" I asked my father, more intrigued than frightened.

"It is Umar. As usual."

Ah, of course. Umar ibn al-Khattab, one of the most virulent of the lords of Mecca in his opposition to God's Messenger. I saw him across the open space, towering like a giant over a small African man I immediately recognized as a former slave named Bilal. My father had bought Bilal's freedom from his ruthless master, Umayya, who had tortured the poor man after he had embraced Islam. Umayya had dragged his rebellious slave into the marketplace, tied him to the ground under the blazing Meccan sun, and placed a heavy boulder on Bilal's chest until it cracked his ribs and made it almost impossible to breathe. Umayya demanded that Bilal return to the worship of his master's gods, but all the courageous slave would croak out under torture was "One God . . . One God . . ." Bilal would have died there that day had my father not intervened and paid Umayya's outrageous price of ten gold dirhams for his freedom.

And now Umar tormented the poor freedman, who lay prostrate on the earth before the House of God, a gesture that immediately identified him as a follower of Muhammad's new religion.

"You son of a dog! Get up!" Umar's voice was like an elephant's cry, terrifying and unearthly at once. He was the tallest man I had ever seen, with a bushy black beard that grew down to his waist. His arms were as thick as tree trunks, the muscles bulging clearly from the thin fabric of his red tunic. Umar reached down with hands that were larger than my head and grabbed Bilal by the scruff of his threadbare white robes. Bilal did not struggle but looked into Umar's eyes with a serenity that only seemed to enrage the monster more.

Umar slapped Bilal hard, and I saw a flash of white as one of the African's teeth flew out of his mouth. Alarmed, my father ran over to his side.

"Umar, leave Bilal in peace. Do not profane the Sanctuary with your wrath."

The son of al-Khattab stared at my father, who barely came up to his chest, with contempt.

"It is you who profane the Sanctuary with your lies, Abu Bakr!" his voice thundered. "You spread discontent and rebellion, turning slaves against their masters!"

My father remained calm, refusing to let Umar get a rise out of him.

"Bilal is no longer a slave to any man," he said firmly.

Umar spat in contempt.

"Just because you bought his freedom does not make him any less a slave."

Bilal looked at his tormentor with a steady gaze. When he spoke, it was with a deeply melodious, musical voice. A voice for which he would be renowned in years to come.

"You are right, Umar. I am still a slave. A slave to Allah."

Umar's face reddened until it became the color of an angry sunset.

"You dare speak to me about Allah before His very House!"

Umar kicked Bilal hard in the gut, knocking the small man to the ground. The tiny African cried out in pain, grasping his stomach and writhing in pain. Umar pushed my father out of the way when he leaned over to help Bilal and then kicked him again.

Furious, I ran over to Umar and kicked him in the shin.

"Stop it! Stop hurting him!"

By then, a crowd of pilgrims and locals had formed around us, watching the ongoing drama. When I lashed out at Umar, many laughed at the madness of a child taking on one of the most feared men in Arabia.

Hearing their jeers, Umar looked up and saw the men for the first time. Alarmed at the sudden public spectacle his temper had created during the sacred Pilgrimage, Umar attempted to reassert his dignity and power over the bemused crowd.

"Step back! I am a guardian of the Holy Kaaba!"

But I wouldn't let him get away with that.

"No! You're just a bully!" I threw my tiny arms around his legs to prevent him from kicking Bilal again, causing a greater eruption of laughter from the spectators. I looked up to see that while some were mocking, others, especially pilgrims who were foreigners to the city, were shaking their heads in disgust at the violent display before the House of God.

And then I saw Talha, my favorite cousin, push his way through the crowd. My face lit up. Of all my relatives, he was the one I was closest to. There was a natural sweetness to him, like the honey from a bee's comb. And he was so handsome, with his flowing brown hair and expressive gray eyes that always showed what he was feeling. And in them now I saw terrible anger.

Talha stormed up to Umar, unafraid of the towering blowhard.

"How brave of you, Umar. Fighting a man half your size, and then a little girl. Shall I bring you a cat to test your prowess next?"

Umar stepped back, stunned by Talha's reproach. He looked confused, as if he could not understand how a powerful man like himself had lost control of the situation so quickly. He finally stared down at Bilal, eager to have the last word.

"Leave the Sanctuary and darken not its stones again with your black flesh," he said contemptuously.

Bilal stood proudly, wiping blood from his mouth.

"God made me black and I praise Him for it," he said with dignity. And then he raised his beautiful voice to recite a verse from the Holy Qur'an.

"We take our colors from God, and who is better than God at coloring?"

There was a murmur of interest from the crowd at the lyrical sound of the holy words. I saw several of the dark-skinned nomads, who were accustomed to being treated with contempt, take in these words with a look of delight. They started whispering to one another, and I knew that soon they would learn about the Messenger from whose mouth these strange words had emanated. Words that broke the rules of Arab culture and yet touched the heart. Words that could give a slave strength to stand up to a tyrant. Now the crowd wanted to know more about these words and who was spreading them.

I saw in his sudden flash of regret that Umar had realized this as well. In his explosion of rage, he had only managed to bring attention to Muhammad's message. Shaking his head, he grumbled to himself as he turned away from us.

"You are all mad," Umar said dismissively. And then he faced the crowd and raised his hands for their attention.

"Know all present that I would not have harmed this girl," he said, pointing at me in the desperate hope of regaining some dignity. "Umar ibn al-Khattab does not hurt children."

Umar turned to walk away from the scene, when Talha laughed bitterly.

"Really? So why did you bury your daughter alive, you pagan wretch?"

Umar froze.

Time itself seemed to stop at that moment.

When Umar turned around to face Talha, there was a terrifying madness in his eyes.

"You . . . you dare . . ."

My father realized that Talha had gone too far.

"Leave it be, Talha," he warned.

But my cousin was filled with righteous indignation. It was an open secret in the city that Umar's wife, Zaynab bint Madh'un, had recently given birth to a girl. Ashamed and embittered that Zaynab had failed to produce a son, Umar had taken the infant child into the desert. In accordance with the practices of the idolaters, he had left the child on the searing sand and covered her with stones until she died. The Messenger of God had condemned this horrifying practice, which had further alienated him from the rulers of Mecca, who viewed infanticide as a man's privilege.

"Murderer!" Talha cried, burning with the fire of outrage. "When you are raised on Judgment Day, you will account for your crimes!"

And suddenly, as if a dam had broken, Umar rushed at Talha and threw him to the ground.

Abu Bakr tried to pull Umar off him, to no avail. Umar threw my father aside as if he were one of my rag dolls. I saw him hit his head hard on the ground, drawing blood.

"Father!" I ran to his side in horror. I had never seen my father bleed before and it terrified me. As I helped my father up, Umar violently hit and kicked Talha, who endured his painful blows with dignity.

"Go . . . go find Hamza . . ." my father said softly. "He went to Mount Hira . . . I am too weak . . ."

Hamza was the Messenger's uncle, a bear of a man who was the only one of the believers of sufficient strength and stature to challenge the formidable Umar. I raced out of the Sanctuary toward the surrounding hills that led to Mount Hira.

+ + +

I DESPERATELY CLIMBED THE rocky hills in search of Hamza, hoping that I could somehow get him back in time to save Talha's life. The thought of losing him, the cousin I loved the most, terrified me. Talha was the only one who did not treat me like a baby. He was strong and handsome and charming and always made me laugh. My gossipy friend Rubina thought I had a crush on him and teased me relentlessly that we would marry someday. Once she said this loud enough for him to hear, to my mortification. But Talha did not mock me. Instead he looked at me with a warm smile and said, "It would be an honor of which I am unworthy."

Oh, poor Talha. There are times that I think I should have left him to die at Umar's hand. Then he would have been the first martyr and no man would question his honor or place in paradise.

But I was only a child and did not have the gift of prophecy. All I could see was that he would die at that moment unless I could save him. And I, whose name meant life, would not let him die.

I stumbled on the rocks and cut my hand against the edge of a jagged boulder. A streak of blood ran down my palm, but I ignored it and clambered up toward the hilltop.

And then I saw a sight that has been forever burned into my soul. Two men and a woman, emaciated and roasted by the sun, tied to the thorn trees like scarecrows. I recognized them immediately. Sumaya, who was often in my mother's kitchen, fussing over the proper number of onions to put in the lamb stew. Her quiet, kindhearted husband, Yasir, and their small but stout boy, Ammar.

I stood frozen, my young mind unable to process what I saw.

＋　＋　＋

THIS WAS NOT THE fate Sumaya had wanted for her family when they left their lives as wandering goat herders and sought a more sedentary experience in the city. She had come to Mecca hoping to find a wife for Ammar and steady employment so that her son could build a life for himself and perhaps one day his children. But all they had found was misery.

Sumaya quickly discovered the rule of Mecca that newcomers had no rights unless they secured the protection of a powerful clan. But protection was expensive, and the few goatskins they owned would not suffice. So her family worked like slaves for whoever was willing to offer a few copper coins. Cooking and cleaning were her lot, while her son and husband would tend to the animals of the wealthy or provide help with their hands, laying stone and brick for the expanding mansions of the town's wealthy lords. Sometimes the pay was good. But if their money was stolen, as it often was, they had no recourse. If their employers beat them and refused to pay after a hard day's work, they could not protest or raise any objection. Without the protection of a clan, their lives were worth nothing in Mecca, and if they were killed no one would notice, much less raise a sword to avenge them.

And then Sumaya had met the Messenger of God. She had been warned to stay away from his house by the families she cooked and cleaned for. Muhammad was a dangerous sorcerer, they said, and he would place a spell on any who came near. But after a week without food and no one willing to pay for their services, Sumaya, Ammar, and Yasir wandered over to the forbidden quarter of the city where the sorcerer was reputed to live. She had found a small crowd of beggars gathered outside his house, and saw a lovely woman named Khadija handing out fresh meat to the desperate poor. Sumaya had fallen before the noble lady's feet and begged her for food and work. Muhammad's wife had brought them inside, and given her family warm soup and shelter for the night.

And then she was brought before the Messenger, heard his gentle words of hope, his teaching that the poor would sit on thrones of gold in Paradise if they renounced false gods and dedicated themselves only to Allah. It was a message that Sumaya and her family had embraced eagerly. And it was their embrace of the message that had now brought them here, tortured and left to die in the wilderness.

─ ─ ─

SUMAYA'S SON, AMMAR, GAZED at me, his eyes alert and full of pain.

"Aisha . . . daughter of Abu Bakr . . . help us . . ."

For an instant, I forgot all about Talha. I ran toward them and desperately tried to tear apart their bindings with my small hands. His father Yasir was unconscious. Still breathing but weakly.

"Who did this to you?" I asked, unable to keep the horror out of my voice.

"Abu Jahl . . ."

And then I understood. The Meccan lord who was the most vehement foe of Islam. The monster whose name was told to Muslim children when they were naughty. "Behave, or Abu Jahl will come for you."

Abu Jahl had come for them.

I tore the flesh from my hand trying to break the cruel knots, but to no avail.

"I can't do it!" I felt hot tears coming to my eyes. Today was a day of death and destruction. Everyone I loved was in trouble, and I was powerless to help them.

And then I heard footsteps. Someone was coming. Ammar heard it, too. He looked down the hill and saw a figure approaching.

"It's him! Hide!"

I turned and saw a man dressed in rich purple robes, a lavender turban wrapped across his head, climbing toward us.

Abu Jahl, the monster of my childhood nightmares, was here.

My heart in my throat, I looked around desperately. And then I saw a fallen tree trunk lying to the side. I jumped inside the trunk, ignoring an enraged spider whose web I tore apart as I hid from this demon.

Abu Jahl clambered over the ridge and stood only five feet away from me. He did not look like a monster. In fact, he was quite elegant in his rich robes, laced in gold filigree. His face was handsome and evenly proportioned, his cheekbones high, and his skin unusually fair for a native of the desert heat. He had a small and well-trimmed mustache that gave him a dapper look. His real name was Abu al-Hakam, which meant "Father of Wisdom" but the Muslims always called him Abu Jahl, "Father of Ignorance."

I saw that his hands were full. In his right hand, he held a spear, the jagged head polished to sparkle in the sun. In his left, I saw an idol. A small, curvaceous stone made of shining obsidian. Even from the distance, I could tell that it was an icon of Manat, Abu Jahl's patron goddess, to whom he attributed his remarkable wealth.

He looked at the three prisoners whom he had been left to die here. Abu Jahl smiled almost apologetically.

When he spoke, his voice was soft, almost soothing.

"I hope the sun god has taught you reason, Ammar," he said, without any hint of the rage or madness that possessed Umar.

Ammar looked him in the eye, ignoring the persistent flies that were buzzing around his sweat-drenched face.

"There is no sun god. There is only Allah, the Lord of the Worlds."

Abu Jahl shook his head, looking deeply disappointed. He sighed, as if filled with regret.

"Even to the end, you remain dedicated to your heresy," he said. "Think, boy. If Allah cared about your singular devotion so much, why would He leave you to die in the desert?"

Ammar's lips curled in fury.

"You did that, not Allah."

Abu Jahl shrugged and turned to Sumaya, who looked up at him serenely despite her pain.

"You are Ammar's mother," he said, his voice eminently reasonable. "Tell me, Sumaya. Do you remember his birth? The agony of labor. The pain almost killed you. Yet your midwife prayed to Manat and you lived. Without the mercy of the goddess, how could you have endured those pangs?"

He held up the idol and dangled it right in front of Sumaya's face.

"Manat ended your pain and gave you and your son life that night. And she can give it you again. Right now." He leaned forward, holding the idol close to Sumaya's lips. "All you have to do is kiss her holy image. And I will release you and your family from your bonds."

Sumaya looked at him, and then at the idol.

I held my breath, praying that she would do it. The Messenger had said that anyone who was forced to renounce his faith for fear of his life, but kept it in his heart, would be forgiven by God. My soul screamed to Sumaya from inside the darkness of the tree trunk: Do it! Save yourself! Save your son!

Sumaya smiled at Abu Jahl gently, almost gratefully.

And then she spit on the idol of Manat.

And then I saw Abu Jahl change. Something terrible came over his face. Not rage, like Umar's, but an emptiness. A lack of feeling. In that instant, he looked more like a corpse than a living man. And he frightened me more with the rigid calm of his face than Umar had with all his bluster.

"So you would choose death over life," he said softly.

Sumaya laughed suddenly, as if she finally realized that she had been wasting her time arguing with an imbecile.

"No . . . I choose life . . . eternal life," she said. She steeled her eyes on him, and I saw no fear. "There is no god but God, and Muhammad is His Messenger."

Abu Jahl gazed into her face, and then nodded. He stepped back, locking his eyes on hers.

And then, in one fluid movement that was so fast my eyes barely captured it, he stabbed her through her vagina, pushing the spear up into her womb!

"No!" Ammar's scream was the most terrifying sound I had ever heard. I bit my hand in horror, letting my own stifled cry shudder through my body.

Sumaya cried out in terrible agony. She writhed on the tree trunk as blood poured out from her womb and into a thick crimson puddle at her feet. Abu Jahl continued to push the spear higher, tearing open her intestines and stomach from the inside.

And then her screams ended. And there was only silence.

As Ammar wept, I saw Abu Jahl casually remove the spear. He used Sumaya's threadbare tunic to clean the blood off his weapon, before turning to face Ammar.

"The gods have won," he said simply, as if stating an obvious truth to the child.

Somehow Ammar found his voice in the midst of terrible grief.

"No . . . my mother has won . . . she is the first of the martyrs."

Abu Jahl allowed a small smile to play on his full, sensuous lips.

"She will not be the last."

He turned and climbed back down the hill, whistling a happy tune.

When he was gone, I emerged from the tree trunk. I felt like I was in a dream. The entire day had to have been a nightmare. Nothing I witnessed could happen in the real world.

I stared at the dead woman, hanging ignominiously, her lower body drenched in the blood that had only moments before flowed through her veins.

This was not real. It couldn't be.

And then the screech of vultures tore me out of my trance and I ran away, racing from the specter of death that would forever haunt me, even as the midwife had prophesied the night I was born.

3

*A*lone figure knelt on the sacred ground of Mount Hira, where the Revelation had begun. He flexed his powerful muscles and then raised his hands in prayer to the One God that had chosen his family to redeem mankind.

Hamza had always known that his nephew Muhammad had been destined for greatness. They were close in years and the man who was now called Messenger of God had been more of a younger brother to Hamza than a nephew. But even when they would race each other across the stone alleyways of Mecca, or wrestle playfully in the sand, Muhammad had never quite seemed like a child. There had been a wisdom in his eyes, a sadness that seemed to belong to someone who had already lived a lifetime of struggle, loss, and triumph. Perhaps it was the sorrow of an orphan, having lost his father before he was born and his mother at the age of six.

But there was something else different about the boy. A sense of destiny that hung around him like an aura. It was a power that others in the family had sensed as well, and not all were comfortable with it. Hamza's half brother, Abu Lahab, in particular had taken an early dislike to their nephew, seeing Muhammad as a dreamer and an idealist, someone who refused to adapt to the harsh realities of life in the desert.

When Muhammad had come to Hamza and told him about his vision, in a cave not far from where Hamza sat now, he had been fascinated but not really surprised. Still, Hamza had been set in his ways and found it difficult to renounce the gods of their fathers. But as he watched the growing opposition of the Meccan lords to his nephew's teaching and their increasing cruelty toward his followers, he had felt a growing passion within his breast. Hamza had always believed in living life with honor and justice, and he began to see that the followers of the old ways displayed few of those traits.

And then one day he heard how the wretch Abu Jahl had insulted

Muhammad viciously while he prayed at the Kaaba, raining obscene curses on him and his family, and his nephew had simply taken in the abuse and walked away with dignity. At that moment, Hamza had made a decision. He had taken the powerful bow with which he had famously killed lions and cheetahs in the desert and strode over to Abu Jahl, who was rallying a crowd against the Muslims in the Sanctuary. Without hesitating, Hamza struck Abu Jahl across the forehead with the bow, knocking him to his knees. And then, before the whole city, he proclaimed faith in his nephew's religion.

And now he sat here, praying as the Messenger had taught him, his knees on the ground, his head bowed in surrender to God. He found peace at Hira, and he could understand why his nephew found solace here. The air was pure, crisp and clear, not filled with the smell of the burning offal of the city. And instead of the cacophony of loud voices, squawking chickens, and braying camels that arose from the streets of Mecca, there was silence. It was a silence so deep, so still, that a man could finally hear the beating of his own heart, the gentle whispers of the soul.

And then the silence of mountain was shattered by a child's cry.

"Hamza! We need you!"

He turned and saw me scrambling up the rocks like a redheaded spider. My dress was torn from this terrible journey and my face covered in the gray dust that covered the mountain like soot.

Hamza moved to intercept me. He climbed down several sharply inclined boulders that I could never have scaled. We finally reached each other and I collapsed in his thick arms, panting for breath.

"Aisha? What is it?"

I wheezed, trying to get the words out, as my heart beat in my ears.

"My father . . . Sumaya . . . They need you . . . Abu Jahl . . . Umar . . . No one can stop them . . ."

I didn't make much sense. But I didn't need to. Mention of Abu Jahl and Umar was enough.

"God will stop them, little one."

He rose and took my tiny hand and then gently led me down the rocky slope.

4

There was one more death that day.

Hamza carried me on his iron shoulders as I guided him to the hilltop where the three prisoners of Abu Jahl were still tied to the thorn trees. Hamza checked on them and found that only young Ammar still breathed. His father, Yasir, had succumbed to the heat, having never regained consciousness. Perhaps it was the mercy of God that he had died without knowing the horrific suffering his beloved wife, Sumaya, had endured.

While I stood to the side, sucking my thumb in a gesture of insecurity that should have been long behind me, Hamza released Ammar, who immediately sank to his knees, his body shaking with shock. Hamza poured water from his cowhide flask directly into Ammar's mouth, but the lad barely moved to drink it. His eyes never left the corpses of his parents. The Prophet's uncle then untied the bodies of Sumaya and Yasir and laid them side by side.

"Can you walk?" Hamza asked Ammar gently. "If so, come with me back to Mecca. We will bring a party of believers to bury your parents."

Ammar shook his head.

"I'll stay with them."

Hamza nodded. He put a comforting hand on Ammar's shoulder, but knew there was nothing he could do or say to ease the young man's pain. So he turned to me.

"You are very brave," he said, rustling my hair affectionately.

"We have to go! Talha and my father need us."

Hamza lifted me on his shoulders and stormed off toward Mecca. I looked back to see Ammar stroking his mother's hair, his eyes staring ahead, vacant.

- - -

IN THE END, HAMZA arrived when he was no longer needed. Umar had beaten Talha to a bloody pulp but had spared him his life. Even the fiery son of al-Khattab was unwilling to risk the retaliation of Abu Bakr's clan, the Bani Taym. Not that he was afraid, he boasted loudly to the crowd that watched him ruthlessly break Talha's arm. "But this little worm is not worthy of a challenge to my life." And with that, he had stormed off to get drunk, hoping to erase the memory of Talha's insult—and his wretched guilt over an infant girl who had lovingly squeezed his finger even as he covered her with stones.

When Hamza heard that Abu Bakr had taken the badly injured Talha to the Messenger's house, he left the Sanctuary and strode quickly there. I was slow to follow, my young mind still reeling from the madness of the day's events. As I picked up my pace to catch up to Hamza, I saw an embarrassed-looking Abu Sufyan attempting to convince the grim-faced Bedouin to stay and spend his gold in the marketplace.

"My people have performed their duties and wish to depart," the Bedouin chief said. "Send your son to retrieve our weapons."

"But you have just arrived!" Abu Sufyan gesticulated in exagerated surprise. "Come, I will arrange for guest lodgings."

"That will not be necessary."

But Abu Sufyan had the persistence of a born merchant.

"You must come to the bazaar in the morning," he said smoothly. "We recently received a shipment of the finest silk from Persia."

The Bedouin shook his head.

"My people have no need of silk."

Abu Sufyan's frustration was beginning to show.

"But there is so much more that Mecca has to offer!"

The Bedouin grimaced as he looked back to the scene of the bloody brawl just outside the gates of the Sanctuary.

"I have seen today what Mecca has to offer. I wish to see no more." And with that, he turned his back on Abu Sufyan and rejoined his people, who were already beginning to pack their camels' bags with food and water for the journey home.

Abu Sufyan shook his head in frustration at the loss of commerce. I turned to rejoin Hamza, when my legs froze.

Walking toward me in all his purple finery was Abu Jahl. His face was calm and undisturbed and there was not a shred of evidence that he had just ruthlessly killed an innocent woman.

For a moment a mad terror engulfed me. Had he seen me running down the hill? Would he now seek to kill me to cover up his crime?

Abu Jahl approached and my heart skipped a beat.

And then he walked right past me, blissfully ignorant of a red-headed child who had seen the depth of his evil up close.

Abu Jahl walked to Abu Sufyan, who was still scowling over lost business

"More incidents like today's will drive away pilgrims," Abu Jahl said with a disapproving tut of his tongue. "If these renegades persist in challenging us, the Pilgrimage will end. Without the Pilgrimage, we will be without trade. And without trade, Mecca will vanish into the sands."

Abu Sufyan nodded.

"This has gone too far. It is time to act."

Abu Jahl smiled, his eyes gleaming.

"I agree."

As the two walked away in quiet converse, I managed to regain strength in my knees and I ran off to the House of the Messenger.

5

That night I sat by my father as the Messenger of God held council with his family and most trusted followers.

There were two dozen of us, mainly the original families that had embraced Islam in the early years and had proven loyal to the Prophet in the first days of persecution. My mother, Umm Ruman, sat next to my father, her auburn hair hidden behind a modest blue scarf. To her left was my elder sister, Asma, now fourteen years old, her brown eyes intent and darting about the room like a bird. I was wondering what she was looking for, and then I saw a tall young man with perfect white teeth enter and Asma seemed to stop breathing. It was your father, Zubayr, and I suddenly understood.

We were in what had once been Muhammad's grand guest room, where the family would entertain friends and visiting dignitaries from the trading caravans. The room was vast, at least to my young eyes, forty feet wide and twenty-five in length. Sturdy pillars supported a row of rounded arches that buttressed a circular balcony from the living quarters above. The roof soared thirty feet above my head and was not flat in the ordinary custom of the city but curved upward to form a majestic dome. An architectural style adopted from the Byzantines with whom the Messenger had had much interaction as a merchant in his youth. It would be a motif that would become commonplace among our people in years to come when the lands of the Greeks fell to our swords.

But as I sat there in a clandestine meeting with a handful of believers, such a mighty destiny would have seemed laughable, a fantasy unworthy of even the most foolish drunk sleeping in the gutters of Mecca. Who could entertain thoughts of empire when our movement was pathetically small and now appeared ripe for extinction? Abu Jahl had been right when he said that Sumaya's death would not be the last. The dread of what was to come hung over us like a cloud of locusts, gathering in preparation for an unstoppable swarm.

But when the Messenger of God entered the room, for a moment a ray of light broke through those dark clouds and we felt hope again,

How can I describe to those who were not there what it was like to be in the presence of the Prophet? It was as if I had entered another world or was seeing this world through reborn eyes. In the years that followed, I would share his life and his bed, and yet every time I saw him, my heart would beat faster. It was as if he were life itself.

You will remember him, my nephew, from your own youth. Yes, by then he had changed some, there were a few gray hairs in his beard, caused by the burden of war and politics that would preoccupy his final years. But he was naturally ageless, and as I sat looking at him that night, I marveled to think that he was two years older than my father and yet looked a dozen years younger.

Muhammad, may God's peace and blessings be upon him, was middling in height, but his wide shoulders and barrel chest exuded power and strength. His hair in those days was ebony black, darker than the veil of night, darker than the deepest levels of sleep when even our dreams vanish and only silence remains. His skin was white like alabaster. As I became older and more aware of my own beauty, I prided myself on the fairness of my skin, a rarity in our sunburned land. But the Messenger of God's face was still fairer than mine, almost ethereal, like the sparkling white of the moon.

His hair was not straight but curled gently, flowing like a lion's mane from his forehead down below his ears. His beard curled similarly and was thick and always well brushed. I often wondered at some of the believers who claimed to imitate him by donning beards and then let them grow wild like the quills of a porcupine. The Messenger of God would never be seen looking like a mangy dog dragged in from the desert, although there are many who style themselves worse and proclaim themselves followers of his way, his *sunna*. He was a man of dignity who loved beauty and grace and exhibited these qualities in the way he groomed himself.

But the most striking thing about the Prophet was his eyes, so black that it was difficult to discern his pupils and yet always filled with light. Few men could gaze deep into them for long. It is said that the eyes are the mirrors of the soul. In the case of the Messenger, his eyes were the mirrors of *our* souls. Anyone who looked into those majestic obsidian orbs would see the depths of his own heart reflected back. And not everyone could bear what he saw.

The Messenger smiled often but rarely laughed, although in later years I was one of the few who could make him throw his head back and rejoice with hearty abandon. His laugh, uncommon as it was, was deep-throated and infectious. And when he laughed, few could resist joining in.

The same was true for his tears, which came more often. And tonight he had shed many. After Hamza had returned and told him of Sumaya and Yasir's fate, the Messenger had wept deeply. Together they had led a small band of believers into the wilderness, where they had rescued Ammar, still sitting forlorn by his dead parents, and then buried the first martyrs of Islam.

The Messenger had returned with a heavy heart and had found comfort, as he always did, in the arms of his wife, Khadija. I looked at her now as she sat next to him on the marble floor of the palatial house that she had owned before she met and fell in love with the young Muhammad. Together they looked like king and queen, except that they had no thrones. Most of the luxurious furnishings in the house had long ago been sold, the proceeds given to the poor, and the beautiful mansion with its whitewashed walls and polished floors was almost as empty as a tomb.

The Prophet squeezed Khadija's hand and she smiled at him encouragingly. Looking at them, it was clear that there was a substantial age difference. Muhammad had only been twenty-five when she hired him to manage her trading caravans. Rumor had it that Khadija was a wealthy widow of forty years when she first saw him and that she had been so taken aback by his nobility and generous spirit—and his handsome features—that she had proposed shortly after he had returned from Syria with a substantial profit for her account. Others said she was only twenty-eight, just three years older than him, when she made him her husband, and that her age had been exaggerated by the pious in order to signify her wisdom.

I think the truth is somewhere in between. When I looked at her, she was still beautiful, but her dark hair had turned to silver, although there were only a few lines around her eyes and mouth. She had borne him six children in the first ten years of their marriage—four girls who had lived and two boys who had died as infants. As a woman, I find it hard to believe that Khadija would have been so fertile at an age when most other women's courses had long ceased. But, after living with the Messenger of God myself, I have seen many strange and improbable things, so perhaps the rumors of her advanced age may indeed have been true. And it was certainly the will of God that she alone would bear him children that would survive, while my womb, young and fertile as it was, would remain inexplicably barren.

The Messenger looked at Khadija for a long moment, before turning to those he had gathered in council.

"Today has been a sad day for the believers," he began softly, when Hamza, who had been pacing back and forth with barely restrained fury spoke up.

"They have crossed all boundaries!" the Prophet's uncle said, his face racked with emotion.

My father stirred next to me.

"This day was long coming," Abu Bakr said, trying to calm the agitated giant. "Sumaya and her family did not have the protection of the tribes. Abu Jahl knew he could act without fear of retaliation."

Hamza sat down, growling like an angry lion.

"Now that they have tasted Muslim blood, they will hunger for more."

Across the room I saw Talha, whose face was bandaged and right arm was cast in a sling of leather, lean toward the man who had belatedly appeared to rescue him.

"So what do you counsel?

Hamza looked across the room at the Messenger.

"Emigrate! We must send the rest of our people to Abyssinia," he said forcefully.

There was a murmur of assent among the believers. A year before, several of the poorest Muslims had emigrated with the Prophet's blessing across the western sea to the African nation of Abyssinia. The land was ruled by a wise Christian king called the Negus, who had taken the refugees in and offered them protection. The Meccans had sent Amr ibn al-As, one of their most charming and diplomatic envoys, to the Negus with gold and promises of discounted trade for his people—if he surrendered the Muslims, whom Amr branded as criminals. The Negus had been impressed by the faith and devotion of these Arabs to the God of Abraham and had denied the request. His clemency came despite the grumblings of his Christian priests, who saw the Muslims as troublesome heretics who denied that the prophet Jesus had ever claimed to be divine. The Muslims had been safe for the past year, and Hamza's suggestion was well received by the believers.

But the Messenger turned his attention to his cousin Ali.

"What do you think?"

The lad was now seventeen years old, but his strange and ethereal personality had not changed from his boyhood. The believers still felt a rush of complex emotions when the Prophet deferred to the youth. They trusted the Messenger but found his singular faith in this dreamy young man to be unusual and hard to understand.

Ali stood up, his eyes looking to an empty corner of the room as if he could see something no one else could.

"I do not advise it. Uthman already has his hands full," he said, referring to the Messenger's son-in-law, who had married Muhammad's ravishing daughter Ruqayya before leading the Muslims across the sea to Abyssinia.

I heard a small cough from across the room and turned to see your father, Zubayr, rise. At the same moment, I felt my sister, Asma, who was sitting to my left, tense with excitement, as she always did when the dashing young man spoke.

"The Negus has treated us kindly. Surely it is worth pursuing for those who have no clan protection," he said, his voice measured and calm as it always was. He had great influence over the community as a cousin of the Prophet, the son of his aunt Safiya, and as one of the earliest believers.

Ali looked at Zubayr with his intense green eyes and shook his head.

"The Negus is under pressure from his priests to expel the new-comers. So far, he has restrained them. But under the current climate, it would be unwise to send more refugees into that nation. It could make the situation worse for those already established."

But Zubayr did not give in that easily.

"We must do something. The Quraysh will soon call a counsel against us."

And then a deep voice resonated from the entry hall and we all whirled in surprise.

"They already have."

6

A shadow fell across the doorway behind me, and I looked up to see a bent old man with a frosty beard enter slowly, his hands wrapped around an ivory walking stick. Here was Abu Talib, the Messenger's uncle and father of Ali. He had been like a fa-ther to Muhammad, raising him after he was orphaned and standing by his side as the lords of Mecca turned against his new religion. The Prophet rose when he saw him, a sign of his deep love and respect, even though Abu Talib still clung to the way of their ancestors and worshiped the pagan gods. We all followed suit. Ali walked across the room and helped his father step across the black-and-white marble floor until he came to sit by the Messenger and Khadija.

Abu Talib looked frail and his hands shook, but his voice did not waver.

"The leaders of Quraysh are meeting in the House of Assembly tonight to determine how to deal with your people," he said with an air of regret. "Son of my brother, please listen to reason," Abu Talib said to the Prophet. "Once the fire of Quraysh's wrath is kindled, it will not be quenched. Your followers will all be consumed, as that poor woman was today. If you do not wish to follow our gods, that is your right. But please do not speak out against them anymore. Let the people of Arabia follow their traditions in peace. Despite their misgivings about your beliefs, the Quraysh respect and admire you, and I am sure they will be willing to offer anything you ask—if only you desist from denouncing their gods."

A silence fell over the crowd of believers. We looked at the Messenger uncertainly, wondering how he would respond to a plea from this beloved old man to compromise with the idolaters.

I saw the Messenger turn to Khadija, who looked him in the eye and nodded firmly. Whatever he decided, she would support him as the Mother of the Believers.

The Prophet looked down for a moment, breathing slowly and deeply. When he finally raised his head, I saw a fire in his eyes that both excited and terrified me. He took Khadija's hand in his right, and Ali's in his left.

"By God, even if they place the sun in my right hand and the moon in my left, I will not be dissuaded from my mission."

That was it, and we all knew it. There would be no compromise, even if the Meccans declared war on the Muslims.

Abu Talib shook his head despairingly.

"But my nephew—"

Khadija interrupted, holding the Prophet's hand high for all to see that her fingers remain firmly clasped in his.

"You have my husband's answer, dear uncle. He is *Al-Amin*, the Truthful, and he can no more hide the truth than the sun can rise in the west. God has commanded him to speak the Truth to Mecca and all mankind, and he will do so, regardless of the schemes of those who spin webs in the shadows."

Her words stirred my heart and I could see that they had the same effect on the others. One by one, each member of the community, man or woman, adult or child, loudly voiced assent.

Seeing our unity and determination, Abu Talib finally bowed his head, accepting his nephew's choice. He rose to his feet, gripping his cane as he prepared to leave.

"Then I fear for you. All of you," he said sadly. "May your God protect you from that which is coming."

"But what is coming? What is it that they are planning? If we know, we can protect ourselves." It was the quiet voice of Fatima, the Prophet's youngest daughter. She was a shy girl, about ten years older than myself, with a perpetually sad face. Unlike her older sisters, who were gregarious and full of life, Fatima was like a ghost who appeared and disappeared wordlessly and was rarely noticed by others. I saw several people start at the unexpected sound of her voice and I realized that I was not alone in wondering when she had entered the room or if she had been there the whole time without anyone noticing.

Abu Talib answered the girl by turning to face his son Ali.

"The doors of the Assembly have been shut to me this night. But I fear the worst."

Ali put a kind hand on his father's arm.

"Fear not, my father. God promises us that *'the righteous will neither fear, nor will they grieve,'*" he said, quoting the holy Qur'an.

"I wish I could share your faith, my son," he said, and I heard real regret in his voice. "But alas, I am old and all I know is that nothing good can come out of secret counsels held by angry men."

As Ali led his father out of the room, I looked around. There was a hubbub of commotion as the believers argued and debated among themselves as to what to do. Everyone seemed to have an opinion, but it was all speculation. Without knowing what was said in the Hall of Assembly, there would be no way to defend our people against this new threat.

And then an insane idea came to me. Of course I thought it was ingenious at the time, but I was a child, and did not know the difference between brilliance and madness. There are many who believe I have never learned the difference, and perhaps they are right.

I saw that my father was preoccupied by the debate, and my sister was preoccupied with staring at Zubayr. No one noticed or cared what I was thinking, and no one noticed or cared as I quietly slipped away toward the door.

But as I turned to leave, I thought I saw from the corner of my eye the Messenger watching me with an amused smile.

7

The Hall of Assembly sparkled like ruby in the moonlight. It was the second largest building in Mecca, with only the Kaaba standing taller. It had been built years before by Qusay, one of the most revered of the ancestors of Quraysh, a statesman who had ended the blood feuds of rival clans and created a unified oligarchy that brought stability to the Pilgrimage and prosperity to the city. The Hall of Assembly was the symbol of his legacy. A sprawling complex that spread out over two hundred feet of polished red stone and marble, it was the closest thing to a palace in the wastes between Yemen and Syria and served as a meeting ground for tribal leaders, as well as a festival hall and the seat of rough desert justice.

Normally, the arched doors, inlaid in silver and polished bronze, were flung open to the public, allowing the average citizen of Mecca the necessary illusion that he had access to the corridors of power. In truth, everyone knew that decisions made in the Hall were based on the cold calculations of gold and political expediency; but the semblance of justice was necessary to prevent complete social breakdown.

But today the needs of appearances were secondary to the demands of secrecy and the mighty doors were shut to all except those who wielded unquestioned power. Guards in heavy leather armor, ringed in steel, stood outside each of the doors, bearing long swords held to the ready. The deliberations tonight were essential to the future of the city, and they had been ordered to cut down anyone who attempted to enter without permission.

A sound like a footfall made one of the guards, a grim-faced brute named Husam, turn his head with a start. It had come from around the corner, where a small alley ran between the southern wall of the building and the gated home of Abu Sufyan. The guard signaled to his broken-toothed colleague Adham. Weapons poised, they stealthily turned around the corner, prepared to kill anyone hiding in the shadows.

They saw nothing except a gray cat looking up at them with un-blinking yellow eyes. Satisfied, the two men returned to their posts protecting the eastern gate to the Hall.

→ → →

I LOOKED DOWN FROM my precarious perch ten feet above the ground as the two angry-looking guards exited the alley. I had often played hide-and-seek with my friends and the alley beside the Hall of Assembly was one of my favorite haunts. I had always been a limber child and I had climbed up the iron drainpipe before, confident that the playmates trying to find me would not think to look up. I loved spying on them while they were unaware. That little skill had proved useful to me that night and had likely saved my life.

When the guards had disappeared from my sight, I allowed myself to breathe again. Looking up, I saw a window on the second floor that was partially open, the gap just small enough for a cat to climb through. Or a small child.

My heart beat with the excitement that comes more from doing the forbidden than from any awareness of the danger I was placing myself in. I dug my fingers into the pipe, my fingernails already black with grime and pigeon droppings, and climbed higher, until I was just parallel to the window. If I had looked down, I probably would have fainted from vertigo, but I had always been a focused girl, and right now my eyes were on nothing except the small sill that jutted out beneath the window. I closed my eyes for a second and said the benediction that I had been taught almost as my first words: *Bismillahir-rahmanir-raheem,* In the name of God, the Merciful, the Compassionate.

And then I swung over like a monkey and grasped the sill, clinging to its jagged stone outline. With a grunt that I prayed would not be heard by the nearby guards, I heaved myself higher until my skinny body was lying flat on the sill. Then, with the impossible dexterity of youth, I managed to squeeze through the window opening and tumbled inside.

I blinked, adjusting my eyes to the dark interior. I was on the floor of what appeared to be a circular walkway overlooking the central assembly chamber. Doors spread out to either side, leading to smaller meeting lounges. For an overly inquisitive girl, this vast building, with its many passages, doors and mysteries was a treasure trove of discovery.

But I had a self-appointed mission tonight and exploration would have to wait for another day.

The sound of voices pulled me toward a wood railing made of expensive acacia imported from the Sinai. I peered through the lattices that had been designed in swirling geometric forms—stars, octagons, and other pretty shapes that I didn't recognize—and peered down on the meeting in progress.

I immediately recognized most of the men as tribal chiefs who had come to my father's house at various times to plead with him to end his preaching and abandon the new religion that was undermining their trade. My heart froze at the sight of Abu Jahl, dressed in robes of rich blue, a black velvet vest covering his broad chest. Of course he would be here. His decision to elevate the persecution of the Muslims to murder had been the basis of tonight's emergency council.

And then I saw something that surprised me. Among all the men with their bright turbans and ceremonial daggers tied to leather belts was seated one woman.

Hind bint Utbah, the wife of Abu Sufyan and daughter of one of the most powerful chieftains of Quraysh. I had seen her before in the marketplace, examining jewelry or rows of cloth with an expert eye. Unlike the other women of Mecca, she did not haggle over prices. She immediately knew what an item was worth and never asked the merchant. She would the name the price, and there would be no argument. The traders often gave her an extra discount in a kind of backward negotiation where they sought to gain more in Hind's favor and political patronage than they lost on their merchandise.

She had a proud, steady walk, graceful and terrifying at once, like a lioness in motion. She was the tallest woman I had ever seen, easily dwarfing many of the men in the room. Her hair fell to the small of her back in waves, the dark locks fashionably streaked with henna. Her skin was olive and glistened like a polished mirror. But it was her eyes that always caught my breath. Yellow green like a cat's, piercing in their intensity. They exuded pride and disdain, as well as a clear hint of danger. Whatever demons hid behind Hind's cruel gaze, it was safer to leave them undisturbed.

"Muhammad's followers have become a grave problem for the people of Mecca," Abu Sufyan proclaimed, his voice booming with authority. "It is time that we take action."

Abu Jahl stepped forward smoothly.

"Today the first of their blood was spilled. More must follow if we are to put an end to this."

The crowd murmured its assent and I saw Hind smile. And then I noticed that there was a friend among the gathered nobles.

The Messenger's uncle Abbas rose. While he had not embraced our faith, he was always kind to Muslims and we counted on him to be a voice of reason among the lords. A role that he was clearly alone in tonight.

"It is time for patience, not hasty deeds,'" Abbas said, his silky voice seeking to quench the fire that had been ignited by Abu Jahl.

But his sympathies were an open secret among the chiefs, and Abu Jahl turned to face Abbas with a cold eye.

"Is it patience that stays your hand, or cowardice?"

Abbas bristled with the pride of his clan, the Bani Hashim. He walked right up to Abu Jahl until their beards were almost touching.

"You dare call me a coward? How much courage does it take to kill an old woman tied to a tree?"

Abu Jahl's handsome smile suddenly curled into a cruel grimace. A dead silence fell over the crowd. For an instant, I thought he would draw his dagger and plunge it into Abbas's chest to avenge this open attack on his honor.

And then Hind stepped between the men, her long elegant fingers positioned on the chests of the adversaries as she separated them gracefully.

"Enough! Save your rage for our common enemy, Muhammad."

Amr ibn al-As, the Meccan envoy with the honeyed tongue who had unsuccessfully sought to repatriate the Muslim refugees from Abyssinia, politely raised his hand. I saw that it was covered in silver rings with expensive stones—garnets, carnelian, and amber.

"But alas, what can we do against Muhammad? He is protected by the clan of Hashim."

Even as he spoke, all eyes fell on another member of the Messenger's tribe, his uncle Abu Lahab. Fat, bald, and perpetually sweating, he always reminded me of a garden slug, although with a less appealing personality.

Abu Lahab snorted in contempt at the thought of his wayward nephew. Unlike his half brothers Abu Talib and Abbas, Abu Lahab despised Muhammad, may God's blessings and peace be upon him, and had made no secret of his belief that the Messenger was simply creating a new religion to monopolize the city's lucrative Pilgrimage trade.

"The sanctuary of our clan will not last forever," Abu Lahab said. "My brother Abu Talib is old. When he dies, I will lead the Bani Hashim and will revoke his protection."

Abbas gave his brother a contemptuous stare, which Abu Lahab met with studied indifference.

Abu Jahl shook his head.

"We cannot wait that long," he said bluntly. "The tribes will grow weary of his disruption of the Pilgrimage. They will take their pilgrims—and their gold—to Taif and the temple of the goddess Allat."

Abu Jahl had chosen his words well. Taif was a prosperous trading center to the southeast, on the caravan route to Yemen. The denizens of that settlement had long envied Mecca's preeminence and had built a sprawling shrine to the "daughter of Allah" to rival and, they hoped, one day eclipse the Kaaba. If Muhammad's preaching against their gods made the annual Pilgrimage an inconvenience and source of turmoil for the desert tribes, it made sense that many would switch their allegiance to the goddess. And take their trade with them.

Seeing that he had hit he proper nerve with the other chiefs, Abu Jahl smiled.

"We must make a decisive move now," he said forcefully. "Muhammad must die."

There was an immediate uproar as various members of the Assembly shouted their opinions on this extremely controversial suggestion. I could see Hind smiling, her eyes glowing. She stood motionless in the middle of the loud debate, like the heart of a whirlwind. There was something both terrifying and mesmerizing about her at that moment, and I felt the hairs on the back of my neck tingle.

Finally Abu Sufyan raised both his hands and spoke loudly, asserting his authority over the tumult.

"No," he said firmly. "If we attack Muhammad, his clan will be forced to avenge him against the murderer. It will start a blood feud that will consume Mecca."

He glanced at Abbas, who nodded coldly. Abu Lahab looked to his feet, knowing that no matter how much he wished it were otherwise, what Abu Sufyan said was true. His cousins in the Bani Hashim would slaughter anyone who attacked Muhammad.

Abu Sufyan's calm voice served to quell the passion of the crowd, to Abu Jahl's clear annoyance. But the weight of his words had put an end to this dangerous line of talk. Abu Sufyan, perhaps better than any of them, understood the threat posed by Muhammad's movement, but he also knew that killing him would be like using oil to put out a kitchen fire.

Satisfied that he had cut off Abu Jahl's provocations before they could grow like weeds in a garden, killing the fruits of wisdom that kept the peace in Mecca, he stepped back.

And then Hind spoke, and everything changed.

8

Why do you fear the spilling of a little blood, my husband?" Hind said in a husky voice. "No nation can stand that will not pay the price of order."

All eyes were on her as she moved toward her husband. Abu Sufyan saw the hungry yet terrified gaze of the crowd on his beautiful wife and his face reddened at her blatant defiance of his authority.

"A wise merchant always weighs the price with a cold heart," he said, an edge entering his voice. "He does not allow himself to be swayed by the emotions of a woman."

Hind turned to face her husband and I saw a dangerous look in her eyes. I saw her right hand move back as if to slap him, and my eyes fell on a golden armlet that wrapped around her olive-colored forearm. It looked Egyptian in design, two snakes curling around her wrist, their jaws meeting behind her hand, a glittering ruby held between their savage fangs. It was beautiful and terrifying, much like Hind herself.

But if she had desired to strike her husband in public for his demeaning words, Hind thought the better of it, and she merely turned her back on him in open contempt.

Seeing the spell her sultry voice had cast on the men and their looks of despairing desire as she moved, Abbas walked to the center of the room to regain their attention.

"Abu Sufyan is right," he said loudly. "Killing Muhammad will prove too costly. Even if the blood feud were settled, his followers would proclaim him a martyr. A ghost is the most dangerous adversary, for it can never be killed."

Abu Sufyan nodded in assent, although he could not completely hide his irritation that his wife's gambit had allowed one of his rivals to state his primary case. But before he could add a word in support of Abbas, Abu Jahl clapped loudly, his hands coming together in slow, mocking strokes.

"Spoken like a true advocate for your nephew." he sneered. "I think it is safe to say that your loyalties lie with your kinsman and not with the people of Mecca. And it is the people of Mecca who are suffering under the lies of this sorcerer. Our city cries for a hero, a man who stands tall and does what needs to be done, without fear of consequences."

This high-flown but calculated appeal to idealism struck an immediate chord with the Arabs, a people who prided themselves on their epic stories of heroes who risked their lives for the honor of the tribe. Abu Sufyan watched in frustration as the fire of aggression he had extinguished began to blaze brightly again.

It was a shift in sentiment that Hind sensed as well. She raised her hands above her head, posing like the alluring idol of Astarte, the Phoenician fertility goddess, which stood in the Sanctuary.

"Who among you is a real man? A man who does not fear retribution? A man who will stand for Mecca and the religion of our fathers, even if it means his own death? A man who prefers the honored sleep of eternity to the shameful comfort of a coward's bed? Is there no such man among you?"

Her words were dripping with promise and warning. Even as a little girl, I knew what was being said beneath those words. Who among you is man enough to please me? To give me everything that is inside you, even if it means losing yourself in the flame of my heart?

I saw the lords of Mecca looking at one another in confusion and uncertainty. Hind's passion was too extreme, even for them. And then a man arose, one of the few who stood taller than the queenly Hind. It was Umar. There was a dark intensity in his face similar to what I had seen earlier in the day when Talha had humiliated him.

"I will do it. I will bring you the head of this liar who has profaned the Holy Kaaba."

There were gasps of surprise—or perhaps relief—that Umar had taken up Hind's challenge. He was essentially agreeing to his own death. While no one had any doubt that Umar had the courage and pure physical viciousness to take on the role of assassin, even he would not be able to defend himself against the retaliation of the men of Hashim.

Hind smiled at him and I saw a glance pass between them that I did not understand. But whatever it was that I saw, I was not alone, for Abu Sufyan caught it as well and looked away, his face red from anger. Or humiliation.

Realizing that Umar's declaration meant almost certain death for his nephew, Abbas tried to reason with him.

"Think, Umar, of what you are saying—"

Umar responded by unsheathing his sword.

"No! I have thought enough!" Umar turned to face Abbas and Abu Lahab, the two representatives of the Messenger's clan. "Know, O sons of Hashim, that I fear not your reprisals. I will kill this renegade, and if any among you has the courage to hold me accountable, then do so. You will find my blade a worthy match."

Abbas saw the madness in Umar's eyes and looked down quickly, before the giant brute lost control and smashed that broadsword on his skull. I saw his brother Abu Lahab smirk with glee. If Umar succeeded in ridding Mecca of his troublesome nephew, Abu Lahab would counsel his clansmen to forgo retribution and allow Umar to pay a blood debt to Muhammad's family rather than risk an all-consuming blood feud that would destroy Mecca. With the Prophet out of the way and the clan divided over how to respond to Umar's act of violence, Abu Lahab would be perfectly positioned to seize the scepter of authority from his aging brother Abu Talib.

I watched as Hind moved forward, her body flowing like silk in the wind, and touched Umar on the cheek with affection.

"I always knew you were the greatest man of Quraysh," she said, her words like nectar dripping from her full, red lips.

Her husband Abu Sufyan turned and walked out, unable to bear the humiliation of his wife's open flirtation with the son of al-Khattab. In later years, I would learn that Umar's affair with Hind had been the worst-kept secret of Mecca, but the two had been discreet in public until this moment.

A strange look came over Umar's face as he gazed at Hind. The harshness vanished and for a moment he looked like a child seeking to please his mother. Or perhaps more accurately, a condemned soul seeking forgiveness from his judge.

"Tomorrow, I will end this scourge," he said, his booming voice suddenly soft like a dove. "Muhammad will die. And the gods will be appeased."

He broke free of Hind and walked out, preparing to kill and be killed. And I later learned the thought that tore through his heart at that moment. That when he died under the vengeful blows of the men of Hashim, perhaps the child he had buried alive would be avenged.

9

The next morning Umar set out to fulfill his mission. As he rounded a corner, the Messenger's house came into view and he froze, looking at it with the perverse curiosity of a man peering into his grave. Umar hated Muhammad with a passion and was glad that he would be the one to eliminate this blot on the holy city. It was not that Umar cared deeply for the cult of his ancestors. He was intelligent enough to sense that most of the rituals of worship in the Sanctuary were a cheap amusement offered to the gullible and the hopeless, two categories of mankind that were predominant in Arabia and perhaps in all the world. He didn't care for the crude idols and icons that littered the Haram like prostitutes around an army camp.

But ever since he was a boy, he had felt something special around the Temple, the Kaaba itself. He was not a poet and had difficulty putting the emotions the House of God inspired into words. Perhaps it was impossible for any man to do so when faced with the Divine.

As a youth, Umar and his friends had made a sport of spending evenings inside old caves or abandoned huts that the superstitious claimed were haunted by djinn. But he had never felt anything supernatural at any of those places. Yet whenever he approached the granite cube that soared over Mecca, his heart skipped a beat. Every time he entered the confines of the Sanctuary, he felt as if he were being watched from all sides. Umar had a reputation for being fearless, a reputation that he nurtured and protected with great care, and in truth nothing on earth really did frighten him. Not the sword of an enemy nor the jaws of a lion. He knew how to deal with foes that bled, enemies that had weaknesses, that could be killed by strength and cunning.

But whenever he approached the Kaaba, he was afraid. Whatever spirit was there, it was invincible and could not be killed. And that truly terrified him. The night after he murdered his infant daughter, Umar had gone to the Kaaba in hopes of silencing the guilt and horror that gripped his heart. But when he crossed the circle of the Sanctuary and stood before the gold inlaid door of the House, his knees had given way and he felt something pressing him from all sides.

He was alone in the courtyard, but he kept hearing terrible whispers all around him. Whenever the wind rose, he could have sworn he heard cold laughter in its echo. The world began to dissolve and swim before his eyes and Umar felt as if he were falling. Convinced that he was dying, that the power that haunted the Kaaba had come to claim him, he had cried out to Allah, begging for mercy and a chance to expiate his sins by serving as a protector of the Holy House.

And then the delirium left him and all was silent. Yet he felt that whatever presence dwelt in those ancient stones had heard him and would hold him accountable to his oath. Since that day, Umar had lived up to his vow, standing watch whenever the pilgrims came, a self-appointed Guardian of the Kaaba. If a drunk or beggar profaned the grounds, he quickly tossed them off. Once he had caught and beaten a teenage thief who had picked the pocket of a wealthy pilgrim from Taif who was circumambulating the shrine. When the grateful merchant offered him a reward of silver from his purse, Umar had refused, explaining proudly that he was there to serve the Sanctuary and could not accept any compensation.

With Umar's formidable presence, the Pilgrimage had become a safer experience and the numbers of pilgrims had increased every year.

He had fulfilled his vow to the Spirit whom he could still feel watching him every day.

But now Muhammad and his heretics had decided to use the Pilgrimage as a venue to preach and spread their new religion, and the peace of the Sanctuary was again threatened. Incidents like the one the day before, when slaves spoke arrogantly to their betters, threatened to tear apart the social fabric of Mecca and poison the atmosphere for worship and trade. Umar realized that the Spirit of the Kaaba was testing him and he resolved that would not be found wanting. If killing this sorcerer Muhammad would restore peace to the Sanctuary, then Umar would fulfill his oath—even at the risk of his own life.

With these thoughts raging in his head, Umar stepped onto the cobbled path leading to the Prophet's house. As he approached the gates, his hand moved closer to the hilt of his sword. He would likely have only one chance to tear it loose from the scabbard and strike the deathblow before the sons of Hashim brought him down. But Umar was not afraid. The Spirit of the Kaaba was with him, and it was greater than this magician. He muttered a final prayer to himself as he stood outside the iron gate from which he would likely not emerge again.

"O Allah, give me the strength to do what is right, that Your House may forever be sanctified." With that, he reached to push open the latch.

And then a shadow fell on him from behind.

Umar whirled, his hand reaching for his sword instinctively. And then he saw that it was a member of his clan, a slight fellow named Nuaym who was perpetually cheerful and posed no threat.

Nuaym smiled and clasped his hand and then looked carefully at his tall clansmen's face.

"Umar! Are you all right? You look feverish."

Umar stared at the little fellow with irritation. He was not about to be distracted from his mission by this silly fool.

"I burn with the fire of justice."

Nuaym raised his bushy eyebrows in surprise.

"What are you talking about?"

There was no harm in telling him. He was a member of his own clan and could be trusted. And if Umar did not emerge alive from the house, Nuaym would tell the other sons of the Bani Adi to sing songs of his heroism.

"Today I have sworn a vow to kill that heretic Muhammad and end this sedition in our city."

Nuaym's mouth fell open in shock.

"Are you mad? The Bani Hashim will kill you in retaliation!"

Umar shrugged, his shoulders rising and falling like two mountains in an earthquake.

"So be it."

Nuaym put a friendly hand on his clansmen's arm as if to pull him away from this madness.

"Come, let us return to my house," he said brightly. "The heat of the day makes it hard to think wisely. We can talk about this over a cold drink in the shade."

Umar removed Nuaym's hand, squeezing the fingers painfully in warning.

"Get out of my way, old friend."

"Umar, listen to reason—"

Umar gabbed Nuaym by his collar and lifted the small man off his feet until their eyes met.

"No! I have sworn a vow to set things right today, and no man can stop me."

He dropped his clansman and turned back to face the house. Unsheathing his sword, he pushed open the gate.

"If you wish to set things right, you should look closer to home!"

Umar froze. Slowly, like a stubborn boulder finally giving way under the force of an avalanche, he turned to face Nuaym.

When Umar spoke, his voice was soft. But there was an edge there that was more terrifying than the roar of a thousand charging elephants.

"What are you saying?"

Nuaym looked deeply frightened, but he managed to meet Umar's gaze. He hesitated, his eyes flicking to the sword that now glittered lethally in the assassin's hand.

"Your sister Fatima is one of them."

Umar's eyes went wide. Of all the possible things that Nuaym could have said, this was the one he had not expected.

"You lie!" Umar's sword began to rise into attack position.

"She has embraced Muhammad and follows his path. Ask her yourself."

Umar's face turned bright red. He stepped forward and for a moment Nuaym believed the sword would soon slice open his neck. Umar bent down until his face was right next to his clansman and Nuaym could see the redness that ringed his dark eyes.

"If you are spreading calumny against my family, your blood will join Muhammad's on my sword."

And then, without another word, Umar turned and stormed down the path toward his sister's home.

Nuaym fell to his knees and buried his head in his hands, grateful to still be alive. At that moment, I emerged from the shadows of the alley where I had been secretly watching Umar's approach.

I walked over to Nuaym and saw that he was shaking. Not knowing what else to do, I put a comforting hand on his shoulder.

Nuaym started at my touch, half expecting that Umar had returned to finish him off. When he saw it was just me, he breathed deeply to calm himself. And then he took my hand in his. I could feel the cold dampness on his palm.

"Thank you, little one, for your warning."

Even though I was a child, I knew what Nuaym had done. He had run out of options, but I was still upset that he had betrayed Umar's sister Fatima, who had been a secret believer for the past year and had always been kind to me and my family.

"But Umar's sister—"

Nuaym shook his head, and I could see shame written on his gaunt features.

"I had no choice," he said, regret filling his voice. He stared down the path where Umar had charged off, still bearing his sword. "May God protect her from Umar's wrath."

10

*F*atima bint al-Khattab sat inside the small living quarters of her stone hut in the southern quarter of Mecca. She had covered her mousy brown hair with an indigo scarf that her brother Umar had given her for her wedding. Her husband, Said, knelt beside her, his head bowed reverently as she read from the leather hide that she had received that morning from Ali, containing words from the holy Qur'an that had just been revealed to the Messenger the night before.

She swayed back and forth like a candle rustling in the wind as the Words of God fell from her lips in the form of majestic poetry.

In the Name of God, the Merciful, the Compassionate.
Ta Ha.
It was not to distress you that We sent down the Qur'an to you
But as a reminder for those who hold God in awe
A Revelation from the One who created the Earth and the high Heaven
The Lord of Mercy Established on the Throne.
Everything in the Heavens and on Earth
Everything between them
Everything beneath the soil
Belongs to Him
Whatever you may say aloud
He knows what you keep secret
And what is even more hidden.
God—there is no god but Him
The most excellent Names belong to Him.

As she recited in her soft, melodic voice, she saw Said wipe tears from his eyes. She understood his emotion, although she had always kept a tight lid on expressing her own. A trait learned under the harsh hand of her father, al-Khattab, who brooked no weakness in his off-spring, whether male or female.

Said was so different from him and from her fiery brother, Umar. He had a gentle soul and was more comfortable playing with children and tending to sheep than engaging in the cruelties of war or the hunt. Other women might have thought him weak, but Fatima loved the softness of his heart. For a girl who had been raised in a house where anger was demonstrated more than love, his kindness and sweet touch were like the calm breeze that brought peace when a storm had subsided.

Said gently touched the cowhide parchment in her hands, stroking it like a lover. Like most men she knew, he could not read or write and relied on her to express the sounds that came with the strange lines and jots that he had never been taught to understand. Though Fatima had much bitterness toward her father for the roughness of her upbringing, she was grudgingly thankful that he had forced her and her brother to learn to read and write. Said had long felt ashamed that his wife was better educated than he, but when he discovered that the Messenger of God himself was illiterate and relied on his wife, Khadija, to read to him and write his correspondence, he had been comforted.

"What do those words mean at the beginning?" he asked. "*Ta Ha*. I've never heard that before."

"I don't know," she answered with a small shrug. "I asked Ali and he said they were sacred letters wrapped in mystery, and only God knew what they signified."

Said nodded. He was a simple man and he easily accepted that there were things that were beyond his comprehension. The fact that God was actually speaking to them right now, in their very city, through the mouth of Muhammad, was itself more than his mind could comprehend, and he had no desire to burden himself with deeper mysteries.

"Read it again," he said, and she nodded.

She began to recite again, letting the rhythm of the words flow through her. It was when believers read the holy Qur'an out loud that they were closest to God. The very words that the Lord of the Worlds had spoken vibrated through her being and lifted her soul.

But when she said the words "He knows what you keep secret," the stillness of her home was shattered and her heart jumped into her throat.

"Fatima! Fatima! Come out here!"

Umar's voice boomed from just beyond the door. Panic gripped her. Had her brother heard her recitation? She looked down at Said and saw that his rosy cheeks had drained of color as the same thought crossed his mind.

And then, without any further prompting, she realized that the end was at hand.

"He knows" was all she could say, her throat closing in on her in terror. Umar began to bang on the door and she knew she had no time to place the leather hide with the holy verses in its proper place, a silver jewelry box that she kept on the top shelf of their kitchen cupboard.

Even though she hated treating the Words of God without proper decorum, she had no choice but to slip the parchment inside her dark woolen tunic, close to her breast.

She squeezed Said's hand and took a deep breath, and then opened the door.

Umar stormed inside without any greeting, his face livid. She saw that he was carrying his sword in his hand and her stomach sank. Umar slammed the door behind him and then pushed up uncomfortably close to his sister, his weapon held in a steel grip.

"What was that gibberish I heard you reciting?" There was a dangerous rumble to his voice that Fatima recognized. It was the tremor before the earthquake was unleashed.

"We were just talking," she said with a small laugh that immediately sounded false to her.

Umar grabbed her by the arm with crushing strength.

"Don't lie to me!"

Said stepped forward. Although he was as terrified of Umar as his wife, he knew that his brother-in-law was violating every rule of Arab etiquette and he hoped that a stern call to honor would calm the brute.

"Who are you to come into our home and proclaim us liars?" he said with as much bravado as he could muster.

Umar looked at him incredulously, as if noticing him for the first time in his life. And then he raised his sword threateningly, the razor-sharp edge glistening in the morning light that poured in from the windows.

"I am a Guardian of the Kaaba who has sworn to kill any who follow Muhammad!"

In later years, Said would say that he had no idea where he had found the courage to stand up to Umar. But seeing the look of fear in the eyes of the woman he loved, she whose strength he always admired, set his blood on fire, and he took his hand and pushed the sword out of his way.

"You have lost your mind! Get out of my house!"

Umar was shocked at Said's sudden defiance, as men always are when those they assume are weak finally reveal a backbone.

"Tell me the truth!" he said, and Fatima could almost hear a desperate plea in his voice. And then when Said did not answer, Umar grabbed him by the neck and threw him across the room. Said fell against a table made of carved olive wood, which splintered with the force of his fall. Said dropped hard amid the jagged wreckage and lay there unmoving.

"No!" Fatima could hear herself scream, but it sounded strangely distant, as if echoing across a canyon in the barren wastes of the Najd to the east. Forgetting about her brother's sword, which could at any moment sever her head in the madness of fanaticism, she threw herself on Umar and slapped him ferociously.

Umar pushed her off him and she felt as if she had been grabbed by a dust devil and flung across the sky. And then her flight was cut short by a cold, cruel stone wall. She struck her head on the whitewashed rock and fell to her knees as lightning seared through her skull.

Fatima's eyes blurred and she felt as if warm water were flowing down her face. And then she realized it was blood. She touched her forehead and saw that her palm was stained in crimson.

Umar was looking at her, breathing hard, as if he had climbed high into the mountains. His eyes were fixed on the blood that flowed steadily from the cut just above her right eye.

Fatima saw that his sword was raised and she realized that the demon that had possessed him would soon kill her. She touched her breast and felt the comfort of the leather strip on which the verses of the holy Qur'an were written. If she was going to die, at least the she would meet her Maker with His Words embedded next to her heart.

"You want the truth? Then, yes! We are Muslims and we believe God and His Messenger! Go ahead! Kill me! Kill your sister like you did your own daughter!"

She did not know what madness possessed her to say the last, but

Umar staggered as if he had just been struck by a spear in the gut. He dropped his sword, which fell to the ground with a clang that echoed relentlessly.

Umar sank to his knees and buried his face in his hands for a long moment. And then, when he finally looked up, there was confusion on his face, like a child awakening from a bad dream.

"What is this spell he has cast on you?" he asked, and she knew he referred to the Prophet.

She managed to get to her feet and stumbled over to check on Said. He was regaining consciousness and she helped him sit up slowly. After checking to make sure that no bones were broken, she finally turned to her brother.

"It is not a spell but a Revelation," she said softly as she found a clean rag and wiped the blood from her face. The blood had stopped flowing and had begun to clot. "God himself speaks through Muhammad, and His words can change men's hearts."

Umar looked at her for a long moment. When he spoke, there was weariness in his voice.

"Show me these words and let me judge for myself."

She looked into his eyes and saw no sign of the demon. Fatima hesitated, then reached into her blouse and removed the leather strip.

Umar held out his hand for the parchment, but she shook her head.

"Only the clean may touch the Word of God."

Umar saw that she was serious. He rose and took a jug of water from the kitchen. First he poured it over her wound and helped her wash away the rest of the blood that stained her cheek.

And he followed her instructions as she taught him *wudu*, the sacred ritual of ablution that Muslims performed before praying or reading the holy Qur'an. He washed his hands, face, and feet as she instructed.

Fatima finally handed him the strip of cowhide, the text standing out in bright green paint. Umar looked down at the page, his brow creasing as he read the mysterious letters that opened the text.

Ta Ha . . .

11

We waited inside the Messenger's house in silence, a cloud of dread hanging over the small community of believers. I saw my father looking down at his hands, unable to meet the eyes of Nuaym, who sat across from him on the cold marble floor. It was Abu Bakr who had asked Nuaym to intervene with his clansman after I returned that night, breathless from my tale of intrigue inside the Hall of Assembly. I had expected my father to be angry with me for taking such a mad risk, but he had listened gravely and then gone to the Messenger with news of the plot. My mother, however, had been furious when she heard how I had risked my life and had spanked me until my throat was sore from crying.

My rump still sore from the beating, I sat on my haunches. I had never seen the Messenger so quiet. The Prophet had been deeply distressed to hear that his life had been saved by placing Umar's sister, Fatima, at risk. He stared out a window at a palm tree that grew just outside the wall of his wife's home, as if he could find some hope in its steady defiance of the desert winds that buffeted the city that morning. Perhaps I imagined it, but I did not see him blink at all for minutes. He seemed to be in a trance, but it was not like the terrifying seizures that overtook him when the Revelation came. He seemed like a man sleeping with his eyes awake, his powerful chest moving up and down steadily as he breathed.

The silence in the Prophet's house was so strong that it was an eerie sound in itself. And then a loud steady knock resounded through the hall, like the trumpet of the angel shattering the stillness of death and summoning men to the Resurrection.

Ali rose from his place at the Messenger's feet. He walked over slowly to the main door and peered through a tiny peephole before turning to face the gathered crowd.

"It is Umar," he said matter-of-factly. "He comes bearing a sword."

A murmur of fear spread among the believers. My sister, Asma, suddenly burst into tears, assuming the worst for poor Fatima. The Messenger's uncle Hamza stood up.

"Let him in. If he has come with good intent, we will give him a mountain of good in return. And if his intent is evil, we will kill him with his own sword."

Ali looked to the Prophet, who stood up with dignity and moved toward the door. I noticed again how his strides were not like those of any other man I had ever seen. Though the Messenger was not as tall as Hamza, he walked with a speed and determination that made those with longer legs pant to keep up with him. It was as if he were the wind itself, forever outracing the fastest of the sons of Adam.

The Prophet stopped a few feet away from the door. He was now positioned so that his followers were grouped behind him, as if he would single-handedly shield us from Umar's vengeance. Hamza stood behind his right shoulder and Ali was to his left. The Messenger nodded to his young cousin, who threw open the door.

We all stopped breathing. I thought I could hear the steady thrum of our hearts, as if they were pounding in unison.

And then Umar stepped inside, his sword unsheathed and glistening in his hand. I looked with morbid curiosity to see if there was any blood drying on the blade. But if he had killed his sister, as we all expected, Umar had wiped the sword clean before returning to fulfill his vow.

I watched his face with fascination. He appeared different from the man I had seen only a few hours before. There was no more rage on his face, and he appeared uncertain, almost afraid, as he stood before the Messenger.

For a moment, no one moved. It was as if the slightest tremor would set into motion events that would change everything.

And indeed it did.

The Prophet stepped forward and grabbed Umar by his studded belt, suddenly pulling the giant who towered a full head over the tallest men in the room as if he were an unruly child. He dragged Umar unceremoniously to the center of the hall, where the assassin was forced to stand among a crowd of two dozen believers staring at him with fear.

"What has brought you here, O son of al-Khattab?" the Messenger said, his eyes never leaving his adversary's bushy bearded face. "I cannot see you desisting until God sends down some calamity on you."

Umar hesitated. I saw him move his sword arm and Hamza instantly had his bow in his hand, an arrow nocked and pointed right at Umar's chest.

And then I saw something that made my heart leap into my throat.

Tears welled into the giant's eyes and poured down his weathered cheeks like the well of Ishmael suddenly erupting from the bowels of the desert and bringing hope of life where there had been only death.

Umar dropped the sword at the Messenger's feet and knelt in humility until his head was positioned beneath the Prophet's chest. And then he said words that no one in all of Mecca would have ever expected.

"O Messenger of God, I have come to you that I may declare my faith in God and in His Messenger and in what he has brought from God."

There was moment of stunned silence. This had to be a trick, some ruse Umar had devised to startle us and lower our guard so that he could strike unexpectedly.

But then the Prophet smiled warmly, his face glowing like the sun breaking through dark clouds.

"*Allahu akbar!*" the Messenger cried in a voice that thundered throughout the hall and poured out into the dusty streets of the holy city. "God is great!"

And then Muhammad, may God's blessings and peace be upon him, embraced Umar like a brother whom he had not seen in many years.

We looked at one another in wonder. And then I started clapping, a flurry of giggles erupting from my lips. The sound of my laugh was throaty and contagious, and soon others joined in. We raised our voices in joy, marveling at the power of faith and the inexplicable depths of the human heart.

12

few hours later, Umar strode through the streets of Mecca, walking as if in a dream. Everything had changed the moment he had read the Words of God. It was as if someone had reached inside his breast and torn out a deadly snake that had been wrapped around his heart, squeezing out any love for life or his fellow man. And then he had understood. The Spirit that he sensed around the Kaaba, the Being that he had vowed to serve at the cost of his own life, had a voice, and it had spoken to him through a book revealed to an illiterate man. All this time, he had been fighting the very force to which he had dedicated his soul.

Umar had read the words that were painted on the leather strip and had fallen back as if struck by an invisible hand. He had started shaking with violent tremors and his head had felt warm and dizzy. But he knew that he was not suffering from fever or plague. It was the same dizzying sensation that had torn through him the day he had sought solace for murdering his daughter by kneeling at the Sanctuary. But this time, instead of cruel laughter mocking him, he heard a gentle voice in his heart, filled with compassion, saying: "Go to him."

And like a child who does not dare question his elders, Umar had gotten up without a word to his sister and walked straight to the Messenger's house. When he had declared his newfound faith, he felt as if a stone had lifted from his shoulders and that someone who had been imprisoned inside of him had suddenly been set free. The man Umar had once been was gone, like a shadow that vanishes when light is shone upon it.

He had not cried since he was a child. His father, al-Khattab, would beat him ferociously each time he sniffled, calling him weak and threatening to cut off his male organ if he kept weeping like a girl. But today he had wept for hours, as if a dam had burst and all the pain that he had bottled inside himself for years had come out. He could not control it if he wanted to. And, in truth, he did not want to.

The Messenger had accepted him and forgiven him his treachery, but Umar found he still could not stop crying. He kept seeing the image of his precious baby daughter looking up at him with a smile even as he covered her tiny body with stones. She had kept squeezing his finger until the breath had finally left her and her little hand had dropped.

He had looked at the Messenger and asked that God punish him for his sin. He had handed his sword to Muhammad and begged him to avenge the girl and cut off his head. But the Prophet had put a gentle hand on his arm, his own black eyes welling with tears of empathy.

"You have already punished yourself enough, son of al-Khattab," he had said softly. "Islam is like a river. It cleans those who immerse themselves of their past sins."

Umar had bowed his head, still not willing to accept the forgiveness he was offered.

"You say that all men will be resurrected one day and the girls who were slain by their fathers will confront them on the Day of Judgment," he said, repeating the teachings that he had reviled and mocked only a few hours before. "What will I say to my little girl when I face her?"

The Prophet looked past Umar's shoulder, as if staring at some grand vision on the horizon of his mind's eye.

"I see her holding you by the hand, squeezing your finger, as she leads you to Paradise."

At that moment, Umar ibn al-Khattab was freed. The man he had been, the murderer, the drunk, the adulterer, died. And the man who now walked purposefully through the cobbled alleys of Mecca had been born.

He noticed that people in the streets were staring at him, looking confused as he passed them. And then he realized it was because he was smiling. Not the smile of a man with a deadly scheme in his heart, but one of pure and unconditional joy. As he passed by a street merchant selling coral combs, agate rings, and vials of rosewater perfume to a group of black-veiled Bedouin women, he caught a reflection of his face in the polished silver mirror the merchant had erected to promote his wares to the vanity of his customers.

He did not recognize himself. The cruel scowl that he had once believed to be a sign of power and masculinity was gone, replaced by a look of childlike wonder. Umar grinned and found that he liked the way the lines around his lips and cheeks crinkled when he did so.

And then he forced himself to adopt a serious, stoic face. For now he was on a new mission and he could not allow himself to be distracted by the unfamiliar face that stared back at him from the mirror.

Umar moved forward with steady strides, his eyes focused on a grand house of yellow stone, the walls decorated with carved flowers and wreaths of silver. He knocked harshly on the dark wooden doors made of cedar imported from Lebanon.

He heard the sound of movement and caught a glimpse of a dark eye gazing at him through a tiny peephole. And then the door swung open and Abu Jahl emerged, his face eager with expectation.

"Is it done? Is the man dead?"

Umar looked at him for a long moment. He had once secretly envied Abu Jahl's chiseled good looks, but now he saw only a demon whose ugliness was evident in the cruel gaze of his eyes.

"One man is dead," Umar said slowly, pronouncing each word as if it would be his last. "Another has been born."

Abu Jahl furled his brow in confusion.

"What are you saying?"

Umar leaned close to him, a triumphant smile slowly crossing his face.

"I have come to tell you that I believe in God and His Messenger, Muhammad, and that I testify to the truth of what he has brought."

Abu Jahl stared at him blankly. And then his face twisted into a violent scowl, and his handsome mask was shattered, revealing a darkness that few had ever witnessed beneath his studied diplomatic veneer.

"God curse you, and may His curse be on the tidings you have brought!"

Abu Jahl slammed the door in Umar's face. The redeemed assassin stood quietly for a moment and then burst out laughing, his beard shaking with violent mirth at the precious sight of Abu Jahl's discomfiture.

He turned and walked back toward the Kaaba, where he would proclaim his rebirth before the entire city. And for an instant, he thought he heard in his ears the joyful laugh of a little girl who should have lived to see this day.

13

Abu Sufyan leaned back on the dais as the dancing girls whirled before him. Their dark skin contrasted vividly with their pink and saffron robes, their skirts twirling sensually with their measured steps, revealing just enough to ignite a man's desire before disappearing in a swirl of mystery.

His eye fell on a doe-eyed girl of fourteen who smiled at him, flashing ivory teeth that seemed to sparkle in the torchlight that lit the audience hall of his grand manor. He felt a stirring within his loins and he glanced over to his wife, Hind, who had her eyes on the same courtesan. She met his gaze and winked, and he knew that she would be open to having the harlot join them in their bed tonight.

Normally the thought would have pleased him, but his mind was distracted tonight. He brooded over the mad scene at the Sanctuary that morning, when Umar had proclaimed his conversion to Muhammad's religion and had announced himself a guardian of the Prophet. With Umar and his terrifying sword in Muhammad's hands, the balance of power in the city had shifted decisively. The Muslims were no longer a troublesome cult of dreamers but an influential tribe of their own, backed by the protection of one of the most powerful leaders of Mecca.

As he glanced sideways at Hind, who was watching the buxom dancer like a cat waiting to devour a mouse, he thought bitterly that the only good thing that could come out of Umar's betrayal was that he would no longer be a cloud darkening their marriage. Abu Sufyan had endured the rumors and innuendoes, publicly denouncing any who would sully the reputation of his honorable wife. But he secretly knew that her frequent evening visits to "her aunts" were mere diversionary tactics and that her true destination was Umar's bed.

Why had he put up with it for so long? He had a wise fear of Umar's temper like everyone else. But in his heart he knew that he would not have interfered even if Hind had taken up with some lesser man whose sword was more easily faced in battle. Was it because his marriage to her had sealed his alliance with her powerful father, Utbah, and guaranteed his unchallenged leadership of Mecca? No, he would like to think that he was politically skilled enough to retain his position as the chieftain of chieftains even if he divorced Hind or killed her to restore his honor.

But the thought of leaving her, or worse, murdering her, left him feeling cold and sick. He looked over at her and saw the faint smile on her lush lips, the savage glint in her eyes that hinted at dark thoughts and darker lusts. And he knew the truth, painful as it was. He loved Hind, more than he loved anything else in this world. Abu Sufyan could not imagine life without her, and he was willing to turn away from her dalliances with men—and women—if only to preserve their marriage. Even after all these years, she ignited his passion as no other woman could. And even more important, she comforted his soul with her innate understanding of the difficulties of leadership and the lone-liness of power. She was the only person he could talk to, to unburden his mind when the pressure became too great.

As it had tonight. Abu Sufyan clapped to signal he was tired of the performance. The musicians who had been steadily pounding drums made of camel hide and bone ended their play and the girls stopped their sensual dancing, the rustle of their skirts quieting like the sudden fall of a heavy wind.

Abu Sufyan threw them a handful of gold coins and waved them away. The dark-skinned dancer with the luminous eyes looked at Hind, who nodded, and then she joined her sisters in the adjoining ante-chamber, where they would be fed roasted lamb and poured wine by the servants before being sent on their way.

When the last of the dancers had left and they were alone, Hind turned to face Abu Sufyan, putting her long-fingered hand over his. He always marveled at the heat she exuded, as if she were a walking torch.

"What is wrong, my husband?" she said softly, her piercing eyes tearing into his soul.

"Umar's conversion is a turning point," Abu Sufyan said with a sigh. He quietly noted the flicker of emotion that crossed her face at the mention of the man who had only days before been her lover and was now an open enemy. "These Muslims are no longer afraid. They will spread their poison openly now, knowing that Umar will protect them."

Hind looked away for a second, her eyes on the lush maroon carpet where the dancers had been swaying only moments before.

"Umar is but one man," she said, as if trying to convince herself. "He cannot hold back the wrath of Quraysh."

Abu Sufyan laughed bitterly.

"What wrath? Our tribe is like a hamstrung camel. Even Abu Jahl is now afraid of igniting an all-out war with these heretics. We cannot risk killing any of them as long as Umar's sword hangs over our heads."

Hind turned to face him, and he saw the raw cunning in her eyes that both excited and terrified him. She stroked the golden snake armlet that she always wore, and he felt his desire rising.

"You men always see things so simply. Night and day. Sun and moon. There are no stars in your world, no clouds or mists. You lack subtlety."

Abu Sufyan leaned closer. "What do you mean?"

"One does not need to kill another man in order to wage war on him," she said, squeezing his hand until he winced in pain. "What is Mecca known for, besides its gods?"

Abu Sufyan had learned over the years to answer her questions, as they were usually meant to guide him to a truth he had not yet seen but was already evident to her.

"Its trade. Our merchants are the heart of all commerce between Yemen, Byzantium, and Persia."

Hind leaned even closer and he could feel her firm breasts rub against him, arousing his desire again.

"And what happens when blood from the heart fails to reach an organ?"

His own organ was engorged with blood and he had difficulty thinking because of the pounding in his loins. But as he let her words penetrate the haze of lust, understanding began to dawn on Abu Sufyan.

"It dies," he said simply.

Hind smiled, and her hand touched his excited flesh.

"Exactly."

He ran a finger across her neck, long and elegant like a gazelle's.

"We will use trade as a weapon."

Hind smiled, delighted as always that the pupil had finally caught up to the teacher. She reached over to a basket of red grapes and took one in her lips. And then she kissed Abu Sufyan and let the grape fall into his mouth. He sucked on it and her tongue at the same time.

She finally broke off the kiss and looked him deep in the eyes.

"You do not need to kill them. If you starve them, they will kill themselves."

The full plan was now coming into view, with all its cold brilliance. Abu Sufyan gazed at Hind with admiration.

"If the Quraysh would accept a woman as their leader, they would have chosen you," he said.

Hind did not deny this. She ran her nails across his chest, feeling the harsh beating of his heart.

"But since they would not, I chose you."

Abu Sufyan smiled.

"I thought you married me because you loved me."

She kissed him again, letting her soft pink tongue play across his lips.

"I do."

And then Abu Sufyan leaned back and looked at her as if appraising the true value of a rare gem.

"Is it me, or is it my power that you love?"

Hind smiled mischievously.

"Defeat Muhammad, and you will never need to know the answer to that question."

She leaned forward and kissed him for a long moment. When she broke free, he saw that they were not alone. The dancer with the lustful eyes had returned to the hall unbidden, perhaps summoned by the magnetic heat that Hind's body exuded.

His wife smiled and pulled Abu Sufyan up with her right hand. She held out her left and grasped the dancer's small fingers, and then she quietly led the two back to her bedchamber.

14

I stood holding my father's hand as Abu Sufyan, dressed in the formal black robes of judgment, led a group of similarly clad chieftains before the golden door of the Kaaba. I saw that he held a heavy lambskin parchment in his hand and that Abu Jahl stood to his right, a triumphant smile playing across his face.

When they were all gathered in the courtyard of the Sanctuary, I counted over forty of the most powerful men, not only of Mecca but of the Bedouin tribes who grazed their flocks just beyond the black hills that served as the borders of the city.

My eye caught movement to my left, and I saw Abu Talib, the Prophet's uncle and the head of the clan of Bani Hashim, standing with his brothers, Hamza and Abbas. He looked even more aged and tired than when I had last seen him, and Hamza held his shoulder firmly to help Abu Talib maintain his balance. I saw the three brothers looking at the gathering of the chieftains, from which they had been pointedly excluded, with evident concern.

And then Hamza scowled and I followed his eyes across the courtyard to see his half brother and spiritual enemy, Abu Lahab, standing by his wife, Umm Jamil. She had become one of the most vocal female voices against the Prophet and his Message. Umm Jamil's petty vindictiveness was legendary, and I remembered how the Messenger had limped to my father's house after she had carefully strewn thorns behind him while he prayed at the Sanctuary so that he when finished and turned to leave, his feet had been torn and bloodied.

The persecution by his own uncle and aunt had so upset the Messenger that God had come to his defense, sending a Revelation that condemned both of them to hell for eternity. This had only enraged Umm Jamil even more, and the next time she had seen the Messenger, she had thrown a pot full of steaming goat feces and entrails over his head.

Now she and her slug of a husband stood gloating as the lords of Mecca moved to destroy our faith once and for all.

Abu Sufyan looked sternly at our small crowd of believers, who had been summoned to hear the proclamation that had been decided in secret council that morning. And then he read from the document, his voice firm with authority.

"In your name, O Allah, we the leaders of Quraysh proclaim this solemn oath. The Children of Hashim have harbored a dangerous sorcerer named Muhammad, a madman whose lies defile the sanctity of Your House and Your children, the gods of the Arabs. His sedition has driven men away from the sacred Pilgrimage and has covered Your holy city with the shadow of poverty and fear. As custodians of Your Sanctuary, we can no longer stand by and watch corruption spread through the earth. We therefore proclaim this day that the clan of Hashim is outlawed. No man of Quraysh may marry a woman of Hashim or give his daughter in marriage to a man of Hashim. And no one of Quraysh may sell anything to anyone of Hashim, nor purchase anything from them. And this proclamation shall stay in force until the Bani Hashim lifts its protection of the heretic Muhammad or the sorcerer renounces his false claim of prophecy."

He finished reading and raised his head to face us again.

"So say we all."

The other tribal chiefs loudly declared their support of the proclamation, raising their right hands in affirmation.

I saw my father's face fall as he watched the chiefs move forward one by one to place their individual wax seals on the document. A crowd of hooligans and rabble-rousers had been strategically gathered by the chieftains, and they now played their designated role by shouting practiced curses and slurs at the Muslims, inviting the gods to rain punishment on us from the heavens.

Abu Sufyan bowed to the angry mob with a deep flourish, as if accepting the will of the people. He took the proclamation and climbed the stone steps leading up to the gold-embossed door of the Temple. I gasped, as I had never seen anyone go inside the Kaaba. It was said that the lords of Mecca would enter the Holy of Holies only on extremely rare occasions when the future of the city was at stake, such as when a Yemeni army had besieged Mecca fifty years ago, shortly before the birth of the Messenger.

Clearly, this proclamation of exclusion was seen by the chieftains as requiring the highest divine endorsement. Never before had the lords gathered together to denounce and expel one of their own, not just one man but an entire clan, and deny by common agreement a whole caste of people any source of food or income to survive.

Abu Sufyan entered the Kaaba, his head bowed in humility and recognition of the fact that he was stepping on sacred ground that was normally forbidden. When the doors swung inward and sunlight flooded the normally dark interior, I saw a flash of crimson inside and caught sight of a towering cornelian quartz idol that I had heard about but never seen before.

Hubal, the god of Mecca, an ancient idol that had been brought all the way from Syria hundreds of years before. Its carved right hand had broken off during the long caravan ride from the north, and the ancestors of the Quraysh had fashioned for the idol a new hand of solid gold. The Messenger had said that of all the pagan abominations that corrupted the sacred ground of the Sanctuary, none was more hateful to Allah than this monstrosity that sat inside the House of God, its jagged face smiling obscenely at its usurpation of the authority of the One.

As Abu Sufyan stepped inside and nailed the proclamation to the dark stone wall behind Hubal, I saw his ally Abu Lahab look across the courtyard to Abu Talib, a victorious gleam in his beady eyes. The ban had cut Abu Talib's leadership of the Bani Hashim at the knees, leaving Abu Lahab rich ground to agitate for new leadership. And then Abu Jahl approached Abu Lahab, shaking his black-turbaned head and placing his jeweled fingers on his friend's meaty shoulder. Abu Jahl sighed in exaggerated sympathy, speaking loud enough so that we could all hear him.

"If only your clansmen had your vision, my friend," Abu Jahl said pointedly. Clearly the campaign to replace the head of the Bani Hashim had begun in earnest.

Abu Lahab wrung his hands in mock despair.

"They have been blinded by my nephew's magic. But the ban will wake them from their dream."

"I hope so," Abu Jahl said. "And then perhaps they will choose someone who can lead the clan of Hashim back to its hallowed seat at the table of Quraysh."

Clucking like old women who have been scandalized by the fool-

ishness of the young, they walked away together, leaving us to the jeers
of Abu Sufyan's hired demonstrators.

Abu Talib watched sadly as his estranged brother departed. Having
swallowed the worst humiliation of his years as a chieftain, the old man
turned to leave the Sanctuary. Hamza and Abbas helped Abu Talib
cross the courtyard slowly, his head held high in dignity even as the
drunken crowd flung insults upon him.

I watched as Abu Sufyan emerged from the Kaaba and closed the
glittering doors with reverence. He turned to join the gathered chieftains and thank them for their unified support of his plan to expel
the Bani Hashim from Mecca. And then he saw me, a thin little girl
who would soon be denied food and medicine under his orders, and I
thought I saw a flash of shame and regret on his face before he turned
his back on me.

I was young, but I understood enough of what had happened to
know that the world had changed and that we were in an extremely
precarious situation. I tugged on my father's sleeves.

"If no one will buy or sell to us, how will we eat?"

Abu Bakr bent down and put a gentle hand on my shoulder.

"When the Children of Israel fled Pharaoh and wandered in the
wilderness, God gave them food. Even so, He will feed us."

His face was calm and composed as always. But in his eyes, I saw
fear.

15 Mecca—AD 619

The boycott by the Quraysh forced the Muslims to evacuate
the city. Forbidden to buy food or the basic necessities of
life within the boundaries of Mecca, we sought refuge in
the blackened hills beyond its precincts. But as we quickly learned, the
borders of a city are determined not by walls, rivers, or mountains but
by the sphere of influence dictated by the might of its armies, by the
network of its merchants. And Mecca's circle of power extended well
beyond arbitrary lines drawn in the sands of Arabia.

With neighboring Bedouin herders and passing caravans refusing to take our money or accept our services in trade, the believers were forced to forage in the wilderness like jackals or vultures. We pitched camp by a small wadi owned by my father. A tent city sprang up by the muddy stream that provided our only source of water in the midst of a gray wasteland.

I was only six years old, but whatever innocence of childhood I possessed had died. My pale face had become the shade of burned copper and my small hands were chafed from carrying pails of water that were almost as tall as I was. My knees were perennially scratched and scarred, the tender flesh torn from climbing through the rocky hills looking for precious eggs at the first sight of a hovering pigeon that might have built a nest nearby.

I rarely laughed anymore and had adopted the grim stoicism that I saw carved on my mother's worn face. Her soft skin had lost its luster and had taken on the hardness of dry leather. At night, I could hear her crying in the small weather-beaten tent next to the one where Asma and I slept. Our mattresses were nothing more than a collection of rags that served many purposes in the camp of the exiles. At night we would spread them on the ground and lie upon them. In the morning, they would be rolled up and used to clean any pots that had been fortunate enough to be filled with food the night before. And once they had been washed in the questionably potable water of the spring, they would serve as our change of clothes for the day.

Childhood should be a time of play, of running through the streets with joy in one's heart, of flying kites and letting the soul soar with them beyond the dome of the sky into a world of dreams and possibilities. In my old age, I look back and remember the countless crimes our enemies subjected us to in the early days of Islam. I have forgiven most of these transgressions, as the Messenger enjoined us. But the pain of those childhood years, spent hovering under the shadow of starvation, pestilence, and death, has been so deeply imprinted in my heart that I cannot let it go. Whenever I think back on those dark days, I feel anew the rage and despair that come with being small and powerless in a world that rewards only cruelty and strength.

It was the memory of that deprivation and fear that would drive me in years to come to seek power when I should have sought wisdom. And my grief is that many men would die because of a child's terror of the scorpions that crawled past her as she lay on hard desert ground in the night.

Eventually the end came, as it always does. If I have learned one thing in the years of my existence, one nugget of wisdom from having lived in the midst of disputations over faith and the nature of the world, it is that everything ends. This is both the blessing and the punishment of God upon the foolish tribe that calls itself man. We can embrace the end or we can weep, but the ghost of time closes all doors with a finality that can never be gainsaid.

So it was that one night, I emerged from a torn green tent and looked out at the dozens of believers, dressed in dirty rags, sitting by makeshift campfires along the tiny riverbed. The sparks crackled and flew into heaven, like desperate prayers. I felt a terrible weight in my heart, for I carried news that would extinguish many hopes tonight.

I saw my father at the edge of the camp, gathering acacia leaves from a scattered copse of trees. We had been reduced to rationing these prickly green sprouts that even our animals were dubious of as our supply of dried meat dwindled. Some of the refugees would eat them raw, while others, especially the children, could stomach them only if they were cooked into a thin broth.

Abu Bakr saw the look on my face as I ran over, and he stopped in his tracks, dropping the basket of leaves.

"How is Khadija?" he said, a hint of dread in his voice, as if he already knew the answer.

I had spent the last two days at the side of the Mother of the Believers. She had been struck by the potentially deadly camp fever and had been fading in and out of consciousness for the past hour.

"She is still feverish," I said, panting to catch my breath. I paused, fearful to say what my father already suspected. "Mother worries for her life."

I saw the color drain from his tired face.

"I seek refuge in Allah! Without Khadija, I do not know how he will go on."

Abu Bakr looked across the camp and I saw that he was gazing at the Messenger, who stood alone at the top of the hill, his head bowed in prayer or sadness. Or both.

And then I felt the ground shudder as Umar stormed over. His dark face was contorted in rage as usual. He stared at the emaciated faces of the refugees kneeling by the wadi and then turned to my father with a now-familiar rant.

"It's been two years! When will this end? Where is God's help?"

My father was the only one besides the Messenger who seemed to have a soothing effect on Umar's volatile emotions. Abu Bakr was as much of a doctor as a friend to this volcano of a man, whose fire easily consumed lesser souls.

"Calm yourself, Umar," my father said patiently. "The people need you to be strong." He did not add what I knew he was thinking—especially if the Mother of the Believers died. The Muslims would need men who were made of granite rather than flesh to guide them through the madness and despair that would follow.

But Umar as usual failed to read that which was underneath the words. He was never a subtle man.

"How can you be so calm?" he said with increasing fury, like a child demanding an answer to an inexplicable mystery. "You've lost everything. You were once one of the wealthiest men of Mecca, and now there is no difference between you and the slaves whose freedom you bought!"

Abu Bakr sighed. Even my father's impatience with this moody giant had its limits.

"Whatever I had was on loan to me from God," he said. "Were I given tenfold what I have lost, I would gladly spend it all for God and His Messenger."

Apparently, he had found the words that Umar needed at that moment, and the son of al-Khattab stopped shaking. A gentle calm descended on him. My father looked again to the Prophet, who now sat down upon a mottled gray rock and buried his head in his hands as if weeping. I saw deep pity on Abu Bakr's face. Few knew as well as he the anguish of the Messenger, who had been preaching One God for almost ten years and had achieved nothing but exile and starvation for his followers.

"Go to him," my father said softly. He knew that the Messenger saw me as one of the few bright lights in this vast blanket of night that covered his life. Even though I rarely laughed on my own anymore, I was still a performer at heart, and I had been the only one who could bring a smile to his face with my games and antics.

I walked over to the Prophet and saw that his face was wet with tears. For a moment, I stopped breathing. If the Messenger of God had been reduced to despair, what hope would there ever be that I could find joy in my dead heart again?

I put a hand on his shoulder and tried to keep it from shaking.

"Don't be sad," I said, and it was more of a desperate plea than a compassionate request. "God is with us," I added, despite all evidence to the contrary.

The Prophet raised his head and looked at me for a long moment. He took my hand and squeezed it gently, and I pretended to cry out in exaggerated discomfort and then danced a silly jig at his feet. He laughed, then scooped me into his arms, smiled into my golden eyes. It was as if my presence gave him renewed strength and purpose. Looking at me, he saw the future that he and his followers were struggling to create.

And gazing into his unfathomably dark eyes, I sensed that I had reminded him of the past as well. In later years, the Messenger told me that my childish defiance of the world, my embrace of life when those with allegedly greater wisdom had resigned themselves to death, had taught him again the lesson of his own youth. For I was the same age as he when his mother had died and he lost what little standing and hope he had in the strict social hierarchy of Mecca. It was a harsh lesson that the orphan had learned that night and relearned again and again, every night for two decades, until God had brought him to Khadija and ended one chapter of his life to begin another. It was the cruel but necessary truth that pain is an unavoidable part of any struggle, as are the inevitable defeats and humiliations of the journey. Loss is the fire that tempers steel and forges it into a sword of victory. Failure is the currency by which success is eventually purchased in bulk.

And then I saw the Messenger's face change. The smile that lingered on his lips froze. I watched in shock as his dark eyes flew back up into his head until all I could see was the ivory white orbs that encased them. His hands began to tremble and he let go of me as tremors tore through his body like terrifying bolts of lightning.

I fell to the ground, my throat constricted in fear. I felt rather than saw my father come running up behind me. Abu Bakr scooped me into his arms and held me tight, but his eyes never left the Messenger, whose face was bathed in sweat and who fell to his side, convulsing like a fish that had suddenly been pulled out of the sea.

The Trance of the Revelation.

We had both seen this happen before, but it never ceased to fill us with awe and terror. For we knew that the Messenger's body shook with the unimaginable power of two worlds colliding. Of the entire might and vastness of heaven itself curling into a ball and descending into the tiny and weak form of a mortal man.

It was at the moment of the Revelation that we had a sense of the power of an Infinite Mind that had created the cosmos with a single word. And now that very same power, the overwhelming energy of the Divine Word, was tearing into the sinews and muscles of this one man who had been chosen to be its herald to mankind.

I saw Ali approach with a blanket. He wrapped the Messenger around the shoulders and sat by him, brushing his dark curls lovingly as he shivered and shuddered under the weight of the Revelation.

And then, so fast that I gave a little scream of surprise, the Messenger's eyes flew open and he bolted upright. The tremors immediately ceased, but I could still feel the air around him vibrating, as if the world itself shook with the force that coursed through his soul.

And then Muhammad, may God's blessings and peace be upon him, spoke. But the voice was not his own. It was deeper, unearthly, like an echo rising up from a chasm between life and death. And it said:

"Do you suppose that you will enter the Garden
Without first having suffered like those before you?
They were afflicted by misfortune and hardship
And they were so shaken that even their Messenger
And the Believers with him cried,
'When will God's help arrive?'
Truly God's help is near."

I saw a crowd of believers gathering around us, their eyes wide with wonder as the Words of God descended into their midst. The Lord of the Worlds was speaking right now, through the tortured tongue of the man whom they had followed willingly to what appeared to be their deaths.

People were crying, not from grief or fear but from joy. God had just reminded them that this terrible period they had endured was nothing more than a test that would end at its appointed time.

And strangely enough, they found deep comfort in the admission of despair on the part of the Prophet. God had lifted the stoic veil over their leader's heart, revealing that the doubts they had all secretly harbored were in fact shared by the Messenger himself. Their fears were his.

There is no greater revelation in life than to learn that those whom we admire share our faults and our weaknesses. In that moment, stone idols fall from their pedestals and the gulf between the lover and the beloved vanishes in the joyful embrace of the beautiful imperfection of humanity.

The Messenger blinked and I saw that the angel had departed and his soul had returned to him.

He took me by the hand and ran his sturdy fingers through my crimson hair.

"Thank you," he said.

"For what?" I could not imagine that the most important person in my life, the man whom my father and mother called master, would have any reason to thank me.

He smiled and spoke loud enough for the eager crowd of believers to hear.

"For reminding me that God's help is always near."

And then he stood and raised his hands in gratitude to God. And even though we were all still cold and hungry, standing there on the dead hill that was our wretched home, I felt as if a curtain had lifted. The air smelled different. The stench of disease and decay was gone.

And in its place was the unmistakable, and inexplicable, scent of roses.

16

I walked proudly beside my father as we broke the law and stepped onto the ground of the Sanctuary for the first time in two years. We were followed by several dozen of the believers, as well as a crowd of sympathizers from the city who had grown ashamed of watching their kinsmen struggle like rats in the shadows.

We should have been afraid of retaliation. Of an arrow shot by one of Abu Sufyan's men positioned on the rooftops. Or a turbaned warrior emerging from an alley at a warhorse's pace and letting his sword sing the harsh ballad of Meccan justice.

But we were not. The Messenger, when he had recovered from his trance, had told us that an army of angels would surround us and protect us from the wrath of the idolaters.

I did not see any winged beings of light. But as I looked around at the men and women of the city pouring out when they saw us, many clapping with joy, their eyes wide with wonder at our defiance of the elders, I wondered if he had been talking about them. They were the masses of the poor, the wretched, who had benefited in the old days from the largesse of our charity. The last two years had been hard on them as well. Through us, they had experienced the possibility of another Mecca, one in which the powerful aided the weak rather than exploited them, and then it had been torn away from them. But having seen a few rays of light illuminating their lives, they had been changed forever and would not go easily back into the darkness.

I realized at that moment why we were so dangerous to the lords of Mecca. Once a fire is ignited in the brush, it cannot easily be put out. Perhaps it was for that reason that we were allowed to move through the city unmolested. Whatever guards or assassins had been positioned to stop us saw the enthusiastic crowd that cheered us and realized that swordplay would likely spark a riot and then a revolution. As I was to learn to my grief in later years, once the passion of rebellion has been unleashed, it cannot be easily countered or controlled

As we approached the holy Kaaba, I saw our greatest enemy, Abu Jahl, standing before it, arms crossed, a look of contempt on his face but a hint of fear in his eyes. He was surrounded by seven of the largest men I had ever seen, black as night, their muscles rippling like the flesh of a running lion as they raised their swords to the ready. Abyssinian slaves, but not gentle and small like my friend Bilal. These were warriors who had been purchased specifically for their might and cruelty.

My father stopped and stared at Abu Jahl, who smiled in challenge. Clearly he was willing to risk violence in the streets to maintain the ban. My father let go of my hand and stepped forward alone.

As Abu Bakr strolled toward the House of God, Abu Jahl nodded to his men, who stepped forward in perfect unison. They crouched like panthers preparing to strike, their ugly swords glinting red in the morning light.

And then I saw a flash of indigo robes out of the corner of my eye and saw Abu Sufyan enter the circle of the Haram. I watched him assess the situation. The agitated crowd, the drawn swords facing an unarmed old man. His politician's instincts overcame his outrage at our defiance and I saw his angry face become calm and neutral as he calculated the best way to resolve this standoff to his advantage.

And then Abu Sufyan moved forward, placing himself strategically between my father and Abu Jahl's soldiers.

"What is the meaning of this, Abu Bakr? You are banned from the Sanctuary!"

My father walked confidently until his face was only inches away from his adversary.

"The ban is over, Abu Sufyan," he said, to loud cries of support from our army of beggars.

Abu Jahl went to place his hands on a nearby idol, that of Abgal, a god from the northern sands of Palmyra, a ferocious-looking boar with giant tusks carved out of ivory.

"Blasphemer! The ban was placed in the name of Allah, and only Allah himself can lift it."

My father looked at him with an amused smile that appeared to infuriate Abu Jahl more than his proud defiance.

"You speak the truth for once," he said, pointing his finger at the golden doors of the Kaaba. "Go inside and see for yourself."

Abu Jahl looked at my father as if he were insane, but Abu Sufyan saw something in his eyes that troubled him. And then without any ceremony, he turned and walked up the seven stone steps and pushed open the gate of the Holy of Holies.

Abu Sufyan walked quickly past the three marble pillars that held up the roof from within, toward the crimson idol of Hubal, its gold hand sparkling from the rays of sunlight that poured inside.

He walked over to the back wall, where he had hung the proclamation two years before, and gasped.

The wall was infested with an army of red ants. They marched across the granite interior in majestic unity, coursing right and left as if guided by an invisible hand. The feared desert insects with razor pincers that could tear a man's flesh to shreds in seconds had unleashed their hungry wrath on the sheepskin hide that memorialized the ban. The document was gone as if it had never existed.

Abu Sufyan leaned forward in shock to see that one small section of the parchment remained untouched. Indeed, the ants seemed to be moving around it in a circle, much as the worshipers did around the Kaaba itself.

It was a sliver of sheepskin that simply said: *In your name, O Allah . . .*

17

Despite the objections of Abu Jahl and a few diehards in the Hall of Assembly, the ban was formally lifted that night. Abu Sufyan knew that the passions of the crowd had been excited by word of the "miracle of the ants" and that the superstitious citizens of Mecca believed that God had spoken. In truth, he understood that the shame of expelling a whole clan, including women and children, had burdened the hearts of the citizens. Mecca prided itself on being a city of hospitality, and yet every time a trading caravan or a train of pilgrims approached its borders, they had to cross a pathetic tent city of hungry people who had been driven from their homes. The ban had proven bad for business, and many of the chieftains had been looking for any excuse to end this embarrassing chapter in their history.

The next day, I helped my mother and sister pack what few belongings we still had left—a copper pot, six rusty ladles, a knife whose blade had long since dulled to the point of uselessness, as well as the rags that had once been pretty clothes that Asma and I would proudly wear when we went to visit our friends' homes in the city.

I had never felt such excitement as Asma and I raced down the black hills toward the haze of chimney smoke that covered Mecca. The world felt reborn. The sky was bluer than I had ever noticed, and everywhere I looked, I saw hints of emerald beneath the rocks, as if a new spring had come to the deserts. Even the stones sparkled, their veins of quartz and calcite glittering under the blazing sun.

There were no welcoming crowds when we crossed the threshold of the city. The poor of the town had decided not to press their luck after demonstrating their unity and courage the day before. It made more sense to let the Muslims return and engage in the commerce of the city without further fanfare that might upset the Meccan lords and compel them to reconsider their magnanimity.

Asma and I walked hand in hand through the quiet streets as we headed home. I looked at her and smiled. She winked at me, and then I saw a hint of sadness in her eyes. I realized that returning to the city meant different things for us. She was now sixteen and unmarried, an old maid by the standards of our people. The past two years had been particularly hard on her and had taken away the youthful vibrancy that could have helped her attract a husband. Her curly hair was now a tangled mess of rushes, and I had a sudden image of her wearing a bird's nest on her head that would have made me laugh if I were truly heartless. Her skin had suffered worse than mine in the unforgiving desert air, and there were unhealthy splotches of white across her sunburned face and neck that were never to disappear. Her breasts, once ripe and plump, were shrunken such that her bosom looked more like mine, and I was ten years her junior. Asma had never been beautiful, but now she looked utterly wretched and I suddenly felt sorry for her.

But your mother, Abdallah, was always strong, and if she suffered, she did so in silence. A smile played across her face as she recognized the orange and yellow facades of the stone huts that stood by the cobbled street leading to our house.

"Race you," she said to me with a grin. Asma knew that I prided myself on my speed and I was immediately off and running to our home. She tried in vain to catch up, but I moved like a falcon, soaring with ease over the cracked stones and potholes that lined the route back to our personal sanctuary.

I laughed with delight as I rounded the corner that would lead to our gate. But when I saw our house, I stopped so suddenly that I almost lost my balance.

Our once-beautiful home, with its blue and green walls and lofty marble pillars, was a ruin. Angry vines rose from our weed-infested garden and wrapped themselves defiantly around the gates, which were rusted to an ugly orange. The windows that we had boarded against burglars had been torn open and I could see rats crawling on the sills, watching us approach, without trepidation.

The paint that my mother had so carefully renewed every year was faded and peeling. But there was new and unwelcome paint strewn across the walls by vandals, spelling out words of contempt for my family: *Traitors . . . Gutter filth . . . Blasphemers . . .*

My vision blurred as tears welled in my eyes. I heard Asma come up behind me, panting for breath, the laughter dying in her throat when she saw the building.

In that moment, I realized that Mecca was no longer our home. The ban may have been lifted, but the hate had not been vanquished, and like a stubborn disease, it would reassert itself inevitably. The hope of return to the past was an illusion, and we would now need to find a new home, a new hope. A new future.

That evening, as my family began the arduous process of cleaning and restoring the house to its former dignity, I had a nagging sense that we were wasting our time. Even as I slept for the first night in two years inside the delightfully cool walls, on a soft bed with cushions, my heart felt trapped. The house was no longer our haven but a prison holding us until the day of execution. We had to escape.

As the annihilation of sleep finally took me in its embrace, I had one last terrifying thought. An image, really, but one more vivid than any my childhood imagination had ever conjured.

A vision of Hind standing over me, looking down with a smile that was neither welcoming nor comforting. Then the gray walls were closing in on me until my bed was surrounded on all sides and I was trapped in a constricted space like a shallow grave. I felt my breathing become more desperate. In my mind's eye, I saw Hind raise her long arms and the golden snakes that wrapped around her wrist came to life and slid down into the darkness with me. I could feel their slippery flesh gliding up my hips, their coldness wrapping around my waist as they slithered higher.

I wanted to move, but my legs were tied by the writhing snakes that squeezed as they climbed and wrapped themselves around my throat, cutting off the scream of horror that was struggling to burst free. And then darkness covered me and the steady stream of time dried up forever . . .

18

Death is always a catalyst, and it was death that finally forced the believers to face the truth that my young heart knew already. That we needed to leave the city, before the unsteady truce ended and the dogs of war were unleashed.

A few weeks after we had restored ourselves to the city, Talha ran breathlessly up to our home. "The exiles have returned!" he said, his voice quivering with delight. For a moment, I was confused. What was he talking about? We were the ones who had been exiled to the barren hills, and we had long since come back. And then I remembered.

Abyssinia. Nearly fifty of our people, mainly the weakest and the poorest of the believers who lacked clan protection, had escaped across the sea three years before and found refuge with the kindly Christian king known as the Negus. They included some of my favorite playmates, like Salma, the daughter of an unwed Bedouin woman who had worked the streets as a prostitute before she had embraced Islam. I had despaired of ever seeing them again, and when Talha's words finally registered, a broad smile erupted on my face and I clapped with glee.

My mother immediately packed a shank of roast mutton she had been preparing for dinner into a leather sack and without another word raced out the door toward the house of the Messenger. Asma and I joined Talha on her heels.

The house of the Messenger was livelier than I had ever seen it. Word had spread through the city like a brushfire after a lightning storm and the main hall was packed with well-wishers seeking to welcome our long-lost brethren. I squeezed through the crowd and for a moment I had an uncomfortable understanding of the life of a chicken fighting its way through a coop to peck at a few seeds.

I finally crawled under a pair of stout legs and shimmied between two short women, twin sisters wearing olive-colored *abaya*s. I found myself near the center of the spacious room, where the Messenger was tearfully embracing his reclaimed brood.

I saw the Prophet hug a remarkably attractive young girl whom I did not recognize, and I felt a stab of jealousy that at the time did not make sense to me. I was confused, since the Prophet always maintained a respectful distance from his female followers, and I had never seen him touch a young girl so lovingly before.

And then I saw her intense dark eyes and I immediately realized that she was no stranger for whom the embrace would be a source of rumor and scandal. It was Ruqayya, the Prophet's daughter, who had married the Meccan nobleman Uthman ibn Affan and had emigrated with him when he had been designated the leader of the Abyssinian exiles. The Prophet's other daughters Zaynab and Umm Kulthum were both lovely creatures. Even his youngest child, Fatima, would have been considered pretty had she ever bothered to put on a little rouge or scent her hair like others. But Ruqayya was a woman from another world. She was then, and remains today, the most beautiful woman I have ever seen. Her skin was flawless, even paler than her father's, and her auburn hair peeked out from beneath the modest silk scarf she wore over her head. She had the tiniest waist I had ever seen. Her aquamarine robes did nothing to hide the generous curve of her breasts, and she seemed to exude a natural scent of tangerine. Staring at her perfect poise and grace, I was reminded of the ancient Greek idol of Athena that stood in the Sanctuary, brought by an Arab trader who had found the goddess in ruins outside Byzantium and carted her back to be displayed by the Kaaba.

I caught my own reflection in a bronze mirror that hung on the wall to my right, and I suddenly felt small and ugly. That sensation worsened when I saw a tall man with a perfectly groomed beard step up next to Ruqayya. He bowed his head before the Messenger and kissed his hand. When he rose, I realized that he was Ruqayya's husband, Uthman, and he was a match for her in beauty. A perfectly proportioned face, with steady gray eyes that always seemed misty and sparkling, like the well of Zamzam in the dawn light. He was elegantly dressed, with embroidered green robes that sparkled with the hint of tiny gems set in the hem. When he smiled, he exuded unlimited kindness and compassion.

Admirable traits that would one day be his undoing and would plunge our nation into a chaos from which it has never recovered.

But that future was long away and could never have been divined by any in the room, except perhaps the Messenger himself. In my final days, looking back at my life to see if I could have read the signs better and prevented the bloodbath for which I was partly responsible, I remember that every time the Messenger looked at Uthman, I would see a hint of sadness in his eyes.

Muhammad never claimed to predict the future—only God knew the details of His plan for mankind—but I believe the Messenger had a remarkably astute sense of the men and women in his life, both his friends and his enemies. And in Uthman's case, he may have felt more than known that his generous soul, his childlike innocence, was ripe for being manipulated by the unscrupulous, with terrifying consequences for the *Ummah*.

But that is a tragedy to be told at another time, and one that you know too well in any case, Abdallah. Returning to the events of that day, I watched as Khadija stepped up to greet the newcomers. She looked so old and frail, her once-smooth skin crushed into a sea of wrinkles. Her face was thin, as was her now snowy white hair. The years in the desert, and her recent bout with camp fever, had aged her to a frightening degree. As the Messenger supported her with a loving hand, I saw how he looked more like her son than her husband, his hair still glossy and black, his masculine face unlined and only a strand or two of gray in his beard.

It was a contrast that the exiles had not been prepared for, and I saw tears welling in Ruqayya's crystal eyes. Khadija could see the shock on her daughter's face, and I can imagine that it broke her heart, but whatever pain she felt, the Mother of the Believers was an expert at hiding it behind her gentle smile.

"My beautiful daughter," she said in a hoarse voice and put her arms slowly around the girl, who shook with open grief. Khadija stroked her hair with her bony fingers and then she let go, a look of extreme exhaustion on her face. The Prophet's cousin Ali moved quickly to her side and helped her sit down on a velvet cushion. Khadija breathed in with an evident struggle, and her hand flitted to her chest as if to remind her tired heart to keep beating.

Ruqayya knelt down beside Khadija, alarm clouding her perfect face.

"Mother, what's wrong?"

Khadija smiled weakly, her eyes distant and unfocused.

"I'm just a little tired, dear," she said faintly.

The Messenger's youngest daughter, Fatima, sat beside her, taking Khadija's hand in hers. She was such a remarkable contrast to her glamorous sister Ruqayya, her black hair tied haphazardly in an old yellow scarf, her tunic made of harsh wool, and her face devoid of even the most basic cosmetic enhancements that might reveal her femininity.

"Mother is sick, but she won't admit it," Fatima said reprovingly.

Khadija's eyes flashed and for a moment I saw the strength and dignity that I had long associated with the Mother of the Believers.

"Nonsense!" she said proudly. "My feet are old, that's all. But enough about me. How have you returned?"

Uthman bent down and kissed her on the forehead, kneeling before Khadija like a slave before a queen.

"We heard about the ban and the suffering of the Muslims. We could not sit in comfort in Abyssinia while you starved."

I felt Asma stiffen behind me and I immediately saw why. The Prophet's handsome cousin Zubayr stepped through the crowd and clapped his hands on Uthman's shoulder in greeting.

"By God's mercy, the ban has been lifted. We are free to live and trade in Mecca as before."

Uthman's lovely features lit up with his incomparable smile.

"*Allahu akbar!* God is great!" he proclaimed, hope dancing on his tongue. "The tide has turned, then."

And then my father stepped forward, his face grave. Unlike the Messenger, who was two years his senior, Abu Bakr's now-salty beard could not deny its age.

"I fear that there will be many more turnings of the tide, for good and for ill, before all is done," he said, shaking his head sadly.

As the men began to talk with the newcomers, I found myself gazing at Ruqayya and Uthman like a child pulled into a dream by a campfire. I suddenly heard the rustle of a skirt beside me and looked to see that Fatima had come to sit at my side.

"They are beautiful, aren't they?"

I blushed hot, realizing that my eyes had betrayed me. But Fatima smiled in silent understanding. I looked at the quiet, plain girl and asked an impertinent question that a more mature lady would not have voiced.

"Is it hard, having a sister who looks like that? I mean, when you—" I stopped, realizing suddenly that I was being horribly rude. But the question to my childish mind was a legitimate one. I was the pretty girl in the house, and I often wondered how my sister, Asma, felt, knowing that even as a girl who had not yet bled, I attracted attention from men, who rarely gave her a second look. Still, it was a stupid thing to say out loud, and I immediately regretted my wild tongue.

But Fatima did not seem to take offense.

"When Ruqayya is in a room, all other girls disappear, like the stars vanish when the sun rises," she said with a shrug. "One grows accustomed to it."

There was something so simple, so unpretentious, about Fatima that I felt an immediate liking for her. Seeking to change the topic to more pleasant and hopeful affairs, I turned to face her with an enthusiastic smile.

"Your sisters are all married. When will you join them?"

Fatima looked at me with those dark eyes, so much like her father's. When she returned my smile, there was a sadness in her gaze that chilled my heart.

"I don't know if I will ever marry," she said bluntly.

I was surprised at this answer.

"How can you say that? Every girl gets married!" Which was true. In the end, even the homeliest girl in Mecca eventually found a mate, although he was unlikely to be a prize catch.

Fatima's eyes twinkled mysteriously, as if tears welled in them, although they remained dry.

"I am not like every girl," she said softly.

But before I could ask her what she meant, I heard the harsh croak of painful coughing. I looked up in alarm to see Khadija holding her chest tight, her face drained of all color.

The Messenger was immediately at her side. He leaned down and spoke to his wife in whispered tones that I could not decipher. She nodded slowly and then covered her mouth as another eruption of coughing coursed violently through her chest and throat.

And when she finally lowered her hands, I saw they were covered in blood.

There were screams of horror and everyone came running to her side.

"Stand back!" Ali rose and pushed the frightened crowd back force-fully, giving Khadija room to breathe, however weakly.

Fatima had disappeared from my side, although I never saw her move. It was as if one moment she was sitting beside me, and the next she was holding her mother's hand and helping her to her feet. I always marveled at her remarkable ability to appear and disappear without anyone noticing, but I always dismissed it as a trick of the eye, the inheritance of her father's fast gait combined with her naturally quiet demeanor. Now I wasn't so sure, and looking at this strange, ethereal girl who moved like a ghost, I felt a sudden chill go up my spine.

19

The Mother of the Believers, the foundation stone of our hopes, was dying. As the Messenger and Ali helped her up the winding marble staircase that led to the family's private rooms on the second floor, my father took it on himself to restore calm and order to the gathered crowd of believers.

After clearing the Prophet's house of all except the closest mem-bers of his family and a few trusted advisers such as Umar and Uthman, we climbed upstairs to check on Khadija. I held on to the cold brass banister like a girl clinging to the edge of a cliff. Every footfall I made on the polished stone seemed to thunder like the beat of a war drum, announcing the arrival of death and pestilence in its wake.

When I followed my mother and father into the Messenger's bed-room, I saw that Khadija was lying on a mattress of goose feathers that been imported from the north. The Messenger had rid himself of near-ly all luxuries since the beginning of his mission, but he could not part with this one item that brought comfort and ease to his aging wife.

She looked so peaceful, lying there with her bony hands across her chest, that for a moment I thought she was already dead. But the gentle rustle of her gray tunic as it rose and fell with her breathing said that her soul still dwelled among us for a short while longer. Beads of pearly sweat ran down her lined face and her daughters quickly moved to wipe her brow with a clean rag.

The Messenger dropped to his knees beside her and closed his eyes, his hands uplifted in fervent prayer. I had never seen him so focused, so utterly unmoving. If I had not caught the steady pulse of a vein in his temple, I could have imagined that he had been turned to stone from grief, like the very idols that he despised.

Silence fell upon the room like the closing doors of a crypt. Even the wind outside became utterly still, like the mournful quiet before the rains are unleashed. No one moved; all eyes were on the elderly woman on the bed. Hours passed as if they were moments, and eventually Fatima left her mother's side to light a small copper lantern as the sun's rays dipped beneath the horizon.

When the disk of the sun vanished and the evening star ruled the sky, Khadija's eyes opened and I saw her smile at the Messenger, who was looking at her like a frightened child. Seeing the lost look on his face, this man who was the center of our community, the rock that gave us stability while the deadly waters of the world raged and churned about us, I suddenly felt very small and alone.

I realized at that moment that it was Khadija who had been the heart of Islam the whole time. Without her initial acceptance of his vision, Muhammad would have dismissed his experience on Mount Hira as a dream or a delusion engendered by a capricious djinn. Had she not believed him and encouraged him, he would have eventually become like the madmen I saw wandering the streets of Mecca in putrid rags, whose disturbed minds had tortured them until even their families had driven them out and left them to die. Whatever this new religion called Islam was, whatever it was going to be, was the product of one woman's faith in a man. And now that woman was dying and I was left to wonder whether our faith would die with her.

I saw a figure enter the room, a man with a deeply pockmarked face and thinning hair, despite his youth. It was Zayd ibn Haritha, the adopted son of Muhammad and Khadija. He had just returned from an unsuccessful hunt in the hills where a leopard had been seen the night before and had been told by the believers what had transpired at the Messenger's house this morning.

Zayd leaned down beside Khadija and she ran her hand across his cheek. He had once been her slave, but he had grown so attached to her and her husband that they had freed him and adopted him as a son after the tragic death of their own infant boy Qasim. Next to Ali, Zayd was the closest person to a male heir in the Messenger's household, and many of the believers looked to him as a future leader of the community. The fact that a slave could rise to become a master over the believers was a matter of great pride for the Muslims and a subject of intense mockery for Abu Lahab and our other enemies.

I watched as Khadija gestured to Zayd, Ali, and her daughters to come close. The rest of us kept respectfully back. The fact that we were even allowed in the inner sanctum to share her final moments was enough. Family had certain rights and prerogatives that needed to be respected.

As each member of the *Ahl al-Bayt,* the People of the House, approached, Khadija said a soft, almost inaudible prayer of benediction upon her loved ones and then whispered into each of their ears. I saw them nod and rise after she shared her private farewells, tears streaming down their cheeks. First her eldest daughter, Zaynab, then Ruqayya, even more beautiful as her black eyes shone with grief, followed by rosy-cheeked Umm Kulthum and dour Zayd.

And then she took Fatima's hand in her right and Ali's in her left and kissed them both on the foreheads. When Fatima stepped back, the look of grief on her face was so painful that I dropped my eyes for fear of being consumed by it.

"Aisha . . ."

I was startled to hear my name and looked up to see Khadija looking at me with compassion. She gestured weakly for me to come.

Stunned and unsure as to why I was being included in this special circle of family, I stood there, my finger in my mouth like a shy toddler. My mother, Umm Ruman, took my hand and pulled me to Khadija's side, before stepping back and leaving me alone with her.

The Mother of the Believers ran her hands through my red hair like a child playing with a favorite doll. And then she moved her head a little and I sensed she wanted me to come close so that I could hear her better. I leaned forward until my ears were almost touching her cracked lips.

She whispered, but her words sounded through my heart like a trumpet.

"Take care of him when I'm gone," she said inexplicably. "You were made for him."

I had no idea what she meant, but there was something both exciting and terrifying in her words. As if she were using her final breath to pass on to me a secret that I was to guard with my life.

I sensed the Messenger standing behind me and scrambled back to my mother's side, unsure of what to make of the strange words Khadija had bequeathed me.

When I looked up, I saw that the Prophet was crying. With what appeared to be a difficult effort, Khadija raised her hands and wiped his tears in front of us the way she had wiped them in private all those years. In that instant, I understood the truth of their relationship. The Messenger had seen his mother die when he was only six years old and had longed all his life for the nurturing touch of which he had been deprived. Khadija was more than just his wife and best friend, more than the first Muslim. She was also the mother that God had taken away from him once before, and I realized as I looked at Muhammad's face that he was reliving the horror of the loss that had haunted him since he was a boy.

"I am summoned to the Abode of Peace . . . Beloved, it is time for me to go . . ."

I saw through my blurred eyes the Prophet lean down and place his cheek next to hers.

"I knew the moment I saw you that you were special . . . Had God never spoken to you, even then would I have known that you were His chosen . . ."

She was looking up, her eyes staring dreamily at the ceiling, at something only she could see.

"The men in white are here . . . I see where they are taking me . . . It's so beautiful . . . so full of light . . ."

She turned to face the Messenger, peering deep into his fathomless eyes.

"There is no god but God, and you, my love, are His Messenger . . ."

She sighed and went still.

There was a moment of silence so great that it reverberated like an earthquake. And then cries of grief erupted all around me. I saw the Messenger of God touch the Mother of the Believers' lips, stroking them in final farewell.

He looked like a shadow from another world. When he spoke, his soft voice cut through the din of mourning. He spoke the Words of God that had come to him in a Revelation at the moment of Khadija's death, words that Muslims speak even today to grieve loss and to remember who we are and where we are going.

"Truly we belong to God, and truly to Him are we returning . . ."

＊　＊　＊

IT WAS TIME TO leave Mecca. Shortly after Khadija died, the Muslims were struck with another loss. The Prophet's uncle and guardian, Abu Talib, passed away, and the reprobate Abu Lahab became the chief of Bani Hashim. We could no longer count on the Prophet's clan for protection from the dogs of Quraysh. The persecution would only grow worse and now there would be no recourse to the rough justice of the tribes. But where could we go? The Quraysh guarded the roads to the sea, so Abyssinia was cut off to us. But even if we could escape the nightly patrols and find a boat willing to take us west, the Negus was no longer in a position to give us sanctuary.

The great king had suffered politically for having given refuge to our people once before. The priests of his African nation had decried the Muslims as dangerous heretics, because we believed in Jesus as a human prophet but denied that he had ever claimed to be the Son of God. Our people were branded as the resurgence of the Arians, a group of Christians who had questioned the Church's teachings on Christ's divinity but had been denounced by the Byzantine emperor Constantine as unbelievers. The Negus still sent kindly letters to the Messenger inquiring about his views on matters of theology, but they contained nothing that would suggest an invitation to come in person and debate these great truths.

There was a cloud hanging over the Prophet in those bleak days, and my sister was already referring to it as "the Year of Sadness." The Messenger had been struck by two powerful blows in sequence. The death of Khadija, the source of his spiritual support, and the death of Abu Talib, the foundation of his earthly protection. Having lost both poles of his compass, he walked among us like a man who was unsure of who he was, where he was going. In later years, he admitted to me that he had been crushed with self-doubt during those terrible months.

If these visions were real, if what he saw was truly an angel and not some mischievous desert sprite mocking him, then why had his God abandoned him and left him without any light of hope?

But, as we all learned, the Divine is a teacher who sometimes shows men what they are made of by taking away everything they have, so that the truth of their character is finally revealed. At his lowest moment, the Messenger's soul was now as naked and vulnerable as a newborn baby's flesh.

And it is in that vulnerability, where there are no veils anymore between a quivering, tormented heart and its master, the Lord of the Worlds, that the inner eye awakens from its slumber and true Vision is born.

Perhaps because of a destiny that I did not yet know awaited me, I was given the precious gift of sharing in that Vision. So it was that one night, after a long day of struggling with the monotonous chores of the household, I crept into my small bed to sleep. I was tired and yet I tossed and turned for hours before finally rising to answer the persistent call of nature.

But as I passed a window on the way to the latrine, I saw a flash like a bolt of lightning. At first, I thought it might be the start of a rainstorm, which we desperately needed owing to drought. Pausing to look out the window, I saw that the sky was clear and not a single cloud blotted the twinkling army of stars. The full moon appeared low in the sky, hovering just above the sacred walls of the Sanctuary. And then I realized with a start that it was the twenty-seventh night of Rajab and the moon should have been a thin crescent waning into nothingness.

As I focused my eyes, I saw that whatever it was that rose over the Kaaba was not the pockmarked moon but a blue-white disk with no discernible features. A ball of pure light. And then, faster than any celestial body I had ever seen move across the heavens, the light rose upward like a shooting star in reverse and vanished into the northern horizon.

I stood frozen at the window, my heart racing. I suddenly had no urge to use the latrine and quickly ran back to my bed and hid beneath the woolen coverlet, trying to understand the strange event I had witnessed. I suddenly felt very drowsy and I surrendered as my soul slipped into the void. My last thought was that I would never know for sure if what I had seen was real. I should forget all about the strange light before my parents started worrying and asked the Messenger to drive away the djinn that were haunting me.

I would forget about it, and the world would never know.

But that was not God's plan.

—•— — —•—

THE NEXT MORNING, MY father and I walked to the bazaar after my mother insisted that we trade a recent surplus of eggs from our coop of chickens for some fresh mutton. We walked down the streets carefully, my father's eyes darting back and forth. With the death of Abu Talib, violence against Muslims was on the rise again, but Abu Lahab refused to pursue claims on our behalf in the Hall of Assembly. Just a week before, my poor cousin Talha had been attacked by the thugs in the middle of the street. When my father had sought to intervene and pay them off, they had beaten him as well and taken his purse. Abu Bakr and Talha had been left on the side of the road, tied together and covered in refuse, until a woman of the Bani Adi had had mercy on them and unloosed their bindings.

But there were no such incidents today. In fact, we were surprised at the emptiness of the cobbled streets, which were normally filled with people and animals heading to market at this hour.

And then we heard the sounds of raucous laughter coming from the Sanctuary, and my father turned and saw a large crowd gathered before the Kaaba. Over the din of jeers and catcalls, we could hear the distinctly rich voice of the Messenger.

"Let's go," my father said, and I followed him without hesitation. The Messenger had not preached openly in the Sanctuary since Abu Talib had died and Abu Lahab had warned him that the clan would not protect his followers from violence if they insulted the gods in front of the Holy House. Something had happened that made the Messenger risk a riot and speak before the pagan worshipers who had monopolized the shrine.

As Abu Bakr pushed forward, Abu Jahl suddenly appeared and blocked his way, his handsome face lit with a triumphant smile.

"What do you think of your Prophet now?" he said with unfettered glee. "He claims he went to Jerusalem last night and came back before the sun rose!"

My father paled at this strange news. The Messenger's words always had the clear ring of truth, appealing to reason rather than superstition, and this was too fantastic a story to have come from his lips.

"You lie!" Abu Bakr said, refusing to let Abu Jahl spread obviously malicious stories against the Messenger.

"Don't blame his madness on me," he said with a smirk. "But what did you expect from a soothsayer whose craft is to befuddle simple minds? Yet in this, Muhammad has gone too far and his tall tales have been revealed for what they are. Even a child knows it takes a month for a caravan to travel to Syria and a month to return!"

And then Abu Jahl glanced down at me to further his point. I saw him pause and take a lascivious look at my small body. I realized that the softness on my chest was already becoming noticeable to the eyes of men. My courses had not begun, but I was clearly becoming a woman, and I felt my cheeks flame at his evident lust.

Something about his disgusting stare lit a fire of defiance in me, and I spoke words that I had promised to forget.

"It's true, Father!" I said before I could stop myself. "I saw it with my own eyes last night. A star arose from the Kaaba and flew north! That must have been the Messenger!"

Unfortunately, my passionate defense of Muhammad's audacious claim only increased the amusement of the crowd, and I heard cruel laughter now directed at me, as well as vulgar comments about my maturing body.

My father grabbed me by the shoulder.

"Quiet! Let me handle this."

And then he took the small white scarf that I wore around my shoulders and put it over my head, wrapping the cloth modestly around the budding nubs of my breasts.

My father led me through the crowd until we saw the Messenger standing just outside the golden doors of the Temple. I caught my breath at sight of his smiling face, which looked as fresh and untroubled as a newborn's. Gone was the sad and lonely man who had become increasingly quiet in the days since Khadija's death. The vibrant, masculine man who exuded power and dignity had been resurrected.

Abu Bakr leaned close to him and whispered.

"Is what they say true? Did you go to Jerusalem and return in one night?"

The Prophet nodded. He lowered his voice until only Abu Bakr and I could hear him.

"Yes. And there is more. But they are not ready for it." He paused and looked deep into Abu Bakr's eyes. "Are you?"

My father looked into those bottomless black pools. And then without any hesitation, he turned and faced the jeering crowd.

"If he says he went to Jerusalem in one night, then it is true," Abu Bakr said loudly, his voice echoing across the ancient stones of the Sanctuary.

The laughter of the crowd died instantly and was replaced by surprise and confusion at my father's unashamed embrace of this ludicrous claim.

Abu Bakr strode forward, looking men in the eye as he passed them, his arms sprung wide.

"And why do you wonder?" he asked defiantly. "Muhammad tells me that he receives tidings from heaven every day, and I know that he is speaking the truth. And that is a miracle beyond anything you marvel at!"

There was an uncomfortable buzz, like the confused hiss of a bee that can no longer find the security of its hive. I saw men looking at Abu Bakr as if he were insane. But when he met their glare with utter confidence, they began to look at one another, as if wondering whether perhaps they were the ones who were insane.

The Messenger moved forward and grasped my father's right hand and held it aloft.

"I hereby proclaim Abu Bakr by a title borne by no other man. *As-Siddiq*—the Great Witness to the Truth!"

It was a powerful honorific, and one that my father carried with dignity for the rest of his life. In the years that would come, certain vile men would question his loyalty to the Prophet, accuse him falsely of acting in his own interests rather than in accordance with the will of God and His Messenger. Yet standing there, I saw the look of deep love and trust in the Messenger's eyes as he gazed at my father, and my heart overflowed with emotions that have no name.

If it be true that Abu Bakr was the calculating politician that his detractors have claimed, then I know not what truth there is to anything I witnessed in all my years at Muhammad's side. For those who claimed in the days to come that Abu Bakr became an enemy to the

Messenger, claimed that the Prophet himself was deluded and trusted in a false front. If the Messenger of God could call a man by the great title of *As-Siddiq* and that man proved to be a liar and a thief, then there is nothing to our religion but foolishness and cruel mockery.

They say that I am biased because I am Abu Bakr's daughter. They warn that I am destined for hell for the crimes I have committed in the heat of passion. And for that I have no clear response. I accept their condemnation for my sins, and it may indeed be that I will go to hell for the blood that is on my hands.

But I will not see my father there.

20

When word spread of the miraculous night journey, the tribe of believers gathered excitedly in the Messenger's home. It was the largest such congregation since Abu Talib's death, as it was now considered unsafe for the Muslims to meet in large groups and potentially be accused of plotting insurrection. The main hall was overflowing, and I saw men and women of all ages cramming together to hear the full story. I marveled for a moment at how much we had grown. Despite the Quraysh's best efforts to crush our movement, there were now several hundred committed believers, most still from the poorer classes but a surprisingly large number from the ruling elite.

One of the most improbable converts was a tall and proud woman named Ramla, the eldest daughter of Abu Sufyan. Her conversion had been a shock to the lords of Mecca, and the Messenger had arranged for her to travel across the sea and take refuge with the Negus in case her father sought to force her back into the fold. Though the Muslims could no longer count on his protection as a group, the Christian king had invited Ramla to come as a "princess of Quraysh" and be housed in a palace reserved for foreign dignitaries.

Ramla sat near the Prophet and I could see her resemblance to her father. With her steely eyes that shone with dignity and authority, she had the aura of a queen, even though she was dressed in modest white robes, her light brown hair covered in a blue scarf. I saw the coquettish way she looked at the Messenger, who was now a widower, and I felt my cheeks burn hot with jealousy. I was not sure why I felt so possessive about the Prophet, but Khadija's last words to me kept echoing in my heart. She had asked me to take care of her husband, and I did not feel that letting him fall into Ramla's seductive web was what she had in mind.

Of course, my nephew, you know the bad blood that existed between us in later years, and even now I have difficulty writing her name without my hand shaking in fury. What she did to me, in my moment of terrible grief, may be forgiven by Almighty God, but my human heart cannot extend to her that clemency.

In those early days, I did not know the depth of her cruelty, and yet I still had a visceral dislike for Ramla the moment I laid eyes on her. There was something about her that struck me as dangerous, far more so than open enemies like her father or her conniving stepmother, Hind. In one glance, she sized up others as if weighing them and calculating their worth, and I never knew for what purpose. And yet Ramla was charming and I saw how she could make the Messenger laugh with her worldly stories from her travels to the courts of Yemen and Persia as part of Abu Sufyan's trading ventures. And I hated her.

In truth, I hated her because she was beautiful and young, and her breasts were well shaped and firm, unlike my own, nothing more than tiny buds that barely rose from my chest. Yes, I had childish fantasies that I would grow up and marry the Messenger someday, as did every other young girl among the believers, and seeing Ramla sitting near the Prophet and her cousin Uthman, I felt the cold, harsh flash of reality. I was a child and she was a woman.

When dreams shatter, Abdallah, they can leave mighty scars that are always raw to the touch.

That night we sat and listened as the Messenger told us more about his wondrous journey to Jerusalem. Of how the angel Gabriel had come to the Messenger while he had slept near the Kaaba, leading a wing horse named Buraq. Together they had flown to Jerusalem, where they landed at the ruins of the Jewish shrine the Temple of Solomon, which was called in the holy Qur'an *Al-Masjid Al-Aqsa*—the Farthest Place of Worship. There, amid the fallen stones of God's other House, sister to the Kaaba, the Prophet had prayed with the spirits of Abraham, Moses, and Jesus.

And then he revealed a secret that we were sworn to keep from the unbelievers, who were unworthy of the highest Truth. From a rock that stood at the site of Solomon's Temple, the Messenger had ascended into heaven and traveled through the many realms of Paradise until he stood before the Throne of God. The Prophet had never before claimed to have spoken directly with Allah, who had communicated with him for the past ten years through angels as intermediaries. But this night, he had crossed the farthest reaches of Creation, past the Lote Tree of the Utmost Boundary beyond which even Gabriel could not ascend. And there, outside time and space, where there was neither light nor darkness, Muhammad communed with his Lord.

We listened with rapt attention, and many wept, as he described the glories of Paradise, the rivers of milk and honey, and wine that did not befuddle the senses. Of perfect trees that provided eternal shade and fruits whose scent was enough to quell the hunger of mankind for eternity. And there were youths like sparkling pearls that served the residents of Paradise with any food or drink that they desired, and *houris*, beautiful virgins whose touch made men forget all the earthly pleasure they had ever known.

At the mention of these delightful creatures, I saw many of the women's faces fall. The thought of their men traipsing about in the afterlife with such perfect beauties did not seem like much of a paradise for them. But the Messenger kindly told us that all believing women who entered Paradise would become *houris* themselves and that there would be no jealousy or loneliness in eternity. Men and women would enjoy one another's company and the ecstasies of one another's bodies in a way that would make the coupling of this world seem like brief and fleeting pleasure, like a tickle from a feather.

The Night Journey had given the Prophet renewed hope and faith. Now that he had seen the wonders of the spiritual realm, the daily struggle of life on Earth held little fear. But most important for the community, God had sent the Messenger back from heaven with a new set of rules for our daily lives.

First and foremost, the ritual prayers and prostrations that we had performed haphazardly over the past ten years were now to be organized and made a daily practice. Five times a day—before sunrise, in the early and late afternoon, after sunset, and in the darkness of night—the Muslims would be required to bow before God in formal worship. And perhaps most startling, God had commanded us to face the holy city of Jerusalem when we prayed. We were accustomed to facing the Kaaba, even though the Messenger had never specifically commanded it, but now we were being told to turn to the north, to a city most of us had never seen and knew of only through myth and legend. But the Messenger was clear. Jerusalem was the home of the Prophets, and he was the last in their line. So we grudgingly obeyed.

He listed for us further commandments that he had been given in heaven. We would be required to fast for thirty days during Ramadan, which was the sacred month in which the Revelation had begun ten years before. That meant no food, water, or sexual relations from first light until sunset. I saw the look of general dismay at word that even intercourse would be banned during the fast, and the Prophet smiled gently, reminding us that sexual relations were a blessing from God, just like food and water, and restraining our lust would purify our souls and allow us to couple with deeper meaning and intensity when the fast was over.

And finally, we would be required to pay *zakat*, or alms, to the poor. Before this day, we had been encouraged but not commanded to share our wealth with the less fortunate. But now one-fortieth of every believer's wealth officially belonged to God and the community and must be given freely to feed and clothe the needy. I stole a glance at Ramla to see how this proud woman, reared in the wealthiest home in Mecca, would react to being forced to give up a portion of her riches every year, but she was all pleasant smiles and graciousness, which only angered me more.

These were the Pillars of Islam, the Messenger announced, commanded by God from His Throne. Along with the testimony of faith, that there is no god but God and Muhammad is His Messenger, they would serve as the formal tests of a Muslim's basic commitment to his or her faith.

The Messenger paused and then added that there was one final Pillar, which was obligatory only for those who had the necessary wealth to undergo the journey and were healthy enough to perform its requirements: the Pillar of Pilgrimage to the holy city of Mecca, which every Muslim who was capable should perform once in his or her life.

We all looked at one another, confused.

Finally, Umar spoke up.

"But, Messenger of God, we all live in Mecca," he said with his usual bluntness. "The Holy Kaaba is down the street. Why would we need to travel to perform the Pilgrimage when we do so every year with ease?"

I saw a strange look of sadness cross the Messenger's face.

"It may not be so easy in the years to come, my friend." And with that he rose, and we knew that the audience was over.

As the excited crowd cleared the hall, I saw the Messenger smile at Ramla and speak to her in low tones. A gesture of intimacy. My stomach twisted painfully.

And then, to my surprise the Prophet looked at me across the room and his eyes sparkled. And then he waved to my father to come to his side.

Abu Bakr nodded to my sister, Asma, and me.

"Go home. I will join you soon, *insha-Allah*."

I did as I was told and stepped outside, before I realized that Asma was no longer at my side. I looked up to see her standing beside the gate to the Messenger's house, speaking with his cousin Zubayr. The handsome young man leaned in and whispered something in her ear and she laughed, her cheeks flushing.

I smiled to see them together and walked home alone.

21

That night, after Asma returned home late to a harsh scolding by Umm Ruman for her unseemly flirtations, I sat in a corner of the living room, playing with my favorite dolls, ugly little things made from rags and robe fiber, which I had named Akil and Akila.

I acted out the wedding between these two figures, a favorite game, but in my mind's eye, instead of my dolls, I saw my beloved sister finally wedding the boy she had secretly loved for years. Your father, Zubayr, was considered a great catch by the girls of the city, and I had never really believed that Asma had a chance with him. But the Messenger said that God holds the hearts of men between His two fingers, and turns them any way He wishes. It was evident that God had turned Zubayr's heart to your mother at last.

I heard the door open and saw Abu Bakr return. I rose to greet him, but he looked at me with intense eyes.

"Go to your room, little one."

There was something in his tone that frightened me, and I stood rooted on the spot.

"But, Father—"

"Go," he said forcefully. "I need to speak to your mother."

Somehow I knew that whatever had upset him had to do with me. I scoured my memory for all the naughty things I had done recently and I wondered which of them had finally gotten me in trouble.

Pondering my childish sins, I turned and went to my room and closed the door. But instead of playing with my dolls on my bed, I leaned up against the door to listen. I heard muffled voices and I strained to make sense of them. Finally I decided to risk it and I opened the door a crack, just enough to hear my parents' words with some clarity. I grimaced as the acacia wood creaked against the marble floor and I wondered whether they had heard and knew I was eavesdropping.

"What's wrong?" My mother's voice was hushed but brimming with concern.

"Nothing is wrong," my father said. "I . . . just need a moment."

I heard my mother pour him a glass of water. After a moment, he spoke, and his words were filled with both fear and wonder.

"The Prophet had a dream," he said softly.

"I know. He told us all about the Night Journey," my mother responded.

"No. This was many nights ago," Abu Bakr said. "It was only after his vision during the Night Journey that he decided it was time to share it with me."

My father had always been respected as an interpreter of dreams, even in the days before the Revelation. He was like the prophet Joseph, a man who had been gifted with such a keen understanding of the human heart that he could easily read the symbols locked inside the hidden imaginings of the mind.

"The angel Gabriel game to him carrying a bundle of green silk," Abu Bakr said slowly. "When the Prophet asked what was in the bundle, the angel said: 'Your wife.' And then he unrolled the silk and the Prophet saw a girl."

Abu Bakr stopped. For a moment, I saw an image of Ramla wrapped in Gabriel's silk, and I wanted to vomit. This beautiful and cunning daughter of Abu Sufyan would soon be in the bed of the Messenger of God. My heart beat fast with indignation.

But when my father spoke next, my heart stopped

"He saw Aisha."

For the next several minutes, I heard nothing more. It was as if I had been struck deaf and even the torment of the damned in hell would have passed by my ears unnoticed.

When the world started again, the sounds came rushing at me faster than I could comprehend.

"What do we do?" My mother's voice was shrill, like a lamb bleating at the first sight of the sacrificial knife.

"We obey God," he said simply.

I heard my mother slam something down on the table and the door shook with its vibrations.

"But Aisha . . . she is promised to Jubayr ibn Mutim!"

This was news to me.

I had met Jubayr a few times, but I could barely remember what he looked like. I was aware that he was a cousin of the hated Hind, and I had heard rumors that he had been considering converting after Ramla had joined the new faith. Apparently, I was being used as a negotiating chip by my father to entice this powerful lord of Quraysh to embrace our faith. My heart, which had soared moments before to know that I was chosen to be the Messenger's wife, now sank into rage and despair at the thought that my own family could bargain my life away so casually.

"Jubayr's father has always opposed the marriage and will be relieved when we rescind the proposal," he said matter-of-factly, as if discussing the proper value of onions in the marketplace. "If Jubayr is destined to come to Islam, God will find him a virtuous wife, I'm sure."

I felt rage building in my young veins. Nowhere in this discussion had anyone mentioned or cared what I might have thought of any of this.

I heard my mother's skirts rustling as she paced across the room, a habit whenever she was nervous or unsure.

"She is so young—" Umm Ruman objected, but my father cut her off.

"No younger than most brides these days," Abu Bakr said simply. "The marriage will not be consummated until her cycles begin."

There was a long silence in which the only thing I could hear was the pounding of my heart.

When my mother spoke again, I could hear deep concern in her voice.

"She will become the Mother of the Believers, a role only held by Khadija. How can a child take her place?"

"The Messenger understands the delicacy of her youth," Abu Bakr said. "He will also marry an older, more mature woman who can run the household."

I saw Ramla in my mind's eye and felt my stomach sink. How could I be a cowife to the daughter of Abu Sufyan? She was so much prettier than me and was older, would know how to please a man. The Messenger would grow bored with me and toss me aside for a woman who was more his equal.

"Who?" my mother asked, with the excited curiosity of a gossip-monger.

My father paused, and I prayed to God: *Please, don't let it be Ramla.* "Sawda bint Zama," he said at last.

I fell back with a thud and for a moment I was convinced that my parents had heard and knew I was listening. But they did not come into my room, and I sat in shock, absorbing this information.

And then I bit down on my hand to keep from laughing.

God had answered my prayer.

Sawda bint Zama was a sweet but elderly woman, a widow of considerable wealth, as Khadija had been. She was an excellent cook and would be a valuable addition to the Messenger's household. But she was old and her body worn. If I were indeed meant to marry the Prophet, at least I would not have to compete with her in the bedroom. And even at that tender age, I knew that men valued young and beautiful women who could give them pleasure and bear them sons. Muhammad was the Messenger of God, but he was a man like any other in that respect, and I almost clapped with glee knowing that I could give him joys that Sawda would be incapable of providing.

When I crawled back to the crack of he door and listened, I heard my father speaking.

"I knew the night Aisha was born that she was special," he said wistfully. "When the Prophet told me of his vision, I knew that the moment of her destiny had come."

My mother sighed loudly

"Everything will change." There was resignation in her voice and I knew that she had accepted the will of Allah.

"Everything must change," my father responded. "With Khadija gone, the Muslims are in despair, walking like dead men. Aisha is a fountain of life. She will resurrect them."

My mother was silent for a moment, lost in reflection.

"The midwife said our daughter would bring death."

"Life and death are bound by a power beyond understanding. The power of transformation," Abu Bakr waxed philosophical. "Aisha wields that power. She is the sword of transformation. Some things must die so that others may be born. That is her birthright."

In later years, when my hand held that sword and rained death upon the *Ummah,* I wondered if my father had had some prophetic insight of his own.

"I am afraid," my mother said simply.

And then I heard my father, the bastion of strength in our household, admit something that I could not have imagined.

"So am I, my love. So am I."

I closed the door and crawled into bed. My mind was racing almost as fast as my heart.

God had chosen me to marry His Messenger.

It sounded laughable, but somehow it felt right. As if some part of my soul had always known that was my purpose. I took my dolls and put them aside with a pang of loss that comes when one period of life ends and another begins.

Yet I did not know where I was in the journey of life, or who I was to be, walking the path that I had been set upon.

I felt trapped between two worlds. I was no longer a child, but I was not yet a woman.

And yet, soon, I would be the Mother of the Believers.

22

One night, several months after I learned that I was betrothed to the Messenger of God, my father pulled me out of bed and told me to dress quickly. My mother and sister were still asleep and Abu Bakr told me to move quietly so as not to wake them up. We had an appointment tonight that it was best not to let them know about.

Confused and a little intrigued, I threw on a woolen robe over my cotton tunic. I tied my hair in a yellow scarf, but my father made me take it off and replace it with a black one that would not reflect the moonlight and draw attention to my presence. We tiptoed through the house, past my mother's bedroom, where I could hear her snoring steadily.

I felt a sudden rush of excitement as we stepped out into the cold night. I knew that all this secrecy had something to do with my new status, and I was eager to unravel the mystery.

My father, wrapped in dark blue robes, his mouth covered by a strand of loose cloth from his brown turban, led me through the abandoned streets of Mecca. Normally there would be at least a few citizens sleeping in bunks outside their doors, as was the custom during the summer months when the cooling winds helped ease the raging heat that made sleeping indoors unbearable. But tonight was unusually cold and everyone was indoors.

I could see the air steam from my breath, and the chill only worsened as we left the city behind and crossed into the moonlit hills. I began to feel a tug of fear. What was this all about? Where was my father taking me in the dead of the night? For a moment, I had a terrible vision of Abraham leading his son into the wilderness in order to sacrifice him to God. I loved Allah and I loved my father, but I did not think that I could surrender willingly to the knife as the boy had.

Now that we were far away from Mecca and no one was likely to hear us, I tentatively spoke up.

"Where are we going?"

My father hesitated, as if debating whether to reveal his true purpose yet.

"To Aqaba," he said finally, and pulled me along faster across the rocky earth.

Aqaba? That made no sense. It was barren area at the base of a volcanic mound where caravans stopped to let their camels rest before the final climb through the hills and into the heart of Mecca.

"But there is nothing there except stones and sand!" Suddenly I didn't like this mystery at all.

"Tonight there will be more," my father said. Despite my continuous barrage of questions, he said nothing else.

We climbed over the last hill that formed the official boundary of the holy city. My father stopped at the peak and looked down into the valley of Mina below. I could see a haze of campfire in the distance, illuminating a vast tent city that must have housed a thousand pilgrims. These were people who could not afford lodgings in Mecca itself and camped outside while they were performing the rites of Pilgrimage.

We started to climb down and I nearly lost my footing. My father grabbed my hand and held it tight as I saw a shower of pebbles race down the hill to shatter on the jagged rocks below. When we finally made it to the base of the hill, I started to move toward the tent city on the horizon, assuming it was our destination. But my father tugged on my hand and pulled me back. He started walking across the base of the hill away from the brightly lit camp until we reached a place shadowed between two hills and surrounded by rocky boulders.

The moon was behind the hills and no light shone down upon this craggy section of desert. It was pitch black, nearly impossible to penetrate, even after my eyes had adjusted to the darkness.

As we moved forward into this void that was darker than any cave, I finally saw the outlines of figures up ahead, heard the soft murmur of voices.

I suddenly heard a clink of metal and saw the quick flash of a blade in the dark. My father stopped dead in his tracks as a boulder moved and I realized that it was not a stone, but a mountain of a man—the Prophet's uncle Hamza.

"Who goes there?" he snarled, and I sensed that the sword would slash down without any hesitation if he didn't like the answer.

"Softly, Hamza. It is I."

Hamza leaned forward until he could see my father. He nodded, but then his eyes went wide when he saw me standing beside Abu Bakr.

"You brought this child?" he asked incredulously. Whatever was happening here tonight, it was clearly not the place for a small girl. A conclusion I had already come to on my own.

"She is not like other children, a fact you know well," my father said, a hint of pride in his voice. "It is fitting that she should be present at the Messenger's side tonight."

The mighty Hamza scowled, but he stepped aside.

My father led me toward the voices, and I saw a circle of unfamiliar men, along with a few women I also did not recognize. The Messenger of God was speaking in hushed tones to these strangers. When he saw my father and me, he smiled widely, but he continued conversing with the people in the group.

I tugged on my father's sleeve.

"Who are these men?"

He bent down to whisper in my ears.

"Tribesmen of the Aws and Khazraj in Yathrib."

Of all the possible answers, that was one I did not expect. Yathrib was an oasis ten days' camel ride to the north of Mecca. It had the blessing of fresh water and plentiful date trees and was a regular stop for merchants heading to the markets of Syria and Persia.

But despite its strategic positioning, the city had failed to achieve the level of prosperity of Mecca, which lacked agriculture but had the benefit of peace. Yathrib was a cautionary tale for the people of Arabia. Divided between two rival clans, the Aws and the Khazraj, the city had been consumed by a century of blood feuds whose origins were long forgotten. Several Jewish tribes lived in the vicinity and had survived the constant state of warfare by strategically shifting alliances whenever the balance of power necessitated. I knew little about the politics of Yathrib, but I did know that the men of Aws and Khazraj hated each other, and I could not understand what these bitter enemies were doing here, meeting the Messenger in the dead of night.

"What do they want?" I asked, my curiosity having reasserted itself as apprehension waned.

My father looked at the Messenger with warm eyes.

"An arbitrator."

And suddenly it all began to make sense.

The Messenger finished his converse with these foreigners and waved with his right hand to Abu Bakr to come join him. I walked rapidly by my father's side, almost tripping over a troublesome rock that rolled under my slippers.

When I entered the circle by the Prophet, I saw his uncle Abbas talking animatedly with the newcomers.

"Why is he here?" I whispered. "He's not a Muslim." Abbas was known to be sympathetic to his nephew, but like Abu Talib, he had not formally embraced the new Way and had never been included in the secret deliberations of our community.

"No," my father acknowledged. "But he loves his nephew and will do what he must to protect him."

Abbas looked at the Messenger, who nodded, and the lord of Quraysh turned to address the small crowd.

"People of Yathrib!" he said, and his voice echoed in the small enclosure. "You know the esteem in which we hold Muhammad, and we have protected him from his enemies. But he has resolved to turn to you and bind himself to you. So if you think you can keep your promises to him and protect him, the burden will be upon you. But if you fear that you will betray him and fail in your obligations, then leave him now."

I did not fully understand what he was saying, but the words *he has resolved to turn to you* hit me in the stomach. Was the Prophet leaving us?

A chief of the Khazraj, a thin man with a prominent wart on his left cheek, stepped forward. I would later learn that his name was Bara.

"We are ready, Messenger of God," Bara said solemnly. "What say you?"

The Messenger raised both his hands. And when he spoke, it was as if a lion were thundering through the darkness.

"I make with you this pact on condition that the allegiance you pledge to me shall bind you to protect me even as you protect your women and children."

Muhammad, may God's blessings and peace be upon him, then lowered his left hand and extended his right. Bara stepped forward and took his hand, his head lowered in humility.

"By Him who sent you with truth, we will protect you as you protect him," he said, his voice cracking with emotion. "So accept our pledge of allegiance, O Messenger of God!"

As I watched, one by one the men stepped forward and took the Prophet's right hand and pledged the same. Then my father lifted a silver bowl that was at the Messenger's feet and I saw that it was filled with clear water. Muhammad dipped his right hand into the bowl, and the women of Yathrib came and placed their fingers at the other end of the bowl, the water linking them, a symbolic act through which the Prophet accepted the allegiance of the women while respecting their dignity.

As the women proceeded to make the same oath, I turned to my father, confused.

"What does this mean?"

His answer would change my life. As well as the history of the world.

"It means, sweet girl, that we are leaving Mecca."

23

Despite our best efforts to keep our plans secret, the steady flow of Muslims out of the city soon became evident. An emergency council of elders was called, and the men gathered in Abu Sufyan's sitting room. The chieftains had been summoned hastily when the word first spread of the silent exodus of Muhammad's followers. Normally they would have met inside the lofty-pillared Hall of Assembly, but even the seat of Mecca's power was infested with the spreading disease of rebellion and was no longer a safe haven for discussing matters of state. It was for this reason, more than any other, that Abu Sufyan hated Muhammad. His stubborn movement had forced the tribal leaders to deliberate in secret like criminals, for fear of inciting further strife. To Abu Sufyan, it was a sad—and dangerous— world where kings hid like rodents from their own subjects. And it was a state of affairs that could not be allowed to continue.

Abu Sufyan turned his attention to a tall man with a well-trimmed beard, a scar under his left eye marring his otherwise well-crafted features: Khalid ibn al-Waleed, the mightiest warrior of the Quraysh and captain of its armies. Khalid had been charged with organizing nightly patrols to make sure that no Muslims escaped the city, but his efforts had clearly failed.

"How could this have happened?" Abu Sufyan barked. "Where were the sentries?"

Khalid stepped forward. His robes were of midnight black and silver, and his leather belt was studded with dozens of emeralds—allegedly one for each man he had slain in battle.

"My men were positioned to the west to prevent escape by the sea," Khalid said, no hint of apology in his proud voice. "But the refugees have turned north."

Abu Sufyan raised his eyebrows. There was only one place he could imagine they would go. But it made no sense.

"To Yathrib?"

Khalid shrugged, but his brown eyes suggested that this was his own suspicion.

"The rumor is that they are seeking Muhammad to serve as an arbitrator in their never-ending disputes with each other," Abu Lahab said, rising with some difficulty from the purple cushions that had been crushed by his generous posterior.

Abu Sufyan considered this. It was a surprising development. But perhaps a welcome one. The Aws and the Khazraj had been at one another's throats for a century. Perhaps the gods had given them a great gift. Muhammad would eventually become a victim of their fratricidal hate, and the hands of the Quraysh would be clean of his blood.

"Good. Let them have this troublemaker," Abu Sufyan said.

There was a murmur of agreement among the nobles, and Abu Sufyan saw on their weary faces the same light of hope that had just been lit in his heart. Maybe this nightmare would at last be over.

"Letting Muhammad go to Yathrib is a mistake." Hind chose this moment to speak, and the tentative looks of relief vanished across the room.

"And why is that, my dear?" Abu Sufyan, said, hiding his irritation.

Hind stood up, ignoring her husband and addressing her response to the chieftains. He saw her move among them like a cheetah, exciting their passion as she had the night she had entranced Umar into her web.

"The men of Yathrib have long looked upon this city with envy," she said, her voice cold with calculation. "They could use Muhammad's religion as a rallying cry to attack us."

Abu Sufyan snorted, trying to regain his authority.

"Unlikely," he said flatly. "Mecca has always had good relations with the Jewish tribes of Yathrib, who benefit from the perpetual war between Aws and Khazraj. They will never allow them to unite."

But Hind, as always, cut away at his confidence.

"And what if the Jews embrace him?" she taunted. "His religion is much like theirs, and he claims to be a prophet like their Moses. Would you risk bringing down their wrath upon us as well?"

Abu Sufyan tried to find a response, but for once he was struck dumb. He had never paid much attention to Muhammad's theology. It was enough that his One God would obliterate the multiple deities of the Arabs, leading to the end of the Pilgrimage and Mecca's prosperity. That was all he had cared about. But now, as he thought about what Hind was saying, he was furious to discover that she had a point. The Jews also worshiped One God and were expecting a prophet to come and grant them victory over the nations. If they fell for Muhammad's delusions, a new and more devastating war might be ignited in Arabia.

The grotesquely obese Abu Lahab spoke out loud what Abu Sufyan was thinking but was still too proud to admit.

"Your wife is right," he said. "Letting Muhammad go is too dangerous. Here in Mecca, we have some control over his poison. But once he is free from our watchful gaze, his words will spread like the sands on the wind."

"We've been down this path before," Abu Sufyan said. "Even if Muhammad is killed, the men of your clan will be honor bound to avenge him. Umar was willing to face the daggers of Bani Hashim. But who among us is willing to sacrifice his life to silence this man?"

As he looked at the perplexed men, he realized that there were no Umars among them. Even the brave Khalid had no desire to subject himself to the wrath of Muhammad's fanatics.

He looked up to see Hind scanning their faces. Her cheeks flushed as she came to the same conclusion. Whatever hold her flesh had once held over Umar's heart, she did not have any lovers among these old and tired men, at least as far as Abu Sufyan knew. And if she had bedded any of the chieftains, her charms had clearly proven to be a poor enticement.

Hind suddenly stormed over to Khalid and tore his jeweled dagger from its scabbard. She held it high and let the blade glint in the harsh sunlight. Her pose was like that of a goddess of war in an old Arab poem, and it had its desired effect.

"You men are such simpletons! Why must you send a single assassin to kill this heretic? If one man from each major clan of Quraysh joins in the deed, you will all share the blood guilt. Is there any among Bani Hashim who can take on all of Quraysh?"

She looked directly at Abu Lahab.

"Regrettably, the task would be too great for even the most avid supporter of Muhammad in my clan," he said with an exaggerated sigh. "I would be forced to accept compensation to end the matter."

Abu Sufyan looked at his wife's triumphant smile and he shook his head, both surprised with the simple elegance of her plan and exasperated that it had taken a woman to come up with it. Maybe he should just step aside and let Mecca be ruled by this ruthless queen rather than his circle of impotent old fools.

Abu Jahl clapped loudly his assent, his eyes looking with approval at Hind.

"Then it is settled," he said, beaming with satisfaction. "We will join together and kill Muhammad. And this madness will finally be at an end."

"So be it," Abu Sufyan said, rising to remind them that it was he, rather than his wife, who made the decisions in Mecca.

"When shall we act?" Abu Lahab asked, his pudgy hands clasped in excitement at the thought of his nephew's imminent death.

"Tonight," said Hind. "The new moon will provide a cover of darkness for the assassins."

"Darkness for dark deeds," Abu Sufyan said wearily. "I never thought we, the rulers of Mecca, would be forced to hide in the shadows like thieves in our own city."

Hind reached forward and ran her hand across his leg. Despite his best efforts at control, his member hardened. She took the studded leather pouch from his belt and poured into her hands a dozen gold dirhams. And then with an instinctive flair for drama, Hind turned and threw the gold across the room into the crowd of chieftains. She smiled with contempt as the powerful men fell to their knees to pick up the valuable coins. It was a simple moment that revealed everything, as Hind had intended. For, like Muhammad, the nobles of Mecca had only one god, and they bowed even now before it.

"Never fear, my husband," she said in a soft voice, meant only for him. "Once Muhammad is dead, we shall return to stealing openly under the sun."

It was the sultry tone Hind used exclusively in bed, and suddenly Abu Sufyan had to fight the urge to throw her on the ground and take her like a dog in heat. The lord of Mecca looked at her with both desire and despair. The chieftains worshiped a god of gold. And he, a goddess of fire.

* * *

THE ASSASSINS GATHERED OUTSIDE Muhammad's home, their black cloaks melding perfectly into the shadows cast by the small sprinkling of stars in the overcast sky. The Meccan general Khalid crouched beside his old friend Amr ibn al-As and Hind's arrogantly handsome brother Waleed ibn Utbah. They could see the lights flickering on the second level, in the family living quarters, and the distinct sound of women's lyrical voices could be heard from within. The heavy iron gate, normally left open, had been chained, a precaution that the Muslims were taking in all their homes since the death of Abu Talib.

Waleed argued for scaling the wall and taking Muhammad by surprise. Amr was shocked at the suggestion, reminding Waleed that there were women inside. Waleed sneered at Amr's sense of propriety, but Khalid silenced him.

"Amr is right," the warrior said, his shrewd eyes taking in everything at once as he developed a strategy of attack. "Muhammad's followers will defend him to the death. If we hurt one of the women, the honor of Quraysh will be sullied, and even Abu Lahab will be unable to quell the fire of revenge among his clan."

Waleed shook his head, unconvinced.

"Muhammad emerges every morning before sunrise to pray," Khalid continued. "He uses the well in his yard for ablutions." The Meccan general nodded to an ancient circle of stones at the edge of the property.

"We will kill him the moment he steps outside," Amr said with a smile, satisfied that decorum would be preserved even in the act of murder.

Khalid lay back against the cold pebbles of the earth and slowed his breathing. He needed to preserve his energy for the moment the door opened. Khalid closed his eyes and time passed in silence. The world seemed to slip away from him. And then he jolted upright. The eastern sky was brightening in herald of the sun god. Khalid looked at the others and saw their eyes were closed, too. He stifled a curse. In all his years as a sentry, he had never once fallen asleep as he spied on an enemy camp. His eyes immediately flew to the gate, which he saw with some relief was still chained. Unless Muhammad had scaled the wall as Waleed had planned to do, he was still inside.

He gruffly shook his comrades awake, covering their mouths so that they did not cry out in surprise. The minutes raced by as tension increased, but there was no sign of movement from the house. As a cock crowed loudly somewhere in the city, Khalid sensed that their plan had somehow gone awry.

"We've waited long enough," Waleed said, moving into a forward crouch, his sword gleaming red in the early light of dawn.

This time, Khalid did not argue.

"All right. Do what you must," he said, rising from the ground. "Spare the women and children if you can. But don't let anything get between you and Muhammad."

They moved out of the shade of the trees like black cats. Khalid clambered up the outer wall and jumped down into Muhammad's courtyard, the others following. They landed softly in the carefully tended bushes and raced toward the main door.

Unlike the gate, the paneled wooden entrance was open. Khalid pushed it slowly, hoping that its distinctive creak would not alert the women inside. But no one stopped them. The house appeared almost abandoned, and the three men crept through the barely furnished interior, their bare feet wrapped in soft strips of goat wool to muffle footsteps on the icy marble floor. Khalid climbed the winding staircase, looking for any sign of a concealed opponent on the balcony above. He led the three toward the heavy door made of carved palm wood at the eastern end of the corridor. This was Muhammad's bedroom and the most likely place to find him. As Amr and Waleed stood on opposite sides of the door, Khalid nodded. He raised his sword and kicked it in with such force that it tore off its hinges. The three men rushed inside. The room was bare, containing nothing except a comfortable down bed, the only furnishing of any value Khalid had seen inside the cavernous home. A figure lay in the bed, covered with a green Hadrami cloak that Muhammad was often seen wearing as he preached in the streets of Mecca.

There he was, the man that had caused such *fitna*, such chaos, in Arabia for the past ten years. In seconds it would all be over, and the Meccan lords could begin the process of restoring order to Arabia.

Khalid stooped, watching the cloak rise and fall steadily as the sleeping figure within breathed his last. Obviously Muhammad was so deep in sleep, perhaps under the spell of his so-called revelations, that even the thunder of the door breaking could not awake him.

This would be easy.

Too easy.

Khalid felt his stomach fall as the truth hit his warrior's soul. He lowered his sword, prepared to order his men back.

But before Khalid could stop him, Waleed rushed forward, his weapon poised.

"In the name of the gods!" Waleed threw off the cloak, his sword moving to strike . . . only to reveal young Ali lying in the bed, looking up at Waleed with those strange and frightening green eyes.

Waleed's face froze in shock. And then it twisted with ugly rage. He raised the weapon to strike Ali dead, when Amr threw himself against the youthful hothead.

"No!" Amr managed to knock Waleed's blow to the right, and it slashed down into the bed, releasing a cloud of feathers that glittered in the morning air.

They had been tricked. Muhammad was gone and the assassins had failed. Waleed glanced over at Amr with gratitude, and his friend nodded, panting from the sudden exertion. Had Waleed killed an un-armed Ali, Abu Lahab's promise of accepting blood money in exchange for the death of a clansman could not be honored. Khalid would have spent the rest of his life waiting for the retaliatory strike that would inevitably come from the men of Bani Hashim.

"Let's go," Khalid ordered.

"But Muhammad—"

"He's not here, you fool!" Khalid looked at Ali with grudging re-spect. The boy had risked his life for his cousin Muhammad. And he was known to wield a sword as if it were his third arm. Such a youth would have been an invaluable asset for Khalid's army.

Ali nodded to Khalid, as if reading his thoughts. The *kahina*s, the wandering witches of the desert, sometimes claimed that Ali possessed a second sight that allowed him to see into men's hearts. They even sold bronze charms to shield one's thoughts from the strange youth. Khalid had always laughed at their superstition, but as he looked into those mysterious eyes, he felt a strange chill. As Khalid led the men out of the room, he saw Ali gazing at Waleed, who had almost killed him moments before.

"Next time we meet," Ali said softly, "I will have a sword in my hand. And you will die."

Waleed began to laugh, but Ali's piercing gaze slit the sound from his throat. The proud son of Utbah, the brother of the powerful Hind, suddenly looked confused and uncertain. Ali's tone was not that of a threat or a challenge. His voice was actually filled with an inexplicable kindness. As if Ali had read the book of their lives and seen how it would end for Waleed, and was graciously preparing him for the inevitable.

Khalid suddenly wanted to find one of the wrinkled old *kahina*s. And he was ready to give away his fortune for a charm to protect against this terrifying youth whose eyes gazed into another world.

24

My father knelt in prayer inside the dark cave on Mount Thawr. He had been there now for three nights along with the Messenger, who had joined him at the rendezvous point in the hills outside Mecca in the early morning hours after his escape from the assassins. When he prodded the Prophet about how he had managed to escape the gang of murderers who had surrounded his home, Muhammad merely smiled enigmatically and praised God. Together they had ridden out by camel into the wilderness to the south, in the opposite direction of the road to Yathrib, where they assumed that the Quraysh would be looking for them.

For the past two days, my sister Asma had stolen away in the dead of the night and brought water and supplies to the refugees hidden inside the cave. She had brought along a small herd of sheep to cover her tracks, just as my father had done to hide the footprints of the camels that carried them to Mount Thawr. Asma also carried with her the latest news and rumor from Mecca, which was aflame with word of the Messenger's disappearance.

Abu Bakr had initially been nervous that their simple stratagem would not work, but after three uneventful days, he gave thanks to Allah that the Quraysh had underestimated them. He bowed his head on the cold earth, facing north to Jerusalem, and a part of his soul took delight that he was also facing the Kaaba. He had not questioned the Prophet when the command came to face *Al-Quds*, as the Muslims called the holy city in the heart of Palestine, but like all Arabs, the Sanctuary remained uppermost in his heart.

He finished his prostration and turned right and left, softly intoning blessings upon the guardian angels that accompanied each man. And then he rose to look for the Prophet, who had disappeared deep inside the blackness of the cave to meditate. *Dhikr,* the Messenger called it—the Remembrance of God. But before his eyes could adjust further to the gloom, he heard the sound of men's voices and his heart leaped into his throat.

Moving stealthily, he grasped hold of a thick stalagmite pillar as he slowly approached the entrance to the cave. He did not peer through the shaft of light pouring in from the tiny crawl space, but moved just close enough to put his ear to the gray earth and catch the vibrations.

Footsteps were approaching. The thud of heavy boots against rock. And then he heard the voices rising as their owners approached the crest of stone just below the cave. He prayed desperately that the voices would be those of Umar or Hamza or Ali, but a booming echo tore away at his hopes. It was a regal voice, masculine and tinted with cruelty. A voice that could belong to only one man.

Khalid ibn al-Waleed had found them. And soon they would be dead.

Despite the cool interior of the cave, Abu Bakr felt drops of thick sweat rolling down the side of his face. After everything they had done, after everything they had sacrificed, would this be how it would end?

The Messenger had always said that God did not need man to fulfill his plan. If they failed and were slain today, Islam would continue. The worship of One God was the destiny of mankind, whether they lived to see it spread beyond the wastes of Arabia or not.

Abu Bakr was not afraid to die. But he felt great grief that his friend, who had sacrificed wealth, comfort, and status to take on the thankless burden of prophecy to a barbaric people, would meet such an ignominious end.

As the footfalls sounded perhaps no more than twenty feet away, Abu Bakr hurried back into the depths of the cave. He almost yelped in fright as the Messenger emerged at the same time and the two nearly collided. Muhammad, may God's blessing and peace be upon him, saw that Abu Bakr was shaking and took my father by the shoulders to calm him.

Even in the darkness that entombed them, Abu Bakr could see the Prophet's eyes gleaming.

"O Messenger of God," he whispered urgently. "They have found us! We are lost!"

The Prophet went very still for a moment, his fingers tightening around Abu Bakr's shoulders. My father thought for a second that he was undergoing the Trance of Revelation, and he silently thanked God. The Messenger would lose all awareness of the world when he fell into that mystical state, and if he was destined to die here, Abu Bakr hoped that Muhammad would be taken while in ecstatic communion with his Lord.

"Grieve not, for truly God is with us," Muhammad said softly.

Abu Bakr's heart fell. The Messenger did not understand what was happening.

"But . . . but we are only two men, without arms. We are trapped!"

The Prophet leaned close and whispered in my father's ear.

"What think you of two, when God is their third?"

The serenity in his voice, the absolute trust and surrender of his words, was like the breaking light of dawn after a stormy night. Suddenly my father's fear was gone, like a man awakening from a nightmare and forgetting the dreamworld he had only seconds before taken for reality.

Abu Bakr turned and faced the cave entrance as the voices of Khalid and Amr ibn al-As echoed at the threshold. He was ready for God's judgment.

25

The tracker, a grime-covered Bedouin named Fawad, excitedly pointed to the cave entrance.

"They are in there!"

For the past seven hours, Fawad had led these Meccan aristocrats through the southern wilderness in search of their mad poet. Though their prey had made an effort to cover his tracks, it had been an amateurish effort at best. City dwellers might have been fooled by the sheep footprints, but Fawad's trained eye immediately saw the unique indentations of camel hooves beneath the veneer of a shepherd's crossing.

He had followed the telltale marks to the foot of Mount Thawr, a blackened volcanic peak that was a jumble of jagged boulders. He had studied the dark ash atop the stones and quickly saw the disruption in the layers that had been caused by hands struggling to find a grip, by leather boots kicking small rocks aside to ease the ascent.

Whether or not this Muhammad was a prophet was outside the scope of Fawad's expertise, but he was definitely not an expert in evasion. Any child of Fawad's tribe of Bani Duwasri would have been able to find him before the sun had set.

The Bedouin could see that the trail led to a small cave opening carved into a flat ridge. This was it, the end of their journey. The Meccans had promised him a hundred gold dirhams if he successfully located the renegade. Such wealth was beyond anything Fawad had ever imagined. Hopefully the refugees were still inside the cave (he saw no receding tracks to suggest otherwise) and the Meccans could dispatch them without difficulty. But if Muhammad and his companions were armed and a struggle ensued, Fawad could see four places amid the rocks where he could hide until the matter was resolved with some finality. He glanced at the leather purse on Khalid's jeweled belt and reminded himself to scavenge what he could in the unlikely event that the scarred warrior did not survive the encounter.

Khalid and Amr approached the cave, their swords glinting in the afternoon sun. But instead of crouching and entering, Khalid whirled, his face twisted in fury, his sword pointing accusingly at Fawad.

"You fool!" he bellowed. "How could they possibly be in there?"

Amr tuned to face him, too, and his genial face was dark with anger.

"No one has been here in months, if ever."

Fawad did not understand what they were saying. Clearly they had not seen the tracks that showed human presence within the past few days. He stepped forward, one eye on the weapons that were now trained on him.

And then he saw what they had seen and his face paled.

"I don't understand," he said, panic rising at the irrefutable evidence of his mistake.

Khalid spit at Fawad's feet and began to climb back down the ledge. Despite his rage, the cringing Bedouin was too pathetic to kill with any semblance of honor.

"We have wasted enough time," Khalid hissed. "Let us go back and join the northern search parties."

— • —

Abu Bakr stared at the cave entrance as the men's voices receded and disappeared back down the mountainside.

He turned to the Messenger, perplexed.

"They're leaving. I don't understand."

Abu Bakr sensed more than saw that the Messenger was smiling in the darkness, but he made no reply.

Curiosity finally overcoming his hesitation, my father climbed up to the entrance and peered outside, his eyes blinking rapidly at the sudden intensity of the light. When he could finally see, his mouth fell open and a gasp escaped from between his parched lips.

The Messenger came up beside him and placed a hand on his shoulder. Abu Bakr turned to look at him, his face broad with wonder. And the Messenger grinned, his teeth sparkling in the sun's warm rays.

And he quoted a verse from the Qur'an.

"Glory be to God, who when He decrees a thing, simply says, '*Kun fa yakun.*'

"Be . . . and it is."

26

I hugged my shoulders to fight off the bitter cold of Mount Thawr. The woolen shawl I had wrapped around my bosom could not protect me from the icy wind as we climbed two thousand feet above the sand dunes. I had trekked through the hills around Mecca, but never a mountain this steep and definitely not in the dead of night. As I watched Asma trudging beside me without complaint, the sack of provisions hefted onto her thin shoulders, I wondered how she could have made this difficult journey for the past three nights. I had volunteered to come those times, of course, but my mother had forbidden it. But last night, Asma had returned, looking even more exhausted than usual, her hands scraped and bloody from navigating the sharp rocks, and announced that the Messenger had summoned me. I was so excited at the thought that I was to be included in the Great Secret and would be able to join my father in his hiding place that I jumped up and down and clapped.

I was not clapping now and was deeply regretting my earlier enthusiasm. My hands burned from the bite of the rope that secured the bundle hefted over my back. There were dried meats inside the cloth, carefully wrapped in lambskin, as well as several water skins made of sturdy camel hair that would provide just enough hydration for the torturous journey north.

As I climbed up a slippery rock, the moon disappeared behind a cloud and I tripped. Suddenly the rope slid from my hand, shredding the delicate skin of my palm. I cried out as a sensation of fire surged up my hand. And then I saw with horror my bundle of supplies break open against a boulder, the precious provisions scattering over the side into darkness. Without thinking, I jumped down from my perch and tried to grab hold of the package before it vanished over the mountainside.

And then I felt the earth slipping from my grasp and I was falling, tumbling down the side of the mountain to a grave blanketed in darkness . . .

"Aisha!" I could hear Asma's horrified scream as I fell and it seemed so distant. I wondered in a strange, detached way if death would be painful or if the girl betrothed to the Messenger of God would be allowed a reprieve, like easing gently into slumber as the earth reached up to reclaim one of its wayward children.

"Hold on!" Asma's voice sounded clearer and nearby, and for a second I wondered whether she had jumped after me. And then the moon emerged from the clouds and I realized that I was clinging to a thistle bush, its ragged thorns digging into my hands, but I felt no pain. I was still in a dreamlike state of disbelief, which vanished at once as I looked down to the jagged teeth of boulders that circled the mountain's base, thousands of feet below.

At that moment, I felt the terrible sting of needles in my hand

and my heart exploded in a burst of desperate fire. Somehow I managed to cling to the thistles, and then I felt sturdy hands pulling me up and away from the precipice and I collapsed onto hard stone, which had never felt so wonderful under my feet. I looked up in gratitude at Asma's face, but my sister's mouth was hard and her eyes cold. I realized later that she was doing her best to hold back terror, but I was hurt in that moment to see the angry jut of her chin.

"Are you mad?" she said, pointing to the wreckage of supplies that I had risked my life to salvage. In the bitter moonlight I could see that most of the provisions were scattered within easy reach. Apparently I was the only thing that had gone over the edge in the ruckus.

"I was just trying to help!" I said, but I felt suddenly very stupid and small.

Asma sniffed haughtily.

"You won't get into Paradise by killing yourself."

There are many nights when I wished I had gone over the edge that night and fallen like a rag doll onto the rocks below. There are countless others who no doubt have wished the same. And yet it was not the will of God. I still had a role to play in the history of our faith, and I hope that some of my contributions were of value to our people, despite all the pain and death that I would unleash in the years to come.

Asma got up and brushed the black dust off her hands. She tore a strip of cloth from her tunic and wrapped it around my bleeding hands before turning to gather the dropped supplies. She moved around carefully, testing the ground with each step, as she collected the provisions.

I saw her frown, her forehead crinkling as she looked at the water skins and the various packages of food. Her eyes fell to the torn rope that I had used to bind my bundle and she sighed.

"I can't carry all of this without a rope."

My eyes flew instinctively to her long blue pantaloons.

"Use your girdle," I said after a moment's hesitation.

Asma threw me a sharp glance and I felt my cheeks flush. But then she proceeded to untie the strip of rope that held her pants up and tore it in half. Taking the loose section of her girdle, she tied the supplies together and then pinned her pantaloons to her blouse with a pretty pink brooch that her sweetheart, Zubayr, had given her.

Throwing me a nod that meant "Let's move," my sister took hold of both my bundle and her own and trudged up the mountainside. Her pantaloons sagged and looked in danger of falling down, and she cursed as she was forced to adjust them regularly as we climbed the rocks to the summit.

Despite everything we had just gone through (or perhaps because of it), I could not restrain my sisterly compulsion to tease. When Asma's pantaloons slipped down past her rear, she tried with some effort to cover herself again. She scowled to see me grinning.

"Don't just stand there, help me!" she barked.

"If Zubayr was here I'm sure he'd help," I said with a wink.

Asma gave me a withering look but I could see the flush of color on her face at the thought. She pulled her pants over her exposed buttocks and clambered up the mountain with what little dignity she could preserve.

We finally made it to the ledge near the peak. A conical rock face soared twenty feet above us, and I watched as Asma scoured its base for the cave opening. She stopped, looking confused.

"I thought you knew where it was," I asked. Suddenly I wondered whether this was even the right mountain, and not one of the sister peaks that surrounded Thawr. The thought of climbing another five thousand feet in the dark was beyond daunting.

"I do," Asma replied unconvincingly. "It should be right down there."

Asma climbed down into a rocky crevice and stood before the entrance of what appeared to be a small cave, just large enough for a man to enter if he bent down and ducked.

But it was clearly not the right opening. The entrance was covered with a heavy spider web, and a small nest stood at its base. Two rock doves awakened by the sound of our approach flew off in terror.

There was no way that any man could be inside there. The web would have been torn by anyone climbing in and the nest overturned.

"That can't be right," I said.

Asma leaned forward, confused. She peered at the web . . . when a hand suddenly emerged from inside the cave and pushed it aside!

I don't know who screamed louder, my sister or I. The cries of shock echoed from the mountaintop and shook the very stones around us. Had the searchers from Quraysh been in the vicinity, we would have easily been discovered.

And then I watched in utter surprise as my father emerged from inside the cave, beaming.

"What took you girls so long?" he asked.

We stared at him as if he were a ghost in the night. And then we raced each other to his arms, still strong despite his age.

The Messenger of God emerged from the cave, his eyes on me, and I felt my face grow warm. I had rarely seen him since we had been betrothed, and I felt a new bashfulness in his presence.

Abu Bakr kissed me on the forehead and hugged Asma. And then he glanced down, his eyebrows rising at the sight of her sagging pantaloons.

"What's wrong with your clothes?" he asked, a little scandalized.

"Don't ask," she said through gritted teeth.

Asma handed my father the bundle of supplies, and his eyes went wide when he saw that part of it was tied together with a piece of her girdle.

There was a moment of silence. And then I was shocked to hear the Messenger laugh. He threw his head back, his mouth wide in amusement. The Prophet often smiled, but I had rarely seen him give in to humor so enthusiastically. His laugh was throaty and infectious and soon we were all giggling with him.

The Messenger finally regained his composure and then looked at both of us with twinkling eyes.

"Welcome, daughters of Abu Bakr," he said, as if inviting us inside a grand palace rather than a rocky hole in the earth. "On this momentous night, when Islam itself has been given a new life, you have been reborn. And as such, I shall give you all new names."

The Prophet turned to my father.

"God himself has chosen this name for you, Abu Bakr—*As-Siddiq*— and it has been revealed in the Qur'an," he said warmly. "Henceforth, you will also be known as The Second in the Cave."

I saw tears well into my father's eyes. In later years, he would tell me that his greatest honor was to have spent those days at the Messenger's side in the cave, such that even the Lord of the Worlds had recognized him as Muhammad's only companion when their lives were truly at stake.

The Messenger then turned to Asma and took the bundle that was tied by her girdle. I saw an amused smile playing on his lips.

"And you, Asma, shall be forever called She of Two Girdles," he said, and I saw my sister blush with shyness at the Prophet's attention.

I have always been cursed with impatience, and in those days I had the impetuousness of youth as well. I stamped my foot at being left out of the naming ceremony.

"And me?" I asked fearlessly, ignoring the pained look on my father's face.

The Messenger leaned down next to me and stroked my cheeks, which were red from exertion and cold.

"And you will be my *Humayra*—the Little Red-Faced One."

I heard Asma laugh and I gave her a stare that would have melted steel. The Messenger laughed again, and everyone joined in, including eventually myself.

When the laughter died, I finally asked a serious question that had been haunting me since that night at Aqaba.

"Are we really leaving our homes behind?"

The smile faded from the Messenger's face and I saw ineffable sadness take its place. He turned to look out past the summit into the valley of Mecca, the city's lights twinkling like stars thousands of feet below. In the moonlight, I thought I saw the sheen of tears on his cheeks.

My father put a gentle hand on my shoulder and turned me away, giving the Messenger a private moment of grief at the loss of the city he loved. A city that had rejected him and forced him into exile.

"We will have new homes soon, little one," Abu Bakr said to me reassuringly. And then he raised his head and looked northeast, past the fires of Mecca, into a horizon that was covered in clouds, glittering turquoise with the first hint of dawn.

27

I grimaced as the camel lurched forward. My legs were hurting from days of sitting on the beast's hard back, and my thighs were rubbed raw by the saddle. The journey that had begun ten days before, when my mother had left to follow Abu Bakr to Yathrib, had proven to be less of an adventure and more of a grueling ordeal, as we followed the ancient caravan path north.

My initial fascination with the sprawling sand dunes had turned to boredom as the monotony of the desert took its toll. The fresh, clean smell of the sand had been long overpowered by the musky odor of the beasts that carried us, and I thought with disgust that I would never be able to wash the pervasive smell of camel dung off my clothes.

Even the excitement and intrigue that had surrounded the Messenger's departure was denied us, as the Quraysh had made no effort to intimidate us or block our passage to Yathrib. Now that the Muslims had settled into the oasis, it made no sense for them to antagonize Yathrib by threatening the women and children who went to join their loved ones. And so my mother, my sister, and I had left to join my father in exile, my cousin Talha serving as our guide and protector.

I grimaced as we crossed over yet another mountainous sand dune, only to see more of the same stretching out to the horizon. I had never realized how vast the ocean of the desert was, and I wondered if perhaps it never ended. If Yathrib was just a legend told to little children, like the lost cities of djinn that were said to rule the wastes of the Najd in the east.

"I hate this place," I said with an exaggerated sniffle. "How much further?"

"Patience, little one. Yathrib is just beyond those hills," Talha said with a smile.

I should have let it go, but my stomach was rumbling from a nasty case of the runs, putting me in a particularly crabby mood.

"You said that three hills back," I said resentfully. "And then seven hills before that."

Talha laughed. "I forgot that you have a memory like a hunting falcon," he said, and bowed his head to show that he accepted my reproach as well earned.

I managed a smile. Talha always knew how to put me in a better mood. He had always been like an elder sibling to me, and when my sister Asma used to tease me that we would marry one day, I was always appropriately mortified. He was like a brother to me. In the days before my betrothal to the Messenger, Asma would laugh and say that I might see Talha as a brother, but he definitely did not see me as a sister. I had never taken her seriously. Looking back at the terrible direction our lives were to take and the loyalty that Talha showed me even as I led him into a valley of darkness, I sometimes wonder whether my sister saw more than I wanted her to.

I gazed out across the horizon and tried to imagine a world beyond this vast nothingness. A world of majestic cities with towers and paved streets, gardens and fountains. A world where women dressed in flowing gowns and men rode magnificent stallions, carrying flowers to woo the beautiful maidens. It was a peaceful world, one where Muslims could walk down the street without fear of being molested, robbed, and beaten. The cold brutality of Mecca could not live up to the world of my imagination, and I did not know if our new home would be anything like that as well.

"Will we be safe there? Yathrib, I mean," I asked my cousin who rode beside me.

Talha shrugged.

"As safe as any can be in this changing world."

His words opened a strange thought in my heart. The question that I was too young to understand was the oldest question of the human race, perhaps first asked by our parents Adam and Eve when they were expelled from the Garden.

"Why do things have to change?"

A thoughtful look crossed Talha's thinly bearded face.

"I don't know, Aisha. But sometimes change is for the best."

I did not know if I believed that, and I could not tell if Talha believed it himself.

"I miss our home," I said simply.

Talha looked away sadly.

"I do, too. But we will build a new home in Yathrib."

"Will we have to stay there long?"

"Yes, in all likelihood," Talha said firmly. "But it is a beautiful city with abundant water and tall trees. You will get to play in the shade. And one day, your children will do the same."

I made a face.

"I'm never going to have children," I said provocatively, knowing full well that my parents were hoping that I would quickly give the Messenger a son once we were married.

Talha gave me a strange look, more intrigued than reproachful.

"Why would you say that?"

I shuddered, remembering the babies that I had assisted my mother in delivering. The screams of the women were terrifying, and the blood and gore of childbirth disgusted me.

"It's too painful. And children are a bother. How can you run free if you have little ones clinging to your skirts? I'm never going to have any children if I can help it," I said, speaking with childish impudence. I have often wondered whether God heard my words that day and decided to grant me my impulsive wish, which I would grow to regret as my years increased and my womb remained barren.

Talha smiled at me gently.

"Your husband might have something to say about that."

I knew that my engagement to the Messenger was widely suspected, but it was supposed to be secret for the time being, and I chose not to acknowledge what Talha obviously knew.

"Then I'm never going to get married," I said with a toss of my head, letting my crimson hair fly in the wind.

"I see," Talha said, playing along with my game. "And what will you do with yourself as a spinster?"

I spread my hands wide as I laid out a dream that even then I knew was impossible.

"I will travel the world. I want to fly like a bird and see every nation under the stars. The gardens of Syria. The rivers of Iraq. The streets of Persia, lined with gold and rubies. And maybe even go to China, where they say the sun is born."

When I looked at Talha, I saw his eyes glistening with a sadness that I did not understand. I could see Asma riding to my left, unsmiling, her eyes watching us carefully. I suddenly felt the nagging tug of guilt, as if I had done something wrong, but I could not understand why.

Talha saw Asma's stern glance and he blushed.

"I hope your wish comes true, little one," he said simply, and then rode ahead over a hill and vanished.

I wanted to ride after him, to ask what I had done wrong, when I heard Asma's voice cut like a dagger through the dead air.

"Stop it," she said with a hiss.

"Stop what?" I turned to look defiantly into her eyes.

"Stop torturing him. You are promised to the Messenger. Never forget that."

I was about to retort in anger, when I heard a shout. It was Talha, racing back toward us, pointing to the horizon excitedly.

We spurred our camels up the flowing expanse until we reached the summit of the dunes and could see what lay beyond.

My heart soared as I saw it for the first time. An emerald valley lovingly planted between a circle of volcanic hills, blackened by sun and lava, the majestic palm trees swaying in the wind as if waving to greet us.

There was the sheen of water that I had seen many times in the past few days, but for once it was not a mirage. The flowing wastes gave way to a paved road that wound past the yellow stone walls of a stern fortress, an imposing edifice I would later learn belonged to the Jews of Bani Qurayza.

A crowd of men and women, dressed in flowing white *abaya*s, was moving down the road toward us, bearing baskets of dates and pitchers of cold water. Tears welled in my eyes when I saw the Messenger of God leading the welcoming party, my father at his right hand.

After days of wandering through a hellish wasteland that was home only to snakes and scorpions, we had emerged from the fire and found paradise. My heart filled with glee, I spurred my camel down the hill and raced toward Yathrib, my new home.

28 Yathrib—AD 622

The day my courses began was also the day that Yathrib received a new name—*Madinat-un-Nabi,* City of the Prophet, or Medina for short. Over the past several months, the Messenger had proven to be a just arbitrator and had settled the daily disputes between the tribesmen in a manner that left both parties feeling respected. His growing reputation as a man of honor had opened more and more people to his message of the Unity of God and the brotherhood of man, and the majority of the town had embraced Islam before that first winter. The Prophet had further earned the people's respect by living with modesty, in contrast with their chieftains like Abdallah ibn

Ubayy, who always made a deliberate show of his wealth and power to keep the crowds awed and docile.

When the Muslims decided to build a *Masjid*—a house of worship—the Messenger joined in with the poorest of workers, regardless of their tribes or ancestry, and laid the foundation blocks with the sweat of his own hands. This rejection of class differences and tribal affiliation moved the hearts of the citizens of Yathrib, who saw in Muhammad a chance to end the centuries of division that had led only to bloodshed and grief. And when the Masjid was finished, the Messenger declined the offers of his ardent followers to build a palace for himself, carving out only a one-room stone cottage in the courtyard of the Masjid, where he lived with the elderly Sawda, the only furnishing a straw mat on the ground for sleep.

His personal example of austerity and humility had done more to spread Islam than a hundred preachers, and that day, when the city was renamed in his honor by a council of its citizens, it was clear to all that the Messenger was not just the arbitrator but for all intents and purposes the unquestioned leader of the oasis. I was too young to understand that Ibn Ubayy, lord of the Khazraj, and other rivals were not pleased with this course of events, but it would soon become evident even to those who had no understanding of politics.

In those early days, I lived with my father in a small hut that was nothing like the grand home we had abandoned in Mecca. But that palatial estate had long felt like a prison to me, and I was delighted to be able to run and play openly in our tiny yard without fear of being harassed by an angry Meccan who bore a grudge against my faith.

And so it was that the afternoon my life changed, I was chasing my new friend Leila through the tiny garden my mother had planted in our yard. Leila was the daughter of a widow whose inheritance the Messenger had restored after her father's relatives sought to deny her a claim to a well on the outskirts of the city. Without access to the well, which they rented out to trading caravans that passed through the city, her mother would have had no source of income and would likely have been forced to turn to prostitution, an exploitative (and prevalent) profession that the Messenger was working diligently to eliminate.

In the distance, I could hear the sweet, melodious voice of Bilal, the African slave my father had freed after he had been tortured by his master, Umayya, for renouncing the pagan gods. He was standing on the roof of the Masjid calling out the beautiful, haunting words of the *Azan*, the Muslim call to prayer:

God is Most Great. God is Most Great.
I testify that there is no god but God.
I testify that Muhammad is the Messenger of God.
Come to Prayer. Come to Felicity.
God is Most Great.
There is no god but God.

As Leila and I played a game of tag, racing between the two palm trees that marked the boundary of my father's small property, I laughed with the fearless delight that only a child who knows no concerns can experience. I sometimes think that was the last moment of my life when I was totally innocent and unburdened, and there are days even now when I return to that tiny strip of land, the palm trees long since cut down, and remember.

My stomach had been hurting all day and I guessed that last night's roasted lamb had not sat well with me. But when I ran through the yard, feeling the tiny blades of grass tickling my bare toes, the kiss of budding hyacinth and chrysanthemums at my ankles, I forgot all my discomfort in the unfettered joy of being alive.

I was faster than Leila, as I was faster than almost anyone I knew, and the poor girl was huffing and puffing with exhaustion as she desperately tried to catch hold of my skirt. I feinted and dodged her giggling attack with the agility that would have made a cheetah proud. But Leila was persistent and came after me with renewed vigor, when her foot was caught in the loop of a weed and she fell, scraping her knee against the warm, rich earth.

"Are you all right?" I called as I ran over to help.

Leila cried as if the foot had been amputated and I looked her over to check the extent of the injury. But as far as I could tell, she had just scraped her knee, not even broken the skin.

"Stop being silly," I said, annoyed at her need for drama. "You're not even bleeding."

Leila sniffed and wiped her eyes, and then I saw her look at me with shock.

"But you are."

With those three words, my childhood ended.

I glanced down to where she was pointing and froze. My dress had ridden up as I sat on the grass and a dark trickle of blood was running down my thigh.

╺ ╴ ╸

THE NEXT FEW DAYS were uneventful, and I was in obstinate denial that anything had changed. I could hear my parents whispering urgently late into the night, but for once I was not curious as to what they were talking about. Perhaps it was because I already sensed in my heart that the life I had known was over. I was a woman now, and I was betrothed to a man. It was only a matter of time before those two realities would lead to an inevitable conclusion, but I didn't want to face it. I kept playing with Leila and my dolls and stubbornly refused to don the scarf that adult Muslim women used to cover their hair in modesty. My mother decided not to press the point, letting me have a few days where I could pretend to be a child still.

Of course, in truth I was still a child. At the age of nine, my menses had come a year or two earlier than most girls', which perhaps should have been anticipated, as my breasts had begun budding in earnest a few months before. But my heart was that of a little girl. And my father and mother had gone out of their way to let me stay that laughing, dancing child who could put a smile on their faces when the burdens of age pressed down upon them.

But everything comes to an end. We can either fight that truth and be consumed in grief, or we can surrender and flow to the new world that the river of life is taking us. Surrender is what I had been taught since my earliest days, for that was the meaning of *Islam* itself—surrender to the Will of God.

I was playing on the seesaw with Leila when the time came
"Aisha! Come inside!" my mother called one afternoon.

I could hear a catch in her throat, a suppressed welling of emotion. In that moment, I knew what was happening, and I surrendered. I climbed down from the seesaw and kissed Leila tearfully, as if saying good-bye forever, and then walked with my head bowed back into the house.

29

My mother and Asma washed my face with clear well water they had gathered in an iron pot. They made me change out of my play clothes and helped me put on a new red-and-white-striped gown that they said had been imported from the tiny island kingdom of Bahrain to the east. This was to be my wedding gown. I would be married tonight to the Messenger of God. And at the tender age of nine, I was about to become a Mother of the Believers, a revered status in this world and the hereafter. Yet I felt small and unworthy, unready for the responsibility.

My mind raced with questions to which I had no answer. How was I going to be a wife in any sense of the word to a man over forty years my senior, whose own daughters were older than me? And how could I, who barely knew a handful of verses of the Qur'an by heart, serve as any kind of spiritual guide or mentor to the Muslims? I remembered my parents' conversation from years before, when my father had said that Gabriel had announced my wedding to the Prophet in a vision. Surely the angel had a made a mistake! For the past three years, I had let that story of the Messenger's dream puff me up with vanity and pride, but now I wanted nothing more than to be forgotten and ignored.

As my mother closed the clasp of my dress around my neck, it felt as if she were putting a shroud over me. She kissed me on the forehead and smiled, and I wanted to smile back but I could not remember how.

My father entered, wearing a long yellow robe and turban. His shoulders were stooped lower than usual, and he nervously pulled at his wispy beard, which was dyed red with henna. Abu Bakr looked at me in my striped dress, a saffron veil covering my hair, and I could see tears welling in his eyes.

He held out his hand. I clasped his palm, felt the familiar roughness of the calluses that cracked even as he squeezed my fingers. He said nothing, and neither did I. We walked out, hand in hand, followed by Umm Ruman and Asma, and strolled through the gently paved streets of Medina. I could smell jasmine in the air, sensuous and pleasing. But it did not alleviate my fear, the fear of every virgin on her wedding night. I had learned the facts of life by watching the stray dogs in the alleys of Mecca and had always found the idea that men and women did the same both amusing and repulsive. I had heard that the first night was painful for many women, and I was suddenly terrified of whatever lay ahead. I wanted to run back to the safety of my bed and have my mother sing me to sleep with a lullaby.

As we walked through the streets, I saw eyes on me from every direction. Women wearing aprons emerged from their homes to gawk, and men in colorful tunics stared at me and then whispered to one another, perhaps acknowledging that the Messenger's new wife was indeed as beautiful as rumor had it. I noticed that their eyes never went to plain Asma, and I felt a pang for her. I prayed in my heart that Zubayr would emigrate to Medina and marry her, so that the old matrons would stop clucking their tongues. The fact that I was ten years her junior and was marrying the most respected man in the city, while Asma lived alone pining for a love that might never be, added fuel to their catty gossip. The injustice of how women are judged, by their features rather than the character of their souls, never outraged me more than at that moment.

And then my thoughts stopped along with my breath as we stood before the Masjid. It was more of an open courtyard than a building proper, with walls made of mud brick and the trunks of palm trees. The sun had set an hour before and the *Maghrib* worship ceremony was finished, so the prayer ground was largely empty, except for a few devout men and women who were still kneeling in prayer. Their devotion and focus on Allah were so great that they paid no attention as my wedding party entered the courtyard.

I saw Sawda's tiny brick hut that had been built on the southeast corner of the courtyard and then gasped when I noticed that another brick cell had been hastily built adjoining it, a structure that I had not seen a week ago when I came with my father for Friday communal prayers. I realized that this must be my new house and noticed with a little dismay that, like Sawda's modest dwelling, the entire building was a single room, not much larger than my bedchamber back in Mecca.

I could see the flickering of candlelight from within and my heart pounded as my father led me to the place that would be my new home. As we approached, I noticed for the first time a group of women gathered outside, wives and daughters of the Prophet's closest Companions from among the *Muhajirun* (the immigrants from Mecca) and the *Ansar* (the helpers who protected them in Medina).

"For good and for happiness—may all be well!" they called out cheerfully. I followed my father inside and saw that the Messenger was sitting on a small spread of soft lambskin that I realized with some trepidation would be our bed. His dark eyes were glowing with that strange fire and I immediately looked down, feeling my face raging with the heat of my emotions.

The women who had come to greet us decked me out in small ornaments—a thin coral bracelet, an ivory brooch for my hair, a ring made of silver with a tiny bluish gem that might have been an amethyst or a sapphire.

When they were done, they took me to the Prophet's side and placed me on the lambskin, the only furnishing inside that tiny cell. The Messenger smiled at me gently and then opened his hand. In it I saw a necklace made of onyx beads. My frightened eyes must have sparkled with a little life when I saw the pretty black stones flecked with white and gold, because everyone in the room laughed as if the tension had been released.

The Messenger tied the necklace around my throat, which was, even in my tender youth, long and elegant. He fumbled with the clasp for a second before finally managing to seal it. I thought for a second that he might be as nervous as I was, but of course that was ridiculous. He was a grown man who had already been married twice and had four daughters who were old enough to give him grandchildren.

When he let go, my hand was drawn like a magnet to the necklace, which was Muhammad's first gift to me as my husband and lover. In the years to come, I would treasure that necklace above all my other possessions, and it would repay my devotion by leading me into scandal and grief. How strange it is now to think that such a small thing could change a girl's life? But that necklace had a terrible destiny, one that would change not only my life but the history of the world.

But none could have foreseen that, except possibly the Prophet, and I often wonder if he ever knew what destruction would come from that little present. The necklace that began as a blessing, a symbol of love, would end as a curse and a harbinger of death.

The Messenger raised a small wooden bowl filled with clear milk, the curds and fat having been carefully strained away. He sipped it and then looked into my eyes as he offered it to me. As I met his gaze, I felt a flash of something I did not understand in my foolish youth but I now know to have been desire. My body grew hot and I could feel my stomach flurrying as if overrun by tiny hummingbirds. I looked down, embarrassed and intrigued by this strange new sensation, and refused the bowl with a terrified shake of my head.

The Messenger nonetheless brought it to my lips and spoke softly. "Drink, *Humayra*."

There was something about the way he spoke his pet name for me that set the hummingbirds fluttering again. I could feel a bead of sweat drifting down the nape of my neck past my shoulder blades.

I looked at him again and he nodded. I bent forward and kissed the edge of the bowl, letting the icy cool milk flow down my throat. My heart began to beat faster as I did so, and it was no longer just with fear.

When I had drunk my fill, I passed the bowl to my sister, who sat beside me. Asma took a sip and then handed it to our mother, and then it was passed along among all who were present. When the bowl returned to the Messenger's hand, I was surprised, because it did not look as if the liquid were any less than when we had first tasted it, but I dismissed the thought as just a fantasy of my excited mind.

The ceremony was over and I was now Muhammad's wife. I had become what the angel had promised and what every other girl I knew secretly wished to be.

I was the Mother of the Believers.

My father arose. He kissed the Prophet's hand and then placed his warm lips on my forehead.

"May Allah bless the two I love most in this world," he said. And then he turned to leave, as did the women.

The simple door of palm wood closed behind them and we were alone. The Messenger smiled at me and took my hand in his. I noticed that despite the lingering heat of the evening, his hand was unusually cold, as if cooled by some mysterious breeze. I could feel the steady calm beat of his pulse. Its gentle rhythm soothed me, and the pounding in my chest gradually slowed until it was as if we shared one heart, one breath.

I gazed into his ebony eyes, blacker than midnight, and could see my own reflection in those bottomless pools. But it was not the reflection I witnessed every morning in the mirror. I looked older, wiser, my girl's body blossomed to full womanhood. My hair was no longer crimson like the sunset but a warm auburn like embers of a dying fire. But I was not smiling. There were pride and righteous anger in my golden eyes that I could not understand. And then I watched as I aged, my hair turning to silver, my face lined but still regal in its beauty. My eyes seemed even older, now filled with regret and shame. And then the vision changed and I was something else, both human and angel, my body at once young and ancient, my hair and the bones of my face glittering with moonlight that seemed to emanate from within. As I looked into the eyes of this otherworldly woman, this spirit from beyond time and space, I saw that there was no more anger or sadness.

Only love.

The vision ended and I was alone with the Messenger. He was looking strangely at me, and for a moment I wondered if he saw what I had seen. But he said nothing about it and simply ran his hand across my face, savoring the delicate softness of my flesh that no man had ever touched before.

He leaned close to me and whispered softly.

"Don't be afraid."

I looked into those unearthly black eyes and answered truthfully.

"I'm not."

He smiled warmly and took me in his arms.

I let myself go and fell into his embrace, losing myself in the wondrous sensuality of his body pressed against mine.

There was no fear. There was no pain.

There was only light.

Book Two

Birth
of a
City

1 Mecca—AD 623

The Muslims had escaped Mecca, but our enemies gave us no respite.

The establishment of an independent Muslim community outside the control of the Arab oligarchs was an even greater threat than the presence of believers inside the holy city. From our new vantage point in Medina, we were strategically placed to block caravan routes to the north. The Muslims had gone from being a persecuted rabble to an organized force with the ability to cut off the lifeblood of Meccan trade. Realizing that confrontation between our communities was inevitable, Abu Sufyan decided to take preemptive action.

And so it was that one day Umm al-Fadl, the comely wife of Muhammad's uncle Abbas, stood outside her home, gazing in shock at the scene playing out before her. A group of men, their faces covered in dirty cloths and scarves, had broken open the sealed doors of the Muslim refugees. The houses of her kinsmen and friends had been locked since they had fled to Medina, and the property was under the protection of her husband's clan, until they returned one day to reclaim it.

She watched in growing outrage as these thieves brazenly violated the honor of the Bani Hashim in broad daylight. The bandits kicked down doors, smashed windows that had been boarded with planks of acacia bark, and threw their ill-gotten booty into the street. Everything that her kinsmen owned—carpets, mirrors, tables, chairs, even cooking utensils—was removed and cast onto waiting donkey carts.

Umm al-Fadl saw the men of the clan standing by, their heads hanging with shame, as these sword-wielding burglars plundered freely. She could not let this go on. Her throat constricting with rage as well as terror, she stepped forward, blocking the path of a particularly loathsome-looking bandit, his cheeks scarred with a thief's brand he had probably received as punishment in Taif or one of the southern towns.

"Stop! What are you doing?" She cast a sideways glance, hoping that the frightened men of her clan retained a few shards of masculine honor to protect her if the burglar turned violent.

The branded thief, his mouth reeking of onions and cheap wine, just looked at her for a moment, then snickered and went about his business. He tossed a silk-cushioned chair onto his cart and turned to go back inside one of the houses his men were ravaging, when Umm al-Fadl ran over and stood in the door frame. Her brown eyes challenged him to touch her, the wife of one of the most respected members of Quraysh. The bandit rubbed his scar in irritation and then decided not to risk inciting an honor feud.

"The goods of the heretics are to be sold in the market," he said through a nest of broken and blackened teeth.

"Under whose authority?" she said, like a teacher scolding a naughty child.

The thief looked over his shoulder at the crowd of nervous onlookers and then spoke loud enough for everyone to hear.

"Abu Sufyan."

Umm al-Fadl felt the color drain from her face. If Abu Sufyan could act with such impunity, then her clan was in severe danger. With the most influential Muslims gone, her husband would not have the backing to protect the community if Abu Sufyan decided to unleash vengeance on those who remained. It would start with stealing the property of the refugees. And it would end with the expulsion of her people. Or worse.

"These are the homes of the Bani Hashim," she said, her outrage heightened by fear. "Abu Sufyan has no authority over our clan."

And then a familiar leering voice she hated came from behind her. "But I do."

Umm al-Fadl turned to face the wormlike face of Abu Lahab.

Her brother-in-law, the chief of Bani Hashim, had always repelled her with his crude comments and suggestive glances at her breasts, which were still shapely and firm despite the onset of her middle years. His betrayal of his own nephew Muhammad, whom Abbas loved and who was always kind to her, had sealed her loathing for Abu Lahab.

"Go on with your work," he said, in his high-pitched, almost effeminate voice.

"How can you let this happen?" she asked indignantly, even though her heart knew the answer. "These goods belong to men of your own clan!"

Abu Lahab shrugged. The sickly odor of his sweat was overpowering and she wanted to retch.

"Men who have renounced the gods and have fled our noble city like petty criminals have no clan," Abu Lahab said loudly, ensuring that the crowds could hear his rationale. "Their goods belong to Mecca and will be sold to promote its commerce."

Umm al-Fadl bit her lip hard, trying to restrain the compulsion to strangle him in the open street. She tasted blood in her mouth, like hot iron scathing her tongue. And then she turned to face the crowd, beating her chest in an ancient gesture of mourning.

"Is this what you have fallen to, Abu Lahab? Sanctioning theft and robbery as commerce?"

There were murmurs of shame among the men, and she saw several of the younger clansmen looking at their leader with open reproach.

Abu Lahab's face turned dangerous. He suddenly grabbed her by the arm and pushed her against the stone wall of the house.

"You should learn to respect your elders, wife of my brother," he said, a red glint in his tiny eyes.

Umm al-Fadl felt her skin crawl at his touch and she shook off his clammy hand with revulsion.

"A man has to earn respect, brother of my husband," she said with as much dignity as she could muster. "It is gained through honor—which you have long since traded for power."

There was a strange flicker his eyes and his tongue flitted in and out of his mouth like a hungry snake.

"Since you are so concerned with matters of trade and commerce, may I propose a business transaction to satisfy the debts of our wayward clansmen?"

She didn't like where this was going. No one ever did business with Abu Lahab and profited. Umm al-Fadl knew that she had to take control of the conversation and the terms of any negotiation if she wanted to help her kinsmen.

"Abbas will ransom their goods," she said with more confidence than she felt. Her husband was wealthy, but even he did not have the resources to buy back all of the stolen property in the marketplace.

Abu Lahab smiled. "It is not from my brother that I seek to collect payment."

He ran his pudgy fingers, slick with the oil and sweat, through her hair. He leaned close to her, and she could feel the nub of his aroused member pressing against the thin cotton of his robe.

She slapped him, letting years of disgust pour through her hand.

Abu Lahab stepped back, stunned. His pale cheeks burned with surprise and embarrassment as the crowd of onlookers murmured at her audacity. The chieftain of a clan was a tent pole of Mecca's social structure, and striking one in public would have many consequences. None of them good.

Abu Lahab's eyes narrowed so much that she could no longer see his pupils. And then he struck back, slapping her with such force that she spun and struck her head hard against the stone windowsill behind her right shoulder.

The world scattered for a moment and she felt fiery needles pushing into her skull. Umm al-Fadl reached for her forehead, which was throbbing from the blow. When she looked down at her hand, she could see it was covered in blood.

Abu Lahab smiled viciously at the sight of his sister-in-law's wound.

"Alas, it appears that we cannot agree to the terms of a deal. Pity."

With that, the giant snail of a man turned and walked away, waving absentmindedly to his hired thieves to continue their work.

Umm al-Fadl looked at him through eyes that blurred with pain.

"Abu Lahab!"

The chieftain turned to face her, his eyebrow raised contemptuously.

"Every debt is repaid, brother of my husband," she said coldly. "Remember that. Every debt."

Abu Lahab snickered. But when he saw the darkness in her eyes, his smile faded and he hurried away.

2 Medina—AD 624

crawled across the floor of my small apartment, the wooden
horse gripped in my hand. It was a toy that belonged to my
sister, Asma, from her own youth, part of a collection of farm
animal figurines that my father had purchased as a present on a trading
mission to Sanaa two years before the Revelation. When my father had
embraced Islam and destroyed the idols in his house, he had prepared
to throw the tiny figures made of sandalwood into our fireplace. Asma
had sat outside and wept at the loss of her toys to the new faith, and the
Messenger had seen her crying and told Abu Bakr to give her back her
playthings. Dolls and toys were not idols meant to represent false gods
but simply amusements that gave children comfort.

In later years, when zealous believers began to prohibit all forms
of images as idolatry, I shook my head in frustration as I remembered
the gentle wisdom of my husband, who had always preached a religion
of moderation. The stubborn resistance of some Muslims to common
sense and their obsession with the letter of the law while ignoring its
spirit has always been the bane of our community. With the Messenger
no longer alive to restrain such foolishness, I fear that dogmatism and
extremism may only worsen with time.

But in those days, with the Messenger's tolerant and patient approval, I could still play with my toys and did so with abandon. My
friends Leila, Munira, and Reem visited me that day, and we had spent
the morning giggling and teasing one another as we had done before
I married the Prophet. The three of us were on the cold stone ground,
chasing one another's toy animals in a mock race, when a shadow fell
over the threshold.

I looked up to see the Messenger watching us, an amused smile
on his face. The other girls shrieked with embarrassment and tried to
run past him out of the house, but he blocked the doorway with his
powerful legs.

"What are you doing?"

The girls blushed and mumbled terrified apologies, but I could see that he was not angry.

"We're playing," I said breathlessly. My friends had given me a brief and desperately needed respite from the serious responsibilities of my new role in the community. They had made me feel like the child I still was, and I did not want to go back to being a married woman and Mother of the Believers just yet.

The Messenger leaned down to see what I was holding. His eyes fell on the horse and he smiled, perhaps remembering how he had made Asma clap with joy when he had saved this little toy from the fire.

He took the horse in his hand and examined it, as if admiring the delicate Yemeni craftsmanship that made the little figure so lifelike.

"What game?" he asked simply.

I picked up the other farm figures that had been scattered on the floor—cows, camels, a lamb that had been covered in a thin layer of real wool—and showed them proudly to my husband.

"It's called Solomon's horses," I said.

The Messenger's smile made my heart quicken and a familiar quiver in my stomach reminded me that I was a woman and not just a girl, no matter how much I pretended otherwise.

The Prophet could see the look in my eye that always came with the surge of desire, and he winked playfully. And then he waved to the other girls, who were quivering in a corner, to come over.

"Solomon is my brother," he said, getting on his hands and knees and grabbing one of the toy horses, which had been painted white. "Come, I will join you."

My friends looked at him, startled. The Messenger of God wanted to play with them?

And then the Prophet lined up his white horse with my tiny black stallion. And he raced across the floor on his knees, daring me to catch up. I laughed and crawled after him, my horse moving swiftly to overtake his in the race.

The girls stared at us in disbelief. And then they laughed and joined in the play. Soon the Messenger's steeds were being chased by a handful of small animals as Solomon's horses galloped toward victory.

I beat the Prophet to the far wall of our tiny apartment, which was still furnished with the lambskin bedspread, along with the addition of a small wooden tray that served as our dining table. I leaped my toy stallion over the table as if it were flying like the winged horses of Paradise and raced toward the door.

And then I froze when I saw it was blocked by a towering figure, whose thick body eclipsed all the sunlight. Even before my eyes adjusted to make out his face, I knew that it could only be Umar ibn al-Khattab. He stood with his arms crossed across his powerful chest and looked down at us playing with the Messenger, his face twisted into a disapproving scowl.

My little friends shrieked and raced for the door again. Umar stepped aside and let them run past in terror. I scrambled up from the ground and ran to the corner where my head scarf lay discarded. I quickly covered my crimson hair under the midnight blue cloth as Umar bent down to speak to the Prophet, who was still on his knees, the toy in his hand.

"O Messenger of God, we need your counsel," he said, and the gravity of his voice caused a change in my husband's demeanor. He was again the leader of a desperate community that had been facing disease and starvation ever since seeking refuge in the oasis. I saw in an instant the weight of the world fall on his shoulders, and I suddenly understood why the Messenger took such delight in playing with innocent children. In a world where the shroud of death hung over his people daily, where any mistake he made could tear apart the fragile peace we had secured at such a terrible cost, the children made him forget the burdens of leadership for just a few wonderful moments.

The Messenger walked out grimly into the courtyard. I sat by the open door, looking out at the walled, dusty field that served as both house of worship and hall of assembly for the nascent community of believers. A crowd of prominent Muslims was gathered, and I could feel the cloud of tension that hung over the *jamaat*.

As the Messenger sat in a circle with his followers, Umar spoke of the current crisis.

"We have received troubling word from Mecca," he said. "The Meccans have stolen the property of the Muhajirun and have sold it in the marketplace."

There was angry murmuring at this news, until the mighty Hamza raised his hand for silence.

"They have used the profits to buy goods in Damascus," Hamza said, his booming voice vibrating into the palm trunks that supported the walls. "The caravan returns from Syria in a fortnight."

Umar pulled at his thick beard with rage.

"The Meccans grow fat off our belongings, while the believers struggle to find enough food to end the ache in their stomachs!"

The Messenger looked at the men, staring at each of them for a long moment as if reading the secret book of their hearts.

"And what counsel do you seek?" he asked quietly.

Umar stood up and began to pace around the circle, the nervous anger in his joints needing to be released.

"We seek to retake what belongs to our people!" he said. "The caravan is rightfully ours. We must seize it!"

I watched from the doorway of my apartment as the men nodded their heads, their voices rising in firm agreement.

But then I saw Uthman, the handsome son-in-law of the Prophet, rise, his face troubled and sad.

"The Meccans will not surrender their goods without a fight," he said with a gentle voice. "Are we ready to wage war upon them?"

Ali, who sat at the Messenger's feet, rose and faced Uthman.

"It is not a question of readiness," he said, his mysterious green eyes unreadable as always. "Every man here is willing to fight and die for God and His Messenger. But we cannot do so without the permission of our Lord."

With that, Ali looked at the Messenger. My husband met his glance and then glanced down at his hands without answering.

Abu Bakr touched the Prophet's shoulder. When he spoke, his voice was calm and firm.

"For the past fourteen years, we have stood back and responded to every provocation with patience and forbearance," my father said. "But our restraint has only emboldened the idol worshipers further. They have driven us from our homes. And now they seek to deprive us of our means to live. We do not seek war. But it is upon us."

The Messenger looked into his friend's eyes for a long moment. And then he turned to Hamza.

"What say you, Uncle?"

Hamza lifted his heavy bow from across his shoulders and laid it in the Messenger's lap.

"There is a time for peace. And a time for war."

When the Prophet said nothing in response, Hamza knelt before him and took his hands in his. "I know that you hate bloodshed. But if we do not stand firm now, the Meccans will see it as weakness. And their armies will be soon be on the doorsteps of Medina. It is time to fight."

My husband finally rose to his feet.

"I will pray to my Lord for guidance."

And without another word, the Prophet left the gathering of men and walked back to my apartment, closing the door behind me as I followed him in.

I saw the conflict on his face and it tore my heart in two. Muhammad, may God's blessings and peace be upon him, was not a violent man. I had never seen him strike anyone, and his anger was rarely voiced and could be read only by the frown on his beautiful face. He told me once that when he was a child, he had been mocked by other boys for refusing to brawl with them in the streets. His gentleness had no place in the harsh desert, where men were taught that cruelty and masculinity were one and the same. Muhammad had lived for over fifty years according to a code of pacifism that was becoming more and more difficult to uphold.

The influx of the refugees had taxed Medina's resources to the breaking point, and a poor date harvest had only worsened the lot of the newcomers. Food was as valuable as gold, and without more resources, famine would decimate Muhammad's followers. Men, women, and children who had lost everything because they believed in him. People who had followed him across the desert wastes and were now facing the certitude of a slow and painful death as hunger set in.

Attacking the Meccan caravan and taking its goods would alleviate our immediate desperation, with the added wealth purchasing food and medicines from visiting traders. But it would open us up to retaliation from Mecca. And the Messenger knew that once the drums of war began to pound, their thunder would echo for eternity.

My beloved husband lay down on our lambskin bed, his eyes closed as he pondered what path to take. Do nothing and watch his people die in quiet dignity, the faith of One God stillborn and buried in the sands of hunger and disease. Or unleash the sword and let forth a spring of blood that might one day become a raging flood. There was no easy answer, and I did not envy the choice that was before him.

Not knowing what else to do, I crawled up beside him and put my arms around his chest. I pressed my small breasts against his chest, hoping the nurturing comfort of my budding womanhood would bring him some peace.

I felt him grow still as slumber came upon him. My own eyes were heavy and I began to drift away. As I fell into the strange shadow land of dreams, I could hear the thunder of hooves as Solomon's horses raged across the earth, and I sensed that they were charging toward war.

3

I awoke in the middle of the night as the Messenger shook violently in his sleep. His face was bathed in sweat, despite the coolness of the hour, and I felt a flash of fear that he had been struck ill by the oasis fever. I shook him with increasing agitation, but he did not respond.

And then, without any warning, his eyes flew open and I could see them shine with the terrifying fire of Revelation. His mouth moved and I could hear that strange Voice that was his and not his emerge from Muhammad's lips. And he spoke the Words of God that would forever change the course of history.

Fight those who fight you, but do not commit aggression.
Truly God does not love aggressors.

Tears welled in my eyes. The choice had been made, and the simple purity of Islam would now be tinted forever with the crimson hue of blood.

━ ‐ ━

THE NEXT MORNING I stood behind the Messenger with my elderly sister-wife, Sawda, as he announced God's will to a packed crowd inside the courtyard of the Masjid.

"And behold!" the Messenger said, a sword raised high in his hand for the first time in my memory. "God has revealed these words in his Book:

"And slay them wherever you find them, and turn them out from where they have turned you out, for persecution is worse than killing.
But do not fight them at the Sanctuary
Unless they first attack you there
But if they attack you there, then kill them.
Such is the reward of disbelievers.
But if they cease, God is Forgiving, Merciful.
And fight them until there is no more persecution and worship is only for God.
But if they cease, let there be no hostility except for those who practice oppression."

I saw the excited looks on the faces of the worshipers, who murmured in delight that Allah had given them permission to fight back against their persecutors. The verses were repeated and passed among them, although I noticed that the words counseling restraint were not mentioned as readily by some believers as those counseling military action.

It was a fact that was noted by Uthman, who shook his head at the fury he saw in the eyes of some of the younger men. Ali, who stood beside him, saw Uthman's gesture of disgust and looked at him sharply.

"Why do you not rejoice at the commandment of God?"

His voice rang out in the Masjid and suddenly everyone's attention was on Uthman.

"I rejoice at the words of God, but I sorrow for this *Ummah*," the kindhearted man said. "I fear that once blood has been spilled by the believers, it will flow with no end."

The Messenger met his eyes and I could see the sadness in his glance, as if in his heart my husband feared the same outcome.

But Uthman's words of gentle reproach were seen by some of the hotheaded youths as treason.

"You are a coward, old man," said a brown-haired boy who could not have been older than thirteen. "The only blood you are afraid of spilling is your own. May Medina be washed in it one day!"

The youth's words were met by a stream of laughter from some of the people in the crowd, and a few of the urchin's friends spit at the helm of Uthman's rich blue robe. The Prophet's lovely daughter Ruqayya put her hand protectively on her husband's arm as the jeering worsened into threatening catcalls. She had been ill for several days with the oasis fever. Her normally rosy cheeks were pale, and dark circles marred the beauty of her eyes. But I saw in the firmness of her jaw her defiance of those who would insult her husband or malign his loyalty.

In the sudden rage of that mob, for the first time in my young life I saw the possibility that Muslims might turn against Muslims. And my stomach was sick with the thought that the bloodlust that had been kindled to defend our community might one day tear it apart. Standing there, my heart pounding in self-righteousness disgust at this rabble, I could never have imagined that I would be the one who was destined to release that dam of death upon on us.

I saw Muhammad's face grow dark, and he suddenly moved with his lightning speed to stand at Uthman's side. He took Uthman's right hand in his and sheathed the sword that he had been bearing moments before. The Messenger raised the red leather scabbard for all to see.

"Know that God has a sword which remains sheathed in its scabbard as long as Uthman lives," the Messenger said sternly. "If he is slain, then the sword will be drawn and it will not be sheathed until Judgment Day."

His powerful words immediately silenced the crowd, and I saw Uthman's eyes well with tears. This gentle man who alone among the Quraysh shared my husband's revulsion at bloodshed was horrified to be the cause of turmoil in the community. Seeing the anger in the Messenger's eyes and the sorrow in Uthman's, the believers were ashamed and began to disperse.

As the crowd parted, my eyes fell on the urchin boys. These young troublemakers, whom the Prophet had reprimanded in the past for their antics, stared at Uthman with undisguised hatred. And a chill closed in on my heart. A premonition of something terrible to come.

I fervently prayed to Allah that the preparations we were making for war would prove unnecessary. The Messenger was dispatching a raiding party to the outskirts of Medina. Once the Syrian caravan passed by, the men would surround it with their horses and disarm the guards, taking the goods back to Medina. If this could be accomplished without the loss of life, perhaps wiser heads in Mecca would prevail.

The Meccans knew they had stolen from us and we were retaking what was ours, so perhaps they would consider the matter closed with honor. As long as no blood was shed in the raid, there was hope that war would be avoided and the sword would forever remain in its sheath.

I raised my eyes to heaven and saw storm clouds gathering on the horizon, and I knew in the cold pit of my stomach that my prayer would not be answered.

4 The Wells of Badr—March 17, AD 624

In the end, war came to us with the dread certainty of death itself. It could no more be resisted than the angels who arrive at the appointed hour to claim the soul. And like the inexorable force of death, the war brought both an end and a beginning for our people.

The caravan, with its riches of gold and spices from Jerusalem and Damascus, had been a ruse to bring us out of our homes onto the battlefield. Abu Sufyan had followed Hind's carefully crafted strategy to the letter. Instead of passing by the black hills of Medina along the normal trading route, he had ordered the caravan to follow the coastal road along the great sea that separated Arabia from Egypt and Abyssinia.

And even as the Messenger ordered a small party of three hundred men to lie in wait for the caravan at the outskirts of Medina, an army of a thousand heavily armed Meccans was marching north to trap us.

We would meet our destiny on a rocky strip of land to the southwest called Badr. It was a regular stopping point for traders headed toward Yemen, as it contained reliable wells of clean water that could replenish a caravan's most precious resource. The Messenger set out with his raiding party, which was equipped for only a minor skirmish and was woefully unprepared for what was awaiting us. We were accompanied by a train of seventy camels and three horses, and I rode behind my husband on his favorite red she-camel named Qaswa. Though it may have surprised the sheltered ladies of Byzantium and Persia, used to hiding behind perfumed walls while their men risked their lives, Arab women regularly accompanied our warriors to inspire them and remind them what they were fighting for. It was a tradition that the Messenger respected, and as a result, I would be witness to many battles over the years to come. It was perhaps this comfortable familiarity with the heart of warfare that would cause me to overreach on that day of infamy that was still decades away.

We rode through the northeast mountain pass until we entered the valley of Badr. It was almost completely surrounded by hills and there were only three gateways into or out of the watering hole—the route we had come upon, a pass leading northwest toward the Syrian road where we expected the caravan, and a southern track that faced Mecca. The valley itself was surprisingly cheerful, with verdant foliage watered by the rich collection of wells. The Messenger pitched camp near the Medina road and the men set up a cistern with which they could more easily access the well waters. A small command station was established by placing several poles made of palm trunks in a circle and then covering the top with a black canvas to shield it from the cruel sun. Here the Prophet held strategic meetings with his generals, while I looked to the north, my heart racing with the nervous anticipation that is the breath of a battlefield.

We were elated. The wells had fallen to us with ease and the caravan would follow suit soon. And then word came from a pair of sentries we had sent to check on the caravan's progress that Abu Sufyan had diverted his train, and excitement turned to frustration. The Messenger had been prepared to pack up the camp and return home, when the steady roll of drums echoed from the south.

The trap had been sprung and Mecca's armies were at our doorstep.

Soon the southern pass was swarming with warriors in glittering mail, waving defiant flags of red and blue. Their cries of challenge and their mockery of our puny force echoed across the valley and a terrible dread fell upon our camp.

I sat beside the Prophet, who had retired to the command station at first sight of the Meccan expedition. He knelt on the ground in quiet prayer, his eyes closed and his brow furrowed as he attempted to contact the angels and find some guidance. My father stood behind, a heavy broadsword in his hand, ready to defend the Messenger should the Meccans break through the line of defense that was even now forming around the command post.

As I shaded my eyes from the blazing sunlight, I looked down at the advancing Meccan army and my heart fell. We were heavily out-numbered, although the haze that covered the southern passage made it difficult to determine the true numbers of our adversaries. I guessed that Mecca had a two-to-one advantage (I would later learn that it was three to one) and the odds of victory against this numerically superior and better-armed foe were not worth calculating.

A sad thought crossed my mind. After everything I had been through in my young life, at only eleven years of age it might all come to an end right here, before the sun went down. Though even the pa-gans did not condone killing women and children (I was both), I could smell the bloodlust from across the valley—feral, animal, unthinking. When the fire of war was ignited in men's hearts, women and children could and would die, as they always had throughout history, and I had no guarantee of clemency. Then again, perhaps death beside my hus-band and my father would be preferable to what would be done to me if I were captured and taken back to Mecca as a slave.

And then I heard a shout from the enemy lines. I looked across the valley and saw three men step away from the Meccan forces and walk fearlessly into the rocky plain between camps. I recognized them immediately as three of the most prominent leaders of Mecca. Utbah, the father of Hind, led his brother Shaybah and his son Waleed, their swords sparkling under the glare of the cloudless sky. This was an an-cient ritual of warfare that I had heard about but never witnessed with my own eyes. Before the Arab tribes fought, they always sent their most feared warriors to face each other in a duel of honor. And the Meccans had sent Utbah, whose yellow-green eyes were so much like his daugh-ter's that I wondered if Hind herself had come disguised as a man.

As Utbah approached the middle ground between armies, he looked over the rows of Muslim men, wearing old leather armor and carrying rusty blades and spears, and laughed. He spit at the ground before him, as if challenging men of this lowly caliber were an insult to his honor. And then I saw his eyes fall on a young man who stood by Hamza at the front line and Utbah's sneer twisted into a gape of shock.

And then I realized that the thin and tall youth he gazed at was Abu Huzayfa—his son. Like Abu Sufyan's daughter Ramla, Utbah's son Abu Huzayfa had defected to the Muslims, adding to the enmity between Muhammad and the tribal chiefs, who accused him of seducing their children with sorcery. I saw the troubled look on my husband's face as he saw father and son stare at each from across the battle lines, and I realized that the Messenger would never have allowed Abu Huzayfa to come with the raiding party had he known this would be the outcome.

But then Utbah regained his composure, a mask of iron covering his raging emotions. He waved his sword defiantly and issued the ancient words of challenge.

"Muhammad! Here stand the lions of Quraysh," Utbah said. "Send forth worthy men to face us—or surrender in shame."

To my horror, I saw Abu Huzayfa unsheathe his sword and move forward, ready to duel his own father to the death. And then Hamza caught the stern look on my husband's face and he put a restraining arm on the boy's shoulder.

"No. Not you."

Abu Huzayfa stepped back and his own mask of defiance fell, and I saw in his eyes terrible grief.

And then I felt a rustle of movement beside me as the Prophet rose and chose the champions who would defend the Muslims. He gazed at the eager faces of his warriors, and then made a decision that I knew was tearing his heart in two. The best men to face Utbah's challenge were those who shared his own blood. He pointed to three of his most beloved family members—his cousin Ubayda ibn Harith, his uncle Hamza, and Ali, the boy he treated like a son. I felt tears burning my eyes. I could not imagine how hard it was to send the people he loved the most to face the possibility of death before his very eyes.

The three chosen ones of the *Ahl-al-Bayt*, the House of the Prophet, stepped forward proudly onto the field, facing their opponents. Hamza had tossed aside his bow for a broadsword, and Ubayda held aloft a saber with a jewel-encrusted hilt that shimmered in his hands.

And then Ali unsheathed his sword and I heard a gasp and realized with some surprise that it was my own. He held in his hand a blade unlike any I had ever seen. Two blades actually, for the sword split in half as it tapered to the point, making it look like a forked serpent's tongue. The hilt was made of polished silver, and gold filigree was etched onto the dual blades, which had a black sheen that suggested they were forged not from steel but from some other metal I had never encountered. I would later learn that this sword was called *Dhul Fiqar* and belonged to the Messenger himself. Whenever I asked him in later years where he had acquired such an unusual and magnificent blade, he merely smiled and changed the subject.

Ali flicked his wrist and *Dhul Fiqar* cut through the air, making a strange singing sound that added to its mystery. He moved forward to face his opponents, and I saw his eye fall on Waleed—one of the men who had tried to assassinate the Prophet the night he escaped Mecca. There was a strange look between them, and I remembered what Ali had said of that night and the promise he had made to Waleed that the next time they would meet, the brother of Hind would die.

A shadow fell over the battlefield and I looked up to see that a heavy cloud blanketed the sun. Which was peculiar, as the sky had been absolutely clear only moments before.

There was a moment of terrible silence, as if history itself were holding its breath. And then, with a cry of fury, Utbah rushed at the men who had answered his challenge. Ubayda moved to intercept him and their swords met with a terrifying crash. And then Hamza was upon Shaybah and Ali faced young Waleed.

Sparks flew as the three men struck at one another, and there was a terrifying beauty to their dance. Despite his age and bulk, Hamza spun and parried like a youth, and Ubayda struck at Utbah's sword with such fury that I was surprised it did not shatter under the blows.

My eyes flew to Ali, who seemed to be moving at a different speed from the others. It was as if time around him slowed; his sword movements were elegant and beautiful, like those of a fish swimming in a gentle stream. Waleed looked confused as he met Ali's attack, as if he also sensed something was different about his opponent. I saw the looks of consternation from men on both sides of the divide as Ali fought from inside the strange dreamworld that he alone seemed to inhabit.

And then I thought the sun must have emerged from behind the cloud, as *Dhul Fiqar* began to sparkle and glow, the blade shining brightly as if it were a torch in Ali's hand. But I soon realized with some shock that the field was still covered in shadow and I could not account for the strange light that was emanating from the sword.

Waleed saw it, too, and his mouth fell open in shock. And at that moment, Ali raised the sword and, with the grace of an eagle racing toward its prey, he ran the blade through Waleed's neck. The young man's head fell cleanly off its shoulders with one stroke and blood erupted like a volcano from the severed neck. Waleed's headless body stood frozen as if in disbelief and then fell to the side.

Ali's prophecy had at last come true.

I heard a soft moan and saw that Abu Huzayfa was struggling to keep his composure at the sight of his brother's decapitation. And then the cloud that had unexpectedly covered the sun evaporated just as mysteriously, and the field was burning with light again. I saw Utbah's face go white as he saw his son's head lying only a few feet away from him, and then, with the terrible cry of a man who no longer wished to live, he threw himself at Ubayda.

An instant later I saw Hamza slash down onto Shaybah's shoulder. Hamza's broadsword tore through muscle and bone until Shaybah's sword arm was ripped away, and the champion of Quraysh died in a flood of blood and convulsions.

Utbah now stood alone against three men, and yet he continued to fight as if he were supported by an army. There was a madness in his eyes that gave him a ferocity I have never seen before on any battlefield. The Prophet's cousin Ubayda fell back under Utbah's furious blows and then suddenly made a swift kick with his leg, catching the Meccan chieftain behind the ankle. Utbah stumbled and fell.

But as he did so, he swung his ugly sword and cut off Ubayda's leg above his knee. Ubayda screamed in agony as a river of gore erupted from his stump, and I heard a terrible sound of grief erupt from Muhammad's throat.

Utbah managed to get to his feet and moved toward Ubayda, ready to deliver the deathblow. He raised his sword high . . . and Ali threw *Dhul Fiqar* across the battlefield. It spun in the air like a disk, flying with perfect precision, until the double blades connected with Utbah's sword arm and severed his wrist.

Utbah did not cry out, did not appear to feel any pain. He stood weaponless and alone, his eyes glistening as he stared at the headless body of his beloved son. And then Hamza was upon him and the mighty broadsword tore through Utbah's rib cage and emerged from his back, like a knife cutting through a milk curd.

Utbah stood there, impaled through the heart. I saw him gaze across the field to his surviving son, his traitorous boy who had chosen Muhammad over him. Abu Huzayfa's face was frozen in horror as he met his dying father's gaze.

And then Utbah did something that I will never forget or perhaps understand. He smiled at Abu Huzayfa and nodded, as if he were proud of him. With a final shudder, the father of Hind fell to his knees and returned to the God he had denied.

Silence reigned over the battlefield as the horrified Meccans dispatched sentries to recover the bodies of their slain champions. Hamza and Ali lifted Ubayda, who was swimming in a pool of his own blood but somehow managed to live. They carried their kinsman to the Messenger's command post, resting his head in my husband's lap. My father immediately knelt down and tried to bandage the stump and cut off the bleeding, but we all knew that Ubayda had lost too much blood for Abu Bakr's efforts to matter.

A shadow fell over us and I saw Abu Huzayfa standing there, looking down at the men who had killed his father, uncle, and brother. He reached for his belt, his hand floating toward the hilt of his own blade. I felt a scream of warning rising in my throat . . . and then Abu Huzayfa removed a wolfskin flask that was buckled near his scabbard. And he knelt down and poured water into Ubayda's lips, giving him one final drink before the angel took him.

Ubayda sucked on the flask, and then coughed up blood. He looked gratefully at Abu Huzayfa, and I thought I saw in his eyes a plea for forgiveness. Abu Huzayfa did not smile in return, but he nodded slowly and walked off to grieve alone.

Ubayda turned to his cousin Muhammad, whom he had followed to his death.

"Am . . . am I not a martyr . . . ?"

I saw tears glistening in my husband's black eyes.

"Indeed you are."

Ubayda smiled at that and went still.

The Prophet closed Ubayda's eyes with his hand and then rose to face the Meccan army. The ritual of challenge had been completed.

The Battle of Badr was about to begin.

5

gazed across the field to the massive army that was ready to move and avenge the deaths of its heroes. The acrid smell of blood was in the air, and I could taste the sweat and fear that covered the valley like the cloud that had appeared during the challenge.

And then I saw a tall and handsome figure emerge from the Meccan lines and my blood ran cold. Abu Jahl moved forward with dignity to stand near the pool of blood that marked Utbah's fall. He stared across the field to the command post and then clapped his hands contemptuously.

The Prophet met his gaze without a word. And then I saw Abu Jahl's eyes fall on me and a smile played across his sensuous lips. I wrapped my scarf closer across my breasts, and he smiled wider at my discomfiture, like a wolf that had found the weakest lamb in the flock. I suddenly had a terrible image of what would happen if our men were defeated and I was taken back to Abu Jahl's tent as a slave. The memory of how his well-manicured hands had torn apart Sumaya's womb without any hesitation haunted me.

"It appears that consorting with pretty girls has not drained you Muslims of your valor," Abu Jahl said with an exaggerated bow. "But three against three is an even match. Is your puny band ready to face the might of a thousand? You will all die before the sun sets."

The Messenger bent down to the ground. I watched in confusion as his sturdy fingers reached for the earth underneath my sandals. He picked up a handful of orange pebbles and then closed his fist around them.

And then my husband rose and stepped forward until he, too, stood alone on the battlefield, his eyes locked on Abu Jahl only twenty feet away from him.

"By Him in whose hand is the soul of Muhammad," he began, "no man will be slain this day, fighting against them in steadfast hope of his reward, advancing, not retreating, but God shall straightaway enter him into Paradise."

His words reverberated throughout the plain as if the rocks themselves were speaking. And then I saw the front lines of our raiding party move into perfectly straight formation behind the Prophet, heads held up, weapons at the ready. The contrast between them and the disorganized and slouching Meccan soldiers was striking. At that instant, I understood why the Prophet had insisted that men and women line themselves in perfectly straight rows every Friday for communal prayers. The discipline and the unity they had practiced for the past few years was now second nature. The Muslims were not three hundred individual men facing a thousand. They were one giant body that moved and acted in unison. As I witnessed the martial discipline on display, I felt a stirring of hope in my heart that we might just survive this encounter.

The Messenger stepped forward and raised his clenched fist as if he held an invisible javelin. Abu Jahl moved back warily, sensing something was about to happen. His eyes darted to the Muslim archers, whose deadly arrows were all trained on him.

At that instant, the wind rose and began to howl like a jackal. The sudden gusts stirred the sands, causing clouds of dust to rise from the rocky earth.

And then I saw Muhammad, may God's blessings and peace be upon him, shake his fist and then throw the pebbles he had gathered from beneath my feet toward the army of Quraysh. The tiny rocks flew across the plain like a thousand spears hurtling forward to rain death.

"Defaced be these faces!" The Messenger's words rang with authority, and I felt a flash of awe when I recognized the Voice that came during Revelation thundering from his lungs.

And then all hell broke loose. The Muslims charged straight at the Meccan army even as the wind raged and sent a cloud of sand toward the Quraysh. I heard screams of rage and triumph as our soldiers tore across the field and engaged the surprised enemy. The Meccans fought back desperately, but their efforts were impeded by the sudden raging sandstorm that had descended on them from all sides.

I strained to see what was happening, but the whirling clouds of dust made it almost impossible. I could hear the clang of metal and the painful screams of the injured. The dry air was suddenly filled with the terrible scent of blood, gore, and feces, the three odors that dying men exude as their final curse on a cruel world that brought them this fate. My mouth was painfully dry and I could taste fiery salt from the wind as it tried to find its way into my lungs. I fell back, coughing and struggling to breathe. The earth beneath me felt cold and clammy, as if I were already locked inside a grave.

The madness of battle always plays tricks on the mind, and as I staggered to find refuge from the biting wind, I thought I heard the sound of horses thundering all around me. Since we had brought only three and the Quraysh had dozens in their camp, I felt a flash of panic as I looked around for any sign of enemy horsemen racing up to deliver death.

But the whinnying and hooves that I heard seemed to be moving toward the Quraysh, not away from them. I looked up in confusion and for a moment the cloud of dust parted and I thought I saw men dressed in white riding mighty stallions racing through the sand, trampling the Meccans under their relentless assault.

Whatever it was that I saw, whether an illusion of the wind or a ghostly army riding down from heaven, Abu Jahl seemed to see it as well. I could see him standing alone amid the chaos, looking around in disbelief as his men fell to the slaughter. And then he dropped to his knees amid the whirling sand and raised his hands to the sky, calling out to his gods.

"Allat! Al-Uzza! Manat! Daughters of God, help us!" he cried out in despair. "Hubal, lord of Mecca, vanquish your enemies!"

And then I thought the wind changed and I could hear cold, terrifying laughter in its midst. The sand flew around us and it appeared that we were alone in the center of a dust devil that swirled up into heaven. I struggled to stay standing as earth and air became one flowing dune.

As I fell to my knees and tried to cover my face from the burning sand, I saw something that I will never forget. Abu Jahl was kneeling, his hands in front of his face, his mouth contorted in horror. And then out of the wall of flying sand, I saw what looked like a figure emerge, dressed in a gown of flowing white and gold.

It was Sumaya.

The phantom raised a hand and reached out to the man who had ended her life. But I saw no anger or bitterness in her gaze. Just an infinite compassion that overwhelmed my heart.

Whether it was the product of my fevered imagination or a vision from the afterlife, perhaps I will never know. But Abu Jahl recoiled as if he, too, saw something in the veil of dust. I heard him scream and strike out at the ghostly figure with a sword.

Sumaya, if that is truly who it was, lowered her hand sadly and vanished into the ethereal swirl from which she had emerged. And then the sands parted as Muslim soldiers of flesh and blood, not these strange hauntings of the wind, descended on Abu Jahl from all sides and cut off his head.

I saw the disembodied head fly across the sky, carried by the unearthly wind, until it landed at my feet. I stared down at Abu Jahl's face, his thick lips curled in fear, and then saw a hand reach down and grab the grisly remains by a tuft of gray hair.

It was the Messenger of God, who held up the decapitated head of his worst enemy, blood still pouring from the severed neck tendons.

I recoiled in horror at the sight of the man I loved holding this macabre trophy. And then the Messenger turned to me and I saw that he was not exulting in the downfall of his foe. Instead he looked sad.

"He was my friend once" is all he said. And at that moment, I realized the true burden that he carried.

The wind died down and I could see that Muslims had broken through the Meccan defenses. The enemy camp was uprooted and the pagans were in disarray.

The Messenger turned to the southern face of the valley and held up the head of Abu Jahl for all to see.

"Behold the enemy of God!"

The sight of Abu Jahl's severed skull cheered the Muslims and sent the Meccans into a panicky retreat. I watched as our enemies, armed with the finest weapons and sparkling ringed armor, fled over the southern pass, leaving the field of Badr covered in a sea of corpses.

— — —

EVERY VICTORY HAS A price.

That night we returned to Medina, the younger men joyfully boasting of their prowess, while the more mature thanked God for His miraculous aid on the battlefield. We had killed over seventy of the most prominent leaders of Quraysh, the "best morsels of Mecca's liver," as the Messenger called them. Aside from Abu Jahl and Utbah, the day had seen the death of Umayya—at the hands of his former slave Bilal, whom he had once tortured in the public square of Mecca. The gentle African whose beautiful voice summoned us to prayers had avenged himself on the battlefield, impaling his former master on the end of a spear.

Along with the mighty lords who had been slain, we had captured over fifty of the highest-ranking noblemen of the city, who were now tied together like common slaves and dragged back to the oasis. Some would be ransomed in the weeks to come. And others would be executed for their past crimes. In one day, nearly the entire leadership of Mecca had been killed or captured.

We were giddy with joy, overwhelmed with our feeling that God was truly with us. As the men sang songs of victory, I ignored the demands of modesty and loudly joined in. Only the Messenger remained silent, pensive, although he finally smiled when we entered the streets of Medina and were met with the jubilation of the crowds.

The captives were taken away to be temporarily housed in barns and storage rooms, since the city as yet had no prisons. Those who were to be spared execution would eventually be allowed to live with some dignity in the houses of Muslim families until their people ransomed them. The Messenger had made it clear that prisoners of war were guests and had to be treated with the Arab tradition of hospitality until their fate was determined.

The Prophet led the joyful warriors to the Masjid, where he was planning to deliver a sermon to mark this momentous occasion. But as he approached the courtyard, I saw him stop in his tracks and grasp at his heart.

For a moment, terror gripped me that he was ill or had been injured unknowingly during the battle. But then he stood up tall and turned, his face full of grief more than physical pain. And then I saw a man standing alone by the doorway of a grand house that stood near the Masjid. It was the kindly Uthman, who had been excused from battle to take care of Ruqayya, whose fever had returned.

I saw tears glistening on Uthman's cheeks and felt a terrible sense of foreboding.

"What has happened?" the Messenger asked, his voice cracking.

Uthman bowed his head, breathing in rapid gulps of grief.

"Your daughter Ruqayya . . . she fell ill . . . and . . . and . . . I'm sorry . . ."

I suddenly felt my husband teeter, as if his legs were giving way. I grabbed him from behind, but I was too small to keep him standing. Umar saw what was happening and grasped the Messenger by the shoulders to keep him from collapsing.

And then a sudden scream erupted from inside Uthman's house. The doors flew open and I saw Fatima emerge. Faster than my eye could capture, she was in the Messenger's arms, crying out in such horrifying wails of grief that my blood filled with ice.

There was something so visceral about Fatima's screams that I felt myself being swept up into another world. A primordial realm where the idea of sorrow itself is born in the mind of God. Her wails spread like a brushfire and suddenly all the women in the city were caught in her grief, beating their breasts and weeping for the Prophet's daughter.

Ruqayya, the most beautiful woman I have ever seen, was gone.

As the Prophet held Fatima close, I looked at her in awe and fear. The unearthly sounds that were coming from her throat had a power unlike any I had ever heard before.

It was as if when Fatima wept, the world itself wept.

6

Muawiya, the son of Abu Sufyan, watched as the defeated Meccan army sulked back into the city. The men looked more confused than humiliated, unable to understand what had happened on the battlefield of Badr. The exhausted soldiers, dehydrated from the long trek through the desert, slumped toward the well of Zamzam, ignoring the accusing looks of the women who had heard of their devastating defeat at the hands of a pathetic little raiding party.

His father gazed at his vanquished comrades in shock. Abu Sufyan looked through the crowd, stinking of blood and urine, for the other leaders of the Assembly. But he saw no sign of the great lords who had controlled the city for decades.

"Where is Abu al-Hakam?" he called out loudly for the man whom the Muslims referred to as Abu Jahl.

A young man whom Muawiya recognized as a silversmith named Nawaf bin Talal stumbled by with the help of makeshift crutches of palm wood. His right foot had been shattered by a spear and had turned an ugly green, almost definitely requiring amputation.

"Slain" was all Nawaf said as he stopped to rest against a wooden post used to tie camels.

Muawiya's eyebrows rose. This was an important development. Abu Jahl had been his father's long-standing rival for control of the council. With him out of the way, there were few impediments to Abu Sufyan seizing total control over Mecca. Perhaps, he thought with a secret smile, his childhood dream of becoming the king of the Arabs might still be realizable.

And then Muawiya felt the air grow colder around him as it always did when his mother appeared. Hind had heard the news of the Meccan defeat and had come to personally release her rage on the incompetents who had ruined her well-crafted plan.

She spit at the train of wounded and tired soldiers and let her voice rise until it resounded off the stone walls of the ancient city.

"Maybe next time we should send the women of Mecca to fight, since there are clearly no men among you!"

Nawaf's weary face contorted and he stepped forward, despite the obvious agony of his crushed heel. And then he did something that no one had ever dared.

He spit in Hind's face.

"Hold your tongue, woman, for you speak ill of your own father."

Hind stood there, her mouth open. The glob of mucus hung from her cheek like a yellow tear. Muawiya had never seen her so taken aback. All the blood drained from Hind's face, leaving her olive skin a sickly green not dissimilar to Nawaf's dying foot.

"Father . . . no . . ." She gripped her chest as if she had to pressure her heart to keep beating.

"Not just your father, Utbah." Nawaf sneered. "But your brother Waleed and your uncle Shaybah as well."

Hind's eyes flew to the back of her head, and she fell to the ground, wailing like a madwoman. She tore her clothes with her talonlike fingernails and poured sand over her hair in grief.

"Who did it?! Who killed my father?!"

Nawaf gathered his crutches and began to hobble away, undoubtedly toward a surgeon who could do the ugly work that was needed to save his life. He turned back and threw out a name, like a man tossing scraps to a dog.

"Hamza."

Hind's face went from green to bright red as her fury built inside her. She began to dig her nails into her own cheeks, drawing blood.

Muawiya saw the crowd's fascination with his mother's performance, both riveted and repulsed, and decided that it would be a good time to announce what needed to be said at long last in public.

"We must end this before more good men of Quraysh die. It is time for a truce with Muhammad," Muawiya said, his young voice echoing through the streets. He saw the warning look on his father's face but ignored it. If he were ever going to fulfill his destiny as the leader of the Arab nation, he had to reach an accommodation with the man who was doing the hard work of uniting the desert tribes for him.

There were loud murmurs of assent from the people, but his words were like a hot needle tearing into Hind's wound.

"No!" she screamed, more demon than woman. "There will be no truce!"

And then she was on her feet and racing toward the Sanctuary. She tore open her robes, exposing her perfectly rounded breasts to the idols. She ran her bloodstained hands across her flesh sensuously.

"Hear me, O sons of Mecca!" Hind cried out in a voice that was not quite human. "The martyrs of Badr will be avenged! The enemy will be crushed beneath our feet! If you do not have the courage, then your women will march without you! We will tear their eyes from their skulls! Rip off their ears and wear them on our necklaces! We shall eat of their flesh! Their hearts! Their livers! Who among you is man enough to join us?!"

Her throaty screams, her sheer insane passion, boiled the blood of the Meccans. Muawiya watched in despair as the crowd fled from his side and surrounded her, spinning and dancing with the frenzy she inspired. Soon, both men and women were chanting along with Hind, mesmerized by her spell.

Muawiya shook his head, awed and frightened by his mother's ability to capture the minds of the masses. They were like flies caught in a glittering web as she steadily crept up to feed upon their souls. He turned to Abu Sufyan, who had just been handed the keys of Mecca with Abu Jahl's death and yet looked increasingly old and irrelevant.

"Behold, Father, how a woman steals your throne," Muawiya said contemptuously. "But fear not, one day I shall regain the honor of the House of Umayya."

And with that, the brooding young man walked away, his mind racing with thoughts of how to turn the troubling course of events to his advantage.

7

Even as our enemies plotted against us in Mecca, a new threat was rising on our very doorsteps. The Muslim victory at Badr had changed the political map of the peninsula. The *Ummah* had been transformed from a small and insignificant community into a force to be reckoned with, not just for Arabs but for Jews.

Yathrib was the ancient home of three Jewish tribes—the Bani Qaynuqa, the Bani Nadir, and the Bani Qurayza. In the beginning, the Jews had cautiously welcomed the Messenger's arrival as the new arbiter. Muhammad was clearly a man committed to establishing justice and order in the oasis and ending the tribal wars that pitted not only Arabs against Arabs but sometimes Jews against Jews. The Messenger had drafted a treaty of mutual defense whereby the Jewish and Arab tribes would unite against any attacker but both would be free to follow their own religion.

But it was that very matter of religion that had quickly led to strife. My husband claimed to be a prophet in the line of Moses and the Jewish messengers. He had ordered us to pray toward Jerusalem and even fasted on the Jewish Day of Atonement, which they called Yom Kippur and we knew as Ashura. And yet the Jews had made it clear that he could not possibly be a prophet of their God, since they alone were the Chosen

People. The Arabs, even though they were descended from Abraham through his first son, Ishmael, were not included in God's covenant. The Messenger had been shocked and saddened by their rejection. To him, God's message was for all mankind. How could it be that only one tribe would be privy to His Word? And yet the Jews held steadfast to their ancient beliefs and did not shy away from branding Muhammad as an impostor. And the relations between our communities had quickly chilled.

But not all of the Jews of Medina were hostile to us. A rabbi named Husayn ibn Sallam had come to respect the Messenger as a sincere man seeking to bring the Arabs a better religion than the barbaric idolatry in which they were immersed. Ibn Sallam worked tirelessly to build bridges between the two faiths, to the derision of many among his own clan. His public show of friendship with Muhammad had cost him dearly, and the rabbi had become increasingly isolated from his fellow believers.

And there was another, more private, supporter among the Jewish tribes. A beautiful girl named Safiya, daughter of the Jewish chieftain Huyayy ibn Akhtab of the Bani Nadir. When she had first heard that a prophet had arrived from the south, claiming to bring the Word of God to a wayward people, Safiya had been swept away by the romance of the idea. She had always loved her father's tales of Moses confronting the Pharaoh and leading God's people to freedom. Of Elijah standing up to the hubris of Jezebel and her Israelite puppet Ahab. Jeremiah, Isaiah, Ezra—all messengers of the God of Israel who had stood in defiance of power with the humble strength of truth.

Ever since she was a girl, Safiya had fantasized about living in those days, when God spoke to men and the world was renewed by heroes of faith. Growing up as the daughter of a tribal leader and politician, she had watched the difficulties of ordering life in the desert and the troubling choices her beloved father, Huyayy, had to make to keep his people safe in the wilderness. Safiya had longed for God to send another prophet and take away her father's burdens. To clarify right from wrong with the sword of justice so that the shadows of ambiguity that weighed on men's souls would vanish under the rays of divine law.

So when word spread through the oasis of a prophet who spoke words of power that changed men's souls, she had been filled with wonder. Could it be that her prayer had been answered, that she had indeed lived to see the coming of God's Chosen One, the man whom her people had hoped for since the days the Temple walls fell into oblivion? But she had quickly learned that her people did not share her enthusiasm and that her father in particular viewed the rise of this Arab prophet as a threat to Jewish survival.

Safiya had buried her fascination with Muhammad in her heart. She kept wisely silent when she heard her father mock the man, denigrating the claim of this illiterate Arab to divine inspiration. And yet, over the past two years, this illiterate Arab's power had only grown, and her father no longer dismissed him as a madman. Muhammad's movement could not be ignored as a foolish cult anymore. The world was changing around them, and Muhammad's increasing power had become a source of alarm for the Jewish tribes.

And so it was that Safiya watched one night as three men sat glumly in her house, trying to make sense of a world they no longer recognized. Her father had invited Kab, the chieftain of the Jewish tribe Bani Qurayza, as well as their Arab ally Ibn Ubayy for what had become a weekly meeting to discuss the changing political face of Medina. But the three chieftains had sat around Huyayy's elegant cedar table for almost an hour without a word, each lost in his own thoughts about the remarkable Muslim victory at Badr and what it meant for the oasis. Safiya served them honey cakes, which remained untouched. Unable to bear the silence any longer, she finally decided to speak up.

"Why do you not rejoice, Father?" she asked casually, but with full knowledge that the subject was no casual matter. "Your allies have won a victory against the idolaters."

Huyayy gave her a sharp look. "These men of Quraysh I have known for many years," he responded. "Idolaters they may have been, but they were honest in their trade. I take no pleasure in their deaths."

The Arab chieftain Ibn Ubayy grasped his wine goblet and took a long sip. He appeared calm, but anger burned inside him.

"Muhammad's victory has convinced these Muslims that God is truly on their side," he said with an incredulous tone.

Safiya hesitated. She knew that she was pushing her luck, but she needed to say what was in her heart.

"Perhaps he is," she said courageously. "Rabbi Ibn Sallam says—"

Huyayy knocked over his wineglass, the purple stain rapidly spreading over the beige table coverlet.

"Don't quote that old fool to me!" Like many, Huyayy was discomfited by the broad-minded rabbi's willingness to test the boundaries of Jewish tradition and scripture.

Safiya recoiled as if she had been slapped. She could feel her cheeks grow warm with hurt. Her father had changed so much since Muhammad had arrived in Medina. Normally boisterous and kind, he had become increasingly brooding and prickly. And she blamed the treacherous Ibn Ubayy for poisoning his mind with plots and fears.

As Safiya turned to leave, her head held proudly, she was surprised to feel her father's strong hand take hold of her wrist.

"Forgive me, my daughter," he said softly. "The world is changing so rapidly. I feel lost."

It was the first truly honest thing he had said to her in months.

"You should indeed feel lost," Ibn Ubayy said with a sympathetic look. "The balance of power has shifted dangerously. The Muslims have been emboldened by their victory at Badr. They consider it a clear miracle for such a small band to rout a powerful army."

Kab, the chieftain of Bani Qurayza, laughed coldly.

"Miracle? Bah. The Meccans were overconfident and underprepared. There is no miracle in hubris and poor planning."

"Be that as it may, Muhammad's victory will raise his standing among the tribes of Arabia," Ibn Ubayy said pointedly. "He has proven that Yathrib is a formidable threat to the northern caravan routes. Soon the tribes will send him heralds seeking alliance in order to protect their trade. And where will that leave your people, my friend?"

"Where it always does," Huyayy answered bitterly. "As outsiders."

Safiya knew that this Arab was seeking to use her people to advance his own ambitions, regardless of what the consequences might be for the Jews. And she would be damned if she would let him play her father like a Bedouin flute.

"Do not rush to such judgments, Father," she said quickly, ignoring Ibn Ubayy's piercing gaze. "Muhammad has kept his end of the treaty. As long as we remain steadfast to the truce, we will prosper from the trade that these new alliances will secure for Yathrib."

Ibn Ubayy rose and approached her. She instinctively moved back. The chieftain of Khazraj maneuvered himself between Huyayy and his daughter, his eyes never leaving hers.

"You have a good heart, my dear, but alas, you are a rare and precious flower," he said with an air of affected sorrow. "The truth is, most men's hearts are not like yours. They are filled with greed and jealousy. Even if your people prosper under Muhammad's reign, what do you think will happen? The Muslims will resent you for your skill in bargaining. They will claim that you are stealing from them, hoarding the wealth that belongs to their community."

He was, of course, striking the very nerves that had been rubbed raw in the memories of her people. Their history was filled with such betrayals and Ibn Ubayy knew exactly the impact his calculated words would have. And to make matters worse, his old ally Kab, the head of Bani Qurayza, nodded in quick agreement.

"It is what always happens to our people, Safiya," he said, sounding like a wise uncle reasoning with a stubborn child. "Since the days of Jacob and his sons, the world has resented our tribe for its prowess in commerce. Whenever we flourish, the nations conspire to take it away from us."

"You are wise to look at history, my friend," Ibn Ubayy continued. "This is not the first time that an impostor has risen, claiming to speak for your God. And what do your rabbis say must be done when a false prophet is in your midst?"

Kab began to glean where his Arab friend's argument was leading. He leaned close to Huyayy, who looked weary from the weight of the conversation.

"He must be opposed. His lies must be unmasked before the people."

Ibn Ubayy grabbed a velvet-backed chair, plumping himself down next to Huyayy. With Kab to his right and the Arab to his left, Safiya thought her father looked liked a tiny mouse trapped between the talons of a mighty bird.

"Follow the wisdom of your fathers, Huyayy," Ibn Ubayy said, his eyes burning with the fire of intrigue. "Muhammad claims to be a prophet like Moses, your lawgiver. Yet he cannot even read or write. He only knows of your Torah what he has heard from the mouths of others. Fragments of tales, misunderstood and misconstrued. His entire claim to power lies in his alleged revelations from God. Challenge Muhammad on his knowledge of scripture, show that his Qur'an differs from your Torah. Undermine the credibility of his prophecy, and you will defeat him in a way that no army ever could. That is the only way that you will protect your people from this new religion that seeks to dispossess you from your rightful status as the Chosen People."

Safiya knew that what Ibn Ubayy was proposing was far more dangerous than any contest of swords. Men could make war over land, water, or women, and still peace could be achieved, for the underlying matter under dispute was tangible, rational. But if Ibn Ubayy convinced her father to launch an ideological war against the Muslims, if they tried to insult or denigrate their neighbors' faith, then there could be no reconciliation.

If there was one thing Safiya had learned from arguing about the Torah with her own people, it was that fighting over intangible ideas was a losing proposition for all sides. Opinions hardened and conflict became a matter of hazy beliefs, phantoms that could never be satisfied, no matter how much blood was spilled. If the Jews allowed themselves to fall into this trap, they would become like a gazelle prodding a sleeping lion.

"Father, don't listen to him!" she cried, falling at Huyayy's feet and clinging to his knees. "It is not the way of our people! Jews do not ridicule the beliefs of others! Let them have their religion and we ours. Or we risk bringing war upon us."

Huyayy gazed at her and she could see how tired he was. The lines around his eyes had become so thick that he looked like an owl. He ran a hand through her sandy hair as he had when she was a little girl.

"War is already upon us, my child," he said softly. "The Quraysh were the first to fall. We will be next. Unless the fire of Muhammad's religion is quenched, it will consume the world—and our people with it."

Safiya looked at her father with pleading eyes, but he rose and gently nudged her away. The Jewish chieftain turned to his guests with a look of grim determination.

"The time has come to show the world that this Arab who claims to speak for the God of Moses is a liar," he said.

Ibn Ubayy and Kab smiled in satisfaction. They had finally come up with a plan they believed could tear Muhammad off the throne that he had steadily been building himself for the past two years.

The three men turned to walk into the courtyard and continue their conversation. Safiya stayed back, her heart heavy. There was no point in pursuing them, for she had lost the argument. She watched her father step through the carved oak doors into their manicured garden. And she had a vivid image in her heart of Huyayy walking into a lion's den from which he would never return.

8

$\mathcal{I}$ sat near the Messenger in the courtyard of the Masjid as he shared with the worshipers the wondrous tale of Moses and Pharaoh. He was a remarkable storyteller, his hand gesticulating as he drew for his followers a vivid picture of the ancient prophet and his confrontation with the king of Egypt. All eyes were on him as Muhammad recited the newly revealed words of the Book.

Moses said, "Pharaoh, I am a messenger from the Lord of the Worlds
Duty bound to say nothing about God but the truth
And I have brought you a clear sign from your Lord."
Pharaoh said, "Produce this sign you have brought, if you are telling the
    Truth."
Then Moses threw down his staff, and behold, it was a serpent!
And he drew out his hand, and behold, it appeared white to the onlookers!

Gasps of awe spread through the crowd of worshipers at the startling images. As the words of the Qur'an flowed from the Messenger's lips in magnificent Arabic verse, the serpent and the white hand were so clear that we could almost see them with our eyes.

And then I heard a loud cough coming from the back of the crowd. I looked up to see Huyayy, the Jewish chieftain of Bani Nadir, standing near the entrance to the courtyard. In his hand he held what appeared to be a scroll wrapped in blue velvet, although I did not recognize the writing that had been embossed in gold over the coverlet.

There were murmurs of surprise at Huyayy's unexpected appearance. The Messenger had long invited the Jews to come hear him preach, but they had politely refused, saying they did not need him to teach them what they already knew. And now the leader of one of the most powerful tribes had come on Friday, when the Masjid was overflowing with believers who had flocked to hear the Messenger's weekly sermon.

"Excuse me, but may I ask a question?" Huyayy's voice was polite, but I sensed an edge there that I did not like.

I turned to my husband, who looked at the visitor warily before nodding.

"Who did you say it was that threw down the staff before Pharaoh?"

The Prophet met the other man's challenging gaze calmly.

"It was not I that said it, for I only recite the words of God," the Messenger responded. "God says in the holy Qur'an that it was Moses who threw the staff."

Huyayy's face contorted as if he were confused.

"How interesting. And yet the Torah says that it was Aaron that threw down the staff while Moses looked on."

There was a murmur of surprise in the crowd. It was such a minor difference that I did not care—the point of the story obviously wasn't whether Moses or Aaron had thrown the staff but Pharaoh's defiance of God's clear signs. And yet some of the less sophisticated believers, unable to grasp the subtleties of poetry, found this seeming discrepancy troubling.

Sensing that his challenge had the desired effect on at least some of the worshipers, Huyayy stepped closer to the Messenger and held aloft the velvet-covered scroll. He kissed it reverently before removing its wrap and unfurling the parchment to a page of what I assumed was Hebrew writing.

"Perhaps you can show us where in the Holy Torah it says that Moses threw down the staff?"

I felt the Messenger stiffen beside me.

"I cannot read," he said, a matter that had once been a source of shame for him but had since the days of Islam been the one clear sign of God's favor. That a man who was illiterate could suddenly recite such great words of poetry had been the proof for many Muslims of Muhammad's divinely inspired mission. And now Huyayy was using his unlettered past as a sword to mock the Revelation.

"Oh yes, I forgot. I apologize," he said, with no hint of apology in his tone. "But if you would indulge me, I have another question."

I saw the Messenger's dark eyes beginning to narrow in irritation.

"Ask, and if God has revealed it to me, I will answer."

Huyayy looked at the men and women seated on the floor of the Masjid as he spoke.

"How many signs did God send to Pharaoh to let the Children of Israel go?"

That was easy. Even a young girl like me who was not well versed in theology had heard the story of Moses enough times to know the answer.

"The holy Qur'an says nine," the Prophet responded with dignity.

Huyayy made an exaggerated look of surprise, his dark lips curling back to reveal yellowing teeth.

"Really? But the Torah claims that there were ten plagues. Perhaps God forgot one when He spoke to you."

Now I could sense real unrest among the crowd. There was a rumble of conversation as people asked one another how the Messenger of God could have made a mistake like that. Even an illiterate man could still count, they whispered.

"Another question, if I may—"

I had had enough of this uninvited guest insulting my husband. I leaped to my feet and shouted at the top of my lungs.

"No, you may not! You only seek to mock him!"

Huyayy looked at me with amusement, and his contemptuous gaze made my heart pound in anger.

"I did not know that the child bride speaks for the Prophet. It was not so in the days of Moses."

I felt a cooling hand against my forearm. The Messenger shook his head slightly and I felt a flush of embarrassment. I sat back down, suddenly wanting to be unseen and forgotten.

The Messenger turned is attention to Huyayy. He spoke calmly, but I could see the vein at his temple beginning to throb.

"Ask, and I will answer if God has revealed it to me."

Huyayy stepped forward, his eyes glistening like a falcon on its prey.

"Who was Haman?"

The Messenger glanced at his followers, who were looking at him eagerly, pleading with their eyes from him to best this arrogant interloper.

"He was the Pharaoh's adviser," the Messenger said, repeating the verses of a Revelation that had come a few months before. "Haman built a tower of baked bricks so that his king could see if the God of Moses lived in heaven."

Huyayy smiled triumphantly.

"Alas, I am confused. The only Haman I know of in the books of my people is in the legend of Esther. He was the adviser to the Persian king Ahasuerus, many centuries after Pharaoh. And the only tower I know of that is as you described is the Tower of Babel, built in the days when all mankind spoke one tongue. But that was centuries before Moses."

Huyayy turned his attention the crowd with a look of pity.

"Surely if you were the Messenger of God, you would know that which was revealed to the prophets before you."

I could feel a terrible wave of anger and confusion building among the worshipers. It was like the rumble preceding an earthquake. Some of the people looked at the Prophet with newfound distrust, as Huyayy had intended. But most were glaring at the Jew who had come to make a mockery of their most treasured beliefs.

In the dark silence that followed, I heard the rustle of robes as the Prophet rose to his feet. His eyes were shining with a fiery light that suddenly made me feel afraid. I had never seen him so angry.

"I am indeed the Messenger of God, as were my brothers the prophets Moses, David, and Solomon before me." His voice was soft, but there was more danger in his tone than any angry shout.

Huyayy smiled in his sickly sweet falseness.

"You see, that really confuses me. For the books of my people say that David was a king, not a prophet. And Solomon—well, the books say that he was a reprobate who worshiped idols and cavorted with evil spirits."

I had never heard this. The Solomon in the Messenger's stories was always a man of great wisdom and piety.

"If your books say that, then they lie," Muhammad said sharply, as if someone had impugned the reputation of his daughters. "Solomon was a sincere servant of God."

"But how could that be?" Huyayy responded with the rhetorical flourish that now filled me with rage. "You claim that your Qur'an and our Torah come from the same God. Surely they could not contradict each other if that were so."

I looked at the Messenger and saw him struggling for an answer. He was accustomed to defending his claim to prophecy from the pagan Arabs who rejected his words as mere poetic fables. But no one had ever dissected the stories of the Qur'an to show that they differed from the Book of the Jews—whose God the Messenger claimed had sent him. I suddenly realized that Huyayy's gambit was a grave threat not only to the Prophet's credibility but to the entire basis of our faith.

The Prophet's teachings had taken the ancient gods away from us, and we could not go back to them any more than an adult can revert to being an infant. But now, in one fell swoop, Huyayy had threatened to take away also the One God for whom we had suffered for so many years. He was like a thief who steals everything a man owns and then returns one night to take his life as well. If the Messenger was not who he claimed to be, we were worse off than the pagan Arabs who still believed in something, even if it was nothing more than a dream wrapped around rocks and carved pieces of wood.

Without Allah, we had nothing but despair and emptiness. Huyayy wanted to take away the very meaning of our lives.

And then I saw the Prophet go terribly still. His body began to shake violently as the familiar tremors set in. I jumped to my feet as he fell to the ground, convulsing wildly. Sweat poured down his face and neck. I pushed the men around him aside and threw my cloak over him as he shivered violently.

"Stay back!" I shouted with all my authority as Mother of the Believers, and the crowd that threatened to surround him and cut off the precious flow of air obeyed. Through the corner of my eye, I could see Huyayy shaking his head in amusement, as if he had just seen a monkey perform a clever trick.

The Messenger's tremors calmed and then stopped altogether. His eyes opened and I saw peace and tranquillity on his face. Muhammad rose to his feet slowly, and there were murmurs of relief from his followers. He turned to face Huyayy, the confusion gone and confidence shining from his handsome features.

"Behold what God has revealed to me," he said, and then recited new verses of the Qur'an with flowing harmony.

There is among them a section who distort the Book with their tongues
You would think it is a part of the Book, but it is not part of the Book
And they say, "That is from God," but it is not from God.
It is they who tell a lie against God, and well they know it.

Huyayy looked at him with raised eyebrows, as if demanding an explanation of these strange words.

"What nonsense is this?" he said, but I heard the first hint of uncertainty in his voice.

"God has revealed to me a great secret that your forefathers have hidden from mankind for centuries," the Prophet said, his voice raised for all to hear. "The words you claim to be revealed to Moses in the Torah have been changed. Your priests and rabbis have corrupted the Book, distorting the true teachings of the prophets. That is why He has sent the holy Qur'an now, to bring mankind out of darkness and into the light."

There was a moment of utter silence, like the stillness of night before the break of dawn. And then the Masjid erupted in pandemonium as Muslims excitedly repeated his words and debated their meaning.

I saw the looks of distrust vanish, and the confusion was replaced by cries of *subhan-Allah*—Glory be to God.

Huyayy was flummoxed. In this one stroke, the Messenger had taken away his entire argument, and indeed had flipped it on its head. Suddenly the subtle differences between the Book of the Jews and the Qur'an were no longer evidence of forgery on Muhammad's part. Instead they were evidence that the Jews had continued their tradition of rebelling against their prophets and had even altered their own scriptures to suit themselves. Their failures to uphold their own religion had stripped them of their pretentious claim to be God's Chosen, and Allah had sent his Message to a new people who were not trapped in a web of falsehood. The Messenger's claim to prophecy was actually strengthened by the distinctions between his faith and that of his predecessors who had corrupted God's Word.

Huyayy had tried to destroy our religion, but he had given it new life. Islam was no longer an upstart faith forever destined to suck on the teat of another people's past. It now held itself as a restoration of ancient truth, the original religion of Abraham and Moses that had been corrupted over the centuries. Huyayy had tried to show that Islam was a deviation from Judaism, and the Prophet instead had shown that Judaism was a deviation from Islam. Huyayy's people would no longer be looked upon by their Arab neighbors as wise sages whom Muslims should defer to but as heretics who had broken their own covenant with God.

I saw his face betray anger as his stratagem fell apart. As the crowd turned to jeer at him, he squared his shoulders and left the Masjid before the rules of hospitality were forgotten.

I looked at the Prophet, who was beaming like a child. The Revelation had freed him from having to show any deference to the Jews and Islam could now spread on the strength of its own authenticity. The shackles of the past were lifted. Instead of being the moon, shining with the reflected light of the People of the Book, Islam was now the sun. It could burn with its own fire and blot out the other stars, the earlier religions that had sought to illuminate men's hearts.

— — —

A FEW WEEKS LATER, the final break from our Jewish brothers came. The Messenger received a Revelation that the believers were no longer to face Jerusalem in their daily prayers. Instead we would kneel toward the Kaaba at Mecca, the House that had been built by Abraham hundreds of years before the Temple of Solomon rose. It was a welcome change, for our hearts had always belonged to the Sanctuary.

The *mihrab*, the small prayer niche of palm wood that indicated the direction of Jerusalem, was boarded up. A new *mihrab* facing south was carved. As the Muslims bowed to Mecca for the first time in years, I could feel the collective longing in their souls for the city we had lost.

As I bowed my forehead to the cold earth, a thought flashed through my mind that I knew must be in the breasts of my neighbors. Now that the center of Islam was Mecca, we could not let the pagans hold on to the Sanctuary.

Mecca had so kindly brought war to our doorstep, and perhaps the time had come to return the favor.

9

*U*mm al-Fadl, the wife of Abbas, bent down to lift a bucket of water from the sacred well of Zamzam. She passed along the wooden casket to Abu Rafi, a freed slave who had been quietly teaching her about Islam. After the defeat of Badr, more and more people in Mecca were interested in learning about this strange faith that could give three hundred men victory over a thousand. Like her husband, who was an uncle to Muhammad, she had been slow to give up on the traditions of her ancestors, but the deaths of Mecca's ruling elite at Badr had shaken her stubborn respect for the old ways.

As Umm al-Fadl dropped another bucket into the dark waters below, she heard familiar voices approaching. Abu Sufyan, who was now the unchallenged ruler of Mecca, was conversing in an urgent tone with her hated brother-in-law Abu Lahab.

"Our caravans are no longer safe to travel north, even along the coast," Abu Lahab said grimly. "Muhammad's forces control the passes and they have vowed to seize any Meccan goods heading for Syria."

"Then we must take the eastern path through the Najd," Abu Sufyan responded, reaching for a copper jug to lower into the well.

"The Najd is a barren waste with few wells!" Abu Lahab hissed. "Even our sturdiest camels risk death in that terrain."

Abu Sufyan filled his jug and then took a long drink.

"It seems your nephew has us trapped," he said after a pause. "As long as Medina blocks the northern passes, our trade with the Byzantines and the Persians is at a standstill."

Abu Lahab leaned close to him, lowering his voice conspiratorially.

"Your wife is right. We must avenge Badr. We must destroy Muhammad once and for all."

Abu Sufyan's jaw flinched at the mention of Hind, but he nodded.

"I agree. Once the winter has passed, we will launch an attack on

Medina," he said, knowing that he really did not have any other choice. "We will gather our finest men and marshal all of our allies. I hope it will be enough."

Abu Lahab snorted contemptuously.

"What do you mean, 'you hope'?"

Abu Sufyan shrugged.

"Muhammad is a survivor. For almost fifteen years we have sought to defeat him. Yet he only grows stronger with time."

Abu Lahab's tiny eyes narrowed further.

"Well, his reign is at an end. Our men will destroy him!"

Abu Sufyan looked at the fat slug of a man who had never held a weapon his life and shook his head. Abu Lahab was exactly the kind of chieftain he despised. Unwilling to risk his own life but perfectly content to send young men to their deaths.

"Our people fear him," he said. "Whatever happened at Badr, it has left a dark impression on their minds. The men believe Muhammad is a sorcerer who can control the wind. That he has armies of djinn at his command."

Abu Lahab laughed, an ugly sound that lacked any humor.

"Don't tell me you believe that nonsense?"

Abu Sufyan turned his head to face the Kaaba. For so many years, he had felt as if he were trapped in a bad dream, and some voice inside him was saying that it was time to wake up and face the world.

"I don't know what to believe anymore," he said with a sigh. "Men whom I have always considered to be sober-minded came back from Badr weeping in terror over the djinn who they say fought alongside the Muslims. Warriors on white horses who emerged from the wind."

Umm al-Fadl had been listening unobtrusively to their conversation, pretending to be absorbed in the work of filling her water cans. But her ears pricked up at this. She looked at Abu Rafi, who had silently stood at her side, ignored by these noblemen like all low-class workers. But his eyes went wide at the strange story and he spoke before Umm al-Fadl could stop him.

"Those were not djinn! They were angels!"

The chieftains turned and saw the tiny man with the pockmarked face for the first time. Abu Sufyan smirked and turned his back. It was beneath him to address this freed slave who was worth less than the mule droppings that littered the streets of Mecca.

But Abu Lahab was outraged at the stranger's audacity.

"You! You're one of them!"

Umm al-Fadl put a restraining arm on Abu Rafi, trying to lead him away from the confrontation. But he shook her off.

"Yes! I am a Muslim, and I no longer fear to reveal it. Not when the angels themselves descend to the Prophet's aid."

Abu Lahab's face turned purple and he looked like an overstuffed grape, ready to burst.

"Let's see if the angels will descend to your aid!"

And then he grabbed a sharp stone and slammed it into Abu Rafi's face, knocking out his front teeth. Abu Rafi fell to the ground in pain, but Abu Lahab was not finished. He continued to pummel him until his features had devolved into a mass of blood.

Umm al-Fadl watched the unbridled cruelty with mounting rage.

"Stop it! You'll kill him!"

Abu Lahab cast an amused look at his sister-in-law. His eyes locked on the curve of her breasts as they always did.

"So what? I am the chief of the clan! I determine who lives and who dies among the Bani Hashim."

Umm al-Fadl turned to Abu Sufyan, the plea written on her face. But the lord of Quraysh merely turned away with distaste. Abu Lahab kicked Abu Rafi in the crotch, and she could see the poor man crying like a baby.

And then something broke inside of her, like a rusty latch that has kept an old door closed. And like the waters of Zamzam, something bubbled up inside of her that was very cold, very ancient.

She grabbed a tent pole that lay fallen on the ground.

"Abu Lahab!" she cried out in a voice she did not recognize. "Remind me. When you die, who will be the head of the clan?"

Her brother-in-law looked up at her, startled.

"What?"

And then the force that was raging within her took hold of her arm. Umm al-Fadl raised the tent pole and brought it crashing down with terrifying fury on Abu Lahab's head.

There was a sound like a melon falling off a merchant's cart and splattering on the cobbled street. Abu Lahab's skull cracked and a burst of gore erupted from an exposed sliver of brain.

Abu Lahab fell back against the well, his tiny eyes now wide open in shock, as blood and gray tissue streamed out of the wound and down the side of his fat face.

He managed to turn his head and look at Umm al-Fadl, who still held the tent pole in her grasp. Her hand was shaking, but when she spoke, her voice was as clear as the spring waters of Yemen.

"Our debt has been repaid."

Umm al-Fadl dropped the pole and turned away from the dying man. She wanted to run away, but a crowd was forming around her, staring at her in shock. And then a horrible scream pierced the open plaza around the Sanctuary.

A woman with dirty white hair and a face lined like a shriveled pear burst through the crowd and ran to Abu Lahab's side.

This was Umm Jamil, his wife, who had a reputation for petty cruelty that made Abu Lahab seem like a diplomat in comparison. She wailed over her bleeding husband, beating her sagging breasts in fury.

"Who did this?" she screeched.

Umm al-Fadl saw her husband, Abbas, push his way toward them. He looked at his injured brother, the head of their clan, and then at his wife. There was no escaping responsibility for what she had done.

"I did," she said with quiet dignity.

And then Umm Jamil was upon her like a bat, the old woman's clawlike nails trying to tear her eyes from her skull.

Umm Jamil's brother, Abu Sufyan, pulled her off Umm al-Fadl and held her forcefully as she screamed vile curses that even drunken men would hesitate to utter.

"If my husband dies, I will have your head!"

Umm al-Fadl turned to Abbas.

"If your husband dies, I believe the question of my fate will reside with the new chieftain of Bani Hashim."

Abbas was shaken by her words. But she persisted, taking his hand in hers and squeezing it softly.

"What say you, husband? Will you kill me? Or will a blood payment suffice the clan's honor?"

Abbas dropped her hand as if it were made of live coals.

"You women are all mad."

He shook his head and walked away, looking very much as if he wanted to wash his hands of the entire affair.

Umm al-Fadl smiled at the elderly witch triumphantly.

"I believe a hundred camels will settle our debt. Don't you agree?"
Umm Jamil spit in her face.

"I curse you and all the children of your loins!"

Umm al-Fadl wiped off the mucus with her sleeve. She looked one last time at the dying Abu Lahab and his wife, her eyes cold with contempt.

And then she remembered something Muhammad had said years before. At that moment, her resistance was gone and she accepted the truth of the new religion that her nephew had brought.

"There is none more accursed than those who are cursed by God Himself," Umm al-Fadl said.

And then she recited a verse from the Qur'an that had been revealed years before when Abu Lahab had led the persecution of Muhammad. A verse that she had first heard her nephew recite when Umm Jamil had carried a bundle of thorns and had flung them upon him during prayers. A verse that somehow came back to her memory as if it had been branded into her heart.

The power of Abu Lahab will perish, and he will perish.
His wealth and gains will not exempt him.
He will be plunged in flaming Fire
And his wife, the wood carrier,
Will have upon her neck a halter of palm fiber.

She saw the color drain from Umm Jamil's face as the shriveled crone, too, remembered the verses that she had dismissed so many years before.

Umm al-Fadl walked out of the Sanctuary quietly, leaving Umm Jamil to ponder the terrible prophecy that had come back to haunt her.

The old woman suddenly seemed like a lost child, looking around in confusion. She saw people staring at her and backing away. Umm Jamil could feel something happening to her as chills ran up her arms and legs. And then she looked down at her hands and saw ugly red pustules spreading across her flesh like a wild rash.

She turned to her brother, who was looking at her face in shock. Umm Jamil touched her cheeks and could feel the hard bumps that were breaking through the maze of wrinkles that had long since taken away her beauty.

Umm Jamil knew what these pustules were. She had seen them once before when she was a child. They were the markings of the same disease that had destroyed the invading army of Abraha, the Yemeni king who had brought an elephant to lay siege to the Kaaba. That same year that her nephew Muhammad had been born.

It was the plague.

And then she saw with horror that Abu Lahab's blood-soaked face was erupting in the same warts. He, too, was being eaten alive by the monstrous disease that always came without warning and could kill an entire city in a day.

"Help me . . . help us . . ." Her voice sounded distant and small.

But the crowd saw the telltale signs of plague and the plaza was quickly empty.

Only Abu Sufyan stood alone by the well of Zamzam, staring in horror at his sister.

She reached for him, seeking his comforting embrace. Just as when they were children and he would hug her when she skinned her knee and the pain would vanish.

But Abu Sufyan backed away, tears flowing down his face.

"I'm sorry."

She felt as if a hot sword had been thrust through her neck.

"No . . . my brother . . . please don't leave me.. I need you . . ."

And then he was gone.

Umm Jamil stood alone by her dying husband, the ugly pustules racing like ants across her body. And then she fell to her knees and screamed. The terrible wail resounded through the city, carrying her horror across the valley of Mecca.

But her cries soon stopped and the echo vanished in the wind, to be forgotten forever.

10

One night, when the Messenger was out late for a meeting of tribal leaders at Uthman's home, I decided to step outside my tiny apartment, which was beginning to feel like a prison cell.

Covering my hair with a dark woolen scarf and throwing on a cloak of golden camel skin, I slipped out of my house and left the Masjid courtyard by the northern gate. I had lived in Medina for over two years, but I rarely went out alone and there were many small avenues and streets I had not explored. I was not especially nervous, as the avenues of the oasis were patrolled by large numbers of Bedouin guards. The newcomers had sensed that the sands were shifting in Muhammad's favor and they had sworn fealty to the man who was bringing order at least to the northern valleys of the peninsula. Even as Mecca and the cities to the south were suffering from a disruption of trade, the lands around Medina were booming.

As I strolled through the streets, I marveled at how wonderful it was to feel safe. I had been born into persecution and my earliest memories were of death and suffering. But since our victory at Badr, the storm had subsided and I suddenly felt free, like an eagle soaring through the skies unchallenged.

I was admiring the delicate arches of a house that stood on the outskirts of the oasis, where the paved roads melded with the sand, when a group of young men saw me standing alone. They whistled appreciatively and called out a variety of indecent proposals. Shocked at this crass impropriety, I turned to scold them and my face was suddenly lit by the full moon. Instantly their amorous attentions turned to embarrassment and fear as they recognized me. They had just propositioned the Mother of the Believers and risked bringing the wrath of God upon them!

The youths quickly bowed and scraped at my feet, asking forgiveness. I smiled, exulting in my young power, and warned them that if they ever spoke to a girl like that again, they would face grave punishment, which I left sufficiently vague to allow their own imaginations to take hold.

The boys scampered away, terror in their eyes, and I laughed. I was alone again and closed my eyes and let the warm wind caress my skin. I opened them again after a moment and looked north, through a gap in the hills that cleared a view all the way to the horizon. There was a whole world there that I hoped to see someday. Magical cities like Jerusalem and Damascus where the ancient prophets had lived. Or even further, to the famed seat of the fabled Byzantine empire. Constantinople, the largest city on earth, whose streets were rumored to be paved in silver and where the churches were as large as mountains. Or perhaps even beyond, to the ruins of a city called Rome that had once been the capital of the world but was now ransacked and forgotten. And if I made it that far, then I would of course go farther, to the lands where the sun is said to never shine and the world is lit only by stars.

It was a beautiful dream, and in my girlish heart perhaps I believed it would come true. I, who had been born with a wanderlust and a need for adventure, had known only two cities my whole life, both surrounded by sand dunes and policed by vultures and wolves. I longed to see flowing rivers and trees that carpeted the earth with life. To gaze upon mountains crowned in ice, where the clouds themselves fell like the rain. And it all seemed possible. I would never have believed that I would spend most of my life trapped inside the confines not only of this small town but ultimately inside the tiny walls of my home. Had I known what was to come, perhaps I would have kept walking that night into the desert, following the shooting stars to the wondrous world over the horizon. A world that would forever be outside the limits of my destiny.

A sudden cry awoke me out of my reverie. I pushed aside a strand of hair that blocked my ear and then listened carefully. There it was again. It was the distinct sound of weeping. Of a man crying in terrible grief.

I looked around to find its source. The only building nearby was a small barn that stood near the edge of the oasis. As I moved closer to the mud brick stable, the sound became clearer. I felt my heart pounding. Someone was hurt, perhaps had fallen and injured himself. God must have sent me here tonight to help this poor soul.

I approached the barn and pushed open the heavy wooden doors that had been bolted from outside. I was too naive to stop and ask myself why someone would be in a barn that had been locked from without, but I must have reasoned that the poor fellow had gotten stuck inside and had hurt himself trying to get out.

The door opened with a steady creak and the weeping stopped instantly. I waited for my eyes to adjust to the darkness within and then cautiously stepped inside. It was an old structure, supported by beams of palm wood. There were open stalls for horses, the ground littered with fresh grass, but I could see no animals within. I began to wonder if I had imagined the sound when I saw a flash movement against one of the walls. My heart leaped and I cried out.

And then I saw him. A wretched-looking man was curled into a ball inside the stall, his face bruised and caked in dried blood. As the moonlight strengthened my vision, I noticed that his hands were tied with a thick rope and were bound to a post.

He looked at me with wild eyes full of fear.

"Help me . . ."

I had never seen anything like this. Someone had beaten this poor man and left him here to die. I stepped inside cautiously, my eyes looking out for any sign of rats or other unpleasant creatures in the corners.

"Who are you?"

The man spoke with a raspy voice.

"My name is Salim ibn Qusay . . . I am being held against my will . . . please help me . . ."

I saw his face better now. He as young, perhaps only twenty years old, and he had bright eyes that seemed to glitter like a cat's in the dark.

"How did this happen to you?"

Salim bowed his head.

"I was a traveler in the desert . . ." he said slowly. "A merchant from Taif . . . There was a young girl in the caravan . . . Yasmeen . . . I fell in love with her . . . I came to Medina to propose marriage . . . but her father has promised her to someone else . . . When he found us together, he tied me up and left me here to die . . . Please . . . help me . . ."

I felt a flash of righteous anger at his story. Despite the Messenger's best efforts to eradicate the practice, such "honor killings" were still commonplace. The thought that someone could murder another human being for the crime of being in love repulsed me.

With a sudden yearning for justice and the sweet foolishness of a teenage girl who wanted to play a heroic role in this tragic tale of love, I tore my long nails into the heavy knot that bound him. After struggling with the rope valiantly for several minutes, my fingertips were rubbed raw, but I finally managed to loosen the bindings. At last, the rope came undone and Salim's hands were free . . . to wrap themselves around my throat!

I tried to scream but his hands quickly moved to cover my mouth.

"You little girls always fall for the love story." His whimper was gone and his voice was laced with menace.

I struggled as he pushed me against the wall. A flash of moonlight from a crack in the roof above illuminated my face for the second time that night.

Salim's eyes flickered with recognition.

"You . . . you're the child bride of the sorcerer . . ."

But instead of falling to his knees and pleading for forgiveness as the youths had done, he smiled wickedly.

"Well, then I'm truly going to enjoy this."

As he leaned closer to me, I could smell the wine on his breath and the sick aroma of arousal that covered him like a cloud of flies.

He threw me down to the floor and then reached for my pantaloons. My heart pounded with the terrible anticipation of violation.

And then it was as if something took possession of my body. I was barely twelve years old and only half his size, when a fire ignited in my veins, giving me strength I had not imagined hid inside my tiny body.

I bit down against his hand, my teeth tearing a chunk of flesh from his fingers. He screamed and fell off me, and my feet swung hard into his crotch. Salim doubled over in agony. My pulse thundering in my ears, I ran past him. But he threw out his leg and tripped me. I fell face-first into the mud of the stables. Tears welled in my eyes. I could feel his cold hands lock around my ankles as he dragged me back into the cell.

I screamed with such force that I felt like my lungs were flying out of my chest to escape the terrible fate awaiting the rest of my body.

And then I heard the sound of voices. Men shouting from outside! As the steady drumbeat of footsteps raced toward the barn, I felt Salim let go of my ankles. There was a rush of air as he fled past me and escaped into the night.

My vision blurred and I saw no more.

11

$\mathcal{G}$ blinked heavily as sunlight poured over my eyelids. When I opened them, I saw a bright haze that slowly came into focus. A figure moved in front of me and I instinctively backed away in terror. But then his strong, manly features came into view and I gasped.

It was the gentle face of the Messenger smiling at me. He bent down over me and stroked my hair.

"Are you all right, *Humayra*?"

I managed a nod, and then looked around the barn, which had appeared cavernous the night before but was much more modest in the daylight.

"The man . . . Salim . . . where is he?"

A shadow fell over us and I saw my father, his face full of relief.

"He was a thief," Abu Bakr said. "We caught him stealing in the marketplace. This criminal was to be punished tomorrow under God's law, but now someone has helped him escape."

I suddenly felt like the greatest fool on earth.

"Not someone, Father. It was I."

The Messenger stared at me in shock.

"What?" both men asked in unison.

The back of my neck began to burn with shame.

"He told me a story . . . about how he loved this girl . . . and her father was keeping them apart . . . I felt sorry for him . . . So I loosened his bonds . . ."

I suddenly saw a dark cloud cover my husband's face. His smile vanished and there was cold anger in his eyes.

"May Allah cut off your hand!"

I sat stunned for a moment, unable to process his fury. And then tears erupted from my eyes. The Prophet had never been angry with me before and I felt as if someone had just thrust a flaming arrow into my stomach.

The Messenger saw my grief but his anger did not abate. He turned away from me and I saw that there was a group of men standing by the door of the barn, keeping a respectful distance from this unfolding family drama.

"Organize a search party," he said forcefully. "We must find him before he hurts anyone else!"

The men nodded and disappeared. My husband turned to look at me one last time, but I did not see any forgiveness in his glance. And then he stepped through the door and was gone.

I shook violently with grief and I turned to my father for his support. But Abu Bakr looked as stunned as I felt at Muhammad's uncharacteristic rage, and he backed away from me as if I were a demon and not his daughter.

He left me alone on the cold floor of the barn. I stared around me at the gray walls that seemed to be closing in, burying me alive with my shame.

And then I remembered my husband's curse and I lifted my hands and stared at them, waiting for the judgment of God that I knew would come upon me any moment.

⬦ ⬦ ⬦

I WAS STILL SITTING there like that hours later when I heard the sound of men approaching. And then the criminal Salim was dragged unceremoniously past me and thrown back into the cell from which I had freed him.

My father stood over the guards as they held the struggling captive down.

"Tie him doubly and post an armed guard at the door," Abu Bakr said wearily. "He will be tried in the public square after midday prayers, and I would prefer that he actually show up for his judgment."

The men tied Salim's arms and legs, and gagged him for good measure.

I saw all of this from the corner of my eyes, but my focus remained on the palms of my hands.

I felt rather than saw the Messenger enter, for the hot morning air suddenly became cooler, as it always did in his presence. He watched me as I sat unmoving, staring at my hands with horrible anticipation.

"What's wrong with you? Are you possessed by a djinn?"

I did not look at him. I found that I could look at nothing but my hands, which were pale and bloodless.

"I'm waiting to see which hand Allah cuts off."

I heard the Messenger gasp as he realized I had taken his angry words at face value. And then he reached down and took my hands in his. He squeezed them tightly and I saw tears in his eyes.

We sat there, husband and wife, looking at each other. No words were said. None were needed.

And then the Messenger let go of my hands and raised his own upward in supplication.

"O Allah, Merciful and Compassionate Lord, forgive me for cursing this child. Bless her and anyone whom I have ever cursed."

And then he lifted me to my feet and led me out of the barn, his fingers wrapped tightly around mine. As I walked past Salim, bound and guarded by men with swords, I saw the hint of a desperate plea for clemency in his eyes.

But my heart was not as big as my husband's, and I had no forgiveness to offer.

* * *

SALIM WAS PUNISHED THAT afternoon for his crimes. He was dragged out in front of a crowd of witnesses by Umar, who tied him spread-eagled to iron stakes that had been hammered into the dark oasis earth. I watched without any emotion as Umar raised his sword and cut off Salim's hands for theft. He screamed in agony, a sound that would have made me cover my ears and hide my face in horror and empathy the day before. But the girl who came out of the barn that morning was not the same girl who had entered. I watched him writhe like a fish pulled from a stream, blood erupting in thick spurts from his severed wrists. And then Umar raised his sword again and chopped off Salim's head as punishment for assaulting the Mother of the Believers.

The screams stopped instantly and there was only silence in the public square. I looked around to see the men's heads bowed in silent prayer, the women's faces covered in tears. They were all shaken by the severity of the punishment. But now there was no doubt in anyone's mind what the price would be for breaching the hard-won peace of Medina. There would be no backsliding to the days of anarchy. Law had come to Arabia, and crimes carried consequences.

I took one last look at the grisly remains of the man who had taken advantage of my innocence, who had sought to mount me like a pig in the mud. And then I turned and walked away in silence.

12

A few weeks later, I strolled through the central marketplace of Medina with my friend Huda. She was sixteen and almost as tall as a man, with legs that seemed to stretch toward the sky. Huda was everything I longed to be, worldly and sophisticated. She regularly went with her father on trading missions to Persepolis and knew the latest fashions of all the beautiful women to the east.

The bazaar was one of my favorite places in the city. It was full of life and there was always some new merchant there, selling some rare item that I had heard about only in stories from cosmopolitan travelers like Huda. The stands carried everything from oranges and pomegranates that had been shipped from Egypt by sea to colorful spices from the east that smelled sweet and sour at the same time. Sometimes there were pets for sale, and I remember how delighted I was the time I saw a cage full of striped cats that I learned were baby tigers. But my favorite section of the bazaar was the long line of tables displaying jewelry— silver rings, sapphire earrings, and jade necklaces that the merchants claimed came from the mythical land of China, where the sun is born each day.

We passed by the rainbow maze of jewelry stands, cooing at the wonderful items and giggling like little girls, until we reached a table manned by a Jew from the Bani Qaynuqa. They were goldsmiths and master craftsmen, and it was rumored that their unique designs were sought by customers as far north as Babylon.

My eyes fell on a remarkable bracelet made of pressed gold and engraved with lifelike images of doves in flight, emeralds studding their outstretched wings.

I tried it on under the watchful gaze of the old vendor, admiring how beautiful it looked against my skin. It fit my tiny wrist perfectly, as if it had been made for me.

"It looks wonderful on you," Huda said excitedly. "You should buy it."

I felt a pang of longing, but I knew it was impossible. I took off the bracelet and returned it to the shop owner.

"I don't have enough money."

Huda looked at me as if I were insane.

"But your husband is the Messenger of God! Surely he must be the richest man in all Medina. Doesn't he take one fifth of all the booty from the raids on the Meccans?"

This was the normal Arab custom. The tribal chief was allotted one-fifth of any booty secured by a raid or a military operation. With the Muslims adopting a policy of economic siege against Mecca, my husband was in a position to secure tremendous wealth from the successful capture of caravans. Huda was right. I should have been the wealthiest woman in the oasis.

"He gives it all away to the poor," I said in explanation. "The People of the Bench."

The People of the Bench were a group of Medinese beggars who regularly sat near a stone bench that stood in a corner of the Masjid courtyard. Anyone who came there was entitled to a share of food and whatever booty was to be redistributed by the Messenger. His daughter Fatima sometimes spent hours standing in the sun and attending to the long lines that gathered there every morning after *Fajr* prayers. I usually saw the same people, some of them able-bodied men who should have been working instead of begging, and had grumbled to the Messenger that they were lazy scamps who took advantage of his generosity. But he had simply smiled and said that even such men serve a purpose. When I looked at him doubtfully, he explained. "They teach us to give without any expectations. That is true compassion."

I had shaken my head in disbelief, even as Huda shook her head now to learn that the Messenger was as poor as he'd been the day he arrived from Mecca, despite the massive wealth that passed through his hands every day.

"The prophets of the Jews were rich," she said. "Why does the Prophet of the Arabs have to be poor?"

I laughed.

"Maybe the Jews get a better deal because they are Chosen." It was a stupid comment by a girl too young to know that words have power. We laughed at my minor witticism and continued looking around the jewelry stands.

But as we moved away from the table of the Jewish goldsmith, our words lingered. A young man named Yacub, the hotheaded nephew of the old merchant, heard us and was angered. He must have recognized me as the Mother of the Believers and added my comment to the litany of offenses that the Jews of Medina attributed to my husband. The Messenger's unification of the oasis and his successful military expeditions had raised their fears that he would soon turn against them.

If I have learned anything in my life, dear Abdallah, it is that fear is the worst enemy of a man's soul. For whatever it is that we fear comes rushing to us like an arrow across the fields of time.

As we stepped away from the table and turned our attention elsewhere, Yacub took a gold brooch from the stand and in one swift movement pinned Huda's flowing skirt to a wooden post as she passed by. When Huda crossed over to a nearby stall, the thin fabric tore open and her skirt fell to her ankles, exposing her womanhood to the gathered crowd of shoppers.

I heard the sharp rip and then Huda's horrified scream. I whirled to see the poor girl desperately trying to cover her privates, tears falling from her face as men in the marketplace whooped and jeered.

Acting faster than I could think, I ripped the scarf off my head and tied it around my weeping friend's waist. I suddenly saw that everyone's attention had left Huda and all eyes were on me. My scarlet hair glistened in the sun and I felt a flush of horror that strangers were now gazing lustfully at my exposed locks. It was a shameful violation of a woman's honor, but not as shameful as what Huda was enduring. I lifted my head with dignity and met the men's probing gazes with my own defiant eyes.

"Stare at us all you wish, you fools! The sin is on you!"

My words shamed them, and the men quickly looked away. I reached down to pick up the pieces of Huda's skirts and saw the gold pin that was responsible for her embarrassment.

I looked up to see Yacub staring at me with anger.

"I guess it's our turn to laugh, you little wench."

A shadow fell over us and I saw a young Muslim man named Muzaffar standing there. He did not look at me, but I saw that he held out a cloak in his right hand. I quickly took it from him and covered my hair again.

Muzaffar challenged the Jewish prankster, his face red with rage.

"How dare you speak to her that way! She is the Mother of the Believers!"

Yacub laughed with exaggerated bravado. He could see other young men of his tribe watching his confrontation with the Muslim and he was now trapped in a deadly contest of virility.

"You Arabs call your children your mothers." He sneered. "No wonder you can't tell your head from your asses! Although as mothers' asses go, she certainly has a nice one. Maybe next time we'll see hers, not just her friend's."

Faster than my eye could follow, Muzaffar pulled out a small knife and slit Yacub's throat with the practiced skill of a butcher. The boy fell forward, his face frozen in a deadly grin. The blood from his gaping neck wound poured out over the beautiful golden jewelry that his uncle had spent many months crafting with such great love.

I screamed in horror, but my voice was drowned out by the shout of Jewish men rushing to avenge their fallen comrade. They threw Muzaffar to the ground and beat and kicked him until I heard the sickening crunch of his skull shattering.

The marketplace devolved into chaos as Muslims and Jews attacked one another with righteous indignation. As I fled with Huda to safety, my heart tightened at the knowledge that a terrible new day was upon us.

The first blood between the sons of Isaac and Ishmael had been spilled. And I had a dark vision in my mind's eye that the trickle of death would soon become a flood.

13

The peace of Medina had been shattered from within, and retribution was swift. An army of a thousand men surrounded the walled district to the southwest that housed the Jewish tribe.

In the days following the marketplace brawl, the Messenger had sent Ali to negotiate blood payment to resolve the tensions between the Muslims and Jews. Each side had lost a man in the scuffle, and according to the terms of the treaty, the matter had to be submitted to Muhammad for arbitration. But the Jews of Bani Qaynuqa turned back Ali, saying they considered the alliance void after the murder of one of their men by a Muslim.

Tensions had risen as the Jews barricaded themselves inside their walls, and there were rumors that that the chiefs of Qaynuqa were sending urgent messages to Abdallah ibn Ubayy, the treacherous leader of the Khazraj. The Jews allegedly promised that they could marshal seven hundred men to their defense. If the Khazraj matched them, then perhaps together they could wrest the oasis from the sorcerer.

But if such an offer was indeed made, Ibn Ubayy declined it. Though we had heard talk that he had been happy to incite the Jews to do his dirty work in antagonizing Muhammad, Ibn Ubayy was not the kind of man who would be willing to risk his own life to settle their scores.

And so the day had come when the Bani Qaynuqa were friendless and alone. The Messenger considered their renunciation of his treaty an act of war and had besieged the settlement. The Muslims had cut off the roads leading to their sister Jewish tribes, the Bani Nadir and the Bani Qurayza, and the fortress had no independent wells. Soon the Bani Qaynuqa would run out of water, and they would have to fight or surrender.

I watched as the Prophet strode among the Muslim soldiers who surrounded the gates of the Jewish fortress. He was dressed in glittering mail made of concentric steel rings, and his helmet covered most of his face. His black eyes glistened from behind his steel visor.

A battering ram had been devised to tear down the heavy wooden doors that protected the Qaynuqa. It was a long pole made of a series of thick palm trunks tied together and reinforced with steel plates. Thirty of the strongest Muslims would join forces to pummel the gates until they fell and the fortress was overrun. The soldiers had been ordered to kill any man who was armed but to spare the women and the children.

As war drums resounded, announcing to the Bani Qaynuqa their approaching end, I saw a man who was dressed in flowing scarlet robes approach the Messenger. It was Ibn Ubayy come to bargain on behalf of the Jews, whom he would not defend with arms.

He pushed past Umar and Hamza, who scowled at his presence, and walked up to the Prophet, addressing him from behind as he surveyed his men.

"O Muhammad, treat my allies well."

The Messenger glanced at Ibn Ubayy briefly and then continued on his tour of the company, his presence inspiring courage among the warriors.

But Ibn Ubayy was persistent. He followed the Prophet and shouted for all to hear.

"Muhammad! Have mercy on my allies!"

The Messenger pretended not to hear him, even though his cries could have woken the dead in *Jannat al-Baqi*, the graveyard outside Medina.

Frustrated, Ibn Ubayy came up behind the Messenger and grabbed him by the collar of his mail shirt.

"Listen to me!"

Instantly a dozen swords were drawn and held to Ibn Ubayy's neck. And yet he held on firmly. The Prophet turned to face him and a silence so great fell over the field that all I could hear was my pounding heart.

"Let go." There was more danger in those two words than any lengthy tirade could have held.

And yet Ibn Ubayy, for all his flaws, could not be called a coward. Feeling the prick of blades against the skin of his neck and back, he nonetheless refused to release the Prophet's armor.

"By God I will not, until you promise to treat them well," he said, and I saw in his face what appeared to be real pain. "The Bani Qaynuqa have four hundred men without mail and three hundred armored. Not much of an army, but in all the years before you came to Medina, those men were my sole protection from my enemies. This Arab lives because those Jews saved him."

He paused and his eyes glistened with grief. If he was performing, he was an astounding actor.

"Seven hundred men who kept me alive before you brought peace to this oasis," he said, his voice choking. "Will you cut them down in one morning?"

The Messenger looked at him. I could not see his face through the visor of the helmet, but I saw the tension in his shoulders fall as ibn Ubayy's plea touched his heart.

When he spoke, his voice was firm but compassionate.

"I give you their lives," was all he said.

Ibn Ubayy's hand fell and the Messenger walked away. He stood for a while staring after the man who had stolen his crown, who ruled Medina while he watched from the sidelines. I do not know what he was thinking, but he looked shaken and confused. Finally, he turned toward the gates of the fortress and went to deliver the good news to his erstwhile allies.

14

Safiya stood by the desert road, watching her kinsmen from the tribe of Bani Qaynuqa abandon their homes and leave the city forever. They loaded their carpets and small furnishings on the back of hundreds of camels and donkeys, along with whatever household items they could carry—utensils, scrolls, small pots and pans. Heavy bundles contained food for the trek through the wilderness, including stores of dates, olives, and dried meats. Her eyes caught the eye of a young boy sitting on a mule, crying that he wanted to stay, but his mother shushed him and told him to always look forward, never back.

It was happening again, Safiya thought bitterly, just as her father had feared. The world was always changing, but one thing remained the same—Jews were being expelled from their homes. She felt a flash of anger at Muhammad, and she wanted to embrace it and fan its fire until it consumed her heart. But she couldn't silence the small voice within her that said her people were not blameless in this matter. Had they listened to wiser voices like her own, they would have welcomed the Muslims and become their allies in bringing peace and prosperity to Arabia. But their own fears, the centuries of loss and betrayal, had conditioned them to resist change. They had sought to undermine the new order and inevitably brought upon themselves its wrath.

Tears in her eyes, she turned to the elderly rabbi Husayn ibn Sallam, himself a member of the Qaynuqa, but one who had been granted express permission to remain because of his cordial relationship with Muhammad.

"What will happen to them?" she asked softly.

Ibn Sallam wiped his nose on his sleeve. His eyes were red but dry, and she guessed that he had no more tears left to shed.

"They will go north to Syria," he said quietly. "Our people still have a few settlements that survive under Byzantine rule. They will find refuge there."

"But you will stay." It was not a question, and there was no hint of reproach in her voice, but the rabbi flinched as if he had been struck.

"I have to."

She had not expected this as a response.

"I don't understand."

Ibn Sallam sighed heavily.

"The sands of time are shifting, but I fear that our people do not see it," he said as if he had read her thoughts. "The Bani Qaynuqa let their pride blind them to the new reality. I will stay and counsel the Bani Nadir and the Bani Qurayza to flow with the stream of history, not against it."

Safiya watched the lengthy train of her brethren pass outside the hills of Mecca toward an unknown destiny in the north.

"Do you really think our people would risk further confrontation with Muhammad?" she asked wearily. She could not bear to witness this exodus again. "Why would they be so foolish?"

The rabbi smiled sadly.

"Our people take great pride in the fall of Masada," he said, referring to the fortress where Jewish zealots had killed themselves and their families rather than surrender to Roman hordes. "I fear that our hearts secretly long to relive it. To die in glorious sacrifice against an invincible foe."

Ibn Sallam turned his eyes away from the heart wrenching sight of his tribe vanishing forever into the sands of time.

"May God protect us from the folly of our own dreams."

And with that, he walked away, head bowed. Safiya could hear the mournful tune of an old Hebrew prayer on his lips, one commemorating the tragic destruction of the Temple on Tisha b'Au.

Safiya watched as the last of the camels left the precincts of the city, taking a proud people away from everything they knew. She gazed at the yellow walls of the fortress that had housed the Bani Qaynuqa for hundreds of years. Safiya knew that by nightfall the abandoned quarter would be looted, and the empty houses would soon be occupied by Muslim families. Within a few months every trace of the ancient Jewish tribe would be lost and forgotten.

She walked back home slowly, wondering how long it would be before she, too, would be forced to look forward, even when her heart cried like a child to go back, to cling to a past that was no more tangible than a mirage.

Her mother had said before she died that home is where the heart is. Safiya's heart had been made from the dust of Medina, and it deserved to return to the dust from which it had been born.

Safiya made a silent prayer to God, Elohim, Allah, Deus, or whatever it was He preferred to be called:

Even if you wish to take me away from this city, let it be that one day I will return. However the winds of history may blow, let them guide the ship of my destiny home. Lord of the Worlds, King of the Heavens, let me die where I have lived. Amen.

15

*W*hile the Muslims and Jews came close to war in Medina, the Meccan army was regrouping under the watchful eyes of Hind. History follows the deeds of men, but often ignores the women who influenced momentous events, for good or for ill. It is time for me, Abdallah, to reveal more about the queen of Mecca. Many know her terrible crimes, but few understand the woman who perpetrated them. It is not easy to descend into such dark depths. But I have seen a shameful hint of that darkness within myself, so perhaps it is only fitting that I do so for Hind.

Ever since their defeat at Badr, Hind had encouraged the Meccan soldiers to conduct regular drills to sharpen their skills. A second defeat was unthinkable, and Hind had promised that any man who sulked back home bearing the flag of loss would be torn to shreds by the women of city before he entered its holy precincts.

Not that she considered Mecca holy. Hind had long ago given up believing in any divine force, plural or singular. The last time she had prayed was when she was six years old. Her mother was dying of a terrible wasting disease, and Hind had watched in grief as her beautiful face had collapsed in on itself until all that was left was a skull barely covered by flesh. The night her father, Utbah, had told her that her mother was leaving them, she had run to the Kaaba. Having stolen the sacred key from her father's den, she had broken the ancient taboo and had climbed inside, falling prostrate before the crimson idol of Hubal. The little girl had stayed in that position until sunrise, her forehead pressed against the cold marble floor of the House. During that time, Hind had prayed to every god whose icon stood in the sanctuary, begging the deity to spare her mother. She had cried out to the daughters of God—Allat, Uzza, and Manat. The Phoenician goddess Astarte. Nergal, the angry god of war. The sun god Shams. Abgal, the lord of camel drivers. Munaf, the goddess of fertility. Aglibol, the Palmyran god of the crescent moon. The snake god Wadd. Qawm, the Nabatean protector of caravans. Even Isaf and Naila, the lovers who had defiled the Kaaba with their unbridled lust.

And finally, when she had named every god she knew and had heard no response, she had cried out to Allah, the High God who created the heavens and the earth before retiring to his Throne beyond the stars. Surely the One who had made the gods themselves, who had created life and death, surely He could save her mother.

But when the sun rose, Hind felt the gentle hand of her father, lifting her from her prostration. Her mother had passed away in her sleep, he said.

Hind had not wept. She had gone home and played with her dolls, apparently accepting the tragic news with the stoic dignity that was required of a great house of Quraysh.

But the tears that she did not release remained locked inside her, eating away at her heart like a worm at a corpse. The pain inside her breast became like a poison that ate away at her soul, building over the years until there was nothing left inside her but anger.

The gods had abandoned her. And so she abandoned them. A fair trade, all in all.

Over the years, Hind had never paid much attention to the stupid cult of her people, who continued to delude themselves that there was some higher order behind life. Hind had learned that night her mother died that there was no meaning, no purpose to existence. Love was an illusion, a painful trick of an uncaring cosmos. Joy a fleeting moment, lost in the wind. The only thing that was real was the body, for it alone felt pleasure and pain. So she concluded that the purpose of life, if there was any, was to heighten pleasure and deaden pain.

And thus her life had become an endless quest for ecstasy, for stretching the body's ability to experience pleasure to its limit. She surrounded herself with amusements to enhance her senses. The most harmonious music to delight her ears. The softest clothes to caress her skin. She had tasted every wine and every rare meat. And she had spent a lifetime exploring the forbidden pleasures of the flesh, with both men and women and with many partners, often at the same time. She had sworn an oath that if there were any pleasure to be plucked out of life, she would experience it all before the darkness took her and she remembered no more.

The gods of Mecca played no role in her life except as a source of income to support her sensual lifestyle. If there were any part of her that still believed in them after her mother died, it vanished two years later when her father invited a wandering *kahin*, a soothsayer who claimed to commune with the gods, to stay in their home and bless their family with his powers. The man had slipped into her bedroom one night, naked except for an armlet of gold shaped like intertwining snakes, the symbol of his sacred familiar. In his hand, the *kahin* held an ivory idol of some Yemeni fertility god whose name she never learned. He had told her to say nothing about what had happened, for it had been a sacred rite and a curse would fall upon her if she told anyone the mysteries of the god.

Spent from his "sacred rites," the man had slept beside her. The eight-year-old Hind had risen from her bed and crawled into the kitchen, ignoring the stream of blood that ran down her leg. She wordlessly pulled out the sharpest meat cleaver she could find and went back and slit the *kahin*'s throat without any hesitation. She then placed the Yemeni idol under her bare feet and crushed it, ignoring the shards of ivory that tore into her flesh. And then Hind had taken the *kahin*'s armlet, the symbol of his power, placed it on her own wrist, and climbed back into bed, falling into dreamless sleep beside the corpse.

Her father had found the "holy man's" naked body in her room the next day and had quietly buried him in their backyard. Utbah had never spoken about it with Hind, but no more *kahins* were invited to stay with them.

After that incident, she had never paid the gods or their self-appointed mouthpieces any attention.

Until Muhammad, the low-class merchant who had climbed into wealth by marrying a rich old woman, decided to enter the prophecy business. He spoke pretty words of poetry and the fools of Mecca were suddenly willing to give not only their wealth to him but also their very lives. Instead of embracing the only truth of life, the pursuit of pleasure, they adopted his austere teachings, denying themselves the good things and wandering around with empty stomachs and praises to an imaginary God on their lips.

This new religion was more sophisticated in its teaching than the nonsense her people believed, and that was exactly why it offended Hind even more. It was such a well-crafted tale that even intelligent men like Umar, men she had admired and exchanged pleasures with, had given up life in order to embrace its walking death. Islam was exactly the kind of delusion that men craved, with its promises of eternal life and cosmic justice, when neither state of affairs was true.

Hind hated Muhammad for giving false hope to people—a hope that made the strong weak and ensured that men would trade the pleasures of the moment for an illusory promise of reward beyond the grave. Hind had made it her mission in life to shatter this illusion, to take away the lie so that men and women could be free to embrace the world as it was, not as they wished it to be.

Since her father's death at Badr, Hind had been consumed with vengeance. She often accompanied her husband to military training exercises in the desert outside Mecca. Her eyes swept across the field in search of a champion, someone who could strike a blow for truth and reveal Muhammad for the sham he was.

She watched her husband calling out to the men, encouraging them as they practiced sparring with swords and thrusting with their spears.

"Train hard, O sons of Mecca! The day of retribution is coming."

The men responded to Abu Sufyan's cries by accelerating their moves, hoping to please the man who was for all intents and purposes their king. Hind had considered discarding her husband after the disaster of Badr, make his death appear to be an accident. But she realized now that she had been wise to restrain herself. She could see that Abu Sufyan held the soldiers' respect and was still useful to her. Still, she knew that he was old and she would need a more youthful body to advance her cause and please her body.

And then, quite unexpectedly, she saw him.

Hind's eyes fell upon a tall Abyssinian slave. He was as black as night and moved like a panther. In his hand, the slave held a powerful javelin, carved in accordance with the traditions of his people, who were masters of the art of spear throwing. He darted through a crowd of defenders, slipping between men like a snake winding through the rushes.

His eyes fell upon a target, a wooden pole that had been erected in the midst of the rocky field. The slave held the javelin to his shoulder and gracefully threw the weapon a hundred feet across the field. It landed straight in the heart of the pole and tore through to the other side.

Hind felt a swelling in her heart as well as in her loins. She walked over to the slave, and felt her desire growing as his skin shone with sweat and his musky odor flooded her senses.

"What is your name?" she asked.

"Wahsi," he said, panting for breath. "I belong to Jubayr ibn Mutim."

Hind smiled. Jubayr was her cousin and she knew him well. There had been a time when Hind had worried that he would defect to the Muslims after she learned that Abu Bakr, Muhammad's chief syco-phant, had proposed engaging his daughter Aisha to Jubayr. But the lustful Muhammad had decided to take the child for his own bed, and Jubayr had remained loyal to Mecca.

She stepped closer to Wahsi, put a hand on his powerful arm that was almost as thick as a tree.

"Do you know Hamza ibn Abd al-Muttalib?"

She spoke the name of her father's murderer with difficulty.

Wahsi looked uncomfortable, but he nodded.

"I know him," he said, then hesitated. "He was always kind to Bilal and myself."

Hind frowned. Bilal, the slave who had become Muhammad's chief singer, had killed his former owner, Umayya, at Badr. The bond between slaves in the city was as tight as brothers, and it was certainly possible that Wahsi's loyalty had been corrupted by the connection. She would have to gauge where his affinities truly lay.

"Would you consider Hamza a friend?"

Wahsi paused, measuring his words.

"To the extent that a slave and a free man can be friends, yes, I would."

That was disappointing, but not an insurmountable obstacle.

"Tell me, Wahsi, what is your freedom worth to you?"

Wahsi stepped back, his eyes looking over Hind carefully.

"I don't understand."

Hind moved again to his side. This time she let her hand touch his bare chest. She closed her eyes and felt the steady, powerful rhythm of his heart beating against her fingers.

"Is earning your freedom something you would risk your life for?"

"Yes," he said, without any hesitation.

She opened her eyes and looked deeply into his black pupils.

"Is it something you would kill for?"

His eyes narrowed but he did not look away.

"Yes."

Hind smiled and caressed his flesh. The muscles of his abdomen were hard and well defined. She could feel her thighs growing wet, and the salty aroma of her arousal filled the air between them.

"No doubt. But is your freedom so precious that you would kill a friend to secure it?"

Wahsi hesitated for a moment. And then he lifted his shoulders proudly.

"If that is the price for the key to my chains, then yes."

Hind squeezed his forearm, let the tip of her fingernail nick his skin, drawing blood. Wahsi stood impassive as she brought her finger to her lips and sucked the tiny drop of his life fluid into her mouth.

"I will speak to my cousin Jubayr," she said in a husky voice. "He will give you a furlough for the evening. Come to my house tonight. There is much to discuss."

◆　　◆　　◆

AND SO HIND FOUND at last a champion for her revenge. A vengeance that would prove far uglier than any of us could ever have imagined.

You may wonder, dear Abdallah, why I take the time to detail her role in these events. She was a monster, you say, unworthy of being recorded in the annals of our faith. And perhaps you are right. Her crimes have justly earned her the condemnation of history. Hind was indeed cruel, vindictive, and manipulative. And yet she was also more than that. Strong. Proud. Passionate. A woman who refused to let the world conquer her. A woman who could have done so much good had the wound in her heart been healed with the balm of love. And despite my hatred for her memory, I sorrow for the child that still lived within her. A little girl on her knees, crying out to the heavens for her mother. A cry that was met with silence.

16

*J*rested my thighs on our lambskin mattress as the Messenger placed his head in my lap, as he often did when he was having difficulty relaxing after a long day. I ran my fingers through his mass of black curls that had begun to gray in a few patches. He looked up at me with a familiar twinkle in his eye and I sensed that he wanted me. The Messenger had been so exhausted in recent weeks that we rarely made love. The crushing burden of his daily life as prophet and statesman had made him too tired to meet even his personal needs as a man. Every minute of his waking hours was spent either teaching, judging disputes, enforcing new laws that God revealed in the Qur'an, or leading raids against Meccan caravans. The Messenger would come home tired and fall asleep in my arms almost instantly.

I missed our nights of intimacy, the powerful warmth of his body entwined with mine. And I longed to give him a son. We had been married now for almost three years and my courses had continued unabated. I prayed every night for the Lord to quicken my womb, but my supplications had remained unanswered.

I moved to blow out the single candle that adorned the room, as my husband was exceedingly modest and shared intimacies only under the cover of darkness. And then I heard a furious hammering at the door and Umar's booming voice calling out for the Messenger. My husband sighed, and I could sense his desire cooling. At that moment, I wanted to grab Umar by the beard and slap him, but instead I went to a corner, sullenly covering my hair as the Prophet opened the door and let the raving giant in.

"O Messenger of God, the honor of my house has been sullied!" he said dramatically.

"What is wrong?" The Messenger's tone was polite but tired.

Umar noticed me sitting in a corner, glaring at him. He suddenly appeared uncomfortable and looked down at his huge feet without speaking further.

My husband turned to me with a sympathetic grin.

"Aisha, please leave us."

I nodded glumly and stepped outside into the courtyard. The Messenger closed the door behind me. Unable to suppress the curiosity that is both my gift and my curse, I pressed my ear to the door, made of thin palm wood, and listened in to his conversation with one of his most trusted advisers.

"As you know, my daughter Hafsa is a widow," Umar said, speaking rapidly. "I approached Uthman ibn Affan with an honorable offer to marry her. And he refused!"

I smiled. Of course Uthman had refused. Hafsa was a beautiful girl, but her temper was as volatile as her father's and no man who valued peace of mind would take her.

"Uthman is still grieving for Ruqayya," the Messenger said diplomatically. "Do not take it to heart."

He did not mention what he had said to me in private, of his intention of marrying one of his younger daughters, Umm Kulthum, to Uthman. That bit of news might not go over well with Umar.

"Be that as it may, and yet I suffered a second indignity," Umar rambled on. "I went to Abu Bakr and offered him Hafsa's hand and he, too, refused! I thought he was my best friend, but he has left me in shame."

I tried hard not to giggle. The idea of my elderly father marrying this twenty-year-old firebrand was beyond comical. His heart would give out on the wedding night, not from Hafsa's passion but from her ceaseless nagging.

"Abu Bakr loves Umm Ruman very deeply. He could not share his heart with another." My husband, as always, knew exactly the right words to say.

"Be that as it may, and yet I am ruined!" Umar said, panic filling his voice. "Even now the gossips are spreading vile stories in Medina. The rumor that Hafsa has been refused by the greatest men of Islam because she is ill-tempered and mean! How could they say such a preposterous thing?"

I trembled with laughter and had to bite my hand to keep from revealing my eavesdropping presence.

"It is best to ignore the slanders of misguided folk," the Messenger said mildly. "Allah will bring them to account. Gossips and backbiters will eat the flesh of their dead brothers on Judgment Day."

It was a vivid image, but one that did not appease Umar.

"I cannot wait until Judgment Day, O Messenger of God! My daughter's honor has been soiled today! No man will marry her once they learn that Uthman and Abu Bakr have rejected her!"

"Have faith, Umar." I could hear the exhaustion entering the Messenger's voice as his efforts to mollify Umar only made him more agitated.

"I have faith in God, but not in the fickle cruelty of men," Umar said, his voice trembling. "In the days before Islam, I would have challenged Uthman and Abu Bakr to a duel. But now they are my brothers and I will not shed their blood. So I have no choice."

"No choice?" Now I could hear alarm in Muhammad's tone.

"I must leave Medina and take Hafsa with me," Umar explained. "I must go where she can escape the shame and rebuild her life."

Umar paused a moment and then I could hear new excitement entering his voice.

"O Messenger of God, deputize me so that I may serve as your envoy to the disbelievers! To Syria or Persia. Send me to share the Word of God in these foreign lands!"

I could hear my husband clap Umar on the shoulder in support.

"A day shall come when you will go to these lands, Umar, but not as an envoy. *Insha-Allah,* you will enter them as a conqueror."

If the Messenger had meant these grand tidings to lift Umar's soul, his efforts were unsuccessful.

"Then what am I to do? I cannot stay in Medina as long as my family's honor is stained."

There was a long silence and I finally felt the humor of the situation vanishing, replaced with a troubling problem for the community. Umar was a powerful leader who was feared and respected by both friend and enemy alike. If he left the oasis, it would create a power vacuum that would encourage our enemies to make aggressive moves against Medina. I knew that my husband was thinking of a solution to put Umar's mind off his daughter's marital difficulty and keep him focused on protecting the nascent city-state.

"Now I must reveal to you the truth," the Messenger said at long last. "Do not judge Uthman or Abu Bakr harshly. They were acting on my orders."

This was unexpected. I leaned closer to hear better and almost pushed the door open.

"I don't understand." Umar's voice was both confused and hurt.

"When you approached Uthman with the proposal, he came to me and I told him to say no. As did Abu Bakr."

Umar was clearly shocked at this revelation.

"O Messenger of God, why?"

I was eager to hear the answer myself. My husband's natural statesmanship was at work here, and I was always fascinated by his ability to make wise decisions that benefited everyone.

"It is because Hafsa is special. She has been chosen for a higher purpose."

Suddenly I didn't like where this was going.

I heard Umar rise to his feet, his powerful legs creaking like the hinges of a giant fortress gate.

"Are you saying . . . ?"

All at once my heart was racing and I wanted to run back inside and prevent my husband from finishing this conversation. But my legs were frozen to the spot.

"Yes. It is my desire to marry Hafsa and make her a Mother of the Believers. If her father will permit it."

The blood drained from my face. I was suddenly dizzy and I could taste bile in my throat.

"Allah be praised!" Umar shouted wildly. "I would give you my daughter and anything else that you asked!"

I could hear the rustle of robes as Umar gave the Messenger an embrace that would have crushed a lesser man. The two spoke more words, but I did care to listen further.

My heart pounded with jealousy. The Messenger loved me! How could he marry another woman, even as a political maneuver? Suddenly I had a vision of my beloved Muhammad entwined in passion with the beautiful Hafsa, and I felt rage burning inside my soul.

I turned and ran out of the courtyard to my mother's house, where I spent the rest of the night crying in her arms.

17

I watched tight-lipped as a group of workers built another small stone apartment just north of my cell in the Masjid courtyard. They were working quickly, as the Prophet's marriage to Hafsa was set for a week from that day, and they wanted to be finished in time for the mud cement to dry. No one wanted to be responsible for the Messenger of God spending his wedding night in a room that smelled like a tar pit after a flash flood.

I looked at that room and saw again an image of my husband in the arms of another woman and I could feel icy claws closing in on my throat. And then, as if she had read my thoughts, the proud Hafsa stepped inside the courtyard, taking off her dainty thong slippers and storming over to inspect her new home.

I stepped into the shadows of my doorway and hoped she didn't see me. The last thing I wanted to do was exchange pleasantries with this pretty girl with the curly black hair who would soon be sharing the Messenger's bed.

As it turned out, she was so focused on her own concerns that she was unlikely to have noticed me had I stood in front of her naked. Her eyes went wide when she saw the state of disarray around her future home, and she immediately began to berate the poor builders.

"What shoddy workmanship is this!" Hafsa shouted in a husky voice that sounded remarkably like her father's. "No, I don't want a window looking to the back wall! I am to be a Mother of the Believers! My window must face the courtyard!"

The harried workers endured her foot-stomping harangue with weary obsequiousness. Hafsa was not as tall as Umar, but she had broad, mannish shoulders that made her unmistakably his child. Her eyes were light brown, as was her unblemished skin. She had ample curves and wide hips and I felt a flash of terror as I realized that her body was better suited than my own thin frame for carrying a child. If she bore the Prophet a son before I did, then she would likely become his primary consort and my hold over his heart might become as brittle as a rusted lock that shatters under the heavy wind.

"Do not fear, Aisha," a soft voice beside me intoned. "You will always be his favorite."

It was my elderly sister-wife, Sawda, who had read my eyes with the wisdom of a woman who remembers the follies of youth. I smiled at her gratefully, but an ungenerous thought flashed across my mind. Her face was wrinkled and her breasts sagging, and her courses had long since dried up. It was easy for her to speak so confidently, since she shared the Messenger's bed without passion and could never provide him a child. If Muhammad's heart turned to Hafsa, it would make no difference to Sawda's status in the household.

It was a nasty thought, cruel and mean-spirited, and I tried (without complete success) to banish it from my mind.

"What kind of wood is this?" Hafsa shouted, and my thoughts fled under the force of her cry. I looked up to see that she was yelling at the foreman of the workers, a burly man who was almost as tall as her father. "Do you want the roof to fall down on the Messenger when he is in bed?"

The heavily muscled foreman looked as if he wanted to say something unkind to this twenty-year-old girl who was acting like the queen of Arabia. But he bit his lip and restrained himself. At that moment, the Messenger entered the courtyard and the foreman gave him a pleading glance for intervention.

My husband walked up beside Hafsa. I saw him take a deep breath as if he were girding himself for battle. But before he could calm his bride-to-be, his eyes fell on me, standing in the threshold of my tiny room, and he smiled warmly. My heart felt as if it would burst, and I had to stop myself from running into his arms, telling him that I was the only one who could ever truly give him happiness. But something in the way his eyes lit up told me that I didn't need to. That he already knew.

— • —

THE MESSENGER WAS MARRIED to Hafsa in a grand ceremony to which all the leaders of Medina were invited, including the Jewish chieftains, who sent presents of gold and spices but did not attend in person.

Watching the Messenger unite with Hafsa in front of a gathering of honored nobles, the bride dressed in a silk gown of scarlet, I felt a new pang of sadness. A sense of my own smallness came to me. My own wedding had been an exceedingly modest affair and I felt as if I had been cheated out of the pomp and circumstance that was being showered upon the daughter of Umar.

I murmured a complaint to my mother, who gave me a sharp look of reproach.

"This is a political marriage meant to keep Umar happy and the Muslims united," Umm Ruman said in a hurried whisper. "But your wedding was ordained by God and reflected the Messenger's heart, not his needs as a leader. Be grateful."

Of course she was right. But at that moment I didn't care. I got up and stormed off in indignation. I exited the colorful pavilion that had been erected in the marketplace, past a line of beggars who had come seeking alms from the Messenger on this momentous occasion. I hugged my scarf closer to my chest, hoping that it would warm the chill I felt despite the dry heat of the night.

I strode out of the bazaar, walking without purpose or direction. And then I stopped in my tracks as my eyes fell on a young woman leaning against a crumbling wall, staring quietly at the stars.

It was the Prophet's daughter Fatima. I suddenly realized that I hadn't seen her inside the pavilion with her sisters, Zaynab and Umm Kulthum, and wondered why she was not with her father celebrating his marriage. And then I thought that the fact that she was two years older than her father's new bride, Hafsa, and yet had no suitors, must have weighed heavily on her.

Fatima seemed lost in a dream and did not react to the approach of my footsteps. I should have turned away and left her to her thoughts, but I felt drawn to her that night for reasons I could not voice. Fatima had always been so ethereal that she seemed like a spirit more than a creature of flesh and blood, and there was something about her that unnerved me. And yet she was my husband's favorite child, and perhaps I felt a connection to her because I was his favorite wife—a status that I fervently hoped to retain after the Messenger spent the night with his new bride. Along with being older and possessing a more mature body, Hafsa had already been married once and was presumably experienced in the arts of love. My stomach curled at that thought and I forced it out of my heart as I slid in beside Fatima.

The girl looked at me with a ghostly smile, and then turned her attention back to the stars. The Milky Way ran like a vast caravan route through the heavens, and I saw that her attention was focused on the constellation of the *al-Jabbar*, the Giant, that hung low in the night sky. I stared up at the three stars that formed his belt and caught from the corner of my eye a glimmer of the tiny lights that formed his scabbard. But whenever I looked directly at them, they vanished, like djinn in the desert.

The silence between us grew uncomfortable and I groped for something that might spark a conversation.

"So . . . do you still think you'll never marry?" I winced even as I said these words, but it was too late to take them back.

Fatima looked at me and I saw her black eyes suddenly focus as if she recognized me for the first time.

"No. I will actually be married soon, *insha-Allah*."

This was news to me.

"You have chosen someone, then?" I tried unsuccessfully to keep the disbelief out of my voice.

Fatima shrugged and looked back up at the stars.

"No. He was chosen for me."

Now, this was definitely surprising. My heart sank at the thought that the Messenger had not shared his plans for his beloved daughter with me. I wondered if he had told Sawda. Or worse, Hafsa.

"By your father?" I asked, my voice sounding squeaky like a mouse.

"No. By God."

And with those strange words, the mysterious girl smiled sadly and gazed back up to the heavens. I looked down at my hands and pondered her words for a moment. When I turned to ask her what she meant, the hair on my neck stood up. The street was empty. Fatima had vanished.

18

The Messenger consummated his marriage that night with Hafsa, to her quite vocal satisfaction. I covered my ears with a rough leather pillow, but her throaty cries wafted through the thin mud walls between our apartments, adding to my misery.

A few days later, while I was still raw from the addition of this spirited girl to the harem, a second wedding was held. Fatima, I learned, was to marry Ali, and somehow that felt right. They were both strange, otherworldly creatures and their union felt almost destined.

The ceremony was not as grandiose as Hafsa's nuptials, but there was a great dignity to the event. I felt an inexplicable solemnity to the wedding, as if this were something momentous in the history of the world rather than the union of two poor misfits who were lucky to find each other.

The Messenger was solemn and quiet as Ali and Fatima sat before him. The groom was dressed in a simple robe of black, his green eyes sparkling in vivid contrast. Fatima wore a russet gown, her face completely covered by a thin veil. Only a few intimates were invited, the heart of Muhammad's family—his wives and daughters, Uthman the widowed son-in-law, and the Messenger's two fathers-in-law, Abu Bakr and Umar. I was delighted to see Talha there, and my sister, Asma's, eyes never left Zubayr, who had finally emigrated to Medina with a promise to marry her and end her spinsterhood.

Ali and Fatima signed the wedding contract and we all raised our hands to pray the *Fatiha*, as was customary. Normally the ceremony was completed with the supplication, but the Prophet did something unusual that night that I never saw before or again.

The Messenger of God raised a small bowl of carved acacia wood and poured it full of clear water from an earthen jug. He then rinsed his mouth with the liquid and spit the water back into the bowl and it seemed to sparkle as if he had cast diamonds into the bowl. And then Muhammad took the water and sprinkled it on Ali and Fatima, and the strange shimmer seemed now to emanate from then. Finally, my husband reached for a small glass vial of olive oil and touched it to his fingers before anointing Ali's forehead. He then reached inside his daughter's veil and did the same to her. It felt as if he was anointing them king and queen, as the prophets of Israel were said to do with their regal charges in days long past.

"May God bless you and your descendants," he said with a look that somehow managed to combine joy and sorrow at once.

The whole ceremony seemed appropriately ethereal for this enigmatic couple and I was glad when the Prophet rose and kissed them, signaling that we had returned to the world I knew and understood.

The women took hold of Fatima's hand and with the usual giggles and knowing glances led her to the adjoining bedchamber, where a sheepskin mattress similar to my own was laid out on the stone floor.

As I adjusted Fatima's veil, which had shifted awkwardly as we moved her, I saw that her eyes were filled with tears and her mouth was a solid line.

"Smile!" I said with a wide grin of my own, hoping to lift her inexplicable gloom. "This is the most important night of a woman's life."

Fatima looked at me as if seeing me, truly seeing me, for the first time. And then she said words that I would never have expected.

"I wish I could be like you, Aisha."

"Why?" I asked, sincerely surprised.

"You live your life freely, embracing every moment," she said softly. "You are not troubled by the past. Or the future."

It was a strange comment from a strange girl, and I responded as best as I knew how.

"My father says that the past is like a dream from which one has awakened. Why look back on it? And the future is like a mirage in the desert. We keep racing after it, and it keeps running away from us."

I was startled at my own words, which had a flourish of poetry that I had not realized was in me.

Fatima smiled sadly, and there was something so tragic in her look that I felt my heart break.

"And yet sometimes the mirage runs toward us," she said. "And then we see it is made not of water but of fiery sand, sweeping away everything we love into the wind."

I looked at her, confused, even frightened. And then the women ushered me out as Ali entered the room, his green eyes as distant and unreadable as ever.

19 Mountain of Uhud—March 23, AD 625

The day of reckoning came at last, and war was upon us. The Meccans had come to avenge the dead of Badr and destroy Medina. It was the first day of spring and the sparrows sang from the palm trees as our soldiers marched out to defend the oasis from the invaders. Abu Sufyan led a force of three thousand men and three hundred horses, while we were able to put together only seven hundred Muslims, along with three hundred tribesmen allied to the shadowy Ibn Ubayy. Despite the overwhelming superiority of our adversary's numbers, the Muslims remained confident. After all, we had seen the miracle of Badr, where we had defeated an army three times our size.

And there had been a special sign of favor in the days just before the battle. The Messenger's daughter Fatima had given birth to a son, a chubby and smiling little boy named Hasan. The Prophet's own infant sons from his marriage with Khadija had died many years before and Hasan was now the only living male heir to the Messenger of God. His birth had come after a difficult pregnancy during which Fatima had spent weeks confined to her bed. The old women of Medina had begun to whisper sadly that the Prophet's daughter was not strong enough to carry the child to term, and my husband's face had become increasingly bleak and despairing in the days before her labor had set in.

But then, as if God had decided that the poor girl had suffered enough, Fatima's pains vanished and she easily gave birth to the plump, curly-haired boy. The successful delivery of the Prophet's heir represented a clear sign of hope for our *Ummah*. None of the Mothers had borne the Messenger any children, a fact that was the source of my greatest personal sorrow. But I took some comfort in the knowledge that if Hasan lived past the difficult weaning years, when most children succumbed to the cruelties of the desert, he would carry in him the sacred blood of the Messenger and ensure the survival of Muhammad's family. The fact that Hasan was Ali's son had instantly pushed the strange young man to even greater prominence in the community, a reality that was greeted with some bemusement by the elders among the Muslims.

But now all rivalries were set aside, for the enemy was at the gates of the oasis. The two hosts met on a valley just beyond a craggy volcanic mountain called Uhud, where the Messenger made camp and awaited Ibn Ubayy's reinforcements. I sat beside my husband as he looked down from the heights to the plain below. The Meccan forces were like shiny beetles, their mail coats glinting up at us in defiance. With my falcon's gaze, I could see the cavalry being led by a powerful, chiseled face man I recognized as the great Khalid ibn al-Waleed. He raised the visor of his helmet and scanned the battlefield, his eyes expertly following the curvature of the mountain, searching for any weak points in our defenses.

As I looked down at the Meccan camp, with its red, purple, and blue flags bringing color to the dead valley, I remembered how similar the scene was to the one I had witnessed a year before. Except that the enemy had tripled its forces and was motivated by vengeance rather than hubris.

If they succeeded, we all would be dead. And if they failed, they would be back again next year, with a larger force and a greater hunger for vengeance. It was as if every victory the Muslims secured only placed them on a new and more dangerous battlefield.

I sighed wearily and put a hand on my husband's arm, more for my own comfort than his.

"Will there ever be peace, my love?"

"Yes. In Paradise," he responded wistfully. "This world was born in war, and will one day perish in it."

His fingers tightened around mine and I could feel the calluses on his hand from the many months of manual labor that had been required to build walls and strengthen Medina's defenses. Muhammad could have absented himself from bricklaying as the chieftain of the oasis, but my husband understood the power of a leader who joined his men in doing the most mundane tasks. It created a bond of trust and loyalty whose true value could be proven only on a day like this.

I heard the steady crunch of rocks as heavy boots struck on the mountainside. I glanced over to see Umar, his massive body covered in rings of armor, race up toward our position. His face was contorted in rage.

"We have been betrayed! Ibn Ubayy has taken his men and turned back!"

My husband nodded grimly. Perhaps he had expected this possibility. Ibn Ubayy had thought the idea of confronting the Meccan force to be suicide and had argued that we should hide in our homes. Medina, with its winding streets layered with palm trees, would not be easily taken unless the Meccans wished to fight alley by alley, house by house.

But the Messenger had decided that allowing Mecca to cross the borders of the city, where they could wreak long-term havoc by burning our crops and poisoning our wells, was too dangerous. The Muslims had to cut the Meccan advance here. Apparently Ibn Ubayy did not agree and had chosen to abandon us even as the wolf pounced on our doorstep.

"Allah will protect us as long as we remain united," he said calmly, but I could hear the edge in his voice. Even if angels came to help us as they had done at Badr, seven hundred versus three thousand presented unfavorable odds. If we were to hold back the Meccan line, there was no room for the slightest deviation in our strategy.

The sudden thunder of hooves echoed from the valley below, and I saw Khalid lead his horsemen toward a tiny pass at the base of the mountain. The Prophet raised his right fist and Talha grabbed a black flag and twirled it. The sign was seen by a group of archers hidden in a ridge to the east of our position and a volley of arrows suddenly rained down on the Meccan cavalry. The horses reared in surprise and Khalid pulled his men back, his eyes scanning the mountain until he located the source of the projectiles. The cavalry did not retreat to the Meccan camp but held position just outside the range of our arrows.

The Messenger rose and shouted across the hill, his voice echoing to the archers.

"Hold your positions," he cried. "You are the vanguard of the Muslims. Do not lower your bows until I command you!"

The archers nodded and I felt a stirring of hope. As long as they remained in place, Khalid would be unable to ride through the pass and attack our forces from the rear. The Muslims held the benefit of high ground, which somewhat mitigated the Meccan advantage in numbers.

The rumble of drums caused my eyes to flash back to the Meccan camp. As one figure moved forward and I recognized the scarlet-and-gold turban.

"O men of Aws and Khazraj!" Abu Sufyan called out. "Quit the field now and leave my cousin to me. Once we have killed this trouble-maker, Mecca will leave your lands. We have no fight with you!"

Perhaps his offer would have carried weight three years before, when the people of Medina had still seen one another as members of one tribe or the other. But since we had arrived, I heard less and less the mention of these ancient clans as the citizens began to think of themselves first and foremost as Muslims. As if reading my thoughts, the leaders of the Aws and Khazraj responded to Abu Sufyan's chal-lenge with a unified thunder of war drums.

"So be it." Abu Sufyan nodded, as if he had expected this response. As the leader of Mecca turned back to his people, I heard the rattle of timbrels and a familiar sensual voice rose up from the camp, sending shivers down my spine.

It was Hind, leading a group of women in a dance around the sol-diers. They were dressed in tight-fitting tunics and skirts cut high to reveal flashes of their thighs as they whirled and chanted, arousing the lust of their men, a fire that would soon be stoked to white-hot rage.

"Advance and we embrace you, and soft carpets spread," they sang in throaty voices, like lovers crying out at the height of passion. "But turn your backs and we leave you. Leave you and never love you."

It was an ancient verse, sung by women of every generation to goad their men to battle. And I could see its power. The Meccan soldiers clashed their swords to shields and bared their teeth like wolves as Hind ignited their loins and their hearts to a frenzy.

Watching Hind, I was both fascinated and repelled by her power. There was something both beautifully feminine and ruthlessly feral about her. I wanted to run from Hind, and at the same time I wanted to learn from her all the terrible secrets she held, the secrets of women's power over men.

As Hind crouched and spun to the thrumming beat of the women's timbrels, I saw Hamza step forward, watching her. And then Hind saw him, recognized the ostrich feather he always proudly wore on his hel-met, and bared her teeth in what could have been a smile or a snarl. Or both at once, if that were possible.

"That woman is the devil," Hamza said, his eyes focused on her sensuous, swaying form. Bilal stood beside him, his eyes poring over the front lines of the enemy forces.

"They have even brought their slaves today," he said with clear regret. "I see Wahsi, my friend."

Hamza placed a comforting hand on the shorter man's shoulder.

"There are no friends on the battlefield, Bilal," he said without hesitation, but I could hear the compassion in his voice. "If you face him in the heat of war, do what you must."

Bilal nodded sadly. And then the thunder of drums stopped. The women fled from the front lines and disappeared into the Meccan camp as the true dance of death began. As at Badr, the Meccans sent forth a champion, a young man I did not recognize but who strode onto the field proudly, jeering confidently at his opponents. He swung his mighty sword and twirled it like the African fire-eaters I had seen perform when a caravan from Abyssinia stopped at Mecca years before. It was a powerful show, meant to mock and terrify the Muslims at the same time.

The Prophet dispatched Ali, who strode out onto the battlefield, his dual-bladed sword, *Dhul Fiqar,* glowing in the sunlight. And then, without any words or performance, Ali struck out and in one blow tore through the Meccan champion's breastplate. The man fell over dead, the mocking smile still frozen on his lips. I heard a horrified cry, and another man, who distinctly resembled the thin-faced champion, rushed out onto the battlefield. This second warrior, almost definitely the brother of the first, ran after Ali, who was facing away from the attacker. And then Hamza charged out onto the plain and hacked the brother to death with his terrifying broadsword before he could stab Ali in the back.

Silence fell over the battlefield as both sides stared in shock at this duel that had lasted no more than a half a minute. It was such a similar moment to what I'd seen at Badr that I had that strange feeling that sometimes comes when the veil of time is tangled and past and present become one. The Meccans must have felt the same, because the sight of their most feared champions struck down again like unarmed children sent a wave of rage and fear through the enemy camp.

And then, without further ceremony, the warriors of Mecca charged.

This time no cloud of dust arose to block my view of the battle, nor did I witness any ghostly riders come to our aid. What I saw beneath me was raw and brutal and would forever haunt my memory.

The Meccans flew at our men with unbridled savagery. Their swords flashed red as the sun reflected off the volcanic rock and soon the ancient stones were splattered with a darker shade of crimson. The clash of blades against shields was deafening, as if a thousand bolts of lightning had struck at the base of Uhud, the thunder reverberating with such painful force that I covered my ears with tightly clenched fists.

Wave upon wave, they came upon us like an ocean of metal racing to flood the valley with death. And yet the Muslims held their ground. We had the protection of the mountain, and even as our front lines held up their shields to the unrelenting onslaught, those behind them rained spears and arrows upon the attackers.

I heard screams everywhere—the cries of pain and triumph, as well as the whimpers of the dying. To my surprise, many of the mortally wounded who had only moments before fought with such animal ferocity now became like little children, crying out for their mothers as the horror of death came upon them. It was that desperate weeping that shocked me more than anything else I witnessed that day, and suddenly the curtain of glory was stripped away and war was presented in it naked ugliness. As the smell of gore and entrails wafted up to me, I looked away, trying to hide the tears that were welling in my eyes. Tears for an enemy that would have no qualm slicing my body to shreds should any escape death and penetrate our defenses. It made no sense and I felt shame and disgust and horror all at once.

Despite my best efforts to hide my conflicted feelings, the Messenger saw the grief on my face and nodded. He understood.

I forced myself to look, to watch this deadly massacre that was unfolding only fifty feet away from me. I saw Hamza tear through the front lines, his ostrich feather splattered with grime and human remains as he cut down men with the ease of a farmer using a sickle on shafts of grain.

And then suddenly the Muslim defense became an offense. With Hamza in the lead, our warriors began to push through, forcing the Meccans to give ground and tumble back toward their camp in disarray. The reversal of momentum only increased the courage of our forces and the confusion of the enemy, and suddenly the Muslims were streaming across the battlefield and the Meccans desperately seeking to stave off our advance. I heard cries of joy as the stalemate broke and the advantage went to the followers of Muhammad. Despite my own complicated feelings at the sight of the dreadful slaughter, I called out to the warriors, even as Hind had encouraged her own men to fight.

"Victory is within your grasp, my sons!" I cried out, unsure and uncaring whether they could hear me over the din of battle. As a twelve-year-old girl, I always felt awkward referring to grown men as my children. But it somehow felt right at this moment. I saw Talha look down at me and wink, and I flashed him a smile that made color rise to his cheeks.

And then I felt the Messenger stiffen. I thought perhaps I had done wrong by calling out to the troops as Hind had done, but when I looked at my husband, I saw that he was paying no attention to me. His eyes were on the battlefield as the Muslims advanced near the Meccan camp at the other end of the valley.

I strained my eyes to see the source of his consternation. As the armies battled like raging ants below, I saw one figure who stood out distinctly in the chaos. Tall, black, and unarmored, he moved like a bird, flitting through the madness without engaging in combat. It was the slave Wahsi, whom Bilal had sorrowed over, and I saw that he was unarmed except for a long javelin that he held like a third arm.

Down on the battlefield, Hamza was striking down his opponents like a living tornado. He struck off the head of one unlucky warrior and then spun and sliced off the arm of a second, who had tried to stab him from behind. Wherever Hamza went, howls of pain erupted and were quickly silenced.

And then the Prophet's uncle stopped in the middle of a swing of his blade, his head raised as if he had heard something distinct in the midst of that horrible cacophony. He suddenly turned to his left and the jumble of warriors all around him parted for an instant, like the waters under the staff of Moses. And across that gap, less than thirty feet away, stood Wahsi.

And then Wahsi threw his javelin, which flew across the plain faster than my eye could see. In one instant, it was in the black slave's powerful grasp. And then a moment later, I saw it tear through Hamza's abdomen and explode out through the small of his back.

I heard the Messenger sob next to me, but I could not look at him. I was transfixed at the sight of this mighty warrior, standing with absolute dignity as a river of blood poured out of his wound. And then this mountain of a man fell, and my heart crumpled with him.

A shocked silence seemed to descend over the battlefield as soldiers on both sides stared at Hamza's corpse. And then I heard something that made my blood chill. It was the terrifying laughter of Hind and it seemed to echo from every stone in the valley.

But it was laughter that was cut short. For the sight of their commander dead on the field only filled the Muslims with fury. And then, as if Hamza in death had given a share of his lion's heart to each man present, the Muslims charged with renewed passion. There was a frenzy in them that was terrifying. The Meccan forces were unable to defend against this rage and I saw the front lines of our advance break through until the Muslims were swarming the heart of the Meccan camp, dealing out death like children swatting flies.

"Retreat!" Abu Sufyan's despairing and humiliated cry rang out through the valley even as Hind's bloodlust had echoed only minutes before. I saw the Meccan shields shatter and the mighty warriors flee for the security of a mountain pass that would facilitate their escape.

I looked at the Messenger, whose cheeks were stained with tears. Hamza had been his uncle, but they were of similar age and their bond had always been more like that of brothers. Hamza had helped fill the heart of a boy whose mother and father had left him an orphan without any other siblings. I took my husband's hand and squeezed it, and he nodded gratefully.

The Muslims had won the Battle of Uhud even as they had won Badr. But each time there was a terrible price for Muhammad personally, the price of blood that God exacted on him and his family. First Ruqayya and now Hamza. For a man who hated fighting, whose message had always been one of peace, it was as if the cosmos were seeking to ensure that his heart would never become hard to the horror of warfare. Many kings thought of their soldiers as expendable, their deaths on the battlefield no more meaningful than a hill of ants crushed by a passing chariot wheel. But for the Messenger of God, war would always be personal, and the cost would have to be borne by those he loved the most.

Still, the victory was a remarkable one, which made Badr look like a small skirmish. Now the legend of the Muslims would spread throughout the desert and more tribes would join us in alliance. A victory of this magnitude would change the history of Arabia forever. And perhaps it would not be long before the Muslims would lay siege to Mecca and liberate the Sanctuary. And then the war would end and all Arabia would become Muslim.

I tried to think like a man, forcing my reason to subdue my raging grief. I told myself that it was a victory that was worth the terrible cost. But that same day I learned that victory should not be counted until the last man has fled the battlefield.

20

The archers positioned at the eastern ridge of Uhud watched with delight as the Muslims ravaged the Meccan camp, tearing its haughty pavilions to shreds and grabbing weapons and gold dropped by the fleeing pagans. The men cheered as the battle thundered toward its conclusion.

A young archer named Madani threw down his bow and began to climb down the hillside, gesturing excitedly to his colleagues.

"Let's go, or we'll lose our share of the booty!"

Their hearts wild with joy, the archers began to climb after the youth. But their commander, a short Aws tribesman named Safi who could shoot a rabbit a hundred feet away, signaled to his men to halt.

"Hold your positions! The Messenger has not relieved us!"

"No need! The battle's over!" Madani's voice was followed by a loud cheer from his friends as they tore down the mountainside and broke into a run toward the besieged Meccan camp.

Safi stared after them, despairing. He turned to look at the Prophet's base camp across the hillside and saw that Messenger was standing, his face filled with alarm.

"No! Turn back!" The Prophet's voice thundered across the ridge. And then the horsemen under Khalid's command emerged from the shadows at the base of the mountain and rode like lightning toward the tiny pass that would allow them to attack the Muslims from the rear.

Safi fell to his knees in horror, shame and guilt tearing through him at his failure to enforce discipline. Khalid rode up right behind the poor Madani, whose youthful laughter was cut short by one blow from the mighty warrior's blade. The other archers who had broken ranks were either slain or fled in terror at the sight of the Meccan cavalry that their shortsightedness had now unleashed on the Muslim army.

— — —

I COVERED MY MOUTH in horror as I witnessed Khalid's horsemen ride up in a cloud of red dust to strike at our men from behind. There were shouts of confusion that quickly turned to screams of agony as Khalid expertly cut down the surprised Muslims. And then I felt the ground around me shake as the men who surrounded the Messenger raced down the face of Uhud to help their fallen comrades. But they were now trapped between the Meccan army to the south and the cavalry that rode down to them from the north, like mollusks caught between the crushing pincers of a giant crab.

In a matter of seconds everything had changed. A clear victory was beginning to look like a horrific defeat.

And then I saw a cloud of dust heading in our direction and I realized that some of the cavalry had broken off their rearguard assault when they realized that the Prophet's base camp was relatively undefended. My heart flew into my throat as I saw a group of warriors racing toward us, spears drawn.

The few Muslims who remained at the camp included women who had accompanied their husbands to the battlefield and were now in danger of being swept into the heart of battle. Talha leaped to his feet to protect us, as did my elderly father. They were only half a dozen men, but they quickly formed a circle around the Messenger. And then I saw the women grab discarded bows and fire upon the onrushing cavalry. The unexpected rain of arrows from these courageous ladies surprised the horsemen and slowed their advance.

But slowing the cavalry was like trying to dam a raging river. One of the horsemen bravely rode through the wave of oncoming missiles and approached the edge of our camp. His sword was raised in challenge, and the sun illuminated his familiar face. And my heart forgot to beat.

It was my brother Abdal Kaaba, my father's eldest son, who had rejected Islam and his family. And now he was bearing down upon us with deadly hate in his eyes.

"Who has the courage to face me?" he bellowed. The sun was in his eyes and I was unsure whether he recognized the people he threatened, his own flesh and blood. And then I saw my father move faster than I could have imagined possible for a man of his age. Abu Bakr's sword was drawn and he moved to face his son in a deadly duel. I wanted to scream for this nightmare to end, for me to wake up in my small apartment and realize that none of theses horrors existed outside my fevered imagination.

As my father moved forward, I saw Abdal Kaaba look down at him and recognition dawn. A flash of shock lit his features, so similar to Abu Bakr's that it was as if a spirit from inside a mirror had emerged to engage in battle. But then a shadow fell over my brother's face and his shock was replaced by a mask of steel. If father and son were meant to fight to the death in this bitter contest, then so be it.

And then my husband rose and put a restraining arm on Abu Bakr.

"Sheathe your sword," he said gently. "Go back to your place and give us the good of your company."

The Messenger's words penetrated to my father's heart. He dropped his weapon and fell to his knees as if the tendons in his legs had suddenly been cut. I saw tears flowing down his face and I stared across the rocky hillside at my brother, wondering whether he would ride forward and kill us.

Abdal Kaaba looked at my weeping father, and then at me. And then he cursed loudly and turned back, riding away from this madness as if pursued by flying djinn. But even as he retreated, others rode forward and the small company of defenders prepared to engage them. As I looked at the stony faces in our tiny circle, I said a silent prayer to God, telling Him that if I died today, I would be thankful that death came while I had these remarkable people at my side.

Along with the ever-loyal Talha, my sister's newly wed husband, Zubayr, stood at the edge of the circle with a sword in each hand. He was the only man I knew who could use each hand equally well and he had mastered the rare ability to wield two blades at once. As a second horseman galloped up the rocks toward our camp, Zubayr began to spin as if he were a dust devil. And then, with a dancer's grace, he swung with his right hand and struck the approaching stallion in the breast. The mighty beast threw its rider as it flailed in agony, and as the stunned horseman fell, Zubayr continued his spin, his left hand traveling in a smooth arc through the air and slicing the man across the neck. Blood spurted from his severed jugular, and the Meccan warrior was soon lying dead next to his horse.

And then Ali was beside Zubayr, *Dhul Fiqar* glowing with that inexplicable light, and the two fought side by side, cutting down any Meccan foolish enough to ride up that hill of death. They were a wondrous pair, cousins who moved and acted like twin brothers who could read each other's thoughts. There was a symmetry in the way Ali and Zubayr's bodies moved, as if they were two wings of a giant butterfly, flapping with terrifying beauty. I had never seen two men act in such perfect unison and I admired the bond of love and kinship that forged their hearts together.

I regret many things in my life, dear Abdallah, and none more than the dagger I wedged between their hearts in the years to come. Your father was one of Ali's few friends, and the poison that I sowed in that pure field of love would reap a better fruit for our nation. Perhaps God will forgive me. But I do not know how I can ever forgive myself.

That day, trust was not a matter of faith, friendship, or blood. It was a matter of life and death. My heart, which soared to see Zubayr and Ali protect our northern flank from attack, suddenly plunged as I saw a group of men abandon their horses and clamber up the southern rock face to attack us from behind.

I screamed and pointed to the incoming wave of Meccan soldiers, their swords held in their teeth as they spidered up the boulders. Talha was instantly at my side, and when he saw the new threat, he threw himself at the warriors.

I watched in horror as three pagans set upon my beloved cousin, who was now the only shield protecting the Messenger from certain death. Talha fought with madness in his eyes, a ferocity unlike anything I have ever seen. He struck blow after blow, even as enemies' blades tore through his mail, leaving deep red gashes.

And yet Talha remained standing. He spun and lashed out, slicing off the arm of one assailant and then plunging his sword into the chest of a second. Talha's sword caught inside the dying man's rib cage and he could not remove it in time to deflect a blow from the last survivor, which cut cross his back with sickening eruption of gore. I watched in horror as Talha swayed and appeared ready to collapse. And then he somehow found the strength to raise his leg and kick his attacker in the abdomen. The man screamed as he went over the rocks and fell fifty feet, landing with a sickening crunch.

Talha staggered back to the Messenger, who was looking at him in wonder. I have no idea how he managed to walk. His armor was shredded and blood was pouring from a dozen wounds. He smiled down at the Messenger, and then his eyes fell on me. Somehow, Talha managed to wink. And then he collapsed.

"Tend to your cousin!" the Prophet cried, and I was immediately at his side. I checked his neck and felt the vein pulsing weakly with life. My father leaned over Talha, opened a water flask made from camel hide, and sprinkled the contents over his wounds. I tore strips of cloth from my cotton robe and began to bandage his numerous injuries.

Talha had protected our rear flank, but Khalid's men were now charging en masse up the hill from the north. There were too many even for Ali and Zubayr to hold back and several of the riders broke through the pass and thundered toward us. And then I saw two women, Nusayba and Umm Sulaym, who had been firing arrows at the attackers, drop their bows and grab swords. These plump housewives with no training in the art of warfare rushed at the horsemen, swinging their blades with terrifying screams of rage. The Meccans stopped in midcharge, startled to be facing these crazed women. Their hesitation proved fatal, as Nusayba plunged her sword into the neck of one stallion, which threw his rider over the edge of a cliff, while Umm Sulaym lopped off the leg of another. When the horseman fell to the ground in shock, Nusayba cut off his head.

But even these fervent defenders could not hold everyone back. I saw a warrior whose name I later learned was Ibn Qamia ride past Ali and Zubayr, who were occupied with fighting two horsemen each, and thunder past the women, who were forced to jump aside as his warhorse nearly trampled them to death.

And then Ibn Qamia saw the Messenger seated on the rocky ground, and he gave a bloodcurdling cry. My eyes went wide as I realized there was no one to defend us from this onrushing wave of death.

I saw my elderly father reach for his sword and race toward the enraged stallion. But Ibn Qamia swatted out with one hand, striking Abu Bakr on the face with the flat of his sword and knocking him to the ground. I screamed for my father, tears blurring my sight. Ibn Qamia was nearly upon us and I saw the Messenger rise, facing death with a courage that would escape lesser men. I watched Ibn Qamia's sword flash in the angry sunlight as he swung out in a wide arc, aimed perfectly to cut Muhammad's head from his shoulders.

"No!" I screamed so loudly that I am sure my voice rattled the gates of Hell itself.

And then I felt movement beside me, and before I could understand what was happening, Talha's eyes flew open and he jumped to his feet, his left hand rising to block the razor sharp blade.

I watched in disbelief as the sword cut through Talha's palm, shattering the fingers of his hand as if they were made from dried mud. As the warrior tore Talha's hand in half, Ibn Qamia's flawless motion was disrupted and the arc of the sword was deflected higher. Instead of striking the Messenger in the throat, the blade slashed up and smashed into the steel of his helmet.

Blood erupted from my husband's cheek and he fell like a doll thrown to the earth by a temperamental child. The Messenger of God lay unmoving at my feet, his handsome face marred by torn flesh and metal.

Ibn Qamia looked down, stunned at his accomplishment. He had done what the greatest warriors of Quraysh had failed to do over the past fifteen years. His eyes wide with the promise of glory, he raised his sword and called out from the mountainside, his voice carrying across the valley like a trumpet blast.

"Muhammad is dead! Muhammad is dead!"

21

9 could hear the cries of joy from the Meccans and the terrible weeping of despair from our people as the chant of "Muhammad is dead" spread through the valley. As Ibn Qamia rode away in triumph, I stared down at the Messenger, unable to move. If he truly was gone, I wanted to climb to the top of Uhud and throw myself into the darkest gorge below.

And then I saw the impossible. His eyes flickered and opened and he looked up at me in confusion.

"Humayra . . ."

I was suddenly flying, my heart breaking through the boundaries of time and space even as Muhammad had on the sacred Night Journey. My vision blinded by tears, I stood up and cupped my hands around my mouth as I cried out to the valley below.

"Muhammad lives!"

At first my words echoed and were lost in the din of madness below. And then I heard it. The steady thrum of a cry that resounded all around Uhud.

"Muhammad lives! Muhammad lives!"

The earth below began to shimmer with the glint of armor as our surviving warriors, energized by new hope, defiantly fought off the Meccans and climbed back up the side of the mountain.

As the Muslim soldiers returned to the safety of the high ground, I knelt down beside the Messenger and saw that his shattered helmet had absorbed most of the blow. My husband had lost two teeth and a good deal of blood, but he would survive with little more than a scar on his cheek that would be easily concealed under the rich black curls of his beard.

And then I heard the whinny of horses and realized that the danger was not yet over. Khalid's men were regrouping and would launch another raid up the mountainside unless we could get the Prophet to safety.

Ali and Zubayr had returned to his side, and they helped the Messenger to his feet. Working together, we helped my husband climb to higher ground. Zubayr saw the crevice of a cave above us that would provide shelter and hide the Messenger from potential assassins until our army had retaken control of Uhud. Ali climbed up first and held his hand out to the Messenger. But the Prophet was disoriented from the pain and could not navigate the steep rock face to reach the ledge. I saw him desperately search for a handhold as he began to swoon.

And then, despite everything he had already done and sacrificed, poor broken Talha somehow managed to hoist the Messenger on his back and climbed the sheer rock wall until he had cleared the ledge. I cannot imagine the pain that must have racked his shattered hand as he pulled them both up and I felt a deep welling of love for Talha, a bond that would make him closer than a brother in my heart.

With the Messenger safe, I could turn my attention to the world below. The battle was over. The Muslim victory had been reversed and both sides had been left bloodied and exhausted. The last of our survivors clambered up the hill and the Meccans pulled back, realizing that it was futile to pursue the fight further.

I felt my heart pounding in my chest and I had to force myself to calm my breath before I lost consciousness. I had seen too much horror that day and I could not imagine that there was any more evil that could poison my eyes.

But Hind would soon show me that the pit of darkness had no bottom.

22

The battlefield smelled like a corpse that had been rotting for a week. The black volcanic ash mixed with the odor of disemboweled intestines, punctured hearts, and the rubbery gray slime of brain matter. It was a smell that would stay in my nostrils for weeks. It would penetrate my nightmares and cause me to wake up in the middle of the night and vomit.

As I looked down with grief at the many young and old who had suffered gruesome deaths on the field below, the sky darkened. The sun was blotted out by a vast flock of vultures, and the sound of their wings flapping impatiently above the valley made my skin crawl.

And then, as I peered through the battlefield for signs of any victims I knew by name, I saw a flash of color as Hind led her party of brightly clad dancers out among the corpses.

I watched in dread fascination as Hind moved among the fallen, gazing dispassionately at the muck and grime and exposed rib cages, until she found what she was looking for.

Hamza. The man who had killed her father still lay on his side, the javelin embedded deep inside his stomach. She knelt down as if to check to see if he were indeed dead, which was, of course, laughable, as he had lain there, skewered, for hours. And then Hind spoke, in a cold voice that sounded as dead as the men whose remains littered the ground beneath her dainty golden slippers.

"So here is the great Hamza," she hissed like a cobra, her voice echoing through the valley. "They said you had the heart of an eagle and the liver of a lion. Let's see if that is true."

Hind grabbed a bloody knife from among the many weapons that had been dropped in the heat of battle. And to my horror, she cut deep into Hamza's side and tore open his flesh. With her bare hands, she dug into the dead man's flesh like a butcher ripping off fat from a shank of lamb. And then she tore out Hamza's liver.

My stomach quivered violently in disgust as I watched Hind hold up Hamza's liver high for the men of both camps to see. And then she put it in her mouth and ate it, the blood of Muhammad's beloved uncle dripping down the sides of her mouth. She chewed it and swallowed, and then retched violently. Hind doubled over, vomiting back a portion of the human flesh she had consumed before all.

And then her gagging cough turned into a maniacal laugh and she grabbed the knife and proceeded to cut off Hamza's nose and ears.

I heard moans and cries of horror from both camps. The pagan Arabs had strict taboos against disfiguring the dead of their enemies, and what Hind was doing was beyond even the meager moral restraints that their primitive religion imposed on their souls. But Hind seemed utterly oblivious to the disgust of her own people, and she began to sway like a kite in the wind.

And then, human blood still dripping from her plump lips, Hind began to dance and sing around the mutilated body of her enemy. She tore open her robes and smeared the blood of Hamza across her breasts. I could see the curve of her ample bosom as she stripped off her gold necklaces.

"O beauties of Mecca, throw off your jewels! Renounce gold and pearls! For there is no greater treasure than the flesh of our enemies!"

And with these words she whirled victoriously around the corpse of Hamza. Her madness spread to the other women like a disease. Suddenly they, too, descended on the bodies of our martyrs, tearing off their noses and ears. And then following her lurid example, they tied their bloody trophies with string and wore the human remains as jewelry. With their new prizes, they began to spin and swoon, their eyes thrown back so far into their skulls that only the whites remained. Their dance was raw and sexual.

Even though I wanted to close my eyes, it was impossible to stop watching. It was as if I were seeing a ritual so dark and ancient that it outdated the memory of man. The absolute purity of her evil was both revolting and mesmerizing, and I felt my heart pound. It was as if Hind had awakened some dark part of the soul that is buried so deep that touching it would unleash a force of transformation that went beyond life or death. It was at once terrifying and seductive and I felt myself being swept into the maelstrom of her madness.

And then Abu Sufyan rode up beside his wife and the spell was broken. He looked down at her obscene dance with unmitigated disgust.

"Enough! This is beneath us!"

Hind stopped spinning and crouched low on the ground, like a wolf prepared to strike. And then she took her hands, smeared with Hamza's blood, and ran them across her face until her cheeks were streaked in human offal.

Abu Sufyan turned away from her, unable to comprehend how far his wife had fallen. He rode toward the base of Uhud and called out to us.

"War goes by turns, my friends, and today was our day," he said in a booming voice. "All praise be to Hubal and the gods of Mecca! The dead of Badr have been avenged. We are now even."

And then I saw Umar arise from among the survivors gathered on the hill. With Hamza dead, he was now the most feared and revered of our warriors.

"God is Highest, Supreme in Majesty! We are not equal. Our dead are in Paradise, and your dead are in Hell!"

Abu Sufyan stared up at Umar, and then he shook his head as if he would never understand this strange tribe that was in its own way as mad as his wife. He rode back to the camp to begin preparations for the long trek home.

The battlefield was now empty, except for the desecrated corpses. Unable to bear the sight, I turned my attention to Abu Sufyan, who was leading his forces out of the pass, and saw the different flags and markers of the tribes. I recognized the symbols of the clans of Mecca like the wolf of the Makhzum and the eagle of Bani Abd ad-Dar. But other pennants belonged to the rival tribes that had little friendship with Mecca, from the double-headed snake of Taif to the horned rams of the Bedouins of the Najd. These old adversaries had come together to defeat their common enemy—Muhammad.

It suddenly struck me that Abu Sufyan had successfully marshaled the warring Arab tribes to the south, even as the Messenger was attempting to unify the north. Arabia was on its way to becoming one nation, and its character would be determined by which alliance ultimately gained the upper hand in this bitter conflict.

In that moment, I realized what we were fighting for. Islam stood as a lonely light flickering in a wasteland covered in darkness. If Hind and her ilk were allowed to win this struggle, barbarism would prevail and eventually spread beyond the boundaries of Arabia like a plague. Our people would become a living curse on mankind, a nation diseased at heart that would pull the world into turmoil from which it would never return.

We had been defeated at Uhud, and now the pagan tribes would see us as weak. They would prepare to pounce on us like hyenas on a wounded lamb. If we surrendered to their combined might, the light of hope would vanish in the sands and something even more monstrous would be born in its wake. Either Arabia would unite under our banner, or it would fight beneath the veil of Hind. And the unsuspecting nations that surrounded us, torn apart by centuries of warfare and corruption, would either be rejuvenated by the message of Islam or fall victim to the unified might of a barbarian horde bent on destruction.

I understood now that the battle for Arabia was not about the survival of a new religion. It was about the survival of civilization itself.

Book Three

Birth
of a
Nation

1 Medina—AD 625

We buried the mutilated dead on the slopes of Uhud and returned to Medina, where news of our loss sent waves of grief and panic among the people. Suddenly small voices could be heard wondering why God had abandoned us on the battle-field, unlike at Badr, where He had sent angels to our aid. Soon the voices become louder and some began to question whether our first victory had been merely the product of dumb luck and there had not been any divine intervention in the first place.

The grumbling was silenced by the revelation of verses in the Qur'an that placed the blame for our defeat squarely on our own shoulders. Had the archers not been overcome with greed and fled their posts, victory would have been certain. We could not blame God for our own failings. It was an important lesson, and the people began to see Uhud as a sign from God that His favor was bestowed on the Muslims not because of who they were but because of how they acted. And this point soon became another way to differentiate us from our increasingly antagonistic Jewish neighbors. The Prophet warned that some of the Jews—although, he stressed, not all—had come to see themselves as deserving of God's blessings as a birthright, without any corresponding moral obligations on their own end, and this had led to their downfall throughout history. Islam had come to erase that sense of tribal entitle-ment and replace it with individual moral responsibility.

The Jews did not deign to respond to this new charge against them, but their leaders made it clear that Muhammad's humiliation at Uhud should serve as a reminder that the future of the oasis was not as clear as the Muslims would like to believe. And they were right.

It was the realization of our precarious position in the aftermath of defeat that forced the Messenger to hold a secret a council of his closest Companions. A handful of the most influential members of our community met inside my tiny apartment, with guards placed in the courtyard of the Masjid to ward off any eavesdroppers.

My father pulled his beard, which had begun to turn from gray to cloudy white.

"Now that the Meccans have tasted victory, they think we are weak," he said grimly. "It will not be long before they attack Medina again with a stronger force."

Umar grunted in assent.

"We must make new allies among the Arab tribes if we wish to mount a defense," he said, leaving unspoken the obvious fact that our Jewish neighbors could not be relied upon to uphold their end of the treaty if Abu Sufyan invaded.

Ali leaned forward.

"The Bedouin tribe of Bani Amir is well armed, and they have no love for Mecca."

I wrinkled my forehead at the mention of the unfamiliar tribe, and then I remembered that the Bani Amir were shepherds who brought their flocks to pasture in Medina every spring. Their wool was actually quite decent, with thick curls that made excellent blankets during the cold winter months, and their shearings sold well in the marketplace. They had remained neutral in our conflict with Mecca, but they definitely had a vested economic interest in the prosperity of the settlement.

Uthman nodded favorably at Ali's suggestion.

"I know their chieftain, Abu Bara. He is an honorable man and would be a useful ally."

My father coughed, as if he often did when he had to make an indelicate comment.

"I have heard that Abu Bara's leadership is in question," he said, choosing his words carefully. "Rumor is that his nephew Husam is seeking to displace him.

Uthman frowned. The complex nuances of such a power struggle could not be grasped by his simple and straightforward nature. A fact that would cause much grief to the *Ummah* in years to come.

"Husam has many friends in Mecca," he conceded with some difficulty. "If he seizes control of the Bani Amir and allies them with Abu Sufyan, we will face a formidable enemy."

Umar banged his hand on his knee.

"Then we must unite his tribe clearly with the Muslims," he said with his customary intensity. "If we can forge relations of blood and marriage between us, it will cement an alliance."

There was a long silence as the Messenger's counselors considered their options. Marriage as a means of establishing treaties between peoples had a long and honored tradition in Arabia. But the question remained as to who among the notoriously independent Bani Amir would be amenable to a match with the Muslims and whom they could be paired with to forge an alliance that would justify the Bedouin risking their lives in Medina's wars.

And then Ali spoke, his voice ringing like a bell in the small room. "Zaynab, the daughter of Khuzayma, is a member of the Bani Amir." Umar's bushy eyebrows rose.

"The widow of Ubayda?"

Ali nodded. And then I had a flash of memory of courageous Ubayda on the plain of Badr, his leg cut off by the dying Utbah. He had been the first Muslim to be killed in battle and had expired with his head in the Prophet's lap. I knew his young widow, Zaynab bint Khuzayma, in passing. She was a quiet soul, who spent most of her time helping Fatima by feeding the People of the Bench or distributing alms to the needy. I had heard the Messenger once refer to her admiringly as "the Mother of the Poor."

Zaynab was a frail woman whose body was malnourished and small, and I found it hard to imagine that this plain, ghostly lady would find a suitor easily. Glancing at the dubious looks on the faces of the other men, I gathered that they were thinking similar thoughts.

Ali turned to face the Prophet, who had sat uncharacteristically silent throughout the entire discussion. My husband looked worn and tired, and I knew that he was still grieving for Hamza and the dead of Uhud.

"Zaynab is a cousin of the chief of Bani Amir and can turn his heart in our favor," Ali said. And then he added words that immediately shook my world. "If the Messenger were to marry her, it would create a powerful bond between the Muslims and the Bedouins."

I felt bile rising in my stomach.

"You are quick to offer my husband's hand in marriage!"

Ali looked at me with those unreadable green eyes. If he was stung by the vehemence of my reaction, he did not show it.

"I meant no offense," he said simply. "But the Messenger is the head of our community. For the Bedouins, only a marriage between leaders of tribes would be sufficient to earn their allegiance."

I sat back sullenly, my arms folded across my chest in defiance. Of course what Ali said made perfect sense from a practical point of view. But I was in no mood for practicality. I had already been forced to contend with one young sister-wife because of the Messenger's political needs. And now I was being asked to accept another woman in Muhammad's bed for the sake of state policy.

The Messenger did not look at me. He sat quietly, considering Ali's words. When he spoke, there was a calm decisiveness in his voice that I had not heard since the tragedy at Uhud.

"Zaynab bint Khuzayma is a good woman," my husband said. "She is kind to the poor. And she is the first widow of Badr. I know of none worthier to become a Mother of the Believers."

I felt my heart sink as the Messenger turned to face Ali.

"Send her my proposal. If she accepts, invite Abu Bara to the wedding and let us make a treaty with his tribe."

Ali nodded and rose to leave. I could not help but give him a furious look as he walked out. He met my eyes, and for a second I saw cold disapproval in his glance. I felt a sudden flash of outrage at his judgmental stare, as well as an inkling of shame at my own jealousy. But as Ali walked out, my wounded pride won the struggle inside me, and I bit my lip in fury until I drew blood.

2

The Messenger married Zaynab bint Khuzayma a fortnight later, and a fourth apartment was built, the newest, just north of Hafsa's stone hut. Abu Bara, the head of Bani Amir, attended the wedding of his cousin and publicly proclaimed that the Bedouin tribe was now bound by blood to Medina. The alliance had been successfully formed, and the Messenger's political marriage had closed the chinks in our armor after the humiliation of Uhud.

And it was an alliance that was tested almost immediately. Abu Bara's ambitious nephew tried to disrupt the pact by leading a renegade group of his tribesmen to attack a Muslim hunting party that wandered into Bani Amir territory. The survivors of the attack hid in the wilderness and took their vengeance on a group of Bani Amir shepherds who were innocent of complicity in the plot.

The dangerous cycle of retaliation had begun and the Prophet wisely offered to ease tensions with the Bedouins by paying a hefty sum to settle the claims of the shepherds' grieving families. The sum demanded—a thousand gold dirhams—was substantial and posed a significant strain on the *Bayt al-Mal,* the Muslim treasury. And so the Prophet sent Ali to seek financial support from the Jewish tribes in accordance with our old treaty.

When I heard this, I shook my head in disbelief.

"The Jews have long forgotten our treaty," I said to him one day as we sat in my room eating roasted lamb from a wooden bowl.

The Messenger's hand brushed against mine as he reached in for a shank, and I could feel the coolness of his fingers beside my own. He took the soft shoulder meat and bit down, savoring its delicate taste.

"If our friends have forgotten the pact, then perhaps it is time to remind them," Muhammad said, as if he were discussing a small bill of goods to be paid in the bazaar.

But I knew that it was not as simple as that. Blood had been spilled and one of the Jewish tribes was now in exile. Pressuring the remaining Jews to pay for a blood feud between the Muslims and the Bedouins would place an even greater strain on relations between the two communities.

And then as I looked into the Messenger's twinkling black eyes, I realized that he understood this. This was a test of Medina's power in the aftermath of Uhud. If the Jews failed to honor the treaty, there would no longer be any question as to where their allegiance lay. And with Mecca now assuredly plotting to fan the brushfire that been ignited at Uhud, we could not afford to have neighbors whose intentions were hostile. The Jewish fortresses guarded the mountain passes into the city. Their disloyalty could prove disastrous should Abu Sufyan's forces again march up the hills toward the heart of Medina.

There was no more time for guessing—the truth of our political situation had to be assessed now. And the blood settlement provided an innocuous means of testing the waters. If the Jewish tribes renounced their obligations under the treaty, the Messenger would have ample reason to expel them from the oasis.

It was an utterly ingenious stratagem. If the Jews paid the Bani Amir, they would be held accountable for any future treaty obligations by a well-armed third party. And if they refused to pay, the Bani Amir would join forces with the Muslims and remove their threat from the doorstep of Medina. I realized that the Messenger would win either way.

I saw the Prophet smile as if he read my thoughts. As he continued to eat heartily of the lamb, I felt a surge of relief that I was his wife and not his adversary.

— — —

THREE DAYS LATER, I was walking alone through the marketplace. My husband had been invited to a dinner at the home of Huyayy ibn Akhtab, the leader of the Jewish tribe of Bani Nadir. His request for their help in paying the blood money to the Bedouins had been received with surprising graciousness. Huyayy had sent word that he wished to begin a new era in relations between their peoples. They worshiped the same God, after all, and both communities had a vested interest in the security and prosperity of the oasis. And so he offered to host a feast of reconciliation at which the Messenger would be his honored guest.

The Prophet had departed to attend the gathering with a small band of his Companions. In his absence, I decided to make a trip to the bazaar and see what new goods had arrived on the morning caravan. As I walked through the paved alleys of the city, I marveled at how things had changed in the past few years. Medina had been a dirty and unkempt town, where the streets were littered with refuse and camel dung. Women could not step outside alone without fear of harassment or worse by drunken tribesmen. The heady smell of *khamr* had hung over the town like a drunken cloud.

But now the cobbled stones were whitewashed and crumbling walls had been rebuilt. Women and children now walked about freely, although the imposition of the Muslim head scarf was still the subject of grumbling by some of the prettier girls, who were accustomed to parading their luxurious locks as a means of enticing a husband.

But the most remarkable change was the ban on wine. Initially Muslims were permitted to drink alcohol, even though the Messenger himself would not touch any strong drink that befuddled the senses. But as the institution of communal prayers was formalized at the Masjid, incidents of believers showing up drunk and disrupting the services had become increasingly problematic. Finally, after a drunken brawl among youths almost erupted into a street battle between the old enemies of Aws and Khazraj, the Messenger received a Revelation prohibiting the consumption of alcohol altogether. Some of the Companions voiced concerns that such a ban would be hard to enforce, as wine and *khamr* were a traditional part of Arab culture. And yet when Ali recited the new verses in the marketplace, the streets were soon running with wine as the citizens emptied their flasks. It had been a remarkable testament to how deeply faith had transformed these people—although I guessed that there were still a few bottles of wine being consumed in secret every night among the less devout.

Still, law and order had been achieved, and the visiting traders who arrived from all over the peninsula departed Medina with a sense of new possibilities. Perhaps the people of Arabia did not have to live like wild animals, crudely struggling for survival in the wilderness. Perhaps they could build cities and roads and establish courts of law that would end disputes without bloodshed. Medina was becoming a model for a new Arabia, and the word that Muhammad's way led to peace and security was already spreading like an unstoppable sandstorm through the lonely wastes beyond the hills.

I walked through the stalls that day feeling happier than I had in some time. The sky was crystal blue with nary a cloud in sight. The air was warm and buzzing with life. Despite the horrors I had witnessed at Uhud, life was moving forward. And now that the Jews had renewed our pact, Mecca was unlikely to attack again. The sweet smell of peace was in the air.

I stopped before a cloth dealer and saw a lovely roll of saffron-colored silk. I ran my fingers through the fabric, letting its softness send shocks of pleasure down my wrist. The merchant, a grizzled old man with one eye, leaned forward conspiratorially.

"The finest cloth from India," he said in a whisper, referring to a mythic land that was said to be south of the even more magical China. A land of vibrant colors and spices that could be found nowhere else on earth. A land where tigers and monkeys roamed the streets and armies fought with the aid of elephants. A land that was said to have so many gods that the idols of the Kaaba were like tiny stars lost amid the glory of the Milky Way.

All rubbish, of course. I doubted that this fabled realm existed anywhere outside the fevered imaginings of campfire storytellers. And in any event, whenever a merchant mentioned India, you knew you were in trouble. Traders always claimed that their goods had been imported from there when they wanted to charge exorbitant prices.

True to form, the merchant smiled widely, revealing a jungle of broken and blackened teeth.

"Only twenty gold dirhams," he said, after glancing around to make sure no one had heard what a magnificent bargain he was offering the pretty young lady before him.

I suppressed a smile at the old fraud.

"I'm just looking. Thank you."

And then I saw the silk dealer's face change. He had recognized me. Suddenly the practiced showmanship vanished and I saw fear and awe in his eyes.

"You . . . you are the Mother of the Believers . . . Please, take it as a gift . . ."

He handed the roll of silk to me reverently, his wrinkled hands trembling, and suddenly it was I who felt like the fraud.

"My husband would not let me take something without paying," I said hastily. I suddenly regretted having come here alone.

I saw tears well in the old man's eyes.

"Then take it in exchange for a prayer," he said in a voice that cracked with emotion. "My daughter Halima is sick with the oasis fever. Please pray for her. I know that God listens to the Mother of the Believers."

I suddenly felt sorry for this kindly old man. He looked at me with the eyes of a child, completely trusting that I could do something for him. But I could not even find an answer for my own fervent prayers. I had now been with the Prophet for almost four years and my womb was barren. I had been praying every night for the past year for God to quicken my body with new life. And there had been no answer.

"I will ask my husband to pray for her," I said softly. "And *insha-Allah* she will be healed."

The merchant's face lit up in a smile of pure glee. He fell to his knees and praised Allah so loudly that people in the bazaar stopped what they were doing to stare.

I felt my face flush red. I wished the old man peace and quickly turned to walk away.

And then I walked right into a tall woman whose face was almost completely covered by a black veil. All I could see were her gray eyes, which pierced into me like an arrow.

"Alms for a poor woman . . ."

She held out her hand and I saw that her fingers were finely manicured, not rough and callused like those of all the other beggars in the town. And yet there was something about the intensity of her gaze that suggested she carried more sorrow than all the hungry women and children who came to the Bench every day asking for food.

I reached into my small leather purse and took out a few silver coins. As I placed them in her outstretched palm she gripped my hand with terrifying strength.

"Let go of me!" I was suddenly afraid, even though I knew that if I cried out, the entire bazaar would rush to the aid of the Mother. But something about the mournful way that she looked into my eyes filled me with greater dread than the violent threats of any enemy.

The woman leaned close to me and I could smell rosewater about her. Even though she was dressed in rags, her flesh had the unmistakable scent of luxury.

"Your husband is in danger."

My heart forgot to beat for an instant, and then made up for it by hammering with wild abandon.

"What are you saying?" I had to raise my voice to hear my own words over the pounding in my ears.

"The Bani Nadir plan to kill him outside the walls of their fortress," she said softly, her gray eyes shimmering with tears. "Save him. Or war will be upon us and Medina will be washed in blood."

I felt all color drain from my face. The woman let go of my hand and I felt my legs moving even though I had not willed them to do so. And suddenly I was racing away from the strange woman, away from the stands of olives and spices and jewelry, away from the cobbled streets of Medina into the palm groves that stood between the oasis and the mighty walls of the Jews.

I did not look back. Had I done so, I would have seen the woman in black bow her head in shame before removing her veil.

And I would have recognized the cold, statuesque beauty of a girl I had seen on a handful of occasions when the Messenger had met formally with the chieftains of the Jews.

A girl named Safiya, who had just betrayed her own people.

3

I tore through the palm grove, blinking wildly as the wind blew grains of dust into my golden eyes. The sun had set and a blanket of darkness was rapidly descending on the grove. I managed to clamber up the path and suddenly I could see the ominous walls of the Bani Nadir blocking my path.

I was relieved to hear the gentle tones of my husband's voice in prayer. He was reciting a sura of the Qur'an that had recently been revealed, a beautiful poetic verse meant to ward off evil.

Say: I seek protection from the Lord of Daybreak,
From the evil of that He has created
And the evil of darkness when it falls
And the evil of witches who cast spells
And the evil of the jealous when he envies.

My eyes adjusted to the fading light and I saw the Messenger leading the *Maghrib* prayers at the base of one of the towers of the wall. I breathed a sigh of relief that he was safe. Suddenly I felt very stupid. I had no idea who the veiled woman was, and yet I had taken her ramblings as truth. Feeling my cheeks flush in embarrassment, I turned to go home.

And then I heard something. A sound coming from above. I looked up and my falcon's eyes fell upon the old turret high above the ground and I saw the distinct outline of figures pushing hard against the old stone from above.

A tiny cascade of pebbles streamed down the side of the tower and then I understood. My eyes went wide with horror and I ran across the path, hurtling toward the Prophet like a crimson arrow.

"No! It's a trap!"

And then I crashed against my husband with such force that I knocked him aside in the midst of his prayers. The Prophet fell backward and his followers immediately stopped the ritual and leaped to his defense.

And then with a mighty roar, an avalanche of stone blocks larger than my head came tumbling down the side of the tower as the turret crumbled and collapsed. The heavy boulders crashed right where the Messenger had been standing and would have buried him in their deadly cascade had God not used me to push him out of the way.

I heard a tumult of cries as the Companions grabbed the Messenger and pulled him back from the wall into the safety of the garden. They took refuge under a thick palm tree and formed a protective circle around him. The men had come unarmed to the feast, but I saw such frenzy in their eyes that I knew they would fight any attackers, using their fingers and teeth if need be.

I looked down at my husband, who appeared to be in shock. And then I saw the familiar tremor racing through his bones and I knew that he was having a Revelation. And then he went still and his eyes opened.

He looked at me in surprise, and then at his followers, and finally at the pile of sharp rocks that covered the space he had occupied only moments before. He blinked rapidly as his sense of self returned.

"Gabriel appeared to me as I prayed and said my life was in danger . . . but God would protect me . . ."

He ran a hand across my face, which was smeared with dirt.

"Thank you," he said softly. I suddenly realized that I was trembling as wildly as he did during his mystical trances, and I hugged myself tight and tried to end the shaking.

I heard footsteps approaching and I saw my husband's face darken. The smile vanished and was replaced by something so terrible that I quickly looked away.

Huyayy, the chieftain of the Bani Nadir, came running to our side.

"My friends! Are you all right?" he cried with an obsequiousness that did not come naturally. "What a terrible accident! I will order our masons to fortify the wall so that something like this will never happen again."

It was such a transparent ruse that I stared at Huyayy in surprise. And then I saw beneath his protestations of innocence a mix of desperation and fear. This mighty statesman, this merchant renowned for his influence in worldly affairs, had been reduced to employing this crude and ultimately ineffective scheme to eliminate the Prophet.

The Messenger looked at him with both pity and contempt.

"You will not need to rebuild your wall," he said, ice in his words.

"I don't understand," Huyayy said, continuing to feign innocence.

My husband stepped forward with dignity and took hold of Huyayy's richly embroidered lapel.

"The Bani Nadir have broken the Treaty of Medina with their treachery. Your lands are forfeit."

Huyayy's fawning mask fell and his face twisted into an ugly sneer.

"You do not have enough men to compel the Bani Nadir to abandon their homes."

The Messenger did not move. His eyes remained locked with his adversary's poisonous gaze.

"Once the Bani Amir learn of your intention to kill a guest under guise of sanctuary, they will stand by Medina," he said with the power of absolute certainty. "As will their allies among the Bedouins. By God, you will leave your homes. Whether alive or dead, the choice is yours."

And with that, the Messenger let go of Huyayy and stormed down the path back to the safety of Medina. The men immediately followed, but I lingered for a second. I stared at Huyayy, who suddenly looked lost, as if he could not understand how the journey of his life had led him to this moment.

I saw the sadness in his gray eyes, and I felt a chill race down my spine as I remembered the veiled woman with the same eyes who had betrayed the Bani Nadir. And then I ran to join my husband, the full tragedy of Huyayy ibn Akhtab branded on my heart.

＊　＊　＊

A FEW DAYS LATER, I stood at the edge of the oasis, watching as the Jews of Bani Nadir evacuated their homes and prepared for the long march north. The rumor was that they would take refuge in Khaybar, a Jewish stronghold at the edge of Byzantine territory. As I watched the men load their possessions on camels and mules, my eyes fell upon a young girl with sandy hair sitting alone upon a horse. Her gaze met mine and I immediately recognized the gray eyes, which now shimmered with tears.

I nodded to Safiya in gratitude, but she looked away. And then the daughter of Huyayy ibn Akhtab turned and rode out into the desert, the secret that we shared a burden that would forever haunt her days.

4

I stood outside the birthing chamber as Fatima's screams of agony echoed from beyond the thin palm-wood door. The Messenger stood by my side, holding his small grandson, Hasan, in his arms. My husband looked even more pale than usual, and his eyes were red from lack of sleep. Ever since his daughter had begun labor three nights before, he had been holding a vigil in her small house. Each of his wives had alternated spending the hours at his side, and I had just arrived to relieve the elderly Sawda, who shook her head wearily as Fatima's cries intensified.

"She is in so much pain," my sister wife said to me quietly. "I don't understand it."

I glanced over at my husband, who held his grandson tight, as if afraid that some evil djinn would appear and spirit him away into the netherworld. The boy was now two years old and his face looked remarkably like the Messenger's, although his eyes were light brown and his curly hair had streaks of gold in it. Hasan looked at us, his grandmothers, with a placid smile, as if he could not hear the heart-wrenching cries from the adjacent room. I was always struck by how perpetually happy the child was. Indeed, I could not remember Hasan ever crying, and he seemed to find every moment of his little life a source of great delight and wonder. The "miracle child," the people of Medina had called him, the boy who should have died in Fatima's mal-nourished and tiny womb.

Hasan's mother had endured great suffering in the final weeks of her first pregnancy and had been unable to rise from her bed, requiring constant attention from the other women of the household. So when we learned that Fatima was carrying a second child, the women of the *Ahl al-Bayt* worked feverishly to prepare a comfortable home and bed for the Prophet's daughter. We expected another difficult pregnancy that would require us to spend many long nights at her side. But this time it was different. Fatima had shown no signs of discomfort in the days and weeks prior to the onset of labor, and we were delighted that our fears had come to nothing.

But the moment her water broke, Fatima had suffered terrifying pain. Her unearthly screams had chilled me to the bone, and for the first time made me thankful that I had failed to conceive a child myself.

My husband saw Sawda and me looking at him and he spoke for the first time in hours.

"It is not her own pain that she feels. It is her child's."

I stared at him in confusion, unable to understand what he could possibly mean. But then I realized I shouldn't have been surprised. Nothing about Fatima had ever made much sense to me.

The Messenger turned his attention to his son-in-law Ali, who sat cross-legged on the hard floor, his head buried in his hands. My husband placed a comforting hand on the young man's shoulders as Fatima's wails continued unabated. It seemed so strange to see this mighty warrior hunched over, as if the suffering of his wife were far more painful to him than any wound he had endured at Badr or Uhud. I suddenly realized with a flash of surprise that Ali truly loved Fatima. I had never thought much about it before that moment. Perhaps I had assumed that the marriage was nothing more than a political union meant to bring the young man closer to Muhammad, his cousin and mentor.

But looking at his sagging shoulders, his body trembling from suppressed grief, I finally understood that the bond between Ali and Fatima was deeper than I understood. They were both misfits, people who did not and could not fit into the cruel world, and in each other's company they must have found solace. And if, as it appeared, Fatima failed to survive the childbirth, Ali would be truly alone. With few friends or supporters aside from the Messenger himself, he would be plunged into a desert of solitude that would make the empty wastes of the Najd look green with life. For the first time in my life, I felt sorry for him.

And then, without any warning, the cries from the birthing chamber ceased abruptly, followed by a terrible silence that was more frightening than all the hours of agony that had preceded it.

Ali lifted his head and met the Messenger's eyes. I saw both men exchange a look of terrible grief and I felt tears welling in my eyes. The Prophet had lost another daughter. Fatima, his most beloved child, who was the plainest and simplest of his girls, and yet the one he treated with such open devotion that it bordered on reverence. Ever since Khadija had died, Fatima had been the rock that held him steady amid the crashing waves of his destiny. Even though I knew that I was his favorite wife, Fatima held a place in his heart that I could never reach. And now she was gone.

I moved to comfort my husband, when, to my absolute surprise, I heard the cry of a baby. The Messenger and Ali both turned to stare at the door to Fatima's chamber, which swung open, revealing an elderly midwife named Malika standing in the threshold, her birthing apron covered in blood.

Malika looked as if her face had aged a dozen years in the past hour. And just beyond her weary form, to my disbelief, was Fatima in her bed, alive and holding a tiny baby swaddled in green.

"Blessings to the *Ahl al-Bayt*." Malika spoke, her voice as heavy and exhausted as that of a warrior crawling back from the battlefield. "The Messenger has another grandson."

As if swimming deep underwater, my husband stepped slowly inside the room, followed by Ali. Sawda and I hesitated and then stepped behind the men, keeping a respectful distance as they leaned over Fatima and stared in silence at her newborn baby boy.

As I stepped inside the birthing chamber, I felt as if I were entering a dream. My vision flickered like a candle caught in a storm and I felt a strange chill even though the night air was unseasonably hot.

I watched in awestruck silence as the Prophet leaned close to the new baby. His elder grandson, Hasan, was still held tightly in his arms, and the smiling boy laughed with delight at the sight of his baby brother. The Messenger held Hasan close to the baby, and the child kissed the newborn on the forehead. And then my husband handed Hasan to his father and took the bundled baby in his arms.

I saw the infant's face for the first time, and I was startled to see that his eyes were already open and were looking at the Messenger with surprising intensity. The Prophet gazed into the baby's eyes, which, I saw, were as black as his own. And then he whispered the prayer call into the child's right ear before handing the baby to Ali, who repeated the prayer in newborn's left ear.

It was a miracle that Fatima and the baby had survived. And it was a blessing that the Prophet had been given another grandson through whom his lineage would continue. But there was no rejoicing. I looked around the room, confused to see the solemn looks on the men's faces and tears of evident sorrow on Fatima's bloodless cheeks.

I felt as if I had walked in on a funeral rather than a birth, and I finally turned to Ali, unable to hold back my unease.

"Why are you not smiling? You have a son!"

Ali looked at me with those mysterious green eyes. As always, I felt he was seeing past me to another place, another time.

"My heart smiles, but my lips cannot. He has a burden I wish for no man."

And then Ali looked down at his son and I was shocked to see a tear roll down his cheek. In all the years that I had known him, I had never seen this strange young man weep, except in prayer.

Shaken, I turned to face Fatima, who was gazing at me as if seeing me for the first time.

"What will you name him?" I asked with a forced smile, hoping to bring some semblance of normality to this otherworldly scene.

Fatima opened her mouth, but it was a long moment before any sound came out. When she finally spoke, her voice was like a whisper carried on the wind.

"He has already been named."

Fatima turned her head to her father. My husband stood at Ali's side, stroking his new grandson's thick black hair with his forefinger. His eyes glistened, but I saw no sign of tears. It was as if a light had been lit in his soul, one that I had seen only during his painful moments of Revelation.

"Husayn," the Messenger of God said. "His name is Husayn."

I looked at the three of them, Muhammad, Fatima, and Ali, and at the two boys, Hasan and Husayn, and suddenly felt as if I were intruding. I was the Messenger's favorite wife, the beloved of the harem, and yet in that moment I was a stranger. My heart ached with the realization that whatever bond linked these five, it was one that I would never truly be able to understand or participate in. Theirs was a world that I could gaze into only from afar, a shore I could never truly step onto because the ocean that divided us was greater than the expanse of the heavens and the earth.

I turned and saw that Sawda and the midwife had already departed, wisely leaving this intimate moment for those in whose veins the blood of the Messenger flowed. I realized sadly that though I shared Muhammad's bed, I could never share in his blood. I did not belong here, either.

Without another word, I walked out of the room and left the unsettling dreamworld of the *Ahl al-Bayt* for the refreshingly familiar streets of the oasis.

5

Muawiya watched with a cold eye as his father hosted a gathering of the allied tribes. The Hall of Assembly had been decked out in flowing curtains of various hues—indigo, emerald, turquoise, and lavender—each representing one of the major clans present at the summit. It was a motley group that included the uncouth Ghatafan Bedouin tribes that grazed their flocks to the north of the enemy in Medina, and their ancient enemies, the proud Bani Sulaym, who had cultivated the lava fields to the east. Muawiya noted with interest that the only thing that unified these disparate and competing tribes was their hatred for Muhammad's steady accumulation of power. The refugee from Mecca was truly bringing Arabia together in more ways than one.

The hall was buzzing with loud gossip about the troubling turn of events. Muhammad's diplomatic efforts, once constrained to the northern tribes of the peninsula, had recently expanded southward. He had forged an unexpected alliance with the Yamama, a tribe that controlled the grain routes from the south. The tribal leaders had adopted the renegade faith and had joined in Muhammad's boycott of Mecca, denying the pagan tribes wheat and barley. Without any warning, one of Arabia's key suppliers of food had joined the enemy, and the threat of starvation for Mecca and its allies was very real. It was this shocking development that had forced Abu Sufyan to call together the heads of the southern tribes in the hope of uniting them in a final stand against the danger of Medina.

Abu Sufyan clapped loudly to gain their attention, and a blanket of silence fell upon the crowd of tribal chiefs. Muawiya read the men's faces and saw anger and fear in their eyes. These were desperate people, ready to take desperate action, a fact that his father relied upon to bring together men whose fathers had been at one another's throats, whose tribes had warred with each other for centuries.

"The situation to the north has become intolerable," Abu Sufyan said without any preamble. "Muhammad's alliance with the Bedouins has choked off all our trade with Syria and Persia. And now Yamama has fallen under his spell and the enemy has brought famine to our doors."

Hind stepped forward, decked in a flowing robe made of red silk that rustled seductively. Muawiya saw some of the men whisper, undoubtedly speaking of her madness at Uhud, which had become the infamy of Mecca. But there was no sign of that crazed demon, hungry for human flesh, and she walked with her usual grace. And when she spoke, her voice was steady and calm, although Muawiya could see an unnerving glint in his mother's eyes.

"The future of all Arabia is at stake," she said. "We will live as free men and women. Or as slaves to Muhammad and the voices in his head."

Her words were met with a loud murmur of assent from the nobles. And then another voice rose above the din. Muawiya glanced over to see that it was his friend, the ever-diplomatic Amr ibn al-As.

"But we have tried military action before, with little success," he said with his practiced silky ease. "Is it not time to reach an accommodation?"

Muawiya smiled in relief. Amr had the respect of many of the tribal leaders. If he had been persuaded to see the reality of their situation, perhaps the fire of this folly could be extinguished before it blazed out of control.

All eyes were on Abu Sufyan to respond. The old man hesitated and then cast a bitter glance at Hind.

"If ever there was a chance for an accord, it is long past," he said with a tone of real regret. "The barbarism shown to the dead of Uhud by our women has inflamed their passions."

Hind turned to face him, one eyebrow raised defiantly.

"Do not place the blame on women for your failure to be men," she said with a dangerous smile.

Muawiya saw his father wince slightly and he shook his head. After all these years, Abu Sufyan remained in thrall to this madwoman. The most powerful man in Mecca had long been enslaved by the chain that she had tied around his heart. Muawiya vowed never to let that happen to him.

"In any event, Arabia is at a crossroads," Abu Sufyan said with a heavy sigh. "We have received word that Muhammad is sending envoys to other southern tribes, asking them to join the Yamama against us. If he forges more alliances to the south, our trade routes with Yemen will be compromised. Without food, without trade, Mecca will die."

His words were meant to silence Amr's dissent, but the son of al-As was persistent.

"Even without allies in the south, Muhammad is well defended at Medina," Amr said slowly, as if explaining a complex matter to a child. "We do not have enough men to challenge him."

His last words were meant to sting, and they did. At best, the Arabs could muster perhaps four or five thousand men. With Muhammad's new allies, they would be matched on the battlefield. And if Muhammad's luck prevailed, a match was as good as a defeat for Mecca.

And then Muawiya saw his mother smile. She nodded to one of her servants, a boy of thirteen, who opened a small door that led to an antechamber. A mysterious figure emerged, his face shadowed by a dark cloak.

Muawiya felt the stirrings of alarm. And then the tall man stepped into the middle of the room, standing between Abu Sufyan and Hind, and threw off his hood dramatically.

It was Huyayy ibn Akhtab, the exiled Jew of Medina.

"The sons of Nadir stand with you," he said in a booming voice.

The room immediately erupted in a tumult of voices, of shock, excitement, disbelief. Muawiya felt the bile in his stomach rising. He was angry at his mother for raising the stakes in this deadly game with Muhammad when the tribes should have been moving toward a treaty. And he was outraged at himself for not having seen this coming, for not having a plan to counter her strategy.

Abu Sufyan raised his hands and shouted over the din.

"Silence! Let us welcome our brother with the dignity of Mecca," he said, and the crowd immediately went still. Muawiya wondered if his father had been privy to Hind's scheme to enlist the support of the Jews of Bani Nadir, but the troubled look on his face suggested that he was as surprised by this development as the other tribal chiefs.

Huyayy cleared his throat. When he spoke, it was with a rich fluidity, the naturally seductive tone of an experienced politician.

"My friends, I have lived next to this Muhammad for the past several years," he said in a measured voice, but his eyes burned with passion. "I have seen his sorcery up close. He claims to be a prophet of my God. But I tell you with certainty that he is a fraud and a liar. He does not even know what is contained in the holy books of Moses, and he contradicts the Word of God with his own fabrications. Such a man is deemed a false prophet in the Torah, worthy of death. And so my brothers in the Bani Nadir stand with you. Together we can wrest Yathrib from the hands of this wizard and restore peace to Arabia."

His words were met with enthusiastic applause. Muawiya cursed under his breath. Huyayy was a fool who had been outmaneuvered by Muhammad. And now they were expected to follow his guidance to bring Muhammad down? It was madness, but as Muawiya looked around at the hopeful faces of the chieftains, he realized that they were all mad. Old men desperate to hold back the flow of time, they were clinging to the sanctuary of their memories rather than facing the truth of the world as it was today. Hind and Huyayy were playing to their false hopes, and the outcome would be devastating for all of Arabia.

Muawiya looked over at Amr, who shook his head in frustration, as if thinking the same thought. And then a deep voice echoed in the grand chamber, and Muawiya's head turned.

It was Khalid ibn al-Waleed, the greatest of the Meccan generals and the architect of their sole victory against Muhammad at Uhud.

"Then let us end this once and for all," he said solemnly. "Let us send against Medina the greatest force ever seen in the sands of Arabia. If Muhammad is a false prophet, as you say, we will prevail. And if he is victorious, then the heavens will have rendered a judgment that can no longer be gainsaid. In any event, let this be the final battle between us."

His words were met with shouts of assent from the weary tribal leaders. As the crowd moved in to surround Huyayy, the nobles vying to offer him lodging and hospitality during his stay in Mecca, Muawiya turned and walked out of the Hall in disgust.

He stood outside, gazing up at the clear night sky. The red flame of Mars, *al-Mareek*, twinkled above him like an angry wasp. It was fitting that the planet of war should rule the heavens tonight. With the Jews and the pagan Arabs united, the bitter skirmishes with Muhammad would now escalate into full-scale war that would tear the peninsula apart. It was not that Muawiya feared war. Conflict was a necessary part of a world where survival itself was a daily battle. What he despised was war conducted under the foolish compulsion of emotion and hubris, the two flags that always led to defeat. A true warrior was dispassionate, saw the battlefield for what it was, not what he wanted it to be. He advanced when the opportunity presented itself and retreated when it was the right thing to do. There was no glory in the reckless death of a warrior. Or of a civilization.

He felt a figure move to his side and glanced over to see Amr. Muawiya nodded to him, and then returned his eye to the stars. Rising across the eastern horizon was the noble star he loved the most—*Zuhal*, the planet the Romans called Saturn. It was the star of destiny, and the *kahina*s said it had shone over him at his birth. And so it was that he had been born with a sense of purpose. Muawiya had known that he had been meant to lead his people, to bring these barbaric, illiterate tribes to greatness. But if his mother succeeded in destroying Arabia with her fanatical pursuit of the one man who was bringing it together, then his destiny would be thwarted.

Muawiya realized in that moment that the time had come for a break from his family, his people. The only way he could save them was to distance himself from their madness. Only when they had destroyed themselves could a man like him move in to build something new from the ruins.

"We must make preparations," he said in a soft voice. Partly to Amr. Partly to himself.

"For victory?" Amr still clung to the false hopes of the masses, even though his diplomatic nature sought conciliation over conquest.

"No." Muawiya's voice was sharp. "For defeat."

Amr stood beside him for a long time before speaking again.

"Khalid has never been beaten in battle," he said softly, as if trying to convince himself that there was still some hope for the survival of the world he knew.

Muawiya turned to face him, his eagle eyes piercing the other man's soul.

"Khalid has never been defeated against men. But we are fighting something greater than any man."

Amr breathed in sharply, surprise lighting his eyes.

"This invisible God?"

Muawiya smiled.

"History. I have read enough of the tales of the past to see when the end of an era is coming. My father is wedded to a dying way. We must be the vanguards of the future. If Mecca is defeated, as I believe it will be, we must secure for its leaders a role in the new order."

Amr bowed his head, realizing the truth of Muawiya's words. The end was coming and they needed to prepare.

"What do you propose?"

Muawiya thought for a moment, letting the quick mind he had inherited from his mother spin its threads. And then he realized that the answer was closer to home than he had expected.

"Muhammad is making alliances through marriage," Muawiya said, his voice rising in excitement. "My sister Ramla is one of his followers, living in exile in Abyssinia. If she marries Muhammad, then the clan of Umayya may yet survive what is coming."

A smile creased across Amr's handsome face.

"I will serve as an intermediary, if Allah wills." Amr had been to Abyssinia before in a failed effort to convince the Negus to surrender the Muslim refugees. He knew the country well, had established profitable relations with its merchants, and could get a message to Ramla without alerting the other Meccans as to Muawiya's plans.

Muawiya placed a friendly arm on Amr's shoulder and smiled shrewdly.

"You said Allah and not the gods," he said.

Amr grinned widely.

6

 I was knitting in a corner of my tiny room when the Messenger's adopted son Zayd entered. It was a bright winter day, the sun streaming in through my window and warming the crisp air. I was in a cheerful mood, as tonight would be my night with the Messenger. My husband followed a strict rule, rotating nights with each of his wives in order to make sure that each was treated equally as commanded by the holy Qur'an. Accordingly, as the harem steadily increased, my limited time with the Prophet was becoming more precious. There were now five women who bore the title Mother of the Believers: the elderly Sawda, myself, the fiery Hafsa, the ghostly quiet Zaynab bint Khuzayma, and most recently Umm Salama bint Abu Umayya. The latest addition to the household was another war widow whom the Messenger had married out of compassion. Umm Salama's husband, Abdallah ibn Abdal Asad, had been killed at Uhud, leaving three children and a pregnant wife with no means of support. The Messenger had married Umm Salama after the four-month-and-ten-day *iddat*, her period of mourning, had ended, and she had given birth to her martyred husband's son Durra shortly after the wedding.

When I had first learned of the Prophet's intention to marry Umm Salama, I had been filled with jealousy. She was a strikingly beautiful woman, with sparkling eyes and a gentle smile. And she was still of age to bear children, and I had failed to produce an heir. But I had grudgingly accepted Umm Salama after the wedding, as it was difficult to dislike her patient and pleasant personality. Unlike Hafsa, who was my chief rival to give Muhammad a son, Umm Salama already had many children from her former marriage and did not appear overly eager to bear more. And so life continued largely as it had for the past few months in the house of the Prophet, with the petty jealousies among wives at a low simmer.

I sat by my husband's side, knitting a woolen scarf for him to keep him warm during early morning prayers. The Messenger was busy with his own handiwork, using a needle and thread to repair the torn leather straps of his sandals. I had never met any other man who enjoyed simple housework like fixing shoes or sewing patches in old clothes. It certainly did not fit the masculine ideals of his followers, who were perplexed by his strange affinity for what they dismissed as women's work. But the Prophet seemed more comfortable around the quiet hearth of the home than around the boastful jousting of the battlefield. As I watched him slowly suture his footwear, his black eyes utterly focused on and absorbed in the task before him, I realized how difficult it must have been for a boy with a gentle temperament to grow up in a world where cruelty and aggression were the proud hallmarks of a man. It struck me in that instant that the Messenger's admitted love of the company of women had less to do with sexual hunger than with an innate comfort with their feminine nature.

But I would soon be reminded that, however gentle and nurturing his soul was, his body still belonged to a man, with all the needs and desires of the masculine flesh.

As we quietly continued on with our work, a shadow fell across the open door and I saw that the Prophet's adopted son Zayd ibn Haritha had arrived. He was tall and lanky, with thinning hair and a face that years of labor under the sun had brutally weathered. His eyes, which always appeared sad, seemed particularly distraught today.

The Messenger caught the haunted look on his face and turned to face him, setting the sandals on the floor with a hard thump.

"What brings you here, my son?" Even as the Messenger spoke, I heard a strange tone in his voice, which in other men I would have recognized as a hint of embarrassment. But that, of course, made no sense coming from God's Chosen One, the most perfect man in creation.

Zayd knelt beside the Prophet, whose slave he had been before he had been freed and inducted into the family. He hung his head, not looking his adopted father in the eye.

"My wife told me what happened between you two."

My heart skipped a beat.

"What happened?" I felt the scarf slip through my fingers. Zayd's wife, Zaynab bint Jahsh, was the Messenger's cousin and one of the most beautiful women I had ever seen, her statuesque features only growing more elegant with age. I had always thought it strange that she was married to the ugliest man I knew. The Messenger had known Zaynab since she was a child and I was always relieved that he treated her like a little sister and was the only man who did not stammer or make a fool of himself in her presence.

The Messenger glanced at me and I could see discomfort in his eyes. And I realized that something had changed.

"It was nothing," he said quickly. "The matter is closed."

His words did not alleviate the growing alarm in my heart.

"Tell me," I insisted.

The Messenger remained silent. And then Zayd spoke up. The Prophet had come to visit him a few nights before, but Zayd had been out. Zaynab had heard the knock on the door and assumed that it was her husband. She had run to the door, forgetting her cloak and dressed in all her finery, her luxurious hair flowing below her waist. But when Zaynab opened the door, she was startled to see the Messenger. He had been struck by her beauty and quickly walked away. But she thought she heard him say, "Praise be to God, Master of the hearts."

I felt my own heart sink. I knew that my husband had always been fond of Zaynab. Could the sight of her in all her bedecked radiance have inspired love?

Zayd looked up and I could see that whatever emotions I was feeling were nothing compared to the poor man's torment. It was well known that Zayd and Zaynab had an unhappy marriage. She was from a proud and wealthy family, while Zayd was a freed slave, a social outcast in Mecca. They had wed after the Messenger had asked Zaynab to marry Zayd as an example to the other Muslims that piety mattered more in a mate than social class. Zaynab had always been fiercely loyal to the Prophet and had acquiesced to his request. It was clear to all of the women of the household that Zaynab was very much in love with my husband. Yet the Messenger had never expressed any interest in her, and she had resigned herself to her fate by marrying poor Zayd. But now, if the Prophet's heart had turned, I knew that Zaynab would seek to escape her loveless union and join with Muhammad.

"O Messenger, you are dearer to me than my family," Zayd said. "I chose you over my own father."

I remembered the story of how young Zayd, who had been kidnapped by slave traders as a boy, had found refuge in Muhammad and Khadija's home. The couple had treated him with great love and respect and he had become for all intents and purposes a son to them after the death of their own infant boys. When the lad's father had finally found him after years of searching through the desert towns, Zayd had refused to go back to his own family and chosen to stay as a slave to Muhammad. My husband had been so moved by the boy's devotion that he had freed him and then taken Zayd to the Kaaba and formally adopted him. It had been a momentous occasion, for in Arab society an adopted son was considered to share a mystical bond that made him the same as a flesh-and-blood child. Zayd had risen in that moment from a lowly slave to the heir of one of the most influential families in Mecca.

I realized with a sick heart that Zayd was the Prophet's son for all intents and purposes. If there were rumors of impropriety between Muhammad and his adopted son's wife, it would be deemed by the people as vile a crime as incest. My husband's standing as the Messenger of God and the moral exemplar of the community would be brought into question, and the foundation of our faith would collapse.

The Prophet must have been thinking similar thoughts, because he looked away, unable to face Zayd. But his adopted son leaned forward and took the Messenger's hands in his, until the Prophet finally met his pleading gaze.

"If it be your desire, then I will divorce her today and you are free to marry her," he said, making yet another sacrifice for the man whom he loved more than his own flesh and blood.

But this was madness. I felt my heart racing and I stood up, facing Zayd with balled fists

"What are you saying?! The Prophet is your father! It is forbidden for a father to marry a woman his son has lain with!"

My voice was shaking and I was unsure as to whether my rage came from horror at the violation of a taboo or from the thought of my husband in the arms of the radiant Zaynab.

Zayd looked at me indignantly.

"Those are the customs of the ignorant," he said sharply. "The Messenger and I share no blood tie."

I felt the bile in my stomach rise.

"That is not how the Bedouins will see it. They will accuse the Messenger of incest and our alliance will be broken."

I looked at my husband, who managed to meet my gaze. I had never seen such shame in his eyes, and I felt suddenly lost.

"Keep to your wife, Zayd," my husband said in a soft voice. "And be careful of your duty to God."

Zayd rose and shook his head.

"Zaynab does not love me," he said, and I could hear the deep pain in his voice. "Every time I lie with her, I will know that she wishes it was you there beside her. That I cannot bear."

He looked at me for a moment and then turned his attention back to the Prophet.

"I will divorce her," he said, with a tone of finality in his voice. "Her fate will be in the hands of God and his Messenger."

The Prophet rose to his feet, alarm on his features. He moved to stop Zayd from leaving. But the tall man simply took the Messenger's hand and kissed it with great love, tears flowing down his pockmarked cheeks. And then he turned and walked out.

The Messenger stood frozen for a long moment. I had never seen him look so confused. He finally turned to me, an abject apology on his face. He looked like a little child seeking absolution from his mother. But I could not bear to meet his gaze and I quickly stepped out and stormed over to Hafsa's house to unburden the rage and jealousy that was threatening to drive me mad.

7

A few days later, my husband called for a gathering of his followers to address the wild rumors that were spreading in Medina over the state of affairs in his household. A crowd of hundreds gathered in the courtyard of the Masjid, and dozens more stood outside, eager to hear what was happening in the strange drama between the Messenger of God, his son, and his daughter-in-law.

While the other wives of the Prophet stood near him as a sign of their support, I stayed by the threshold of my house, watching the proceedings with sullen intensity.

The Prophet looked at me eagerly and I could tell that he was hoping I would come to take my place beside Sawda and Hafsa, but I crossed my arms and held my chin up defiantly. He turned away and brought his attention to the jumbled gathering of believers. There was a crackling in the air like the coming hint of a thunderstorm, and I realized that this incident with Zaynab was the biggest threat to my husband's credibility since the day that the Jewish chieftain Huyayy had tried to mock his knowledge of the ancient scriptures. Whispers abounded about the Prophet's infatuation with his daughter-in-law and the terrible implications for the truth of the Revelation. How could God send a man capable of transgressing one of the most ancient of Arab taboos?

The Messenger raised his hand and the tense murmur of gossip abruptly ended, blanketing the courtyard with a silence so thick that all I could hear was the dull thud of my own heart.

"Today I received a Revelation from my Lord," the Messenger said in a voice that seemed to echo past the mud walls and into the paved streets of the oasis. He hesitated, the first time I had ever seen him having difficulty relaying the Word of God. I saw the color rise in his pallid face and I realized he was blushing like a bride on her wedding night.

And then Muhammad took a deep breath and recited the Divine command:

And when you said to him to whom God had shown favor
And to whom you had shown favor
Keep your wife to yourself
And be careful of your duty to God
And you concealed in your soul what God would bring to light
And you feared men
And God had a greater right that you should fear Him.
But when Zayd had divorced her
We gave her to you as a wife
So that there should be no difficulty for the believers
In respect of the wives of their adopted sons
When they have divorced them
And God's command shall be performed.

I listened to the newly revealed words of the holy Qur'an. And then I stepped back as if I had been struck in the gut. Allah had nullified the oldest of Arab taboos that had made the sons of the flesh and the sons of oath equal in the eyes of men. I looked at the crowd, uncertain how they would react. If the people rejected the commandment, the Prophet's standing in the oasis would disappear. He would be proclaimed a self-serving impostor, legislating away ancient values to satisfy the desires of his own flesh. If the people of Medina denounced this remarkable shift in the definition of family, everything we had worked for over the past decade would instantly dissolve. Abu Sufyan would not need to attack the oasis to kill Muhammad. The people of the oasis would do it for him.

There was a murmur of disbelief from some of the crowd. All eyes fell on Zayd, who stood quietly to the side, looking at his feet. For years he had prided himself on being Muhammad's only lawful son. And now his inheritance had been invalidated by God Himself. If Zayd accepted this, he would no longer be the "son of the Messenger." He would just be another ordinary freedman, a former slave with no money or standing in society. And he would no longer have a wife and family as well. My heart went out to the poor, ugly, unfortunate man. In this one moment, everything that Zayd had, everything that he could have laid claim to in this world, had been taken away.

And then Zayd raised his head and I was stunned to see a wide, genuine smile on his battered face. He fell to his knees and tears of joy were streaming down his cheeks and making the black tufts of his beard glisten.

He raised his hands in supplication and his voice boomed through the courtyard.

"Praise be to God, who honors this unworthy slave with mention in his Holy Book!"

And then Zayd fell prostrate on the ground, his forehead pressed hard against the stone floor of the Masjid. And then I realized that Zayd was right. Allah had mentioned him by name in the holy Qur'an, an honor given to no other Muslim. Even my father was called by his title "The Second in the Cave"—no mention of the name Abu Bakr was anywhere in the text. And as I looked down at the kneeling man, who was crying praises to his Creator even as his face was pressed to the earth in humility, I realized that the former slave had been given something far greater than everything that had been taken away from him.

Zayd ibn Haritha had been given immortality. Long after he died, after his bones had crumbled into dust, his name would be recited by millions of believers with awe and reverence every time they read the holy Qur'an.

As I watched Zayd's complete surrender to the will of God, his joyful acceptance of his fate, a wave of shame and sorrow spread through the crowd of believers who had questioned the Messenger's integrity. And then, one by one, they all fell prostrate in obedience to God's command.

The tension that had gripped my heart vanished like dew exposed to the rising sun. The crisis was over. The people of Medina had been tested, and they had passed.

And then my eyes fell upon the sparkling beauty of Zaynab bint Jahsh, the source of all this madness. I realized that she had been standing discreetly in the shadows, her face covered by a black silk veil that she had lifted when it became clear that the community would not pounce upon her. Even though her hair was still covered by a dark scarf, her perfect features, her upturned eyelashes and thick, inviting lips shone forth. Zaynab stepped proudly to stand at the Prophet's right hand, next to Sawda. I suddenly cursed myself for remaining aloof and giving my space up to this woman. Zaynab turned to face the Prophet and smiled at him, her ivory teeth flashing in the sun. And the fire of rage that had been kindled in my heart burst forth again.

Zaynab saw me looking at her and I thought I saw her lips curl in a victorious smile. She had won. I was no longer the crown jewel of the harem. Zaynab would be the most beautiful woman in the household and the Messenger would soon taste of her flesh and be satiated. And unlike all of his other marriages, his wedding to Zaynab was one that came from the heart. The Messenger wanted Zaynab for herself, not for a political alliance or as an act of charity. He wanted Zaynab's body and soul, even as he had wanted mine.

My heart pounded in despair and I barely heard my father's voice as he politely spoke to my husband.

"May I serve as a witness at your wedding ceremony to Zaynab?"

I flashed Abu Bakr an outraged look, even though I knew that he was being diplomatic. My father full well understood that Zaynab could easily become the Prophet's new favorite and that his status as Muhammad's closest adviser might be diminished as a result. Abu Bakr was trying to show the Messenger that he was a supportive friend, even if he must endure a loss of face for his family. It was a wise and generous act. But at that moment, I felt so alone that I could not bear to see my own father welcome this beautiful interloper and bless her union with my husband.

The Messenger put a gentle hand on my father's shoulder, which had become even more stooped with age and the burdens of life over the past few years.

"There will no ceremony, my friend," Muhammad said. "The wedding has already been performed in heaven, with angels as the witnesses."

At this, I saw Zaynab beam widely. She would not even need to wait for the formalities of a wedding. She could take the Messenger to bed at once and consummate their union that very night.

I felt my face turn hot, and my cheeks burned brighter than my hair. And then I found my feet moving against my will and I was suddenly no longer safely ensconced in the doorway of my little home, but standing in the center of the crowded courtyard facing my husband, the Messenger of God.

"Your Lord is quick to fulfill your desires!" I screamed into his face.

The Prophet stepped back as if I had slapped him. I saw Zaynab's face turn down in contempt, and I caught a look of warning in my father's stern glance. I suddenly realized that every eye in the Masjid was on me, and I felt like the greatest fool on earth.

Somehow I managed to hold my head up in dignity. And then, without another word, I turned and stormed back inside my apartment, slamming the door shut and locking out the harsh world.

At that moment, my legs gave way. I fell to the ground and vomited. My body shaking violently, I crawled to a corner of my room and began to cry at the injustice of life and the cruelties of womanhood.

8

*T*he desert filled with the thunder of hooves as the Meccan army marched steadily toward Medina for the final confrontation. Four thousand men, armored in the finest chain mail from Abyssinia, accompanied by three hundred horsemen and fifteen hundred warriors on camels.

At a wadi four days south of the oasis, they were met by their new allies, the displaced men of Bani Nadir. Huyayy ibn Akhtab led a contingent of two thousand seven hundred infantry and three hundred horses. Joined together, it was the mightiest force ever seen in Arabia.

As the combined juggernaut turned its red eye to the north, a figure hiding in crevices of an ancient lava mound watched their movements carefully. The Muslim scout, a tribesman from the allied Bani Khuza'a, quickly calculated the full extent of the invading army and then crawled back to his horse, which had been tied by the mouth of an old cave that burrowed deep into the ocean of sand.

Saying a silent prayer to Allah to grant him the speed of a falcon, the scout climbed on his mount and raced back toward Medina. If he continued for three days with no sleep, he might be able to get back in time to warn his people. He only hoped that his horse would survive the merciless pace. But if he was forced to complete the journey on foot, he would do so. The scout knew that the dogs of war were bearing down upon the unsuspecting oasis, and if he failed in his mission, the *Ummah* would be consumed in the jaws of their rage.

＊　＊　＊

THE COUNCIL OF WAR gathered in the courtyard of the Masjid. I walked among the worried men, carrying a bucket of water to help them quench their thirst or wet their brows as the cruel sun beat down upon them. The Messenger sat by the *mihrab*, the southern alcove facing Mecca that delineated the direction of prayer. His brow was furrowed and his shoulders bent. His black eyes were upon the dark earth at his feet, where his followers had drawn a rough map of Medina and its surrounding hills.

Umar had just explained that the best strategy would be to evacuate the women and the children into a network of caves in the volcanic fields while the men barricaded themselves inside the houses and prepared for hand-to-hand combat in the streets. There was no talk of moving out to confront the enemy as we had done at Uhud. The scout, before he had died of exhaustion and sunstroke, had given us a troubling estimate of the size of the invading army. Even with our Bedouin allies to the north, we would be outmatched two to one. Though Ali had been adamant that we could beat such odds—we had done so at Badr, and even at Uhud we had been winning until the archers betrayed us—there was another problem.

The Bani Qurayza, the last of the Jewish tribes in Medina, would be directly behind us if we chose to go out into the hills and battle against the invaders. Though the Jews had refused to participate in the past conflicts, even though our treaty required them to join us in the defense of the oasis, there could be no guarantee that they would remain neutral this time. According to the courageous scout, the Jews of Bani Nadir had joined in arms with Abu Sufyan, and it was unlikely that the Qurayza would sit back while their kinsmen fought the Muslims. If we risked going out into the fields, we risked opening ourselves to attack from the rear.

The only plan that made sense was Umar's. But I could tell that my husband was not enamored of the idea of turning the city streets of Medina into a battleground. He had worked for five years to bring order and peace to the chaotic settlement and the thought of blood flowing through its cobbled streets was too painful to bear. But without other options, he had announced to the gathered believers his intention to lure the Meccans into the winding alleys of the oasis, force their troops to divide and scatter, and turn the houses themselves into death traps. It was a butcher's job, but war was ugly no matter how it was executed.

There had been a long silence as the men looked at one another grimly. This would be the last battle. Either the Meccan army would be annihilated in the streets, or the Muslims would be massacred. And if the Muslim men were defeated, the women and children would be hunted down in the neighboring hills and captured or killed. There would be no quarter from the Meccans, not after so many years of bitter conflict. After watching Hind's cannibalistic barbarism, they shuddered to think what would become of any survivors left in the hands of the enemy.

I heard a nervous cough as a man sitting outside the central circle of the Prophet's advisers cleared his throat. It was Salman, a Persian who had been a slave to one of the Jews of Bani Qurayza. After he had adopted Islam, the Messenger had purchased his freedom and the foreigner had lived among the Arabs as one of them. Salman was short and thin, with blue eyes and the handsome chiseled features of his race. When he spoke, it was with a lyrical voice that made every word sound as if it had been sung, and his Persian accent was hauntingly beautiful.

"O Messenger of God, is your strategy revealed by God, or is it a matter of personal opinion?"

Umar scowled and turned red.

"How dare you question the Messenger?"

The Prophet placed a hand on his father-in-law's massive shoulder.

"Gently, Umar," he said with a patient smile, and then turned his attention to the freedman. "It is a matter of opinion. Do you have another suggestion, Salman?"

Salman hesitated and then moved into the circle of the Messenger's closest aides. Umar gave him a furious flash of his eyes, but the Persian ignored it. He leaned down to look at the map of the oasis drawn in the upturned earth and ran a delicate finger through his perfectly groomed beard.

Salman took his fingers and clawed out several deep lines on the ground representing the northern face of the city. The lines connected and formed an arc that encircled the vulnerable northern passes where the Meccan army would be best positioned to invade. Salman finished his work and looked up at my husband with a nervous glance.

"In my native land, we would dig a trench around our cities to protect them from siege," Salman said. "If it pleases God and His Messenger, perhaps a similar strategy would serve in the defense of Medina."

I looked down over the shoulder of my brother-in-law Zubayr and suddenly understood what the Persian was saying. I was not yet a military strategist—my days as a commander of armies were still many years away—but I could see how a ditch dug at the intervals Salman suggested might work.

The Companions looked at one another in surprise but said nothing, each perhaps afraid to be the first to voice support for this unusual stratagem. And then, finally, Umar spoke, his gruff voice rumbling through the courtyard.

"A trench large enough to hold back an army? I have never heard of such a thing," he said, with a hint of grudging respect.

My husband looked into Salman's nervous eyes and smiled warmly, taking the Persian's hand in his.

"Neither have the Meccans."

9

The Confederates, as the unified Meccan and Jewish contingents called themselves, crossed waves of blackened sand dunes as they made their final approach to Medina. The size of the army had swelled to ten thousand as disgruntled Bedouins were recruited to join the behemoth as it marched toward the upstart oasis that had thrown the world into disarray

It had been twenty days since the Arab and Jewish forces had joined together in the wilderness and the steady march through the desert for the army had been exhausting. Water skins were running low, and the first sight of the palm trees that lined the southern boundaries of Medina had been welcome. The men had raided the wells on the outskirts of the town and had been surprised to find them utterly undefended. They had rejoiced, seeing their easy capture of the southern passes as a sign from the gods of imminent victory.

But their commander, Khalid ibn al-Waleed, was troubled. He sat upon his mighty black stallion and gazed out across the horizon, past the lava tracts that served as Medina's natural defensive border to the south. He did not stir, even as Huyayy ibn Akhtab, the leader of the Jewish forces, rode up beside him, beaming.

"Smile, my friend! Victory is upon us." Huyayy gazed across the dark stones that led to his lost homeland and breathed in the salty oasis air deeply. "Soon my people will reclaim their homes. And your people will regain their honor."

Khalid turned to face him at last, his eyes burning darkly.

"Where are Muhammad's advance guards? We are almost to Medina and there has been no sign of even a single horseman."

The chief of the Bani Nadir shrugged, unwilling to let the dour Arab spoil his jubilant mood.

"He has likely taken refuge inside the city, like my forefathers did at Masada," Huyayy said, although he disliked comparing the noble warriors of his ancestors with this self-serving impostor and his illiterate fanatics.

But the reference was lost on Khalid, who gave him a blank look.

"They held off the entire Roman army for years," Huyayy explained proudly. "When the centurions finally breached the walls, they found that all the Jews had killed themselves rather than surrender."

The chieftain's eyes gleamed with pride at the memory of the noble sacrifice, the courage of his people in the face of unconquerable odds.

But if the Jew saw honor in this tale, the Arab found it less appealing. Khalid spit on the ground in contempt.

"The Arabs are not suicidal like your ancestors," he said sharply. "They are nothing if not brave. They will meet us and fight."

Huyayy bit his tongue before he said something that would wreck their hard-won alliance.

"If these Arabs are so courageous, then where are they?" Huyayy tried to keep the poison out of his voice, but he was not entirely successful.

Khalid shook his head

"That is what concerns me."

Before Huyayy could respond, shouts echoed from ahead. Khalid roughly spurred his horse and rode past the front lines of the advancing army. Huyayy quickly followed and saw a group of Confederate scouts standing on top of a large lava tract that would give them a view down into the heart of the oasis.

When Huyayy reached the ledge, he felt his heart miss a beat.

A massive trench had been dug across the northern passes into Medina. From where he stood, Huyayy estimated that it was thirty feet wide and perhaps a hundred feet deep. The cavernous ditch wound across the borders of the city to the west until it vanished into the thick jumble of palm trees and rocky hills to the south.

He had never seen anything like it, and he could see no way to traverse this barrier.

As Huyayy's heart sank, he heard the racing of hooves and saw the Meccan leader Abu Sufyan ride up to join them. The old man breathed in sharply at the sight of this surprising defensive tactic.

"What is this?" Abu Sufyan asked, his voice mixing fury and despair all at once.

And then Huyayy was stunned to hear the sound of deep laughter. He turned to see Khalid's head thrown back in genuine delight.

"A work of genius," the general said, without any hint of bitterness.

And then, like a child racing to collect a new toy, Khalid rode down the ash-covered dunes toward the edge of the pit. The Confederate army followed, although the soldiers' faces were twisted in confusion at the sight of the barrier.

When Huyayy pushed his horse to follow, he saw that the trench was not the only obstacle facing them. The entire Muslim army, numbering perhaps three thousand men, stood on the far side of the ditch, bows pointed at the invading forces, spears held ready to fly across the divide at their adversaries.

And then he saw Muhammad standing there, bare-chested and covered in sweat and dust, and realized that the heretic leader had been among the workers who had torn open the earth in what must have been a backbreaking exercise over many days. Despite his hatred of the man, Huyayy had to admire his willingness to get his hands dirty along with his men. Such leaders always inspired the loyalty of their troops, and Huyayy knew that they would fight to the death for this man should the Meccans somehow break through their defenses.

Muhammad greeted the invaders with a broad smile and threw open his arms in a defiant welcome. Khalid stared across the divide and smiled, saluting his enemy an acknowledgment of a well-conceived plan. Whatever differences of faith divided them, the code of honor between warriors still held its sway.

And then Khalid turned and signaled to his best horsemen. Without a word spoken between them, the cavalry rode forward, knowing exactly what the Meccan general expected of them.

A dozen of the mightiest chargers raced through the desert plain and leaped across the trench. A swarm of arrows met them and the horses were hit in midflight. The terrified screams of the animals ended abruptly as they plunged to their deaths in the pit below. Most of the riders broke their necks in the fall, but those who somehow managed to survive and crawl away from their shattered mounts were immediately struck by a second volley of projectiles.

Khalid held up his hand to prevent more honor seekers from trying to leap across the ditch. As an experienced general, he knew that once a stratagem had failed, it was a waste of lives and resources to repeat it in the hope of securing a better outcome. The horses simply could not leap the distance and land safely on the other side, and if miraculously one or two made it across the chasm, their riders would be alone and surrounded by well-armed enemies.

He looked across the ditch at his adversaries and calculated. Khalid could send his men down into the pit with ropes, but the Muslims held the advantage of the high ground. They would easily cut down his soldiers before they ever managed to climb to the other side. It would be a waste of life with little likelihood of success.

"What do we do?" It was the despairing voice of Abu Sufyan, who looked increasingly too old and weary to lead the Meccans to triumph. Khalid had nothing but contempt for this man who had proclaimed himself king of Mecca and whose only claim to power came from his cowardly avoidance of battle at Badr, where the competing chieftains were killed. There had already been whispers that Khalid should dispatch the elderly fool and take his place in the Hall of Assembly.

But Khalid ibn al-Waleed was a warrior, not a king. He found purpose and joy in the heat of the battlefield among the brave men he loved, not in the coddled life of a ruler surrounded by bureaucrats and sycophants. Khalid had no interest in becoming a king, but he knew that one was needed at the moment. It was kings and chieftains who declared the wars that men like Khalid lived to fight. But in the past several years, he had become increasingly disgusted with the leaders of Mecca, who showed cowardice and avarice, who ruled by bribery and fear, without any sense of honor.

He gazed across the enemy lines at Muhammad again and realized that his enemy had all the qualities that his allies did not. He was noble and courageous and could inspire men to lay down their lives. As he looked at the man who had been denounced as a rebel by the lords of Mecca, Khalid began to wonder what life would be like leading armies under Muhammad's command.

But before he could take the thought further, he heard the insistent braying of Abu Sufyan in his ear, demanding a solution to this unforeseen problem.

Khalid sighed heavily and turned his attention to the fields of grain that stood just outside the borders of the trench, the groves of olive trees that were budding with the coming of the spring. The Muslims had wisely built the trench in a circle as close to the city as possible, limiting the area that needed to be defended. But in the process, they had been forced to cut themselves off from their own farmlands.

Khalid knew what needed to be done. And a part of him regretted that it had to be this way.

He turned to face Abu Sufyan and his Jewish ally Huyayy.

"We wait. Hunger will accomplish what swords and spears cannot."

10

The siege had persisted for ten days and our food supplies were running desperately low. I had spent almost every daylight hour at the front lines, taking water to the soldiers who bravely guarded the trench. The Meccans had been tireless in their efforts to find a way around the obstacle, and we could not afford to let our guard down for a minute. The first few nights, Khalid's warriors attempted to use the cover of darkness to climb down into the ditch. But Zubayr's alert eyes caught sight of the moving shadows and a barrage of arrows and spears quickly put an end to infiltrators. Had it not been for your father's sleepless vigils, Abdallah, a few of the assassins would have broken the perimeter and wreaked havoc on Medina.

By the fourth day, Meccan scouts had spied a small weakness in our defenses. The trench ended at a leafy marsh to the southwest, where the natural barriers of trees and rocky hills made penetration by cavalry impossible. But a few intrepid men, led by Ikrimah, the son of Abu Jahl, and Amr Abdal Wudd, swam through the muddy bog and slipped past our sentries. The band was poised to enter the confines of the city, where they planned to spread fires and breed general chaos, when Ali confronted them at the edge of Medina. Ali and Abdal Wudd engaged in a short but brutal duel, which ended when the glowing *Dhul Fiqar* split the Meccan spy's head in two. The cowardly Ikrimah and his men fled back through the swamp, dodging the barrage of missiles raining down upon them when the alarm was raised.

On the sixth day, the horizon was covered in smoke. Abu Sufyan had ordered the burning of the crop fields that circled the oasis, and I watched with tears as the verdant lands around us were consumed. We had harvested most of the date palms and the grains of wheat and barley in the weeks prior to the attack, but with the destruction of the trees that were the lifeblood of Medina, our chances of long-term survival were greatly diminished.

But by then, few of us were thinking in the long term. Survival had become a matter of getting through each day alive. With trade effectively cut off by the siege, we had no way to replace the rapidly diminishing stores of food. Even though the Messenger had instituted rationing, with women and children given twice the daily portions of the men, there was simply not enough to go around.

And so it was that on the tenth night of the battle, I walked with the other Mothers, going from house to house to check on the needs of the families that had been sequestered away from the front. It had been a difficult evening, for in every household we came upon we found the sick and the dying. The matrons pleaded with me for their children, asking me to relay the distress of their loved ones to the Messenger and begging me to perform some kind of miracle to save their lives. I wanted to run away, to hide somewhere from the desperate looks, the bony hands that reached out to touch me as if my body carried some kind of *baraka*, some miraculous blessing that would take away their sorrow.

I smiled gently at them and spoke words of comfort and hope, as required of a Mother of the Believers. But for all my lofty spiritual trappings, I was only fourteen years old and the weight of the world was crushing me.

As I emerged from a small stone hut that was overcrowded with a dozen women and their children, I let the cool oasis breeze strike my face, felt the tingle of the air against the wetness of my cheeks. This last house had been the worst. Several families were hunched together inside a space that had been meant for three people at most, with barely any room to breathe, much less walk. The house belonged to a carpenter whose wife had recently given birth to a daughter. The man had been injured by an arrow to the shoulder while guarding the trench, and he had been brought back here to heal. But the unsanitary conditions in the tight quarters had made his wound fester, and I could smell the lurid stench of death hovering over him. I thought bitterly that the carpenter's martyrdom would at least somewhat alleviate the space concerns inside the cottage. Perhaps when he was buried, some of the children could move just far enough away to avoid catching the dreaded camp fever that had infected two toddlers, who had been crying nonstop for hours.

It was a heartless thought, but I was tired and hungry. I was angry at life. And perhaps, although I would not have admitted it aloud, I was angry at God for letting this happen.

As I led my fellow Mothers away from the house, my scarved head bowed in fury and despair, I heard Umm Salama, the gentle widow, speak.

"We should tell the Messenger," she said, her voice cracking in sorrow from the tragedies we had witnessed tonight.

I turned to face her and shook my head grimly.

"He has enough to worry about."

The Messenger had not left his post at the trench since the first Meccan horseman had appeared. He had survived on perhaps two hours of sleep every night, and the toll of the siege was clear on his face. His glossy black beard had begun to streak with gray, and new lines had appeared around his dark eyes. It was as if this perpetually young man had aged overnight.

Sawda, my plump and elderly cowife, wiped tears from her eyes.

"But the children are starving. It will not be long before *Jannat al-Baqi* takes them," she said, referring to the graveyard on the outskirts of the oasis.

"There is nothing more he can do," I snapped, suddenly feeling intensely protective of my husband. The last thing he needed right now was to be nagged by his wives about matters that he could not control.

The Messenger knew full well the suffering of his community. Providing grisly details of famine and disease would only shatter his soft heart, making it that more difficult to stand up against this relentless foe.

I saw my young rival Hafsa shrug as if she were not convinced by my words.

"Perhaps he can negotiate a truce," she said bluntly. "Or perhaps a surrender with honor—"

I slapped her.

Hafsa recoiled as if I had cut her with a knife. But the slice of a blade would have been more bearable than the cold fire in my eyes.

"The wolf is at the door and you would deliver us into its jaws!"

Hafsa's face turned bright red, the rage that was the legacy of her father's blood kindled. I steeled myself for a retaliatory blow and prayed that the cover of night would prevent anyone from seeing the Mothers of the Believers fighting like cats in the streets.

But then Hafsa surprised me. The daughter of Umar ibn al-Khattab took a deep breath and calmed herself. With what must have been a monumental effort, she bit down on her lip and then spoke in a calm, steady voice.

"You're right. I shouldn't have said that."

In that moment, Hafsa went from being a dreaded rival in the harem to a woman I could respect. Indeed, as our friendship deepened over the years, we would often laugh that it began because I was the only person ever to stand up to her.

But that night there was nothing to laugh about. The vultures were waiting at the edge of Medina for us to fall prey to starvation and disease. And within ten days, they would have their wish. Unless the Messenger could find a way to dislodge the dogs of war from our doorstep, we were all doomed. And to have any hope of doing that, he needed support from his loved ones in his darkest hours.

I turned to face my cowives. When I spoke, it was with the voice of a strong woman, not that of a little girl. My body was that of a child, but my soul was already aged beyond a dozen a lifetimes.

"We are not like other women, who have the luxury of nagging their husbands with doubts and fears," I said solemnly. "We are the Messenger's last defense against this cruel and mad world. Do you think Khadija ever asked him to surrender when all of Mecca sought his head?"

That last was the hardest for me to say. Even though I had shared the Messenger's bed for five years, even though I had been proclaimed the most beloved and honored of his wives, I had never been able to take the place of Khadija, the first person to believe in him and stand by his side. There were times when I felt him toss restlessly in bed beside me. And I would hear him whisper her name and see tears fall from his sleeping eyes as the pain of loss consumed his hidden mind. No matter how long I stayed with him, no matter how many sons I might bear him, he would never truly be mine.

Hafsa bowed her head and I saw the last fire of pride go out.

"I was a fool. I'm sorry," she sobbed.

And then the radiant Zaynab bint Jahsh put her hand on Hafsa's shoulder in comfort.

"Do not be. The thought had entered my mind as well."

Zaynab looked at me with a raised eyebrow, her eyes challenging me to strike her perfect face as I had struck Hafsa's. There was such power in her gaze, such innate nobility, that I suddenly felt like a child again, my pretense of authority vanishing into the night air.

The kindly Sawda moved to my side, perhaps sensing that my bravado was little more than a cover for the grief and uncertainty that veiled my heart.

"But what do we do?" she asked softly. It was strange, this woman who was well into her sixties turning to a teenage girl for advice. But the world was upside down and only those who could navigate the strange pathways of this nightmare would survive.

"We stand with the Messenger," I said, feeling my confidence return with renewed vigor. "And if our destiny is to die at his side, whether by an arrow or by hunger, we do it with dignity and a smile on our faces."

I took Sawda's right hand as if to swear an oath. Hafsa placed hers atop mine. After a moment of hesitation, Zaynab did so as well.

"We are the Mothers of the Believers," I said, pronouncing each word of our shared title with great dignity. "Nothing less can be expected of us in the eyes of God or man."

The women smiled, their hopes renewed, and even Zaynab gave me a grateful look. I smiled back at her and hoped that her piercing eyes could not see the terrible chains of fear that bound my heart.

11

The black gates of the fortress shimmered in the moonlight. They had stood for a dozen generations, protecting their inhabitants from the wolves that roamed the volcanic hills, whether those beasts were canine or mortal men.

A single man stood outside the protection of those doors tonight, his dark eyes gazing over the tops of the hillocks toward a world he no longer recognized. Kab ibn Asad, the chieftain of the Bani Qurayza, saw the burning clouds of smoke that rose to the north, where an army stood on the verge of destroying the town that had once been called Yathrib. His brothers among the Bani Nadir had returned to reclaim their homes and had brought with them thousands of Arab warriors to support their cause. True, they had been temporarily blocked by the Muslims' ingenious trench, but Kab knew that the moment would come when the barrier would fail and vengeance would be taken.

Almost a fortnight had passed with the army of liberators held back at the gates of Medina, but the delay had served a purpose. The Muslims were like trapped animals, hungry and exhausted, cut off from the necessities of survival by their own hubris. They were hanging fruit, ripe to be plucked. When his spies had confirmed the extent of the famine, the weakness of the Muslim troops, Kab had sent a specially trained falcon to the camp of his kinsman Huyayy, leader of the exiled Bani Nadir. In its deadly claws it carried a small message written in Hebrew, a language none of the enemy would understand if the bird were captured or killed. But the mighty falcon had returned unharmed, a reply written in Hebrew with the answer Kab had been hoping for.

And so it was that he stood alone tonight just past the safety of the fortress walls. He was doing what he had done for many months. Watching and waiting.

And then he saw it. A flicker of movement against the black lava flows that surrounded the southern pass. Kab focused his eyes but could see nothing more in the darkness. For a moment, he wondered if he had imagined it, his eager mind showing him what he hoped to see. And then he heard the steady crunch of footsteps against the cold pebbles and two small shadows broke free of the great black shadow of the hillside.

Kab stood perfectly still as the cloaked men approached him. He glanced up at the walls above. Archers were hidden in the turrets, ready to take action at his signal. If his message had indeed been intercepted by Muhammad's men and these two were assassins sent to even the score, the matter would be dealt with quickly.

The cloaked men stopped ten feet before the chieftain. And then the shorter one spoke, his voice rich and wonderfully familiar.

"You can tell your men to stand down," Huyayy ibn Akhtab said. "Unless they want to do the enemy's work for them."

Kab smiled and raised his left hand. Although there was no sound from the turrets above, he knew that his men had lowered their weapons. And then he turned to greet the newcomers.

Huyayy removed his cloak and embraced Kab warmly. The chief of the Bani Nadir nodded to his companion, who pulled off his hood, revealing the aging but still regal features of the Meccan lord Abu Sufyan.

The Arab greeted the Jew with a sardonic smile.

"It is a changed world where old friends must meet with such intrigue," Abu Sufyan said.

Kab took Abu Sufyan by the hand and led him toward the mighty gates of the fortress, which sung aside with a harsh groan.

"Then it is time to change the world back," he said.

— — —

IT WAS NEARLY FIRST light before the iron gates thundered open again. The three men emerged from a night of negotiations that had not gone as Kab had expected. His offer to work with the Confederates had been welcomed, but Abu Sufyan had sought to place the burden of risk on the Bani Qurayza's shoulders. The Arab chieftain had asked for the Jews to take Muhammad by surprise and attack from the rear. Once the warriors of the Qurayza had spread chaos through the oasis, forcing the defenders to leave their places at the trench, the Confederates would traverse the barrier and come to Kab's aid.

It was a tactic that put the Bani Qurayza's head on the block, with only a hope and a prayer that the Confederates would be able to intervene before the executioner's blade descended.

Kab had been bitterly disappointed by the stratagem. He had waited so many months, patiently praying for deliverance from the sorcerer who had hijacked his home, but now, when the answer had come, it carried too high a price.

But his views were not shared by the other elders of his tribe. Hungry to confront Muhammad and gain revenge for the humiliations the Jews had suffered over the past five years, the shining lights of the Qurayza had embraced this foolhardy plan. Kab had been shouted down in the council of war by old men who dreamed of victory but who would not themselves carry a blade into battle.

But Kab had been able to gain one concession from his allies. The Arabs would be required to send a dozen of their most noble leaders to the fortress of the Bani Qurayza as "guests" during the hostilities. The safe return of these hostages would require the Meccans to take decisive action to end the siege. If the Quraysh failed to speedily come to the aid of the Qurayza, they would risk losing their own men in the fire of Muhammad's vengeance.

Abu Sufyan had reluctantly agreed and offered the sons of the Meccan chieftains who had been killed at Badr and Uhud, the most prominent being Ikrimah ibn Abu Jahl. Kab had made a sour face when he heard the name. Ikrimah was as brutal as his late father but lacked the charm and diplomatic skills to be a leader like Abu Jahl. Kab wondered if anyone would come to his rescue when the flames of chaos were ignited. He had politely asked Abu Sufyan the whereabouts of his own son, the charismatic Muawiya. At mention of the young man's name, Abu Sufyan's face had darkened and he had refused to speak further. Kab had wisely dropped the topic.

As the three men stepped outside, Abu Sufyan turned to face Kab and looked him straight in the eye.

"Do we have an understanding?" he said, in a tone that suggested he was not convinced of Kab's support after the contentious meeting.

Kab felt a flash of fury. He leaned close to Abu Sufyan and spoke slowly, making sure that the Arab understood what was being asked of the Qurayza.

"If my people break the treaty, there will be no turning back.

Should any of Muhammad's men survive our attack, they will seek vengeance."

Huyayy put an arm on Kab and pulled the men apart.

"Then we will leave none alive."

Kab turned to face his old friend. He had been so delighted to see him only a few hours before. And now he was beginning to regret ever letting the chief of the Bani Nadir inside the fortress.

"You seem very sure of yourself, Huyayy," he said sharply. "Considering that your own web collapsed on you, I would think that you'd be cautious about spinning new ones."

Huyayy stepped back as if struck. He looked at Kab as if he did not recognize him.

"There is a time for caution and a time to seize the initiative," Huyayy said coldly, his eyes narrowing. "This is our last chance, Kab. And yours. If Muhammad defeats the siege, he will be emboldened. He will find a pretext to expel the Qurayza and then will wage war on Khaybar. The Jews of Arabia will vanish into the sands of history."

Kab stepped back, let the anger seep out of him until he was calm again. They were both on the same side. Both trying to save their people from extinction. It was true that the Confederate plan placed his tribe at risk of immediate annihilation. But it was also true that should the liberators be defeated, the Qurayza would eventually be destroyed anyway as Muhammad's movement gained supremacy.

The choice Kab faced was stark and cruel, like the wilderness of Arabia he loved with all his heart. Either way, the Bani Qurayza ran the risk of defeat. But if his people were to face death, then it was more honorable to do so fighting by the side of his fellow Jews.

"I will stand by our people," Kab said after a moment of painful reflection. "But you must not tarry. The gates will open tomorrow night when the new moon covers the land in its veil. If you are not ready then, they will be closed to you forever."

Abu Sufyan nodded, satisfied that Kab would uphold his end of the bargain.

"We will be ready."

The two men then slipped on their cloaks and vanished into the darkness, seeking to reach their camp before dawn penetrated the gloom and revealed their presence.

They needn't have hurried, for they had already been detected. As

Kab returned inside the fortress and the powerful gates shut with an ominous boom, a small figure, dressed in robes of midnight black, rose up from a hidden position in the crevices of the lava flow and hastened toward the oasis.

12

I approached the stout housewife and handed her a dagger.

"Take this," I said with as much authority as I could muster. The woman hesitated and I grabbed her by the wrist and placed the hilt of the blade in her hand. "It is not a request."

"Why?" she asked, her voice quivering with fear.

I had spent the entire morning performing this ritual and was weary of the question. I was about to respond with a sharp retort, but I peeked at the woman and suddenly felt compassion for her. She could not have been more than thirty, but years of toiling under the cruel sun had left her as withered and wrinkled as a dried fig, her hair colored red with henna to hide the early streaks of white. She was not ready for what was coming. None of us were.

"The Messenger says we must be ready to fight in the streets," I replied with a conscious effort to be gentle. "Every Muslim, man or woman, who can lift a weapon must do so when the time comes."

The frightened woman—Nuriya was her name—looked closely at the weapon with a trembling hand. I heard the rustle of her skirt and looked down to see a toddler, a boy of perhaps two, clinging to her and staring up at me with wide eyes. The child's cheeks were sunken and his stomach was distended, a sign that famine had struck this home with particular fury.

Nuriya lowered the weapon and looked at me with dead eyes.

"So this is the end."

I reached out and took her bony fingers in mine, squeezing them gently.

"Only God knows."

Fear had gripped the oasis ever since our spies had returned with word that our enemies had been secretly meeting with our putative allies, the Bani Qurayza. The Messenger did not know what their plan was, but one thing was clear. The last of the Jewish tribes had renounced its pact with us and was now poised to help the Confederates. We had to prepare for the worst.

Nuriya began to cry and pray desperately to Allah for the deliverance of her children. She tried to reach out to me, as if she wanted my comfort, but I turned away, ready to continue my rounds. My straw basket was heavy and overflowing with small weapons—knives, arrows, anything that could be spared by the defenders at the trench in order to arm their families. I had two dozen homes to visit before the sun went down and did not have time to soothe this woman any further.

And then the sound of a newborn crying from inside stopped me. From the desperate wails, I could tell that the infant could not have been more than a week old. My heart sank as I wondered whether this poor baby's destiny was to enter this world only to leave it again in a few days in the chaos of flames and destruction. It was an unjust fate and I felt a flash of anger at the Meccans, at the arrogance and heartlessness of men, at the cruelty of life in this miserable desert wasteland.

I looked at Nuriya, saw the terror and uncertainty on her features. And the anger I felt building inside me was suddenly released on the poor, cowering woman.

"Stop it! Stop crying!"

Nuriya looked up at me, stunned and hurt.

I leaned forward to her, my heart pounding in my ears.

"Listen to me," I said with grave intensity. "Your children will not be saved by your whimpering! They need you to be as strong and as cold as a man. If the enemy knocks at your door, do not let the softness of your heart be your undoing. They will give you no quarter. Give them none as well."

The steel in my voice cut through her grief and her tears stopped. I saw a stony mask come upon her lined face as she slew the weak housewife she had been and gave birth to the warrior that is buried inside every woman's heart, one who is unleashed when her children's lives are at stake.

She wiped her tears and nodded, gripping the dagger like a lion locking its jaws on the throat of its prey.

I nodded and moved away. And then, when I could find shelter in the nook of an abandoned alley, I dropped the basket and fell to my knees. My body trembled violently as the emotions I had been suppressing all morning erupted from inside me like a volcano. I vomited and then buried my face in my hands, letting the tears I had forbidden Nuriya to shed flood my cheeks.

A dark cloud covered the sun and the world looked utterly black, without any hint or hope of light.

The shadow of death hung over Medina. War would soon cover the streets in blood. And I could see no escape from the final doom that my people had somehow avoided up until this day. The end was near and I surrendered to despair, closing my eyes and forgetting everything. My duty. My family. My life. I just wanted to go to sleep and never awaken again.

To let the darkness take me into the eternal void.

And then I heard a soft voice. Whether it was in my ears or in my heart, I will never know.

God leads from darkness to light, Humayra.

I opened my eyes in shock. It was my husband's voice, as clear and as loud as if he were standing above me. But the alley was empty, except for a small gray cat that looked at me from atop a pile of rubbish with its mysterious yellow eyes.

The shadow that had covered the city began to lift. I looked up to see small rays of light tearing through the angry clouds. And then, as each ray broke through, opening a way for another beam of light to cut a path out of the gloom, the cloud began to shatter and disperse until the golden disk burst forth in all its glory.

I realized in that moment that the sun was a fire composed of an infinite number of tiny sparks, each playing its role in creating the light that drove away the darkness. Even the tiniest and most insignificant ray had a part in the heavenly dance.

I found myself rising to my feet and reclaiming my store of weapons. The people of Medina needed me. And even if it was all meant to end under the harsh steel of our enemies' blades, I would play my part to the last.

13

Kab stood outside the southern gate as the sandstorm raged all about him. The devil's wind had risen with no warning an hour before sunset, sending a wall of earth crashing down on the oasis like a wave in a turbulent ocean. By nightfall, the winds had worsened and the stars were blotted out by the fury of the desert squall. It had taken ten men to push open the massive doors that protected the fortress as the wind fought back with the force of a thousand battering rams. Kab had managed to step into the chaos, his body and face covered by a heavy woolen cloak, but tiny particles of sand slipped through his protective wrap and stung him like a cloud of angry wasps.

The chief of the Bani Qurayza had stayed by the threshold of the gate for nearly three hours, braving the merciless winds, his burning eyes peering through the maelstrom for any sign of the expected delegation of Meccan lords. It was a futile hope, of course, as no man could have successfully navigated the swirling sand in the darkness of night. The torches Kab had ordered lit on the battlements of the fortress as a beacon had blown out in seconds and proved impossible to ignite again in the midst of the raging storm. If any of the Quraysh had undertaken the journey through the southern passes, they had likely perished as sand clogged their lungs and a rain of tiny pebbles shredded their flesh raw. Their corpses would likely be lost forever in the dunes that would serve as their anonymous graves for eternity.

Kab bowed his head. He had failed. Tonight was their only window for attack. His spies had alerted him to the Muslims' defensive preparations earlier that day. Somehow Muhammad had learned of the Qurayza's intrigues with the Confederates and had begun arming the citizens of Medina in preparation for the invasion. The elders of the tribe had made emergency deliberations that afternoon and had agreed—against Kab's better judgment—to commence the attack that night, even if the

Quraysh failed to send the hostages that would secure their support during the chaos that was to follow.

And then the wind had changed from a gentle spring breeze into an angry tempest and the world had been plunged into darkness even as the sun still kissed the horizon. The offensive was now impossible, and the small window of time the Qurayza had before the Muslim defenses were erected was gone. Even if the sun rose on a clear morning, Muhammad would have shifted enough warriors from the trench to the Jewish quarter to make the initial onslaught a pitched battle rather than an easy victory. With the Meccan forces likely to be in disarray because of the sandstorm, there would be no intervention by the Confederates to shift the scales back in favor of Kab's people.

The battle was over before it began, but the consequences would linger.

Kab finally turned back and stepped inside the protective walls of the fortress.

"Close the gate," he said to the weary men who had braved the elements and kept the passage open for the past several hours. They quickly complied, their dust-covered faces revealing relief that Kab had finally faced reality.

As the mighty doors slammed behind him with a thunderous crash, Kab saw a small figure step toward him, bearing a robe. Even in the dark he caught sight of a lock of flaming red hair and knew immediately who had come to greet him. It was Najma, his beloved niece, who had been like a daughter to him over the years. She wrapped him in the soft linen and led him back home by the hand.

— — —

KAB SAT BY THE stone fireplace, sipping a cup of warm goat's milk that Najma had prepared for him. He stared at the far wall of the chamber, which was lined with tiny cracks that spidered out across the sturdy mud bricks. Najma had insisted for many years that he should refinish this room, which served as his personal study, but Kab had refused.

The chamber was one of the original structures in the Jewish settlement, having been built over three hundred years before when Kab's forefathers had found the oasis after a deadly journey through the Arabian sands. The small room had once housed entire families, before succeeding generations had added a dozen more rooms and turned the modest home of the tribal chief into a palatial estate. The remaining chambers were elegantly decorated with marble tiles and furnished in a style that befitted the prosperity of his people, but this central room, with its plain walls and harsh stone floor, remained as it had in the days when the first Jew had found refuge in Yathrib.

This room had been the seed from which the grand fortress that protected them had grown. And Kab felt that it was fitting that he spend this night, when the fate of their people had been sealed, here.

Najma saw the sadness in his eyes and put a gentle hand on his arm.

"Once the storm ends, we can begin preparations for the liberation," she said with a hopeful smile. "And then you can reclaim the oasis for our people and there will be peace."

Kab looked up and met her dark eyes, saw in them the absolute trust of a child, even though Najma was a grown woman pursued by many suitors. He felt a pang of grief as the thought crossed his mind that he might not get a chance to see her marry. Confronted with her innocence, her misguided belief in his great wisdom and leadership, he suddenly felt very small and alone. Part of his soul wanted to let her keep believing that things would turn out well for their people, that his grand sagacity would turn this minor setback into an easy victory.

But he couldn't. Najma needed to be prepared for what was coming.

"There will be no liberation, my dear," he said, and the words burned his throat more than all the fiery sand he had inhaled that night. "The siege has failed."

Najma's brow crinkled as it always did when she was confused.

"Then we will bide our time," she responded, trying as always to find the flicker of light in the shadows. "God will provide us another day."

Kab hesitated. And then he took her tiny hand in his and squeezed.

"No. There will be no more days."

She sat down beside him, looking up at Kab with uncertainty.

"I don't understand" was all she said. Kab felt his heart break as he gazed into her wide eyes, filled with disbelief.

"Our allies are running out of food and water. The storm will decimate their supplies further. They have no choice but to break camp. And once the Confederates evacuate, Muhammad will turn his dogs on us."

He saw the color drain from her rosy cheeks. She took her hand out of his grasp as if she had been scalded by a flame.

"You can't be sure of that," she said forcefully.

"It is what I would do in his position," he said softly.

Najma rose to her feet and turned away from him. Kab looked away, unable to bear her grief at the revelation that he had led their people to disaster.

And then, after a long moment in which the only sound was the roaring of the wind outside, Najma turned to face her uncle again. But instead of sorrow or recrimination, her eyes burned with an intensity that he had never seen before.

"Then I will stand by your side, as Esther stood by Mordecai in the face of Haman," she said.

Kab felt his eyes water. He rose from his carved cedar chair and put his arms around this beautiful girl who was worth more to him than all the treasures of Arabia.

"I've failed you," he said in a quaking voice.

But Najma wrapped her arms around his broad shoulders and pressed him tight.

"You can never fail me, uncle," she said softly. "Where there is love, there is only victory."

The two stood together, holding each other tight as the roaring winds echoed like the beat of war drums, coming steadily closer.

14

The siege was over and the defeated army of the Confederates had fled the oasis. The sandstorm had devastated their base, killing men and animals and burying precious food supplies under mountainous dunes. Horses had bolted at the first sight of the black cloud racing across the horizon, decimating the ranks of the Meccan cavalry. It had been a final humiliating rout for the forces of the Quraysh and their allies. Despite desperate pleas from Huyayy,

Abu Sufyan had ordered the evacuation, disgust and exhaustion written on every line of his aged face.

Muhammad had won again. But this time the victory was far-reaching. The failure of the unified armies of the Arabs and Jews to dislodge him from Medina had solidified his rule of the northern peninsula. Trade with Syria and Persia was now completely in the Muslims' hands and the entire economic future of Arabia depended on making accommodations with the new city-state. The Muslim nation had survived onslaught upon onslaught and proved itself to be a lasting power that would reshape the course of history in the region.

Only one threat remained to Muhammad's total domination of the northern lands, and his people swiftly moved to bring it to an end.

I watched as the Muslim army surrounded the fortress of the Bani Qurayza. The moment our scouts had confirmed that the Quraysh were in retreat, my husband had ordered the entire defensive force to abandon the trench and regroup at the enemy stronghold. Ali had ridden forward to the grand gates of the citadel and issued a challenge to the leaders of Qurayza to emerge and account for their treachery. His words had been met with an explosion of arrows from archers hidden in the walls. Ali evaded the missiles and turned to the men behind him. The mighty battering ram that had been prepared for the tribe of Qaynuqa years before was brought forth to be used against their brethren, the sole surviving Jewish residents of the oasis.

A dozen armored soldiers took hold of the mighty pole made of palm wood and reinforced with steel. And then they heaved forward, smashing it with terrifying force against the towering gates. The iron doors trembled but held.

As the men pulled back for a second blow, a shower of stones fell upon their heads, and several of the soldiers dropped, blood pouring from their shattered helmets. I looked up to see a surprising sight. My breath stopped for a second as I thought I was looking into a bizarre mirror. A young girl no older than myself, with bright red hair like my own, was lifting rocks that were impossibly large for her tiny size and throwing them down from the turret just above the gate.

Ali signaled and Muslim archers immediately targeted her. The girl dropped beneath the protection of the stone walls just as a curtain of arrows flew high upon the turrets like upside-down rain. For a long moment, there was silence. And then the girl raised her head above the ramparts just long enough to send another boulder crashing down on the head of one of the soldiers. There was a flash of gore as the man's head burst like a squashed grape and he collapsed and did not move again.

The girl ducked as another volley of arrows tore at her position. But when the missiles were past, I could her hear childlike voice, laughing and taunting us.

I shook my head in wonder at this girl's resilience.

Ali approached and filled a stone cup from a bucket I held. He sipped the water and then passed the cup among the men nearest us. I was surprised to see them each drink heartily from the small container and then pass it along as if it were still full.

Ali glanced at the girl high above us, who was still flinging rocks from behind the wall. Our archers had decided not waste any more arrows on her, and two dozen men carrying shields had gone out to protect the troops by the wall as her onslaught continued.

"She is brave," I said.

And then Ali's ethereal green eyes met mine and I felt suddenly uneasy, as I often did in his presence.

"Yes. She is brave. But she is also unwise." He paused and looked at me as if seeing something in my eyes that even I was unaware of. "When a woman fights, she takes away from herself the cloak of honor which shields her. Remember that, young Mother."

I felt a chill as Ali turned his attention back to his men. It was as if his words held a strange premonition, and for a moment I felt the veil of time shift and I saw a vision.

A vivid and terrifying image of me standing in the desert, surrounded by a thousand corpses washed in a river of blood.

I dropped the bucket and hurried back to the oasis. I suddenly wanted to be far away from the battlefield, from the stench of blood and the sickening fog of fear and rage that hung over the oasis. I wanted to be a little girl again, whose only occupations were playing with my dolls and brushing my mother's soft hair.

I ran until I found refuge in my small apartment in the Masjid, far away from the ominous thunder of the battering ram, the singing of the arrows as they cut through the dry desert air. But it was not far enough to escape my destiny.

There are times when I wished that I could have kept on running and never stopped. For it is when we take a moment for breath in the struggle of life, when we let our guard down and allow ourselves a second to exult in a false sense of security, that the terrible wave of our doom is finally able to catch up with us.

15

The Bani Qurayza held out for twenty-five days. But as their supplies of food and water vanished and the pestilence that had struck the Muslims during the siege of the trench migrated to the Jewish quarter, Kab's people were faced with no alternative but to surrender and hope for the Messenger's mercy.

But my husband was not in a forgiving mood. In all the years that I had known him, I had never seen such anger in his eyes as I saw on the day he first learned of Qurayza's betrayal. Had God not intervened with the sandstorm that blotted their plans, the Jewish tribe would have struck us from the rear while we desperately held back the Confederate invaders at the barrier. Our women and children would have been the first casualties, as the homes where they were lodged would have been the first line of attack when the gates of the fortress had swung open.

The Messenger knew that the Qurayza had planned the utter annihilation of his people, and their treachery could not be left unanswered. Muhammad had shown clemency to the other Jewish tribes, guaranteeing their lives and letting them leave the oasis in safety. And they had repaid him by joining with his enemies. If the Qurayza were allowed the same easy fate of expulsion, they would inevitably join their kinsmen at the citadel of Khaybar to the north, where even now Huyayy was plotting to regain his lost lands despite the failure of the Confederate invasion. All of Arabia would be watching how we treated the Qurayza now that they had fallen into our hands. And mercy would be seen only as a weakness to be exploited by our enemies.

As the battered gate of the fortress opened, I watched the weary residents of the Jewish quarter emerge, their necks bowed in surrender. First the men came out, their bodies shorn of armor and their hands held high to show that they carried no weapons. There were at least seven hundred males, and I could see in their eyes the fire of defiance even as Ali, Talha, and Zubayr took them to the side and tied their hands together with sturdy ropes. I shuddered at the thought that these would have been our executioners had the sands not risen in rebellion.

And then, when the final man had emerged, the women and children followed. The women's eyes were filled with grief and rage at the sight of their men bound like slaves, but I also saw a hint of relief in many of their faces. Their children had gone without food for days, and many were too weak even to cry. But now that the end had come, at least they could find a way to feed the little ones.

I quickly led the other Mothers to their side, carrying bowls of dates and figs and buckets of water. The Jewish women hesitated when they saw us, but their children ran forward at the sight of the food, their hands outstretched in desperation. I felt tears welling in my eyes as I saw their parched lips and sunken cheeks. They were the innocent victims of war, too small to understand or care about the differences of politics and theology that had led our peoples to this terrible moment. As the children swarmed around us, I saw their mothers looking at us with gratitude as we poured water into their open mouths and placed small treats in their tiny hands.

It was a heartbreaking scene and I felt numbed. I moved toward a woman of the Qurayza who could not have been older than my mother, her dark hair streaked with gray, and embraced her. At that moment, we were neither Muslim nor Jew, neither friend nor foe. We were just women caught in a world that was bigger than us and we held each other tightly, sobbing in our shared grief at the tragedy of life in this cruel wilderness.

And then I saw a young woman step out of the fortress to join the others and I broke free of the embrace, my eyes wide with concern. It was the redheaded girl who had so stubbornly defied us during the opening days of the siege. She walked slowly, as if in a dream, the fire in her eyes now quenched by hunger and exhaustion. Had this girl, whose name I learned was Najma, been more discreet, had she hidden her face behind a veil during the attack, she might have walked unrecognized among the other refugees.

But her fiery hair, so like my own, burned like a beacon in the crowd and she was immediately surrounded by several Muslim soldiers. I ran over to her side just as Ali arrived, holding a rope.

"What are you doing?!" I cried out as Ali steadily bound the girl's hands.

"She goes with the men," he said simply.

"They will kill her," I said. I did not know this for sure, but I sensed that the Muslims were in no mood to give quarter. Whatever punishment awaited the warriors of the Qurayza, I did not feel that this young and impressionable girl should suffer it.

Ali shrugged as if I were commenting about something as trivial the weather.

"If she wishes to fight like a man, then she must be willing to die like a man," he said. And from the look he gave me, I felt that somehow his words were not meant for the Jewish girl alone.

I stood shaking with impotent rage as Ali led the girl to stand with the male prisoners. Najma did not resist, and she followed like a lamb patiently walking to slaughter. But then, just before she disappeared inside the crowd of captured men, the girl raised her eyes and met mine. I did not see in Najma's look sorrow or anger at her fate. Just confusion, as if she were lost in a strange world that she no longer recognized.

And for a terrible moment, I understood how she felt.

16

That night I accompanied my husband to the granary, where the prisoners were kept. Abu Bakr and Umar joined us, along with a man of the tribe of Aws I recognized as Sa'd ibn Muadh, who walked in great pain, a thick bandage around his gut that was stained with blood. Sa'd had been injured by an arrow during the Confederate attack and the whispers were that he was dying. Why he would leave his bed to walk here tonight was a mystery. But I saw from the grim look on the Messenger's face that my normally inquisitive nature would be unwelcome tonight.

I wasn't sure why I had been asked to come, but some instinct in me said that Ali must have mentioned to the Prophet my compassion for the Jewish girl who was the sole woman to be held prisoner. I sensed that judgment would be rendered against the Qurayza tonight and my husband wanted me to be there to witness it. If not to approve, then, perhaps, to understand.

As we entered the granary that was now a prison, I saw the Jewish men standing in prayer, surrounded by hundreds of armed guards. Their arms were still tied, but their legs had been freed so that they could sway back and forth as the elderly rabbi of the settlement, Husayn ibn Sallam, led them in reciting the ancient Hebrew words that sounded so much like our own tongue and yet were still so foreign

The Messenger stood respectfully, watching the men pray. I caught sight of the girl Najma alone in a corner, her red hair covered by a scarf. She did not join the others in worship but stared straight ahead, unblinking.

When the rabbi finished his invocations, a blanket of silence fell upon the crowd as all turned to face the man who would decide their fate. A tall, thin man with dark eyes who had been standing beside ibn Sallam now stepped forward, his head held proudly, and faced the Messenger of God.

My husband met his eyes for a long moment. When he spoke, it was in a deep voice. His words echoed throughout the vast chamber that had stored our supplies of wheat and barley before they were consumed during the siege and the famine.

"Kab ibn Asad," my husband said, and the tall man nodded in acknowledgment. "You have sought my judgment against your people."

"I have," he said with great dignity.

The Messenger stepped forward, his black eyes glistening in the torchlight.

"Your treachery nearly brought the fire of death into he streets of Medina," Muhammad said. "Had God not intervened, you would have assuredly left none of my people alive."

Kab looked at his adversary without blinking.

"Yes," he said. It was a simple statement of fact, without any guilt or shame.

The Messenger frowned and I could see a hint of the outrage that he had shown when he first learned of the Qurayza's deal with the Confederates.

"It is not for me to judge you," my husband said, to my surprise. "My anger is so great that I fear I will not be impartial."

Kab nodded, no emotion on his face.

"I understand."

The Messenger now turned to the injured Sa'd, who was leaning against a wooden post, his hand covering the bandage. I noticed that the splotch of blood had spread and now the entire wrap was soaked.

"Will you submit to the judgment, Sa'd ibn Muadh?" the Prophet asked.

Kab turned to face Sa'd. I recalled now that the two had once been friends and that Sa'd had served as an intermediary between the Muslims and Jews over the past several years. But if Sa'd had retained any memory of that friendship, I could not see it in his brown eyes, which were burning with anger at betrayal.

"Sa'd has always been a friend to the Qurayza. I trust that he will do what is just." But even as Kab spoke these words, I knew that he, too, understood that whatever courtesies had existed between them, the bitterness of war had erased that past forever.

Sa'd moved forward, grimacing from the pain of his mortal wound. He stepped so close to Kab that that their noses almost touched. Kab did not flinch as Sa'd looked straight into his eyes and spoke.

"You are not Muslims and so you are not subject to the laws that God has revealed in the holy Qur'an," he said, his voice quivering with anger. "I can only judge you by your own laws. Do you understand?"

Kab nodded, never letting his eyes leave Sa'd.

"Yes," was all he said.

Sa'd stepped back and faced the elderly rabbi. Ibn Sallam had been the only one of the exiled tribe of Qaynuqa who had been permitted to stay in Medina, as he had always been respectful of the Muslims' beliefs and had never disparaged my husband's claim to being a prophet. The old sage had lingered in the oasis, ministering to the remaining Jewish tribes, until the Bani Nadir had been expelled and only the Qurayza remained.

"Tell me, Rabbi, what does Moses say is the punishment for a tribe that breaks its treaty and makes war upon its neighbor?"

It was a simple question, asked in a respectful tone, but I saw the color drain from Ibn Sallam's wrinkled cheeks.

"The text is ancient," the rabbi responded slowly, as if choosing every word carefully. "The words refer to a time long past."

Sa'd ibn Muadh turned back to the Jewish chieftain.

"Do you believe, Kab, that the Torah is God's Word?"

Kab smiled softly, realizing Sa'd's intent.

"I do."

Sa'd spoke loudly now, so that his words echoed throughout the granary.

"Then God's Word does not change from day to day," he said. "What was revealed to Moses in days long past will serve as a witness against you tonight."

Kab nodded

"So be it."

Sa'd faced the rabbi and pointed a finger at him.

"Ibn Sallam, what does your Torah say about the fate of a tribe that makes war upon its neighbors?"

Ibn Sallam hesitated. He looked at Kab, who nodded. And then the old rabbi unraveled the sacred scroll of the Torah from which he had been praying and read aloud, a quiver of sadness in his raspy voice.

"In Devarim, which the Greeks call Deuteronomy, in chapter twenty, verses ten through fourteen, the Lord says: 'When thou comest nigh unto a city to fight against it, then proclaim peace unto it. And it shall be, if it make thee answer of peace, and open unto thee, then it shall be, that all the people that is found therein shall be tributaries unto thee, and they shall serve thee. And if it will make no peace with thee, but will make war against thee, then thou shalt besiege it. And when the Lord thy God hath delivered it into thine hands, thou shalt smite every male thereof with the edge of the sword. But the women, and the little ones, and the cattle, and all that is in the city, even all the spoil thereof, shalt thou take unto thyself; and thou shalt eat the spoil of thine enemies, which the Lord thy God hath given thee.'"

I felt a chill as I heard these words and realized that the fate of the Qurayza had been set. They had been doomed by their own scriptures to suffer the fate that their ancestors had unleashed upon others a millennium before. The men would be all killed, and the women and children would live as slaves in the land they had once ruled.

Sa'd nodded and met Kab's eyes.

"Your Book has spoken," he said.

Kab did not flinch at the cruel sentence but simply nodded in resignation, as if he had expected no less.

As we turned to leave, I heard the rabbi lead the prisoners in a haunting chant that I could not understand but whose intonations, rife with weariness and sorrow, did not need to be translated. I cast a final glance at Najma, who continued to stare straight ahead as if locked in her own dream, and then stepped outside.

We walked back to the center of the city in silence. When we reached the Masjid, the Messenger embraced Sa'd and thanked him for bravely pronouncing the judgment. The dying man nodded, and my father and Umar helped carry him back to his bed. I had no doubt from his gaunt and yellowing skin that he would not live long enough to see the punishment of the Qurayza carried out.

That night, I lay by my husband's side, facing away from him rather than nestling against his bosom as was my habit.

"You are angry at me," he said gently.

I hesitated, unsure of what I was feeling in the hollow of my stomach.

"No," I said at long last. "They would have killed all of us had they been able to attack. If we let them leave as we did the Qaynuqa and the Nadir, they would have come back to attack us. The judgment is cruel, but they cannot complain. The Qurayza have been punished by their own traditions."

The Messenger took my hand in his.

"Not quite."

I looked up at him in confusion. In his dark eyes I saw no more anger, but a profound sorrow.

"The rabbi read the wrong section of the Book, as I had asked him to."

My eyes went wide.

"I don't understand."

The Messenger squeezed my fingers and I could feel the depth of emotion that he was suppressing.

"The law of Moses he read was a punishment only for distant tribes who fought the Children of Israel from other lands. It was not the punishment for a neighboring tribe."

I looked up at my husband, unsure of what he was holding back.

"What would have been the punishment in the Torah for a neighboring tribe?"

The Prophet looked at me and I saw lines of great sadness in his eyes.

"The rabbi read to me the verses that followed," he said. "The Book says that in the cities that are near, the judgment is to kill everything that breathes."

I was stunned and shuddered at the horror. Could the God of Moses, the God of love and justice that we worshipped as Allah, be so cruel that He would call upon the Children of Israel even to slay women and children?

It was a barbaric code for a barbaric world, and I began to understand why God had sent a new prophet to mankind. A new Book that sought to restrain and regulate the madness of war for the first time. In a world where greed and lust for power were enough to justify bloodshed, the holy Qur'an said *"Fight those who fight you, but do not commit aggression."* In a world where soldiers raped and killed innocents in battle without any guilt, the Revelation had established rules that prevented such atrocities from happening. Women and children could not be killed under the rules of Islam, and protection was extended to the elderly, as well as to the priests and monks of the People of the Book.

Allah had even forbidden the destruction of trees and the poisoning of wells, tactics that were widely employed by so-called civilized nations such as the Byzantines and the Persians. And the Messenger did not permit us to use fire as a weapon, for only God had the right to punish His Creation with the fires of Hell. Flaming arrows would have helped us burn down the houses of the Qurayza and end the siege, but the Prophet rejected the horror of burning people alive in their homes, even if it was the accepted practice of warfare throughout the world.

We had shown restraint, but in a world where death hung over the sands like a bitter cloud, bloodshed was inevitable. I looked up at my husband and realized from the sadness in his face that he did not relish the massacre that was to come. He had done what was necessary to save his community from extinction, and the death of the warriors of Qurayza would send a clear message to all the neighboring tribes that treachery would be punished. Once the Qurayza had been dispatched, more chieftains would realize that it was in their best interest to join the alliance. A state was being born out of chaos, and the price of establishing order was high.

I leaned close to the Messenger and buried my face in his breast, letting the gentle pulse of his heart lull me into a dreamworld in which there was no death, no blood, no tears. A world in which love alone could end tyranny and save the weak from the depredations and cruelty of the strong. A world where there was no war and men could lay down their swords and live without fear of attack from their neighbors.

It was a world that could exist only in dreams.

17

A mass grave had been dug in the marketplace, ten feet wide and nearly thirty feet deep. It looked like a miniature of the mighty trench that had protected the city from the invaders. And it was perhaps fitting, if macabre, that the men who had betrayed us would now be buried in a ditch that resembled the very defense they had sought to undermine.

The prisoners were brought forth in small groups, starting with the tribal leaders whose intrigue had brought this disaster on their people, as well as those who had been identified as having actively fought against the Muslims during the siege of the Jewish fortress.

I accompanied Najma, the sole woman among the seven hundred men who had been sentenced to death. I tried to remind myself that this girl who looked so much like me was no innocent. She had chosen to participate in the battle and had injured several good Muslim soldiers, killing one man who had left behind a wife and three children. And yet in my heart I knew that she was simply acting in defense of her own community. With my fiery spirit, I expected that I would have done the same if the situation had been reversed.

I led Najma out of the granary, holding on halfheartedly to the rope that bound her by the wrists. I was prepared for tears and shouts of rage, anything except what I found. The girl was in the best of spirits as we walked down the paved streets of the oasis toward the spot that would soon be her grave.

As we approached the marketplace and the crowd that had come to see justice against those who had committed treason in the midst of war, Najma smiled broadly and began to laugh and wave to the startled onlookers. Seeing the girl gaily walking to her death, people looked away and I saw a few women wipe tears from their eyes.

Najma turned to me and I saw in her eyes a terrifying madness. It was as if some djinn had come and possessed her, buried her mind beneath the veil of insanity so that it would sleep through the horrible moments to come.

She smiled at me broadly and glanced at my saffron-colored robe, the hem lined with brocaded flowers in red and green.

"Your dress is beautiful. Is it from Yemen?"

It was, but I could not find any words to respond. Her madness frightened and confused me, and I suddenly wanted to be anywhere but here.

Najma shrugged at my blank stare.

"I was planning on having a dress ordered from Yemen," she said in a high voice. "For my wedding one day. Oh well. I won't need it now."

I felt my throat constrict and I forced myself to speak.

"I'm sorry," I croaked.

Najma laughed as if I had told her the most wonderful joke.

"Don't be silly," she said. Najma paused and then looked at me closer. "You're married to Muhammad, right?"

I nodded.

Najma smiled and then picked up our pace. As the colorful pendants and dainty tents that lined the marketplace came into view, she began to skip, pulling me forward with her little dance.

And then, just as we approached the grounds where the grave had been dug, she stopped and turned to face me.

"Is he good to you? Your husband, I mean."

I felt tears blurring my vision.

"Very," I managed to whisper.

Najma clapped her hands awkwardly, the bindings on her wrists stymieing her efforts to express her glee.

"Wonderful! How many children do you have?"

I shook my head.

"None."

Najma's mouth widened in an expression of genuine compassion.

"That's too bad," she said, leaning close to me in sympathy. "You'd be a good mother. But I'm sure it will happen soon. And then you can sing your baby a lullaby. Here's one my mother used to sing to me at night."

And then the poor girl started to sing some quiet, haunting verses about a bluebird that built its nest only in the moonlight because it loved to work beneath the canopy of the stars.

She continued to sing even as we walked into the central plaza, where the massive ditch had been cut out of the earth. I saw the first group of three men who had been set for death led toward the grave. Their faces were stoic, but I could see terror in their eyes as they faced Ali, Talha, and Zubayr, their executioners

The men did not protest as they were made to kneel before the pit and bow their heads over the dark chasm. Talha and Zubayr lifted their swords, and I saw Ali raise the glittering *Dhul Fiqar*.

And then the three swung their blades down and sliced off the traitors' heads with a sickening crunch. The decapitated bodies writhed as blood exploded from the severed necks. And then the corpses fell forward and vanished into the darkness of the grave.

I watched, sickened and fascinated, as three more men were brought forward to meet judgment. Najma had continued singing unabated when the first executions were performed, but she suddenly stopped and I saw her looking at one of the men being led to the pit. I recognized him as Kab, the chieftain of Qurayza, who I understood was her uncle.

For a moment the cloud of madness in her eyes lifted and I saw the true face of the young girl whose life was coming to its end. Horror and grief shattered her pretty features as she watched her beloved uncle fall to his knees before the grave.

While the other two men loudly said prayers to the God of Moses, Kab turned to face the niece who was about to watch him die.

"Forgive me, sweet girl," he said. And then he bowed his neck over the edge of the pit and closed his eyes.

Ali moved forward, and with one swift blow, Kab ibn Asad lost his head, his body rolling over the edge to join the corpses below.

I heard a terrible sound from Najma, something that made my blood curdle. It was not a scream or a cry of sorrow, but a wild and insane laugh.

"Look at them! They fall down like dolls thrown across the room by a naughty child! How silly!"

Her laughter became more manic as Ali approached her, his forked blade still dripping the blood of her uncle.

And then the Prophet's cousin leaned down beside her and looked into her eyes, and I saw in them a gentleness that seemed utterly out of place.

"It will not hurt. I promise," he said softly.

Najma threw her head back in raucous laughter, her crimson hair flying in the wind.

"Oh, silly boy. You can't hurt me! No one can hurt me!"

And then she moved toward the pit. I suddenly stepped forward and grabbed her hand and squeezed it.

The girl turned and looked at me. We stared into each other's eyes for a moment that seemed like an eternity. Two young women, enemies by fate, yet sharing the common bond of girls who had been swept into something that was far greater than themselves. The terrible, unstoppable flood of history, which destroyed all hopes and dreams that stood against its mighty flow.

And then she winked at me as the madness that, paradoxically, kept her sane in these final moments returned.

Najma laughed and skipped all the way to the grave's edge. Her laughter grew louder as she knelt and looked down into the chasm where her loved ones now lay. I heard her guffaws grow mightier and more shrill and soon I could hear nothing else, not the raging wind, not the steady murmur of the crowd that had come to quench its thirst for blood. Not even my own heart, which I could feel pounding in my ears.

Her laughter accelerated, vibrating faster until it sounded like a primordial scream from the depths of Hell itself.

And then Ali raised *Dhul Fiqar* and Najma's laughter abruptly ended.

A silence fell over the execution ground that was even more terrible than the madness of the young girl's cries. I turned and ran away, unable to watch anymore. I raced through the streets of Medina, the terrible silence enveloping me like a thick blanket.

I ran to my mother's house, as I could not bear to go home. I was afraid that my husband would read my heart and divorce me for the blasphemies that were raging in my soul. I was trembling with anger. Anger at the cruelty of life, anger at the pride of men that divided tribes and nations. Anger at a God that had given us free will and left us to destroy ourselves with our own stupidity.

In my mind's eye I saw again and again Ali's blade falling on that foolish, treacherous girl's neck and I felt a flash of rage at this man who could perform his grisly duty with such quiet calm. Many have wondered about my estrangement from the Messenger's son-in-law, a divide that would one day cost the lives of thousands of men and plunge our nation into civil war. Although the greatest wound between us was yet to be inflicted, I looked back and realized that my feelings for Ali changed that day from guarded admiration to a quiet dislike, a tiny flame in my heart that would one day be kindled into a fire that would consume the *Ummah*.

What I had witnessed that day in the marketplace had scarred me more than the cut of any earthly blade. Of all the horrible things I have experienced in my life, my dear Abdallah, none has stayed with me as vividly as Najma's laugh. I sometimes think I can hear it again, echoing across time and space, full of despair and madness, begging for a chance to live and to love, to marry and bear children and sing lullabies to the little ones that would never be.

The lost cry of a girl who had made the terrible, unforgivable mistake of defying the flow of history.

18

The Bani Qurayza had been destroyed and the Messenger of God was now the unchallenged ruler of Medina. His victory, as expected, led to the arrival of delegations from all over Arabia. Tribal chieftains sought to forge alliances with the rising Muslim state through bonds of trade and kinship. Envoys came from both north and south. And, to my surprise, a delegation came from Mecca itself, from the house of our greatest enemy.

I felt fury building in my heart as I looked upon Ramla, the beautiful daughter of Abu Sufyan, who had arrived at long last to make my childhood nightmare come true. She had aged well in the past seven years, and even though there were lines around her eyes, her cheeks were still rosy and her skin soft and unblemished. I had thought I was rid of her when the Messenger had married her off to his cousin Ubaydallah ibn Jahsh, the brother of my rival Zaynab. Ramla had been openly disappointed in Muhammad's failure to embrace her charms in the aftermath of Khadija's death and had reacted with caustic bitterness to the news that I would become his wife instead. Perhaps sensing her hurt feelings, the Prophet had wisely sent Ramla and her husband away to join the refugee community in Abyssinia, where she had remained safe during the terrible years of conflict.

But now she was back, come to claim the position that she had always desired and felt entitled to. She was to become the newest Mother of the Believers. Her husband, Ubaydallah, had proven feckless and weak-minded, and had abandoned Islam for the Christian faith while he stayed at the court of the Negus. Under the law of God, Ramla could not remain married to an apostate, and her divorce left her and her infant daughter, Habiba, in a precarious situation, living in a foreign land without economic support and protection.

The Messenger had heard of her predicament through the most unlikely of sources—her brother Muawiya, who had sent his friend Amr ibn al-As on a secret mission to the oasis in the aftermath of the Battle of the Trench. The Prophet had immediately agreed to take responsibility for Ramla and her child, and Muawiya himself had brought her to Medina for the wedding.

And so it was that I sat inside the spacious manor of Uthman ibn Affan, the Prophet's gentle son-in-law, as the Messenger greeted the son and daughter of his greatest enemy. I saw many of the Companions looking at Muawiya with open distrust as he moved forward to kiss my husband's hand. He had been a child when I last saw him and had changed greatly since then. Gone was the perpetual gloom that had followed him in youth, replaced by an energy and eagerness that was seductive.

As the grand hall was set for the wedding festivities, Uthman's white-clad servants rushing to and fro with baskets of dates and jars of honey, Muawiya mixed easily with men who should have been his enemies. He had a natural tact and grace of movement that was disarming, and I could feel the steady heat of his gregarious charm cause the initial cloud of suspicion that hung over the room evaporate. Even Umar seemed impressed with Muawiya's courage in coming alone to the oasis, without the retinue of bodyguards that one would expect to protect the boy who was for all intents and purposes the heir to the throne of Mecca.

As the son of Abu Sufyan, he was, of course, well aware of his potential value as a hostage, but Muawiya moved among us with the confident ease of a trusted guest rather than an open enemy. He spoke to each man as if he were an old friend rather than an adversary and even congratulated the Muslim elders on their brilliant defensive tactics that had thrown off the Meccan invasion.

I was impressed with Muawiya's diplomatic genius. Within minutes of arriving at the oasis, he had won over many of his detractors with honeyed words and carefully calculated compliments. Watching Muawiya charm his opponents was like watching a master swordsman in action—each stroke was both beautifully executed and perfectly timed.

Ramla, for her part, had nothing to fear, for she had long earned the trust of the community, if not my own. Many had once believed that her conversion had been some kind of tactic conceived by Abu Sufyan to infiltrate the Muslim ranks. But word from Abyssinia was that she had shown commitment to the faith over the years and had proven a tactful advocate in the court of the Negus, protecting Muslim interests in the foreign land. Even I did not really doubt the sincerity of her spiritual convictions, but I hated the hungry way she looked at my husband, as if he were a prize that she had been long denied. Her bright eyes met mine and she raised an eyebrow in defiance, and I frowned. Ramla would be a true rival in the harem, one who combined beauty with a deadly sharp mind, and I knew that I would have to keep a close eye on her. And then I saw the Messenger looking at me with an amused glance as if he could read my thoughts.

My husband smiled knowingly and then turned to his young guest, who had just finished making the rounds of the Companions, healing old wounds and cementing new alliances. Muawiya turned to the Messenger and bowed his head low.

"I am honored that my sister has found such a noble match," he said in a rich voice that was deep and masculine.

The Messenger took the youth's hand in his and squeezed it tight.

"May this wedding be the first step in ending the long enmity between your clan and mine," he said.

As the Prophet went to stand by his new bride, wrapped in a wedding dress of dark blue, a red-striped veil covering her dark hair, Muawiya lifted a bowl of goat's milk in honor of the nuptials and then drank with a slow flourish.

A shadow fell over him and he looked up to see the towering form of Umar ibn al-Khattab, the man who, before his defection, had been Mecca's greatest hope of destroying Muhammad.

"Your father must be angry that you came," Umar said, looking closely into the eyes of the guest as if searching for any hint of deception or intrigue.

"He was livid," Muawiya said with a broad smile filled with devilish amusement. "But I am my own man. I realize that the old ways are dying. The Quraysh must accommodate the new reality or vanish into irrelevance."

Uthman, our kindhearted host, came up to the young man's side and put an affectionate arm around him. Muawiya was a distant cousin of his and Uthman had always been close to the boy in his youth, before the divisions of faith had torn apart the clan of Umayya.

"You always had great foresight," Uthman said warmly. "The river of the world is changing its course, and only the wise anticipate its new direction."

And then I saw Ali approach. He alone among all the Companions had remained aloof, despite Muawiya's persistent efforts to charm him.

"It is one thing to foresee the course of a river," Ali said softly. "It is another to foresee the fate of one's own soul."

Silence fell over the room and I could suddenly feel the tension that had abated over the past hour reassert itself like a cold wind. Ali and Muawiya stood in the center of the room, looking at each other without speaking. Even though they were only a few feet apart, there seemed to be a divide between them that was greater than the distance between the east and the west. Between heaven and earth. Ali was from another realm, a strange bird soaring above mankind, observing but never quite participating in the world. And Muawiya was his direct opposite, a man who had mastered that world and had little interest in the ethereal dreamland that Ali called his home.

And then I saw the Messenger step between them, as if to place himself diplomatically in the path of any confrontation between these young and passionate men that would mar the wedding.

But as I saw my husband come between them, smiling graciously as he placed a hand on each man's shoulder, I suddenly realized that there was another meaning to the scene before me. Muhammad stood between these two poles as no other man could. He was both a resident of the ethereal realms of the spirit and a master of the worldly plane, and he alone understood how to bridge the gap between these opposing realities. In the years that would come, after the Messenger had returned to his Lord, the precarious bond that he had forged between these planes would shatter, and the history of Islam would forever be a war between the soul and the flesh.

And then Muawiya turned away from Ali and the spell was broken. The Meccan prince smiled brightly at the Messenger and spoke loudly, as if intending everyone in the hall to hear his words. It was unnecessary, as there was absolute silence at that moment and his words would have carried to each corner even if they had been whispered.

"The fate of my soul I leave to the judgment of my Creator," Muawiya said with dignity. "But this I know. Before you came, O Muhammad, none of our people ever thought about a world different from what they had experienced for centuries. A world of barbarism, cruelty, and death. But you have given them a vision that has brought them together. Forged them from warring tribes into a nation. I know of no man who could have done this without the aid of God."

And then to everyone's shock, Muawiya stretched out his right hand in the formal sign of allegiance, and the Prophet clasped it in his own. Muawiya knelt down and kissed the Messenger's hand. And then he spoke the words that would change everything.

"I testify that there is no god but God, and that Muhammad is the Messenger of God."

The room exploded in a commotion of cries. Surprise, disbelief, and jubilation mixed together in an air of heady celebration. Abu Sufyan's son, the heir of our greatest enemy, had embraced Islam, and in that one instant, the two forces that had torn the peninsula apart were reconciled. I felt my heart racing in excitement. Once the other tribes learned of Muawiya's conversion, the final vestiges of support for Mecca would collapse and the war would end.

It was the thought on everyone's mind, except perhaps for Ali, who continued to gaze down at the young man with those unreadable eyes. But Muawiya ignored his stare and kept his attention focused on the Prophet.

"If it please you, O Messenger of God, I wish to stay here and support your cause," he said. Which was, of course, what was needed. If Muawiya settled in Medina, his superb political skills and vast network of allies would help bring order to the nascent state. With Muawiya's crafty guidance, we would bring together the recalcitrant tribes and then wage a final battle against Mecca. We had hidden in our homes in terror so many times as the armies of Arabia came down upon us that it seemed like justice that Hind and her followers should do the same now.

And then the Messenger of God said something utterly unexpected.

"No. Return to your father and tell no one of your faith," he said, and the rejoicing in the room stopped cold.

Muawiya's brow wrinkled.

"I don't understand," he said, sharing our surprise. "I am prepared to shed the blood of my father's men so that you may be triumphant."

"You will prepare the way," the Messenger said gently. "The day is coming, *insha-Allah*, when we will meet in Mecca. But there will be no bloodshed."

Muawiya appeared confused, but he lowered his head in acceptance. I saw his cousin Uthman give the Prophet a grateful look. The destruction of Mecca's forces would mean the annihilation of Uthman's own clan, and the softhearted nobleman was clearly delighted that the Prophet intended to find another way to retake the city.

The room now buzzed with a flood of conversation, as Companions and their wives talked animatedly, trying to understand what the Prophet's words meant. And then Uthman rose and clapped his hands to end the sudden tumult of conversation.

"Come, my friends, let us feast, for there is much to celebrate tonight."

19

*W*e all gathered in Uthman's spacious dining hall. The walls were covered in delicate floral tiles made of ceramic, said to have been imported directly from Constantinople, and the arched ceiling was held aloft by sturdy marble pillars. It was a palatial room set for banquets that would have made the kings of Persia feel welcome. I wondered at Uthman's good fortune.

Even though much of the oasis remained mired in poverty, wealth seemed to flood him wherever he went. The Prophet had given Uthman the title *Al-Ghani*, which meant "the generous," and he was always ready to share his vast stores with anyone who needed help. But no matter how much he gave away, more money seemed to rush toward him and his coffers were always overflowing. There was a legend I had heard of a Greek king whose touch could turn anything to gold, and I would joke that Uthman was the Midas of our people.

And for the Prophet's wedding to a woman of Uthman's own clan, he had thrown together one of the most extravagant banquets I had ever seen. The Messenger himself appeared uncomfortable with the vast wealth on display—the silver bowls filled with succulent red grapes, trays stacked with fresh breads steaming from the ovens, delicate raisins on plates decorated with fresh desert roses, their tiny leaves spiraling toward the soft petals. Goat stew, spiced with saffron and rich salts. Cakes dripping with honey and powdered with a sugary substance said to have been brought from Persia. And a seemingly endless supply of roast mutton, cut thin, the meat mouthwatering and tenderized to perfection.

The Companions, many of whom had never eaten anything beyond coarse bread and grizzled meat, stared at the feast in awe, and a few threw jealous glances at Uthman, who sat beside the lovely Umm Kulthum, the Prophet's daughter whom he had married upon the death of Ruqayya. It was as if this gentle pacifist of a man had everything any of them could ever want, and yet he seemed blissfully unaware of how lucky he truly was. In the years to come, the feelings of resentment that I sensed from some of the younger men would worsen, and Uthman's opulence would come with a price that would be paid by an entire civilization.

I walked among the believers, carrying trays of spiced chicken, a highly prized delicacy as the fowls were rarely found in the desert wastes and were mainly shipped from Syria. And then I saw Ramla looking at the Messenger with her delicate eyes and I could tell that my husband was smitten.

The thought of him spending the night with her, exploring the arts of love with this cosmopolitan and sophisticated woman, made me sick. A flash of jealousy raged inside me and I found myself turning to the man closest to me, the giant Umar, who was hungrily tearing off pieces of a chicken bone with his fingers.

"Why bother, Umar? Just swallow it whole already!" I said in my best teasing voice. He looked at me with surprise and then burst out laughing. I made the rounds of the men at the long cedar table, cheerily mocking them for their uncouth manners and desert coarseness. But I would follow my harsh words with a coquettish smile, a wink of my golden eyes, and they would respond as all men do to the flirtation of a beautiful woman. With zest, amusement, and subtle desire.

I soon found myself the center of attention at the banquet as I traded jokes with Talha or mocked Zubayr's tales of his adventurous exploits as a youth before my sister, Asma, had turned him into a trained kitten. I caught Ramla looking at me with irritation for having stolen all her thunder on her wedding day, and I smiled at my little victory against my rival.

As I made the rounds of the men playing my childish games, I saw from the corner of my eye my husband watching me with a stern look. I knew that I was making him jealous, something that I had never tried to do before, and I thrilled secretly at the thought that I could still sway his heart. Even as he took Ramla in his arms tonight, part of his mind would be consumed with the memory of my little performance, my demonstration that I was still the youngest and most desirable of his consorts in the eyes of the world.

I was a silly girl of fifteen and thought nothing more of my behavior than I did of the daily gossip sessions I held with the other

Mothers. I had no idea that my little game would have such dire consequences, that my foolish flirtations would change my life so drastically. And I could not have foreseen that the freedom I had treasured from birth would soon end behind the walls of a prison forged from my own folly.

20

Talha let the loud commotion of the marketplace, the crowing of merchants, and the laughter of children run through him. He was feeling dejected, and a walk through the bazaar did him good. Though there was much jubilation among the believers these days, Talha was farsighted enough to see that the Messenger's efforts to forge the Arabs into a nation would not end the war but were likely expand it. But their new enemies would not be a few thousand poorly armed desert dwellers. They would be the legions of Persia and Byzantium, empires that had mastered the art of warfare over centuries of bloodshed.

That terrible day of imperial conflict was coming upon them fast, and the Muslims would need the best and the brightest of the Arab nation to hold their ground. Men like the fearsome general Umar ibn al-Khattab and now the brilliant politician Muawiya. The role that these great leaders would play in the war to come was clear.

But the role that he would play was not.

Talha, his hand forever shattered by the sword that had been meant for the Messenger, was no longer an able warrior, like his friend Zubayr. He was not a revered statesman like his cousin Abu Bakr or a wealthy merchant like Uthman, who could single-handedly fund an entire military campaign.

He was a poor cripple who could barely afford to keep food on the table for his wife, Hammanah, and his infant son, Muhammad. His wife was a sweet and gentle woman and had never complained. But he felt like a failure. One of the first Meccans to embrace Islam as a young man, he remained the only one of that inner circle who had failed to turn the poverty of the early years into prosperity in Medina. It was that perpetual struggle that prevented him from being of greater service to the cause. And it had prevented him from proposing to a young girl before she had been chosen for a greater destiny.

Although he never said it aloud, everyone among the Muslims knew of his feelings for me. He had tentatively approached Abu Bakr to ask for my hand when I came of age. But my father had been reluctant to engage his precious daughter to a boy whose hard work had never quite lifted him from the ranks of the poor. Instead, he had promised me to Jubayr ibn Mutim in the hopes of enticing the influential young Meccan aristocrat into Islam.

Talha had been bitterly disappointed, but he had held hope that Jubayr's loyalty to the old ways would prevent the wedding from ever happening. And he was proven right. But when my betrothal to Jubayr had indeed been abrogated, Talha had been stunned to learn it was because I had been promised to a husband with whom he could never compete, even if he had all the wealth of Arabia. And so he had forever closed that door in his heart. For Talha revered the Messenger, and he accepted God's will, sacrificing one love for another.

Talha tried to turn his thoughts away from the past. But the world would not let him.

"The daughter of Abu Bakr was in fine form last night," a deep voice said.

Talha looked up to see two merchants standing beside him. They examined a parcel of leather goods that had recently been smuggled from Taif in defiance of the Meccan ban on trading with Muhammad.

Talha stared at the two figures, who were conversing nonchalantly, a richly dressed tribesmen from the Khazraj named Sameer and his friend Murtaza, a Bedouin clansmen from the tribe of Tayy to the east. They were men who had some business dealings with Uthman ibn Affan and had been invited to the Prophet's wedding to Ramla the night before.

"The Messenger is truly lucky," Sameer said with a wink to his colleague.

"She is the most beautiful girl I have ever set eyes upon," Murtaza responded with a lascivious smirk. "Is it true that she was still a virgin on her wedding night?"

Talha felt his heart thunder with rage. He stormed up to the men and pushed himself between them, his eyes burning.

"What shameful talk is this? She is your Mother!"

Sameer looked at Talha, in his faded wool tunic and dusty pantaloons, and his eyes mocked him with the casual cruelty of a rich man.

"Only as long as she is married to the Messenger," Sameer said.

Murtaza stepped closer to Talha, his sunburned face smelling of oil and *qat*, the Yemeni leaf that was said to make men dream while awake.

"What if the Prophet dies or divorces her?" Murtaza sneered. "What will become of this delicate flower then?"

Talha's heart was pounding. And then he spoke before he could stop himself.

"Then I will marry her, if only to protect her honor from scum like you!"

Talha froze, horrified that he had spoken aloud his darkest, most private desire, one that never should have been voiced in this world or the hereafter.

"It sounds like you have feelings for the pretty lady you call your mother," Murtaza said.

The Najdi Bedouin put an arm around Talha in false comradeship.

"Don't be ashamed, boy," Murtaza added, amusement dripping from his lips. "If a son had a mother who looked like that, he'd be forgiven if he entertained a dirty thought now and again."

And then, as if he were being moved by a force greater than himself, Talha swung forth with his scarred fist and smashed Murtaza's teeth with one brutal blow. The stunned Bedouin fell back, blood exploding from his mouth.

Talha stood perfectly still, unable to move, despite the pounding agony in his ruined hand. And then Sameer was on top of him and he was being punched and kicked into the ground. Talha stopped fighting and absorbed the enraged merchant's blows without crying out, even as he had done years before when Umar had beaten him in the Sanctuary. He could hear his ribs crack under the onslaught, the pain almost as intense as the agony that emanated from his deformed and brutalized hand.

Talha did not move, did not breathe. He let Sameer crush him into the earth. His eyes blurred and darkness flew toward him like a gentle blanket, come to cover him in the sleep of unconsciousness. If this was death, he could think of no happier end than to die protecting the honor of the Mother of the Believers.

21

I sat nervously inside my tiny apartment, which felt even smaller than usual, as all the other wives had gathered here tonight at the command of the Messenger. The harem had grown prodigiously over the past several years and now included six women—Sawda, myself, Hafsa, Zaynab bint Jahsh, Umm Salama, and Ramla, the most recent addition. The other Zaynab, the daughter of Khuzayma whom the Prophet had married to bring the Bani Amir into alliance, had passed away a few months before. Her loss had been hard on the lower classes of Medina, as Zaynab's tireless efforts on behalf of the weak and the indigent had earned her the sobriquet "Mother of the Poor."

I look back and realize that in some ways Zaynab bint Khuzayma was the luckiest of us all, as she left the world long before the terrible trials and sorrows that were to besiege the Muslim *Ummah*. And, perhaps most poignantly, she had passed on to the next world after having lived a life that was full and free of undue restriction or limitation. The simple normalcy of her daily existence, the pleasure of walking in public under the full light of the sun, would soon become a luxury for the rest of us—another disaster that was forged by my passionate and willful soul.

The tension in the room was thick, like smoke from an oven that has been left unattended for too long. The fires that were being contained behind the cool glances of my cowives was about to burst.

None of them was looking at me, except for Hafsa, whose furious gaze summed up their feelings succinctly. My flirtatious spectacle at Ramla's wedding had brought shame upon the entire household, as well as violence to the streets of Medina. Poor unlucky Talha had been beaten senseless defending my honor from crass talk among the merchants, and the ensuing struggle had erupted into a vicious melee as outraged Companions had rushed forward to avenge him. Though no one had been killed, the ruckus had been a terrible reminder of the fragility of peace in the oasis.

What would happen next was unclear. But there would definitely be consequences, and the Prophet's terse summons to all the Mothers suggested that they would all pay collectively in some fashion for my foolishness.

I looked away from Hafsa's accusing eyes and stared up at the roof of palm leaves, where a gray moth was sleeping amid the crevices of a frond. I suddenly wanted to be that moth, hidden in shadows and ignored by the world, but free to fly away at the slightest impulse.

And then the door swung inward and the Messenger of God entered the room. He looked at the Mothers and nodded to each of them in turn without smiling. But when his eyes fell on me, he simply blinked and looked away without acknowledgment. My heart shattered like a mirror dropped from a treetop.

The Prophet closed the door behind him and then sat cross-legged on the floor. He breathed in deeply and then sighed wearily. But still he said nothing.

Moments passed, but the Messenger did nothing to assuage our growing anxiety. He simply sat, looking at us with a terrible patience that was somehow more frightening than any anger he could have expressed.

My mouth was painfully dry, as if I had eaten a brick of salt. And still my husband said nothing.

I could take it no longer. Even at the risk of igniting the rare fire of his wrath, I forced myself to speak

"Is Talha all right?" I croaked as if I had not spoken in years and my tongue had forgotten its cunning.

I could feel every eye on me now. The other Mothers glared at me in anger, but I did not return their cruel glances and focused my attention solely on the man who held my destiny in his hands.

The Messenger stared at the opposite wall for a long moment before he finally turned to face me. I braced myself for an outburst. Perhaps I even hoped for an explosion of outrage, a flash of passion that showed he still cared for me.

But when he finally met my eyes, there was no punishment in his gaze, no flames of wrath.

"Talha will heal in due time," Muhammad said softly. "But the wounds to the *Ummah* will take longer."

He sighed again, a sound that was laced with exhaustion. I suddenly saw the tiny new lines around his dark eyes and realized that he had not been sleeping well. Just as suddenly I felt regret that among all the responsibilities of leadership he carried, worry over the trouble I had foolishly caused should add to his burden.

"I have worked for so many years to bind these quarrelsome people together as a family," he said, his eyes never leaving mine. "Yet it takes only one small incident to tear them apart."

The room blurred as tears flooded my eyes.

"I'm sorry, I never intended—"

"It was not your intention, but the damage is still done," he said abruptly, and I felt as if I had been slapped. The Messenger was always exceedingly courteous and considered interrupting others to be the height of ill manners. The fact that he would cut me off so forcefully, especially in the presence of my rival wives, revealed how far I had fallen in his estimation. I felt my throat constrict painfully as the thought that he would divorce me stabbed into my heart.

And then another voice sounded through the small apartment, the gentle motherly tone of Umm Salama.

"We are your wives and your partners in this world and the next," she said steadily. "What is it that you wish us to do, O Messenger of God?"

She had chosen her words carefully and in doing so had taken the brunt of responsibility for the day's events off my lonely shoulders and placed them squarely upon the Mothers as a group. I looked across the room at her, my eyes brimming with unspoken gratitude for her decision to end my solitude.

The Prophet hesitated, and when he spoke, it was with the unyielding authority of the leader of a nation, not with the gentle tones of a family patriarch.

"God has revealed these words to me," he said, and my blood began to race. A Revelation had come to address the chaos I had created, and the thought that God Himself would intervene in this earthly affair terrified me.

And then the Messenger of God began to recite the lyrical words sent down from heaven, and I forgot everything except the haunting beauty of his voice:

O wives of the Prophet, you are not like any other women.
If you fear God, do not speak softly
In case the sick at heart should lust after you
But speak in a firm manner.
Stay at home and do not flaunt your finery
As they did in the Days of Ignorance.

The Messenger stopped and let the holy words sink in. I blinked and suddenly felt a flash of relief. The commandment was not onerous, and surely God could not mean this literally. The Messenger had often said there was much in the holy Qur'an that was symbolic and a dogmatically literal adherance to the law would undermine God's purpose. The commandment to stay at home, locked away in this tiny room with clay walls, while the world buzzed around about me, could not possibly be a strict rule that was meant to be applied with fervor. It had to be a general admonition, to curtail the kind of social impropriety that could lead to scandal and violence, as my stupid behavior at the wedding had done.

But when I looked at the Prophet, the intensity in his eyes froze the smile that was forming on my lips. Something dark still hung between us, and I suddenly felt frightened again.

"You should not leave your houses unless necessary. It is for your good and for the good of the *Ummah*," he said, and I felt my breath stop. The Messenger was serious about applying the commandment. We were now expected to stay inside our homes like prisoners.

"There is more," he said grimly. "God has issued a command to the believers as well."

He took a deep breath and then recited the flowing verses:

When you ask his wives something, do so from behind a curtain.
This is purer for your hearts and theirs.
It is not right for you to offend God's Messenger
Just as you should never marry his wives after him.
That would be an enormous sin in the sight of God.

The Messenger stopped and we looked at one another in confusion, unable to comprehend what was being asked of us. I understood
the prohibition against marrying another man after the Prophet—the
rivalries and divisions that would erupt over the honor of securing the
hand of a queen of the realm would tear the nation apart. But the notion that we could only speak to men from behind a curtain was startling to Arab women, who were accustomed to living in the open air.
We all wanted to believe that we had misunderstood the verses. It was
one thing to stay inside our homes under the compulsion of necessity,
but to cut ourselves off from our fellow believers in this manner was
incomprehensible. Surely this rule would be liberally interpreted.

But the Messenger quickly put an end to our hopes.

"From this point on, you may not speak to any man who is not
mahrem except through a veil or a curtain," he said forcefully, his eyes
locked on mine, and I felt my heart sink.

The *mahrem* referred to any man whom we were forbidden from
marrying because of the laws of incest. Our brothers, our sons, our
fathers, our uncles, and our nephews were our flesh and blood and
outside the possibility of sexual relations. But all other men, including
close friends like Talha, fell outside the taboo—and now we could no
longer talk to any of them except from behind a barrier. It was a stunning and extreme change, one that I had not been prepared for, and I
could not imagine how I could possibly comply with God's commandment.

The Messenger stood up to leave and we all watched him go as
if we were in a dream. But as he opened the door, I saw a flash of the
outside world, of the hustle and bustle of the Masjid and the streets of
Medina, and suddenly felt tears in my eyes as the realization struck me
that I would never be able to venture out into that world as I had done
all my life, free and proud.

From now on, my life was to become a prison, even when I was not
confined to the tiny apartment whose mud walls seemed to be closing
in on me. For whenever I ventured out into the sun, my face would be
hidden away behind a veil. The bars of my jail would follow me everywhere and were unbreakable, forged from a tiny strip of cotton that
was stronger than the mightiest Byzantine steel.

22

The next several months were among the most difficult of my young life. Accustomed to freedom of movement in the oasis, given deference and right-of-way anywhere I went as a Mother of the Believers, I was suddenly trapped inside the confines of my tiny chamber. The small window that looked on the Masjid courtyard was covered with a thick black curtain made of coarse wool, and a similar sheet blocked the threshold of my door. Not that it mattered. Once the commandment of the veil had been revealed, the men of Medina had assiduously avoided my company, fearful of bringing the wrath of God down upon their heads. Even if the walls of my apartment had been torn down and I sat open and exposed to the sun, not even a blind man would have dared approach me.

Even the women of Medina were now nervous about keeping my company, and I had few visitors aside from my sister, Asma, and my mother. The other wives, similarly trapped behind the veil, blamed me for their predicament. Even Hafsa, with whom I had developed a friendly alliance against our beautiful rival Zaynab bint Jahsh, was bitter and rarely spoke to me anymore.

My lonely days were spent reading the holy Qur'an, which was no longer being secretly inscribed on palm leaves or the shoulder bones of goats but was being preserved on pieces of sturdy parchment bought from Egyptian traders. I found comfort in the stories of the prophets who had endured great tribulations during their sacred missions, men like Moses, who had been forced to leave behind the riches of his princely life and flee into the desert, where he would hear the Voice of God. Or of my forefather Ishmael, who had been expelled from a life of comfort in Abraham's home and sent into the arid wastes of Arabia to found a new nation that would renew God's covenant with man. These stories of exile and redemption had always held great meaning for the Muslims, who saw in the painful journeys of the past an echo of their own lives. But they began to take a greater personal meaning for me, as I found some comfort in the hope that even as these holy ones of God had endured deprivation and loss in the service of a higher cause, perhaps my own confinement would serve some purpose beyond a punishment for my sinful flirtations.

In those difficult weeks, the Messenger continued to follow his policy of spending alternating nights with each of his wives. Even though he had been clearly angered by my behavior, once the commandment of God had come, the Prophet had been conciliatory, recognizing that any further harshness would only add salt to our wounds. I would look forward to our time together once a week and would inundate him with questions about life outside my prison walls, the state of affairs in Medina, and the ongoing war with the Meccans. The Prophet seemed surprised and even delighted by my interest in political matters, something he rarely discussed with his other wives, and he was able to release the weight of his daily life as a statesman in my presence. So, despite my resentment at the new limitations placed on my life, I found that my relationship with my husband actually improved in the aftermath of the veil.

Our hours of conversation were my only relief from the monotony of my life, and I found our bond growing deeper, more intimate, even as the demands of the world grew heavier on his shoulders. For the past several years, I had been afraid that I was becoming less important to the Prophet, as his harem steadily expanded and every beautiful woman in Medina vied to become one of the Mothers. Yet the irony of my caged existence was that the love between us was reignited, and the rumors that I had been displaced as the Prophet's primary consort were replaced by whispers of envy at my unbreakable hold on his heart.

One day, the Messenger came and asked if I would join him on an excursion into the desert west of the oasis. His spies had learned that one of the Bedouin tribe of Bani Mustaliq had reached a pact with Mecca and was planning a raid on Muslim caravans returning from Syria along the seacoast. The Prophet had decided that the best course of action was a preemptive strike against the tribe. The Muslims could no longer afford to cower behind a defensive posture. In the aftermath of our near extermination during the Meccan invasion, we needed to take the offensive at the first sign that our enemies were regrouping.

And so the Muslim army would go out and defeat the Bani Mustaliq before they could prepare their attack. And the Messenger wanted me to accompany him on the expedition.

I felt a flush of joy that brought tears to my eyes. This would be the first day in weeks that I would leave the confines of my home and see the world again. Even though I would be required to wear a full veil, hiding my face from mankind, I would at least be able to walk again in the sun and breathe the rich musky air of the desert. And most important, I would have several nights alone with the Messenger.

I jumped up and down like a little girl, clapping my hands, and my husband smiled at my enthusiasm. And I could see the flame of desire lighting in his eyes and my heart pounded faster. I ran to the small acacia chest in the corner that held all of my meager personal belongings and removed the long dark cloak and veil that had become my prison outside my prison. The cloak was made of thick cotton that covered my body like the black shadow of an eclipse, the flowing robes specifically designed to hide any hint of my delicate curves. It was like a shroud for a living corpse, which is what I had come to feel like in the lonely days of the past month. But I donned it now with pride and excitement, as if it were a glorious wedding dress made of silk and gold. And in a way, it was. For tonight I would have a chance to bind myself to the Messenger all over again, to convince him with my persistent kisses that he was the only man I would ever love.

I slipped on the heavy curtain that was my shield against the world and was about to close the chest when I saw something glittering to the side, beneath a pair of pretty bronze bangles and a coral comb that my father had given me upon my arrival in the oasis. It was the onyx necklace, the Messenger's wedding gift.

I reached down and took the necklace in my hand and tied it above my slender collar. A smile of memory played on my lips as I wrapped my face behind the black veil, the *niqab*, such that only my golden eyes peeked out from behind the soft cotton. The Prophet reached out and took my hand before opening the door. I blinked for a second, blinded by the ferocity of the now-unfamiliar daylight.

And then I took a deep breath and strode back out into the world from which I had been banished. The Masjid courtyard was full of worshipers who turned with surprise to see me emerge. Some quickly looked away, while others gazed in fascination at the bulky black mass that had once been a beautiful girl. A girl whose familiar face none of them would ever see again as long as they lived.

The Messenger led me through the throng of believers who always crowded about him, hoping to touch his hand or the hem of his robe and absorb the *baraka*, the divine blessing, that emanated from his body.

As my husband led me through the streets of Medina that seemed so alien to me now, I had a strange thought that the disorientation I was feeling was akin to the confusion of a soul resurrected from the grave and wandering toward the terrible Throne of God's Judgment.

It was an impression that would prove far more apt than I could have ever known.

23

The attack on the Bani Mustaliq was a resounding success. The Bedouin tribesmen had been caught wholly unprepared for the assault, and their raiding party was no match for the thousand well-armed Muslim warriors who descended on their camp at the break of dawn.

I witnessed the battle, such as it was, from the back of my she-camel, a sturdy beast I had nicknamed Asiya, after the wife of the Pharaoh who had secretly embraced the religion of Moses. I was inside a heavily armored howdah that had been specifically built for the protection of any of the Prophet's wives who accompanied him on a military expedition. I peered through the curtain of steel rings into the heart of the blazing desert, where the Messenger's troops struck down the treacherous Bedouins. The fighting lasted barely an hour, and the Bani Mustaliq capitulated after their chieftain, al-Harith, was decapitated by the sword of a Companion named Thabit ibn Qays.

I watched with grim satisfaction as the Bedouin fighters dropped their weapons in despair and fell to their knees, prostrate in surrender. The Messenger strode out on the battlefield and walked up to the nearest man, a dark-skinned warrior with broken teeth, and lifted him to his feet.

"Do not prostrate yourself before men," he said to his defeated adversary. "Bow only before God."

The enemy soldier looked at him in gratitude and I knew that the Bani Mustaliq would soon be won over to our cause. They were a clan of mercenaries who blew with the wind, and the surprise attack by Medina had shown them that the climate in Arabia had changed permanently. The Prophet had wisely shown them that their future lay with us rather than Mecca. The loss of nearly two dozen of their warriors was a heavy blow, but had they made the mistake of serving as Abu Sufyan's proxies, they would have lost many more.

As Umar and Ali began the process of herding the defeated tribesmen into rows and binding them with solid ropes, I heard a cry of anguish and saw an old woman emerge from the dusty tent city that served as the shelter of her people. She was elderly and her face was lined with years of struggle against the cruel life of the desert. But she moved with startling speed for her age and raced across the blood-stained sand toward the headless corpse of al-Harith. I realized from her piercing wails that she was the chieftain's wife, and I felt sorry for her.

And then another woman, a girl of about twenty years, emerged from the brightly colored pavilion that must have been al-Harith's dwelling and ran over to the old woman. The girl looked away from the sight of the dead chieftain, but she did not cry out. Instead she put her arms around the old woman and comforted her, whispering softly into her ear until the elderly lady stopped shaking and collapsed into her arms, resigned to the loss that had struck their tribe that morning.

I saw the men staring at the girl, who had flowing brown hair, flecked with gold, and olive skin that matched the color of her eyes. She was quite attractive, and I realized that the Muslim warriors would soon be competing to lay claim to her as a captive of war.

The girl sensed their eyes on her and stood tall, throwing her head back in defiance.

"I am Juwayriya, daughter of al-Harith, whom you have slain," she said without any hint of fear. "This is my mother and the mother of my entire clan. Treat her and her kin with dignity if you fear Allah."

Her words were brilliantly chosen and had the desired effect. The

lustful men turned their heads away, embarrassed at their own crass-
ness, and I grinned inside my armored howdah. The girl had spirit.

And then I saw my husband watching her intently with a smile,
and my own quickly vanished.

◆   ◆   ◆

WE CAMPED NEAR THE tents of the Bani Mustaliq for two days, during which the booty was divided among the troops. The tribe had been
successfully raiding caravans for years, and their robbery had brought
them considerable wealth that would soon be apportioned among their
conquerors. A fifth of the spoils would go to the Messenger, including the tribe's store of rare gems—opals, emeralds, and sapphires that
made my heart stop with their glittering beauty. I touched the jewels
with a wistful sigh, knowing that they would soon be redistributed to
the needy and the Prophet's own household would remain as impoverished as ever.

The thorniest issue remained the fate of the captives from the tribe,
especially the proud Juwayriya. Arguments erupted over who had the
best claim to the daughter of the chieftain, who had shown the greatest bravery and prowess on the battlefield to merit a slave girl of such
rare beauty. The rivals turned to Umar, who had been designated by the
Messenger as the judge over all disputes regarding division of spoils.
The grim-faced giant listened impatiently to each man, cutting him
off when he had heard enough of his case, and then made his decision
without hesitation. The girl belonged to Thabit, the man who had personally killed the chieftain of the Bani Mustaliq, her father.

While the other claimants were disappointed, none had the courage to grumble about the judgment before the mighty Umar, and the
matter was resolved in everyone's eyes.

Everyone except Juwayriya herself. When informed of her fate, she
loudly demanded to speak with the Messenger of God himself. Her furious and stubborn insistence made even her captors cower, and shortly
thereafter I accompanied the Prophet to the slave tent where she and
the other women were being housed.

The moment we entered, Juwayriya was transformed from a
haughty and demanding princess into a humble slave girl, her head
lowered, tears instantly flooding her cheeks as if by command. She
begged the Messenger to save her from her ignominious fate. She was

the daughter of one of Arabia's chieftains, a princess of her people. It was the height of degradation and shame for her family that she should now become the property and sexual plaything of a lowly soldier in the Muslim army.

I watched her through the heavy cloth of my veil, grudgingly impressed with her performance. Juwayriya alternated between sorrowful dignity and emotional hysteria as she made her case, and I could see my husband was moved by her pleas. I could feel the familiar sting of jealousy as the Messenger agreed to free her from her bondage—on the condition that she marry him and serve as a voice of conciliation that would bring the remainder of her tribe into a treaty with Medina.

Juwayriya readily assented to the proposal, and I shook my head in wonder at what a strange day this girl had experienced. She had risen with the dawn as a Bedouin princess. By midday, she was a captive and a slave. And by sundown, she had become a Mother of the Believers, one of the queens of Arabia.

That night, as I slept alone in my tent and the Prophet enjoyed the charms of his beguiling new wife, I fingered the onyx necklace, letting all the fury and envy in my heart flow into the dark beads. No matter how hard I tried, I could never be the center of Muhammad's life. He was too vast for any one woman, and his life's mission was greater than the call of any marital union.

I wanted desperately to be the most important of his wives, the one who would even replace Khadija in his memories, but I knew this would never happen. I would have to settle for being the first of an ever-expanding circle of consorts, one name lost among many in the annals of history.

I felt my angry heart scream at the injustice of my life. The most shining star in the firmament of Arabian women, I was nonetheless being buried like a diamond in a sand dune, my delicate beauty hidden from the world, my sharp mind unable to sparkle in the open light of the sun. I was more than this fifteen-year-old girl wrapped in a black veil and sleeping on a rough mat in the desert. But the world would never see me as such. I was a queen who could never claim her crown.

I made a silent oath that of all the Messenger's wives, I would be the one whom the world would still talk about a thousand years from now. The one whose name would play on the lips of men and women when all the others had been forgotten.

It was a terrible vow, and one that should never have been made. For the Lord heard my dark prayer that night and granted it, but not in any way that I could have hoped or desired.

24

The morning that changed my life, as well as the history of the world, was unremarkable. I woke at first light to the haunting sound of Bilal's voice calling the believers to prayer. I had slept fitfully and had been troubled by dreams that immediately fled as I rose from the straw mat. I performed my ablutions from a pail of water that had been left discreetly outside the entrance to my tent by a soldier.

I let the soothingly cold water flow through my hands and then washed the sleep out of my eyes and dabbed my hair and feet according to the proper ritual of *wudhu*—the lesser ablution that one normally performed before any prayer. Only after sexual intercourse was one required to take a *ghusl*, a full bath in which every part of the body had to be cleansed before one could stand in worship of the Lord of the Worlds. The thought flashed through my mind that the Messenger would, of course, have to perform the *ghusl* after spending the night with his new bride, and I felt the pangs of jealousy tighten my chest.

When I emerged, fully veiled and covered head to toe, as was now required of me, I saw the Prophet was gathering the men in single lines facing south toward the Holy Kaaba. He smiled when he saw the black bundle that was me, but I looked away, unable to meet his eyes. I saw from the corner of my vision that his smile widened just slightly, as if he were amused by my clear annoyance at his marriage to Juwayriya, and I had to bite my tongue before I said something out loud that would be unworthy of a Mother of the Believers.

After we had performed the *Fajr* ritual, before the disk of the sun had yet emerged on the horizon, the men began to break down our camp for the journey home. I went off to brood by myself, staying aloof from Juwayriya despite her glances in my direction. She was now wearing a purple veil that matched her flowing robes, and even in her modest dress she seemed to exude great sensuality. She was taller than me and her bosom was round and firm, her thighs shapely—a girl who was clearly capable of bearing the Prophet children.

I seethed as I realized that Juwayriya would now become the new hope of the community, since I had failed to give the Prophet a son despite the six years we had shared a bed. The tongues of cruel gossips wagged that I was infertile, and yet my courses came every month without fail. It was true that the Prophet now spent only one night a week with me, so the chances of conception were accordingly lowered. There was, of course, still hope that my womb would bear fruit in the years to come. Yet some part of me had begun to believe that it was not the will of Allah that I should carry my husband's son. The only thought that caused me more grief was that God might choose one of my rivals for that honor.

As I sat by myself in a corner of the camp, brooding over my lot in life, I felt the arid desert air suddenly cool around me, even though no wind rustled my robes. I looked up to see the Messenger of God standing above me, the infuriating smile still on his lips.

"Come, let us have a race," he said, reaching out his hand to me.

I stared up at him in complete surprise, and then I felt my anger evaporating under the warmth of his gaze. In the early days of our marriage, when I was still a girl in body and heart, the Prophet would often play such games with me. He particularly loved to race, as I, with my lightning speed, was the only person who had any chance of beating him.

It was a tender offer, a reminder of days long past when it was just the two of us, before his harem was filled with beautiful women whose charms were an easy match for my own. I took his hand and rose, following the Messenger past the bustling crowds who were taking down tents and untethering the camels for the voyage. I saw Juwayriya standing by her widowed mother, watching us like a hawk, and I smiled beneath my black veil.

My husband led me to a hillock where a lone oleander bush stood in defiance of the wilderness, its pink-and-yellow buds shimmering in the early morning light. I saw him gaze across the landscape until he found a suitable landmark, a cactus tree near a ledge, beyond which was a sharp drop into rocky gorge.

"There," he said, pointing to our finish line. "Don't fall over the edge. The angels might not catch you in time!"

I narrowed my eyes at him and he laughed heartily. The Prophet waited with an amused grin as I girded my robes above my ankles to make sure I didn't trip—there were no men in the immediate vicinity, and he did not object. I then kicked off my sandals and let the coarse sand caress my feet as I used to do when I was a child.

I saw the Messenger's face change and the teasing look left his eyes, replaced by genuine fondness. I suddenly realized that he, too, missed the days when the world was simple, when it was just a handful of us speaking truth to power. Now we had become the power in the land and nothing was simple anymore.

The Messenger faced straight ahead, bending down in preparation. And then without the customary countdown from three, he simply cried, "Go!"

And the race was on.

I tore past him with the vibrancy of youth, my bare feet flashing beneath me. The hot air smashed against my face, pressing the heavy cloth of my veil against my mouth. I could feel my heart pounding as I pushed every sinew in my legs to the utmost. I could see the cactus growing closer, even as the empty desert appeared to stand still, and for a moment I had the strange thought that I was stationary and the plant was running toward me.

I could see no sign of my husband from the corner of my eye and wondered whether he had even left his position. And then I felt a rush of cold wind to my right, and the Messenger of God thundered past me, his black hair flowing wildly in the wind, the thick curls of his beard shaking from his hearty laughter.

And then he was at the cactus and he turned to face me triumphantly as I arrived a second later. We both dropped to the ground, gasping for breath and laughing with a joy that neither of us had expressed in so many months. The joy of being together, bound by destiny, this great man and this little girl, the most improbable of couples.

He held me close to him and I could feel the steady, comforting beat of his heart. I realized in that moment that no matter how many women entered his bed, I would remain special. I would never replace

Khadija, his first love. But I would assuredly be his last. And in the end, what more could any woman ask of a man?

After we had caught our breath, I lowered my skirt and we walked back, hand in hand, to the camp, which was by now almost completely dismantled. My tent had been taken down and I went obligingly to Asiya, my she-camel, while my husband rejoined his men and helped them complete the preparations for the journey.

I sat inside the armored howdah and placed my hand across my heart, feeling the wonderful pangs of love renewed. And then I realized that something was wrong. My onyx necklace, which should have been lying on my bosom, was missing. I quickly searched through the howdah, but the tiny compartment was empty. I gingerly climbed out and looked around the camel, but all I could see was yellow sand and orange pebbles. The distinct black stones would have stood out like a blot on the sun, and yet there was no sign of them.

And then I remembered. I had last felt the necklace on my bosom during the race, the sharp beads pressing against my delicate flesh as I ran toward the cactus. It must have fallen off near the ledge where we reclined after the Messenger had beaten me to the finish.

I cursed the faulty clasp that had always given me trouble and began walking away from the camp in search of my wedding present. The onyx necklace was the first gift the Messenger had given me, and every time I felt it around my neck, I would remember that special night when I became a woman. I treasured it above all of my meager possessions and was not about to let it vanish into the sands for all time because of carelessness.

I climbed over the hillock and soon lost sight of the base camp. My eyes scanned the ground as I carefully retraced my steps, but there was no sign of the necklace. Frustrated, I looked around the base of the cactus, and still the necklace eluded my search. I stubbornly crossed the path again and again, kicking aside stones and overturning an anthill in my quest to find my wedding present. I became increasingly agitated and wondered how I would tell my love that his special gift to me was lost forever.

And then I saw it. Partially buried under a small mound of sand, a black stone winked out at me, its white flecks glittering in the harsh sunlight. I smiled in delight and thanked Allah for helping me find the necklace. I quickly pulled it out of the ground and wiped it clean. I held it close in my palm rather than tie it to my neck and risk having it fall off again. And then I looked up at the sky and realized that the sun was now far above me. I blanched—how long had I spent out here, alone in the wilderness? Had it been hours? I cursed my own foolishness. The Muslims should have been on the road to Medina by now, but my little excursion had delayed the entire army. Scouts were probably searching frantically for me, and the whole camp would be in disarray at my disappearance. My heart racing, I ran back to the hillock and climbed down, practicing a thousand apologies in my head for having held up the entire expedition.

And then I froze as the campground came into sight.

The area was deserted. There was not a single human being or animal left of the entire armed contingent. I stood there in utter shock, my breath caught in my throat. They were gone. The Muslims had broken camp and left without me.

I looked around desperately and called out for help. But there was no sign of any stragglers, and the only answer was the mocking call of my own echo.

My vision blurred as I stood forsaken in the empty wasteland where no man or woman could survive alone for more than a few hours. Tears fell readily from my eyes and I could feel their bitter salt on my tongue. The mad thought crossed my mind that the only water I would ever taste again would be that which flowed from inside me.

I sat down in despair, the necklace falling from my hand and landing on the dry earth that would soon become my grave. I looked in fury at the simple onyx beads whose pursuit would now cost me my life. And then I felt all the color drain from my face.

The necklace had fallen in such a fashion that the beads curled up to form a smile, a cruel, mocking jeer. And then the wind rose and I thought I could hear a terrible, inhuman laughter echoing all about me.

25

Iwandered alone in the desert for hours, following the tracks of the camels eastward toward Medina. The dromedary beasts moved like falcons through the shifting sands and the army was in all likelihood already most of the way back to the oasis. If I continued on my present course, I would be able to reach home on foot within six days. Which was, of course, six days longer than I could survive without any food or water. And yet something kept pulling me forward, some desperate hope that my absence from the caravan would be noticed and a search party sent back. But as the sun fell toward the horizon, my hopes began to dwindle. And when the last light disappeared from the sky, they died with the sunset.

A blackness fell over the wilderness that was so thick that even the sea of stars above me could not shed any light on my path. The air that had sizzled with merciless wrath during the day now became still and deathly cold. I lay down on the coarse sand and hugged myself tight, hoping to keep my body warm enough to survive until the sunrise. But my teeth chattered viciously and tremors of ice ran through my veins.

The world began to darken further, and even the stars faded from my view. My head began to spin and my breathing slowed to a soft whisper. I could feel my heartbeat wane and I no longer had the strength to fight.

I was falling into a chasm that had no bottom and I finally surrendered and gave myself to the void.

— — —

I AWOKE WITH A start at the sound of drums pulsing in the distance. The world remained black all around me, and when I looked up into the sky, I could see no stars. For a moment, I was confused. Had I died? Was this the *barzakh*, the barrier between worlds where souls were stored until the Day of Resurrection? I looked around in trepidation, expecting the terrifying forms of Munkar and Nakir, the angels of death with black faces and piercing blue eyes, to appear at any moment and begin the solemn questioning of the soul in the grave. The angels were said to ask three questions: "Who is your Lord? Who is your prophet? What is your religion?" Those who answered correctly—"Allah, Muhammad, and Islam"—would be granted peace in their graves until the Final Judgment. And those who answered with falsehood would suffer torment that would prefigure the horrors of hell.

I gripped my hands to my chest, waiting and watching, the sacred words of the *Fatiha* repeating on my parched lips. And yet no angels appeared. But I heard the thunder of drums grow louder and a red glow appeared on the horizon. But it was not the welcoming glare of sunrise, but something else, for the sky remained black save for the throbbing, pulsating halo beyond the hills.

There was something that was both enticing and terrifying about that light. It beckoned to me and I felt drawn toward it. And yet a voice inside my heart said to stay where I was, to avoid the mysterious light and all the secrets that it offered. I struggled with myself, but my curiosity finally took hold of my heart and I walked toward the unearthly glow.

I climbed up a tall dune, struggling with the shifting sand beneath my feet that kept threatening to pull me back. But I finally managed to make it to the top of the hill and was able to look down at the source of the light. My eyes grew wide as I saw a campfire burning in the distance, the flickering flames dancing and calling out to me with the hope of rescue.

I began to run, joy in my heart. God had heard my prayers and the danger was over. Where there was fire, there were people. I should have hesitated, wondering who would be out here in the middle of the night, whether they were friend or foe. A pretty girl alone in the wilderness would be easy prey for the Bedouins, who followed no law save the call of their lust. And yet some part of my heart reasoned that I would be safe once they knew who I was. Even a bandit would find more value in ransoming the wife of Arabia's most powerful man than in taking her virtue.

As I ran closer to the fire, the drums grew louder. I saw figures milling about the light and I slowed, my prudence finally reasserting itself. I crept closer to the burning pyre until I could get a clear look at these people and decide whether it was indeed wise to reveal myself.

And then I froze when I saw who they were. It was a group of women who looked disturbingly familiar, dressed in robes of scarlet and gold, their anklets jingling as they danced around the fire. They were led by a tall woman whose face was covered by a veil and who was beating a timbrel with intensity. The strange women swayed and swirled by the fire, their bodies shaking in an ecstasy that would have made me blush had I not been so disoriented. What were these women doing out here in the middle of the night, dancing and throwing themselves about as if they were making love to unseen spirits? My blood began to chill and I suddenly regretted having followed the light.

I was ready to crawl back over the hills and take refuge from these strange and alluring figures when I saw the veiled woman who led the dance raise her arm. A golden armlet reflected the raging fire and I could make out a distinct shape—two snakes winding about each other, and where their jaws met, a glistening ruby sparkled in defiance.

I stopped breathing as I realized who this woman was.

Hind. The mad wife of Abu Sufyan, who had eaten the flesh of the martyrs.

I wanted to run but my legs were rooted to the spot. And then I saw a flash of light above me and heard the terrible crash of thunder. And I realized that the reason I could see no stars was that the heavens were covered by thick, rolling storm clouds. The lightning flashed again, and a sudden torrent began, rain plunging down from the angry sky and flooding the earth around me.

I felt the hard drops hitting my face like tiny pebbles and I opened my mouth, desperate for water after hours of wandering in the desert. But the rainwater tasted different, salty and vile, and I retched violently. And then the sky was lit by a dozen terrible jagged bolts and for a moment I could see the world clearly about me.

The raindrops were not clear, but crimson.

The sky was raining blood.

As my heart pounded in horror, the unholy torrent struck the campfire. But instead of extinguishing the flames, it was as if oil had been poured upon them, and the fire burned higher and brighter, illuminating the desolate valley as bright as day.

And then I saw a sight I will never forget. All about me the ground was littered with corpses from a battle. Men in armor, their breastplates pierced by dozens of arrows, arms and legs dismembered and thrown to the side like refuse. The terrible stench of rotting flesh engulfed me and I wanted to scream, and yet no sound emerged.

And then I watched with horror beyond horror as the veiled Hind stopped her dance and turned to look in my direction. In the light of the raging fire she could now see me, and she suddenly laughed with bloodcurdling viciousness. Her maidens, whom I now recognized as the same madwomen who had danced over the body of Hamza, pointed at me and sneered.

And then Hind was walking toward me and I saw that the timbrel in her hand had become a mighty sword, the blade curved and cruelly jagged. At that instant, my terror overcame my shock and I began to run. Yet everywhere I turned, I was blocked by a sea of corpses, and I had no choice but to step on their bodies, feeling the sickening sensation of my feet sinking into their rotting flesh.

I could hear Hind's laughter growing closer but I dared not look behind me. I needed to get away, far away from this madness. Every prayer I knew was on my lips, and yet the nightmare continued, my supplications met only with the terrible roll of thunder from above.

And then my sandals jammed inside the open mouth of a dead soldier whose skull I tried to run over, and I tripped, falling hard on my face. I desperately tried to move, to pull my foot free from the teeth of the poor man whose corpse I had no choice but to desecrate. I managed to pry my foot loose from the jaws of the unlucky soldier and crawled away, shuddering in disgust. I was ready to get back to my feet when lightning flashed and I saw the face of the poor man clearly.

It was the face of your father, my sister's husband, Zubayr ibn al-Awwam.

My eyes went wide in horror and I could not move. Zubayr lay on the ground and I saw that his head had been severed from his body. In each of his hands he held a sword, even as he had that fateful day he had protected our lives at Uhud.

I wanted to scream, but it was as if my tongue had been ripped from my throat.

And then I saw a figure lying beside him, pierced with a dozen arrows shot through his breast, his eyes looking up at me accusingly.

It was my sweet cousin Talha, the one man who loved me more

than himself and had nearly died fighting those who sought to sully my honor.

Tears exploded from my eyes and I felt myself swooning. And then, in that terrible moment, Hind appeared, standing above the bodies of two of my dearest and closest friends, laughing in contempt. I threw myself at her, clawing at her veiled face with my fingers. She appeared startled by my onslaught and raised her sword to strike me. Somehow I found the strength to kick her in the womb, and she doubled over in pain, letting the blade fall from her grasp. I immediately took up the weapon, which felt surprisingly light and natural in my hand, and in an instant I was standing atop the fallen Meccan queen, the blade at her neck.

The terrible image of Talha and Zubayr dead before me consumed my eyes and I raised the weapon, ready to strike.

"You did this to them!" I screamed.

And then Hind spoke words that have never left me and haunt me to this day.

"No. You did."

I did not understand what she meant and I did not care to. Screaming with animal rage, my heart crying out for vengeance, I sliced the blade down and cut Hind's head from her sensuous body.

As her decapitated skull rolled away, the veil fell off.

And I dropped my sword in horror.

For I was looking at my own face.

26

I screamed with such intensity that I woke myself from the nightmare, the cry still echoing from my lips even as my eyes blinked in confusion. There was no battlefield, no sea of corpses. My beloved Talha and your father, Zubayr, were nowhere to be seen, nor was the ghastly demon image of Hind—or was it myself?

I was alone where I had collapsed hours before, in the middle of the empty desert, with only scorpions and lizards to keep me company. For a moment, a wave of relief ran through my veins and I said a silent prayer thanking Allah that what I had seen was just a dream, a delusion arising from the terror of my predicament.

And then my relief faded and the stark realization of my situation came back to me like a kick to the stomach. I was alone and lost in the wilderness, and had not had a sip of water since noon the day before. My head was pounding and the world swam before me as I tried to rise to my feet. I would not able to survive another day out here like this, and by the time the search parties reached me from Medina, I would be a desiccated corpse, partially consumed by the sands and the ferocious insects that hid in the shadows of the wastes.

And then I turned my head and saw the red glow on the eastern horizon. At least the sun would be up shortly and the icy air would give way to its unrelenting fury. I held myself tight, trying to warm my bones as the winds slapped at me from all sides, like an angry mother chiding a troublesome child. I had no choice but to keep moving toward the sun, hoping against hope that the caravan had returned for me during the darkness, that soon I would be home again in my small but comfortable little chamber in the courtyard of the Masjid. How I had longed to escape that tiny room as if it were a prison! And now I would have traded my soul for a chance to sleep inside its sturdy walls, free of wind and rain and the raging furnace of the sun. During the worst moments of my confinement, I had dreamed of running off into the open desert, letting the sands caress my bare feet and the air wash freely over my uncovered tresses. But now I hated this vast openness, this stark emptiness that was a dungeon far worse than any designed by man.

As I stumbled forward, memories of my family came back to me. My beautiful mother, softly whispering a lullaby to me as I fell into safe slumber in her arms. My father, hunched and careworn, yet always smiling at me with sparkling eyes that knew only kindness. My sister, Asma, whose plainness and strength and quiet dignity gave her more beauty than all the flighty girls whose glitter faded with time. As I coughed up dust from my battered lungs, I said a silent prayer that they would not grieve for me for long. Their lives were difficult enough without the weight of heartache and the bitter poison of loss.

And then the crimson disk of the sun broke over the horizon and

I blinked in surprise. A figure was silhouetted against the heavenly fire, a man on a camel, riding steadily in my direction. No caravan, no contingent of soldiers that would have normally made up a search party for so august a person as a Mother of the Believers. Just one man, moving inexorably toward me.

I looked around, but there was nowhere to hide in the vast nothingness. And then I moved out of pure instinct. I grabbed a sharp rock whose cruel edges looked as if they could tear open flesh down to the bone. And then I pulled up the veil that I had tied around my waist and hastily covered my face.

And then the sun rose higher and I saw the man's face and recognized him. He was a youth of twenty years named Safwan who had often come by the Masjid to help the Prophet's daughter Fatima feed the People of the Bench. He had no wealth or social position, but his darkly handsome features always set my girlfriends giggling in his presence. Safwan was the source of many unspoken fantasies among the women of Medina, although he was remarkably pious and seemed utterly unaware of the heated thoughts he inspired in others.

And now he was here in the desert, and we were alone.

As the climbing sun illuminated the world about us, Safwan stopped his camel and stared down at the tiny figure standing inexplicably on the desert plain. I saw him blink several times as if he was trying to convince himself that I was not some sort of mirage or twisted vision of his mind.

And then I saw his dark eyes fall upon my onyx necklace, the accursed object that had brought me to this wretched place between life and death. And then I saw the color drain from his face.

"*Inna lillahi wan inna ilayhi rajioon,*" he said, reciting the prayer in the Qur'an that is said when man faces adversity or a situation beyond his ability to handle. "Truly we belong to God and truly we are returning to Him."

I stared up at him, unblinking, utterly unable to speak. And then Safwan climbed off his camel and approached me slowly, one hand on the hilt of his dagger.

"Are you . . . are you the Messenger's wife? Or a djinn sent to lead me astray?" There was fear and wonder in his voice, and I realized that he had not been sent to look for me. Somehow, by the strange hand of fate, this lone warrior had been wandering through the desert wastes and had come upon me at my moment of dire need. If ever there had been any small part of my heart that had questioned or doubted the existence of God, it vanished forever in that remarkable moment in the desolate wilderness.

My vision blurred as tears of joy and disbelief flooded my eyes.

"I am no djinn," I managed to croak out. "Please . . . help me."

27

$\mathcal{I}$ had awakened from one nightmare and found myself in another. Within hours of my miraculous return to Medina, the daggers of envy were bared against me. The Messenger had dispatched search parties when he learned that I was missing from my howdah. But when the people of Medina saw me returning in the company of Safwan, salacious talk of my time alone with the attractive soldier began to spread like a brushfire. Nervous whispers fanned into open word in the marketplace that I had arranged to fall behind the caravan so that I could tryst with my young lover. Even though I was secluded again inside my tiny apartment, the rumors were so prevalent that they quickly reached my shocked ears.

The Messenger of God reacted swiftly, calling the believers to a *jamaat* at the Masjid where he openly declared his rejection of such gossip, which was apparently being fomented by Abdallah ibn Ubayy and his disgruntled cohorts among the Khazraj. The gathering had become heated as members of the rival tribe Aws openly accused Ibn Ubayy of slandering the Mother of the Believers, and there had been a tense moment when it appeared that the ancient hatred between the clans had been rekindled and could lead to open warfare. Sensing the dangerous mood of the crowd, the Messenger had called for calm and forgiveness and then quickly dispersed the gathering. And yet the reopened wounds between the tribes did not heal so easily, nor did the accusation against me die with the Prophet's defense.

And as the evil tongues continued to spill their poison, even my husband's trusting heart was no longer immune to the lies. He stopped visiting me on our appointed days and I realized with horror that the seeds of nagging doubt were beginning to germinate in his mind.

And so it was that I sat weeping in my tiny home, the mud walls that I had despised as a prison now my only protection from the crowds that gathered daily in the courtyard to mock my honor. My mother sat beside me, holding my hand and brushing my hair as she had when I was a little girl a lifetime before. I was grateful for her soothing presence and yet troubled by her inability to look into my eyes. The thought that she, too, might quietly doubt my integrity was more painful than I could bear.

The door opened and I looked up to see my father enter. He appeared to have aged a dozen years in the past few days, and his graying hair was now almost completely white.

I wanted to get up, to run into his arms, but there was a terrible cloud over his face. And then I realized with dread that he was looking at me less in sympathy than in anger, as if I were somehow to blame for this calumny, and I felt the sting of new tears in my eyes.

"What has happened?" he said softly, looking at my mother rather than me. But I spoke up quickly, refusing to let others talk of my situation as if I were not present.

"The Messenger bade me stay with you until he decides what to do," I said, trying to keep my voice from cracking under grief.

My mother patted my hand and stared up at the ceiling.

"Do not fear. This will all pass soon," she said, her voice sounding distant, as if she were talking aloud to herself rather than to me. And then she looked over at my father, who was still avoiding my eyes. "You are a beautiful woman and the wife of a powerful man. Those who speak against you are filled with envy."

Her words were meant to comfort, but I could hear the hint of doubt in her voice and could see her looking at Abu Bakr as if for reassurance. But he simply stared at his feet without responding.

"But what am I to do?" I cried out in agony, begging for them to set aside their hesitation, to save their daughter from this cauldron of sorrow. "What if the Messenger divorces me? Or I am put on trial for adultery? The punishment is death!"

The horror of my words seemed to break through the ice between us and I saw the first hint of compassion on my father's tired face.

"Do not fear, my daughter," he said, finally moving from the doorway to sit by my side. "He is the Prophet of God. If you are innocent—"

All the color drained from my face and then came flooding back in a rush of anger that made my skin burn.

"*If* I am innocent?"

"I only meant . . ."

I rose to my feet and moved away from him.

"I know what you meant! You don't believe me!"

My father tried to take my hand, but I pulled it away as if he were a leper.

"I didn't say that," he said meekly, trying to undo the damage of his careless words. But it was too late.

"You don't have to!" I raged at him. "I see it in your eyes!"

My mother tried to intervene. She took a deep breath and then finally looked at me directly.

"Aisha, you are a young girl who has been through so much," she said softly, and I could see that she was struggling with the words. "You are such a vivacious child with a love for life, and you have been burdened with more responsibility than any girl should bear at your age." She hesitated and then said the words that would tear my heart in two. "I know the veil has left you feeling lonely and trapped. It's perfectly understandable to seek an escape, even for one night . . ."

I felt my heart miss a beat, and for a second the world spun around me. I was drowning and there was no one to save me. Not even my mother, who was intent on pushing my head farther into the rancid waters of shame and scandal.

And then I heard myself speaking, but it was not me. A voice unlike any that had emerged from my throat echoed in that room. It was deep and harsh, like a man's, resounding with power and terror.

"Get out!"

Umm Ruman's mouth dropped open in disbelief, and her eyes bulged from her lined but still elegant face.

"Don't talk to me that way! I am your mother!" There was more fear than anger in her voice, as if she did not recognize this strange djinn that had taken possession of her precious daughter.

And yet the voice I could not control would not be silenced.

"No! I am yours!" I could hear it say. "I am the Mother of the Believers! I am the Chosen One, brought by Gabriel himself to the

Messenger of God! You must obey me as you would obey my husband! Now get out!"

Tears welled in my mother's luminous eyes and yet I felt no sorrow for her. I felt nothing but outrage and righteous indignation.

My mother looked as if she were about to retort. I saw her hand trembling as if it took every last thread of willpower to refrain from slapping me across the face.

And then my father rose and touched her on the shoulder, shaking his head. My mother's fury collapsed like a dam and the flood of grief that was inside her was released. She wept violently, her face buried in her hands, her body shaking with such violence that I thought her delicate bones would shatter.

I gazed down on her grief and turned my back, preferring the sight of the dull brick wall to that of my own flesh and blood who had betrayed me. I heard the rustle of cotton robes as Abu Bakr rose and helped my crying mother to her feet. Their footsteps echoed coldly on the stone floor and then I heard the door slam behind them.

I was alone now. More alone than I had ever been. Even though sunlight streamed in through the tiny cracks in the sheepskin covers over my window, I could feel a curtain of darkness falling over my life. A blackness so thick that even the shadows of the grave seemed to burn like torches of hope.

And then, with nothing else left to do, I fell to my knees and prayed.

And then, in that lonely silence where the only sound was the sullen tremor of my heart, I heard a voice inside my mind. It was gentle and soft, like the whisper of a spring breeze, and it recited the words of the holy Qur'an.

God is the Protector of those who have faith. From the depths of darkness, He will lead them forth into light . . .

28

I sat close as my maid Burayra whispered to me what she had heard outside the door of Zaynab's apartment. She was one of the few members of the household who had stood by my side as the scandal had spread and I counted her as my one true friend in what was becoming the darkest hour of my life. Her plump arms were soft as cushions and I would lean into them and weep every night as I awaited news of my fate. I had come to rely on Burayra's persistent cheer to keep me from surrendering to despair. But tonight her chubby face was downturned with the weight of the words she carried.

"Zaynab bint Jahsh spoke in your favor with the Messenger," she said, to my sincere surprise.

"Zaynab?" It was hard to believe that my greatest rival had spoke in my defense. And I suddenly felt exceedingly cheap and small for all the dark thoughts and bitterness I had harbored about her over the years. "Then I have been wrong about her. May Allah bless her."

I would later learn that as the whispers of infidelity had grown louder, as the whiff of scandal had become a cloud of stench over the sacred household, some of Zaynab's friends had told her to rejoice. The daughter of Abu Bakr, her chief rival in the harem, would soon be undone by the sword of shame, and Zaynab would become the principal wife, the most revered of the Mothers in the eyes of the community. My downfall would be the catalyst that would raise Zaynab's sun in the eyes of God and man, and she would quickly fill the void in her husband's betrayed and broken heart.

Such was the excited chattering of the other women of standing in Medina, women from powerful and noble families who had welcomed the wealthy Zaynab as one of their own even as they scorned me as an ambitious upstart. To these ladies, I had finally received my long-overdue comeuppance, and they were eagerly awaiting the final act in this sordid drama, a denouement that would end in my disgrace and divorce from the House of the Messenger. The fact that my end could be met under a pile of stones in the desert, the ancient punishment for adulterers, did not seem to concern these catty gossips. They were too busy savoring the spice of scandal to consider that a young girl's life was at stake.

Perhaps not too long ago, Zaynab would have happily done the same, delighting in my fall. The humiliation of a woman whose childish games had brought the curtain of the veil down on all of them, cutting Zaynab and her sister-wives off from the world forever. She should have taken justified pleasure in my predicament as the proper retribution for a life of entitlement and unearned distinction as the Messenger's only virgin wife.

And yet now that her rival was in the center of a maelstrom that would in all likelihood consume me, Zaynab felt no joy. She had never liked me, that was true, and my hold on Muhammad's heart would always be a source of jealousy for her. But in her heart, she knew that I was innocent of the slander. For all my faults, my arrogance and quick temper, Zaynab knew that I was utterly besotted with the Messenger of God and would not willingly submit to the charms of any man, even one as dashing and virile as Safwan. No, in Zaynab's eyes, I was not guilty of adultery. Idiocy, yes. Immaturity, yes. But she knew that I would not, could not, be unfaithful to Muhammad, any more than the moon could refuse to follow the sun.

And so it was that Zaynab bint Jahsh, my chief competitor for the heart of God's Messenger, made a decision, one that would perplex her friends but one that was made because it was the right thing to do.

I listened intently as Burayra shared with me what she had heard.

◆　◆　◆

"O Messenger of God, may I speak?" Zaynab had been sitting by the Prophet's side for some time before summoning up the courage to raise her voice.

The Prophet looked up at her, his eyes weary. He had sat by Ali for nearly half an hour without either man speaking. Zaynab had watched the two, more like father and son than cousins, as they gazed at each other as if communicating without words. To anyone outside the confines of the sacred household, the persistent silence would have seemed awkward. Yet those in the inner circle of the family had come to understand that the relationship between Muhammad and Ali was special. The normal rules of social propriety did not seem to exist between them, as if they were one person rather than two, part of each other in some mysterious way that was beyond the understanding of mere mortals.

"Speak, daughter of Jahsh, for I would hear your counsel," the Prophet said softly.

Zaynab hesitated, afraid that she was inserting herself into matters that were dangerously outside her purview. But as she looked at the pain in her husband's eyes, she knew what she had to do.

"Aisha and I have never been close, for many reasons that do not matter anymore," she said, cautiously at first, as if every word were a step onto a deadly battlefield. And then the words came rushing from her lips, as if something greater than herself had taken control of Zaynab's soul and was speaking through her. "But I can say this. She loves you and you alone. It is a passion that is so fiery that it consumes her with jealousy at times, to the grief of your other wives. But it is that very same passion that makes it impossible for her to have done the things she has been accused of."

She stopped, almost afraid to breathe. The Prophet looked at her and she saw the flicker of gratitude in his eyes.

"Thank you, Zaynab."

He spoke like a patient thanking a doctor for a desperately needed salve. Her words had lessened his pain, his isolation. But she could see that the torment of doubt still raged in his heart.

"Even if I believe Aisha, the scandal threatens to consume the *Ummah* like a wildfire," the Messenger of God said with a sigh, "I don't know what to do."

Zaynab's eyes fell on Ali, who looked down at his hands for a long moment before finally raising his head to speak.

"There are many women besides her," Ali said gently.

Zaynab saw the Prophet stiffen as if he had been stung, and then tears welled in his black eyes. The Messenger looked at his younger cousin, who shrank back slightly from his gaze, as if in apology. And yet Ali did not retract his words.

In the years to come, Zaynab would remember this simple exchange between two men. A few words between family members dealing with an embarrassing scandal, words that would have had little impact beyond the moment had they been said by other men with more modest destinies.

Ali's advice was well intentioned, she knew. His suggestion that Muhammad should divorce Aisha was likely being whispered by many other Companions. They were words that were said out of love for Muhammad and a desire to protect the honor of his household. But words are like sparks, and these would kindle a flame that would forever change the course of history.

✦ ✦ ✦

I WAS STUNNED WHEN Burayra told me of Ali's advice to divorce me. The Prophet's cousin had betrayed me. The man who was closest to my husband's heart had tried to use his powerful influence to have me expelled from the People of the House, have me cast out like a leper into the wilderness. He had judged me guilty without evidence and had cast his lot with the evil men and women who were spreading lies to destroy me.

I felt my heart begin to pound, and the blood rushed so quickly to my head that I reeled as if I had been slapped. In that one moment, every complex feeling I ever had toward this strange and unearthly young man coalesced into one emotion.

Hatred.

" Ali . . ." I said his name out loud with difficulty, my voice shaking with anger so hot that it burned my tongue white. And then I made an oath that would change everything. The course of my life and the destiny of Islam itself turned on the words that exploded from my lips like a raging flood, destroying everything in their path.

"By God, I will humble his face to the ground . . . I will tear him from his seat of honor if it's the last thing I do . . ."

I saw the terrified look on Burayra's face and I did not care. She stared at me as if she did not recognize me, and she was right. For in that moment, Aisha bint Abu Bakr, the frivolous, warmhearted girl who loved life, was dead. I had been reborn as a woman of ice, whose cold heart beat for only one purpose.

29

After I had heard that the Prophet was being advised to divorce me by his closest allies, I left the confines of my apartment and returned to my mother's home. It was not that I felt safer or more accepted there. On the contrary, my parents' doubts were like claws scratching at my heart, and it was difficult for me to look either of them in the face. But I could not continue to dwell in the household of the Messenger, sleep in the bed we had once shared, as long as there was a cloud of suspicion hanging over me. And if I were to be cut off from the marriage bond—or worse, placed on trial for adultery—then I did not want to face the indignity of being taken forcefully from my own house. And so I donned my veil and left of my own accord one morning, with Burayra my only protection against the accusing stares of the crowds as I walked down the cobbled streets of Medina.

My mother gave me a small room in the back of her stone hut, little larger than the cell that had been my apartment in the Masjid. She tried to comfort me, but I brushed aside her clumsy efforts at reconciliation and kept to myself. I spent the days in prayer, kneeling before God and asking Him to remove this lie that had been branded on my name. And every night I slept alone on the rough cot, the mattress made of knotted palm fiber that cut my skin raw as I tossed and turned with a thousand nightmares. But no matter how horrible the dreams were, the faces of djinn and demons that haunted my nights, I preferred the troubled madness of sleep to the greater nightmare that awaited me when I awoke.

I remained in that room for six days, emerging only to visit the rickety toilet shed behind the back wall of the house. My mother tried to coax me to join the family for meals, but I would simply take rough pieces of meat and bowls of wheat porridge back into my room and eat alone. After two days, she stopped asking me to come out and simply left the food on a tray by my door.

And then, on the seventh day, I heard a knock and my father's voice asking me to let them in, for he had brought a visitor. The Messenger of God had finally arrived to speak with me. And I could tell from my father's grave tone that he feared the worst.

I was numb from the unrelenting pain of the past few weeks and I felt nothing in my heart as I went to greet my husband. No anger, no fear. No despair. And even the love that had always bonded us was hidden so deep in the void of my heart that I could not find it. I was a corpse, without life or sensation, a dead tree whose branches rustled under a cold wind.

I opened the door to see the Messenger of God, his face drawn and solemn, looking down at me. I offered a perfunctory greeting of peace and then sat down on the hard cot and stared straight ahead, ready for whatever judgment he had brought.

The Prophet entered, followed by my mother and father, who looked more frightened than I had ever seen them. Even during the tense flight from Medina, their faces had been calm, their demeanor untroubled and steady. And yet now they looked as if everything they had was about to be taken away from them. I would have appreciated their fear for my future, a sign of their love for me despite their doubts and misgivings about my character. But my heart was like winter frost on the palm leaves, sharp and unyielding.

My husband sat beside me and looked at my face for a long moment. His dark eyes were impenetrable, and the hint of rose normally found on his cheeks was gone, leaving him as pallid as a ghost.

When he finally spoke, I barely recognized his voice, for its fluid melody had been replaced by a hoarseness, as if he had not spoken in years.

"O Aisha. I have heard these things about you, and if you are innocent, surely God will declare your innocence," he said, measuring every word carefully. "And if you have done wrong, then ask forgiveness of God and repent unto Him. Truly if a servant confesses to God and repents, God relents toward him."

So here it was. The Messenger of God was sitting beside me, asking me if indeed I had betrayed him with Safwan in the desert. After all our years together, after everything we had endured, he still did not trust me. His words cut through me and suddenly a hidden well of emotion was unleashed. Tears welled in my eyes and fell down my cheeks, but I made no effort to wipe them away. My eyes were blurring wildly, as if I had been thrust face-first into a river, and for an instant I thought I might go blind, like the prophet Jacob, whose grief at the loss of his son Joseph tore away his sight.

I turned my face to my father, who stood by the doorway.

"Answer the Messenger of God for me," I said, pleading with Abu Bakr to intervene and save me from this final disgrace.

But my father bowed his head.

"I don't know what to say."

Through my tear-filled eyes, I could make out the figure of my mother standing behind him, her hands held to her breast in a sign of terrible grief.

"Mother . . . please . . . tell him . . ."

But Umm Ruman turned away from me, sobbing.

I looked at my parents and realized that I was truly alone in this world. And then something strange happened. I could feel a warmth spreading in my breast, a fire that had been kindled in my heart. The flame of dignity and honor that was my birthright.

I wiped my tears and stood up, my head held high.

"I know you have heard what men are saying, and it has settled on your souls and you believe it," I said with pride, my eyes passing from my parents to my husband. "If I say to you that I am innocent—and God knows that I am innocent—then you will not believe me. But if I confess to something of which God knows I am not guilty, then you will believe me."

And then I remembered again the prophet Jacob and his response when confronted with the lie that a wolf had eaten his son.

"So I will say as the father of Joseph said. *It is best to be patient, and God is He to whom I ask help against what they say.*"

And with that I climbed back onto my hard bed and turned my back to them, lying crumpled in a ball like a baby in its womb, my arms wrapped around my shoulders in an embrace that no one else would give me.

I heard the Messenger of God stir, and then I felt the bed shaking violently. It was a sensation that I immediately recognized, having experienced it so many times when he was lying beside me.

It was the convulsion of the Revelation.

I felt him slip off the bed and heard a thud as he fell to the ground.

Despite my anger, despite my feelings of loss and betrayal, I turned to see if he was all right. The Prophet had fallen on his side and I saw him bent and shivering, his knees pulled up to the chest. Sweat poured down his face, even though the air was so cold that I could see the mist of his breath.

Abu Bakr and Umm Ruman were immediately at his side, but there was nothing they could do but gaze in awe as the divine communion played out before their eyes. The Messenger's shaking slowed and finally stopped, and his eyes blinked open. He looked around, disoriented as he often was after a Revelation. And then he saw me on the bed and his face broke into a wide smile.

The Messenger struggled to rise to his feet, and my parents helped him as he steadied himself. And then he laughed, the first sound of joy that I had heard from his lips in weeks.

"O Aisha, praise God, for he has declared you innocent!"

The words hit me in the pit of my stomach. The world spun around me and I suddenly felt as if I were about to faint.

My parents stared at the Prophet with wide eyes and then embraced each other with joy. I saw the relief on their faces, but I did not move. My legs felt dead beneath me, and my heart pounded so loudly that I could feel my bones shake.

My mother looked at me with a broad smile and then bent down to kiss my forehead. And yet even then I sat still, staring at the three of them without a single word.

"Rise and thank the Messenger of God!" my mother said, with both joy and a hint of reproach in her voice.

And then I felt my face turn hot red, and all the poison of the weeks before came rushing into my veins. I rose to my feet and threw my hair back in defiance.

"No!" I shouted in a deadly voice that even I did not recognize. "I will not rise and go to him, and I will not praise anyone except God!"

God had believed me even though the whole world had turned against me, including my own flesh and blood. Including the man I loved. Had it not been for the Creator of the heavens and the earth intervening in this sorry state of affairs, I would have lived my life and possibly met my death under the cloud of a lie.

I turned and stormed out of the room, wishing to escape all those who had not believed me and bow my head to the One who had. To the only one whom I could trust unconditionally, the only one who mattered. A Being whose Face was everywhere I looked and nowhere at the same time. A God whose words I read every day and yet whose voice I had never heard.

I realized that day that Muhammad was exactly what he claimed to be—a man and nothing more. I had loved him with such youthful ferocity that I had turned him into an idol, a pristine icon of perfection, when in truth he was of the same flesh and blood as the rest of us, with the same doubts and fears that plagued the hearts of other mortals. I knew that when the fire of my anger had faded, my love for my husband would return, as it always does between those whose souls are bonded. But it would be a healthy love, of two people learning to live together in an imperfect world, not of a trembling supplicant bowing before an angel.

It would be a human love from that day forward, without the taint of idolatry, a sin that had been cleansed from my heart through the fire of scandal and injustice. And though the mystique of girlish romance, of a union that was a rose free of thorns, was lost forever to me, it had been replaced with a steady and honest view of life and the difficulty of living and loving in a broken world.

As I look back upon my life in these final hours, I realize that at that moment, I truly changed from a girl into a woman.

—   —   —

I RETURNED TO MY apartment that afternoon, and word spread throughout Medina of my divine vindication. Not only had God cleared me of the false charge, He had commanded a new law in the holy Qur'an, which required that anyone accusing a woman of adultery must produce four eyewitnesses to the act itself. And if four witnesses do not step forward, then the accuser himself must be lashed eighty times for besmirching the honor of an innocent woman.

But in the immediate aftermath of my own rehabilitation, the Prophet urged me to forgive the gossipmongers and end the rift that had threatened to tear the nation apart. I agreed, and a parade of apologetic men and women came to my door, weeping and begging my forgiveness, which I readily gave. The matter was closed, and I had no desire to pour further poison onto the wounds of the community.

But when the final supplicant came, I found that my heart had run out of generosity. Ali arrived at the threshold of my apartment and gently sought my pardon.

I stared at my nemesis through the curtain of my thick veil. His humble gestures of regret were sincere. And yet his apology did nothing to lessen the rage burning inside me. Ali, alone of all people, had the power to sway my husband's heart for good or ill, and he had chosen to use that power against me.

Staring at Ali, his head bowed before me in apology, I felt as if talons were closing around my neck, and the ugly taste of bile rose in my throat. And then, without responding to his repeated requests for forgiveness, I rose and closed the door in his face.

30

Khalid ibn al-Waleed, the general of Mecca's forces, stared out at the approaching throngs of his enemies. But they were not garbed in steel armor or carrying mighty weapons of war. Instead they were clothed in the *ihram,* the simple white linen of pilgrims coming to visit the Sanctuary at the heart of Arabia. The men of Medina wore a two-piece costume, a sheet wrapped around their loins with a second draped across their shoulders, while the Muslim women wore flowing robes and head scarves.

Khalid sat on his mighty stallion, his eyes fixed on the sea of fourteen hundred Muslims marching unarmed and defenseless on the sacred city from which their leaders had been expelled almost a decade before. He heard their emotional cries of the ancient Pilgrimage evocation: *Labayk, Allahumma, labayk!* "I answer your call, O God, I answer!" And even his heart, which had little room for sentiment, was moved.

But though his emotions may have been softened by this remarkable sight, his duty as a warrior remained unchanged. Khalid clicked his tongue and spurred his horse forward and raced to the approaching throng of worshipers.

The leaders of Mecca had just received word of this incoming wave of Muslims and the city was in a frenzy. It was a sad testament to the fall of Mecca's prestige since the failed Siege of the Trench that none of the allied Bedouin tribes had bothered to give Abu Sufyan and his cronies sufficient warning of the approaching pilgrim caravan from Medina. Perhaps their spies in the neighboring hills did not think the arrival of unarmed worshipers to Mecca posed any threat, but Khalid wondered whether the same silence would have greeted Muhammad's arrival on a mission of war.

Muhammad. Khalid shook his head in admiration. The man had proven to be not only an inspiring teacher and political leader but also an apt general and a truly brilliant military strategist. This most recent surprise tactic, of sending his people out to join the Pilgrimage like the other Arab tribes, was a brilliant stroke, the play of a master at the top of his game. For even as Khalid rode out to meet his foes, he knew there was little he could do to stop them. Pilgrims were protected by the ancient taboos of his people, and he could not lay hands on them without inciting the wrath of Mecca's few remaining allies.

Which, of course, Muhammad understood. He was sending to Mecca a force large enough to invade and occupy the city, but one that carried no weapons that could invite retaliation. Muhammad would in essence bind Mecca with a chain of peace and there was nothing that Abu Sufyan or the elders could do about it.

As Khalid rode over a hill, he heard the thunder of hooves behind him and could smell the sweat of his men who were riding out to support their commander. Two hundred of the finest cavalry of Mecca would be behind him in moments, and the dust of their approach was likely already visible on the horizon to the approaching pilgrims. And yet the crowd did not slow its advance, and the Muslims continued walking toward the sacred city from which they were banned.

As his legion of horsemen raced toward the peaceful invaders, Khalid rode forward until he was within shouting distance from the men at the front lines. He recognized Umar ibn al-Khattab, the fierce warrior who had abandoned his people for this new faith, and he spurred his horse toward the towering figure.

Umar must have seen him ride up from over the dunes, even as he must now see the oncoming wave of Meccan horses. But the grim man simply stared straight ahead, chanting the pilgrim's call even louder as the rumble of hooves echoed closer.

Khalid rode up straight to him and called out.

"I have been sent by the lords of Mecca to say that you are not welcome here. Go back to your land and disturb not the Pilgrimage."

Umar finally looked at him, but there was no fear in his eyes, only mild contempt, as if he were being barked at by a rabid dog. And then Umar strode forward and continued to walk past Khalid as if he did not recognize the most acclaimed soldier of their nation.

Khalid reared his horse, which struck out its hooves defiantly at Umar. A single blow from his stallion's powerful legs could easily kill a man. And yet Umar continued to ignore him and raised his voice louder in prayer.

Khalid watched as the throng of Muslims passed around him as if they were a raging river and he a mere stone that could in no way inhibit their flow. And then he felt a welling of deep respect for the heretics who had turned his world upside down.

The warrior pulled on his reins and his horse began to move through the crowd. As he rode back up toward the hill, he saw that his men were waiting at its top. They were gazing down in awe at the confident progress of the crowd, and even though each man was armed with a bow and arrows that could easily decimate their enemies, his soldiers did not move to challenge the Muslims.

As Khalid reached the front lies of the now-impotent Meccan defense force, he saw his old friend Amr ibn al-As at its forefront. Khalid saw in Amr's eyes the same respect that he had felt, and he knew that he could share his innermost thoughts with his comrade.

"These men are braver in their rags than a thousand soldiers hiding behind armor and blades," Khalid said.

Amr kept his eyes on the mass of thousands, moving in perfect unison, their march steady and timed with almost military precision. And then he turned to face Khalid, a glint in his eye.

"Imagine what such bravery could accomplish if they had the power of armor and blades as well," Amr said.

Khalid smiled as he suddenly understood what Amr was thinking. And for a second, he no longer felt the weariness of his years of leading Mecca in a losing war against a smarter foe. His heart swelled with unexpected pride that his kinsman Muhammad had somehow united a raggedy band of disorganized Arabs with such bonds of power. It was an ambition that Khalid himself had always nurtured, of forging the barbarian desert tribes into a nation worthy to stand against the mighty armies of the surrounding empires. Of harnessing the ferocious, warlike blood of his people with the military discipline that they had lacked for centuries. But he had dismissed the notion as an empty dream of his youth, a monumental task that was beyond the skills of any man.

Any man except Muhammad.

And as he gazed down at the steadily approaching, utterly fearless legion of men, the warrior of Mecca had a vision of the future that made his heart race faster in excitement.

"They would conquer the world," he said, his eyes growing wide in wonder, as if a lifelong riddle had been answered in the most unexpected of ways.

Amr smiled at him knowingly, and then the two men led the Meccan cavalry back to the stables, allowing the Muslims to approach the holy city unmolested for the first time in a decade.

31

9 gazed across the pilgrim camp at the outpost of Hudaybiyya to the distant hills that delineated the formal border of Mecca. The Messenger had ordered us to stop here and wait for the Meccans' next move. Khalid's horsemen had turned back, but there was no guarantee that Abu Sufyan would not send a new force that had less respect for the ancient taboos of the Pilgrimage.

As the hours passed and there was no sign of any attack from the Meccan forces, the excitement that we had felt over the long journey back to our homeland gave way to boredom and growing frustration. Many of the pilgrims began to beseech the Prophet to continue on toward the city, but he remained steadfast in his belief that it would be unwise to cross the boundary without a clear understanding of how Mecca would react. But he agreed to send his son-in-law Uthman, a highly respected nobleman of Quraysh, to speak with Abu Sufyan and secure assurances of our safety.

Uthman had left the night before and had been expected to return before sunrise. But it was already late in the afternoon and there was a growing sense of alarm that he might have fallen victim to Abu Sufyan's wrath. As rumors began to spread that the gentle-hearted ambassador had been killed by the lords of Mecca, my husband's patient stoicism was shaken, and he gathered his closest Companions underneath the shade of a *ghaf* tree, its bluish green leaves sparkling in the harsh sunlight. He appeared deeply agitated at the possibility of Uthman's execution, and I suddenly remembered his warning to the youths of Medina that Uthman's death would unleash the mighty sword of God's vengeance upon the world.

The men approached him one by one, grasping Muhammad's right hand and pledging to fight to the death to avenge Uthman if indeed he had been martyred. I could see the grim determination in their eyes and my pulse quickened at the thought that this peaceful journey was about to erupt into terrible bloodshed. Since the Muslims were unarmed, they would have to face down the Meccan army with only their hands and their feet as weapons. In such a scenario, it was likely that these brave men who swore themselves to the Prophet would die before they ever laid eyes upon the Holy Kaaba that they all longed to see after so many years.

And then, when the last of the Companions had sworn the oath, I felt a strange sensation. It was as if a gentle rain were falling all around us, even though the sky was clear. The punishing heat of the desert vanished, replaced by a delightful coolness, and yet the sun blazed high above us and there was no wind. It was as if a blanket of mysterious tranquillity had descended upon us, and I could see on the surprised faces of the others that they sensed it as well. Whatever it was that was happening, the tension in the camp vanished, replaced by a powerful sense of peace that was unlike any I have ever experienced in my life.

I looked at my husband in confusion, and he smiled softly.

"God is well pleased with those who have taken this oath," he said, and his voice was as soothing as the invisible cloud that had fallen among us. "He has sent down His *Sakina* to bless us."

Sakina. The Spirit of Peace and Tranquillity. I would later learn that the Jews had a similar word. *Shekhina* they called it in the language of the Hebrews, and it was the feminine face of God, the indwelling Presence that had once been found in the Temple of Solomon and was now hidden from mankind. Whether what I experienced was the same as what the Jews believe, I cannot say. But something magical happened in that moment, and all anger and fear left us.

And so it was that I gazed now across the plain toward Mecca without any worry as to what would come next, for I knew that God was with us. The sun began to dip toward the horizon, the disk turning from blinding gold to dull ocher, and then I saw it.

A figure riding on a horse over the hills of Mecca, the billowing purple standard of an emissary held aloft in his hand.

✦ ✦ ✦

WE GATHERED TO MEET with the ambassador of the Quraysh, a honey-tongued nobleman named Suhayl ibn Amr. The Messenger had greeted

Suhayl graciously, and after ascertaining that Uthman was still alive and securing an agreement for his safe return, he invited the emissary to negotiate an end to the impasse.

I watched from a corner of the tent as Suhayl raised his manicured hand, each finger wearing a ring of precious stones, and laid out the Meccan proposal.

"We will not begrudge you the rites of Pilgrimage," he said calmly. "But your arrival is unexpected and we need time to calm the passions of the people. So we are willing to let you perform the *Hajj*—next year."

There was an immediate grumble of outrage from the Companions. Never before in the history of Arabia had a group of pilgrims been turned back from the Kaaba and told to return at another time.

The Prophet appeared ready to answer Suhayl's proposal, when hot-headed Umar stepped into the negotiation with his usual bluntness.

"You have no right to turn back peaceful pilgrims!" he shouted, the soothing effects of the *Sakina* having apparently worn off. "We will enter Mecca, and I dare you to stop us!"

My husband raised his hand and turned to Umar, who was seated on his left.

"Gently, Umar," Muhammad said pleasantly, but I knew my husband well enough to note the edge of warning in his voice. The Messenger turned his attention back to Suhayl and smiled.

"The son of al-Khattab is correct. We are within our rights before all Arabia. But we are reasonable men. What could you offer us to forgo our rights and turn back?"

I saw Umar and several other men look at the Prophet in shock. They had expected him to negotiate their entry into the holy city, not their retreat.

Suhayl hesitated, as if he was having difficulty saying the words out loud.

"A treaty," he said, and I saw his cheeks pinch inward as if the very word were as sour as lemon on his tongue.

I heard several gasps of surprise from the men seated around the Prophet, but he himself betrayed no emotion. The Muslims had been at war with the Meccans for so long that no one had ever expected a treaty between us. We had always assumed that victory would be absolute, with one side destroying the other, even as the Bani Qurayza had been annihilated for their treachery.

My husband leaned closer, his handsome face passive and impossible to read.

"What are your terms?"

"We will secure a truce between us of ten years, during which neither of our people nor our allies will attack each other," Suhayl said swiftly, as if each word were a hot coal that he needed to expel from inside his mouth. "Starting next year, you will be allowed to perform the Pilgrimage. We will evacuate the city for three days so that there are no . . . misunderstandings . . . between us."

The Companions spoke loudly their opinions of Mecca's proffered terms, but Suhayl raised his hand and again silence fell.

"And one more thing," Suhayl said almost apologetically. "If, during this period, any man among your people wishes to return and subject himself to the authority of Mecca, we will not be obliged to return him. But if any man leaves Mecca against our wishes and seeks refuge with you—you must return him to us, even if he is of your faith."

There was dead silence for a long moment. And then I heard Umar laugh, but there was no humor in the sound. The towering man pulled at his gray beard in fury and appeared ready to speak, when he saw the stern glance from my husband that conveyed a command to be silent.

The Messenger sat looking at Suhayl for a long moment. And then, to everyone's surprise, he leaned forward and took the pagan emissary's hand in his.

"I accept your terms."

There was an immediate explosion of voices as the Companions registered their shock and dismay. How could the Prophet accept such a blatantly one-sided agreement? The Meccan offer was a clear insult, one that even a poorly skilled negotiator would have seen as an opening ploy in what was meant to be a long and complex discussion. And yet the Prophet had accepted the initial terms without protest.

The Messenger seemed utterly oblivious to the cries of his followers, and I saw a strangely triumphant smile play on his lips as he looked at Suhayl, who appeared as shocked by his acquiescence as we were.

Umar stood up and towered over the Messenger. He ignored Suhayl and vented all his fury at the man whom he had only hours before sworn to stand beside, even if it meant death.

"This is outrageous!" Umar shouted at the Prophet, his voice booming so loudly that all other conversation stopped. "We will not make peace with these murdering idolaters!"

I felt a sudden tightening in my throat. Umar, the most fanatically loyal of the Muslims, was now openly disparaging the Prophet's judgment. The Prophet frowned at him and said nothing, but I saw the vein in his forehead throb as it did whenever he was angry. And then my father, who sat to the right of the Messenger, rose and stared up into Umar's eyes. When he spoke, his words were simple and yet carried the weight of terrifying authority.

"Be quiet, Umar," Abu Bakr said, and I saw Umar step back as if he had been slapped. The son of al-Khattab moved away from the Messenger and Abu Bakr and stood alone in a corner, like a child who has been punished for naughty behavior.

Suhayl watched this entire exchange with clear fascination. Once my father had silenced Umar, Suhayl cleared his throat and lifted a sheet of parchment from inside his fine silk robes.

The Meccan emissary unrolled the sheet, which was blank, and placed it at the Messenger's feet.

"I have been authorized to draw up a document of truce," Suhayl said, and I could hear the eagerness in his voice. He clearly wanted to get the terms down in writing before the Messenger changed his mind.

My husband looked across the room to Ali, who stood alone by the entrance to the grand tent, his hand on the hilt of *Dhul Fiqar*.

"Ali will serve as my scribe," the Prophet said.

I had been ignoring Ali's presence until then, and I felt a flash of dislike as he went to sit beside my husband. Suhayl produced a quill pen made from the feather of a gray heron and offered it to Ali, along with a small clay vial containing ink.

Ali took the writing implements and began to make marks on the parchment as the Prophet dictated.

"*Bismillah Ar-Rahman Ar-Raheem.* 'In the name of God, the Merciful, the Compassionate—'"

Suhayl interrupted with a cough.

"I'm sorry, I don't know who this *Ar-Rahman* is," he said in a tone dripping with mockery. It was an old joke, as the Meccans had claimed in the early days of the Prophet's mission that *Ar-Rahman*, a name for God in the holy Qur'an meaning "the Merciful," was actually the name of some secret teacher, Jewish or Christian, who had been allegedly supplying the Prophet with his knowledge of their Book.

I could feel the heat in the room rising, but Suhayl continued, apparently enjoying playing with the Prophet's patience.

"We would prefer the traditional honorific—*Bismik, Allahumma,* 'In Thy Name, O God.'"

At this instant I saw Talha rise and shake his scarred fist at the emissary.

"You swine! You mock the holy words of God Himself!"

The Prophet smiled at Talha, but there was steel in his eyes, and my sweet cousin blushed bright red and sat back down. The Messenger then turned to Ali.

"Write 'In Thy Name, O God,'" he said softly.

Ali hesitated and then complied, his fingers moving swiftly across the sheet as the Prophet continued.

"These are the terms of the truce between Muhammad, Messenger of God, and Suhayl, son of Amr . . ."

Suhayl giggled, an obnoxious sound that made me want to slap him.

"Pardon me, but if we believed you to be the Messenger of God, we really wouldn't be in this position, would we?"

The Messenger looked at him, and I expected his patience to finally break. But I was surprised to see my husband's eyes twinkle, as if he were a child playing a game with a mischievous friend.

"Strike out 'Messenger of God' and replace it with 'Muhammad, son of Abdallah,'" the Prophet said to Ali.

Ali looked up at him and I saw the young man's mysterious green eyes filling with surprise. He lifted the pen and brought it to the parchment, and then lowered it again without making a mark.

"I . . . I cannot."

There was a murmur through the crowd, as some whispered their shock at Ali's uncharacteristic defiance of his elder cousin, while others expressed their pride in his refusal to give in to Suhayl's offensive niggling.

The Prophet sighed in exasperation and looked around at the men as if peering into their souls to see who would assist him. And then his eyes fell on me.

"Aisha, show me where the words are," he said.

I felt every eye in the tent on me and for once I was glad that my face was hidden behind a black veil. I did not want the Companions to see the wicked smile on my face as I walked past Ali and leaned over the Prophet's shoulder. I stared down at the page and saw where Ali had written my husband's name and his title as Messenger of God. And then I pointed my forefinger at the simple swirls of the Arabic alphabet, indicating to the Prophet where the troublesome language lay.

The Messenger took the pen from Ali's hands and without any hesitation crossed out his sacred designation. My task fulfilled, I stepped back, but my eyes locked with Ali's, and I savored my tiny victory over the man who had sought my downfall.

Muhammad handed the pen back to Ali, who bit his lip and wrote over the deleted honorific "the son of Abdallah" . . .

— — —

A SHORT WHILE LATER, the treaty was signed and Suhayl departed to take the news of the Prophet's capitulation to his masters in Mecca. I saw the sullen and disappointed faces of the Companions, but none had the courage to press the matter further with my husband.

None except Umar.

The Prophet sensed Umar's eyes on him and he turned to face the father of Hafsa, the man who had once been considered the most stalwart of his followers. My husband raised his eyebrows and stood patiently, waiting for Umar to explode.

But when the giant of a man spoke, it was not with outrage but with deep confusion and mistrust.

"Are you truly the Messenger of God?" he said softly, a question that was shocking in its implications. I heard several Companions gasp loudly. Had Umar lost his faith? Had the great defender of Islam become an apostate?

Whatever thoughts may have run through his mind, the Prophet merely raised his head with dignity.

"I am" was all he said. All he needed to say.

"Your promised us victory!" The fight had seeped out of Umar and his usually deep and raging voice was now more like the whine of a disappointed child.

The Prophet stepped forward and put a gentle hand on Umar's forearm.

"And I have delivered it you," he said confidently. "This treaty will be the greatest victory of Islam."

Umar's shoulders fell, as did his voice, which was now almost a whisper.

"But you said that God promised us we would conduct the rites of Pilgrimage . . ." he croaked out.

The Prophet turned to my father, and Abu Bakr spoke loudly, as if he intended his words to be heard by all the secret doubters in the tent, not just by Umar.

"God did not promise us that it would be this year," Abu Bakr said, and I saw people lower their heads in shame as his soothing voice put out the last fires of rebellion in their hearts.

As my father's words sank into his heart, Umar knelt down at the feet of the Messenger and kissed his right hand, tears streaming from his face.

"Forgive me, O Messenger of God," he said, his voice trembling with grief.

My husband took Umar's hand and helped him rise to his feet.

"You are forgiven, my friend," he said warmly. "Come, let us spread the good news to the pilgrims. The war is over. Peace has come to Arabia at last."

At these words, I saw the sad looks evaporate, replaced by beaming faces and mouths opened wide in laughter. I suddenly felt a rush of joy as the truth of it came home to me at long last. We had made a treaty with the Meccans. A peace treaty that would end a war that now spanned almost two decades. There would be no more horrific battles, no more agonizing cries of mothers as they looked down upon the corpses of their sons. There would be no more Hamzas struck down in the prime of their lives, their bodies mutilated and dishonored. No more Talhas to lose the use of their hands and be forced to live like cripples, the cruel repayment for heroism in this world. My heart soared at the thought that the ten-year truce could become permanent and that Arabia would never be cursed with the misery of bloodshed again.

But I was wrong, and I would soon learn that the peace we embraced that night, like the gentle caress of the Divine *Sakina*, was a fleeting moment to be savored but could no more be held in one's grasp than the fickle kiss of the wind.

32

*W*ord had reached the Jewish fortress at Khayber of Muhammad's peace treaty with the Meccans, and Huyayy had raged and cursed for days about the betrayal of the Quraysh. The Arabs were two-faced dogs, he had ranted, and they had abandoned their promises to their allies in the hopes of securing some temporary security against the expanding influence of Medina.

Safiya had tried to calm him, but her father had refused to listen. The Treaty of Hudaybiyya was the proof that Huyayy had been seeking of the treachery of his erstwhile Meccan allies. Ever since the failure of the Siege of the Trench, Huyayy had become obsessed with speculation that Abu Sufyan had betrayed him and made a secret agreement with the Muslims to withdraw, leaving his Jewish compatriots of the Bani Qurayza to face annihilation. She knew that the guilt he felt about the destruction of the last remaining Jewish tribe of Medina weighed heavily on her father's heart, and the only way that he could bear the pain was to find someone besides himself to blame for the tragedy.

Though few among her people shared in Huyayy's increasingly elaborate conspiracy theories, there was no denying that the treaty between Muhammad and his pagan enemies had forever altered the balance of power in the peninsula. And the new reality did not favor the people of Khaybar, the last remaining Jewish settlement in Arabia. Without the support of the Meccans, the tiny enclave was isolated and exceedingly vulnerable to conquest by the ambitious Arab prophet.

And so it was that the elders of Khaybar opened their ears to the words of the Byzantine envoy. Donatus had arrived earlier that morning at Khaybar with a small contingent of Syrian guards bearing the seal of Heraclius, Emperor of Constantinople. Even though Heraclius was no friend of the Jews, Safiya's father had convinced the elders of the settlement to offer him a dignified welcome, for they shared a common enemy.

Safiya eyed the Byzantine emissary with a mixture of curiosity and contempt. He was dressed in the flowing dalmatic of the Romans, the long-sleeved robe partially covering his brightly striped tunic and tight breeches. A blue Phrygian cap covered his flowing brown hair and bracelets of gold glittered on his wrists. All in all, Donatus looked more like a primped and pretty girl than a man of power, and his authority was based on aristocratic blood rather than achievement. She had no patience for such weak men, especially after her father had compelled her to marry Kinana, a prissy nobleman of Khaybar whose touch she found repellent.

Safiya listened intently as Donatus explained how the Byzantine emperor had become aware of the new power rising on his southern borders. Apparently Muhammad had himself reached out to the imperial court with a letter inviting the Romans to surrender to his God. News of this startling development set the council room ablaze with excited talk until Huyayy called for silence so that Donatus could give more details.

According to Byzantine intelligence agents, the Arab prophet had similarly written to the Persian emperor Khusro at Ctesiphon, who had been so stunned at the audacity of this illiterate Arab chieftain that he had the letter torn up.

Though the Persians had laughingly dismissed the idea that the newly rising power in Arabia was of any concern to them, the Byzantines had been sufficiently alarmed by the speed of Muhammad's consolidation of the tribes to decide that it merited a response. Heraclius had instructed his generals to begin preparations for a preemptive invasion of the peninsula before its ambitious prophet-king became a problem for the empire's lucrative trade routes. And the Byzantines wanted the help of the people of Khaybar in mounting their attack.

"Your fortress would be an important staging ground for the imperial army," Donatus said in his awkwardly accented Arabic, clearly taught to him by those who spoke the dialects of the Syrian desert.

There was a moment of tense silence as the elders considered the ramifications of the proposed alliance. Safiya saw that all eyes were on Huyayy, whom the Jewish chieftains deferred to as the most experienced man in dealing with Muhammad and his troublesome religious movement. As the rapid spread of Islam was now the primary topic of conversation among the political elites, her father had become the de facto leader of the Khaybar community, even though he was a refugee who had survived only because of the generosity of local citizens.

Huyayy eyed the Byzantine ambassador coolly, his brows knitted in deep thought. Safiya knew that her father was glad to have found a potential new ally against Muhammad, but his inherent distrust of Gentiles was holding him back from embracing the envoy's offer.

"Forgive me if I hesitate, but your people have shown little respect for mine before this day," Huyayy said. "You have butchered us under the lie that we killed your Christ."

There was a murmur of surprise at Huyayy's bluntness, but Safiya knew that her father was saying aloud what everyone was thinking in their hearts. The Jewish experience under Roman rule had been exceedingly painful, culminating in the destruction of Jerusalem and the Diaspora, which had sent her people out of Palestine and forced them to settle all over the world. Centuries of history could not be erased overnight, whatever the immediate political needs of the moment.

If the Byzantine emissary was offended by Huyayy's lack of diplomacy, he was too experienced in his profession to show it. Donatus made a face of practiced grief and bowed his head before the Jewish elders.

"What you say is regrettably true," he said, to the surprise of his audience. "There have been many injustices under the reign of our forefathers. Men blinded by faith or seeking an easy scapegoat to cast the troubles of the empire upon. But the great Heraclius is not like those men. He reveres the Jewish people, for is it not true that Christ himself shared your blood?"

It was a perfectly worded response, and Safiya could see that the men of Khaybar had been put at ease by his feigned contrition. Of course no one believed for a moment that the Roman envoy felt any guilt for the crimes of his people, but he obviously needed their help enough to wear a mask of calculated humility.

"What guarantees would we have if allied with your emperor?" Huyayy asked.

"Once you have helped us clear Arabia of this madman, you will be appointed His Majesty's viceroys to rule the new province in the emperor's name."

Safiya saw her husband, Kinana's, watery eyes light up at the offer of dominion over the Arabs, and her dislike for him only increased.

There was a clear buzz of excitement at the envoy's words, but if Huyayy shared the sentiment of his people, he was too masterly a statesman to show it. Safiya's father stepped forward, his face stern, until he was uncomfortably close to the envoy. Donatus, to his credit, did not flinch under the old man's withering stare but met it head-on.

"Your emperor can find someone else to rule this desolate waste," Huyayy said after a dramatic pause. "My people's heart belongs elsewhere. In a land where we are not permitted to go."

Safiya knew that Huyayy was playing a dangerous game here, but it was a gamble that could change the history of her people if he won. For there was, in truth, only one thing that any Jew desired, and it was the one thing that had been denied her people for over five hundred years. The chance to return to their homeland from which they had been barred since the days of the Jewish revolt against the Romans under Simon Bar Kokhba, the false Messiah who had led their people to tragedy.

The Byzantine envoy stood motionless, his face a controlled mask, impossible to read. Finally he spoke. "I have been authorized by the emperor himself to guarantee that if your people join forces with Byzantium, he will rescind the ban. Once this Arab king is defeated, your people will be free to emigrate to Palestine."

There were cries of disbelief and shouted prayers to God, who had shown their people a way at last to end the tragedy of exile. Safiya was torn by a confused upwelling of emotion. A deep longing to see her people return to the Holy Land, mixed with grief that the price would be to destroy a man whose only apparent desire was to bring the Gentiles to God and a better way of life.

Though the excitement in the many-pillared hall was almost palpable, Huyayy remained calm and seemingly unimpressed.

"And what of Jerusalem?" he said loudly, his simple question immediately silencing the agitated crowd.

And for the first time, Donatus appeared taken aback, as if he had not expected the Jews to press their demands further. He hesitated and then shook his head.

"I regret that I cannot offer you full access to the holy city," he said, to the dismay of the crowd. "It is still a very sensitive matter for the Holy Church."

Huyayy shrugged and turned his back on the ambassador.

"Then we have no arrangement," he said, and began moving toward the carved bronze door of the chamber, as if the matter had been concluded. And then, to Safiya's amazement, the other elders of Khaybar rose and moved to follow him. A mass exodus signaling the failure of Byzantine diplomacy.

Donatus blanched, his eyes wide with surprise and a hint of fear. Safiya suddenly felt sorry for the feminine little man, who would likely face terrifying consequences if he returned to Heraclius empty-handed. But she knew her father was doing what he had to as a politician, using whatever leverage he felt he needed to achieve his objectives.

As the leadership of Khaybar approached the exits, Donatus shouted for them to wait.

"I believe that I can convince the emperor to make certain exceptions," he said, his silky tone gone, replaced with agitation. "An annual pilgrimage to your holy sites. But that is the furthest I can go."

Huyayy stopped and turned to face the envoy, his eyes bright with renewed interest. Donatus took a deep breath and regained his composure.

"If that is unacceptable to you, then I will return to His Majesty with your regrets," he said coldly. "But please keep in mind—when the soldiers of Byzantium enter these lands, you will not be afforded the protection of an ally."

It was an open threat, and one that weighed heavily on everyone in the room. The legions of Constantinople were coming, whether the Jews eased their way or not. They could either help Heraclius eliminate the Muslim threat or face elimination in turn.

Safiya watched her father, who moved back to stand before Donatus. He did not seem afraid of this man who regularly stood in the presence of kings, whose words could mean life or death for his people. Whatever she may have thought of her father's politics, he could never be branded a coward.

And then Huyayy held out his hand and grasped the palm of the Byzantine ambassador.

"Tell your emperor—we have an arrangement."

— — —

THAT NIGHT SAFIYA HAD a troubling dream. As she tossed and turned beside Kinana on their wide bed made of carved pine, she dreamed that she was walking down the paved roads of Khaybar, the city that had become her home since her tribe's expulsion from Medina. But instead of the brightly painted stone houses, she saw only smoking ruins, the mighty walls of the citadel shattered and crumbling. And instead of children running and laughing through the streets, she saw only corpses rotting in the alleyways.

Safiya tried to run away, but wherever she turned, she saw only death and devastation. The stench of decay was overpowering and her stomach trembled with nausea. She finally fell to her knees in grief and raised her eyes to the heavens, pleading for help from a God who had chosen her people and then cruelly forgotten them.

The full moon sparkled above her, and for a second Safiya stared at it in confusion. For the face she had always made out in its shadows had changed. It was no longer an indistinct outline, and the features were clear and recognizable.

It was the face of Muhammad.

As Safiya stared in shock, the moon fell from the sky, a sparkling ball of pure light that lowered itself into her lap. And as the ethereal light from the heavenly orb flooded her, the pain vanished and her grief became a distant memory.

And then Safiya heard it. The sound of children's laughter.

She gazed up through the circle of ethereal light and saw that the city had come back to life. The walls stood strong and firm, and there were no corpses. Everywhere she looked, there was rebirth. The flowers bloomed and the gentle trickle of water from a nearby fountain gave her hope. And then she saw the hustle and bustle of crowds as her people walked through the marketplace, apparently unaware of the devastation that had been there only moments before.

As the mysterious light around her grew brighter, her eyes fell on a group of children chasing one another gleefully. They stopped their games to stare at Safiya and then waved to her with a smile.

And then the magical moonlight became as bright as a thousand suns and the world dissolved into its warm bliss.

33

*O*watched from the Messenger's battle tent set high in the hills of Khaybar as the Muslim army launched its surprise attack on the Jewish fortress. We had been warned by spies among the neighboring Bedouin tribes of the Byzantine army's intention to use the oasis as a launching ground for an invasion of the peninsula and the Prophet had made immediate plans to take the city before the Romans could dispatch soldiers.

I was accompanied by my sister-wife Umm Salama. Together we were charged with the duty of caring for the wounded, and we had already spent much of the morning bandaging wounds and applying ointments made from crushed belladonna leaves to ease the pain of the dying.

The Muslim army was a small force of just over fifteen hundred soldiers and one hundred horses, but men and animals had been chosen specifically for their speed and agility. We knew that the fighting men of Khaybar numbered nearly ten thousand, so victory would come not by brute force but by craftiness and unpredictability. The Messenger intended to mount a series of raids on the oasis, which was guarded by three separate walled encampments, forcing the enemy to engage us on our terms. The hope was that our seemingly puny force would make the Jews overconfident and that our hit-and-run tactics would keep them confused as to our real plan of attack. My husband reasoned that the defenders of Khaybar would expend their energy fighting on several small fronts rather than concentrating on a single battlefield, disorienting them long enough for us to make a break in their defenses. It was the strategy of the bee, buzzing around its victim just long enough to confuse him before delivering the sting.

And so far, it was working. Ali had been placed in charge of the army that laid siege to Khaybar, a controversial decision that had caused some discontent among the Muslims. Though no one could argue with his military prowess, many felt that placing a man who was not yet thirty in charge of older and more experienced fighters would damage morale. There were many rumblings that an elder statesman such as Abu Bakr should lead the battle, but my father had quickly silenced the talk as he had silenced Umar at Hudaybiyya. Abu Bakr unquestioningly accepted Ali's leadership on the battlefield, and my husband, natural diplomat that he was, gave his house a special honor. The Messenger had taken one of my black cloaks and had it fashioned into the war standard for the army, giving both my father and myself a special distinction in the eyes of the soldiers. And yet the rumblings against Ali did not fully subside, a fact that gave me secret pleasure.

But once the swords were unsheathed, all such idle talk ended and the blood rush of war replaced political posturing. Ali led the first wave on the surprised stronghold, and the Muslims advanced as far as the city walls before we were met with a shower of arrows. The archers of Khaybar were the finest in all of Arabia, and nearly fifty of our men were hit, forcing Ali to withdraw as thousands of defenders spilled out of the fortress of Natat on the outskirts of the settlement.

After our initial advances on the field, we were pushed back into the hills. But the Prophet's strategy was working. The Muslims would emerge from different locations every hour, first from the east, then north, then southwest, and hit the enemy's forces with lightning speed before vanishing like ghosts into the wilderness. The Jewish fighters became increasingly frustrated at our unpredictability and they were forced to divide their forces to patrol the countryside, which was exactly what the Prophet had expected.

The on-again, off-again battle had now been raging for six days, and we could tell that our adversaries were becoming exhausted by the intermittent raids followed by hours of wasted efforts chasing us into the shadows. We had enough food and water to keep up our pinprick attacks for at least another week, but I knew that we would not need that long. For last night, Umar ibn al-Khattab had captured one of the Jewish commanders in a surprise raid, and the man had saved his own life by betraying his people's one military weakness. The castle of Naim was a small outpost at the western edge of the settlement that was not as well guarded as the other links in the defense chain. And it apparently contained stores of hidden weapons that would help us break through the walls into the heart of the oasis.

And so Ali had led a surprise attack on Naim this morning while the rest of the Muslim army engaged the sons of Khaybar at the eastern wall as a diversion. The fighting had been brief but vicious. Ali had dueled the famed Jewish champion Marhab at the gates, and as was the usual outcome of any encounter with the glowing *Dhul Fiqar*, Ali had sliced his enemy's head off in seconds. Zubayr had joined Ali on the field and dispatched Marhab's equally well regarded brother Yasir, swinging a blade in each of his hands as only Zubayr could. The death of the Jewish heroes had led to disarray among the small band of protectors at the castle and the Muslims had managed to break through its fortified gates and storm the outpost.

And then Ali emerged with a triumphant smile and returned to the Messenger's base camp, where he advised my husband that the breach of Naim had provided the Muslims a back door into the oasis. But more important, the intelligence Umar's captive had provided was accurate. Hidden inside storage rooms underground was an array of weapons that would facilitate our efforts to take the city, the most important being a ballista, a small Roman catapult that the Byzantines had apparently given as a gift to their new allies. And there were two testudos, covers of overlapping shields that the Romans wheeled up to walls to defend themselves from attackers. In a delicious twist of irony, these foreign contraptions that had been stockpiled for use against the Muslims would now be used against our enemies to break through the walls.

My father rose to congratulate Ali on the victory that had changed the course of the battle, as did the other Companions. As the men embraced and clasped hands with the young hero, the Prophet beamed like a father who had finally seen a misunderstood son receive honor in the world.

Ali's sparkling eyes fell on me and in them I saw the desire for reconciliation, for an end to the rancor between the two of us who were beloved by the Messenger of God. But whatever grudging respect I could give him for his prowess as a warrior, I could not forgive him for his betrayal, which had nearly cost me my marriage and my life.

I turned my back on Ali and went to help Umm Salama comfort a youth who had lost his hand in the siege.

34

Safiya gazed out in grief across the ranging maelstrom of death that had once been a city. The Muslims had breached the outer walls and had brought the battle to the heart of the oasis. Her people had been taken by surprise for a second time in the past week, and most of the Jewish army was scattered outside the fortified battlements in a fruitless hunt for an attacker that was hiding in plain sight.

With the fall of the defensive outpost at Naim, the dam had been broken and the flood of Arab soldiers had reached the streets near the grand council chamber where, only days before, the elders had been celebrating the new alliance with Byzantium. Even as the elite soldiers led by Ali decimated the few Jewish defenders inside the beleaguered city, other Muslim troops were busy securing the wells and taking positions on the mighty walls, where their archers were busy raining death on the surprised warriors of Khaybar, who were now trapped outside their own walls. It was a humiliating turnaround, as Jews desperately attempted to get back inside the homes that were now occupied by the Arabs they had been pursuing.

Safiya stood on the roof of the council chamber, staring down over the stone ramparts as her people emerged from their homes in surrender, begging Muhammad's men for clemency. On the horizon she could see clouds of black smoke hovering over the mighty castles of Natat and Shiqq, and she knew the battle was over. The fortresses were the pride of the people of Khaybar, capable of resisting any attack from without. But no one had thought to protect them from within, and the Jewish defense was now overrun.

She looked over to her father, who was staring in utter shock at the ruins of the city that was to have been the capital of the new Byzantine province of Arabia. Huyayy's gray eyes were brimming with tears, as the complete defeat of his people could no longer be denied. And she knew that he realized, at long last, that there was no one to blame for this tragic outcome but himself.

Safiya should have felt sorry for him. She should have reached out and embraced him like a dutiful daughter, succored him as he faced the failure of his life's work. But there was no sympathy left in her heart for Huyayy, a man who had stubbornly marched his nation over a precipice. Her father had deluded himself into imagining that he was capable of orchestrating the defeat of all their enemies, not only conquering Arabia but restoring the Jewish birthright to the Holy Land.

Huyayy knelt down and began to pray fervently to God, asking for mercy on the Jewish people. And then her miserable husband, Kinana, knelt beside him and patted Huyayy's hair like a woman comforting a child.

"Do not despair," Kinana said in his lisp that she found so repulsive. "There is still hope for victory."

Safiya finally exploded. "No!" she screamed, with such ferocity that Kinana recoiled in surprise. "There will be no victory! Have you men learned nothing? We were the last Jews of Arabia and you have brought doom upon us with your intrigues!"

"None could have foreseen this," Huyayy said, desperately trying to shirk responsibility for the disaster that he had wrought.

Safiya had had enough. She grabbed her father by his robes and lifted to him to face her.

"Only a fool could not have foreseen this!" she said, no patience for self-deception left in her heart.

Kinana placed a cold hand on her wrist and pushed her away from the old man.

"How dare you speak to your father this way!" he said, his lips curled into an ugly snarl.

But Safiya no longer cared what he or anyone else thought. If she was to die today as Khaybar fell to the invading forces, she would die with truth on her lips. Consequences be damned.

"I wish I had spoken this way years ago!" she said, spitting at Kinana's feet. "Then perhaps my father would have listened to reason and we would not be facing extinction!"

Her husband moved forward, his hand raised to strike her, but Huyayy stopped him.

"She is right," the Jewish chieftain said, his voice trembling with shame. "My pride has brought us to this place."

Kinana looked at him in shock. "It is not over!" he shouted, stamping his foot like a spoiled child. "The soldiers of Byzantium will soon come to our aid!"

Huyayy shook his head.

"No. It will take weeks for Heraclius to mobilize his army. Even if we push the Arabs back outside the walls, we will run out of food and water long before then."

Safiya saw that her father had finally accepted the truth. The fire of her rage flickered and went out, and she was left with a dull emptiness in her heart. Anger and grief were pointless now. All that was left was to do her duty, to save as many of her people as she could in what little time they had left. Safiya stepped forward, taking her father's hand and looking into his eyes, to help him do what needed to be done.

"We must negotiate a surrender," she said, and her voice sounded very tired and old.

Huyayy blinked as the truth of her words began to sink in. But even as her father faced reality, her accursed husband fled into delusion.

"Surrender? And suffer the fate of Bani Qurayza? Never! We will defend our homes to the last man!"

"And I'm sure you will live long enough to be that last man, considering what a coward you are!"

Kinana's face turned an ugly purple, but she ignored him, her eyes focused on her father.

"Let me go to the Muslims. I can speak with Muhammad. He will listen to me," she said.

Huyayy stared at her in confusion. And then she described the dream she'd had, of the moon resting in her lap and bringing life again to the oasis.

"It is a sign from God. A portent." She hesitated and then said the words that had been imprinted on her heart since the night of the strange vision. "It is my destiny."

Huyayy looked at her with wide eyes. But before he could respond, Kinana grabbed her by the hair and slammed her face against the brutal stones of the parapet. Safiya cried out in agony and for a second the world spun around her as blood poured into her eyes.

"You treacherous whore!" he screeched like a vulture. "All of this time you lay in my bed, you have been dreaming of that desert snake! Go to him, then! You are no longer one of our people!"

As pain flooded her senses, Safiya felt Kinana grab her hand and push her down the stairs from the roof.

"Father!" she managed to cry out. "Please! Help me!"

But Huyayy simply stood there, looking alone and confused as the world he had fought so hard to create came crashing down all around him.

— —

THE HEAVILY GUARDED DOORS of the council chamber were flung open for a brief instant and Safiya was thrown unceremoniously into the middle of the street, where the battle raged with fierce intensity. Swords clashed with terrifying brutality as Muslim men and their Jewish adversaries fought house to house, hand to hand, for control of the governing seat of the oasis.

Safiya screamed in horror as a turbaned horseman rode toward her, his sword glinting unnaturally bright as if it reflected a thousand suns. And then she recognized the legendary dual blade of *Dhul Fiqar* and knew that she was in the presence of the famed Ali, the legendary warrior who had single-handedly slain many of the Muslims' most hated enemies. Her heart leaped into her throat as she wondered if her name was about to be added to that long and illustrious list of kills.

But the sword did not come down on her head. Instead, Ali lowered the blade and climbed down from his black stallion. He looked at her with no surprise, as if he had somehow expected her to be there, lying in the middle of a blood-soaked avenue as the Angel of Death claimed its victims all around her.

And then he offered a gloved hand to her and helped her to her feet.

"Do not fear, daughter of ibn Akhtab," he said, and she wondered in shock how he knew her name. "I have been sent to offer you sanctuary."

Safiya was too stunned to ask who had sent him, who could have known that she would be out here in the midst of this deadly fight at this exact moment. But as men from both sides fell about her in a maelstrom of carnage, she decided it was not the time to ask such questions.

As she climbed onto Ali's horse, she turned a pleading face to the noble warrior, whose green eyes seemed to shine with a light of their own.

"My people . . . please have mercy on my people."

Ali leaped onto the saddle in front of her and kicked his horse forward just as a spear struck the spot where he had been standing only seconds before.

"Only God and His Messenger can decide their fate," Ali said, seemingly unperturbed by the madness of death all around them. He paused and then glanced back at her. "But you can plead their case before him."

And with those words, Ali took Safiya away from the eye of the storm and rode through the chaos back to the Muslim camp. As Safiya passed through the devastated streets, riding with the man who had defeated her people, she should have felt a rage of emotions—confusion, guilt, shame. But instead there was a quiet serenity even as the cries of the dying echoed all around her.

It was as if some part of her had known that this day would come. That she would leave her father and go to the man he hated the most. It was a destiny that had been written that first day when Muhammad had arrived in Yathrib, when Safiya had refused to condemn him because he sought to remind the sons of Ishmael of the God of their father Abraham. Her empathy for the Arab prophet who had turned the world upside down had created a rift between her and her family, between her and her people, a divide that had grown so large that she no longer felt that she belonged with them. But if she was no longer a Jew, then who was she?

It was a question that she had found troubling and painful, and one that she could never voice aloud with anyone. For the answer was one that she could not face without cutting the final bond between herself and the only world she had ever known. But that world was dead now, consumed by the fires of its own hubris. Her family, her home, her nation were all gone forever. She had lost everything that had mattered to her, everything except the truth of who she really was.

And so it was that when she finally stood before Muhammad, his black eyes looking at her with deep compassion, she understood the role she had been destined to play in the history of nations. She knelt before the man who should have been her enemy and softly said the words that she realized had long been branded into her heart.

"There is no god but God, and Muhammad is His Messenger."

35

The battle was over and Khaybar had surrendered. The Jewess named Safiya had served as a mediator between the Prophet and the people of the besieged city, convincing them to lay down their arms on the promise of clemency for the local populace.

With the clash of swords silenced, I helped an elderly Jewish woman step over the grisly carnage in the streets of Khaybar and guided her to the pavilions that had been hoisted for the sick and the injured on both sides. She held me tight, her skeletal fingers cutting into the flesh of my wrist, and whispered her gratitude repeatedly. And then she asked me if I knew what had happened to her son, a young soldier named Nusayb, who had raced from her house to fight the first wave of Muslim infiltrators pouring in through the breached walls. I gently told her that I would find out and reassured her that he was probably with the other prisoners of war. I did not have the heart to tell her that none of the warriors who had thrown themselves at Ali and his men had survived the initial foray.

I left the elderly woman in the care of Umm Salama, who gave her a bowl of water and a small plate of figs. The pavilion smelled of the sickly musk of the dying, a stench that I had come to despise over the past several days, and I quickly turned to exit. Wrapping my cloak against the bitter chill of the morning, I wandered through the devastated alleys as Muslims and Jews worked together to pick up the bodies that littered the streets and haul them away for burial in a cemetery on the outskirts of the oasis.

I stopped before an open field where the prisoners were being held, tied and surrounded by hundreds of Muslim soldiers. A quick round of questions confirmed what I had suspected—the old woman's son was not among them and had probably already been buried in the mass graves, which were overflowing.

I looked at the center of the field and saw that new graves had been dug here, ditches like the ones in the marketplace of Medina where the Bani Qurayza had been buried. The Prophet's truce with Khaybar promised amnesty only to the citizens of the town. But the men of Bani Nadir who had taken refuge with them and then incited them to war with the Muslims received no such guarantees. And I could tell from the grim look on the faces of the captives that they knew their fate had been sealed.

As I turned away, I saw my husband approaching with Ali, followed by the Jewish woman Safiya who had helped bring the fighting to an end. She was as I remembered her, tall and statuesque, her bones delicate and perfectly crafted. But her gray eyes were reddened with tears. I saw her look upon her father, Huyayy, who stood proud, exuding dignity even in captivity, and I could not imagine the pain that she must have felt, seeing bound him like an animal for sale in the marketplace.

Ali stepped forward, his black hair glistening like a lion's mane in the morning sunlight.

"O men of Khaybar, the Messenger has spared your lives because of the pleadings of one whom you cast out," he said, looking pointedly at Safiya. "The good people of Khaybar are not responsible for the treachery of your guests, and so your prisoners will be set free. And you may retain your lands unmolested upon payment of a tribute of half your annual produce."

As Ali spoke, I saw the Muslim soldiers move forward and cut the bindings of the prisoners who had been identified as native to the city. The men of Khaybar were stunned to be set free, and many wept and kissed the hands of their captors.

And then Ali turned to face the remaining prisoners, the exiled men of the Nadir whose machinations had led them to this awful place from which there would be no further escape.

"But your brethren among the Bani Nadir have broken every covenant and spread discord through the land," he said forcefully. "They will be held to account. Such is the command of God and His Messenger."

I glanced at Safiya and saw tears streaming down her pallid face. And then she ran forward and embraced Huyayy and wept. The guards moved to push her off, but one stern glance from the Messenger caused them to relent. She stood there, holding her condemned father and weeping in his arms, until Huyayy kissed her on the forehead and gently pushed her back.

"I tried to save you . . ." I heard her say through the chokehold of grief.

Huyayy smiled at her softly, no blame or recrimination in his eyes. "I know . . ."

Ali's men stepped forward, prepared to lead the chief of the Bani Nadir to the grave that would soon be his eternal home.

As the guards gently pulled Safiya away, Huyayy gazed at his daughter. I could see deep regret on his lined face, the look of a man who had realized too late that he had been wrong about everything that truly mattered in life. And then he looked at the Messenger of God, his rival and nemesis who had finally bested him after a decade of bitter conflict.

"I was reading last night a story from the Torah," Huyayy said, his voice thoughtful, bearing no hint of malice. "About the death of Abraham. His sons Isaac and Ishmael, estranged for many years, came together and buried him in the cave of Hebron."

The Messenger smiled gently at the reference and nodded.

"I'd like to think that story is a prophecy," Huyayy said, a warm grin playing on his lips at the end. "Perhaps one day our nations will find a way to bury the past together."

And with that, Huyayy ibn Akhtab turned and knelt before the ditch as Ali raised *Dhul Fiqar* and Safiya's cry of sorrow echoed around the ancient stones of Khaybar.

36

Safiya and the Messenger were married in the days following the defeat of Khaybar. The Prophet told me that it was an act of mercy for a girl who had lost her entire family to the vengeful swords of the Muslims. And it was a political marriage as well, he explained, since Safiya would continue to be a helpful diplomatic link to the remaining Jews of Arabia as the Muslim state consolidated its power. All of what he said was true, but I saw the way his dark eyes looked appreciatively at her flawless skin and the ugly demon of envy was ignited yet again in my soul.

Even though Safiya had embraced Islam, I always called her "the Jewess" and was not above making snide comments in her presence about her ancestry and the duplicity of her people. When she complained to the Prophet about my denigration of her kinsmen, he told her to respond that she was the daughter of Aaron and the niece of Moses, which she invariably did with great pride, increasing my jealousy toward her.

The addition of Safiya to the harem increased our number to eight Mothers, along with Sawda, myself, Hafsa, Umm Salama, Zaynab bint Jahsh, Juwayriya, and Ramla. As mentioned before, the kindly Zaynab bint Khuzayma, the Mother of the Poor, had died of fever, and her calming influence over the household was missed. Despite our years living together, and despite the Messenger's best efforts to treat us as equally as he could, petty rivalries still existed. The hot-tempered Hafsa and the Bedouin princess Juwayriya often locked horns, as did the haughty Ramla and the down-to-earth Umm Salama. But not everyone in the harem was at war. I had made my peace with Zaynab after her kind support in the days of the false accusation against me, and the grandmotherly Sawda was loved by all.

Our arguments were over the petty things—who had said what about whom, who was trying to take too much of the Prophet's time and attention. Who had the prettiest clothes and jewelry, although the reality was that we all lived spartan lives and had few adornments. And in truth, our rivalry was no longer over who would be the first to become pregnant, as we had all quietly given up the hope of carrying the Prophet's heir. He had had six children with Khadija, and both sons had died. Since then, God had not blessed him with any more issue, despite the fact that he was married to several young and fertile women.

There were whispers among the believers that God did not wish the Prophet to have a male heir. Many said it was because the Muslim *Ummah* was not meant to be ruled by a monarchy, as would inevitably happen if the Prophet had a son, who would be expected to succeed him as leader of the community. And a few speculated that it was because God had already chosen the male lineage of the Prophet by favoring his cousin Ali, who had fathered Muhammad's two grandsons, Hasan and Husayn. Those who held this viewpoint were a tiny minority of the believers, but in the years to come, they would become a powerful voice whose message would tear apart our nation.

But those years of strife and division over the Messenger's legacy were still far off. With the pacification of Khaybar and the treaty with the Meccans, peace had come to the peninsula. And as the Messenger had predicted at Hudaybiyya, the truce proved to be a greater victory for Islam than any of the battles we had fought over the past decade. With hostilities ended, trade flourished between the northern and southern tribes, and Muslims now regularly made the Pilgrimage to Mecca, where they were finally able to preach the oneness of God without fear of reprisals.

It was in that atmosphere of peaceful commerce and dialogue that the message of Islam began to spread rapidly through the desert, and it was said that in the two years that followed the agreement at Hudaybiyya, more people embraced Islam than in the two decades prior to the treaty.

As the power of Islam spread through the peninsula, the wise among the Quraysh began to realize that the old days were gone forever. Though some of the elders like Abu Sufyan stubbornly refused to join the Prophet's movement, the next generation of leaders realized that the future of Arabia was in Medina, not Mecca. The cracks in the dam of Meccan unity became a flood after two of the most prominent nobles of the holy city defected. Khalid ibn al-Waleed, the commander of Mecca's armies, and Amr ibn al-As, the city's most respected diplomat, rode to Medina and gave their allegiance to God and His Prophet, and there was much feasting in celebration of their conversion.

Medina became a bustling metropolis where goods from all over the region were traded, and the tiny oasis began to expand and look more and more like the capital of a prosperous nation. And we, the Mothers of the Believers, found our hands overflowing with work on behalf of the growing Islamic state. Whether it was organizing delivery of food and medicine to the needy or teaching other women and their children about the moral principles of our faith, our hours were increasingly filled with the demands of our role as Mothers. We did not have time to indulge in our habitual cattiness, and peace began to reign in the Prophet's household even as it did throughout Arabia.

All that changed with the arrival of a slave girl from Egypt.

Mariya was a Coptic Christian, a gift to the Messenger of God from an Egyptian governor who had the political foresight to realize that Muhammad's vision was on the way to triumph in neighboring Arabia. She was a girl of shocking beauty, her hair a flowing sea of soft brown curls, her eyes shaped like perfect almonds, and her breasts generous. She was soft-spoken and majestically feminine, more womanly than any other girl I have ever known.

The moment the Messenger of God saw Mariya, he was besotted, and the rest of us were filled with despair. Sensing that she would be the unwelcome target of much jealousy if she were housed near his other wives, the Prophet had a special home built for her on the outskirts of Medina, where he would spend increasingly large amounts of time, to the growing alarm of the Mothers.

And so it was that the wives of the Messenger came together and asked me for help. They feared that the Prophet's love for Mariya would displace all of us, and they asked me to intervene as the one who still, in theory, remained the most beloved of the consorts.

One night, when the Prophet was relaxing with his head in my lap after a long day of dealing with the affairs of state, I sprang my trap. Muhammad looked up at me with his soft smile and stroked my hair. But when he leaned up to kiss me, I turned my head away.

"Don't. Please," I said, with intentional sharpness.

The Messenger sat up and looked at me with his obsidian eyes.

"What's wrong?"

I turned my back to him and began to sob. Though I was definitely acting in accordance with my plan, the tears and the pain in my heart were real.

"You don't love me anymore!"

The Messenger placed a hand on my shoulder and I could feel that strange cooling sensation that always seemed to emanate from his presence.

"How can you say that? I love you first among all my wives."

I turned to face him, the tears still flowing down my cheeks.

"Your wives, perhaps. But not among the women your right hand possesses."

My husband stiffened and I saw his kindly smile fade.

"Mariya gives me comfort," he said slowly, as if measuring every word with due care. "But she does not take your place in my heart. No one can."

I took his hand in mine and squeezed it.

"Then prove it."

The Prophet sighed and he suddenly looked very tired.

"What do you want of me?"

I leaned closer, my eyes fixed on his.

"Leave this slave girl! Promise never to see her again!"

The Prophet blinked in surprise at the audacity of my request.

"*Humayra*—" he began, but I cut him off by removing my hand from his and shifting away from him.

"Promise, or you will never have my assent to touch me again! If you take me, it will be by force and not love."

The Messenger looked as shocked as if I had slapped him. In all the years of our marriage, I had never threatened to withhold the intimacies of our bed from him, no matter how fiercely we had argued or fought. Even after the Messenger harbored doubts of my fidelity, I did not punish him by denying my embrace, and through the gentle warmth of our union, we had begun to repair what the gossips had shattered.

The Prophet stared at me with those powerful, unreadable eyes, but I met his gaze defiantly. For a long moment, the only sound that I could hear was the rhythmic call of the crickets and the gentle rustle of palm leaves in the wind.

And then the Prophet spoke and I could hear the frustration he was trying to suppress.

"I promise," he said, although I could tell he was bitter at having to take this oath. "I will not go to Mariya again. Are you happy now?"

I felt a rush of excitement at my little victory and I smiled like a little girl who had finally been given a much-sought-after toy. But when I moved forward to kiss my husband, it was his turn to back away.

"Did the other women of the household put you up to this?" he asked, and I realized that he knew us too well to be deceived. I did not respond, but he seemed to find the answer he was seeking in my guilty face.

The Messenger of God stood up and shook his head, and I suddenly had a strange sinking feeling in my stomach, a sense that my victory was a mirage and that I had actually brought defeat down upon myself and my fellow wives.

"You are like the women who threatened Joseph with prison if he did not give in to their demands," the Prophet said with a weary sigh, and I felt a sting of humiliation at being compared to the sinful ladies who had tried to seduce the son of Jacob.

And then without another word, the Messenger of God turned and walked out, leaving me feeling suddenly very alone and helpless. There was something in the way he closed the door behind him, a finality in his stride, that made me feel as if he were gone for good and would never return.

New tears welled in my eyes, tears of shock and loss, as I suddenly realized that I had made a terrible mistake.

37

The Messenger sent the Mothers a message through the fiery Umar. He would not speak to any of us for a month. He retired alone to a small tent at the edge of the Masjid courtyard and refused our desperate entreaties for reconciliation.

The next month was one of the most miserable in my life. The

Prophet was true to his word and did not speak a single word to any of us for the entire time. And to make our punishment sting deeper, we received word that God had absolved his Messenger of his hasty oath and my husband was spending his nights solely in the company of the slave girl Mariya. As usual, the other wives blamed me for our collective predicament, although in this instance we all shared responsibility for pushing Muhammad too far. They avoided me as if I carried a disease, and I was more isolated than ever.

The only company I found during those miserable days was that of my sister, Asma, who would often bring you, Abdallah, to play in the corner while she comforted me. You were still a small boy, not yet five years old, but you had a seriousness and wisdom about you even at such a tender age. When I cried, as I often did during your mother's visits, you would invariably put down your toys and come over to me, placing your head in my lap until the gentleness of your presence calmed me. I knew in my heart that I would likely never have a child of my own, and you became a son to me in those moments, a bond that I still feel as readily today, nearly fifty years later, as I did then. And it is perhaps for this reason that I open my heart to you now, for you have always been a salve to the pain of your aunt, whom destiny has chosen to be both blessed and cursed.

Time lost all meaning during those weeks, and yet I did not stop counting the hours before the ban would be lifted and—I hoped— my husband would return to us. Still, I was terrified at the thought of where we would go from there. Would he still love me, or had Mariya forever taken my place in his heart? Would the glorious fire that had once linked our souls be reduced to a smoldering ember, a pale echo of days long past?

And then one night, as I sat alone in my room, looking down at my husband's threadbare mantle, the musky scent of his flesh still emanating from its fibers, I heard the sound of footsteps. And then the door opened, revealing the silhouette of a man standing on the threshold. Startled, I reached for my veil, and then the figure stepped inside and I saw that it was the Messenger of God.

For a moment, I sat utterly still, convinced he was just a waking dream, a shadow of my imagination. He looked down at me for a quiet moment, and then his pale face broke into a small smile.

I rose to my feet, my heart caught in my throat.

"But . . . it's been only twenty-nine days . . ." was all I could croak
out.

The Prophet raised an eyebrow in surprise.

"How do you know that?"

I moved toward him, pulled like a drop of water toward the ocean.
"I have been counting the days. And the hours."

And then I realized that this month, Rajab, had only twenty-nine
days instead of thirty because of the early sighting of the new moon.
The Prophet had waited exactly as long as he had promised and not
a moment less. And he had chosen to come to me first of all of his
wives.

The Messenger of God took my hand in his and squeezed tightly
until I could feel the steady pulse of the blood in his veins, matching
the rhythm of my own heartbeat.

"Aisha, God has revealed these words to me," he said gently, but I
sensed a hint of sternness still lingering in his glance as he recited the
newest verses of the holy Qur'an.

O Prophet, say to your wives
If your desire is for the present life and its finery,
Then come, I will make provision for you
And release you with kindness.
But if you desire God, His Messenger
And the Home of the Hereafter
Then remember that God has prepared great rewards
For those of you who do good.

I listened with my head bowed as Allah presented me with two
paths, the way of the world or the way of eternity. The God who had
rescued me from disgrace, who had saved my honor when even my
husband had doubted me, was now warning me that my future with
Muhammad and the believers lay on the path toward which I turned
my heart at this instant.

"So, *Humayra*, what do you choose?" the Messenger asked in a
voice that was a whisper.

Hot tears ran down my cheeks and I looked up into the obsidian
eyes of my husband, and I knew there had never been any choice in the
matter.

"I choose God and His Messenger, and the Home of the Here-after," I said, trembling with an ache that threatened to tear my heart in two.

And then the Prophet smiled warmly. He took me in his arms and kissed me, and the waves of passion soon took us beyond the veil of this harsh world into the timeless mystery of man and woman and the infinite joy of their union.

→ → →

A WEEK LATER, I learned that the slave girl Mariya had missed her courses for the second month in a row.

She was pregnant with Muhammad's child.

38

Seven months later, the wives gathered around Mariya as she went through the final, horrific pangs of childbirth. I held her hand while Hafsa wiped the flood of sweat that bathed her soft curls and Umm Salama crouched low over the birthing chair, gently coaxing the poor girl to push just a little harder.

Whatever jealousies we had felt—whatever lingering bitterness had hung over the household of the Messenger since we'd heard the news of the slave's conception—all of it had finally been forgotten in the long hours we'd spent beside Mariya since her water broke. The girl was as fragile as a bird, and each contraction produced such wrenching screams that the coldness of our hearts melted in the flame of empathy. She was no longer our rival for the love of the Messenger, no longer the usurper who had come in and taken the honor that was meant for one of the noble women of free birth who had shared Muhammad's bed. That night, she had become just another terrified girl, enduring the agony that was also the glory of womanhood.

I looked into Mariya's soft eyes, as kind and lost as those of a doe in the wilderness, and tried to send into her soul the strain of indomitable strength that flowed in my own blood. She looked up at me, confused and frightened, but I could see a light deep inside her eyes that said we had made a connection and I could see a hint of gratitude in her bloodless face.

And then Mariya clutched my hand with such fury that I thought she would shatter my fingers, and gave a scream that was more horrible than any cry of a dying man I had heard on the battlefield.

And then a new sound filled the stone barn that now served as a makeshift birthing chamber. The wondrous, improbable, heart-stirring sound of a baby crying.

I turned in awe to Umm Salama, who was kneeling on the ground, holding the child who was the hope of a nation. And then the gentle woman with the motherly smile looked up at us with reverence, thick tears welling in her eyes.

"Tell the Messenger of God . . . he has a son . . ."

◆ ◆ ◆

I HAD NEVER SEEN such rejoicing in Medina. In the days that followed, the sober oasis was transformed into a city of grand festivities as the Muslims celebrated the birth of Muhammad's son, who had been named Ibrahim. Hundreds of camels, sheep, and oxen were sacrificed by overjoyed believers, the meat distributed to the poor. Merchants heavily slashed prices in the marketplace and sometimes simply gave away their goods as gifts. Poets raced to compose verses in honor of the new boy in whose blood lived the hope of the entire Muslim *Ummah*. Had alcohol not been banned by the holy Qur'an, the streets would have been flowing in beer and *khamr*, and I suspected a few of the less pious were secretly toasting away in the privacy of their own homes.

It was a glorious time, and the joy was shared by all in the Prophet's household, including the Mothers. Our envy of Mariya had been replaced by a fierce protective instinct toward her and the baby, who had become the son of us all. I remember the first time I held Ibrahim, after his mother had suckled him and the Messenger had wept over his tiny fingers. The Prophet had given him to me first in a sign that, even now, I remained foremost among his consorts.

I had held the tiny bundle in my arms as if he were a precious jewel and looked down at his face. Ibrahim's hair was a mass of brown curls like his mother's, but his eyes were indisputably those of his father, gazing up at me like black pearls filled with ancient wisdom. His skin was softer than a dove's, and he radiated that mysterious coolness that always surrounded Muhammad, even in the hottest days of summer. And then those mesmerizing eyes seemed to twinkle at me as he smiled, and I fell in love with Ibrahim in that instant. It was a love as ferocious and all-consuming as I had for the Messenger, and I vowed that I would lay down my life to guard him and his mother, even if all the demons of Hell were unleashed upon us.

On the seventh day of Ibrahim's life, the Messenger held the ceremony of the *aqiqa,* where the baby's hair is cut for the first time and weighed, with the weight in gold then passed along to the poor. The People of the House gathered to celebrate this first milestone in the child's life, and a pavilion of green and yellow stripes was placed outside the Masjid, where the faithful could come see the beautiful boy and the indigent could find alms.

The women of the household were gathered in a closed section in the back, separated by a woolen curtain from the excited crowds. Along with my fellow sister-wives were the daughters of Muhammad—Zaynab, with her little daughter, Umama; the childless Umm Kulthum, who had married Uthman after Ruqayya's death; and the Prophet's favorite, Fatima, with her sons, Hasan and Husayn. All of us gathered reverently around Mariya as if she were the queen of the nation, jostling with one another for a chance to hold the baby, the little Chosen One who was the light of the *Ummah.* I heard Hasan giggle as he chased his little brother, Husayn, around the room and I glanced at Fatima, who for once did not look sad and distant but was laughing heartily as her new baby brother looked up at her with the utter trust and absorption that only infants untainted by the world possess.

In the early days of Mariya's pregnancy, some gossipmongers had spread vicious tales suggesting that Fatima and Ali were sad about the news that the Prophet would soon have an heir, displacing their own sons as the sole custodians of Muhammad's bloodline. But despite my own unwavering antipathy for Ali, I did not believe for one second that he or his wife held anything but happiness for the Messenger, and, seeing the sincere look of joy on the normally taciturn Fatima's face, I knew that such talk had been malicious and misguided.

And then the curtain parted and my husband walked inside the women's chamber, his eyes twinkling. He went over to Mariya, kissed his infant son on the forehead, and then whispered something into the Egyptian girl's ears. She giggled mischievously and nodded as the Prophet turned his attention to us. And I saw for the first time that he held in his hands a pretty necklace—an emerald pendant on a silver chain.

"In honor of my son's *aqiqa*, today I will give this necklace to the girl I love most," the Messenger said, holding the pendant aloft for all to see.

There was an immediate rustle of excitement and I suddenly felt my heart pounding in my chest. The Messenger glanced at me for just a brief moment and then began to walk slowly past each of his wives, dangling the necklace near their eager faces.

I saw Hafsa turn to Zaynab and whisper. Her voice was too low for me to hear, but I had mastered the art of reading lips during my years of fending off—and participating in—harem gossip.

"He will give it to the daughter of Abu Bakr," Hafsa said, and I could see the irritation on Zaynab's beautiful features as she nodded her agreement.

I felt a flash of pride as the Messenger walked by all of his wives and approached me. For a moment, he lingered before Safiya and I felt my heart sink. And then he passed by the disappointed Jewess and strolled toward me, the last in the circle of the Mothers.

I smiled triumphantly and raised my hand to take the jewel ...

... and the Messenger walked right past me! I flushed red, shocked and confused. He had gone by each of his wives and yet the necklace remained in his hands. And then I saw him approach little Umama, who was sitting in her mother, Zaynab's, lap. The Messenger bent down and tied the necklace around his granddaughter's neck, then kissed her on the lips.

We all groaned, realizing that the Prophet had played a poignant little joke on us, the women of the household, who were perennially creating drama in our rivalry to be the first in his heart.

The Prophet looked at me in amusement. I crossed my arms in mock irritation, but I could not suppress the smile on my face. I finally burst out laughing, and soon everyone joined in.

And the mirth of the afternoon was interrupted by the sound of a dog barking wildly nearby, and I saw the Prophet's face grow dark. He began to tremble and I saw beads of sweat on his forehead, and I leaped to my feet on the assumption that the tremors of Revelation had set in.

But the Messenger did not fall to the ground in convulsions as often happened during these moments of spiritual ecstasy. He stood where he was, his eyes gazing out across the pavilion as if he were looking through the cloth walls and seeing something far beyond the confines of time and space.

And then the moment passed and the Prophet blinked rapidly, looking around as if trying to remind himself where he was. He turned to face us, his eyes gazing long and deep at each one of his wives, his handsome face suddenly tense with anxiety. His gaze fell upon me and I felt a strange chill in my heart.

"O Messenger of God, what is it?"

The Prophet continued to look at me, as if his eyes were peering deep into my soul.

"The dogs of al-Haw'ab . . . they bark so fiercely . . ."

Al-Haw'ab was a valley to the northeast, on the caravan route to Iraq. I did not understand why the Prophet was mentioning this remote and desolate place, but there was something about his tone that suddenly frightened me. I looked at my sister-wives and saw that they were unnerved as well.

The Prophet now looked away from me and stared across the room. He continued to speak, but it was to himself and not to us.

"They bark at the Angel of Death . . . who follows her skirts . . . so much death in her midst . . ."

A terrible silence followed and the only thing I could hear was the pounding of blood in my ears. And then the Jewess stood up, her eyes filled with the terror that we all now felt.

"Who is she? Who do the dogs bark at?"

The Prophet stirred from his silent reverie and then looked again at each of us, sorrow etched on to his features.

"I . . . I don't know . . . but I grieve for her . . ."

The air of festivity was gone, replaced by a terrible sense of doom hanging over us. The Messenger of God shook his head as if trying to free himself from the awful vision that had captured his heart. He turned to leave and then stopped, his eyes suddenly focused on me. He leaned close so that only I would hear.

"Please, *Humayra,*" he said softly. "Don't let the dogs bark at you."

He walked out, leaving me with an unearthly sense of foreboding. I suddenly threw on my veil and ran outside. As I fled the pavilion and raced back to the security of my little home, I felt like a terrified gazelle charging through the wilderness, escaping an unseen predator that was coming closer every moment.

In years to come, when the Messenger's prophecy came true, I learned that we are all gazelles, and the lion that is bearing down upon us is the heartless hunter called fate. And the tragedy of life is that no matter how fast we run, no matter how far we go, the lion always wins.

39 Mecca—AD 630

On the eighth year after we had emigrated to Medina, when I was seventeen years old, the Meccans broke the truce of Hudaybiyya. Men of Quraysh helped a group of hotheads from the Bedouin clan of Bakr attack Muslims from the Bani Khuza'a. It was some foolish quarrel, a blood feud over a woman from a pagan clan who had fallen in love and run off with a Muslim boy. But it was a clear violation of the peace that had stood for two years, and the Prophet ordered the army of Islam to march out to Mecca in response.

By now, we truly could be called an army. Having been battle-tested in dozens of increasingly complex skirmishes, the barbarian tribes were now a powerfully disciplined and honed fighting force, one that had in recent months had its first confrontation with the legions of the Byzantine empire. After the failure of the Roman alliance with Khaybar, the day had been rapidly approaching when the imperial troops would engage our men. The Byzantines had precipitated the crisis by capturing the Prophet's emissary to Syria and brutally killing him. The murder was a ruthless violation of the ancient diplomatic sanctity of envoys and was no doubt intended to show the Byzantine contempt for the rising Muslim power and to provoke a response.

The Messenger had sent a force of three thousand to avenge his ambassador's death, led by his adopted son, Zayd. The resulting battle against Byzantine troops at the valley of Muta'h was the first in a war that would soon see the mighty Roman empire collapse at the hands of a group of desert warriors. The fighting was brutal and Zayd was killed. The death of Muhammad's beloved kinsman had caused the Muslims to fight with such ferocity that the overconfident Byzantine legions were forced to retreat. The Meccan defector Khalid ibn al-Waleed took the standard of the army and fought the stunned Byzantine forces back to the Dead Sea before pulling his men into the safety of the desert. Though the battle could at best have been called a draw, the Byzantines were horrified. Their elite forces, which had ruled much of the earth for almost a thousand years, had been checked by lightly armed horsemen who had been outnumbered three to one.

When the survivors returned to Mecca, the Prophet had congratulated them for their courage and awarded Khalid with the title "the Sword of Allah," by which he would forever be known. And then the Messenger had retreated to the privacy of Zaynab's apartment to weep bitterly over the death of Zayd, who had been a son to him and a husband to her.

The Muslim army had faced down the Byzantines and was now ready to face its most important challenge—the conquest of the holy city of Mecca. The Messenger brought together ten thousand of his finest warriors and marched to Mecca in response to the treaty violation. Many of the men were filled with righteous indignation and a burning desire to avenge years of humiliation and death at the hands of the Quraysh. But the Messenger calmed their hearts, saying that he would prefer to take the city without bloodshed. Even though it had been the base of operations of our enemies, Mecca remained a sacred city and the Prophet had no desire to stain the Sanctuary of Abraham with blood.

And so, as the Muslim army camped in the hills outside the ancient city from which we had been exiled, he ordered each and every one of the men to light a small campfire, rather than a few large bonfires around which the army would gather. And so it was that the night sky of Mecca was illuminated crimson with the combined flames of ten thousand fires, creating the terrifying impression of an army of one hundred thousand camped on the edge of the city. It was an effective ruse, and the citizenry of Mecca devolved into panic at the illusion.

I stood by the Prophet's side at the edge of a hill, my skin tingling with the waves of heat emanating from the burning camp behind us. The smoke from the fires made my eyes water and I was perennially terrified that a stray spark from one of the thousands of burning pits would consume the Prophet's pavilion, which he had pitched just outside the perimeter of the camp. Though Umar and the other commanders had objected to the Messenger's command center being established at the base of the hills, where it would be easy prey for the first Meccan attack force, my husband did not seem in the least bit afraid. And looking back at the flaming horizon, which seemed as terrifying as the gates of Hell, I understood his confidence. There would be no attack.

Two men approached our camp, carrying the flag of heralds. Unlike the Byzantines, Muslims respected the immunity of envoys and these men did not need any protective force. As the tall figures clambered down the hill toward the Messenger's simple green tent, my eyes went wide with recognition. These were not simple ambassadors. They were the lords of Mecca itself.

Abu Sufyan had come, along with his son Muawiya, who had been a secret convert for several years. From the smile on Muawiya's face and the tired and defeated look on Abu Sufyan's, it was clear that there was no more need for pretense. Mecca had been defeated, and all that was left was to settle the terms of its surrender.

The Messenger stepped forward with a warm smile and extended his hand to the man who had been his enemy for twenty years. Abu Sufyan looked at him wearily and then shook the Prophet's hand with dignity.

⸺ ⸺ ⸺

OVER THE NEXT HOUR, the Messenger and Abu Sufyan negotiated a permanent end to hostilities between our peoples. The Muslim army would enter the city in the morning with the guarantee of a general amnesty for its populace. This was a remarkably magnanimous gesture on my husband's part. He had defeated the people who had persecuted him for two decades, the people who had killed his family members and loved ones and had nearly exterminated the entire Muslim population at the Battle of the Trench. And he would forgive them and grant them privileged membership in the Muslim *Ummah*. The Quraysh, the tribe that had expelled Muhammad from its bosom, would retain control of Mecca and their traditional right to administer the Sanctuary and the Holy Kaaba in the name of Islam.

All of this the Messenger offered with a smile and an open hand. Abu Sufyan sighed, shaking his head at his enemy's generosity, which he himself had failed to show over the years.

"Perhaps I always knew this day would come," he said after a long moment of silence. His hair was now as white as the clouds, and his once-handsome faced was lined heavily with creases, the shrewd eyes weighed down by dark circles. He looked more like an old beggar than the would-be king of the Arab nation.

The Prophet leaned closer to him, took his hand in his as if they were old friends and not mortal enemies.

"Then why did you resist for so long?"

Abu Sufyan looked at his son Muawiya, his hope and pride, who had betrayed him and joined forces with his adversary. The dignified young man met his gaze and I could seen in them a glint of triumph, as if he had finally been proven right in an old family argument.

"Pride," Abu Sufyan admitted at last. And then he turned his eyes on the Messenger. "And perhaps jealousy. That Allah had chosen you over me."

The Messenger smiled.

"You said Allah, and not 'the gods.'"

Abu Sufyan shrugged and rose to his feet.

"If my gods were real, they would have helped me over the years."

The old man turned to leave, and then, almost as an afterthought, he turned to look back at my husband, an ironic smile on his lips.

"I testify that there is no god but God, and that you, Muhammad, are the Messenger of God."

And with that, the last of Muhammad's old enemies became his follower. Muawiya rose to help the old man limp out, when the Prophet called after them.

"Tell your people to stay indoors and abandon their weapons," he said slowly, making sure that every word was understood. "No man will be harmed who does not resist."

Abu Sufyan nodded. He was about to step out into the desert air, heated to frenzy by the thousands of campfires, when he looked one last time at the Messenger of God.

"Congratulations, Muhammad. You have defeated Quraysh at last."

And then I saw the Prophet turn his gaze to Muawiya and for a second there was that strange and chilling flash of premonition in his black eyes. And then the Messenger smiled, and I was surprised to see a hint of sadness on his face.

"No. I have given the Quraysh victory."

40

The next morning, Muhammad entered as a conqueror the holy city from which he had been expelled. Khalid ibn al-Waleed had led an advance guard to secure the city, but there was little resistance. The exhausted citizens of Mecca stayed inside their homes, quietly praying to their gods that the man whom they had persecuted would show them the graciousness that had escaped them when they held the reins of power. And their prayers would be answered, but not by the idols that they had fought and died for. The days of Allat, Uzza, and Manat were over, and Allah had emerged triumphant. The many had been defeated by the One.

My husband rode his favorite camel, Qaswa, back into the city that had been his home until he had questioned its ancient taboos and challenged its powerful elite. My father, Abu Bakr, rode at his side, followed by the ranks of the Muslim army, marching forward with dignity and discipline down the paved streets toward the Sanctuary.

I was on my own camel, riding in the covered howdah that been the source of so much trouble when I had been left behind in the desert. The Muslims had a policy now that they would not break camp until the Mothers had all been safely tucked away in their honored carriages and accounted for. Normal decorum required that I sit behind the heavy curtains of the howdah until the company had come to a halt, but the excitement of the day won out and no one objected when I peered through the woolen covers at the glorious sight of the Sanctuary, which I had not seen since I was a little girl.

The Kaaba was as I remembered it, the towering cubical temple covered in rich curtains of multicolored silks. The circular plaza around this holiest site of the Arab people was still littered with the three hundred and sixty idols that represented the different gods of the tribes, but this abomination would soon be at an end.

The Messenger rode ahead of us and circled the holy house seven times while proclaiming God's glory. He then stopped his camel and climbed down, approaching the Black Stone that was placed inside the eastern corner of the building. The Stone was said to have been lodged there by Abraham himself when our forefather had built the original temple with his son Ishmael. According to the Messenger, the Black Stone had fallen from heaven and was the only remnant of the celestial paradise from which Adam had been expelled.

The Messenger kissed the Stone of Heaven with reverence. And then he signaled to Ali, who strode forth with his mighty sword and began to slash away at the idols that had polluted the House of God from time immemorial. He tore down the ancient statues of the Daughters of Allah, followed by the grinning carved faces of the Syrian and Iraqi gods who had been imported into the Sanctuary when their images were no longer welcome in the Christian world. As the idols fell, a tremendous chorus of chants rose from the Muslim ranks, cries of *Allahu akbar* and *La ilaha illallah*. "God is great. There is no god but God." From this day forward the Arabs were no longer a disparate group of competing tribes, each with its own customs and beliefs. They were a single nation, united under one God.

And then, when the plaza was covered in rubble and the last of the idols had been smashed to dust, the Messenger of God opened the doors of the Kaaba and gestured toward us, his family and closest followers. My father and Ali came to his side, as did Umar, Uthman, Talha, and Zubayr. Fatima joined them, holding the hands of her little sons, Hasan and Husayn. And then Prophet looked at me and nodded. I hesitated, feeling my heart pounding with anticipation, and then I led my sister-wives to the entrance of the Holy of Holies, where the Spirit of God dwelled for eternity.

The Messenger stepped inside and we climbed the stone steps, following him into the darkness. There were no torches inside the Kaaba and for a moment I was blind and lost. And then my eyes adjusted to the gloom and I could see the three marble pillars that held up the stone roof of the temple. And on the far wall towered a mighty carnelian statue of Hubal, the god of Mecca.

The Prophet stared at this icon for a long time, the symbol of everything that he had spent his entire life fighting against. And then he raised his staff and pointed it at the idol, and for a moment he looked very much like Moses confronting the hubris of Pharaoh. And then the Messenger of God recited a verse from the Holy Qur'an: *Truth has come and falsehood has vanished. Verily falsehood always vanishes.*

I heard a rumble and I suddenly felt the ground beneath me shaking. And then as the tremors intensified, the majestic icon of Hubal shuddered and pitched forward on its face. The idol fell to the ground and shattered like a crystal vial thrown from a great height.

The ground became still and a deep silence fell over the Kaaba.

And then I heard the voice of Bilal, the Abyssinian slave who had been tortured in the Sanctuary so many years before. He was calling out the *Azan*, the call to prayer, summoning men to the Truth that could no longer be denied.

There is no god but God, and Muhammad is the Messenger of God.

41

The Messenger of God pitched his tent on the outskirts of the city, where each and every one of the residents of Mecca came to give him their pledge of loyalty. Abu Bakr sat at his right and Umar at his left hand, while Uthman stood to one side and gave to each of the new converts a gift of gold or jewels from the *Bayt al-Mal*, the Muslim treasury, a gesture of reconciliation and welcome to the new order. Ali stood behind the Prophet, *Dhul Fiqar* unsheathed and held aloft, a warning to any who might try to take vengeance on the man who had defeated the proud lords of Mecca.

It was not idle posturing, for the Messenger had recently survived an assassination attempt. During a visit to the conquered city of Khaybar, the Prophet had been welcomed by the Jewish chieftains who were eager to keep the peace after their humiliating defeat. But not everyone in the city shared their leaders' sentiments, and a woman of Khaybar had poisoned a feast of lamb that had been prepared for the Prophet by his hosts. The Messenger had tasted the meat and immediately sensed that something was wrong. He had spit out the poisoned morsel, but several of his Companions had been less fortunate and had died painfully at the table. The terrified Jewish leaders, fearing that their tribe would be annihilated in punishment, had found the cook and forced her to confess that she had acted alone. Ali had been prepared to execute her on the spot, but the Prophet had restrained his outraged cousin. My husband had asked the defiant Jewess why she had tried to kill him, and she had responded with her head held proudly that she was merely avenging the deaths of her kinsmen at Muhammad's hand. And to everyone's surprise, the Messenger had nodded with understanding and pardoned her.

As I looked at the faces of the defeated Meccans lining up before my husband, I did not see what I had glimpsed on that Jewish woman's angry face. I saw no fire of defiance, no hint of rebellion still in their hearts. They were humbled and weary, tired of fighting, tired of losing, tired of being on the wrong side of history. I felt a particular flash of satisfaction when I saw Suhayl, the pretentious envoy who had negotiated the Treaty of Hudaybiyya, bow his head before his new master. There was no insouciance in his voice, no flash of contempt in his dark eyes. Just eager gratitude that the Messenger had chosen to show clemency to men like him who did not deserve it.

And there were moments of sincere reconciliation and joy. The Prophet's uncle Abbas, who had been his secret ally inside Mecca all these years, could finally embrace his nephew openly. And to my great joy, my estranged brother Abdal Kaaba, who had nearly killed his own father at the Battle of Uhud, rejoined our family. The Messenger embraced my brother and gave him a new name, Abdal Rahman. I had never seen my father so happy as on the day that his eldest son returned to his bosom, and it was as if years of pain fell off Abu Bakr's face and he was a young man again.

My half sister, Asma, also received a blessing when her elderly mother, Qutaila, came and finally embraced the faith that she had rejected years before. It was a tearful reunion, and I wondered how Asma had endured all those years cut off from the woman who had given her birth and then rejected her when she chose her father's religion over the ways of the ancients. I suddenly realized how lucky I really was to have had a loving family that remained intact despite all the hardships we endured, and how brave my sister had been all these years when her heart had been weighed down with such unspoken sorrow.

And then a towering black man stepped forward and I felt my breathing stop. I recognized him immediately, for his visage had been burned into my heart since the disaster at Uhud. He was Wahsi, the Abyssinian slave who had killed the Messenger's uncle Hamza with a javelin.

I saw the Prophet stiffen as the hulking African knelt before him, his right hand held aloft. My eyes flew to Ali and I could see his green eyes burning with anger, and for a second I wondered if *Dhul Fiqar* would slice Wahsi's head from his muscular shoulders.

The Messenger leaned forward.

"You are the one who killed Hamza, the son of Abdal Muttalib. Is that not so?" There was a hint of danger in my husband's voice, and I could see a line of sweat drip down the Abyssinian's broad face.

"Yes," he said softly, his head bowed in evident shame.

"Why did you do this thing?" my husband asked, his black eyes unreadable.

"To secure my freedom from slavery," the African said, his voice trembling.

The Prophet looked at him for a long time. And then he reached forward and took Wahsi's hand in acceptance of his *baya'ah,* his oath of loyalty.

"We are all slaves to something," he said. "Wealth. Power. Lust. And the only freedom from the slavery of this world is to become a slave to God."

Tears welling in his eyes, Wahsi clasped the Messenger's hand. He recited the testimony of faith and the Prophet nodded, accepting the conversion of this man who had murdered his beloved uncle Hamza, his childhood friend and the only older brother he had ever known.

And then I saw my husband's eyes glisten with tears and he turned away from the African.

"Now let me not look upon you again," Muhammad said, his voice caught in his throat. Wahsi nodded sadly and departed, and I did not see him again for all the days that the Messenger lived.

- - -

As the sun set, the last of the Meccans stood before the Prophet, ready to accept membership in the *Ummah*. Among them was an old woman, hunched over and covered in a black *abaya*. Her face was covered by a black veil, but there was something hauntingly familiar about her eyes.

Yellow green and piercing like daggers. The eyes of a snake that was poised to strike its prey.

I felt a wave of alarm rising in my heart, but before I could speak, she knelt before the Prophet and placed her long fingers in a bowl of water, and the Prophet dipped his own fingers in the bowl in formal acceptance of her allegiance.

"I testify that there is no god but God and that you, Muhammad, are the Messenger of God. And I pledge my allegiance to God and His Messenger."

The voice was hoarse but unmistakable and I saw my husband's eyes narrow. His smile was gone and his face now rigid as stone.

"Remove your veil," he said in a powerful voice that sent a chill down my spine. There were murmurs of shock from some in the tent, as the Messenger was always respectful of the modesty of women and had never before asked anyone to remove her *niqab*.

The old women hesitated, but Muhammad continued to stare at her without blinking. Ali stepped forward, his glittering sword raised menacingly.

"Fulfill your oath. Obey the Messenger," he said, and the tension in the air became unbearable.

And then the woman raised her hand and ripped off the veil, revealing the face of the Messenger's greatest enemy. Hind, the daughter of Utbah, the most vicious of his opponents, the cannibal who had eaten the liver of Hamza as the ultimate sign of her contempt for the believers.

I gasped when I looked upon her, for I barely recognized her. Her dangerous eyes were unchanged, but her once-beautiful face had been cruelly ravaged by time. The perfect alabaster skin had turned a sickly yellow and was scarred with deep lines. Her high cheekbones, which had highlighted the chiseled perfection of her features, were now skeletal crags. She looked like a corpse, and the only evidence of her living spirit was the steady rise and fall of her sagging throat as she breathed with some difficulty.

The Prophet looked at her with his eyes brimming with anger.

"You are she who ate the flesh of my uncle," he said simply, no accusation in his voice, just a harsh statement of fact.

I saw the revulsion on the faces of the Companions, and I glanced at Umar, who had been her lover in the Days of Ignorance. The horror in his eyes at the sight of the decrepit woman he had once loved was palpable.

Hind ignored the stares, the cruel whispers, and kept her eyes on my husband.

"Yes," she said simply, acknowledging before the world the crime that easily merited her death.

My eyes fell on Ali and I saw *Dhul Fiqar* glowing red. I would have dismissed the vision as an illusion created by the flickering torches, but I had seen enough to know that the sword burned with its own anger.

And then I realized that Hind was looking at the weapon as well and her ugly face curved into a truly terrifying smile.

"Do it. Kill me," she hissed defiantly, and yet I could hear what I thought sounded like a plea beneath the affectation of pride.

There was a hush of silence as the Prophet looked at his adversary, a trembling sack of bones who had once been the most beautiful and noble woman among the children of Ishmael. And I saw a sudden softening in his eyes that mirrored the change in my own heart, for in that moment I truly felt sorry for her.

"I forgive you," he said simply. And then he turned away from her and placed his attention on a mother who was standing behind her, a young woman carrying an infant in her arms.

Hind looked at him, confused. Her eyes went to Ali, who had lowered his sword, and then to Umar, who refused to meet her gaze. She stared at the other Companions and then at the men and women of Mecca around her, but all chose to ignore her. In that moment, I realized that Hind had been both pardoned and condemned. For she had gone from the most feared and hated enemy of Islam to a nobody, a woman who was irrelevant to the new order, who had no power or say in anything that happened in Arabia from that day forward. As she turned and hobbled away, I realized that my husband had given her the one punishment she could not endure. The curse of anonymity.

The defeated old woman skulked away and left the tent, her head bowed. I should have stayed inside by my husband's side, but something in my heart compelled me to step outside, to see for myself the final end of my greatest nightmare.

Hind was already past the guards who had been placed at the perimeter of the Messenger's tent when she suddenly stooped and turned. Her yellow-green eyes met mine and for a second I saw a hint of the pride and dignity that she had always carried. The old crone hobbled over to me and looked at me closely. My face was hidden behind my veil, but my golden eyes shone forth unmistakably.

"You are the daughter of Abu Bakr," she said, with an unnerving smile, the look of a cat as it plays with a mouse it has caught in its paws.

"Yes," I said, suddenly regretting my decision to come outside.

"I always liked you, little girl," Hind said in a raspy voice that still tinkled with seduction. "You remind me of myself."

I felt my face flush at her words and my pulse pounded in my temples.

"I seek refuge in Allah that I should ever be like you!"

Hind smiled broadly, revealing a row of cracked and blackened teeth.

"Even so, you are," she said with a laugh that lacked any joy. "There is a fire inside you that burns very bright. They can cover you with a hundred veils and it will still shine through. But know this, my dear. The fire of a woman's heart is too hot for this world. Men will fly to it like moths. But when it burns their wings, they will snuff it out."

I felt the hair on my arm standing up and chills ran through me. I turned to leave, when Hind reached forward and took my arm in her bony grasp. I tried to pull free, but her fingers were like the jaws of a lion, crushing down on my bones. And then she put something in my hand, something that sparkled under the evening stars that were slowly taking possession of the sky.

It was her golden armlet, the band of snakes intertwining until their jaws met to encase a glittering ruby.

I stared down at this strange and awful symbol of Hind's power, a totem that she was now passing along to me as the sun of her life set into the horizon of history. It was a gift with terrifying implications, and one that I had no desire to accept.

But when I raised my head to protest, Hind was gone.

42

It was my husband's distinct tragedy that soon after each victory he was given in his mission, God always exacted a terrible price from among his loved ones. Shortly after we returned to Medina and the city was alive with rejoicing at the final victory of Islam, the Messenger's infant son, Ibrahim, fell ill and began to waste away.

Despite the desperate prayers of the community and the efforts of those who were skilled in medicine, the poor boy deteriorated rapidly, his tiny form ravaged by the camp fever that few grown men could survive.

I watched through eyes reddened by tears as Muhammad stroked his dying son's curly hair in farewell. A steady flow of tears ran down his face, causing one of the men present, a Companion named Abdal Rahman ibn Awf, to raise his eyebrows in surprise.

"O Messenger of God, even you? Is it not forbidden?"

The Prophet spoke with some difficulty, his eyes never leaving the face of Ibrahim as the flow of life seeped out from the child.

"Tears are not forbidden," the Messenger said softly. "They are the promptings of tenderness and mercy, and he who does not show mercy will have none shown to him."

And then my husband leaned close to the little boy, who was looking up at him with dreamy eyes as his soul began to detach from this valley of sorrow.

"O Ibrahim, if it were not that the promise of reunion is assured, and that this is a path which all must tread, and that the last of us will overtake the first, truly we would grieve for you with even greater sorrow. But we are stricken indeed with sadness for you, Ibrahim. The eye weeps and the heart grieves, but we say nothing that would offend the Lord."

I felt my heart quiver in grief as Ibrahim smiled up at his father, his tiny hand wrapped around the Messenger's finger. I saw the little boy squeeze one last time and then his eyes closed, and Muhammad's son passed away into eternity.

+ + +

WHEN WE HAD WEPT all the tears we could, the Messenger covered Ibrahim's face with a sheet and stepped outside to address the agitated crowd. I looked up in the heavens and saw that the sky was dark, and realized that the sun was in eclipse and the stars were shining in the middle of the day.

The Muslims were gazing up in wonder at the thin crescent where the sun had been only moments before, and I heard a man cry out.

"Behold! Even the heavens weep for the Prophet's son!"

I did not doubt that this was a sign from God for the poor, innocent child who would never have a chance to experience the joys of life and love in this world.

But even at this moment, when grief had overpowered us all, the Messenger remained true to his faith.

"No," he said loudly, his voice echoing through the streets of Medina. "The sun and the moon are signs of God. They are eclipsed for no man."

And with that Muhammad reminded us that he was no more than a man himself and that his own son was no more special than the hundreds of children who died every day in the cruelty of the desert, whose families were forced to grieve alone, without the loving support of an entire nation.

My husband turned away, his face looking very tired and old. I reached over and took his hand, and he held mine tightly, his eyes brimming with gratitude. And then we walked back inside and began the preparations for the funeral.

43

The next several months were a flurry of diplomatic activity as the Messenger dispatched envoys throughout Arabia. With the fall of Mecca, the ancient pagan cult had breathed its last, and it was time to bring the remaining tribes under the governance of Medina. A nation had finally been forged, and the Prophet was busy making plans for its survival. I did not understand the urgency in his daily letters to the varying provinces of the peninsula that now swore allegiance to him, perhaps because I did not want to face the truth. My husband was over sixty years old and had lived a hundred lifetimes in one. But he was not immortal, and as the weight of his age grew upon him, he was making plans for the survival of the *Ummah* once he was no longer there to guide it.

With the death of Ibrahim, talk had begun among the people of Arabia about the successor to the Prophet now that he had lost his direct heir. Many names were whispered, most prominently that of my father, Abu Bakr, who was an elder statesman and held the respect of the entire community. My father always angrily dismissed such speculation and yet it persisted. A few voices suggested that young Ali, who was now just over thirty years old, would be a natural choice, as the closest living male relative to the Prophet and the father of his grandsons. But there was a natural dislike among the independent-minded Arabs for monarchy, and the idea that the leadership of the community should be based on the right of bloodlines left a sour taste in the mouths of the tribes.

It was significant that of the few Companions who spoke in favor of Ali, the most prominent was Salman, the Persian hero who had devised the strategy of the trench that had saved Medina from invasion. The Persians were an ancient people who were proud of their long lineage of philosopher-kings and looked upon the Arab custom of choosing tribal leaders by an assembly known as a *shura* as a crass system that could be manipulated by the powerful to oppress the weak. For the Persians, the qualities of leadership, the instincts for justice and honor, were sacred traits that were passed along by blood and upbringing and should not be bartered away for the mercurial passions of the mob. It was a passionate and proud stance, but one that was utterly alien to the freethinking Arabs, who were only now becoming accustomed to being ruled by a single man.

My husband was certainly aware of the talk, but he made no effort to end it or to clarify his own preferences in the matter of succession. In the years that followed, I have often looked back and wondered why he was so circumspect. In all other areas of life, he was a clear and commanding guide, one whose words were carefully chosen to limit the possibility of misinterpretation or confusion. Yet when it came to the matter of succession to the leadership of the *Ummah*, he was stubbornly silent, and much of the chaos that was to emerge would arise from our best efforts to understand his ambiguous pronouncements on this subject.

It is my belief that my husband did not announce his intentions clearly because his heart was torn, even as the *Ummah* itself would one day be torn apart. The death of Ibrahim had taken away his last hope for a son to carry his lineage, which would now pass through his daughter Fatima and her sons, Hasan and Husayn. Ali was indeed the closest of his living male relatives and had been in many ways both a brother and a son to him. The Messenger spent a great deal of time talking in private with him, and none except Fatima would be permitted to join them in those moments. What was said between them was always a mystery, and there were rumors that my husband was passing along divine secrets that were too weighty for the common Muslims, even for pious men like my father or Umar, to hear.

This speculation added to Ali's reputation for otherworldliness, and many of the Muslims became increasingly uncomfortable around the strange young man. No one would deny that he was a mighty warrior and an eloquent speaker, but it was this peculiar sense that he was not like the rest of us that estranged him from the hearts of many. And it is for that reason that I have difficulty imagining that my husband expected the Muslims to follow Ali unquestioningly, as his supporters would claim with increasing vehemence in later years. Muhammad was a statesman above all, one who understood the nature and character of the people he had been destined to lead. It was his diplomatic wisdom that had caused him to agree to a truce with Mecca, even though the Muslims were in open revolt at the idea. My husband had seen further than the rest of us and had known that Islam would grow rapidly in peacetime and that Mecca would one day fall without bloodshed. And it was that same visionary thinking that had caused him to pardon his worst enemies and offer the leaders of Quraysh prominent roles in the new state. Even though many Muslims resented the lords of Mecca, the chieftains retained the broad respect of the Arab tribes and their support would bring unity to the nation

My husband, who saw so much, must have seen that his beloved Ali was a polarizing figure, one who brought about intense reactions of both love and hate. My own antipathy to him was visceral, and I knew I was not alone. Muhammad must have known that Ali would never be able to unify the Arabs, and it was the unity of the *Ummah* that was his primary concern in all the years that I knew him. Others, like my father and Umar, had the respect of the entire nation and could easily hold the community together when Muhammad was gone. And yet my husband did not openly proclaim in their favor either.

As I look back in my own twilight years, dear Abdallah, I believe that my husband's heart and his mind were divided on the matter. In his heart, perhaps he would have preferred Ali and his grandsons to be the leaders of the community. And yet his intellect saw that the Muslims would probably not support his family's claim to power, and everything that the Messenger had worked for would shatter upon his death. That truth, the vast chasm between his preferences and those of his own people, was so painful that I believe he intentionally left the matter unresolved in those final days of his life. Perhaps he was hoping that God would give him a Revelation that would clarify the issue of succession, which would absolve him of having to make a choice that could lead to discord and civil war. But when the day of the last Revelation came, the matter remained unsettled.

Those final verses came down upon him during his participation in what would later be called the Farewell Pilgrimage. My husband led tens of thousands of believers to Mecca to perform the rites of Abraham, during which he established forever the rituals according to the laws of Islam. Gone were the old superstitions of the desert, including the pagan custom of circumambulating the Holy Kaaba naked. In their place were the simple acts of piety that reminded us of our connection to our father Abraham.

Along with the ritual encircling of the temple, the Muslims retained the practice of running seven times between the hills of Safa and Marwa. This rite, whose meaning had long been forgotten by the Arabs, commemorated our mother Hagar and her desperate search for water. She had sought to save her dying son Ishmael, and at her moment of despair in the arid valley, God had caused the well of Zamzam to miraculously appear at Ishmael's foot. As my husband explained the meaning of the ritual to the masses of pilgrims, many of whom were recent converts, I remembered how I had told Abu Sufyan the same story when I was a little girl almost fifteen years before. Abu Sufyan, who had then been the proud king of the idol worshipers, the same man who now stood humbly dressed in a pilgrim's loincloth near the Prophet, a follower instead of an enemy.

The next day, the Prophet had led his followers through another ancient rite, the stoning of three old pillars in the desert that had stood since time immemorial. The ritual was meant to commemorate the three times that Abraham was tempted by Satan and how he had driven away the devil by stoning him in the desert.

And then, finally, the Messenger led the throngs out into the vast desert plain of Arafat toward the mountain from which he would deliver what would prove to be his final sermon to mankind. I gazed down at the thousands who had come to hear him speak, the crowd stretching from horizon to horizon, and I had a persistent thought that what I was seeing was a small precursor of the awe of the Day of Judgment, when mankind will rise from their graves and stand side by side before the Throne of God.

As I looked upon the sea of white-garbed pilgrims, all dressed in equal humility regardless of wealth or status, with fair-skinned and dark-skinned believers praying side by side to the same God, I was struck by my husband's remarkable triumph. He had taken a group of fiercely divided tribes, at war with one another for centuries, and had forged them into a single nation. A community that valued moral character over material success, an *Ummah* in which the rich eagerly sought to alleviate the suffering of the poor. Such a feat could not have been accomplished by a thousand great leaders over a thousand generations. And yet my love had done it single-handedly over the course of one lifetime.

As the Messenger stood atop the ancient mountain of Arafat, I heard his voice echo to the thousands who eagerly stood under the punishing sun to hear his words.

"O people, hear me well as I speak to you, for we may not meet again in this place after this year. O people! Your lives and your property are as sanctified to each other as the sanctity of this day, and this sacred month. Have I given the message? O God, be my witness."

At his words, the Pilgrims cried out in unison, "Yes!"

The Prophet raised his hand and continued.

"So let whoever has been given something for safekeeping give it back to him who gave him it. Truly, the usury of the Era of Ignorance has been laid aside forever. And truly, the blood vengeance of the Era of Ignorance has been laid aside forever. Truly, the hereditary distinctions that were the pretense of the Era of Ignorance have been laid aside forever."

He paused and then laid out his final commandments for the people, even as Moses had done at Sinai.

"O people: truly you owe your women their rights, and they owe you yours. They may not lie with other men in your beds, let anyone into your houses you do not want without your permission, or commit indecency. You in turn must provide for them and clothe them fittingly. So fear God in respect to women, and concern yourselves with their welfare. Have I given the message? O God, be my witness."

The crowds cried in assent again, their voices thundering through the valley with such power that I could feel the earth beneath me tremble.

"O people, believers are but brothers. Your Lord is One, and your father is one. All of you are from Adam, and Adam was from the mud of the earth. The noblest of you in God's sight is the best in conduct. An Arab has no merit over a non-Arab, nor a white man over a black man, other than in his moral conduct. Have I given the message? O God, be my witness!"

As the crowd shouted again its agreement, I saw a strange light surrounding the Messenger, like a circle of fire. I told myself it was just the punishing desert sun playing tricks on me. And yet the light persisted and grew gradually brighter.

"Today I received these words from God, which the angel Gabriel has told me will be the final Revelation from the Lord of the Worlds."

There was stunned silence and everyone listened carefully as the Prophet recited in his beautiful flowing voice the Word of God.

Today the disbelievers have lost all hope that you will give up your faith.
Do not fear them, but fear Me.
Today I have perfected your religion for you
Completed my blessing upon you
And chosen for your religion Islam—the Surrender.

We all stood there in awe as God's final words to mankind sank into our hearts. And then the Prophet raised his voice and asked the question one last time.

"Have I given the message? O God, be my witness!"

And as the cries of affirmation echoed all around us, I saw tears flowing down my husband's face. For in that moment, I realized that he had finally completed his life's work. There was nothing more left to be done.

"Then let whoever is present tell whoever is absent. And peace be upon all of you, and the mercy of Allah."

Even as he spoke these words, the strange light around him appeared to intensify and for a moment it seemed as if my husband were made of light itself, shining brighter than the sun. I looked down, unable to bear the blinding rays emanating from about his noble figure.

And then I gasped, for my eyes fell on the earth around where he stood. And I could see no sign of a shadow. My father and Umar were right beside him, and their shadowy outlines fell away from them as the sun slid toward the horizon. And yet Muhammad alone among all those who stood at the peak cast no shade.

And then the mysterious light around my husband vanished, and his shadow reappeared against the craggy rocks as if it had always been there. And without another word, the Messenger of God climbed down from the mountain peak and immersed himself in the adoring masses.

◆ ◆ ◆

As we returned to Medina at the end of the Pilgrimage, two events occurred that would change the course of Muslim history. First was the birth of my half brother Muhammad. My father had taken a second wife in his old age, a war widow named Asma bint Umais, who had become pregnant with his last child. Even though she was late in her term when the season of Pilgrimage had come, my stepmother had insisted upon accompanying my father to Mecca. She had performed all the rituals admirably and without complaint, but soon after we left the precincts of the holy city, her water broke and my baby brother was born.

I fell in love with little Muhammad the moment I saw him, for he had my fiery red hair and adorable dimples on his cheeks whenever he smiled, which was often. In the years to come, Muhammad ibn Abu Bakr would become like a son to me, even as you have been, Abdallah, and it is my greatest regret that I was not able to restrain him or guide him away from the terrible destiny that awaited him.

And though I did not know it then, the man who shared responsibility for my brother's destiny was among us, and it was because of the events that occurred on that road home from Mecca that their souls would become intertwined.

Our pilgrim caravan stopped for water at a pond located in a small valley called Ghadir Khumm, a barren place of no significance that would later be remembered as the home of the great schism that drove the Muslims apart forever, shattering a unified *Ummah* into sects that were perennially at war.

As the camels and horses drank at the pond and the believers re-filled their water caskets, a man approached the Prophet and loudly complained about Ali, who had been his leader in a recent military command and had been seen by the men as too strict in enforcing discipline.

I saw the patient smile on my husband's face vanish and a dark look cross his features. I knew that he was very sensitive about Ali, and I had learned through experience to keep my own rather dismal opinions of the Prophet's son-in-law to myself. Of course the Messenger was aware that Ali was unpopular with some of the Muslims, but hearing that the soldiers under Ali's command were now openly agitating against a man whom Muhammad loved like a son inspired in him a rare fury. He suddenly summoned all the believers to gather about him and then called forth Ali, who had been sharpening his sword against the jagged rocks of the valley.

The Messenger of God held Ali's right hand aloft and called out loudly, his black eyes shining with a frightening intensity.

"Hear, O Muslims and do not forget. Whosoever holds me as his *Mawla*, know that Ali is also his *Mawla*. O Allah, befriend those who befriend Ali, and be the enemy of whosoever is hostile to him!"

It was a powerful pronouncement and one unlike any I had ever heard my husband say. He had clearly exalted Ali in a way that he had never done for any other man among his followers. And yet the words themselves were unclear and open to interpretation, for the word *Mawla* means many things in Arabic, including master, friend, lover, and even slave. But whatever my husband meant, it was clear that he was tired of the grumbling about the young man who had fathered his grandchildren and wanted to put an end to the cheap gossip about his closest relative.

Whether Muhammad intended anything more in that moment than to remind us to respect and honor his cousin would become a matter of passionate debate in the years to come. And one day the argument would devolve into open warfare.

44

Several months after we returned from the Pilgrimage, the Messenger entered my house one day when I was sewing. I looked up from the patch that I was applying to my old cloak to see him gazing at me serenely, a soft smile on his lips.

"Is it not Maymuna's day?" I asked, referring to the most recent of my husband's wives, Maymuna bint al-Harith, an impoverished divorcée whom he had married shortly after the truce with Mecca. She was a kindly woman in her thirties who was always seeking ways to raise money to free slaves, as she believed that no man should be a slave to anyone except God. Maymuna was an aunt of Khalid ibn al-Waleed, the Sword of Allah, and many believed that she had influenced her nephew to abandon Mecca and defect to the Prophet's side.

The Prophet had continued his policy of spending one day with each of his wives to ensure that they were all treated equally. Today was dedicated to Maymuna, and my husband was normally meticulous about spending all of his allotted time with the wife whose turn had come, so I was surprised to see him in my room.

"I just wanted to look at you," he said simply, but there was something in his voice that worried me. It was the tone of a man who was about to leave on a long journey and was unsure when he would see his loved ones again.

The Messenger walked toward me slowly. He looked weak and tired, and I sat him beside me on a small cushion. He smiled warmly as I ran my hand through his black curls, which were now peppered with strands of silver.

As I looked into his eyes, I sensed he wanted to say something, and yet he was holding himself back.

"What is it?" I asked, despite my growing apprehension about whatever it was that he was hiding from me.

"You will live long, *insha-Allah*," he said rather elliptically. "But there are times that I wish you would have passed away before me."

I was shocked at these words. My husband wanted me to die before he did?

"Why would you say that?" I asked rather sharply, not bothering to hide my hurt.

The Prophet ran his hand across my face, like a blind man trying to recognize someone's features. Or a traveler who was leaving and wanted to imprint a memory onto the tips of his finger.

"So that I could pray over your body and ask forgiveness for you."

I gave him a surprised and perhaps ungracious look, as my pride managed to twist his words into some kind of insult. But in the years to come, there would be many times that I wished that I had indeed died that day, and that his blessing could have protected me from the Day of Judgment, when the true burden of my guilt will be weighed by God.

But alas, that was not my destiny, nor his. The Messenger of God took no offense at the rather sharp glance I had given him. He smiled again and rose to his feet to leave . . . and then collapsed to the floor!

"My love!" I cried out in shock, forgetting to be angry at his enigmatic words. The Messenger had fallen as if his knees had been cut from beneath him, and he lay curled at my feet like a baby in a crib.

I quickly bent over and touched his forehead. He was burning up. And then I felt his body shake with tremors, but they were not the unearthly convulsions of the Revelation; they were the very human shivers of a man consumed by fever.

→   →   →

FOR THE NEXT THREE nights, we gathered around the Messenger as he lay in Maymuna's bed. The Mothers had been at his side nonstop since the moment I had cried out for help and Ali and Abbas had arrived to aid their kinsman. We had kept a vigil into the late hours, applying cold rags to his forehead to lower the fever and feeding him bowls of soup and broth to give him strength. But the days passed and my husband's state only worsened.

"It will pass . . ." I would reassure the other Mothers. "It always does . . . He is the Messenger of God . . . the angels will heal him . . ."

But even I had difficulty believing my own words.

→   →   →

ON THE FOURTH NIGHT of the Messenger's illness, a council of his inner circle gathered at his bedside to debate the future of Islam. With the Prophet incapacitated and steadily deteriorating, the future of the entire *Ummah* was at stake. The fragile unity that the Messenger had forged among the Arabs by the sheer strength of his personality was now on the verge of collapsing. Rumors were coming that some of the Bedouin tribes were considering renouncing their pacts of alliance with Medina. And the Byzantine empire was allegedly massing its forces for an invasion.

While these were the kinds of political and military threats the Muslims were accustomed to facing, there was a more troubling development. A group of pretenders to the mantle of prophecy was rising, each trying to steal some of Muhammad's success to enhance his own glory. A rogue named Musaylima had proclaimed himself a new prophet of Allah. He had written to my husband in the months past calling on his "brother" to recognize Musaylima as his fellow Messenger of God and suggesting that the two should divide the world between them. Before he had fallen ill, Muhammad sent a response to Musaylima branding him a liar and proclaiming that all the world belonged to God alone. But the false prophet was undeterred and had begun to raise a following from among the superstitious clan of Bani Hanifa on the eastern edge of the Najd desert. And a woman of the Bani Tamim named Sajah, a *kahina* who was rumored to be versed in dark magic, had similarly proclaimed herself a prophetess and was busy gathering a small but fanatically loyal group of disciples. Had the Messenger not been confined to his sickbed, the defeat of these new threats to Islam would have been his priority.

The council of believers had arrived, hoping to find the Messenger in a rare moment of lucidity in which he could guide them as to how to run the affairs of state. The small band consisted of my father, Umar, Uthman, Ali, Talha and Zubayr, along with Muawiya, a new member of the Messenger's inner circle. The son of Abu Sufyan had emigrated to the oasis after the surrender of Mecca and had been chosen by the Messenger as his personal scribe, an honor that had formerly belonged to Ali. Muawiya's sudden rise to prominence in the community had startled some Muslims, but my husband had wisely realized that an overture to this scion of the Quraysh would accelerate the process of reconciliation. And the honey-tongued young man had quickly proven his skills as a politician, winning over skeptics with gifts and sweet words. Umar in particular had taken a liking to the former prince of Mecca and had taken him under his wing. Muawiya's star was rising rapidly in the heavens of Islam, and it appeared that the only one who remained suspicious of his intentions was Ali, which was perhaps understandable.

The Companions waited quietly by the Prophet's side for over an hour until his eyes opened briefly. My poor husband looked at them all for a second as if he did not recognize them, and then his black eyes finally kindled with their mysterious inner light and he sat up slowly in bed.

My husband must have guessed why these men were here, as he spoke before any of them could greet him. His eyes focused on Muawiya as he gestured with his hand.

"Bring a parchment and pen . . ." the Messenger said, his voice hoarse and trembling. "I have something to dictate . . . As long as the Muslims follow my command, they will prosper . . ."

Muawiya rose and removed a sheaf of parchment from inside his rich emerald robes. But before he could move to the Prophet's side, Umar put a restraining hand on his arm. I saw the troubled look on the towering Companion's face when he glanced at the Messenger, whose eyes were struggling to stay open as the delirium came back with a vengeance.

"The holy Qur'an is enough for us," Umar said, clearly nervous that the Messenger was in no state of mind to give commandments.

But Ali stepped forward, his green eyes flashing.

"Obey the Messenger of God," he said to Muawiya sharply. The hawk-faced young man met Ali's gaze without flinching and then turned his attention back to Umar, who shook his head gravely.

"He is sick and his words may be confused. Do you want to bring *fitna* on the people?" Umar said sharply, using the Arabic word for chaos and political strife.

Ali did not back down.

"You are bringing *fitna* by disobeying the Prophet!"

I felt the tension in the room rise, and my father quickly moved between the men and tried to calm them.

"My brothers, please, lower your voices," Abu Bakr said, glancing at the Messenger, who was struggling to speak but was unable to form the words.

And then Talha rose and took Ali's side.

"Do as the Messenger says," he said quietly, but there was an edge I had never heard before in my gentle cousin's voice.

Your father, Zubayr, who was Talha's closest friend, inserted himself into the debate, taking the opposing position.

"Umar has a point. If the fever sways his words, the people will be misguided," he said grimly.

As the argument grew heated and voices rose in fury, I glanced at my husband, who was now fully awake and aware of the rapidly deteriorating situation. And I saw that his face had become hard and angry, and his black eyes blazed with a fury that frightened me.

"Enough!" the Messenger said, his voice echoing like a blast of thunder in the small room. The men immediately fell silent, but I saw that their tempers were still smoldering. Muawiya, ever quick to gravitate toward authority, was at my husband's side in an instant, pen and paper in hand to record whatever commands his master issued.

There was a tense moment of silence as we waited for what we assumed would be his instructions about the succession of leadership. Would he order the Muslims to obey Ali, even though many would do so halfheartedly? Would he appoint my father or Umar to take charge and risk forever denying his own bloodline a claim to authority? Or would he devise another solution that satisfied all parties in the Muslim *Ummah,* an answer that only a visionary statesman like Muhammad could find amidst the chaos of competing interests?

After a long moment spent looking at the men he had led to victory, men whom he loved like children and who had now been behaving like children, Muhammad finally shook his head and sighed wearily. Muawiya leaned closer, but my husband waved him away.

"Leave me. All of you," he said with a trace of bitterness. And then the Messenger of God rolled over in bed and closed his eyes, refusing to divulge his final testament to a people who had proven unworthy.

I saw the fire of contention go out in the Companions' eyes and they all looked ashamed. One by one, the men who held the future of the *Ummah* in their hands walked out with their heads bowed, leaving the wives alone with their sick husband.

I have often wondered what the Messenger of God would have said that night and whether his words could have spared us the horror and the bloodshed that was to come. Looking back, I realize that of all the mistakes the Muslims made in the course of our history, none was graver than the pain we caused an old man that night, a man who loved his people and who wanted for them only peace.

45 June 8, AD 632

On the seventh day of his illness, the Messenger awoke in the middle of the morning and looked around at the Mothers in confusion.

"Whose day is it?" he asked softly, his voice barely audible.

Zaynab bint Jahsh took his hand in hers and smiled. Even in the midst of his raging fever, he remained concerned that each of his wives be treated equally.

"Mine, O Messenger of God," she said.

The Prophet looked at her for a long moment as if trying to remember her name. And then he gazed around at us again.

"And tomorrow?"

Ramla stepped forward.

"Mine, my husband."

The Prophet's eyes fell on me and I saw the confusion in his face fade.

"And the day after?"

And then I and the other women understood. Even as his mind burned with fever, even as the Angel of Death hovered in terrifying proximity, the one thing Muhammad cared about was when he would be able to spend the day with me, the most beloved of his wives.

I felt tears pouring down my cheeks and I could not speak. And then the elderly Sawda put a gentle hand on my shoulder.

"The next day is mine. But I give my day freely to my sister Aisha."

And then one by one, each of the other wives said the same thing. I looked at them in shock, and my tears now flowed in gratitude.

My husband tried to rise to his feet, but he could not.

"Help me . . . go to Aisha . . ." he said, his voice cracked and trembling.

Ali and Abbas, the Prophet's closest living kinsmen, were the only men with us that day. They stepped forward and helped the Prophet to his feet, holding him up by the shoulders as they gently guided him out of Maymuna's house.

There was an immediate roar from the Masjid courtyard, where hundreds of believers had held a vigil since the news of the Prophet's illness. The faithful cried out to him like babies calling out for their mother. The Messenger smiled weakly at them but did not have even the strength to raise his hands to wave in acknowledgment. And then a terrible silence fell over the crowd as they watched the Messenger limp toward my house. It was a shocking and tragic sight, and I saw many grown men weep openly at the Prophet's deterioration.

The Messenger looked at his people and tried to smile encouragingly, but I could see the sadness in his eyes. This was not how he wished them to remember him, and yet he was a mortal man and no more immune to the ravages of time than the least of his followers.

Ali and Abbas led the Prophet into my room and helped him lie down on the soft lambskin mattress where we had spent so many nights wrapped in love. The moment his back touched the soft, familiar fur lining, I saw him breathe deeper and the muscles in his face relax.

Whatever else happened now, he was home.

I sat down beside him and brushed his hair. He looked at me with deep love and then ran his fingers across my cheek. And then he stirred, as if finally remembering something he had long forgotten.

"Is there any money left in the house?" he asked, and I heard a strange urgency in his voice.

"A few gold coins. Nothing more," I said, surprised by his question. The Prophet did not need money to purchase anything. He was the master and lord of the Arab nation, and whatever he desired his followers would have gladly given him without recompense.

But he was, as usual, not thinking about himself.

"Give them to the poor," he said, and I saw in his eyes that he wished his request to be carried out immediately.

I rose and went to a corner of my apartment. Under a loose stone I had buried a handful of coins that were the sum total of the wealth my husband, the king of Arabia, possessed.

I took the gold and saw Ali step forward, ready to take the coins from me and fulfill the Messenger's wishes. But I turned away from him and placed the coins in the hands of Abbas, who nodded and left to hand them out to the poor souls who still gathered at the Bench seeking alms.

I could feel Ali's intense green eyes on me, and then he turned and followed Abbas out without a word.

― ― ―

A FEW HOURS LATER, I heard the melodious voice of Bilal echoing in the courtyard as he summoned the believers to noon prayers. At the lyrical calls of the *Azan*, my husband's eyes opened and he rose from the bed. I looked at him in surprise and saw that his face was bathed in sweat and his graying hair shimmered with perspiration. And then I clapped my hands in joy and praised God.

The fever had broken. The Messenger of God had recovered.

I went to his side and wiped his brow with the hem of my skirt. I urged him to lie back down and rest. But he ignored me and changed into a clean white robe and reached for a stone pitcher from which he performed his ritual ablutions.

And then my husband stepped outside, standing tall and erect like the man he had always been. The worshipers had already gathered in

straight lines behind Abu Bakr, who had led the prayers at the Masjid
in the Prophet's absence. But at the surprising sight of the Prophet
emerging from my room, looking refreshed and recuperated, there was
a tumult of shouts as the believers broke ranks and hurried to surround
the man who had become the center of their whole world.

I watched from behind my hastily donned veil as the Prophet
strode through the excited crowd to Abu Bakr's side. My father looked
at him with tear-filled eyes and stepped back, gesturing for the Messenger to take his place at the head of the *jamaat*. But my husband
shook his head.

"Lead the prayers," Muhammad said to my father, clasping his old
friend's shoulder.

Abu Bakr blinked in confusion.

"I cannot lead you in prayer. You are my master," my father said, his
voice trembling with emotion.

"Lead the prayer," my husband repeated.

Abu Bakr hesitated and then returned to his place as imam of
the Masjid. The worshipers quickly gathered behind him in perfectly
straight lines, shoulder to shoulder, the feet of each man touching the
feet of his neighbors in spiritual equality.

And then the Messenger of God moved to sit to the right of my
father and prayed beside him. It was a strange sight, for never in my life
had I seen the Prophet, our leader, pray beside any man. And then I felt
my stomach twist in apprehension as I realized how the community
would interpret this action and what it would mean for my gentle-
hearted father, who had no desire for any authority in this world.

When the prayer was over, the Messenger rose and embraced Abu
Bakr, kissing his cheeks warmly. And then he walked slowly back to
my apartment, surrounded by throngs of adoring followers. As he
approached the threshold of my door, I saw his face and my breath
stopped. There was a white light shining on his features unlike any I
had ever seen before. It was as if he were glowing like the moon, and
suddenly the years fell from Muhammad's face and he looked younger
than I had ever known him. He was no longer a stately old man but a
youth filled with boundless life and energy. It was as if I were seeing
him in the days before the Revelation, as Khadija would have seen him
in the early days of their union almost forty years before. He smiled at
me, and in that moment I fell in love with him all over again.

The Messenger stopped at my door and turned to face the excited crowd of believers. He looked at them with such joy, as if each of them were the most precious person on earth to him. He raised his hand to them as if waving farewell and then turned and joined me alone in our apartment.

46

The Messenger lay down with his head against my breast. He breathed slowly and deeply, as if savoring every single breath. I felt his hand searching for mine and I squeezed his palm. His fingers caressed mine steadily, and then he lifted his face for a moment to look at me.

I looked into his black eyes, which seemed farther away than ever, and I had a strange sensation that wherever he was, I would not be able to join him. Gazing into those obsidian pupils, I saw myself reflected in their unblinking gaze. How different I looked from that little girl on her wedding night! I was nineteen years old now, tall and slender, my waist tightly curving into the muscles of my hips, my breasts full and generous, yet still untouched by an infant's lips. It was strange seeing myself as a woman and stranger knowing that in my heart I was still a child.

The Messenger leaned close to me and we kissed. It was long and deep, and I felt my heart pouring into him. I held him close, not wanting to ever let him go. And after an eternity that was only a moment, he broke away and leaned his head so that his face was pressed against my gently beating heart.

I heard footsteps and I saw my elder brother, reconciled with his family and renamed Abdal Rahman, enter the room and greet the Messenger. Seeing my husband and me entwined in an embrace, he flushed in embarrassment and turned to leave.

And then I saw my husband raise his hand and point toward something Abdal Rahman held in his grip. A *miswak,* a rough toothbrush carved out of olive twigs. I saw my husband looking at the small instrument with surprising intensity and I gently asked my brother to hand it to me. Abdal Rahman did so readily and kissed the Messenger's hands before leaving us alone.

I chewed on the *miswak* and moistened the rough bristles with my saliva. And then I handed the toothbrush to my husband, who began to brush his teeth with great vigor.

When he was done, he handed this *miswak* back to me and leaned against my bosom, closing his eyes. His breathing slowed and became rhythmic, and I assumed he must have fallen asleep.

I don't know how long we lay like that together, two lovers who had been thrown together in a mad world and had somehow managed to come out of the chaos still bonded at the heart. After so many years of hardship and struggle, I finally felt at peace.

It was a moment that I wanted to last forever. And yet, like everything in this fleeting world, it came to an end.

I felt my husband stir and he opened his eyes. But instead of turning to me, his gaze fell upon an empty corner of the room. And then I had a strange sensation that we were not alone. There was a Presence in the apartment, and I felt the hairs on my neck stand up.

And then the Messenger spoke, his voice loud and clear and strong.

"No," he said, as if responding to a question. "I choose the supreme communion in Paradise . . . with those upon whom God has showered His favors . . . the prophets and the saints and the martyrs and the righteous . . . most excellent for communion are they . . ."

And then I remembered what he had said to me years before. That prophets were given the choice at the moment of death whether to remain in the mortal realm or return to their Maker.

My heart began to pound wildly as I understood that the angel had given him the choice at last. And he had chosen eternity.

I wanted to scream, but no sound came out of my throat. I was frozen to the spot, unable to move as the shock of what was happening hit me in the stomach.

Muhammad, the Messenger of God, the man I loved more than any other in the world, was dying in my arms.

"O God . . ." I heard him say, his voice now faint and distant. "With the supreme communion . . . "

And then Muhammad's eyes closed and I felt the last breath

emerge from his breast and fly away to heaven, like a caged dove set free, soaring back to the openness that was its joyous home.

His head grew heavy against my heart and he was gone.

I held the lifeless body of Muhammad in my arms. Tears streamed down my cheeks in rivulets, and I rocked back and forth, like a mother singing a lullaby to her baby.

I don't know how long I sat there. But something in my broken heart finally moved me to let him go, to let my love lie in peace. I pulled away from him and set his corpse down on the lambskin mat that had been the sanctuary of our love. His face looked up at me, more beautiful in death than it had been even in life, the lips curled slightly in a serene smile.

And then the dam of grief burst and I screamed, my cries echoing through the streets of Medina and telling the whole world the tragic news.

Muhammad ibn Abdallah, the last Prophet of God to mankind, was dead.

47

Abu Bakr pushed his way through the crowd that had flowed out from the Masjid into the streets of the oasis. He managed to jostle his way into the courtyard, where he found Uthman sitting on the ground, sobbing like a little boy.

"What has happened?" Abu Bakr's heart filled with dread at the answer he feared was coming, but Uthman remained silent, wiping his eyes and looking around like a lost child seeking its mother.

Realizing that Uthman was in no state to talk, Abu Bakr turned and saw Ali standing nearby, oddly looking away from the crowd and staring across the horizon. The old man moved to Ali's side, pushing aside a youth who was laughing like a madman even as thick tears flowed from his eyes.

Ali stared straight ahead, as if gazing into eternity with his other-worldly vision. He did not seem to notice Abu Bakr come up to him, and the elderly minister finally laid a hand on Ali's shoulder and shook him as if awakening him from a reverie.

"Tell me," Abu Bakr said simply.

Ali blinked several times, but his green eyes still flickered with confusion. And when he spoke, his voice sounded odd and distant.

"They say the Messenger—may God's blessings and peace be upon him—has passed away," Ali said, confirming Abu Bakr's worst fears. And then he returned his gaze to the horizon. "But that is strange . . . because I can still see him . . ."

Abu Bakr felt a chill go down his spine. And then a loud shout caused him to turn his head and he saw that Umar was standing on the *minbar*, the small platform from where the Messenger had given his sermons. He brandished a terrifying sword above his head and called for the attention of the believers, who soon massed around the towering figure.

"It is a lie!" Umar bellowed, his eyes bulging with madness. "The Messenger lives! He has only gone to commune with his Lord! Even as he did when he rose to heaven on *Lailat-ul-Mi'raj*!"

The crowd rumbled at Umar's words, and many cried out in support of his claim. The Messenger of God was not dead. His soul was traveling through the heavenly spheres as it had done before and would shortly return to revive his body.

It was a dream and a fantasy, and it was what they wanted to hear. And yet Abu Bakr had long ago learned the painful lesson that wishful thinking and reality were often desperately at odds.

He turned and stepped inside his daughter's home to see the terrible truth for himself.

◦ ◦ ◦

I SAT IN THE corner, shaking violently as the other Mothers gathered around me, their loud wails tearing the hole in my heart even wider. And then a shadow fell across the threshold and I saw my father enter, hunched and weary with age. His eyes immediately fell upon the figure of the Prophet, which lay on my bedspread covered in his favorite green cloak.

Somehow I managed to get to my feet and run into his arms. He held me tight as I wept like a little girl, patting my hair gently as he used to do when I would skin my knee racing down the streets of Mecca a lifetime ago.

And then he stepped back and let me go, his attention fully on the unmoving outline of the Messenger's body. My father approached the shrouded corpse slowly, and then, with great reverence, he lifted the cloak from my husband's face. I watched through blurred eyes as Abu Bakr leaned close and checked the vein in Muhammad's neck for a pulse and then his chest for any fleeting heartbeat. Abu Bakr finally put his ear close to my husband's lips in search of any sign of breath. My father finally sighed and lifted his head, gazing down at the body of the man who had changed his life and the world.

And then he leaned down and kissed the Messenger on the forehead.

"Dearer than my mother and my father, you have tasted the death that God has decreed for you," he said as tears streamed down his wrinkled cheeks. "No death after this will ever befall you."

My father placed the cloak back over the body and turned to walk out. Not knowing what else to do and not wishing to spend another moment in the grief-stricken company of the other wives, I wrapped my face behind my veil and followed him into the courtyard.

The first thing I saw was Umar, waving a sword from the pulpit and shouting like a madman, his voice became increasingly hoarse from his cries.

"Those who say the Messenger of God is dead are like the Children of Israel, who proclaimed Moses dead when he climbed the mountain to speak with his Lord! And like those faithless cowards at Sinai, those who spread the lie against their Prophet will be killed! We will cut off the hands and feet of the traitors!"

My father stepped forward and called out to his friend, who had by now clearly taken leave of his senses.

"Gently, Umar. Calm yourself."

But Umar ignored him. He continued ranting and raving about the various creative tortures he would impose on any man who dared to say that Muhammad had died.

My father shook his head sadly and then raised his voice, his measured words booming with authority.

"Listen to me, my brothers," Abu Bakr called out, and suddenly all attention was upon him. I saw the terrified and grief-stricken people of Medina look upon my father, the first adult man to embrace Islam and Muhammad's childhood friend and closest adviser. Their eyes were pleading for him to end their pain, to show them light and lead them out of the darkness of uncertainty that covered them from all sides.

And then my father spoke the words by which he would be forever remembered, the words he had been born to say.

"If anyone worships Muhammad, know that Muhammad is dead. If anyone worships God, know that God lives and will never die."

A deep silence fell upon the crowd as the awesome, undeniable Truth was said at last aloud.

And then my father recited a verse from the holy Qur'an that had been revealed years before, during the aftermath of Uhud, when the Messenger had nearly met his death on the battlefield. It was a verse that I knew by heart, but it had somehow been forgotten in the midst of the madness of the past few hours.

Muhammad is just a messenger
And messengers have passed away before him.
If he dies or is killed
Will you turn on your heels?
Whoso turns on his heels will not hurt God.
And God will reward the thankful.

The Muslims gazed at one another in wonder, as if they had never heard these verses before. I saw the desperation in their eyes fade away, replaced by deep sadness that was nonetheless buttressed by the indomitable power of faith. And then I heard a terrible cry like that of a cat being strangled and my eyes flew to Umar. The power of God's Word had penetrated the cloud of his madness, and he was standing bereft and alone on the *minbar*. And then the sword slipped out of his grasp and landed on the earthen floor of the Masjid with a clang. Umar fell to his knees and buried his mighty face in his hands and wept like a child.

As the truth finally sank into our souls, the claws of panic released their grip on our hearts, and then the flow of tears began in earnest. Tears of loss, but not of despair.

We knew now that the journey of Muhammad had come to an end.

But the journey of Islam was just beginning.

Book four

Birth
of an
Empire

1

uhammad was dead, but the *Ummah* was very much alive and in desperate need of leadership. The next several hours were chaotic, as word spread through the oasis of the Prophet's passing and various factions attempted to assert their own agendas. And then word came to the Masjid that the tribal elders of the oasis were gathering in the ancient meeting hall of the Bani Sa'idah, where they had forged their ever-shifting allegiances in the days before Islam. The old clans of Medina were apparently planning to choose one of their own for the leadership of the community, and they had pointedly met without inviting any of the immigrants from Mecca, those who had stood by the Prophet from the beginning.

Upon hearing this, Umar flew into a new rage and grabbed my father by the arm, urging him to go and intervene before a decision was reached that would tear apart the *Ummah*. A Companion named Abu Ubayda, a respected Muslim from the tribe of Quraysh, joined them as they turned to face this new crisis. As my father and the other men hurried along to the old meeting hall, a thought flashed through my mind that Ali would likely have desired to attend as well. He had retired to grieve in his house with Fatima and their sons, and Talha and Zubayr were with him. For an instant, I wondered if I should send a messenger to Ali's house to inform the others of the tribal conference under way. And then I felt that old flash of bitterness at Ali's betrayal, and the thought quickly fled my mind.

＊　＊　＊

UMAR PUSHED HIS WAY through the heavy bronze doors that had been closed as the elders of the oasis gathered to discuss what to do now that the Messenger of God was dead. The issue that they had all been avoiding for the past several months could no longer be tabled, and a successor to the leadership of the community had to be selected.

And it was an issue that remained as contentious as it had always been. Umar scowled at the sight of the tribal chiefs arguing angrily, each selfishly asserting his own claims to power. The room was packed and tempers were clearly rising as the rival tribes of Aws and Khazraj jockeyed for position. The Prophet had spent years working master-fully to bring these disparate and antagonistic peoples together, and the moment he was gone, they were ready to backslide into old feuds and enmity.

Abu Bakr stood beside him, looking at the loudly arguing men with sadness. Umar knew that his friend's heart was broken to see the cruel divisions of the past reassert themselves. Abu Bakr had always seen himself as a doting father over the Muslim community, and it must have been agonizing for him to watch people he loved like chil-dren fighting bitterly, the civility of the recent years torn apart with the opening of old wounds that only Muhammad had been able to heal.

The stone hall was held up by dozens of sturdy pillars, and Abu Bakr leaned against one to steady himself.

"Listen to me, my brothers," he said. But his hoarse voice was lost in the tumult of dispute and heated emotion. The old man took a deep breath as if trying to find the energy to speak over the maddening roar of the crowd, and then tried again, but to no avail.

Umar felt his blood pound in his ears, and then he strode for-ward into the middle of the room and raised his thick hands above his head.

"Silence!" he cried out with such thunder that the windows shook. A pall instantly fell over the startled crowd and all eyes were upon him. He noticed that some of the tribal leaders were surprised, even irri-tated, to see that the Meccan immigrants had learned of this semisecret council. But if any wished him to leave, none had the courage to say so now.

Umar turned to Abu Bakr and nodded. The old man strolled for-ward into the room, his back hunched over more than usual, as if his bones could no longer hold up the weight of responsibility that he had carried for so many years.

"Listen to me, brothers," Abu Bakr said, his voice hoarse but clear. "We are at a dangerous moment, when Satan will seek to mislead us, to tear apart what God has brought together. It is the time for measured judgments, not decisions made in the heat of passion."

At Abu Bakr's carefully chosen words, Umar felt the tension in the crowd ease slightly. Abu Bakr continued, gently praising the Ansar, the natives of Medina who had taken in the Prophet and his sorry band of refugees a decade before. He acknowledged that had it not been for the generosity of men like the tribal elders who were gathered here now, Islam would have died. Instead, the religion had prospered and had conquered all of Arabia, and Medina had gone from a backward and forgotten town to the capital of a new nation. A nation that was now facing new threats, from both rebels within and the great powers on its borders. What was needed now was a leader who could hold together the disparate tribes and guide the Muslims through the uncertain days ahead.

"Medina is the capital of Arabia, but the nation's heart remains in Mecca," my father said slowly, his eyes peering at the faces of the elders. "If the Arab nation is to remain unified, its leadership must remain in the hands of Quraysh, the only tribe that has the prestige and the resources to keep the smaller tribes united under its command."

Abu Bakr's words were met with silence. Then a tribal leader named Sa'd ibn Ubadah stepped forward. He was the head of the Abu Sai'dah clan, in whose hall they were meeting, and he had been one of the most prominent candidates for leadership whose name was being bandied about by the council before Abu Bakr had spoken. Umar tensed, knowing that Sa'd held in his hands the ability to rip apart the Muslim community or to bring it together

And then, to Umar's surprise, the tribal elder chose the latter.

"You're right," the gray-haired Sa'd said, nodding to Abu Bakr. "The men of Medina have played their part in the destiny of Islam, and it is a hallowed role for which we will be remembered. But our hands are too small to hold the reins of Arabia."

It was a stunning admission and a capitulation of authority that would have been unthinkable years before. At that moment, Umar realized that the Prophet's legacy was very much alive and their people would survive. Islam was like the sea—even when the surface appeared torn apart by the storms of time, at its heart it remained calm and serene.

There was silence for a long moment. And then other chieftains stepped forward and nodded, accepting the truth of Abu Bakr's words and joining Sa'd in renouncing their claims to power.

And then Umar felt Abu Bakr take his hand and pull him forward and he turned to see that the old man had done the same with their friend Abu Ubayda.

"I offer you these two men from Quraysh, men of nobility and character who can keep the *Ummah* united and spread the message of Islam to the world," Abu Bakr said, holding Umar and Abu Ubayda's hands high. "Pledge your allegiance to whichever you will."

Umar was shocked, and he glanced at Abu Ubayda, who looked utterly terrified. Neither of these men had expected that Abu Bakr would nominate them for the leadership of Islam. Umar felt tears welling in his eyes at his friend's loyalty and belief in him, this gentle old man who had no ambitions of his own, no desire for power over others. A man of such honesty and integrity that the Prophet had named him *As-Siddiq*, the Witness to Truth, and had trusted him as his sole companion in the cave while the assassins hunted him in the desert.

Abu Bakr. A man whom the Prophet had made his right hand in administering the daily needs of the *Ummah*, a man who had been wealthy and had given everything he had to free slaves and feed the poor. A man who lived like a pauper when he should have been clothed in the riches of power. A man who was loved by everyone and hated by none.

A man whom the Prophet had appointed to lead the prayers just before he died. A man for whom the Messenger of God had set aside his own position as imam and had prayed beside in the final hour of his life.

And then, like a bolt of lightning striking his heart, Umar knew what needed to be done. He lowered his hand and spoke words that seemed to come from someplace deeper than his own heart.

"O Ansar!" he cried out, his voice trembling with emotion. "Do you not know that the Messenger of God himself ordered Abu Bakr to lead the prayer?"

There was a stir of assent, and Umar saw Abu Bakr frown, giving him a warning look to stop. But Umar could not have stopped even if he'd wanted to. Something had taken possession of his soul, and the words erupted from inside of him, like the first shoot of life rising up from the dead earth after a rainstorm, signaling the beginning of a new era.

"Then who among you would dare take precedence over him?" Umar asked. There was a moment of awed silence as Umar's words sank into their souls. And the son of al-Khattab, a man who had been a monster and a murderer in another life and was now a revered and honored leader among men, took Abu Bakr's right hand in his and proudly pledged his allegiance to his friend.

Abu Bakr turned pale white and began to protest. But it was too late. Umar's actions had stirred the emotions of the crowd, and suddenly the entire room descended on Abu Bakr. The reluctant old man was surrounded by the elders of Medina as they unanimously pledged their loyalty to him and proclaimed him *Khalifat Rasulallah*, the Caliph, or Vice-regent, of the Messenger of God.

——— • ——— • ———

I WAS KEEPING VIGIL over the Messenger's body when I learned of the council's decision to elect my father as the new leader of the community. And I grieved. For he was an old man, tired and weary of the world, with no love of power. And yet his new role as Caliph would place him in the deadly path of others whose ambitions had been frustrated. Every decision he made would be scrutinized by his rivals and he would inevitably be compared unfavorably with the Messenger, who had been the most brilliant statesman the Arabs had ever seen. Ruthless men would be eagerly waiting for him to make a mistake, their daggers sharpened both figuratively and literally. It was a terrible and thankless position.

But whatever my doubts, the men of Medina did not appear to share them. As word spread of Abu Bakr's accession to power, crowds gathered outside his house and mobbed him with their enthusiasm, the Muslims lining up to pledge their loyalty to the man whom the Messenger had honored in the final moments of his life.

Every household in Medina sent representatives to pledge their fealty and support of the new Caliph. Every household except one.

Shortly after Abu Bakr had been chosen, Umar and the crowd of elders exited the ancient hall and headed immediately toward the small stone hut where Ali and Fatima lived with their sons. Umar pounded on the simple door of palm wood, demanding that Ali come out and pledge allegiance to my father, whose face was dark with embarrassment at the fervor of the mob.

When Ali emerged, he looked at the Muslims with his unreadable green eyes and listened as Umar announced what had transpired.

"Abu Bakr has been chosen," Umar said. "Give him your hand."

Ali remained rooted to the spot and made no sign of moving to my father's side.

"You have made this decision without consulting the Family of the Messenger," he said softly, a hint of hurt in his voice. The matter that had been on the minds of everyone that day, whether Ali would assert his own claim to power, had been settled in the least gracious fashion possible—by excluding him from the deliberations and denying him the opportunity to make his case.

Umar scowled, realizing that Ali had reason to feel insulted but refusing to budge from the conviction of his own heart.

"Even so, the decision has been made," Umar said. "Give him your pledge of loyalty." A hint of danger had entered his voice. If Ali chose now to challenge Abu Bakr's appointment by the council, the *Ummah* would be torn apart and the demons of civil war would soon be upon us.

Ali looked at the towering Umar, gazing deeply into his eyes. Few men would have been able to withstand the glance of either of these powerful men, and seeing them staring each other down was like watching two rams preparing for battle.

And then a shadow fell between them and the Prophet's daughter Fatima appeared as if out of nowhere. She took her husband's hand in hers and squeezed it tight, and then turned to face Umar, who towered a head above her.

"Leave us," she said, her eyes burning with an anger that no one had ever seen before on her gentle face. Umar stepped back as if he had been stabbed in the gut

My father immediately placed himself between them, seeking to prevent the tensions from escalating

"I apologize to the People of the House," the new Caliph said. "May God shower his blessings forever on the Family of the Messenger."

Fatima looked at Abu Bakr, her black eyes still burning. And then, without another word, she guided her husband back inside and slammed the door on the crowd.

- - -

ALI DID NOT PLEDGE his allegiance to my father that day, a fact that only increased my dislike for him. As long as he stood aloof, Abu Bakr could not reign in security, for the threat of rebellion from the Prophet's bloodline would hang over him like a bitter and deadly sword. His legitimacy would remain in question, and the vultures that were even now gathering would move closer, ready to swoop in and destroy him.

But as the sun finally set on that terrible day, Ali emerged from his household and came to my apartment to help make plans for the Prophet's burial. Fatima was with him, and though I refused even to look at Ali, I gave the Messenger's daughter a deep embrace. Whatever poison existed between her husband and me, Fatima had always been kind to me and I felt nothing but respect for this sweet girl. She held me tight as I wept over the loss of the man we had both loved, but she did not tremble with tears like the other women and was, in fact, strangely calm. I assumed that she was in a state of shock or denial and that the tears would come when the truth finally sank into her heart. But as the hours passed and she remained resigned and dignified, I finally asked her about her restraint in the face of her father's death. She gave me a strange smile and said she had no reason to grieve, as she would be joining him soon. It was an odd and unnerving comment, but then she was an odd and unnerving woman, and I decided to leave her be.

The immediate concern was what to do with the Prophet's corpse. In normal Muslim tradition, the body of the deceased was washed ritually before it was shrouded, except in the case of martyrs, whose blood was considered a sign of eternal glory. The Prophet had not died on the battlefield and yet there was much hesitation to strip him bare and wash him like any other man. I myself had never gazed upon the Prophet's naked body, for he was exceedingly modest, as I have said, and even when we made love, it was under the cover of darkness.

As the men stood and argued about what to do, we heard a voice say loudly: "Wash the Messenger with his clothes on." It was a deep voice of great authority and I thought at first that Umar had entered while we were talking. And yet when we turned to look, there was no one there but us. I felt my heart begin to race and I saw the frightened look on the others' faces. But the words had been distinct and clear, and Zubayr went out and filled a pail of water from the ablution pool, which Ali then poured over the Messenger's body, washing him and his garments clean one last time. The men then shrouded my husband in three layers of cloth, the first two of plain white Yemeni linen and the third a green-striped mantle that the Prophet had often worn.

I watched with a broken heart as Ali, Talha, and Zubayr placed the soft cloth over Muhammad's gentle face, and I felt my eyes blur with grief as I realized that I would never see those beautiful features again, at least not until Judgment Day.

And then, when he was completely covered by the shroud, a new and more animated argument began as to where the Messenger of God should be buried. Some suggested that he should be placed in *Jannat al-Baqi*, the main cemetery of the oasis, next to his son Ibrahim. Others suggested that we take his body back to Mecca, where he could be buried beside Khadija. But the teachings of Islam called upon believers to inter the dead within one day, and the journey to Mecca was at least twenty by camel. A few contended that he should be buried by his uncle Hamza on the battlefield of Uhud or that a separate tomb should be erected at the outskirts of the city.

And then I heard a voice behind the men, and this time it was no mysterious angelic presence. My father stepped into my crowded apartment and wiped his eyes as he looked down on the shrouded figure who had been his best friend and master.

"The Messenger of God once told me that no prophet dies except that he is buried where he dies," Abu Bakr said softly and then glanced at Ali. After a moment, the young man nodded his agreement.

That night, my apartment was turned into a tomb. Abu Bakr organized a small group of trusted Muslims to bring shovels and pickaxes, and they dug a grave directly under the spot where the Messenger had passed away in my arms. There was no grand ceremony, and most of the city was unaware of what was happening. Abu Bakr had wisely reasoned that emotions were still running high and a public funeral could still incite passions that would be difficult to contain.

The handful of believers privy to the secret burial stood behind the Prophet's body and prayed the funeral prayer. My father refused to lead the *janaza* prayer over the body, an act of presumption in his eyes, and he moved to stand beside Umar, Uthman, and Ali in a straight line behind the shrouded corpse.

And then, when the rituals were complete and there was nothing left to be said or done, Ali climbed down into the grave and my husband's body was gently lowered into his arms. He placed the body on its right shoulder, as was the custom, with the face pointing south to Mecca.

And then as the believers poured dust over the body until it was completely covered, Muhammad vanished into the earth from which our father Adam had been born.

2

𝓘n the months following the Messenger's death, my father was forced to face the first challenge of his caliphate: the rebellion of the Bedouin tribes. With Muhammad dead, many of the southern tribes declared that their treaties with the nascent Arabian state had been nullified and that they no longer felt bound by the authority of Medina. Some openly declared their apostasy, returning to the worship of the old gods. Others, perhaps realizing that the ancient practices were pointless now that Mecca itself had banned all idols, declared that they remained believers but refused to pay the *zakat,* the tax that was levied on the citizens to provide for the poor. But a few posed a greater problem, for they had joined forces with Musaylima and Sajah, the two false prophets who now declared themselves to be speaking in God's name. The two pretenders to the mantle of prophecy had married and had brought their followers together in an alliance against Medina.

Of all the troublesome rebels, that last group was the most immediate danger. For the central tenet of Islam was that Muhammad was the final prophet of God. Any who arose after him were impostors who had to be defeated before they misled the people. And Musaylima was no wandering madman spouting prophecies. He had gathered the disaffected tribes of the eastern Najd to his side, and our spies estimated that he was amassing a force of almost forty thousand tribesmen, the largest army ever to assemble in the sands of Arabia.

And so my father dispatched Khalid ibn al-Waleed, the man my husband had proclaimed as the Sword of Allah, to face this new and grave threat to the future of Islam. Khalid's forces confronted Musaylima's armies at Yamamah, in the heart of eastern Arabia. Although numbering only thirteen thousand men, Khalid's forces were better organized and disciplined than the tribal fighters. Khalid divided the troops into three wings and took personal command of the center. The battle was brutal, but the Muslims had the advantage of zeal and an utter fearlessness in the face of death that unnerved the Bedouins. The tribesmen scattered, leaving Musaylima only seven thousand fanatically loyal men, who walled themselves inside a garden. A foolish mistake, for now they were trapped and surrounded on all sides. Muslim warriors scaled the walls and broke down the doors, flooding into the enclave, which would forever after be known as the Garden of Death. The followers of the false prophet were massacred, and Musaylima himself was killed, struck down by Wahsi's infamous javelin. The Abyssinian slave who had murdered Hamza had finally cleansed himself of his sin. Sajah, Musaylima's wife and fellow claimant to prophecy, was captured and quickly embraced Islam. Khalid let her go, and she vanished into the desert.

With the death of Musaylima, the fire of the old pagan ways was quenched in Arabia. My father had successfully managed to quell the revolt of the Arab tribes. He had gained the trust and respect of the Muslims and was now busy administering the affairs of state. One of the thorniest issues he faced was dealing with my husband's estate. Though Muhammad had died having given all of his worldly wealth and possessions away to the poor, there were several tracts of land, small gardens in Khaybar and the nearby oasis of Fadak, that had been spoils of war after the defeat of the Jews of Arabia. My husband had administered these lands while he was alive, feeding his family and the needy with the produce of the gardens. One day Fatima came to Abu Bakr and asked that these gardens be relinquished to her and her children as her inheritance. The People of the House were desperately poor, despite being the only surviving bloodline of the Prophet, and the gardens would help them ease the daily struggle to put food on their table.

My father was in an awkward position, and he gently told Fatima that the Messenger had once said to him that prophets leave behind no inheritance, that all their wealth should be given to the community. It was a comment that Muhammad had made to me in passing as well, and I spoke up in support of my father's judgment. But Fatima was livid, claiming that Abu Bakr was stealing her patrimony, and she stormed out of my father's house, leaving him heartbroken. He had done what he thought was the right thing according to his best understanding of the Prophet's wishes, but it had only increased the chasm of pain that had opened up between him and the Messenger's family.

Shortly thereafter, my father tried to reach a compromise. He learned that a Jew from Bani Nadir who had converted to Islam had died childless and had left the Prophet seven small garden plots in Medina in his will. Abu Bakr appointed Ali and the Prophet's uncle Abbas to administer the gardens on behalf of the Messenger's descendants. But Fatima refused to be reconciled by this gesture. She never spoke to my father after that day when he had first refused her claim to inheritance, despite his repeated overtures. Abu Bakr once told me that of all the things he had lost in the course of his life—his wealth, his youth, his health—nothing grieved him more than his estrangement from the sweet girl whom he had always loved like his own daughter.

+ + +

ONE NIGHT, SIX MONTHS after Muhammad died, I lay in my bed, hovering on the edge of sleep. I tossed and turned on the sheepskin mattress on which I could still sometimes smell the scent of my husband, the strange aura of roses that always seemed to follow him in life. It had taken me some time to get used to sleeping in my apartment again, knowing that the Messenger was buried only a few feet away. But I had eventually grown accustomed to the strange feeling that I was never quite alone, that he was very much there with me, and not just in a metaphorical sense.

There was a heaviness in the room, as if the air itself had changed since the day he died, and eventually, as I learned to fall asleep again in the apartment, I started having vivid dreams, filled with strange and beautiful lights and colors I had never imagined. I would often wake up in the middle of the night thinking I had heard his voice or felt the touch of his cool hand on my hair. Over time, these experiences became part of my daily life and I eventually accepted them without question, if only to keep my sanity. But in the early days, it had been difficult and frightening, as if I were living in a portal between two worlds, and I was never quite sure which one I was in at any given moment.

And then on that cool winter night, something happened that I have never forgotten, something that still sends chills down my spine when I think of it. The heaviness in the air had grown almost intolerable, and I found that I had to breathe in deeper and deeper just to fill my lungs. It was as if a thick curtain were falling down on top of me, and I found it hard to move, as if I were being tied down by invisible ropes.

I struggled against the pressure, like a drowning woman deep underwater and desperately trying to rise to the surface to breathe. And then I heard a woman's voice, which I thought must be coming from the courtyard of the Masjid. But the voice grew closer and clearer and I realized that it was whispering right beside me. Despite the heavy air that was holding me down, I managed to turn my head and look.

And I saw Fatima standing a few feet away. She was dressed in silvery white robes, her hair covered in a scarf that seemed to be glittering with stars. She was standing above her father's grave, speaking words to him that I could not understand. The language was not Arabic, nor did it sound like the foreign tongues I had heard spoken in the marketplace—Persian, Greek, Amharic, Coptic. In fact, I could not say that she was speaking words at all. The sounds that were coming out of her lips were rhythmic and lyrical, almost like a song rather than speech.

I wanted to call out to her, to ask why she had come in the middle of the night, whether everything was all right for her and her children. But no words came out of my mouth. I simply stared at her, transfixed, until she finally turned to look at me.

And then I felt my breathing stop altogether. I recognized her and yet, at the same time, I did not. I somehow knew that the woman standing before me was Fatima, but her face had been wondrously transformed. Gone were the plain, harsh features, the long face that was always drawn in sadness. And in its place was the face of a new Fatima, a woman of such intense beauty and perfection that she no longer looked human. She had become what I had imagined an angel to be when I was a child. Her skin, which had often suffered from rashes and pimples, was now flawless and her cheekbones were crafted with such perfection that she looked like a living statue. Her eyebrows, once thick and unruly, looked as if they had been painted on her face. Her lips were no longer chapped, but full and sensuous, and her unruly hair now flowed like honey around her delicate shoulders, which had once been mannish and square.

The only thing about her that was unchanged was her eyes, the same black eyes that had belonged to her father, eyes that looked as if they could see deep into the farthest reaches of your soul.

She looked at me with those luminous eyes and smiled. And when she spoke, her voice sounded like the tinkling of bells.

"Tell your father that I understand now," she said, and her words echoed as if she were calling to me from across a great chasm. "I understand and I forgive."

Then she raised her right hand to me as if waving farewell. And my heart skipped a beat when I saw that in the center of her palm was what looked like a glowing blue orb shaped like an eye.

I stared into the swirling light at the palm of her hand as it grew brighter and brighter, until my entire room was bathed in its ethereal shine. The darkness of my room vanished in the cascade of wondrous azure light, as bright as heaven itself on a cloudless summer day.

⇀ ⇀ ⇀

I WOKE WITH A start to hear cries of grief from the courtyard. I looked around in confusion, expecting to see Fatima standing in the corner, but I was very much alone. As the sound of weeping intensified, I threw on a cloak and wrapped my face hastily behind a veil before peering outside.

A crowd of what looked like mourners had gathered in the courtyard, tearing at their clothes and wailing in sorrow.

"What is it?" I cried to them. "What has happened?"

A middle-aged woman stumbled toward me, slapping her breast and pulling at her hair.

"O Mother, the *Ummah* is bereft! Fatima the Shining has returned to our Lord!"

I felt my knees grow weak.

"When?" I managed to croak out. "When did this happen?"

An elderly man looked at me, his wrinkled face twisted in pain.

"Our master Ali said she died at sunset yesterday," he sobbed. "He buried her in secret so that no man would worship her grave as the ignorant did of old."

I sank to the ground, not able to comprehend what he'd just said. If Fatima had died the evening before, who had I seen in my room later that night?

No. I had imagined it. It was a dream, I told myself, nothing more, nothing less.

And then I remembered something that Fatima had said to me once when we were young girls in Mecca, a lifetime ago. I had told her that I had suffered through a bad dream the night before, one where I was being chased by a frightening old hag wearing a golden snake on her arm.

Fatima had simply shrugged and said not to worry. It was just a dream and no more real than anything else in life.

"What do you mean?" I asked, questioning her strange comment.

And then Fatima had fixed me with those powerful black eyes and spoke words that now echoed across the bridge of time.

"Life itself is a dream. When we die, we awake."

3

Shortly after Fatima passed away, Ali went to my father and publicly reconciled with him. He told Abu Bakr that he bore no bitterness toward him and did not dispute his right to authority. He had withheld his endorsement, Ali said, as he felt that the family of the Prophet had been excluded in the handling of the succession. But the matter was done and Ali wished no more ill will between the House of the Messenger and the House of the Caliph. With the loss of Fatima, the Prophet's young grandsons were motherless and Ali wanted to dedicate his time to raising them and spreading Islam through teaching. Abu Bakr was welcome to shoulder the burdens of the nation in his stead.

My father had wept and embraced the young man, and even my stone heart softened toward him slightly. Despite my inability to forgive him for betraying me, I felt sorry for Ali, who had, in the aftermath of the Prophet's death, lost everything. As long as the Messenger had been alive, Ali had been one of the most prominent and influential members of the community. But since my husband's death and the controversy around Ali's refusal to swear allegiance to Abu Bakr, he had become increasingly isolated. His strange and awkward personality, tolerated during Muhammad's lifetime, now made people wary, and he spent most of his days alone, tending to the plot of land that Abu Bakr had agreed to give him in trust. Ali had few friends, and only Talha and Zubayr could be considered regular visitors to his home. And now, with the death of Fatima, he was truly alone.

Abu Bakr led Ali out before the believers in the Masjid after Friday prayers, and the son-in-law of the Prophet clasped the right hand of the father-in-law of the Prophet and swore his loyalty. There were audible sighs of relief and cries of praise to God, for the uncertainty that had hung over my father's reign, the nagging question of legitimacy, had finally been resolved.

At least in the hearts of most people. A few passionate supporters of Ali continued to grumble that the right of Muhammad's bloodline had been usurped and that Ali remained the rightful claimant to the throne of the Muslims. Ali himself did not publicly endorse such talk, but I remained suspicious that he was not doing enough to silence these malcontents.

And then news came from Khalid in the east that made us all forget our squabbles and turn our gaze to the future of Islam.

+ + +

The Muslim defeat of Musaylima had placed our armies directly on the borders of the ancient Persian empire. The Sassanid kings had ruled this great nation for almost four hundred years, and at the height of their power, their empire held dominion from Anatolia to the Indus River. But over the past several decades, the Sassanid shahs had been locked in a brutal and destructive war with the Byzantines for control of the region.

For most of my young life, the Christians had been on the defensive. Antioch and Alexandria had fallen to the Sassanids. And then the Christians suffered the ultimate humiliation when the fire worshipers conquered Jerusalem and stole the sacred relics of the Church, including what was alleged by their priests to be the True Cross of Jesus. The Byzantines had been demoralized until the rise of the Emperor Heraclius, who had valiantly fought back against the Persians and expelled the invaders from the holy city.

The victorious Heraclius had rallied his people to take the fight to the enemy, and the Byzantines had attacked the very heart of the Persian empire, marching down the length of the Tigris River and sacking the Sassanid palace at Dastagered. Heraclius had nearly achieved his goal of taking the Persian capital at Ctesiphon, but the Persian defenders had destroyed the ancient bridges over the Nahrawan Canal, frustrating his advance. Heraclius had returned triumphantly to the seat of his own empire, but his victory was ultimately hollow. Though he had succeeded in pushing back his ancient adversaries, his army was broken by the constant warfare and the Byzantine treasury depleted.

The Sassanids were in even worse disarray, and the Persian king, Khusro, was overthrown and murdered by his own son Kavadh, who negotiated a shaky truce with the Byzantines. I remember when I first heard the news of Khusro's death from a Yemeni merchant in the marketplace of Medina. I had smiled behind my veil, for Khusro had rejected my husband's call to Islam, tearing up his letter in contempt. As the Messenger had prophesized then, his kingdom had been similarly torn in two.

The grand political events to the north provided interesting gossip, but they had been of little practical interest to the Muslims in the early years, as survival had been our primary focus. But now that Islam was established as the sole ruling force over a united Arabia, we could no more ignore the empires on our borders than they could us. These two great nations—Persian and Byzantine—had exhausted each other through centuries of warfare, and the rise of a new state in their midst presented an unexpected and dangerous threat to their delicate balance of power. Neither of the empires had the resources or energy to engage us directly, whatever threats may have rumbled from their envoys, and they were forced to use proxies in their effort to keep us in check. The Byzantines had tried to ally with the Jews of Khaybar, forcing my husband to conquer the city and use it as a defensive shield to the north. And the false prophet Musaylima was rumored to have received financing and training from the Persians to the east. But with the defeat of these quislings, the day was fast coming when our forces would come into direct contact with those of the rival empires.

And then one warm morning, a year after my husband had died, that day came. Acting upon orders from my father, Khalid sent an army of eighteen thousand men from Yamama into the fields of Persian Iraq, claiming them for Islam. The Persians responded with a force of nearly twice that size, led by elephants armored in steel. The Sassanid army was a terrifying juggernaut, the likes of which the Arabs had never before encountered, and the Arab swords and spears looked like toys compared to the mighty honed blades of the ancient Persian empire. But Khalid knew that this monstrous foe had one weakness. Mobility. The heavily shielded horses and elephants could not march for long under the hot desert sun without succumbing to exhaustion, and so he utilized the hit-and-run tactics the Messenger had perfected at Khaybar. The Muslims would ride out into the field and engage the front lines of the Persians, and then escape back into the wilderness, having goaded their adversaries into pursuit. The farther the Muslims drew the soldiers of Persia into the sands, the slower and more confused they became. By the time the Persian general Hormuz realized his tactical error, it was too late.

Khalid led the Muslims in one final charge, during which the tired and bewildered Sassanids used a standard defensive tactic that had worked for them in the past but would lead to tragedy that day. The Persian soldiers linked themselves together with chains to hold back Khalid's cavalry. They stood united like a rock in the face of the Muslim charge. This tactic had been successful against Byzantine soldiers, who had decided that a frontal attack against the chain was nothing less than suicide. But the Persians did not understand that the guarantee of death on the battlefield did not deter Muslims but only encouraged them with the promise of eternal life. To the shock of the Persian defenders, Khalid's horsemen crashed against the chained warriors without fear, immolating themselves on the lances of the Sassanids. As the Muslims continued to charge despite the wall of death, the Persians became frightened by their intensity and commitment, and panic began to spread among the dehydrated and exhausted troops. And then, when Khalid slew their commander, Hormuz, the Persian warriors tried to flee, but the chains that had been meant to hold back their enemies now became shackles that led them to their deaths.

Khalid's men destroyed the Persian force in what became known to us as the Battle of the Chains. Thousands of the Sassanids' best troops fell that day, and the Arabs had opened a door into the east. The

Muslims exploded out of the desert and soon descended on the city of al-Hira, the capital of Persian Iraq, which had been administered by Arab Christians known as Lakhmids. Khalid showered the people of al-Hira with gifts and promised the Christians that their right of worship would be protected under the laws of Islam, a guarantee that had never been given by their Persian overlords. The Lakhmids quickly capitulated, and the boundaries of Islam had in one stunning swoop extended outside of the Arabian peninsula and reached the banks of the Euphrates.

Our nation had just become an empire.

— ◆ — ◆ —

THE REJOICING IN THE streets of Medina at word of Khalid's victory was soon followed by sadness. My father fell deeply ill, and he was confined to his bed. I sensed the cloud of death that was hanging over Abu Bakr. I could not imagine a world without him any more than I could one without my husband. But in truth, I could still feel Muhammad's presence in my room and found some comfort in the intuition that he was still with me. Yet my father was just an ordinary man, and when he passed away, he would truly be gone.

Asma and I stayed by his side, night and day, nursing him through the fever. And then one morning, I saw a look on his face, a serenity and resignation that told me that his time had come.

"Call Uthman," he whispered to me.

I immediately dispatched a messenger, and within a few minutes the son of Affan arrived. As Uthman knelt beside my father, he looked older but was still remarkably handsome, and I noticed the sparkle of generosity and kindness in his eyes.

"What can I do for you, old friend?" he said, running a hand through my father's thinning white hair.

"I have a testament for the people, a final command as Caliph that I want you to deliver to them," my father said, enunciating every word carefully, his breath wheezing.

Uthman lowered his head. For a moment, I wondered if he would object, as had the Companions during Muhammad's last illness. I trembled at the thought of another chaotic struggle for succession. The Muslims had established order only because of my father's statesmanship. Would we have to endure another round of tribesmen jockeying for position? With the Muslim nation now expanding into the heart of the Persian empire, with enemies circling us like vultures over a battle-field, we could not afford another dispute over authority. And my heart chilled at the thought that the small but vocal faction that favored the right of Ali and the Prophet's grandsons might not choose to acquiesce as easily as they had done before. If Uthman refused to pass along my father's wishes, the *Ummah* could descend overnight into civil war.

Uthman finally raised his head and looked into Abu Bakr's eyes. He squeezed my father's gnarled hands and nodded.

"I will do as you wish."

My father sighed in clear relief and then gave me a glance that I understood. I went and retrieved a piece of parchment and gave it to Uthman, along with a quill pen that was one of Abu Bakr's few earthly possessions.

And then my father recited his last testament.

"In the name of God, the Merciful, the Compassionate. This is the order of Abdallah ibn Abu Quhayfa, known to men as Abu Bakr. Whereas . . ."

And then he stopped. I looked at my father and saw that he had fallen unconscious. My heart skipped a beat. If my father died before he could state his wishes, *fitna* would be upon us. I looked at Uthman and saw from his pale face that he was thinking the same thing.

I looked around and saw that we were alone. Asma had returned home to feed you, Abdallah, and there was no one present in the Ca-liph's quarters to witness what happened next.

"What do we do?" Uthman asked me in a voice that sounded like a frightened boy's.

I could hear the blood pounding in my ears, and my mouth was as dry as salt. And then I made a decision for which I could have been killed on the spot.

"Write in 'I appoint Umar ibn al-Khattab as my successor among you,'" I said, fighting off the terror of my own presumption. Of all the men left in Medina, I knew that only Umar commanded the fear and the respect of every faction, and he could be counted on to hold the people together.

I looked at Uthman, my gold eyes focused on him like a hawk. If he objected and word spread that I had usurped the Caliph's power and forged his final command, nothing would save me from the fury of the mob. The Mother of the Believers would be torn to shreds in the street by her children.

But Uthman's saving grace, and his fatal weakness, was his trusting and gentle nature. He was like a little child who saw only the best in others and had no understanding of the machinations of politics or the treacheries of the human heart.

He looked at me for a moment and then nodded and wrote in the words in Abu Bakr's name.

I felt the world spin around me. Had I just done this thing? Had I actually seized my father's mantle and spoken on his behalf, single-handedly appointing the next Caliph of Islam? And then I began to tremble in fright at my audacity and wondered what madness had taken hold of me.

And then a miracle happened. Of all the wondrous and inexplicable things I witnessed during my years with the Messenger of God, none was as remarkable as the sudden sound of my father's voice.

"Where was I?" Abu Bakr said, his eyes blinking away the sleep that had taken hold of him.

The blood drained from my face, and I shot Uthman a warning look, but it was too late. The gentle and unpretentious man simply handed over to the Caliph the sheet on which he had written in the words I had instructed him.

My father looked at the parchment in surprise, his eyes narrowing. And then he turned to Uthman, and, to my shock, a warm smile spread on his face.

"I think you were afraid that the people would dispute among themselves if I died in that state," he said, no hint of accusation or outrage in his voice.

Uthman looked at me, and for a moment I expected him to reveal my presumption. But his eyes twinkled and he simply nodded in affirmation, and I realized that my secret was safe with him.

Abu Bakr nodded and praised God.

"You have done well," he said. And then his eyes turned to me and he held out his hand.

I leaned close to my father and held his hand in mine.

"I have no love for this world," he said softly. "But I am glad to have been in it for two reasons. One is that I knew and befriended the

Messenger of God. And the second is that I have been blessed to call you my daughter."

Tears welled in my eyes and I struggled to speak, but my father shook his head and I knew that there was nothing I could say with words that he did not know full well in his heart.

His hand fell from mine and his eyes slipped back into his skull as I heard him whisper his final words. *There is no god but God, and Muhammad is His Messenger*. And with that, Abu Bakr, the Witness to the Truth, the Second in the Cave, and the first Caliph of Islam, passed away into eternity.

✦ ✦ ✦

THAT NIGHT, THE MUSLIMS buried my father in a grave next to my husband. Abu Bakr was laid to rest behind his master, his face near the Prophet's shoulder. Ali led the funeral service and was kind and gracious in his eulogy.

And then, in accordance with my father's last wishes, the Muslims gathered and paid allegiance to Umar ibn al-Khattab, who became the second and perhaps greatest of the Caliphs.

4 August 26, AD 636

Muawiya gazed out at the mighty Byzantine army gathered at the river of Yarmuk and felt a rush of fire run through his veins. This day had long been coming. The initial Muslim victories under Abu Bakr had been highly improbable. The subsequent conquests under his successor, Umar, should have been impossible. Khalid's brilliant entry into Iraq had placed the Muslims like a dagger aimed at the heart of Byzantium. Within a few months, the Sword of Allah had crossed the desert and come west. Khalid's lightly armed and highly mobile horsemen descended on the plains of Syria without warning. The Byzantine commanders dispatched ten thousand local men to hold off what they thought were disorganized bandits seeking booty. They did not expect to find an efficient and highly disciplined Arab force that outnumbered them two to one. The hubris of the Byzantines led to their massacre at the Battle of Ajnadayn, and the Muslims exploded through the hills of Syria unchallenged until they surrounded the ancient city of Damascus. The stunned Byzantine commanders who had underestimated their foes were suddenly cut off from reinforcements and forced to evacuate what had been the proud capital of the imperial province. Within weeks, Damascus fell and Muslims were suddenly the rulers of all of Syria.

The unexpected loss of Damascus caused the Byzantine generals in neighboring Palestine to panic, and they sent a force to the valley of Jordan to confront the invaders. But Khalid had anticipated the attack from the south and the Muslims met and crushed the Roman troops at the village of Fahl. And then, like the gift of rain coming down from the heavens after a long drought, the Holy Land of Abraham, David, and Solomon, the land of the prophets and of Jesus the son of Mary, was now in the hands of Islam. Only Jerusalem itself remained in the possession of the stunned Byzantines, who desperately holed themselves up and prepared for a siege they knew was coming.

Heraclius had realized belatedly that he was dealing not with tribal marauders but with a highly organized army bent on conquest. The Arabs, with their light arms and camels that moved like a flash flood, were unlike anything he had faced in decades of warfare with the lumbering Persian juggernaut. His commanders had no experience in battle against such a mobile foe, especially one that did not appear to fear death, and they were at a loss for a strategy to rout the Muslims. So Heraclius decided to unleash the combined forces of the entire Byzantine army on Syria and crush the invaders. The time for gamesmanship was gone, and the moment of brute strength had come.

And so it was that Muawaya stood among the Muslims as they faced the greatest army ever gathered in the region. Over one hundred thousand of Rome's elite warriors had been sent to crush the Muslim forces. The army of Islam was outnumbered four to one. Survival for the Arabs, let alone victory, should have been impossible and yet Muawiya felt excited. His men had seen so many impossible victories that even the most cynical of the Quraysh were now convinced that God was on their side. And if Allah, the Lord of the heavens and the earth, was with them, who could possibly withstand them?

The Muslims had one advantage—cavalry. Heraclius had sent primarily infantry soldiers with a small but sturdy contingent of horsemen for support. If the Byzantine cavalry were destroyed, the Muslims would be able to take on the massive fighting force with the benefit of superior horsemanship. It would mean taking a tremendous risk—to ride out and concentrate all their cavalry's power on engaging the enemy's horsemen. A horseman would always be superior to a foot soldier, but two horsemen were equally matched. If the Muslims won, they would have a chance to overwhelm the Byzantine infantry. But if they lost, then the battle was over. Without the shield of their horses, the Muslims would be slaughtered mercilessly.

It was a gamble, and the stakes could not have been higher—all or nothing. In the days before he had embraced Islam, Muawiya had been an avid gambler, known to take risks in games of chance that would have shocked the faint of heart. But if the son of Abu Sufyan had learned anything from his years of observing Muhammad's improbable string of successes against his enemies, it was that fortune favored the bold.

And so it was that day that Muawaya sat on his stallion beside the greatest warriors of Islam, including Khalid ibn al-Waleed and the famed swordsman Zubayr ibn al-Awwam, and looked into the face of death. Once they charged into the heart of the Byzantine cavalry, there would be no retreat. Either they would emerge victorious, or they would never emerge at all.

Khalid met his eyes and Muawiya could see that he was thinking the same thing. The two Meccans grinned at each other like boys on the playing field. And then the Sword of Allah raised his blade and called the battle cry that had changed the world forever.

"Allahu akbar!"

As horses raced into the whirlwind of death, as swords clashed and arrows buzzed about him like angry bees, Muawiya laughed and thanked God for giving him a chance at glory.

—   —   —

THE MUSLIM CAVALRY DESTROYED the Byzantine horsemen that day, and the battle was over. Without the protection of their mounted troops, the enemy soldiers were crushed under the hooves of eight thousand Arabian stallions. The mighty legions of Constantinople scattered, fleeing back over the Yarmuk River or escaping into the desert.

In six days, an empire that had inherited the scepter of Rome was gone.

As Muawiya gazed out at the carnage on the battlefield, at the thousands of broken bodies carpeting the earth, he smiled to himself. How foolish the Arabs had been to resist Muhammad for all those years. He had given them a faith and then forged them into a nation. And now he had bequeathed them an empire. The only question now was whether his people had the courage and willpower to sustain their success or whether they, too, would disappear into the scrolls of history like the men they had just defeated. Was Islam a passing wave in the ocean of time, or could they turn it into a civilization that would out-strip all the nations that had fought for dominion over these lands?

As the sun set over a day that had changed history, Muawiya gazed up into the heavens and he saw a sign that caused his breathing to stop.

The new moon was shining high above him in the fading twilight. And *al-Zuhra*, the shining star known as Venus to the Romans, glit-tered closer than he had ever seen to the horns of the crescent. It was a beautiful and stirring sight, a conjunction unlike any in the memory of men, and his soldiers soon stopped what they were doing and stared up at the sky in amazement.

Muawiya joined them, gazing up at the strange celestial phenom-enon, and then he felt a sudden chill go down his spine. A sense of wonder that had always been foreign to his fiercely practical—some would say cynical—heart.

And then he understood. The crescent and the star were a sign from God, an answer to the secret thoughts of his heart. Allah had showered his blessings on the Muslim *Ummah* that day and had shown Muawiya that His hand was indeed guiding the forces of history.

In that instant, Muawiya knew that Islam would triumph and the nations of the earth would turn and face the Kaaba. And he knew with even greater certainty that he was destined to lead the Muslims to their glorious victory. Muawiya's childhood dream of becoming king of the Arabs would be fulfilled, but on a scale far greater than he could have ever imagined.

The Battle of Yarmuk was just the beginning.

5

The conquests that had begun under my father continued with miraculous speed during Umar's reign. Damascus fell, as did Palestine. The Byzantine humiliation at Yarmuk had effectively destroyed Roman imperial power in the region after almost a thousand years of dominance. The Prophet's command to treat conquered peoples with leniency, giving them the right to worship and live their lives as long as they paid the *jizya* tribute to the state, was a decisive factor in the ease of our victories. When word spread that the Muslims did not plan to impose their religion on the defeated peoples, quick and painless surrender became preferable to extended resistance. Our generosity toward our subjects was unusual in a world where conquerors were expected to vanquish and crush their opponents and played a major role in ensuring peace in the lands we took long after the last sword had been sheathed.

This was particularly true of Jerusalem, which finally fell after months of siege. Umar himself traveled to the holy city to formally accept its surrender. The Christian patriarch of Jerusalem had led Umar through the ancient streets where the prophets of old had walked, until they reached the sacred site where the Temple of Solomon had once stood. It was a place that was deeply sacred for Muslims, not only because it had once been the House of God but because Muhammad had ascended to heaven from its stones during the Night Journey. But when Umar arrived, he was shocked to discover that it was a garbage dump. Literally. The Christians of the city had dumped hundreds of years of sewage on the holy site, under the misguided belief that they were honoring Jesus, who had prophesied that the Temple would be destroyed. As long as the plateau was left in disarray, the prophecy would remain in effect and the truth of Christ's words would be evident for all to see.

Outraged at the Christian desecration of the Sanctuary, Umar had personally cleansed the site with his own hands, carrying out rubbish in the folds of his cloak until the platform had been cleared and a small house of worship could be built. When the Sanctuary was again purified, Umar signed a treaty with the defeated Christians of Jerusalem, guaranteeing the safety of their lives and property and their right to worship freely. The Christian patriarch had politely asked that the Muslims continue the Byzantine policy of banning Jews from the holy city, but Umar refused. And so, for the first time in centuries, the Children of Israel returned to the Holy Land from which they had been expelled, ironically at the generosity of a religion they had rejected.

And our policy of religious tolerance was soon to have a proactive effect in generating support for our expansion. After the fall of Palestine, the Meccan emissary Amr ibn al-As led a small force of a few thousand horsemen into the Sinai and invaded Egypt, which had been traded back and forth by Persians and Byzantines during their all-consuming war over the past century. Neither side had shown much compassion to the people of Egypt, who were merely pawns in the great game of empire. The Persians were fire worshipers and had no love for the Christianity of Egypt, which missionaries and warriors had been trying to impose on their ancient people for centuries. And the Byzantines looked upon the Coptic Christians of Egypt as heretics who had been misled from the true teachings of Rome and Constantinople. Both nations had brutally persecuted the Egyptians and tried to erase their religious identity. And so it was that when Amr's forces appeared on the horizon, the local populace rose up against the last of their Byzantine rulers and helped the Muslims take control of the land beyond the Nile. The Muslims did not understand, nor did we care for, the minute differences of theology that divided the Copts from their fellow Christians. They were all People of the Book as far as we were concerned, and as long as they paid their taxes, we didn't bother with what they believed or how they performed their church services. Thus it was that the Holy Qur'an's commandment *Let there be no compulsion in religion* became the rallying cry that brought the oppressed peoples of North Africa into our fold. And it was the great irony of God's purpose that the Muslim prayer call of *No god but God* was at last heard to echo at the Pyramids, where Moses himself had sought to convince Pharaoh of this truth in a world long gone.

And even as the west fell to the forces of Islam, the east opened to our armies like the petals of a flower in the springtime. The defeat of the Persians in Iraq had rumbled through the Sassanid provinces like a landslide, and under Umar's command, the Muslims tore through the heart of Persia. We crushed the last of the Sassanid troops at the Battle of Qadisiya and soon Ctesiphon, the mighty capital of Persia, fell to Islam and the ancient empire of the shahs vanished into the annals of history.

As nations fell before us with stunning ease, the coffers of Medina began to overflow with gold and jewels, tribute coming in from all over the world to the new empire that had slain the old. I heard one account that said that the storehouses of the *Bayt al-Mal* held tens of millions of gold dirhams, more wealth than had ever physically existed inside all of Arabia. It was a bounty beyond comprehension, and Umar was rightly concerned that such a concentration of wealth would corrupt the hearts of the Muslims. He ordered wide distributions from the treasury to the poor and placed the elderly and the sick on regular pensions to ensure that they were provided for. But no matter how much Umar gave away, more kept flowing into our coffers, as the borders of Islam expanded from the deserts of Africa to the mountains of the Caucasus.

It was an exciting time to be alive, and every day news came to Medina of some stunning victory of the Muslim armies. And yet I can only write of those battles as others have relayed them to me, for in all those years, I did not cross the borders of Arabia. With my husband's death and then my father's, I found that my role in the life of the Muslim *Ummah* was becoming circumscribed to Medina. During the Prophet's life, I had traveled with him on his battles and had been his constant companion on diplomatic journeys to unite the Arab tribes. But after his passing, I rarely left the confines of the oasis except to go to Pilgrimage in Mecca, and then only under a heavy honor guard of the Caliph's soldiers. The freedom that I had loved as a child was gone, and for all intents and purposes, I had become a prisoner to my honored status as Mother of the Believers.

Since there was nothing I could do to change things, I decided to make the most of the role that was given me. I became a teacher to both men and women, and every day prominent Muslims would come to my apartment and speak to me through the curtain, asking for spiritual and practical advice. My prodigious memory proved to be a valuable asset to the believers, as I could easily recite word for word conversations that I had had with my husband years before. I became one of the most trusted narrators of *hadith*, oral traditions about the life and teachings of Muhammad, which were soon being passed by word of mouth over the vast distances of the Muslim empire. Whenever the people wished to know what my husband had said regarding anything from how to properly cleanse themselves after defecation to the appropriate inheritance shares for their grandchildren, they came to me and I told them what I knew.

My reputation as a scholar had led Umar to rely on me heavily for advice during his reign, and I felt great pride that a young girl in her twenties had become an influential voice in the court of the Caliph, who was fast becoming the most powerful man on earth. Yet despite his unquestioned authority, Umar remained a deeply humble and austere man, wearing patched clothes and sleeping on the floor in his tiny hut. When envoys from conquered nations arrived in Medina, they were invariably shocked to find that their "emperor" lived like a beggar, without even the security of personal bodyguards.

But even as my prestige in the community rose, my loneliness increased. I and the other Mothers had been forbidden by God to marry again after the Messenger's death, and so we lived alone in our apartments, the old jealousies fading away under the bond of shared boredom. In truth, even if God had permitted us to remarry, none of us would have done so. It was impossible to love any man other than the Messenger.

It would have been an easier life had we been blessed with children, but that was not to be for any of us. And so I contented myself with the company of the children of my loved ones. You, Abdallah, my sister's son, became the closest thing I would ever know to a child of my own, and I loved you accordingly. I took great pride in watching you grow from a carefree child into a mature and responsible young man, and I know that as long as Islam is led by men like you, our nation will be safe from the temptations of power.

I also spent a great deal of time with my younger brother, Muhammad, who had been born during the Prophet's final Pilgrimage to Mecca. After my father died, his mother, Asma bint Umais, married Ali, and Muhammad was raised beside Hasan and Husayn, who were also like children to me. Though I had no affection for their father, the grandsons of the Prophet were innocent and sweet, and whenever I saw them, I was reminded of my gentle husband. Hasan was a fun-loving youth who was always climbing trees and racing with the other boys, and his handsome face, so much like his grandfather's, was always bright with a smile. Husayn was the more serious of the two, shy and reserved, his eyes exuding a deep compassion and sadness that reminded me of his ghostly mother. My little brother, Muhammad, was their constant companion and protector. If any of the naughty boys ever acted up or played rough with the Prophet's grandsons, Muhammad was there to teach them a hard lesson in playground manners. He had always possessed a passionate sense of justice, a quality that would sadly lead to tragedy for him and the whole *Ummah* one day.

Though I loved the children of Ali's house, my relationship with the Prophet's cousin was still strained. We were always formally cordial in each other's presence, but the chasm between us continued to grow over the years. My refusal to forgive Ali for his suggestion that the Messenger divorce me had become a matter of stubborn habit now, a fault of my pride that would be the cause of much sorrow.

But despite the minor frictions between members of the Prophet's household, the life of Medina was one of peace and placidity. The excitement and the terror of my youth were replaced by a pleasant monotony of quiet days, each little different from the one before or the one to come. It was utterly safe and utterly boring, and some part of my adventurous spirit longed for a return to a time when every day was a matter of life and death, when the future was covered in mists and clouds and my heart beat loudly in the thrilling anticipation of change.

And then one cold winter day, when my twenties had at last given way to my thirties, the golden age of Islam ended with a single act of violence. Umar was standing at the head of prayers in the Masjid when a Persian slave sought revenge for the conquest of his nation. He rushed the Caliph and stabbed him viciously in the gut, before taking his own life.

Umar was mortally wounded by the assassin, but he lived long enough to appoint a small council of believers to choose a successor. As he lay dying in great agony, I saw him look up and smile and I heard him whisper something that I did not catch. When I turned to your father, Zubayr, who had leaned close to Umar and caught his words, he was pale.

"He said he sees his daughter holding out her hand," Zubayr

recounted, and I felt a chill go through me as I remembered the stories of the little girl he had buried alive during his days as a pagan. Umar raised his hand weakly and I watched him curl his fingers as he took hold of something I could not see. And then the Caliph of Islam, the most powerful and noble leader I had seen next to my own husband, passed away to his eternal reward.

That night, Umar was buried alongside my husband and my father, and that day, I erected a curtain inside my apartment, separating their graves from the tiny space where I lived.

The council of believers had no time to grieve, for the fate of the empire was at stake. After three days of secret consultation, the elders of Medina emerged and proclaimed the sweet-hearted Uthman to be the next Commander of the Believers.

It was a decision that made political sense, since Uthman was a prominent leader of Quraysh and could be expected to keep the nobles of the far-flung empire in check. But in the end it would prove to be a disastrous mistake, one that would lead to the horror of blood flowing through the streets of Medina.

6 Medina—AD 656

The first several years of Uthman's rule were unremarkable. The conquests of Islam continued unabated. The Muslim armies pushed west out of Egypt and seized control of most of the Mediterranean coastline. On the eastern front, our soldiers pushed through the dying remnants of the Persian empire to seize the Kerman province, where a race of fierce tribesmen called Baluchis reigned. To the north, Armenia and the mountains of the Caucasus came under our dominion. Following my husband's commandment to *seek knowledge even if you must go to China,* Uthman sent an envoy to the Emperor Gaozong and invited him to accept Islam. The Chinese overlord politely declined to convert but was shrewd enough to open trade with the Muslim empire and allowed our people to preach and propagate our faith inside his borders.

Perhaps most significantly in the realm of international relations, Uthman supervised the building of the first Muslim navy. His kinsman Muawiya, who had become the highly respected governor of Syria, soon led a naval attack on the Byzantine forces off the coast of Lebanon. The Muslims, filled with the brash confidence of decades of success, rammed the Byzantine ships, bringing their own vessels so close to the opposing fleets that their masts were almost touching. And then our warriors leaped across decks and engaged in ferocious hand-to-hand combat with the Greek sailors, using their fiercely honed skills from urban warfare on the ocean.

The Byzantine marines were accustomed to shooting at their enemies from a distance with arrows and launching flaming pellets at rival ships, but they had never fought in this fashion, with ships used merely as bridges for foot soldiers. Their confusion quickly devolved into chaos, and the sea was stained crimson with the blood of imperial sailors. Muawiya emerged triumphant, his prestige rising like the sun among the Muslims. In later years, we would learn that the victory could have been even greater, for the emperor himself had been on one of the Byzantine ships that Muawiya's men had boarded. The lord of Constantinople had escaped certain death only by disguising himself as a common sailor and jumping into the sea, where he was rescued by his men and rushed to safety on the island of Sicily.

Uthman continued and expanded upon his predecessor's military success, but it was in the spiritual realm that he left his greatest legacy. As the caliphate continued to grow by leaps and bounds and the number of Muslims went from thousands to millions, the need to present the standard written copies of the holy Qur'an became pressing. The Holy Book had never been compiled into one document during the Prophet's lifetime, primarily since he was illiterate, as were a great many of the Arab tribesmen, and symbols on a parchment were meaningless to them. Because of this stark reality, Muslims committed the Qur'an to memory and relayed its teachings orally. This system worked well in the early years of our faith, but as we came into contact with highly advanced civilizations where literacy was the norm, the need to present the Word of God to the new believers in written format became a priority.

My father had kept a private copy of the Qur'an in his study, one that he had compiled after the Garden of Death, where many of the

Companions who had memorized the entire Qur'an had been killed.
Before his death, Abu Bakr had passed along his personal compilation
to Umar, who had subsequently left it to his daughter Hafsa. When
Uthman learned that she still had the folio in her possession, he asked
her to submit it to him for verification. And then he summoned those
in Medina who were known to have memorized the entire Qur'an,
forming a committee in which I and my sister-wife Umm Salama par-
ticipated. We were given Hafsa's codex, which was a jumbled collection
of verses written on parchments and palm leaves, and asked to verify its
accuracy. Once it had been confirmed by all those in the holy city who
knew the Qur'an by heart, Uthman ordered copies of the authorized
text to be made and sent to the capitals of every province of the empire.
And thus he ensured that the Word of God would not be changed according to the desires of men, as the Prophet had claimed to have happened with the scriptures of the Jews and Christians. And in doing so,
Uthman fulfilled the prophecy of God in a verse of the Qur'an itself:
Truly We have sent down this Reminder, and truly We will preserve it.

I have often thought that Uthman would have been fortunate if
he had passed away shortly after issuing the standard written text of
God's Word. He would have been remembered purely as a man of great
wisdom and vision, whose life had been of great service to the cause
of Islam.

But, alas, this was not meant to be. His memory has been tainted
by the actions of evil men and fools. And I grieve to say that I count
myself among them.

— — —

As the years of Uthman's reign grew, so did the wealth of the Muslim empire—and the ambitions of its leaders. Uthman had increasingly relied on members of his own clan, the Umayyads, to administer
the business of the rapidly expanding state. Some of his kinsmen, like
Muawiya, were efficient and respected governors who were loved by
their subjects. But as the empire grew ever wider and the supervision
by Medina became more difficult, local politicians from among the
Quraysh, many of whom had embraced Islam only when Mecca fell
and they had no choice, became increasingly free to rule as they wished.
And in a world where gold was flowing in rivers, corruption and venal-

ity began to set in. Complaints arose over the self-serving conduct and brutality of some of the Umayyad governors, but the Caliph himself did not hear of the growing unrest until the sparks of discontent had become a raging fire.

For Uthman had made one terrible mistake in choosing his own inner circle. He had appointed a young cousin named Marwan ibn al-Hakam to serve as an adviser. Both Marwan and his father had the dubious distinction of being cursed by my husband, who had expelled them from Arabia because he saw in their hearts the disease of grave treachery. They had remained in exile until Uthman took power. Feeling great sorrow for his kinsmen, the old man had pardoned them and recalled them to Medina in the hope of rehabilitating them. It was a foolish mistake, motivated by the softness of his heart, for the moment the bitter young man returned, he quickly sought to achieve power over those who had humiliated him. Using honeyed words and feigning humility, Marwan rose to power as Uthman's personal scribe, thereby becoming responsible for writing—and reading—all of the Caliph's correspondence. Using his newfound power, Marwan began issuing commands under the Caliph's seal without his knowledge, furthering the interests of corrupt members of the Umayyad clan while keeping word of the growing unhappiness in the empire from the old man's ears.

But even if Uthman remained oblivious to the rising cries of discontent, word was rapidly spreading to others in Medina, and our alarm at the deteriorating situation began to grow. My brother Muhammad, now a handsome and passionate young man, had emigrated to Egypt and had become embroiled in the political strife there. He was an idealistic youth who was ready to fight against injustice wherever he saw it, and his status as the son of Abu Bakr gave him immediate standing among the Egyptians. Within a short time, my brother became a vocal leader of the opposition, and he gained the support of Amr ibn al-As, the revered conqueror of Egypt, whom Uthman had displaced as governor in favor of his own kinsman.

The unrest in Egypt soon boiled over into rioting, during which the Umayyad governors brutally suppressed the protesters. Muhammad sent several letters to Uthman demanding that he address the grievances of the Egyptians, but they quickly disappeared into the void through Marwan's machinations. Convinced that the Caliph had himself become corrupt, my young and idealistic brother led an armed band of rebels to Medina to demand Uthman's resignation.

It was a foolish act, the tactic of a young and misguided man who wanted only to do the right thing. For that, I hope he is one day forgiven. But the one person I cannot forgive in the drama that subsequently unfolded is myself.

— — —

I WAS NOW A woman in my forties and I thought I had gained the wisdom necessary to intervene in these dangerous affairs of state. As word of the uprising in Egypt came from my brother, I went to Uthman to plead with him to replace the corrupt governors who were fomenting chaos. Marwan attempted to deny me an audience, but when I stormed inside Uthman's palatial home, his guards stepped aside, afraid to lay a hand on the Mother of the Believers.

When I saw Uthman, he looked old and very tired. I could see a hint of confusion in his eyes as he looked at me for a long moment. It was as if he did not recognize me, a woman he had known from birth. Even though my face was veiled, my golden eyes still sparkled. But his mind soon cleared and he smiled, his face still beautiful despite the weight of decades. He listened to me patiently for some time, but I could tell that he did not understand what I was saying. And then I realized to my horror that Uthman had absolutely no idea that the situation in Egypt had changed, that there were men marching in the streets of the province calling for the ouster of his appointed envoys. He kept looking to Marwan for confirmation, but that wily rat shrugged as if this were all news to him. At the end of our audience, Uthman politely rose and asked me to give his regards to my mother, Umm Ruman, and all blood drained from my face.

My mother had been dead for over twenty years.

I left the Caliph's manor with dread in the pit of my stomach. Not only was Uthman being manipulated by corrupt officials, he appeared to be suffering from dementia. The future of the empire was at stake and I had to act fast.

— — —

I BEGAN TO SPEAK to the elders among the Companions. Talha and Zubayr, who were revered by the community as two of its greatest war

heroes, were sympathetic to my concerns but were wary of openly challenging the Caliph. I finally turned in frustration to Ali, who sternly
warned me to stay out of political affairs.

"You are playing with a sharp sword, my Mother," he said. "It is a
weapon that could cut you in turn."

My face grew red at what I perceived to be his condescension, and
I stormed out of his house. I returned to the Masjid and shared my
concerns with the other Mothers, but they all joined Ali and the other
elders in warning me to stand back. Ramla was especially caustic in her
words, which was no surprise, considering that she was the daughter
of Abu Sufyan and a kinsman of Uthman. Umm Salama was kind but
firm, saying that our place as the Mothers of the Believers was to teach
and nurture the Muslims. Politics was the domain of men. Even Hafsa,
who had gone from a bitter rival to a close friend over the years, was
nervous and refused to commit herself to supporting me against the
Caliph.

Angered by my failure to drum up support among my peers, I decided to turn to the masses. I began to appear regularly in the marketplace, standing veiled but proud and calling out to the men to pressure
Uthman to step down. It was a dangerous act of rebellion in the heart
of the city, and only my honored status as the Prophet's wife kept me
from being arrested by the Caliph's men. As I shared my concerns with
the people of the city, I lit a fire that I hoped would smoke the old man
out of his home and cause him to see the truth of the world. But it became a fire that soon threatened to consume everything I had worked
for my entire life.

For my brother Muhammad arrived with hundreds of armed and
angry young men from Egypt and the rebellion I had sought to incite
suddenly became a terrifying reality.

-- -- --

MUHAMMAD MET WITH ME and explained that he did not seek violence, but he was willing to defend himself and his men. Realizing
that my young brother's veins ran hot with the fire of justice and that
his emotions were ruling his reason, I tried to mediate. I arranged for
a private meeting with the Caliph, who listened patiently to the litany
of complaints from the Egyptians—how Umayyad officials were stealing from the local treasury, how wealthy and well-connected criminals

were being pardoned in exchange for bribes while the poor suffered the lash, how taxes were being levied unfairly on the populace without their consent. Such behavior might be the norm of other nations, Muhammad argued with passion, but we were the servants of God. If the *Ummah* turned a blind eye to injustice, the incredible wealth and power God had given us would be taken away,

Uthman nodded throughout the meeting, but his eyes looked glazed and I wondered how much of my brother's speech the old man truly heard or understood. But in the end, the Caliph surprised me by agreeing to Muhammad's request that the Umayyad officials in Egypt be replaced. And then he summoned the wretched Marwan to draft a letter to that effect, removing the Umayyad governor and replacing him with my brother. I saw Marwan's eyes narrow, but he complied. I read over the letter myself to make sure that he had obeyed the Caliph, and I saw no irregularities in it. The parchment was signed by Uthman and sealed in wax with his insignia, and Muhammad rejoiced. He had come to Medina prepared for a fight, and the Caliph had instead given him everything he had asked for.

I was delighted but not completely surprised. Uthman had always been an exceedingly kind and generous man, and in truth, I could not remember him ever denying a request by anyone. Indeed, it was his complete openness that had been the cause of the current scandal, for he had never turned down the request of any man—including those who sought to use him to their advantage.

I embraced my brother and led him back to his men. When they learned that the Caliph had capitulated, there was much rejoicing and a few danced with joy, until stern looks from some of the more pious fellows quickly sobered them all up.

As Muhammad rode back into the desert for the long journey to Egypt, the nation he now ruled, I decided to go to Mecca on Pilgrimage and thank God for bringing the troubling crisis to a peaceful resolution. As I rode out in my armored howdah, surrounded by the Caliph's finest guards, I did not see a lone rider emerge from the stables and ride north, carrying a secret letter that bore Uthman's seal.

— — —

THE ENVOY WAS INTERCEPTED by my brother's men after one of their intrepid sentries realized that they were being followed. They caught the rider and searched him until they found the letter bearing the Caliph's mark. When my brother read the secret dispatch, he turned bright red with rage. For it was a letter purporting to be from Uthman, ordering the governor of Egypt to arrest Muhammad and execute him as a rebel the moment he returned.

Muhammad's men raced back to the city and immediately laid siege to Uthman's house. I was already on my way to Mecca and was utterly unaware of the horrifying turn of events. I have often thought that the world would be a different place today had I just stayed home a few more days. But such are the pointless musings of regret.

Even as I traveled to the holy city of my birth, blissfully ignorant of the sword that now hung over the Muslim nation, my brother's men proceeded to take control of Medina. They bullied their way into people's homes and took whatever provisions they deemed necessary to support their "holy cause." When other nations later heard about the course of events in the Muslim capital, they must have been shocked that a small band of rebels could have taken over so quickly. And yet there was no standing army inside Medina, as there had been no need for one for the past twenty years. The Muslims ruled the world from horizon to horizon, and the thought that Medina could come under attack had been laughable.

But no one was laughing now. My brother confronted Uthman with the letter and the old man denied any knowledge of it, despite the parchment carrying the Caliph's seal. But Muhammad was not satisfied.

"Then you are either a liar or a puppet being used by others," he retorted. "In either event, you are unworthy to lead Islam."

The gentle Uthman was deeply saddened by these words, perhaps because he heard the ring of truth in them. Of course I have never believed that the Caliph ordered my brother's death. The vile monster Marwan had clearly written the letter, but it would be the old man who was held responsible for it. And perhaps Uthman finally saw the reality of what had happened and his heart had shattered with the realization that he had been duped by a young man he loved like a son. He retired to his home and did not come out again, leaving his fate to God.

The rebels grew increasingly agitated as the days passed and Uthman neither emerged nor responded to their demands for his resignation. It soon became clear that tempers were boiling, and the threat of violence was no longer just an unfortunate possibility. Ali dispatched his sons, Hasan and Husayn, now grown into fine young men, to guard the Caliph's doors, and the presence of the Prophet's grandsons held back the spreading wave of anarchy for a time.

But as the weeks passed with no resolution, the Egyptian rebels decided to force the issue. They cut off all delivery of food and water to the elderly Uthman, who was a prisoner in his own home. The Jewess Safiya, my sister-wife, tried to save the beleaguered Caliph. She owned a house that bordered his and she set up a plank on her roof by which she would pass across food and water to Uthman's young and pretty wife, Naila.

On the forty-ninth day of the siege, a group of men led by my brother stormed the roof of Uthman's house and broke in. The gentle old man sat on the floor in his study, reading the holy Qur'an. He seemed utterly unafraid of the rebels who were ransacking his house, bloodlust flowing through their veins. My brother Muhammad, filled with the fire of idealism and pride, finally came upon Uthman and raised his hand to deliver the deathblow. He grabbed the Caliph by his beard, at which point the elderly leader looked up at him and smiled softly.

"Son of my brother," he said, his warm eyes gazing into my brother's soul. "Let go of my beard. Your father would not have done this."

It was a simple statement, said without malice or accusation. And in that instant, his words penetrated my brother's heart and Muhammad fell back, as if waking from a dream. Shame and horror filled him, and he realized how far he had fallen.

My brother turned back, ready to order an end to the attack. But it was too late. Several of his men broke into the room, the bloodlust burning wild in their eyes. Seeing the Caliph alone and unarmed, they raced to him, swords raised.

"No!" Muhammad ibn Abu Bakr screamed. But the rebels ignored him and threw their leader aside. And then they descended on the softhearted Uthman, who loved peace and could not bring himself to harm even his enemies. His wife, Naila, threw herself as a shield on top of her husband, but the rebels sliced off her fingers and tossed her aside like a rag doll. And then they stabbed the Caliph nine times, their blades slicing through his neck, his heart, and his skull with monstrous brutality. Uthman fell over dead, the pages of the holy Qur'an he had so carefully compiled stained with his blood.

Even as I write this, dear Abdallah, tears stain these pages. It was a brutal murder of a good man, and I cannot hide from God the truth that I share some of the blame. Had I not spoken out against Uthman in public, had I instead used my influence to calm the fire in my young brother's soul, perhaps he would have lived. And I shudder as I remember the terrible words of my husband so long ago, his warning that the sword of God would be unsheathed against the Muslims should harm ever befall Uthman, a sword that would consume our nation until the Day of Judgment.

May God forgive me for what I did, for I acted then out of passion for justice, even if I was misguided. But for the actions I would take next, Abdallah, I do not know if pardon is possible. What I did in the aftermath of Uthman's murder came out of the blackest pit of my own soul, a crime for which I can never forgive myself, even if God and the angels grant me reprieve.

7

𝓘 was in Mecca when I first heard the news of the siege of Uthman's home. I had just finished the Pilgrimage, along with my sister-wife Umm Salama, who had joined me. We were planning to return after completing the rituals at the House of God, when envoys sent by Zubayr advised us to remain in Mecca until the rebellion was over. My heart had sunk when I heard word of my brother's actions, and I desperately sought to return so I could calm him and arrange some kind of reconciliation. But Umm Salama begged me to stay away from the chaos and our guards pointedly refused to permit me to leave until peace had been restored to the capital.

The weeks dragged on without word and I began to have a terrible feeling in my heart that things had gone wildly wrong. And then two men rode in from the desert, bearing news that horrified me and brought my blood to a boil. They were not envoys—the matter was too urgent for messengers. They were my closest friends, my beloved cousin Talha and my brother-in-law Zubayr. One look on their ashen faces and my worst fears were confirmed.

We gathered in the old Hall of Assembly, where I had spied on Hind and the council of Mecca a lifetime before. The stone walls looked as they had almost forty years before, cold and proud, untroubled by the vagaries of time. As we sat inside the chamber that had once been the throne room of our enemies, Zubayr revealed all that had happened. His once handsome face was now heavily lined, and a mighty scar ran down his right cheek. Your father had fought in so many battles that I could not even remember where he had earned this mark of heroism.

Talha, for his part, had been unable to fight in the later wars of conquest because of his shattered hand. Instead, he had spent his years working as a merchant. His brilliant negotiating skills and his talent for learning the languages of our conquered subjects had allowed him to build a vast business empire, and he had been transformed over the years from an impoverished cripple into one of the richest men in the empire. And he had spent much of his vast wealth on spoiling his beautiful daughter, whom he had named, perhaps not surprisingly, Aisha. She was a vivacious young woman who had captured the hearts of many of the young men of Medina but had a shocking reputation as a flirt who enjoyed leading boys on. I had often sternly lectured the girl about social proprieties, and she had simply laughed and said I would have done the same had I not been married as a child and hidden away behind a veil. I would always give her a tongue-lashing for her impudence, but in my heart I loved her like a daughter, and I knew there was more than a little truth to what she said.

It was to Aisha bint Talha that my thoughts turned now as my friends revealed the shocking news of Uthman's murder. I grieved for the old man who was a victim of his own kindness, and I feared for the people of Medina now that the blood of the Caliph had been spilled. According to Zubayr, Uthman's cousin Muawiya was dispatching a mighty contingent from Syria to avenge the Caliph's death. Apparently Marwan had been able to get word of the siege to the Umayyad leader, and when Uthman was killed, his blood-soaked shirt had been sent to Damascus, along with the remains of poor Naila's severed fingers. The outraged Muawiya had held aloft these grisly relics in the newly constructed Grand Masjid of Damascus, built next to the church where the prophet John the Baptist was buried. With his brilliant oratory, he had riled up the passions of the crowd, and the cry for vengeance was rapidly spreading through the empire, especially after news of how the rebels had treated Uthman's corpse

"What happened to Uthman's body?" I asked and then saw Zubayr's face grimace with pain.

"They threw his body in the trash heap and refused to let him be buried," Zubayr said, horror welling in his eyes. "Safiya finally intervened and convinced them to let us bury him. But they would not allow us to inter Uthman with the Prophet or with the other believers in *Jannat al-Baqi*. So Safiya arranged for the Caliph to be buried in the Jewish cemetery near her ancestors."

I hung my head in grief. I had one more question, but I was afraid to ask it. And then Umm Salama spoke up, her voice soft, almost a whisper.

"Who is in charge?"

It was a simple question, but the fate of an empire that ruled half the earth turned on the answer.

There was a moment of long silence, and then finally Talha spoke, a hint of bitterness in his voice.

"After the Caliph's murder, there was chaos in the streets," he said. "Ali, Zubayr, and I gathered in the marketplace and called for calm. It was then that the rebels arrived, their swords drawn, and your brother said that he would recognize no man as master except his stepfather, Ali."

I felt as if someone had punched me in the stomach. Seeing the look of shock on my face, Talha nodded in understanding.

"We had arrived there, the three of us, with the understanding that we would call for an election by the elders of Mecca," he said, his voice rising. "But the rebels surrounded the crowd, their weapons in view, and it was no surprise that the vote went unanimously for Ali. Even Zubayr and I pledged our loyalty to him. We had no choice."

I could tell that the brutal way in which my brother's men had secured Ali's election haunted Talha and Zubayr. The three of them had been close friends for years, but this incident had clearly created deep ill will. They, like Ali, were two of the most revered leaders of Islam, men who had fought beside the Prophet and had been serious candidates for the position of Caliph after Umar's assassination. They had

accepted Uthman's election and had supported him loyally. But now, in
the face of Uthman's murder, they had been denied the opportunity to
assert their claim to the throne of Islam by the murderers themselves.
It was a bitter pill to swallow, and I could sense their anger at Ali for
going along with the tainted election.

And then I felt something grow inside me, something cold and
ugly. The old wounds were opened all at once, and I could feel the poison of the past flowing through my veins. I remembered how Ali had
nonchalantly convinced the Messenger to marry Zaynab bint Khuzayma in order to secure a political alliance, offering up my husband's
hand to another woman in my presence as if my feelings were worthless. I remembered how he had led that tragic girl of the Bani Qurayza
who looked just like me to her execution and how the young woman's
mad laughter still haunted my dreams. And then I remembered most
vividly how he had tried to get Muhammad to divorce me when I was
falsely accused of a shameful crime.

"Now that he has finally received his lifelong wish and crowned
himself Caliph, what has Ali done to punish the assassins?" I asked
through gritted teeth.

My friends looked at each other and hesitated.

"Nothing," Talha said coldly.

The world around me seemed to change colors, and suddenly I saw
everything through a veil of red.

"Then Ali has failed in his first task as Caliph. To enforce justice."

I saw the men look at me, and there were uncertainty and fear in
their eyes.

"What are you saying?" Zubayr asked slowly.

"I am saying that Ali cannot be put on the throne of the Muslims
by the murderers of the Caliph!" I felt my bones tremble with fury as I
convinced myself of the justice of my position. "And even if his election
were legitimate, he cannot lay claim to authority until he punishes those
who have committed this vile crime. Otherwise the Caliph is complicit
in the murder of his righteous predecessor, and God help the Muslims
if we should fall that low to accept such a man as our master!"

The words came out of my mouth with such ferocity that both
Talha and Zubayr sat back as if I had slapped them. And then my
sister-wife Umm Salama rose, her eyes wide with anger.

"Stop this! End this mad talk at once!"

"What madness? Is there any greater madness than to let a criminal rule over the believers?" Any other woman—or man, for that matter—would have been terrified by the dangerous look in my eyes, but Umm Salama refused to back down.

"Remember yourself, Aisha," she said, her voice stern. "You are the Mother of the Believers. You are meant to guide the Muslims, to heal their wounds, not inflict new ones. Do not go down this path, or the wrath of God will be unleashed on the *Ummah*."

I had never heard this matronly and warmhearted woman speak in such an outraged tone, and I would have been stung had there been any feeling left inside me except rage.

"It is Ali who will bring down the wrath of God upon us if he holds on to his blood-soaked throne," I said, my voice soft but dangerous.

Umm Salama turned to Talha and Zubayr but saw that they had been moved by my words. And then she shook her head in despair and stormed out of the Hall of Assembly.

As I sat there in triumph, a memory came back to me of the last time a woman had convinced men in this room of the justice of her argument. It had been Hind, who had called for the murder of Muhammad. It was a troubling thought and I quickly pushed it out of my head.

— ◦ —

OVER THE NEXT SEVERAL weeks, I convinced Talha and Zubayr, along with many other Muslims in Mecca, that we had a moral responsibility to challenge Ali. My cry for justice on behalf of the murdered Uthman stirred the hearts of the people of the city, who had benefited tremendously from the old man's generosity. As more and more men gathered to our cause, it became clear that we had enough to form an army, one strong enough to challenge Ali and force his abdication.

And then word came to us that Ali had raised his own troops to try to secure peace in the troubled empire. Although many of the Muslim governors in Yemen and the eastern provinces of Persia had accepted Ali's claim to authority, Muawiya refused to acknowledge him as Caliph. Ali's army of supporters included many devout Muslims who revered him for his reputation for wisdom and moral character, while others, known as the *Shia*, or Partisans of Ali, believed that he had always been the rightful leader of the Muslims through the claim of his lineage. And a rather shady group among his followers included the rebels of Egypt, who had a vested stake in ensuring that Uthman's clansmen did not get a chance to avenge the death of the Caliph.

As Muawiya gathered his forces in Syria, Ali had decided to leave Medina and move north into the green fields of Iraq. He sought both to spare the holy city the horror of further bloodshed and to garner the support of the Iraqi provinces in what would likely be a protracted war with Muawiya.

When word came to us that Ali's army was on the move, it became clear to Talha, Zubayr, and me that our moment had come. By then, our call for justice had attracted many of the most prominent Muslims to Mecca, and I remember with great joy the day that I saw you arrive, Abdallah, on horseback from Medina. You had grown into a dashing young man, so much like your father, and yet whenever I looked upon you, I saw only the little boy who'd played in my sister's lap. Your support meant more to me than that of all the gathered nobles of the tribes, some of whom I did not trust but whose help I desperately needed.

The worst of these was the rat-faced Marwan ibn Hakam, whose machinations had brought all this evil upon us. Not surprisingly, he had fled Medina after the rebels killed his sponsor, Uthman, and had sought refuge in Mecca, which was still governed by one of Uthman's appointed viceroys. I despised Marwan, but I kept my hatred in check, for he still commanded the loyalty of the Umayyad clan, whose support I needed to bring down Ali. Unfortunately Talha was less able to hide his feelings, and he openly insulted the young manipulator and publicly humiliated him by reminding the nobles of Mecca that Marwan had been cursed and expelled by the Messenger of God himself. It was a disgrace that Marwan never forgave and that would lead to tragedy for my beloved cousin.

During the weeks that our group planned its revolt against Ali, my fellow Mothers arrived from Medina, sent by the new Caliph to dissuade us from taking any rash actions. Umm Salama rallied my sister-wives to try to change my mind, but their voices fell on deaf ears. I had convinced myself of the righteousness of my cause, and my passionate defense of my actions nearly swayed Hafsa to join us. But her brother Abdallah ibn Umar, a stern and powerful man like her father, convinced her to stay clear of my ambitious and dangerous plan.

And so the day came when our army prepared to journey north

into Iraq and intercept Ali. I alone of all the Mothers of the Believers joined the men, who had prepared for me a special camel that was carrying an armored howdah. I often look back and call that day the Day of Tears, for I remember how my fellow wives wept and begged for me to stay. And yet my heart had been turned to stone by my hatred for Ali, and their words did not reach my soul.

Talha, Zubayr, and I rode out from Mecca with an army of three thousand and began a march that would forever change the destiny of Islam and the world.

— — —

AS WE PASSED OVER the deserts of Arabia and entered the rolling plains of Iraq, I gazed out from my howdah in wonder at the vast fields of green all about me. Tears welled in my eyes as I realized that this was the first time I had ever crossed the boundaries of the peninsula. I was over forty years old and the queen mother of an empire greater than any known to human history. And I had never set foot outside the desolate patch of sand where I had been born. I wondered what would happen once we had defeated Ali, whether the new Caliph (in all probability either Talha or Zubayr) would permit me at last to fulfill my childhood dream and wander free, to see the world that I knew of only through tales told by travelers and merchants in the marketplace. I imagined reclining in the gardens of Damascus under the shade of pink cherry trees or climbing through the snow-covered mountains of Persia. Or perhaps gazing upon the ancient pyramids that towered over Egypt and the mysterious lion's head that gazed out from the sands of Giza, as I had heard my brother Muhammad describe. My poor, idealistic brother whose cry for justice had set in motion the terrible events that had brought me here.

And then I heard a dog bark and I snapped out of my reverie. I peered through the heavy metal rings of my armored curtains and saw that our caravan had entered a valley. The sun had fallen behind the mountains and the earth was draped in shadow.

And then I heard a chilling howl, followed by another. I looked out from my howdah as dozens of vicious dogs ran out from behind the rocks and crevices and raced around my camel, barking wildly. There was something unearthly and terrifying about them, and I felt my bones grow cold.

And then I felt the stirrings of memory and my blood fled from my face.

The dogs of al-Haw'ab . . . they bark so fiercely . . . my husband had said. *They bark at the Angel of Death . . . who follows her skirts . . . so much death in her midst . . .* And then he had turned to me, fear in his black eyes. *Please,* Humayra . . . *Don't let the dogs bark at you.*

And then, at that instant, the demon that had possessed my soul departed and I became the Mother of the Believers again.

I called out to Talha in desperation. He rode over immediately at my cry for help.

"What is it? Are you all right?"

I peered out from my howdah, so agitated that I forgot to put on my veil. I saw him look at my face in stunned surprise, and I realized that he had not seen my features since I was a teenage girl. Talha immediately looked down and I felt my face flush in embarrassment and shame as I quickly wrapped my face behind the *niqab*. And some small part of me wondered if I looked ugly to him, a middle-aged woman who no longer possessed the vibrancy of youth that he remembered. But then the memory of the dark prophecy came to mind and all thoughts of vanity disappeared.

"We must turn back," I begged him.

"Why? What's wrong?"

"This is the valley of Haw'ab!" I shouted to him. "The Messenger warned me against it! Please! This mission had been cursed! We must abandon it!"

Talha looked up at me in confusion. And then I saw the hateful face of Marwan as he rode up beside my camel.

"You are mistaken, my Mother," he said. "This is not Haw'ab. That valley is miles to the west."

"You lie!" I cried out, but Marwan simply smiled and rode off, pointedly joining the train of his fellow Umayyad lords who had financed this expedition. Even if I wanted to turn back, the men whose gold had brought us here wished to continue. And one woman's voice of conscience had no weight on the scales of power.

Talha gazed at Marwan and I saw a defeated look cross his face.

"I'm sorry," he said, and then rode back to join Zubayr.

I felt steel talons gripping my heart, and I began to pray to Allah for protection from the darkness inside my own soul.

＊　＊　＊

AND SO IT WAS that we at last came upon Ali's encampment, deep in the heart of southern Iraq at a town called Basra. We had recruited sympathizers among the Bedouin tribes and some disgruntled Iraqis, and our army had now swelled to ten thousand, nearly equal to the fighting force of the Caliph.

Ever since the incident with the dogs of al-Haw'ab, the bloodlust had seeped out of my veins and I had no more desire for battle. And I could tell that Talha and Zubayr shared my feelings. The sight of an opposing army consisting of our fellow Muslims, the idea of shedding their blood, revolted us. And then an envoy from Ali arrived asking for a private meeting with me and the two Companions who led the army of Mecca.

＊　＊　＊

OVER THE NEXT SEVERAL hours, we met in Ali's simple command tent, not as enemies but as old colleagues who sat in wonder at how things could have gone so wrong between us. Ali apologized to Talha and Zubayr for the ungracious way in which he had assumed power, but he said quite convincingly that he felt there had been no other choice. With the death of Uthman, chaos had reigned, and he had sought only to reestablish order and justice to the caliphate.

"If you sought justice, then why did you not punish the assassins?" It was a question that came out of my mouth before I could stop it, and I saw that Talha and Zubayr looked relieved that I had said aloud what they had been too diplomatic to mention.

Ali sighed wearily.

"I am well aware that the assassins still live, and some of them have even joined my army, thinking that I am their patron when in truth I hold them in contempt." He paused and then looked into my eyes, green meeting gold. "But what did you expect of me? I had no soldiers at my command at Medina. How could I have enforced the law and held these murderers accountable, when they held the entire city hostage? I needed to bring together the forces of the *Ummah,* and then I would have the power to avenge Uthman's death."

It was a simple statement of fact, said with such clarity that we realized at once that he was right. And then I bowed my head in shame, for I realized that I had been in the wrong the whole time.

And then a thought came to me and I suddenly felt my heart beating faster.

"You have the power now," I said, a smile suddenly spreading beneath my veil. "We have ten thousand men under our command who are eager to hold the assassins accountable. And of the army you have gathered here, the rebels can only be a few hundred. If we combine forces, we can easily arrest them with little bloodshed."

Ali looked at me for a long moment, and then he smiled, his mysterious eyes twinkling.

"Then perhaps all of this has happened for the best," he said. "Satan tried to divide us, but God has brought us together again."

And so it was decided that day that we would join forces and avenge the death of Uthman. The Umayyads would be satisfied with the trial and execution of the rebels (Ali had pardoned my own brother, as he had renounced the actions of the killers). And Ali could then reign legitimately as Caliph under a united empire. This terrible moment of *fitna* would be over, and the Muslims would continue to expand and grow as one community, spreading to every corner of the world the message of unity—*there is no god but God.*

We retired that night to our separate camps, praising God for saving us from the folly of our own passions. But even as we slept in security, thinking that civil war had been averted, Satan had other plans.

— — —

THE NEXT DAWN I awoke to shouts and cries of horror. I leaped up and threw on my veil, staring out from the opening of my private sleeping tent at the plain of Basra. And raised my hand to my mouth in shock at what I saw.

A contingent of Ali's men had raided our camp, setting fire to tents and killing our soldiers in their sleep. The men of Mecca poured out onto the field, quickly donning their armor to respond to this treachery. For an instant, I thought Ali had betrayed us, but then the rising sun revealed the faces of the marauders and I recognized them as the accursed Egyptian rebels whose penchant for violence had brought us to this terrible place. I realized that they must have learned of our plans to turn on them, and they had attacked preemptively, seeking to turn our armies against each other before we could unite against them.

I raced out into the field, calling for the men to stop fighting. But it was too late. Blood had been spilled and the madness of battle was flowing through their veins. Our soldiers raced across the field to avenge themselves on Ali's men, and the nightmare that we had sought to avert was upon us.

Civil war.

As arrows and spears began to fly all around me, I raced to the safety of my armored howdah. My brave camel rose and tried to pull me to safety, but there was nowhere to run. The fighting had begun in earnest, and the two armies of Muslims came rushing out into the field, hatred consuming them as they fought their brothers like savage beasts.

I felt tears flowing down my face as I saw swords clashing and the beautiful emerald grass turn dark with the blood of the believers. Blood that had been spilled not by idolaters or the hordes of foreign empires but by their fellow Muslims. I screamed at the top of my lungs, calling out to the men whom I called my sons to stop killing one another, but my voice was lost in the terrible din of war.

As the madness spread, my camel was soon swimming in a sea of twenty thousand men who clashed brutally all around. Arrows struck my carriage from all sides, and yet the multiple layers of ringed armor saved me, even though my howdah was beginning to look like the shell of a porcupine.

I managed to watch the unfolding battle through a small hole in the curtain, but all I could see was a blur of blood and death, and the terrible stench of defecation and decay made me want to wretch.

My camel tried to shift away from the carnage, but everywhere it went, waves of enemy soldiers were upon us. And then I realized with deep horror that they were *chasing me*—the warriors of Ali were hunting me down. Somehow I had become the symbol of the entire rebellion, and they had made me the vaunted prize, the target of their fury.

I had become a vortex of death.

And then I heard in my head a terrible cold laughter and I felt something burning on my forearm. I looked down and my eyes went wide in horror.

I was wearing Hind's gold armlet.

She had given it to me that day when Mecca fell, the last day I had seen her. I had wanted to throw it away, but some small part of me was fascinated by the dark beauty of the entwined snakes with their ruby heart. I had told myself that it was just one small, meaningless trinket, and I had locked it away inside the trunk that held my few valuables, including the onyx necklace that had nearly destroyed my life. Over the years I would look at the armlet from time to time, examine its fine craftsmanship, but I had never worn it.

And now, somehow, it was there on my arm. And it burned like a torch, as if the ruby at its center were a live coal. Frightened, I tried to tear it off, but it was seared to my flesh.

And the laughter in my head became a voice. A clear distinct voice. Hind's voice.

I always liked you, little girl. You remind me of myself.

I screamed in rage.

"I am not like you!"

And then the laughter grew louder and I thought I would descend into madness. I was trying to fight this monster that was inside me, and it was winning.

And then I heard another voice, a voice that was soft and gentle and familiar. The Voice of the Messenger.

Do not fight anymore. Surrender.

I closed my eyes and let go. Let the rage and the guilt and the horror wash through me like rain running down a gully in a mountainside. I felt myself fall, as I had done that fateful night on the mountain where Muhammad and my father were hiding from the assassins. I was falling deeper and deeper, my shame and anguish tearing through me. And yet I did not resist. I let myself feel all the anger and doubt and misery and loneliness and regret that I had locked inside myself, let it all flood into my heart, until I felt swelled up with its bile.

And then I said aloud the words that Adam had said after he had been expelled from Paradise. The words that had reconciled him to his God. The words that even now could free me from the weight of the million sins that were poisoning my soul. The words that my husband had come to remind mankind of, one last time.

"Forgive me, Lord, for I have sinned."

And then the darkness took me, and I knew no more.

Epilogue

The End
of the
Beginning

What is faith?

It is a question that I asked at the beginning of the end, and I ask it once again now, at the end of the beginning. The setting of one world and the dawn of another.

Perhaps I have written this account, this collection of my memories, for no other reason than to answer this question that has haunted me over the years.

Nearly twenty years have passed since that fateful day in Basra when I faced my darkest demons, and the world has moved in directions that none of us could have expected.

Ali is dead. Muawiya reigns unchallenged as the Caliph of the Muslim empire.

It was an outcome that none of us could have foreseen on that terrible, blood-soaked plan in Iraq. Ali emerged victorious in a battle that he had never wanted to fight. The worst fighting had centered around my camel, as Ali's men sought to bring down the most visible symbol of the enemy, while my own soldiers had fought to the death to make sure that the Mother of the Believers was unharmed. In the end, the last of my protectors was killed and the poor camel's legs were hamstrung. When my howdah crashed to the ground, the Meccan resistance collapsed and Ali's men held sway over the battlefield.

I lay inside the upturned carriage in shock, an arrow having torn into my shoulder. My mind was still reeling from the strange vision I had experienced at the height of the battle, but I felt no fear in my heart. Even though I was facing almost certain death at the hands of my enemy, I was calm, serene, for I had surrendered my fate to God. I had become, in truth, a *Muslim*.

And then the steel curtains parted and a gentle hand reached inside to see if I was still alive. My brother Muhammad had ridden out into the field when he saw my camel fall, and he alone had the courage to peer inside the sacred carriage and see if the Messenger's most beloved wife still lived. I held him tight and wept, and the tears cleansed my heart as the rain would soon cleanse the green fields of Basra of the stain of blood.

After Muhammad had removed the arrow point from my shoulder and bandaged my wound, he picked me up like a little girl and carried me back to Ali's tent. The Caliph looked at me with great sorrow, and I could see that his green eyes were now crimson from grief.

"Zubayr is dead," he said simply, and I felt my heart crumble. They had been best friends and had fought beside each other, and now he was gone.

Somehow I managed to find my voice.

"And Talha?"

Ali turned away, unable to answer. Muhammad took my hand in his and shook his head, and I felt a scream rising in my throat.

"How?" was all I could choke out. It did not matter, but I needed to know.

"It was not one of our men," my brother said softly. "A soldier of the Bani Tamim in our ranks said that Talha was betrayed by Marwan, who shot him in the back in heat of battle."

The world was vanishing in a veil of tears.

And then Muhammad leaned close to me.

"My witness said that Talha spoke before he died, but the words made no sense to him," he whispered.

"What did he say?"

"She is still so beautiful."

- - -

ALI PARDONED ME IN public and announced that he had nothing but respect for the Mother of the Believers, the wife of Muhammad in this world and the hereafter. He led funeral prayers for the dead on both sides of the conflict. And then he sent me back to Medina with an honor guard.

I returned to my home in silence, unable to share with anyone the depth of pain that I carried. The other Mothers avoided me for a time, and the only person I could turn to for support was my sister, Asma. She was kind to me, although I sensed that there was a distance between us.

She did not say it aloud, but I always believed that she never truly forgave me for having led her beloved husband, Zubayr, to his death.

Isolated from family and friends, I focused on doing what I could to repair the damage I had inflicted on our faith. I returned to teaching and sharing the hadith that contained my beloved husband's words. But I renounced any involvement in politics.

The Battle of the Camel was not the end of the civil war, just the beginning. Muawiya refused to make peace with Ali, and their struggle erupted into open warfare on the plains of Siffin near the Euphrates. The brutal battle between the Muslims led to thousands of dead on both sides. And then Ammar, one of Ali's soldiers and a man from my childhood memories, was slain. Yes, Ammar, whose mother, Sumaya, had been the first martyr; Ammar, the youth whom Hamza and I had rescued from the wilderness. The Messenger had once prophesied that Ammar would die a martyr, like his mother, and that his killers would be wrongdoers. When word spread that Ammar had been killed in battle by Muawiya's men, some of the rebels lost heart, fearing that the Prophet's words now branded them as the unjust party.

Ali gained the upper hand. But as his forces were poised to annihilate Muawiya's regiments, the crafty politician sued for peace, sending out troops who held pages from the holy Qur'an high on their spears. Ali was tired of warfare between brothers and accepted Muawiya's proposal to arbitrate their rival claims to the leadership of the community.

It was a decision born out of compassion and statesmanship, but some of Ali's partisans were shocked to hear that he was willing to negotiate what they believed to be his divine right to rule. Ali himself had never publicly claimed any such right for himself or his heirs, and some of these partisans turned against him like spurned lovers. They renounced their support and branded him a traitor. These fanatics decided that they alone possessed the true understanding of Islam, which had been corrupted by men like Ali and Muawiya. And these self-proclaimed true believers, known as the *Khawarij*, were now dedicated to cleansing Islam by destroying anyone who failed to embrace their uncompromising vision. The *Khawarij* sent spies with poisoned daggers to rid the Muslim world of its competing claimants to the throne. They struck Muawiya in his palace in Damascus. The son of Abu Sufyan was grievously wounded but survived.

Ali was not so lucky. A *Khawarij* assassin named Ibn Muljam stabbed him in the head while he was leading the prayers in Kufa in southern Iraq. Ali lived for two days in excruciating pain before dying a martyr. His final wish had been that his assassin be tried fairly and that the Muslims should refrain from torturing him. In this last request, he was ignored, and his followers made Ibn Muljam's final hours on earth horrifyingly painful.

In the aftermath of Ali's death, his son Hasan was briefly elected Caliph in Kufa but abdicated under threat of attack by Muawiya. The Syrian governor quickly declared himself Caliph, and the Family of the Prophet did not oppose him. Muawiya was gracious in victory and treated the People of the House magnanimously. He gave them great wealth and generous pensions, on the condition that they stay out of politics and not challenge his rule. The Prophet's grandsons, Hasan and Husayn, agreed, and they withdrew from public life to the quiet sanctuary of Medina. They lived in peace in the oasis, and I saw them regularly, always greeting them as if they were my own sons.

And then a few years ago, Hasan unexpectedly fell ill and died. There was much weeping in Medina for the son of Fatima and Ali, and there were rumors that he had been poisoned by Muawiya's corrupt son Yazid, who had feared that Hasan would challenge the power of Damascus once the Caliph died. I do not know if this is true, but I have learned that the Umayyads are a cruel and vicious clan.

For in the midst of all this madness, I faced my own painful tragedy at the hands of the Bani Umayya. My fugitive brother, Muhammad, was finally captured by Muawiya's men. The lord of Damascus wanted my brother sent to him so that he could face trial for his involvement in the events leading to Uthman's death. But my proud and fiery brother taunted his captors with such intensity that they disobeyed Muawiya and killed him on the spot. Even as I write this, my hand shakes in horror at their vile actions. For the Umayyad commander added desecration to the crime of murder. The odious man took Muhammad's corpse and threw it into the carcass of a dead mule, and then set it on fire.

I wept for many days when I heard the terrible news. And then, in the midst of my grief, Ramla, the daughter of Abu Sufyan who had married my husband, made a vicious gesture to rub salt in the wound. She ordered her servants to cook a lamb and then deliver the meat to my door, with a note saying that it had been roasted just like my brother.

I have not touched meat to this day. And I have never forgiven the heartless Ramla, nor will I look upon her again, even if we are reunited as Mothers of the Believers on Judgment Day.

+ + +

LAST NIGHT THE MESSENGER of God came to me in a dream. He was clothed in green and surrounded by a golden light. I bowed my head, too ashamed to look at him. But then he took my face in his hands and raised my eyes to meet his.

"What will happen to me, my love?" I asked. "For I fear that when my time comes, my sins will grab hold of my soul and pull me into darkness."

Muhammad smiled at me, his eyes twinkling with an ethereal radiance.

And then he said to me the words of the holy Qur'an that I had heard before, at a time when hope had been clouded by fear of death.

God is the Protector of those who have faith. From the depths of darkness, He will lead them forth into light.

And then he vanished and I awoke knowing that the day of my death was fast approaching.

+ + +

AND SO WE COME to this moment at long last, beloved Abdallah, son of my sister.

What is faith?

It is a memory. Of a time when all was perfect in the world. When there was no fear and no judgment and no death.

It is a memory of a time before we were born, a beacon to guide us back from the end to the beginning, to the memory of where we came from.

It is a memory of a promise made before the earth was formed, before the stars glittered in the primordial sea.

A promise that says that we will remember what we have learned on this journey so that we may return full circle, the same and yet different.

Older. Wiser. Filled with compassion for others. And for ourselves.

What is faith?

It is the memory of love.

Afterword

I, Abdallah ibn al-Zubayr, add these closing words to my beloved aunt's account of her life. It has been over a decade since the death of Aisha bint Abu Bakr, but I still remember her final moments as if they were yesterday. As her kinsman, I was one of the few men living who could look upon her face, which was still remarkably beautiful and largely untouched by the ravages of time. Her skin was still pale and soft like a baby's, with only a few lines to mar her statuesque features. Even though she was nearly seventy years of age, her golden eyes were still vibrant and filled with life, as well as a hint of the sorrow that she had carried with her since the Battle of the Camel.

The final illness had been hard on her, her fingers cracking with pain, and yet she somehow managed to finish this record, driven by some need within her to tell her tale before others told it for her. When she finished the book, she gave it to me and then retired to her apartment, from which she would never emerge again. As her illness took hold of her, my mother, Asma, and I spent the final hours at her side, even as thousands of believers, both men and women, gathered outside the Masjid to pray for her recovery.

I remember how frightened she looked as the moment of death approached, and it was deeply painful for me to see a woman who had always been so strong curled up in terror like a child. I reminded her that she had nothing to fear, that she was the beloved of the Beloved of God, and that whatever mistakes she had made would be forgiven.

And yet she seemed oblivious to my words, and she muttered over and over again, *"Astaghfirullah"*—"I seek the pardon of God."

And then, as the sun began to set and the sky turned the crimson hue that had once been the color of her hair, I saw Aisha's breath slow and I knew that the time had come. My mother, Asma, her elder sister, took Aisha's hand in hers and squeezed reassuringly.

And then I heard the wind rise outside and the heavy curtains that hung on my aunt's door began to rustle. And for an instant, I could have sworn that I heard a voice tinkling through the veil. A gentle voice that called out the name given to Aisha by the Messenger of God.

Humayra.

It was a name that had not been spoken aloud since Muhammad's death, may God's blessings and peace be upon him. Perhaps I imagined it, but if I did so, I was not alone. My aunt stirred upon hearing the voice in the wind. And it was as if the memory of joy returned to her, for Aisha's fearful prayers stopped. She looked across the room, to the curtained section of her apartment where the Prophet, my grandfather, Abu Bakr, and the Caliph Umar were buried.

And then I saw her smile, her face as radiant as that of a girl on her wedding night, and she spoke to someone whom neither my mother nor I could see.

"My love . . ." Aisha said.

And she was gone.

We buried her in *Jannat al-Baqi,* the cemetery that is now the resting place of most of those who knew and lived beside the Messenger of God. With Aisha's passing, there were few left on earth who had seen and spoken with our beloved Prophet, and all that was left were the accounts of his life, the hadith, they had so meticulously related for future generations.

Over the past ten years much has changed, and not for the better. By the grace of God, the Muslim empire continues to grow and now stretches from Kairouan in North Africa to the Indus River. Constantinople still stands, but the Muslims remain committed to taking the seat of Christendom. For now, we are content to control the islands of Rhodes and Crete, from where the believers will expand into the northern realms of the Romans, *insha-Allah,* if God wills.

Yet even as our empire eclipses those of Alexander and Caesar, there is a growing sickness at its heart. For since the death of Ali, whom, I am ashamed to say, I fought against in my youth, the spiritual core of the Muslim leadership has been replaced by men of cunning and zeal but questionable morals. The Caliph Muawiya succeeded in bringing order and prosperity after years of civil war, and his rule was for the most part benign and wise. And yet under his command, practicality and expediency became the primary motivators in dealing with affairs of state, and the ideals of our Holy Prophet degenerated into mere platitudes on the lips of corrupt governors. I grieve to say that the Muslims now fight for wealth and glory rather than in pursuit of justice and a better world for mankind.

I did not object to the rule of Muawiya in his lifetime, and I prayed for him upon his death. And yet he, who was famed as the great uniter of the Muslim nation, made one terrible mistake that would plunge our *Ummah* into its second civil war. In the final years of Muawiya's life, the love of fatherhood overcame his wisdom. The Caliph appointed his hated son Yazid to succeed him, a youth who was better known for drinking and carousing than for statesmanship, and many among the Muslims were horrified. Muawiya had taken great pains as a leader to publicly uphold the laws of Islam and respect for the Prophet, but his worthless son now openly used his inherited throne to engage in debauchery and composed blasphemous poems denying the truth of the holy Qur'an.

And then it was that my friend and master Husayn, the last surviving grandson of the Messenger of God, rebelled against Yazid's tyranny. The most beloved of the Prophet's household left the safety of Medina and went to Iraq, as his father Ali had done. He hoped to garner support from the people to stand against this dark cloud that sought to block the light of God from illuminating the *Ummah*. And then the greatest of tragedies occurred, for at the small town of Karbala, Yazid's forces fell upon the tiny band of seventy-two worshipers led by the Prophet's grandson. They slaughtered these holy men, who had sought only to remind the Muslims that wielding power without faith would corrupt and destroy us, as it had done to every empire in history.

My master Husayn was beheaded, and most of his family was killed, including his infant son, Abdallah. Even as I write these words, the pages are stained with my tears, for I could not have imagined that men who called themselves Muslim could have laid hands upon Husayn, the boy whom the Prophet had carried on his shoulders, the man in whose blood the blessing of the Revelation still ran.

Husayn's tragic death lit a fire that still burns today. When I saw how the reprobate Yazid had treated the Messenger's grandson, I lifted my head in Mecca and denounced his regime. With none of the Prophet's bloodline left to lead—Husayn's one surviving son, Ali Zain al-Abideen, was being held hostage in Damascus and had been forced to renounce politics—I proclaimed a new caliphate that would return to the moral example set by the Messenger and his first four successors, who were now being called the Rightly Guided Caliphs.

My rebellion in Mecca has brought down the wrath of the Umayyad army, and although my men have resisted bravely for seven months, I fear that the city will soon be conquered by Yazid's forces. Led by his monstrous general, al-Hajjaj ibn Yusuf, they have ruthlessly breached the boundaries of the holy city and have besieged even the Sanctuary with their catapults. They have shown neither mercy to the people nor reverence for the holy sites, and my heart grieves to write that this morning the warriors rained down fiery debris upon the center of the city, and the Holy Kaaba itself has been set aflame.

It is clear that the forces of Yazid will take Mecca before the sun falls and I will be killed soon thereafter. With my death, only my mother Asma remains of the generation of the *Sahaba*, the Companions who lived alongside the Messenger of God. She is nearly ninety years old, but she stubbornly clings to life, even as she stubbornly stood beside the Prophet, her father Abu Bakr, and her sister Aisha, in the cause of justice so long ago.

The battle is lost today. But as I gaze out at the burning ruins of the Sacred House, I realize that the war will continue long after I and all those who knew the Messenger have passed away. For the fight is no longer between pagans and believers in the one God. That argument has been settled forever. The new war is now between those who fight for the religion of love and justice that Muhammad taught and those who hide behind the trappings of Islam to commit murder and atrocity.

And though I grieve that there are some who will always twist the Word of God to justify their crimes, I cannot hold myself above them, for even the righteous can fall victim to that temptation. My aunt Aisha allowed the passions of her heart to consume her in her conflict with Ali, as did good men like Talha and my father Zubayr. And as did I on that tragic field at Basra. But unlike these marauders who cloak themselves in the name of Islam today, we were wise enough to recognize our mistakes and repent of the *fitna*, the chaos, we caused.

And if there is one thing that I have learned in Islam, one principle that gives me hope on this sad day as the holy city burns all around me, it is this. That God is Merciful and Compassionate and accepts the sincere repentance of His servants. That no matter how far they fall into darkness, He is always prepared to lead them back to light.

And it is that knowledge that gives me hope for my people. For no matter how many false preachers arise to spread death and corruption in the name of Islam, the true message of our beloved teacher Muhammad ibn Abdallah, the Prophet of God, will never be lost. The message of unity and love for all mankind.

And so, as my life draws to a close, I will take these writings of my beloved aunt Aisha, Mother of the Believers, and bury them deep beneath the sands of Mecca, hoping that they will be uncovered one day when their message will be most needed.

If you have found them, dear reader, then it means that day is today.

Peace be upon you. And may the blessings of God be upon our holy Prophet Muhammad, and upon his family and his Companions.

Amen.

Acknowledgments

Publishing a first novel is an act of faith. A great many people came together and put tremendous time and effort into this project, solely because they believed in me and in my book. I would like to take a moment to give special thanks to a few of those who have played a pivotal role in this adventure.

First and foremost, to Rebecca Oliver, the most remarkable literary agent any author could hope for. There are only a handful of people who have single-handedly changed my life. You are at the top of that list.

To Judith Curr and the extraordinary staff at Atria Books for championing my work. In the current political climate, many publishers would be nervous about promoting a book of fiction about the birth of Islam. And yet Judith has shown once again that she is a visionary who has the courage of her convictions.

To Peter Borland, my editor and friend, who has patiently and enthusiastically guided this novel to publication. To Rosemary Ahern, whose detailed advice helped me craft the book into final form. And to Suzanne O'Neill, who first fell in love with the idea of a novel on Aisha and set the wheels into motion.

To my television agent, Scott Seidel, for passing along my initial manuscript to his colleagues in New York. When I told Scott I wanted to publish my novel, he said he would do everything he could to make it happen. He proved to be a man of his word, a rare quality in Hollywood.

To my managers, Jennifer Levine and Jason Newman, who supported me during the long and arduous process of crafting this work while balancing a hectic film and television career. And to all my agents at Endeavor, who have opened so many doors for me as a writer: Tom Strickler, Ari Greenburg, Bryan Besser, Tom Wellington, Hugh Fitzpatrick, and many others. Thank you for taking me seriously every time I come to you with a crazy new idea.

To my elder sister, Nausheen Pasha-Zaidi, the first published author in my family. Her beautiful novel, *The Colour of Mehndi,* inspired me to stop procrastinating and start writing. To my younger sister and best friend, Shaheen, who patiently read through every single page of this book as it evolved and never feared to give constructive criticism.

And to my parents. For encouraging me to dream.

Mother of the Believers

Kamran Pasha

Readers Club Guide

INTRODUCTION

In the desert of seventh century Arabia, a new prophet named Muhammad has arisen. After he beholds a beautiful woman in a vision and resolves to marry her, the girl's father quickly arranges the wedding. Aisha becomes the youngest of Muhammad's twelve wives, and her fierce intelligence establishes her as his favorite. But when Aisha is accused of adultery by her rivals, she loses the Prophet's favor—and must fight to prove her innocence.

Pardoned by her husband after a divine revelation clears her name, Aisha earns the reluctant respect of fellow Muslims when their settlement in Medina is attacked and she becomes a pivotal player on the battlefield. Muhammad's religious movement sweeps through Arabia and unifies the warring tribes, transforming him from prophet to statesman. But soon after the height of her husband's triumph—the conquest of the holy city of Mecca—Muhammad falls ill and dies in Aisha's arms.

A widow at age nineteen, Aisha fights to create a role for herself in the new Muslim empire—becoming an advisor to the Caliph of Islam, a legislator advocating for the rights of women and minorities, a teacher, and ultimately a warrior and military commander. She soon becomes one of the most powerful women in the Middle East, but her passionate nature leads to tragedy when her opposition to the Caliph plunges the Islamic world into civil war. Her legacy remains one of the most compelling stories of Islam.

1. "God had chosen me to marry His Messenger. It sounded laughable, but somehow it felt right. As if some part of my soul had always known that was my purpose." To what extent does Aisha feel conflicted about her sudden transformation from child to Mother of the Believers? In what ways does her betrothal and marriage to the Prophet challenge some of his most faithful believers? What accounts for the unique nature of Aisha and Muhammad's emotional connection with each other?

2. How do the climactic events of the Battle of Badr—particularly the deaths of many prominent Quraysh leaders—serve to galvanize the Muslims in their efforts to rally future believers? What does the defeat of the Meccan army by the vastly outnumbered followers of the Messenger represent to leaders of the Assembly? How does the Meccan defeat further empower Hind, the lascivious wife of Abu Sufyan, to incite further violence against the Muslims?

3. Aisha finds herself in trouble with the Messenger and her faith when she ventures places she shouldn't go, such as when she comes to the assistance of Salim ibn Qusay, a thief who attempts to rape her; when a young Jewish goldsmith, Yacub, is punished with death for insulting her honor; or when she is suspected of infidelity for having gotten lost in the desert. To what extent can these mishaps can be attributed to Aisha's youth and inexperience? What role does her personality play in leading her into these morally compromising situations?

4. "The whole ceremony seemed appropriately ethereal for this enigmatic couple and I was glad when the Prophet rose and kissed them, signaling that we had returned to the world I knew and understood." Why does the marriage of Ali to Fatima seem symbolic to Aisha of some more momentous alliance than that of a customary wedding ceremony? How would you describe the roles Ali and Fatima play in the life of Muhammad and in the history of Islam? What accounts for Aisha's troubled relationship with Ali?

5. What role does a young Jewish woman named Safiya, the daughter of the prominent Jewish leader Huyayy ibn Akhtab, play in alerting Aisha to an assassination plot against Muhammad by the Bani Nadir? How does the treachery of the Bani Nadir lead to an affiliation between the Arab and Jewish forces against the Muslims? What does Muhammad's later marriage to Safiya suggest about his ability to accommodate marriage to his political advantage?

6. "You should not leave your houses unless necessary. It is for your good and for the good of the *Ummah,* he said . . . We were now expected to stay inside our homes like prisoners." What does Muhammad's commandment to his wives to veil themselves to strangers and to stay confined to their homes reflect about his culture and society? How would you describe the modern-day effect of this commandment on faithful Muslim men and women?

7. Why does Muhammad's death, after several days of illness, lead to unrest and uncertainty in his immediate circle? How does his lack of an immediate male heir complicate his succession? What does his death, as witnessed by Aisha, reveal about his spiritual nature?

8. "And so, for the first time in centuries, the Children of Israel returned to the Holy Land from which they had been expelled, ironically at the generosity of a religion they had rejected." How do the actions and policies of Muslims, even in the midst of conquering territories and transforming regions, reflect the tenets of their faith? To what extent does the spread of Islam across the Middle East unite former enemies and transform the city of Medina?

9. How does Aisha's political alignment with her brother, Muhammad, challenge the rule of the Caliph Uthman and lead to his death? To what extent does Aisha's subsequent rejection of Ali as Muslim leader stem from her longstanding grudge against him for suggesting to the Prophet that she was an expendable wife? How does the civil war that arises between Muslims lead directly to Aisha's renunciation of involvement in politics, and how does it connect to a foreboding prediction made by her husband?

10. At the opening of *Mother of the Believers*, Aisha poses the rhetorical question, "What is faith?" But by the end of her memoir of her life, she has answered her own question in her letter to her nephew. How does her answer relate to her experiences as the beloved wife of Muhammad? Based on what you know about her faith, how would you characterize its role in her life?

A Conversation with Kamran Pasha

Q: *Mother of the Believers* **is your first novel. What first drew you to Aisha and her remarkable story?**

A: I have always been fascinated by strong women, and growing up as a Muslim in the United States, I found myself intrigued by how Aisha breaks every negative stereotype that Americans have about Islam and women. A scholar, a poet, a statesman, and a warrior, Aisha lived a life that rivals those of the greatest men in history. She was a passionate and fiercely intelligent woman who changed the course of human civilization, yet has received almost no attention in Western literature. It has been a lifelong dream to write a novel about Aisha, and I'm frankly still a little stunned that I have been given the opportunity to actually make that dream come true. I always wanted to highlight those aspects of her character that make her stand out among the accounts of early Muslims—her powerful will, her sharp mind, and the intensity and depth of her emotions.

In researching Aisha's life, it became clear that she possessed rare gifts that made her destined for greatness—traits that Prophet Muhammad, a master judge of human character, would have noticed immediately. His decision to marry young Aisha and bring her into the center of the community was, I believe, motivated in part by his recognition of her genius and his desire to place Aisha in a position where she could fulfill a destiny that would have been otherwise stifled in the primitive desert world in which she was born. And the fact that the Prophet loved her first and foremost among all his wives in Medina reveals a great deal about how forward thinking he was. In many ways, Prophet Muhammad can be considered a proto-feminist, and the fact that he loved Aisha's fiery nature and independent spirit reveals his own progressive attitudes toward women. In Aisha, we see a mirror of the Prophet's own revolutionary nature, as well as a glimpse of the reverence for the sacred feminine in Islam that many contemporary Muslim men have perhaps forgotten.

Q: What were some of the challenges you experienced as an author in getting into the perspective of a female protagonist?

A: It is of course impossible for a man to truly know how a woman sees and experiences life, and it would be disingenuous for me to claim that I have accurately done so. But I have the benefit of being raised in a family of powerful Muslim women who continue Aisha's legacy of independence and intellectual curiosity. A lifetime of conversations with my mother, sisters, and other Muslim women gives me at least an observer's insight into the challenges faced by women in society, both in the Islamic world and the West. To the extent that I succeeded in creating an authentic female voice for Aisha, the credit belongs to all the women in my life who guided me over the years. To the extent that I failed, I hope the reader will excuse it as the natural shortcomings of the masculine perspective in that regard.

Q: Why did you decide to frame Aisha's narrative in terms of a memoir and letter to her nephew?

A: I felt that Aisha's voice is so unique that the novel had to be presented from her point of view. She was such a complex person whose attitudes and opinions evolved so much over the course of her lifetime that the only way I felt I could do justice to her tale was to set it as a memoir. Aisha on her deathbed looking back at a life of great triumph and tragedy allowed me to explore her passionate youthful nature, as well as the more sober perspective of a mature woman who has had a chance to consider her legacy. Many readers may be surprised at how sad and wistful the memoir seems to be at times, but I am only following Aisha's own accounts, where she admitted in later years to regretting many of her youthful follies. But it is that regret, that poignant longing to correct the mistakes of the past, that makes her especially human for me. Aisha, by her own admission, was a brilliant but flawed human being, and it is that stark humanity that brings her closer to us. Aisha was no plastic saint. And that is exactly why we can learn from her and honor the remarkable things she accomplished. If Aisha, with all her passions, jealousies, and rage, can become the most beloved and revered of the Prophet's wives, there is hope for all of us in finding redemption.

Q: You are well acquainted with fictional portrayals of Muslims from your work as a writer and coproducer of the television series *Sleeper Cell*. How would you compare the experience of writing historical fiction about the earliest Muslims with the process of creating portrayals of Muslims in the modern world?

A: I think one of the biggest differences is that *Sleeper Cell* dealt with the modern phenomenon of Muslim terrorists, villains who are attempting to hijack the beautiful religion of Islam. This novel, on the other hand, focuses on the revered heroes of my faith. What became evident as I researched this tale is that Prophet Muhammad, Aisha, and the rest of the early Muslims would have been horrified to learn that Islam would one day be painted as a religion of terror. Islam began as a pacifist movement that only took arms after being pushed to near extinction by the idolaters of Mecca. Even after military engagement became part of Muslim experience, strict rules of war were adopted. Women and children were to be spared in combat. Priests and rabbis of the People of the Book were protected from attack. Environmental warfare, including burning trees and poisoning water supplies, was forbidden, even though such tactics were considered acceptable by neighboring cultures (and remain common today). Muslims throughout the past 1,400 years took great pride in following strict rules of war, even as many in the West justified indiscriminate slaughter from the Crusades up until modern day. It is an incredible tragedy that there are people in the Muslim word today who feel that the only way they can fight political oppression is to engage in terror against civilians, which goes against the vast corpus of Muslim tradition and history. In writing this book, I have sought to remind both Muslims and non-Muslims that Islam stands for justice and human equality, as evidenced by the lives of the Prophet and the early community. The word "Islam" derives from the Arabic root meaning "peace." The idea of "Islamic terrorism" is as much of a non sequitur as the phrase "loving murder." I hope that this novel will inspire people to reexamine what Islam has stood for throughout history, and what it offers humanity today.

Q: **How do you respond to critics who contend that fictional accounts of religious figures are potentially blasphemous?**

A: I think such accusations are misguided and fail to understand the magnificent role literature and storytelling have played in Islamic civilization throughout history. Muslims have been telling stories about Prophet Muhammad, his wives, and companions around campfires and in books for centuries. The Modern Library has recently published *The Adventures of Amir Hamza*, a beautiful translation of a medieval Islamic epic about the Prophet's uncle Hamza. The book contains dozens of incredible—and fictional—adventures that Muslim storytellers attributed to Hamza over the centuries. Like *The Arabian Nights*, the stories about Hamza were hugely popular throughout the Islamic world as tales of wonder and faith, both serving to entertain and educate the masses. One of my favorite books of all time is *Yusuf and Zulaikha*, an epic tale written in the fifteenth century by the Persian poet Jami (translated in English by David Pendlebury). It is a fictionalized account of the story of the prophet Joseph in the Qur'an and his star-crossed romance with an Egyptian princess. The tale is treasured by Muslims as both a beautiful love story and a deeply mystical allegory of worshippers seeking the Divine. The Muslim community has always understood that stories can teach and inspire us and that the line between historical fact and creative imagination is less important than the wisdom one gains from the tale. I have written my novel as part of that proud literary tradition, and I hope that many more historical fiction accounts about the great figures of Islam will be published to enlighten new generations about the richness of Muslim civilization.

Q: **Your portrait of Muhammad's relationship with Aisha emphasizes the uniquely mystical nature of their connection as husband and wife. How much of that relationship did you base on historical accounts of their marriage?**

A: I have tried to base my story on as many historical accounts as feasible. According to early Muslim traditions, Prophet Muhammad was told in a mystical dream by Gabriel that Aisha was destined to be his wife. And the Prophet is reported to have said that among all his wives, he only received divine revelation when in bed with Aisha. She served as a profound inspiration to the Prophet, and it is not surprising that as he felt death approaching he chose to spend his final moments in Aisha's arms. Their spiritual bond was clearly unique, and I have tried to capture the essence of their relationship in this novel.

Q: What did you discover in the course of researching and writing *Mother of the Believers* that surprised you?

A: I was surprised and delighted by how deeply human and relatable the great heroes and heroines of Islam were according to early historical accounts. Aisha's triumphs and tragedies were recounted by Muslim historians without any effort to sugarcoat or mythologize her or the other founding figures of Islam. Love, passion, jealousy, hate, and forgiveness all played very real roles in the lives of these remarkable people. It is that humanity that makes Aisha and her contemporaries accessible to modern readers. And, on a personal note, it is the stark realism of the depictions of the early Muslim community that strengthened my own personal faith. That God can speak to and through fallible human beings like ourselves adds to the appeal of Islam as a practical revelation for the real world, not a fairy tale set in the clouds.

Q: To what extent is the intense jealousy you depict among Muhammad's many wives something that you extrapolated from historical accounts?

A: The jealousy among the Mothers of the Believers is well documented, with Aisha by her own admission being particularly guilty. There are accounts that she would actually secretly follow Prophet Muhammad around at night to see if he was going to spend the evening with one of his other wives. It is that passionate, stubborn nature that both bonded her deeply with the Prophet and also led to some of the terrible mistakes she made in the first Islamic civil war. But it is that fiery personality that also makes Aisha the most endearing of his wives. In her jealousy and possessiveness, we see our own insecurities, fears, and desires. And it is the Prophet's incredible patience with the rivalries between members of his household that reveals how remarkable a man he was. Prophet Muhammad was a spiritual teacher to thousands, as well as a politician, statesman, and military commander, and yet he managed to find time to bring together not only the warring tribes of Arabia, but also the competing groups inside his own home with expert diplomacy. The Prophet truly serves as an example to human beings of how to master challenges in all aspects of life, public and private.

Q: **As a Muslim yourself, what kind of obligation did you feel as an author to your representation of your faith in this novel?**

A: I feel a great burden of responsibility in writing this tale. Islam is the most misunderstood religion on Earth and is subject to a great deal of propaganda in the media today. As a believer I am aware that anything I write could be misconstrued or used by anti-Muslim bigots to advance their agendas. And there are, of course, a few radical Muslims who might take offense at something I have written and denounce me. But at the end of the day, I cannot predict every possible outcome that could arise out of the words I have put on paper. My intention is simple and straightforward—to write an exciting work of historical fiction that educates readers about Islam and honors the legacies of Prophet Muhammad, Aisha, and the early Muslim community. How the world responds to my efforts is beyond my control. But I rest secure in knowing that my intentions are good and sincere. The rest I leave in God's hands.

Q: **If you could have been present for any event of early Muslim life that you describe in your novel, what would it be?**

A: It is hard to choose any one moment, as there are so many remarkable events that I have chronicled and would love to have witnessed with my own eyes. But if I can single out any moment in this history of early Islam that I would have liked to have seen, it would be the peaceful fall of Mecca to the Muslims in AD 630. I can only imagine what it must have been like for the Muslims to return to the holy city from which they had been expelled, and to do so with such honor. The Prophet could have massacred the entire city for its crimes, and yet he chose in victory to be magnanimous, establishing a general amnesty that spared the people who spent years trying to kill him and murdered his loved ones. I would have loved to walk at his side into the courtyard of the Holy Kaaba and watch as the Muslims destroyed the 360 idols that littered the Sanctuary, rededicating it to the One God. I think our forefather Abraham would have been proud to see his children through Ishmael renounce idolatry and return to the pure monotheism that he had expounded to mankind. Even now, I get emotional at the image of Islam's final—and highly improbable—triumph against all the forces that had been aligned against it for decades. The Prophet's victory over the idolatry of Mecca is one of the greatest spiritual moments in history, and I would have loved to see it with my own eyes. The victory of Islam was the victory of human unity over tribal division, the triumph of equality and brotherhood over racism and class distinctions. That to me is the greatest gift of Islam to the world.

In December 2008, I went to Mecca for the first time to participate in the Hajj, the grand pilgrimage. And there I saw the Prophet's triumph in full glory—four million people, of every nation, every skin color, every language on Earth, together. Mankind in all of its wondrous diversity coming together to worship One God in love and companionship. The desert wastes became a paradise of human unity, a beautiful sign of what men and women could be if they chose to transcend superficial distinctions and embrace a common destiny. This was the greatest legacy of Prophet Muhammad, Aisha, and the early Muslims to mankind. And in that moment, I truly understood the power of the sacred words that define my faith.

There is no god but God, and Muhammad is His Messenger.

1. Are you interested in learning more about Kamran Pasha, the author of *Mother of the Believers*? To read about Pasha's recent visit to the plain of Arafat during the Hajj, or to find out more about his experience in paying homage to his novel's heroine, Aisha, at the site of her burial, visit the blog on his website: http://blog.kamranpasha.com/.

2. *Mother of the Believers* offers Aisha the opportunity to reflect on her life and her many experiences in the form of a memoir that she shares exclusively with her nephew. Have you ever considered your own life experiences in light of your successes and failures? To whom would you choose to address your final remarks? If you already keep a diary or journal, you may want to revisit it and chart some of the many important moments in your life. Consider sharing your findings with your fellow readers. Aisha marks the important events of her life in terms of private rites of passage and victories for Islam. How do you mark your most significant moments?

3. How has your knowledge about the religion of Islam changed or been affected by reading *Mother of the Believers*? Would you like to know more about the underpinnings of this faith, or about its practice around the world? If so, you may want to arrange to visit a mosque in your community. For a virtual exposure to the many facets of Islam in contemporary society, visit http://www.islam.com/, which is a wonderful reference for thousands of subjects inspired by and directly related to Islamic worship.